BEST SELLER ROMANCE

An Awakening Desire

HELEN BIANCHIN

Harlequin Mills & Boon

SYDNEY ❀ AUCKLAND ❀ MANILA
LONDON ❀ TORONTO ❀ NEW YORK
PARIS ❀ AMSTERDAM ❀ HAMBURG ❀ MILAN
STOCKHOLM ❀ MADRID ❀ ATHENS ❀ BUDAPEST
WARSAW ❀ SOFIA ❀ PRAGUE ❀ TOKYO ❀ ISTANBUL

First Published 1987
This Edition 1998
ISBN 0 733 51143 0

Published by
Harlequin Mills & Boon
3 Gibbes Street
Chatswood, NSW 2067
Australia

HARLEQUIN MILLS & BOON and the Rose Device are trademarks used under
license and registered in Australia, New Zealand, Philippines, United States
Patent & Trademark Office and in other countries.

Printed and bound in Australia by
McPherson's Printing Group

For Danilo, Angelo and Peter

CHAPTER ONE

'DARLING, are you quite sure about this trip?'

Emma secured the lock on the expensive piece of luggage and bit back a strangled sound as a tiny hysterical laugh rose and died in her throat. She wasn't *sure* about anything, much less flying half-way across the world, but indecision at this late stage was impossible.

A wry smile tugged at the corners of her generously curved mouth. Maternal devotion could prove daunting, especially when its entire gamut was focused on one sibling.

'I'm twenty-four, not seventeen,' she reminded her mother gently, and Mrs. Templeton lifted a hand only to let it fall again in a gesture of helpless self-defeat.

'If you'd waited, we could have taken a holiday together, Hawaii, Hong Kong—anywhere.'

Which was precisely the reason Emma had insisted on taking a break *now*. The need to get away on her own had become increasingly necessary over the past few months as familial solicitude threatened to destroy each renewed attempt at independence.

Emma refrained from commenting as she crossed to the dressing-table to add the finishing touches to her make-up. Via mirrored reflection she glimpsed the anxiety clouding her mother's attractive features, and for a brief second she was consumed with guilt.

Damn! Why did leaving have to prove so difficult? Her

lipstick slipped, and she plucked a tissue from its nearby box with shaking fingers.

'It's only a year since——' Mrs Templeton's voice faltered to an awkward halt, and Emma finished quietly,

'Since Marc died.' Her eyes captured her mother's and held them with a steadiness that was uncontrived. 'Believe me, I won't go to pieces if you say it.'

There was a measurable silence, one she didn't attempt to fill as she finished outlining her mouth. Mascara came next, and she applied the brushed wand to her lashes with skill before capping and tossing it among the array of cosmetics in her make-up pouch.

'Your father and I are concerned you're attempting too much, too soon.'

Oh, lord, what could she say? Admit her mother was voicing her own uncertainties? No, she reflected wearily. For both their sakes, she had to project enthusiasm. Anything less would be intolerable. 'Three weeks is hardly a lifetime,' she chided gently.

Standing back from the mirror, she viewed her image with critical appraisal, studying the dark auburn curls with something akin to resignation. Reaching her shoulders, the tapered length of her hair was an encumbrance she'd learnt to bear with over the years. Expensive experiments by a number of hair designers had elicited the unanimous opinion she should retain her natural curls, and for the past seven years she'd opted for a casual windswept style which served to highlight her delicately boned features.

Of average height and fashionably slim, she bore feminine curves in all the right places. Tawny-coloured eyes were set wide apart above a *retroussée* nose and a soft, curved mouth. Identical dimples deepened whenever she smiled, alluding to a captivating personality whose warm spontaneity was totally without guile.

Selecting something suitable to wear for the long flight had afforded more than scant deliberation, and she viewed the emerald-green dress in uncrushable silk with approval. Elegant, slim-heeled black shoes completed the outfit, and her only jewellery—aside from her wedding ring—was a gold roped chain and matching bracelet. The overall effect portrayed designer *élan* at its most chic.

Emma fastened her make-up pouch and slipped it into her overnight bag, checked her travel documents, then she slid her arms into a fine wool coat that was light, yet warm, and could be discarded on arrival in Rome.

'Shall we go?'

It would take thirty minutes to reach Sydney's International Air Terminal, and a further half-hour to check in her luggage and attend to formalities.

However, two delayed flights resulted in the passenger lounge being overcrowded, and Emma felt as awkward as her parents did, uttering inanities that had little perspective and merely served to compound her own insecurity.

'I'll send you a postcard every few days,' she promised with a shaky smile as the threat of tears added impetus to the need for a swiftly taken farewell.

Once past the security barrier and out of their sight she was able to regain a measure of control, although her emotions seemed caught up in an unenviable tangle, conversely urging her to *stay* now that she was actually going.

A hollow laugh rose up in her throat as she joined the queue of passengers waiting to complete the electronic check of hand-luggage prior to boarding the huge

Boeing. If she didn't summon some semblance of inner calm, she'd soon be reduced to a quivering mass of nerves!

Her designated seat was next to a window, and as soon as they were airborne she ordered a vermouth and soda, glad of its relaxing effect as she gazed sightlessly at the pale grey sky with its heavy banks of slow-moving cloud.

Despite a determination not to lapse into retrospection, it was all too easy to recall a multitude of bitter-sweet memories centred around one painful figure.

Dear, sweet Marc. Loquacious, fun-loving, endearing. Why *you*? she demanded silently.

Two of Sydney's élite families, the marriage of the year between respective only children, their future had promised so much. A fatal car accident a mere week after their wedding had robbed her of childhood sweetheart, husband and lover, in one brutal swoop, whereas she had been pulled from the passenger seat virtually unscathed apart from some lacerations, two cracked ribs and severe bruising.

After her release from hospital and necessary convalescence, her work as a fashion co-ordinator to an exclusive designer became all-important, and during the ensuing months she devoted long, hard hours in an effort to dull the edges of an inconsolable loss.

It hadn't needed a physician to point out the telltale signs of exhaustion, both mental and physical. His cautioning merely aided her decision to get away from loving, over-protective parents and parents-in-law, as well as a cluster of well-meaning friends whose combined solicitude enveloped her like a shroud, almost to a point whereby she thought she might suffocate from so much caring attention.

'Please fasten your seat-belt.'

The hostess's smooth reminder jolted Emma out of her reverie, and she automatically attended to the clasp as the Boeing began its descent towards Melbourne's Tullamarine Airport, the last Australian port and the shortest of three scheduled stop-overs.

The adjacent seat became occupied by a sweet-faced woman of middle years who regaled Emma with the life history of her five children and four grandchildren all the way to Singapore where she disembarked, and Emma took the opportunity while the jet was stationary to stretch her legs and freshen up. She felt tired and had the vague beginnings of a headache. With luck, the seat next to her would remain empty. If not, she'd feign sleep all the way to Bombay!

Fate elected to be unkind, and she cursed beneath her breath as a tall, masculine frame eased itself down beside her just prior to take-off.

Perhaps if she immersed herself in a magazine he would correctly assume her disinterest in indulging in polite conversation and leave her alone? With that thought in mind she reached into her overnight bag, selected one of three glossy magazines, and began studiously leafing through its pages.

After a while her attention wandered, drawn as if by some elusive magnet to the man at her side, dispassionately noting the quality and cut of his dark grey business suit. The faint aroma of his aftershave teased her nostrils—Yves St Laurent's *Kouras*, she identified, reluctantly approving his choice. A gold Rolex graced his wrist, and she saw that his hands were broad with strong, tapering fingers and clean square-cut nails.

A man who spent his time jetting between one country

and another, closing corporate deals? Emma mused speculatively, assessing his age to be in the vicinity of mid-to-late thirties. He extracted a folder from his briefcase and became engrossed for the next few hours with an impressive sheaf of papers. Perhaps a member of one of the accepted professions embarking on a conference? Somehow he looked more like a high-powered executive—in control, rather than beneath directorial domination.

A faint smile lifted the edges of her lips. People-watching could be an absorbing pastime, allowing one's imagination to weave a fantasy that was in all probability the antithesis of reality.

Choosing another magazine she selected an article and read it, then another, before settling for an unconventional short story which proved interesting, if a trifle avant-garde for her taste.

She must have dozed, for she came sharply awake at the faint thudding sound of the jet's wheels touching down on the runway, followed within minutes by the discovery that her seat-belt had been fastened while she slept. By whom? The man at her side? Somehow the fact that he'd reached across and calmly tended to the task without her being aware of it was vaguely disturbing.

The need to freshen up elicited a murmured request to slip past him, and as he stood to his feet and moved into the aisle she registered that even in three-inch heels her eyes were barely level with the impeccable knot of his dark silk tie.

Emma's cool 'Thanks' evoked a vaguely mocking smile, and in those few seconds she was made aware of strong, arresting features: a composite of chiselled bone-structure and smooth tanned skin, dark, well groomed hair, and a pair of wide-set, piercing brown eyes.

Ten minutes later she resumed her seat, relieved that this was the final stop-over. It brought her destination closer, despite the sad reminder that Marc should have been sharing this trip as a celebration of their first wedding anniversary. Now she was doing it alone, and she hadn't been able to explain to anyone precisely *why*.

'A pleasure trip?'

At the sound of that deep, slightly accented drawl Emma schooled her expression into a polite mask, not really wanting to converse with him at all; and she glimpsed his lips twist into the semblance of a smile as she accorded him a faint nod in silent acquiescence.

'I shan't eat you.'

He sounded *amused*, and it rankled unbearably. With considerable coolness she let her eyes sweep his features in deliberate appraisal. 'Whatever makes you think I'd allow it?' she inclined with arctic civility, her dismissal containing such crystal clarity that only the most audacious male would have dared pursue another word.

His gaze was assessing beneath its indolent veneer, yet strangely watchful, almost as if he sensed an acute vulnerability beneath her icy façade, and after seemingly endless seconds her lashes slowly fluttered down as her ability to out-stare him diminished.

A prickle of unease slithered the length of her spine, and she shivered, instinctively aware that he was the sort of man who commanded most women at will, and took pleasure in every sensual pursuit.

Perhaps if she adjusted her seat and leaned back against the cushioned head-rest she might manage to escape into sleep. Surely she should be able to? Her body clock was attuned to another time sequence, and she closed her eyes in the hope of drifting into blessed oblivion.

The touch of a hand on her arm caused her to stir, and she blinked, disorientated for a few seconds by her surroundings. Then she became humiliatingly aware that her head was resting against a hard, muscular shoulder!

She moved at once, conscious of a faint tinge of pink colouring her cheeks as her fingers sought the appropriate button to restore the seat to an upright position.

'I'm sorry.' The words emerged scarcely before she could give them thought, and she felt flustered and curiously fragile. *Why*, for God's sake? The man was a stranger, and the chance of them meeting again had to be in the vicinity of one in a thousand.

'Whatever for?' His voice held quiet mockery, and to Emma's ears it sounded impossibly cynical.

Perhaps he was so used to women flinging themselves at him, using every known ruse, that he thought she was merely trying to gain his attention.

Deep inside a tiny seed of resentment flared into antagonism, and for the remainder of the flight she alternately read, became lost in reflective thought, and obviously slept, for when she woke the sky beyond the window was tinged with the first opalescent glow of a new day's dawn, and she watched in idle fascination as the deep blue gradually lightened, casting a pale, eerie illumination of the jet's silver-metalled wing.

Breakfast was served an hour before their scheduled arrival in Rome, and Emma eyed the array of food with uninterest, selecting a croissant which she broke in half and spread with apricot conserve. After drinking a second cup of coffee she silently admitted to feeling almost human.

Disembarkation at Fiumicino International Airport and dealing with Customs took considerable time. There was a brief glimpse of her companion's tall frame as he joined a separate queue, then when next she glanced into the bustling crowd he was no longer in sight.

At last she was free to emerge into the Arrival Lounge with her luggage, and she stood searching for a familiar face in the sea of waiting people, wondering whether Marc's grandparents would come to meet her themselves or despatch their chauffeur.

'*Emma!*'

She might be in a strange city—*country*, she amended silently—but the elderly man threading his way towards her was endearingly familiar. For as long as she could remember, Marc's grandparents had regularly flown to Sydney each year to spend Christmas with their son and his family.

'*Cara!* It is so good to see you.'

'And you,' Emma greeted shakily, blinking quickly as she became enveloped in his embrace.

'Come, the car is outside,' Enzo Martinero bade, taking charge of the luggage trolley, and she walked at his side to a large saloon car parked at the kerb, with a chauffeur at the wheel.

The air was hot and dry, and filled with a cacophony of sound. Jarring hornblasts as taxis jostled with privately driven vehicles for space; voices raised in voluble Italian, altercations which, if Emma's reasonable command of the language proved correct, questioned parentage and managed to blaspheme the Deity with formidable disregard.

Within minutes her luggage was stored and, seated in the rear beside Marc's grandfather, Emma watched as the chauffeur eased the car clear of immediate traffic.

This was *Rome*! Where great emperors had ruled and been defeated, she mused, and ancient civilisation dated back to the years before the birth of Christ. Little wonder they called it the Eternal City.

'Rosa would have accompanied me to meet you, but Annalisa, our young guest, was not feeling well when she woke this morning.' A smile creased Marc's grandfather's kindly features. 'The result of too much excitement, I think.' As if he sensed her curiosity, he sought to elaborate. 'Annalisa is the daughter of our nephew and godson.' He paused fractionally and gave a slight, philosophical shrug. 'Each year Annalisa travels from Milan with her governess to spend the summer holidays with us.'

Emma was intrigued. 'How old is she?'

'Nine. Nick is a devoted father,' Enzo hastened to assure as he caught her perplexed frown. 'Unfortunately his business interests demand much of his time, hence Annalisa attends a boarding school run by the good Catholic Sisters.'

Emma conjured up a picture of a child trapped in a strict scholastic regime, and felt her interest quicken. 'Surely a governess is superfluous?'

They were skirting the city, their progress often slowing to a complete standstill in heavily congested traffic, and although Enzo's luxurious vehicle was air-conditioned the outside noise filtered through the closed window, punctuating their conversation with frequent blasts on the horn by a host of impatient drivers.

'Perhaps governess is the incorrect term,' he declared

with thoughtful contemplation. 'Silvana Delrosso is many things. A distant cousin related to Nick by marriage, she is tutor, companion; the one woman constant in Annalisa's life since the death of her mother.'

'I see.' Did she? Silvana could be a martinet or an angel.

'Nick arrives tomorrow. I am sure you will get on well together.'

Heavens, she didn't know whether to be pleased or dismayed at the prospect. 'You should have said you were expecting guests,' she demurred, unsure now if her visit was convenient.

'Nonsense,' the older man reiterated at once, his pleasant features creasing with genuine concern. 'We are overjoyed for you to be here. Our home is large, with many rooms.' He reached out and took hold of her hand, enfolding it within his own. 'You must not think for one minute, one *second*, that your visit is ill-timed. We adore to have family around us.' His expressive eyes were eloquent in their sincerity. 'And you, sweet Emma, are special. You are the wife of our only grandson.'

She felt a lump rise in her throat, and she swallowed it convulsively. Then she leant forward and brushed her lips against his weathered cheek. 'Thank you.'

CHAPTER TWO

THE Martinero villa was large, nestling high against one of the many rolling hills that encompassed Tivoli. Set in spacious grounds and commanding a spectacular view, its neo-classical exterior had become mellowed with age. Scrupulously tended gardens, blooms ablaze with riotous colour abounded within symmetrical borders and sat like semi-precious gems against a green, velvet smooth-lawn. Shrubs were clipped with expert precision to retain a conic shape, and a fountain, complete with statuary and cascading water, graced the circular courtyard.

Emma slid out from the car and stood hesitantly as Enzo crossed round to her side, then together they moved forward and mounted the few steps leading to the main entrance.

Almost at once the solid double doors were flung open and she found herself drawn into a warm, welcoming embrace by Marc's grandmother.

Elegantly slim, Rosa Martinero possessed a sparkling vivacity that belied her age. 'Emma. Let me look at you.'

Held at arm's length for a few seconds, there was little Emma could do but offer a tremulous smile as kindly brown eyes searched her features in caring appraisal.

'I cannot believe you are actually here.' Rosa shook her head slightly and gave Emma an affectionate hug. 'And you are even more thin than when we last saw you.' She lifted a hand and lightly traced Emma's cheek.

'Come inside, my dear. It has been a long flight, hmm? Accustomed as I am to them, they are incredibly wearing. You will want to shower and change.'

The foyer was magnificent. Marble floors, cool painted walls displaying several exquisite works of art, and a central double staircase provided an impressive backdrop for a white three-tiered fountain, above which a sparkling crystal chandelier hung suspended in dazzling splendour.

'I have put you in the eastern wing,' Rosa conveyed as she led the way upstairs. 'It has a lovely aspect, and I am sure you will be comfortable there.'

'You have a beautiful home,' Emma declared sincerely as she was ushered into a generously proportioned room furnished with gracious rosewood pieces. A large four-poster bed was a focal point, furbished with dusky pink brocade, satin and lace. It was delightfully feminine and bore a slight air of granduer.

'Thank you, *cara*.' A twinkle gleamed in the older woman's eyes as she indicated a door to Emma's left. 'The villa may be old, but we have modern plumbing. Each guest room has its own bathroom.' She turned at the sound of a discreet knock on the outer door. 'Ah, here is Carlo with your luggage. Maria will unpack while you bathe, and afterwards you must come down to the *sala*. Lunch will be served in an hour.'

Alone, Emma extracted toiletries and fresh underwear, then she made her way into the adjoining bathroom. Sheer luxury, she decided as she filled the capacious spa-bath, adding bath oil with a delicate floral fragrance. It would be all too easy to close her eyes and drift into blissful sleep, letting the gently pulsing water soothe her tired body.

Fifteen mintues later she emerged into the bedroom with a towel fastened sarong-wise around her slim curves to discover the contents of her luggage reposing neatly on hangers in the wardrobe and in drawers of the delicately carved rosewood dressing-table.

Of Maria there was no sign, and Emma quickly donned clean underwear, then she selected a pale blue silk dress with a swirling skirt of tiny pleats and slipped it over her head, securing the zip fastener with ease. Sleeveless, it looked cool and fresh and showed her fine-textured skin to advantage. Make-up was kept to a minimum, and after pulling a brush through her hair she stood back, well pleased with her mirrored reflection.

A swift glance at her watch revealed it had been over half an hour since she'd begun her ablutions, and, stifling the sensation she should be retiring rather than dining, she turned and left the room.

It seemed for ever since she'd last slept in a bed, and as for *sleep*—a few hours of intermittent dozing aboard the plane could scarcely be termed adequate rest.

'Ah, there you are, my dear. I was just coming to fetch you.' Rosa's smile gentled as she slipped a hand through the younger girl's arm. 'I expect you could do with a drink. Enzo is waiting for us in the *sala* with Annalisa and Silvana.'

Together they descended the curving staircase and moved along a wide hallway whose walls were studded with beautiful tapestries.

Situated on the southern side of the villa, the *sala* was a large room with high ceilings and several french doors opening out on to a wide, balustraded terrace from which steps led down to a rectangular-shaped swimming pool. From this distance the tiled depths looked infinitely cool and inviting, Emma decided wistfully as she dragged her eyes back to the room. Casually furnished, it bore a light airiness that was enhanced by ceramic urns containing masses of leafy green foliage and indoor flowering plants.

'Emma, allow me to introduce you to my great-niece, Annalisa. And her governess, Silvana Delrosso.'

Dear heaven, the child was exquisite! A Botticelli angel! Emma smiled and gravely took the small hand extended in formal greeting.

'I am very pleased to meet you.'

'Hello, Annalisa.' Her voice held genuine warmth as she met solemn interest reflected in a pair of unblinking hazel eyes. The young girl looked more suitably dressed to model a junior *Miss Pears* soap commercial than to greet a distant relative all the way from Australia.

Dragging her eyes away, she met the carefully schooled features of the child's tutor and proffered a polite smile.

'Silvana.'

'Signora Martinero.'

Oh dear, she sounded rather austere, Emma decided involuntarily, wondering why Silvana insisted on formality when she looked to be only in her early thirties.

'Oh, please,' she demurred out loud, 'call me Emma.' Her smile widened as she glanced towards Rosa. '*Two* Signora Martineros in the same household can only lead to confusion.'

'May I call you Emma, too?' a young voice queried, and Emma was about to agree when Rosa inclined with accustomed gentleness,

'*Piccina*, I think it must be *zia*, yes?'

'But *you* are my *zia*,' Annalisa declared seriously.

'Cannot it be Zia Rosa, and Zia Emma?' Enzo suggested quizzically, and was the recipient of a solemn unwavering gaze.

'If you say so, *Zio*.'

Enzo leant forward and lightly touched the young girl's cheek. 'Perhaps we can let your *papa* decide, hmm?' He straightened and moved towards a lacquered cabinet. 'Now that everyone is here, we shall have some wine.'

Emma accepted a crystal goblet filled with Moselle and sipped it slowly, aware that its effect could be potent combined with jet-lag.

Lunch comprised a beef consommé, followed by a selection of cold meats and varied salads served with crunchy bread rolls, and a *compote* of fresh fruit for dessert. Emma sipped iced water between each course and joined in the conversation, becoming vaguely fascinated by Annalisa's exceptionally good manners. Behaviour so faultless in such a young child was laudable, but Emma couldn't help feeling it would have been more natural to glimpse a slight lack of restraint, although the reason was self-evident when, at the end of the meal, the young girl folded her napkin carefully and replaced it on to the table before politely requesting to be excused.

'Make ready for your siesta, Annalisa,' Silvana instructed with quiet authority.

'*Si*, Silvana.'

'*Yes*,' the governess corrected. 'It is luncheon, Annalisa. During which we speak English, do we not?'

'Yes, Silvana.'

Emma experienced a mixture of mild irritation and

barely contained surprise as she hastened to assure gently, 'You mustn't feel obliged to speak English solely for my benefit. My command of Italian is reasonably fluent.' Her eyes softened as she met Annalisa's solemn gaze. 'Do you learn English at school?' she queried with genuine interest. 'You speak it very well.'

'No, Zia Emma. We begin English next year. It is *Papa* who insists I must speak English and French. To practise, I speak French at breakfast, English at lunch, and Italian at dinner.' The round hazel eyes widened even further. 'Do you speak French?'

For heaven's sake! Annalisa's father and Silvana Delrosso would make a good pair, she decided wryly. 'I am able to comprehend a fairly extensive menu written in French,' she declared with a deprecatory shrug, then added with a smile, 'I shall have to be silent at breakfast, and only offer a Gallic *non* or *oui*—hopefully in the right places.'

Annalisa blinked twice, then offered with the utmost politeness. 'I could help you learn, if you would like to.'

Why, in the name of several sacred saints, did the child have to have lessons during the holidays? 'Thank you,' she acknowledged, not daring to glance at Rosa or Enzo. 'It's very kind of you, but I'd prefer to brush up on my Italian than attempt to learn a third language.'

'You may speak with Mrs Martinero tomorrow, Annalisa,' Silvana reproved firmly. 'Please go to your room.'

Emma felt her eyes drawn to the small, dark-blonde-haired figure, watching as the young girl obediently excused herself and walked from the room.

There was something poignantly *lonely* about the

child—never alone. Who, after all, she decided with a hint of cynicism, could be *alone* in a house filled with servants and doting relatives?

Unconsciously her eyes slid back to the table, and she glimpsed Rosa's eloquent gaze, then it was masked, and afterwards Emma wondered if she'd imagined it.

'Perhaps you'll excuse me?' She removed her napkin and placed it on the rich damask. 'I'm very tired, and I'd like to rest for a few hours.'

'Of course,' Rosa acceded at once, her kindly expression softening with sympathy. 'You must telephone your parents.' She spared a glance at her watch. 'Just before dinner, I think. Then it will be morning in Australia.'

It was a relief to escape, and when Emma reached her room she closed the door and sank down on to the bed, tired to the point of exhaustion.

Slipping off her shoes, she eased the counterpane to one side, then lay down. The pillow was soft, the mattress seeming to mould itself to her slight weight. Her eyes felt weary, almost gritty with tiredness, and she closed them in a gesture of self-defence.

It would be dark and cold in Sydney, the city's streets slick with winter rain. Quite suddenly she wished she was back there, in her parents' home and in her own bed.

When Emma woke there was light filtering through the drapes, a faint stirring of movement as the silken folds parted beneath the slight breeze wafting in through the open window.

Emma blinked slowly, disorientated by her surroundings for a few scant seconds until memory surfaced. Just how long had she been asleep, for heaven's sake?

A knock at her door was immediately followed by entry into the room by a young woman carrying a tray, and Emma looked at her with dawning dismay. It couldn't be *morning*, surely?

'*Buon giorno, signora.*'

A hollow groan left Emma's lips as she struggled into a sitting positon and took the tray.

'Zia Emma? May I come in?'

A smile widened Emma's generous mouth as she caught sight of Annalisa standing anxiously just inside the doorway. 'Of course.' The little girl looked perfectly groomed from head to toe, her gleaming hair caught with a ribbon each side of her face.

'Zia Rosa said I could come and tell you that breakfast will be ready in an hour.' Her forehead creased with earnestness at the importance of her mission. 'We thought you would be hungry, so that is why Maria has brought croissants to have with your coffee.'

'*Scusi, signora.*' Maria poured steaming, aromatic liquid into a cup, then moved quickly from the room.

Croissants and a choice of three fruit conserves. Emma broke one and spread it with plum jam, then took an appreciative sip of coffee. Absolutely delicious.

'Will you have some with me?' She proffered a portion to Annalisa, who looked doubtfully unsure. 'One mouthful won't spoil your appetite.'

'*Papa——*'

'Isn't here to object,' Emma declared quietly. The more she thought about Annalisa's father, the more she was disinclined to meet him. An austere businessman too immersed in financial pursuits to bother about his daughter wasn't an appealing prospect.

'*Papa*,' Annalisa persisted hesitantly, moving a step further towards the side of the bed, 'and I often share breakfast together when I am not in school.' Her eyes were incredibly solemn. 'Sometimes,' she paused, as if imparting a secret, lowering her voice until it was scarcely more than a whisper, '*Papa* gives Silvana the day off, and we go on a picnic.'

'Really?' Emma tried hard not to smile at such a revelation, for the vision of father and daughter indulging in such frivolity was difficult to comprehend. 'That sounds like fun.' She broke off the end of a croisssant and spread it with strawberry jam, then offered it to the young girl. 'If I eat any more, I won't have room for breakfast.' Pushing the near-empty plate to one side, she sipped what remained of her coffee.

'You will want to shower and dress,' Annalisa stated, taking a few backward steps, and Emma nodded in silent agreement.

'I won't be long.'

As soon as the door closed she pushed the covers aside and slid from the bed. In the adjoining bathroom she reached into the shower recess and turned both crystal knobs, then she quickly slipped out of her dress and stepped beneath the warm spray of water.

Twenty minutes later she was dressed in a pale honey-coloured sleeveless dress with a scooped neckline and slim-fitting skirt. A wide leather belt skimmed the top of her hips, accentuating her small waist, and she slid her feet into low-heeled soft leather sandals before crossing to the dressing-table to tug a brush through her hair in an attempt to restore some kind of order to the curling tresses. Making-up came last, and she patted a light dusting of powder over a thin film of moisturiser, added a touch of clear pink gloss to her lips, then she turned and left the room.

Despite the relatively early hour, the heat of the sun was beginning to make itself felt as it streamed in through the high-sashed windows and open french doors, fingering the marble floors with bright, geometrically patterned light.

Various beautiful antique pieces bore a rich patina from years of loving care, and there were freshly cut flowers arranged in numerous vases at every turn.

Emma's footsteps slowed almost to a halt as she admired the soft-brushed pastels of a misty Monet, and an equally superb Renoir nearby.

'You are interested in art, *signora*?'

She turned slightly at the sound of a feminine voice and met Silvana's carefully assembled features.

'From a purely aesthetic viewpoint,' she concurred, wondering why she should sense a faint feeling of antagonism emanating from Annalisa's governess. Surely it had to be the result of her overly sensitive imagination?

'I favour Picasso, or the tortured Van Gogh. So much brilliance and flair.'

It depended whether she meant the former at his conventional or flamboyant best, and Emma merely inclined her head in silent acknowledgement.

'I believe Signora Martinero has instructed breakfast to be served on the terrace.'

Minutes later Emma walked through wide-open french doors leading from the *sala* and was greeted with hearty enthusiasm by Enzo, followed by a warmly affectionate hug from Rosa.

'You slept well? Ah, let me look at you. Yes, better, much better.' Enzo pulled out a chair and motioned her to take a seat. 'Orange juice?'

He filled a glass and handed it to her, then resumed his position at the head of the table, content to leave the serving of food to Rosa.

Numerous covered platters reposed on a mobile trolley, together with a steaming pot of coffee, and after refusing a variety of tempting hot dishes Emma settled for a small serving of muesli, followed by toast and coffee.

Silvana studiously monitored Annalisa's fare, insisting on a nutritional balance with muesli, soft-boiled egg and toast, together with a glass of milk.

'It is a beautiful day, so warm already,' Rosa intimated with a charming smile. 'After breakfast you might like to use the pool.' Her gaze shifted towards Annalisa, and her eyes softened. 'Perhaps you could entertain Zia Emma this morning. Would you like that?'

'Oh, *yes*!' The young girl's elated agreement made Emma smile. 'If Silvana has nothing planned,' she ventured hesitantly, her expression assuming diffident solemnity.

'Very well, you have my permission.'

Annalisa's eyes shone. 'Thank you.'

'I will be in my room attending to correspondence, if you should need me.' Silvana declared, cautioning her young charge. 'Try not to chatter too much, or bother Mrs Martinero with too many questions.'

'Yes, Silvana,' Annalisa responded meekly, and immediately the governess was safely indoors she finished her milk and sat almost breathlessly still, her hazel eyes round with barely suppressed excitement.

Emma didn't have the heart to dally over a second coffee, and some ten minutes later she traversed the wide steps leading down towards the pool with Annalisa close by her side.

'Tell me what it is like in Australia, Zia Emma. Is it true there are cattle stations with thousands of acres?' Her young face was alive with curiosity.

'Millions,' Emma corrected softly. 'Some are so large it takes several stockmen weeks to inspect boundary fences.'

'Don't they use helicopters?'

'Sometimes. It depends on their financial status. Helicopters and planes used for aerial surveillance are expensive to maintain. Owners often prefer four-wheel-drive vehicles, trail-bikes, or stockmen on horseback.'

'I thought men who owned that much land must be rich!' Annalisa declared, clearly astounded, and Emma laughed.

'Not always. Severe drought can have a disastrous effect, and the farmer must manage to pay for feed and the men's wages. If the drought doesn't abate, as it sometimes doesn't for years, it becomes a vicious circle in the struggle to survive.'

'It doesn't rain for *years*?' Annalisa repeated incredulously.

'Some areas in the Outback haven't seen rain for up to seven years,' she replied solemnly.

'But what happens to all the cattle? So many must die.'

'Australia is a land of many contrasts, where the centre is mostly desert. Dark red sandy soil whose natural vegetation is mainly wild scrub and spinifex.' If she was going to impart an informal geography lesson, she may as well do it properly. 'There are goannas, which look like miniature prehistoric monsters, snakes and lizards, several species of kangaroo, together with the marsupial koala.'

'Where do you live, Zia Emma?'

'In Sydney. While not the capital, it is certainly Australia's largest city,' she explained quietly, aware they had skirted the white-painted balustrading surrounding the pool and were descending a set of stone steps leading down to a terraced garden.

'I have seen pictures of Sydney. It has a large bridge spanning the harbour, lots of tall buildings, and several bays and inlets. It looked pretty.'

'It is,' Emma agreed, visualising the city's landscape without any difficulty at all. 'The harbour is often host to various sailing craft all year round: yachts, cruisers. Most Australians adore the outdoor life—swimming, boating, surfing—sport of one kind or another.'

'Italy is beautiful, too. There are so many places to see,' Annalisa enthused, quite carried away with numerous plans of her own making. '*Papa* telephoned last night from Milan, just before I went to bed. He will be here soon; before lunch, I think.'

A faint fluttering of annoyance stirred deep inside her, then Emma dismissed such a feeling as totally uncharitable. After all, it had been she who had chosen the timing of her visit, not Rosa, and no blame could be attributed to Marc's grandmother. As Enzo had so charmingly pointed out, the villa was large enough to accommodate several guests, and although *she* was family, Rosa's nephew and his daughter were equally family and just as entitled to receive hospitality. Except, if she had known in advance, she would not have come. *Why?* an inner voice demanded. Annalisa is a delightful child, even if Silvana Delrosso appears rather stiff and unfriendly. If the truth be known, it was the imminent appearance of Annalisa's father, Nick—— A faint frown creased her forehead as she realised she didn't even know his surname, and a grimace momentarily twisted her lips. She didn't want to meet any eligible member of the opposite sex, for the simple reason she didn't feel equipped to deal with the consequences when projected charm was met with polite rebuff. The male ego was incredibly fragile, she'd discovered, unable to comprehend why a courteous rejection should elicit on most occasions such wounded reaction.

'I'm sure your *papa* will want a relaxing holiday,' Emma reiterated quietly, unwilling to dampen the young girl's enthusiasm by openly refusing the invitation to be included on any excursions.

'But he does relax,' Annalisa hastened to assure. 'He says to stay in one place and not be for ever boarding planes *is* relaxing—by comparison, that is.'

The vision of a jaded jet-setter sprang immediately to mind, and Emma wasn't sure she liked the projected impression. He probably had a number of mistresses in capital cities throughout the world, she decided dourly, while purporting to be a doting father on his own home ground.

'I think he would prefer to spend as much time with you as possible,' she demurred, only to hear Annalisa reassure quickly,

'But he *will* be with me. We will be together just the same if you are there, too. Except it will be better. Please,

Zia Emma. You will come, won't you?'

Oh dear! To be implored so eagerly was flattering, but nevertheless she was non-committal, tempering her words with a faint smile. 'I'll think about it.'

'If I ask *papa* to invite you, he will,' Annalisa declared with sureness, and Emma's expression assumed a certain wryness.

'And will you tell your father that you have already issued me an invitation, and convey that I might agree?'

The young girl's features became grave as she met Emma's questioning gaze. 'You think I would play each of you against the other in order to get my own way?'

Damn! Why did it have to prove so difficult to opt out of something she instinctively felt might be misconstrued? Seeking a change of subject she inclined an arm towards various statuary gracing the gardens, their symmetry enhanced by a stand of majestic pines. Every statue bore a graceful beauty, despite being weathered with age.

'Do you know whom they each represent?'

'Of course,' Annalisa answered politely. 'Silvanus is the first; he was the mythological god who protected forests, fields and gardens. It must be true, for the gardens here are very beautiful, are they not?'

Emma had to agree as she took in a variety of multi-coloured carefully tended flora. From brilliant reds to palest pink, with splashes of white, grown in beds banked between terraced paths leading down the gentle slope to the southern boundary.

It was hot, the sun's heat seeming to have intensified in the short time since they'd left the villa. With a rueful glance she caught sight of the slightly pink skin on her arms and knew that if she didn't seek the protection of sunscreen cream soon, she'd burn.

'Would you like to join me for a swim?' The thought of slipping into the pool's cool, sparkling depths held infinite appeal, and she was heartened by Annalisa's enthusiastic response.

'I was hoping you would ask. I don't enjoy swimming on my own. It's not nearly as much fun.'

By tacit agreement they turned and retraced their steps indoors, mounting the curved staircase together.

'I'll meet you downstairs in five minutes,' Emma suggested as she reached the door to her bedroom. 'OK?'

'OK.' Annalisa's dark eyes sparkled with anticipatory pleasure. 'I will tell Zia Rosa where we will be.'

In the bedroom Emma moved quickly across the room and pulled open a drawer, extracting a bikini in bright gold synthetic silk before tossing it to one side in search of the one-piece she'd packed on the spur of the moment. A *maillot*, it was simple but daringly cut, and black, flattering her pale skin—milk-white, she amended somewhat wryly several minutes later as she checked her appearance in the mirror. Picking up a short beach jacket, she slipped it on, caught up a towel, then she made her way from the bedroom.

The water was refreshing and deliciously cool, and she surfaced from a neat shallow dive to hear a splash close by as Annalisa followed her lead.

For more than an hour they alternately swam or floated atop body-length rubber cushions. Emma emerged to re-apply sunscreen cream to her body, then she slipped back into the water to leisurely stroke several lengths of the pool, deliberately pacing her own style to match that of Annalisa, who was making an admirable effort to keep up.

'I think I've had enough,' Emma vouched as she reached the pool's edge a few seconds behind her young companion. 'How about you?' She lifted a hand and smoothed water from her hair, wishing now she'd thought to wear an adequate cap instead of the silk scarf she'd tied round her hair.

'It was wonderful,' Annalisa enthused vivaciously, a wide smile almost stretching her mobile mouth from one ear to the other. 'I won! I really beat you, didn't I?' For a moment a faint frown clouded her attractive features. 'You didn't let me win, did you?'

'Now why would I do that?' Emma parried as she placed her hands on to the slate tiles and levered her body up in one fluid movement to sit on the pool's edge. Then she leaned forward and took Annalisa's outstretched hand and pulled her up to sit at her side.

'Because you are taller than me, and your arms are longer,' the young girl declared solemnly, watching with fascination as Emma untied the scarf and released her hair.

It sprang vibrantly free and with a faint grimace she squeezed the excess water out and pushed her fingers through its thickness in an attempt to restore a modicum of order.

'I'm also unfit,' she offered lightly, all too aware of the faint pull of muscles sadly out of tone. It didn't pay to remember that she'd been something of a fitness fanatic, loving to participate in several sports, particularly tennis, netball and aerobics. Marc had been equally avid, and they'd shared work-outs together, revelling in maintaining a physical peak. In the past year she hadn't played a single game of anything, although she'd resorted to gentle yoga exercises, preferring solitude against partnered competitiveness.

A faint sound alerted her senses, followed by the distinct chink of ice-cubes as a tray was set down on to the table behind them.

'Oh, good,' Annalisa sighed blissfully. 'Maria has brought us something to drink.'

Emma reached for a nearby towel as Annalisa scrambled to her feet, suddenly aware of a slight prickling sensation at the base of her neck as if some sixth sense had extended its antennae and become acutely attuned to an entity she had yet to recognise.

'*Papa! Qui arrivato!*'

The animated excitement in the young girl's welcome was explicit, and Emma registered a deep, slightly accented voice issue an affectionate paternal greeting in response.

She turned slowly, her gaze travelling towards a tall male frame standing several feet distant. Something about the dark slant of his head, his height, was vaguely familiar, and she lifted a hand to shade her eyes from the sum as Annalisa launched herself into his arms.

Aware that an introduction was imminent, Emma slid to her feet and reached for her beach jacket, unsure as she slipped it on why she should suddenly feel so reluctant to meet the man who was gently disentangling himself from his daughter's embrace.

'Zia Emma, this is my *papa*, Nick Castelli.'

Emma felt her eyes widen with shocked disbelief as she met his faintly mocking gaze, and her stomach lurched in sickening unison with the knowledge that the compelling stranger who had shared part of her flight less than thirty-six hours previously and Annalisa's father were one and the same.

CHAPTER THREE

'MR CASTELLI,' Emma acknowledged formally, unwilling to take his outstretched hand.

He was aware of her reluctance, damn him! It was there in his eyes, the faint, challenging gleam that dared she flout convention and refuse.

'I've heard so much about you,' she remarked with distant civility, placing her hand in his for a few brief seconds. The enveloping warmth of his clasp sent a slight charge of electricity tingling through her veins, and she snatched her hand back in angry confusion.

'Indeed?' His voice was silky-smooth beneath its veneer of musing indulgence, and for some unknown reason an icy frisson of fear slid stealthily down the length of her spine.

There was an elemental ruthlessness apparent beneath his sophisticated façade, a latent strength that was impossible to ignore. A man, she perceived with instinctive insight, who knew exactly what he wanted and pursued his objective with single-minded determination.

'Annalisa and Rosa have spoken of you with the highest regard,' Emma continued with deceptive coolness.

Why should she feel so *betrayed*, for God's sake? Because, a tiny voice whispered insidiously inside her brain, it was impossible to believe *chance* had anything to do with a Martinero nephew and a Martinero granddaughter-in-law sharing adjoining seats on the same long intercontinental flight. That was stretching coincidence a bit too far. Yet with whom could she lay the blame? Her parents, Marc's, Rosa? Nick Castelli for his complicity? It was inconceivable he had been unaware of her identity, for there were sufficient family photographs on display in various rooms within the villa, and a framed enlargement of Marc's wedding held pride of place atop a *chiffonier* in the *salone*.

'Should I be flattered?'

Resentment flared briefly as she met his steady gaze and saw the cool, assessing quality apparent, the strangely watchful element that bore distinct resemblance to a jungle animal at prey.

'Familial devotion is second to none,' Emma accorded with seeming lightness as she became aware of Annalisa's intense interest in their exchange.

'And therefore prejudiced,' he alluded with faintly mocking cynicism.

'I wasn't aware that that was what I implied.'

'No?'

Determination was responsible for the slight, almost winsome smile that widened her generous mouth. That, and a refusal to allow him to best her. 'I wouldn't presume to judge, Mr Castelli. I barely know you.'

A dark gleam momentarily lit his eyes, then it was gone. 'Perhaps we could walk back to the villa together. Rosa dispatched me to tell you that lunch will be ready in half an hour, and you will both need to shower and change.'

Emma had, perforce, to measure her steps with his as they moved up through the terraced gardens. Every instinct bade her break into a run and race as fast as her legs would carry her into the villa, up the stairs and into her room away from this man. Preferably, if it were possible, take flight on the first available jet out of Rome!

'*Papa*, what do you think? Should I call Emma, Zia Emma, or just Emma?' Annalisa queried, hurrying her words quickly together before he could answer, her voice sounding incredibly earnest. 'Zia Rosa does not mind, but Silvana says it should be Mrs Martinero.'

'Which does Emma prefer?' Nick Castelli countered, shooting his daughter a musing glance before shifting his attention to the subject of their conversation.

'Oh,' Annalisa hastened, 'Emma says I should ask *you*.'

'I see.' He sounded grave, as if he was giving the matter serious consideration. 'I imagine it should be Emma's decision,' he drawled at last, watching the play of emotions flit briefly across Emma's expressive features.

He would pass the ball into her court, wouldn't he? 'I prefer Emma,' she acceded quietly, although it was an effort to keep her voice steady.

'Oh, *good*,' Annalisa enthused, her face wreathing with a series of delighted smiles. 'These holidays are going to be such fun, are they not, *Papa*? We can take Emma to Naples, and have picnics together.'

Emma had serious doubts about such arrangements, and it was on the tip of her tongue to demur, except she was keenly aware that that was precisely what he expected her to do.

They reached the terrace, and with a murmured excuse she broke away and moved indoors.

In her room she showered and changed into a blue sleeveless dress whose soft, rolled neckline and flared skirt accentuated her slim curves and tiny waist. Make-up was confined to moisturiser and a touch of colour to her lips, and, despite a vigorous brushing, her hair sprang away from her head in a mass of wayward curls, affording Emma a faint grimace as she ran a final check on her appearance. Slim-heeled sandals in white leather completed the outfit, and with a quick glance at her watch she smoothed a shaky hand over her hair, then took a deep breath and made her way downstairs.

Lunch. Emma wasn't even hungry, and she could easily have existed on a piece of fruit instead of the beautifully presented three-course meal served in the *sala*.

As it was, she dutifully ate the avocado vinaigrette, forked a few mouthfuls of salad, declined the sliced ham and cold chicken and refused dessert.

Throughout the meal she became an interested spectator, aware that the image she'd conjured of a cold businessman too caught up with corporate wheeling and dealing to devote much time to his daughter was unfounded.

If she was honest, she'd *wanted* to find fault, a flaw that would give her a legitimate reason to dislike the indomitable man seated diagonally opposite her at the table.

Not that she needed a specific reason, for he represented most things Emma disliked in a man. He was too attractive and far too self-assured, with a degree of weary cynicism that was vaguely frightening. Dangerous, she amended. He undoubtedly ate little girls for breakfast! A sudden shiver feathered up from the base of her spine and she tensed her shoulders in order to suppress it. Somehow she doubted his penchant for feminine companions extended to *girls*; sophisticated socialites well versed in pleasing a man were more likely to be his style—the type he could love and leave with little or no commitment. To become involved with someone of Nick Castelli's calibre would be akin to attempting to tame a prowling tiger.

Heavens, what on earth was she thinking of? The last thing she needed was to foster imaginative speculation over any man, much less Rosa's and Enzo's formidable nephew. Yet, of its own will, her attention was continually drawn towards him as she became startingly aware of what he could represent to her peace of mind.

Annalisa's presence at the table provided a necessary distraction, for the young girl's pleasure was patently obvious, and even Silvana's occasional faint frown couldn't dampen her enthusiasm.

It was a relief when the last plate was removed, and Emma declined wine in favour of chilled water, sipping it slowly as Annalisa chattered with her father.

'Silvana is pleased with my results at school. Even Sister Margherita said I did very well. Didn't she, Silvana?'

Emma saw Silvana's lips tighten a fraction, then relax into a courteous smile. 'Indeed. However, your written French could do with some improvement, and there are a few factors of English grammar which you have failed to correctly grasp.' She turned her attention to Nick Castelli, and the subtle change in her expression, a softening that was meant to convey the depth of their long association was plainly evident. 'I have taken the responsibility of ensuring Annalisa does a few hours' study each day. I trust this meets with your approval?'

Annalisa appeared to be sitting on the edge of her seat, her expression one of unconscious pleading as she gazed at her father, and Emma waited with interest to see whose side Nick Castelli would take.

'Perhaps we could reach a compromise?' His voice was silky beneath the smile he projected. Smooth, yet denoting a will of tensile steel. 'As Silvana will be vacationing in Venice until the last week of the school holidays, I suggest studying be relegated until then. How does that sound?'

Annalisa clapped her hands together in delight. 'Thank you, *Papa*.'

'An excellent idea,' Rosa approved. 'Don't you think so, Emma?'

Oh lord, why involve me? Emma queried silently. Yet she was aware of Annalisa's intent air of expectancy, an eagerness for Emma to add her approval. 'Yes, of course.' She deliberately refrained from looking at Nick Castelli, although she sensed his gaze and forced her expression to remain serene. It still irked her that he'd known precisely who she was on that long flight, yet had chosen not to introduce himself. And if he had? What would have been her reaction?

'What plans do you have for tomorrow, *Papa*?' Annalisa began, her eyes sparkling with anticipation. 'Emma can come with us, can't she?'

'That would be nice,' Rosa interceded quickly. 'Silvana's flight leaves early in the morning. You could begin exploring the city itself, or take a picnic lunch into the hills. I have a few days planned for Emma, myself. Shopping, a few fashion showings at some of the famous design houses. Annalisa shall accompany us, if she wishes.'

'I shall be delighted for Emma to join us,' Nick drawled.

'How very kind of you, Mr Castelli.'

'Nicolo,' he corrected imperturbably, and she could have sworn there was an indolent gleam apparent in the depths of his eyes. 'My family and friends call me Nick.'

Her lashes swept up with complete lack of guile as she silently appraised his enigmatic expression, and his eyes held hers in mesmeric confusion, daring her to refuse.

For a moment she almost did, then she caught sight of Annalisa's anxious expression and she experienced a twinge of remorse.

'Really, Nick,' Silvana reproved. 'I am sure Mrs Martinero has plans of her own.'

'Why so formal?' He flicked his attention from one to the other and raised a quizzical eyebrow in Emma's direction. 'You can't want to be referred to as Mrs Martinero for the duration of your stay?'

It would be churlish to respond that she wanted to put up an impenetrable barrier and remain aloof from any extended friendship where he was concerned. Then a hollow laugh died in her throat at the mere thought. Nick Castelli would never be any woman's friend. Such an appellation was far too insipid! Somehow she doubted there was a woman alive who could fail to be aware of the powerful magnetism he exuded. And how did he regard his daughter's governess-companion? Were they bound together merely by virtue of being related, however distantly? Somehow she imagined Silvana retained an affection for her employer that wasn't motivated entirely by her position or connection to the family. Yet there was a resignation apparent and a degree of vague irritation, almost as if Silvana recognised she would never be anything to Nick Castelli other than Annalisa's tutor and companion.

'No,' Emma agreed, and incurred a long, level stare from Silvana.

'I am relieved,' Nick drawled.

'Shall we adjourn to the *salone*?' Rosa suggested. 'Then Maria can clear the table.'

It was an excellent excuse to escape, and Emma used it shamelessly. 'Would you mind if I went to my room and rested for an hour or two?' She still felt tired from the long flight, the dramatic climatic change, and the tension Nick Castelli was able to evoke without any seeming effort at all.

'Of course not, my dear. In fact, we always observe an afternoon siesta,' Rosa explained kindly as she stood to her feet and moved away from the table. 'The shops—everything, in fact, even the business sector—close at one, then re-open again at four, usually until eight.' She reached out and touched Emma's arm. 'Come downstairs whenever you feel like it. Dinner isn't until nine.'

A perfectly civil meal, Emma discovered, during which she ate little and allowed herself to be drawn into conversation with Rosa, Enzo and Annalisa. Nick Castelli she largely ignored, except when good manners demanded otherwise, and it was an immeasurable relief to escape to her room and blissful solitude.

'Please come with us, Emma,' Annalisa implored as she polished off the remainder of her toast and then proceeded to empty the milk in her glass. 'After we see Silvana's flight depart, we could go into the city. You could toss a coin into the Trevi Fountain.' Her eyes lit up with pleasure, and her mouth curved into the most beguiling smile. 'I am sure *Papa* would not mind if we visit some of the famous boutiques along the Via Condotti.'

It sounded tempting, although Emma wasn't sure Silvana would approve, or even if Nick Castelli seconded his daughter's invitation.

'I can see Annalisa has nothing less than the grand tour in store for you,' Nick drawled as he poured himself another cup of coffee, and Rosa added her support.

'I think it is a splendid idea.'

She would be perfectly safe, she determined, with Annalisa in tow. Besides, she really did want to explore, and who better to act as her guide than Nick Castelli?

'Thank you,' she acquiesced politely, blithely ignoring Silvana's faint frown.

Two hours later they set out in Nick's car, a sleek Ferrari Mondial, Emma noted with concealed admiration. Annalisa's animated chatter more than made up for any lack on the part of her governess, and Emma concentrated her attention on the passing scenery for the time it took to reach the airport.

After Silvana had departed, Nick steered them, at Annalisa's insistence, to a café for a thirst-quenching drink, then they drove into the city.

Together they walked at a leisurely pace until they reached the base of the Spanish Steps.

'They are French and Italian,' Nick informed as Emma centred her attention on the broad travertine steps. 'Not Spanish at all.'

The baroque staircase was crowded with lounging teenagers, vendors and souvenir-hawkers, and Emma bore their open admiration with vague embarrassment.

'You have gone pink,' Annalisa declared. 'All Italian men express their appreciation of a pretty girl,' she explained with a warm smile. 'You must not think anything of it.'

She felt Nick's light clasp on her elbow, and quelled an initial instinct to withdraw. Perhaps he sensed it, for his fingers tightened fractionally, and every nerve-end in her body quivered into vibrant life.

'There is the *Trinita dei Monte*,' Nick declared, directing her attention to the twin-belfried French church.

He didn't intimidate her, Emma assured herself, at least not in the accepted sense, yet it was almost as if there was a generation of electricity between them, creating its own shockwaves and pitching her into a state of confusion.

They wandered at will along the Via Condotti, where she looked with envy at Gucci's renowned leather emporium and lingered to admire the jewellery displayed in Bulgari's famed store.

She could have spent *days* just browsing, she decided, determined to return when there was more time. Rosa was sure to have included this glamorous area in one of her planned shopping excursions.

Lunch was a leisurely meal eaten in a pleasant *ristorante*, air-conditioned, Emma discovered much to her relief, for her skin felt flushed with the intense heat. Being plunged into a northern hemispheric summer after experiencing a cold winter in southern climes took some adjustment.

'What will you have, Emma?' Annalisa queried, openly delighted to be sharing her father's company. 'I will have pasta, I think. Their spaghetti is very good, isn't it, *Papa*?'

'Indeed it is,' Nick responded easily. 'Some wine,

Emma? Or perhaps you would prefer chilled mineral water?'

Alcohol in the middle of the day would go straight to her head, especially in this heat, and instinct warned she needed every faculty intact to deal with Annalisa's inestimable father!

'Mineral water, please, and a light garden salad.'

They had almost finished when Annalisa spared her father an imploring glance. 'Can we visit the Trevi Fountain this afternoon, *Papa*?'

Nick afforded her an indulgent smile, as with childish simplicity she set about lining up a number of possible outings that would easily take care of several days.

It was obvious they shared a close bond, but Emma suppressed a faint feeling of unease at the thought of spending so much time in Nick's company. Not that she wasn't grateful, she assured herself, just mildly resentful. Apprehensive, a tiny imp taunted.

'Why don't you invite Emma out to dinner tonight, *Papa*? She has come for a holiday, not to stay at the villa every evening.'

'Why not?' Nick responded before Emma had a chance to refuse.

Damn, she cursed silently. How did she get out of this one? Perhaps she could plead exhaustion, or an aversion to the day's heat, and decline?

It was late when they returned to the villa after a pleasant number of hours spent exploring the city's streets and *piazzas*, where, much to Annalisa's expressed delight, they tossed coins into the Trevi Fountain. Something, Annalisa assured fervently, she always did so that she would return next summer for a vacation with her adored Zia Rosa and Zio Enzo.

Nick brought the car to a halt outside the villa's entrance and Emma slid out, a polite few words of thanks hovering on her lips, followed, she determined, by a suitably regretful excuse not to dine with him.

'Will an hour be sufficient for you to shower and change?'

Her eyes flew to meet his, and she realised at once the subtle taunt beneath his query was meant to convey that he knew she intended to opt out if she could.

'Can I help you choose what to wear?' Annalisa begged, and as Emma glanced from father to daughter any words in excuse of the invitation died as she caught sight of the young girl's enthusiasm.

Afterwards Emma could only query her own sanity as she showered and attended to her toilette. Slipping into fresh underwear, she donned a silk wrap, then at the sound of a tentative knock she crossed to the door and welcomed Annalisa into the room.

'This cream frock, I think,' the youngster declared at last, after admiring the classic lines of an expensive Zampatti original. 'It's beautiful.'

'Are you sure?'

Annalisa's head moved in quick averment. 'Yes,' she declared seriously, watching with intense interest as Emma applied the finishing touches to her make-up.

It was fifteen minutes before they descended the staircase and entered the *salone* where Rosa and Enzo were sharing a pre-dinner drink with Nick.

He looked devastating in impeccable evening attire, Emma decided as she declined Enzo's offer of wine.

For some unknown reason she seemed to have developed a heightened sensitivity where he was concerned that confounded even her as she attempted to analyse its cause.

'Shall we leave?'

There was little she could do but bid Rosa and Enzo goodnight and thank Annalisa for her assistance. Except there was a vague flaring of resentment apparent at his high-handedness.

The Ferrari was parked immediately outside the main entrance, and Emma slid into the front seat whilst Nick crossed round the front of the car and slipped in behind the wheel. With a deft flick of his wrist he fired the engine, then eased the vehicle down the long, curving driveway.

As it paused momentarily at the gates he slanted her a dark glance. 'You are annoyed,' he remarked drily.

'At being railroaded into accepting an invitation I never wanted?' Emma parried, thrusting him an arctic glare. 'Did you expect me not to be?'

The car gathered speed with smooth precision, traversing the winding road with ease beneath Nick's competent expertise.

'I had thought you might enjoy seeing some of Rome's nightlife,' he declared silkily.

'*La dolce vita.*' She hadn't meant to sound quite so cynical, and he spared her a look that was infinitely mocking.

'That particular axiom has acquired a rather unsavoury meaning over the years. I had something more——' He paused.

'Refined?' Emma responded archly.

'In mind? You can be assured of it,' Nick declared and she proferred a smile that was a mere facsimile.

'What if I said I was feeling adventurous?'

'Are you?' There was no doubting his meaning, and Emma didn't dare look at him for fear of glimpsing the amusement she felt sure must be evident. Fool, she accorded wryly. Bandying words with Nick Castelli could only prove to be her undoing. Yet she was darned if she'd let him gain the upper hand.

'Not in the way you imply.'

'Pity.' He caught her outraged expression and offered a twisted smile. 'Relax, Emma. All I have in mind is the enjoyment of some fine wine and excellent cuisine in the company of an attractive companion.'

Relax? How could she *relax*, for heaven's sake? As urbane as he appeared, there was an animalistic sense of power beneath the sophisticated veneer, an inherent vitality that was arresting. Unleashed, whether in anger or passion, it would prove a force she felt ill-equipped to deal with.

'Why me?' she queried simply, sparing him a steady glance. 'I don't want to be entertained. I'd be more than happy to remain at the villa. Rosa and Enzo are delightful company.' Once she started, she couldn't stop. 'I'm sure you can't lack—amenable female companionship.'

'You expect me to deny it?'

'Not at all,' she responded evenly. 'I'm puzzled why you should waste your time.'

'With a woman who is the antithesis of amenable, hmm?'

'I don't want you to feel obligated in any way.'

'What gives you that idea?'

'It would be very easy for Rosa and Enzo to ask you to take pity on their grandson's widow,' she said stoically, and unbidden her chin lifted fractionally as she became aware of his deep, probing glance. 'I left Sydney to get away from over-solicitious family protectiveness.' Her eyes darkened with remembered grief. 'Two sets of parents who treated me like a piece of precious Dresden china, watching and analysing every move I made. I thought I was going to suffocate!'

Her outburst was greeted with silence; then, after what seemed an age, he voiced quietly, 'We are almost there.'

Emma took note of her surroundings, and was unable to contain her surprise. 'I thought we were going into the city.'

'I don't remember saying so.' He eased the car off the road and parked it close to a cluster of time-worn buildings. The pavement was filled with tables and chairs, pottery urns overflowing with flowering plants of various hues which, together with bright-checked tablecloths, green and white striped umbrellas, provided a colourful backdrop to what she identified as a small, bustling *trattoria*.

'I thought you would find it amusing to eat here. The food is extremely good, and the atmosphere informal and friendly.'

It was so different from what she had expected. Somehow she'd envisaged Nick Castelli choosing an elegant restaurant where the city's social echelon wined and dined in sartorial splendour.

'The chef excels with pasta—his *pasta al forno* cannot be bettered anywhere.' He slid out of the car and crossed round to open Emma's door, reaching forward to take hold of her arm as she stood to her feet.

Although it was quite early by Roman standards, there were several patrons seated and she was acutely conscious of their scutiny as she allowed Nick to lead her towards an empty table.

'They are admiring your hair and pale complexion,' Nick murmured with a faint smile, and her lashes lowered in a gesture of self-defence, aware that she provided a startling contrast to the tall, dark-haired man at her side.

'Would you like some wine? Or perhaps you'd prefer a *chinotto*?' he asked as soon as they were seated.

Emma chose the latter, for it was an innocuous beverage, not unlike Coca Cola, and very palatable. The chatter of voices mingled with music emitting from nearby stereo speakers, conspiring to provide a relaxing atmosphere.

'We should have brought Annalisa. She would have enjoyed it.'

His dark, gleaming gaze rested on her expressive features, and a smile tugged the edges of his mouth. 'Yes. However, my daughter considered I deserved to have you to myself.'

What would he say if she revealed she'd prefer Annalisa's company to his? Or at least be able to utilise the young girl's presense as a protective buffer. Sagely she declined to comment, and when they were each handed a menu she took time to study the selections and eventually ordered *pasta al forno* as a starter—only because she enjoyed it, she assured herself firmly, and not due to any recommendation Nick had accorded the dish. Electing to follow it with an individual tossed green salad, she declined dessert.

Nick joined her with the starter, decided on veal *parmigiana* as the main course, and opted for the cheese board.

Emma watched him surreptitiously as he took a measured sip of his wine, and wondered at her sudden lack of *savoir-faire*. There was something vaguely threatening about her companion, a quality she couldn't quite pin down, and it bothered her more than she was prepared to admit. Consequently she felt ill at ease and slightly on edge. There was no recollection, ever, of having been so acutely aware of a member of the opposite sex. It made her feel breathless, heightening the reality by monitoring every single breath she took, which was crazy. The act of breathing was an automatic reflex, for heaven's sake!

'You live in Milan, I believe.' The words were a civil attempt at conversation, a need to say something to fill an empty void, and it irked her that he knew she felt gauche in his company.

'My business interests are centred there.' A slight smile curved his sensuously moulded mouth, and one eyebrow slanted in quizzical amusement. 'Would you like a résumé of my life-style? It might save me answering endless questions.'

Her eyes widened slightly, and a delicate pink tinged her cheeks. 'It wasn't my intention to pry.'

'But you feel vaguely uneasy in my presence,' he persisted musingly. 'And aware of the need to indulge in polite conversation.'

There was a measurable silence, during which she fought to regain her composure, and she viewed the waiter's appearance with relief, glad to have something to do with her hands as she picked up her fork and began to eat.

'You speak English with very little accent at all,' Emma commented, more as an observation that from the need to determine the reason why.

'The result of a comprehensive education,' Nick told her lazily. 'I studied at universities in Milan and London.'

That would account for it, she allowed silently. 'I see.'

'Do you, Emma?' His smile held an element of mockery, and she looked at him carefully.

'What do you want me to say?' she replied quietly, hating his verbal thrust and parry.

'My business interests take me all over the world,' he enlightened her with a certain wryness. 'Despite the rapid advancement of electronic technology in assessing and relaying relevant data, there remains the necessity for personal negotiation.'

'And while you are flitting from one continent to another, Annalisa is well cared for in an educational institution during semesters and she has Silvana to fall back on in between.'

'You don't approve?'

He had finished his pasta and was leaning back in his chair with indolent ease as he sipped his wine.

'It isn't my business to approve or disapprove,' Emma declared evenly, biting into a slice of delicious garlic bread and following it with some *chinotto*.

'You do, however, show some interest in my daughter's welfare.'

She met his gaze with equanimity. 'Are you seeking my opinion, or simply stating an assumption?'

The arrival of the waiter precluded an immediate

answer, and she watched with detached interest as their plates were removed.

'You find it surprising that I might seek your opinion?' Nick drawled, and Emma's stomach gave a slight lurch as she recognised the faint cynicism apparent in his voice.

'If you genuinely want it,' she offered calmly, and watched as his mouth curved into a sardonic smile.

'Now why should you suppose otherwise?' His eyes became faintly hooded, and she could sense their brooding assessment.

It was difficult enough simply sharing his company, without being subjected to an analytical appraisal!

'Because I think you're playing a game,' she responded levelly. 'One in which you intend to amuse yourself at my expense.'

'You're sure of that?' The silkiness evident in his voice set her nerve-ends vibrating in instinctive alarm, despite his apparent indolence.

'Will you deny it?' she countered as she fearlessly met and held his gaze. Her fingers smoothed the napkin on her lap, unconsciously examining the stitched edge before curling into a tight ball.

'The summer holidays are long,' he reflected deliberately. 'During which I arrange to have several weeks free to spend with my daughter. Silvana accords that the process of learning is an ongoing occurrence, no matter how briefly or in what manner the lesson. Hence the adherence to a daily study period prior to my arrival in Rome. Once Silvana departs on her vacation I ensure Annalisa enjoys a relaxing break, and we spend most of the daylight hours together.' One eyebrow rose quizzically, and he queried tolerantly, 'Perhaps we should declare a truce, and begin again?'

'Or you could take me back to the villa.'

'And spoil what promises to be an enjoyable evening?'

'You might take pleasure in baiting me, but I find it distasteful.' She didn't really care if he took umbrage; he had no right to treat her as an interesting specimen and attempt a dissection.

Hidden laughter gleamed from the depths of his eyes, and she became so incensed she was tempted to hit him.

'Silence?'

He was amused, and she seethed inwardly as the waiter appeared with her salad and Nick's veal dish. The atmosphere between them must have been apparent, for the waiter looked momentarily startled as he set both plates down on to the table before he made an unobtrusive but hasty retreat.

The salad looked fresh and inviting, but if she ate one mouthful she would choke! Yet if she pushed it to one side the action would be tantamount to an admission of sorts, and she was darned if she'd give him that satisfaction. Instead she stabbed her fork into the crisp curl of lettuce, fervently wishing that it was Nick Castelli.

Studiously she avoided sparing him so much as a glance, although half-way through her salad she found the temptation unbearable and risked a covert peek beneath long, fringed lashes. To witness, even so briefly, his obvious enjoyment of his meal was sufficient to enrage her further, and at that moment he sensed her regard and levelled a glittering glance that left her in little doubt of his amusement at her antipathy.

Her eyes widened infinitesimally, then warred openly with his own, and it took considerable effort not to pick up her glass and toss the contents in his face.

As if aware of her train of thought, he held her gaze,

deliberately daring her to carry out her silent threat, yet managing to project just what form his retribution would take if she did.

A sudden chill invaded her veins, slipping like ice through her body and cooling her temper. God, what was the matter with her? She had to be mad to even contemplate tangling with him. He seemed curiously intent on unsettling her, arousing anger and a latent animosity she had never even known she possessed.

With a trembling hand she pushed her plate to one side and pretended an interest in their fellow patrons, hearing the quick, fluid chatter, the muted laughter, yet barely registering it as she let her gaze rove sightlessly from table to table.

For one wild moment she considered getting to her feet and walking away, hailing the first taxi that came along and instructing the driver to take her back to the villa. However, such an action would be childish, and she doubted Nick Castelli would permit her such an easy escape. In any case, the evening was still young, and how would she explain to Rosa that she'd chosen to return alone?

It took all her will-power to remain seated in her chair and continue evincing a preoccupation with her surroudings. A lump rose up in her throat, and she swallowed it painfully. It isn't fair, she raged silently. *He's* not being fair. Yet how could she expect a man like Nick Castelli to play by her rules? He was a force unto himself; indomitable and obdurate. If he wanted something, he'd permit no obstacle to stand in his way. Yet what *did* he want? Her companionship for Annalisa in the absence of Silvana? Somehow that answer appeared too simple.

The nerves in her stomach activated themselves and twisted into a palpable knot, pulling cruelly as her emotions began to shred and the pain became a harsh reality that was impossible to ignore.

'Coffee?'

The sound of Nick's voice made her jump, and she missed his narrowed gaze as she kept her head averted.

'No, thank you.' She'd never be able to hold the cup, let alone drink its contents!

The evening dusk had slowly diminished, leaving a velvet sky studded with minuscule far-away stars. Coloured lights suspended at regular intervals provided adequate illumination, and candles flickered inside their ballooned-glass containers on each table.

The long, light, evening hours were difficult to assimilate, together with the continental habit of dining late. The numerous restuarants and bars probably didn't close until three or four each morning!

Emma's thoughts wandered idly to her parents, and she wondered if they were missing her as much as she missed them. The past twelve months had been harmonious, yet at twenty-four she could hardly expect to remain living at home indefinitely. It had been a refuge, a sanctuary where she'd voluntarily given herself into their protective custody, grateful to be shielded from the harsh aftermath of Marc's tragic accident. Perhaps when she returned to Sydney she should think seriously about getting her own apartment.

'Tell me about yourself.'

The soft query startled her, and it took considerable effort to look at him. Only a modicum of good manners was responsible for an attempt at civility, although the words emerged stilted and husky.

'I imagine Rosa and Enzo have already supplied you with a number of pertinent details.'

She saw his eyes darken fractionally, then assume inscrutability.

'Don't be so defensive. It isn't my intention to elicit information you are not prepared to divulge freely.'

'No?' Oh, this was impossible! Here she was, ready to put a cynical connotation on every word he uttered. Drawing a deep breath, she expelled it slowly, then began with contrived politeness, 'I grew up in Sydney, attended private schools, took dancing and music lessons, played tennis in summer and netball in winter. During my mid-teens I developed an interest in co-ordinating fashion accessories with designer garments, and eventually made it my career.'

Nick regarded her silently for several long seconds. 'You have never travelled before?'

'My parents presented me with a return air ticket to London for my twentieth birthday. It was a gift to mark the end of my education, and, they insisted, for being a model daughter.'

A faint gleam of amusement lightened his dark gaze. 'I see. Despite auburn tresses, there were no teenage tantrums, no rebellion against parental authority?'

'We had a few differences of opinion,' Emma allowed. 'But the ground rules were fair, and I saw no reason to thwart them.'

'No boyfriends other than Marc?'

Perhaps she should have been prepared for it, but the query temporarily robbed her of breath, and her lashes fluttered, then lowered, creating a protective shield from his scrutiny.

'When we were young, he was the brother I never had.

We did everything together,' she revealed slowly, hating his imperturbable probing.

'And fell in love.'

Her eyes closed with momentary pain. 'Yes.'

There was a long silence, one that became increasingly difficult to break. Perhaps she should ask a few questions of her own, create an about-face and re-open a few of *his* wounds.

'What of your wife?' She had wanted to hurt as she'd been hurt, but there was no relish in her statement, no demand for his explanation.

'Anna died from a complication associated with Annalisa's birth. She never left the hospital.'

He'd had nine years to recover from the loss, and there was the living bonus of his daughter. Emma had nothing.

'You've never sought to provide Annalisa with a mother?'

He took his time answering, and for a few minutes she thought he wasn't going to; then a wry smile tugged the edge of his mouth.

'One must first find the right woman to marry,' he declared with thinly veiled mockery, and she held his gaze without any difficulty at all.

'Somewhere among the countless number of eligible females beating a path to your door there must be a sincere soul who will love you for yourself and not your worldly possessions.'

'I'm working on it,' Nick drawled, and she effected a faint grimace.

'And enjoying the process of elimination.'

'Are you suggesting I should not?'

His cynicism struck an antagonistic chord, causing her to employ unaccustomed flippancy. 'I hope you've assured whichever young woman I've supplanted this evening that your position as my escort is merely an obligatory duty.'

For a brief second Emma thought she glimpsed anger in the momentary hardening of his eyes, then it was gone, and he leaned well back in his chair to regard her with deceptive indolence.

'I am answerable to no woman.' The words were soft, yet beneath the silk was tensile steel.

Naturally, she agreed silently. There probably wasn't a woman alive who could tame him.

'Perhaps if you've finished your coffee, we could go home,' Emma ventured quietly. 'We've enjoyed a pleasant meal, but it's quite late, and——'

'You need your beauty sleep,' Nick intervened imperturbably.

'Yes.'

'As well as a number of hours in which to fortify yourself against my presence tomorrow,' he added sardonically, and she offered him a brilliant smile.

'Ah, but Annalisa will be with us.'

His eyes gleamed with hidden laughter as he collected the bill and extracted his wallet. 'And her company is infinitely preferable to mine, hmm?'

'I won't answer that.'

He got to his feet and beckoned the waiter, handing over a generous tip—if the man's almost obsequious gratitude was any indication. Then he lightly clasped her elbow and escorted her out to the car.

The drive home was achieved in less than fifteen minutes, and once within the electronically controlled gates he negotiated the driveway and slid the car into the garage situated at the rear of the villa, taking the furthermost bay from a gleaming Alfa Romeo, a Porsche and a functional Fiat.

There was a path leading to a side entrance into the villa through a rose garden, and Emma made her way towards it as Nick secured the garage doors.

Electric lanterns provided a soft, illuminating glow, and the trees lining the boundary seemed to loom incredibly tall in the enshrouding darkness.

A faint prickle of apprehension shivered through her slender frame at the almost eerie stillness, and she wondered if there were spirits of a past civilisation haunting the grounds. Fanciful thinking, she dismissed in self-admonition.

A touch on her arm caused her to jump imperceptibly, and she offered little resistance as Nick fell into step at her side. His nearness was protective, yet she was supremely conscious of him, aware of the faint aroma of his aftershave in the clear evening air, his sheer masculinity and the threat he posed to her equilibrium.

The walk was an incredibly short one, and she released an inaudible sigh as he reached out and unlocked the door.

'Would you care for a nightcap?' he queried as they reached the main hallway. The wall sconces were all alight, but she couldn't detect any sound. 'I doubt Rosa and Enzo will have retired.'

'I'd prefer to go straight to bed,' she declined, unwilling to prolong the evening any further. 'Thank you for taking me to dinner.'

He reached out a hand and trailed his forefinger down the length of her nose. 'Spoken like a well behaved child.'

To stand here like this was madness, and she took a backwards step as he bent his head to bestow a fleeting kiss to her lips; light as the brush of a butterfly's wing, yet it released a flood of warmth that slowly swept through her entire body.

'Ah, there you are! We were about to go upstairs,' Rosa's voice intruded, and Emma looked stricken, her eyes widening with a mixture of guilt and remorse.

For a few timeless seconds she'd been enmeshed in an irresistable pull of the senses, without thought to anything except the moment.

'We have just this minute arrived,' Nick announced smoothly, turning slightly so that his frame provided a partial shield.

Emma took a deep, calming breath and attempted to present a relaxed, smiling façade as she stepped forward. 'It was a lovely meal,' she imparted quietly. 'Nick was right, the food was delicious.' She spared him a quick glance, then she moved forward to touch her lips lightly to the older woman's cheek. 'Goodnight, I'll see you at breakfast in the morning.'

She moved quickly towards the stairs, and had to refrain from running up them as if a hundred demons were chasing at her heels.

It wasn't until she was safely in her room with the door closed behind her that she slumped in a heap on to the bed and buried her face in her hands.

She couldn't be susceptible to Nick Castelli! It was simply a natural feminine reaction to a very attractive man. Even as the thought surfaced, a hollow laugh rose and choked in her throat. There had to be a logical reason for the way she was feeling, yet the only one she recognised had its roots buried in the most base of human needs. Up until now she had thought sex and love went hand in hand; inseparable entities that became entwined in the sexual act itself.

Perhaps, she decided with a sense of desperation, the deep, aching void she experienced could be attributed indirectly to a need for what she had tragically lost.

However, it wasn't Marc's face that clouded her vision, and that seemed to be the ultimate sin.

In a daze she rose to her feet and crossed to the dressing-table. The drawer slid out smoothly, and she extracted a framed photograph. The laughing, boyish face stared back at her, the wide-spaced, bright eyes so alive, his mouth parted in an affectionate, teasing smile.

It was only an image on celluloid. Marc belonged in the past, where perfection ruled, and the present was part of a horrid nightmare.

With careful fingers she placed the frame on the pedestal beside her bed, then she discarded her clothes and slipped between cool percale sheets to lie staring at the ceiling until sedative-induced sleep lulled her into merciful oblivion.

CHAPTER FOUR

DURING the following days, Emma didn't know whether to be pleased or irritated by the number of sightseeing excursions suggested by Annalisa and indulgently fostered by Nick. Certainly she was grateful for their company and factual knowledge as they visited the Sistine Chapel, the Vatican Museum, the Roman Forum and the Colosseum. All were steeped in history, and there was a natural awe in treading such hallowed ground.

There were also scenic trips by car which inevitably included a picnic lunch or a meal eaten at a convenient *trattoria* en route.

Annalisa was a delight, her laughter warm and infectious, regarding everything with such natural enthusiasm it proved to be increasingly difficult for Emma to refuse Nick's continued hospitality. Even Rosa unknowingly aided Annalisa's collusion by developing a mild virus which kept her indoors and thus delayed her own plans to escort Emma to a number of fashionable boutiques.

As for Nick, he was the perfect host and companion; amusing, informal, and Emma found him increasingly impossible to ignore. No matter how she tried to convince herself she was immune to his particular brand of masculinity, each passing day brought an elevated awareness that was positively maddening.

That he *knew*, angered her unbearably, and it was

almost the final straw when, at the conclusion of one breakfast in the second week of her stay, Annalisa excused herself from the table and went in search of a clutch of brochures from which to plot out the day's outing.

'I really can't continue to impose on you like this,' Emma ventured, and incurred his dark, steady glance before he picked up his cup and drained what remained of his coffee.

'My dear Emma, how can your company be an imposition? Besides, think how disappointed my daughter will be if you don't come with us,' he remarked musingly. 'Tomorrow you are to visit some of the city's famed fashion houses with Rosa,' he reminded with unruffled ease. 'Annalisa will have to make do with me, so why not indulge her today?'

His gaze was level, yet his eyes held latent amusement and an element she was unable to define. Damn him, she cursed beneath her breath. He was steadily infiltrating her life, placing her in an increasingly invidious position, where to refuse made her seem exceedingly rude and ungrateful. And he had supposedly innocent assistants in his subterfuge, for if it wasn't Rosa urging her to accept, Annalisa was the mastermind of all matchmakers!

'I would be quite happy to spend the day here, and swim,' she said evenly.

'Is it your intention to be contrary?' His deep, husky laugh was almost her undoing, and she shot him a look of mild antipathy.

'You flatter yourself if you think I sit here quivering at the mere thought of your invitation.'

'*Quivering*, Emma? What an evocative thought,' Nick

mused with a degree of cynicism, then he added softly, 'You sound almost afraid. Are you?'

'Of course not,' she retorted swiftly. Yet deep inside she wasn't so sure. *Damn him!* Who did he think he was, for the love of heaven? Then a hollow laugh rose in her throat. He knew exactly who he was. Not only that, his every action was calculated with implacable precision.

Her eyes slid over his broad shoulders, down to his tapered waist, noting the lean hips, the forceful thrust of muscled thighs beneath the fine material of his trousers. Just by looking at him she could almost feel again the touch of his mouth on hers and, as if possessed of some diabolical form of mental telepathy, he caught her eyes and held them, his gaze steady, missing nothing as they swept her expressive features.

The mere sight of him stirred her senses, reawakening the seeds of desire, and she experienced a feeling of shocked disbelief at the wayward trend of her thoughts. Perhaps it was the aura of power which surrounded him, an elemental magnetism that combined self-assurance and latent sexuality; a dramatic mesh of male charisma that was infinitely dangerous.

'Shall we endeavour to get away about eight-thirty?'

His voice was a mocking drawl, and she was darned if she'd meekly comply. Unbidden, the germ of an idea took root in her mind, and she directed him a look that appeared completely without guile.

'Very well, if you insist.' Her eyes assumed a deep tawny hue. 'Will you mind if I browse among some of the boutiques and shop for clothes? A devilish imp prompted her to offer him a singularly sweet smile. 'You'll probably be bored to death.'

'Annalisa, however, will be in her element,' he responded lazily, and without a further word she rose to her feet and made her way upstairs to change into suitable attire, hollowly aware that she had been defeated.

Three hours later his arms held a variety of multi-coloured packages and carrier-bags, and the sight of such an obviously masculine man thus encumbered brought forth a devilish smile.

'Are you suffering?'

'Wasn't it your intention that I should?'

That he was aware of her perversity merely made her determined to prolong the shopping expedition. 'I haven't finished yet,' she declared blithely as she caught sight of a shop displaying exquisite lingerie. 'Perhaps you'd prefer to wait outside. I won't be long.'

One eyebrow rose with quizzical mockery. 'Why should you imagine I will be embarrassed? The female form adorned in such wispy fripperies holds no surprises for me.' His eyes gleamed with merciless humour. 'You may even appreciate my opinion.'

Before she had the opportunity to demur he moved into the shop, utilised deliberate charm with the young assistant, then proceeded to indicate a selection of garments which he considered flattering—for Emma, as well as Annalisa.

It left her feeling helplessly angry, although she had no intention of letting him guess he'd got beneath her skin.

'Shall we deposit these in the car, then find somewhere to have lunch?' Nick suggested blandly when they emerged out on to the pavement.

'Yes, please, *Papa*. I am *hungry*,' Annalisa agreed with alacrity.

Food. Now that she gave it some thought, she was ravenous. Besides, the heat was beginning to have an enervating effect, and the thought of walking the city's streets no longer held any appeal, especially as everything would soon close for the afternoon.

'Thank you.' She even managed a faint smile.

Nick chose a charming *ristorante* and ordered wine while Emma perused the menu, selecting after very little deliberation a portion of *lasagne* which, when it duly arrived, proved to be utterly delicious.

'I adore the dress you bought,' Annalisa enthused as she forked pasta into her mouth. 'I can't wait until I am old enough to wear something like that.'

'A few years yet, *piccina*,' Nick commented indulgently, and Emma offered the young girl a sincere smile.

'You'll knock all the boys for six,' she assured her gently, adding with a touch of humour and a quick glance towards the man at her side, 'and doubtless give your father a few extra grey hairs in the process.'

'Do you think so?' Annalisa asked, clearly intrigued.

'About the grey hairs? Assuredly,' concluded her father wryly.

'I have just had a wonderful idea. Why don't you take Emma out to dinner tonight?' Her eyes sparkled with youthful enthusiasm and the sureness of one who is convinced of success. 'Emma could wear her new dress.'

'Why not, indeed?' Nick concurred smoothly, and Emma met his gaze, her eyes cool and infinitely clear.

'Perhaps we should first check with Rosa? She may have made plans which include us.'

Rosa hadn't, and expressed delight that her godson intended escorting Emma to dinner—so much so that, between Rosa and Annalisa, Emma didn't stand a chance.

The calf-length dress in deep turquoise silk-textured fabric possessed a pin-pleated skirt which floated softly with every movement she made, while its camisole-styled bodice with twin shoestring straps over each shoulder lent emphasis to her slim curves and accentuated the delicate glow of her skin. Slim-heeled gold evening sandals, a gold chain at her throat and matching bracelet at her wrist added understated elegance, and to complete the outfit she added a silk beaded evening jacket in matching turquoise. The whole effect was stunning, and she stood back, pleased with her mirrored image.

Nick was waiting in the lounge, a crystal tumbler in one hand, looking the epitome of male sophistication in a dark superbly tailored evening suit, pale blue shirt and a black bow-tie. He exuded more than his fair share of raw virility, and Emma felt her pulse-beat quicken and begin an erratic, hammering tattoo.

'This is becoming something of a habit,' she declared almost ten minutes later as Nick eased the Ferrari through the impressive gates guarding entrance to the villa.

'Hardly that. This is only the second occasion we have dined out in the evening. Most nights have been spent at the villa in the company of Rosa, Enzo and Annalisa, have they not?' he queried smoothly.

It was true, for she had enjoyed the family atmosphere generated by Rosa and Enzo, the games of cards and the lengthy discussion over a leisurely meal.

'Where are we dining?' she queried lightly.

'I've reserved a table at a restaurant on the *Piazza Navona*,' Nick informed, concentrating on urging the car through the flow of traffic. 'Parking within walking distance will be almost impossible, and the attempt merely time consuming. Hence the need for a taxi for a minimum few kilometres.'

The establishment he'd chosen was well patronised, its décor steeped in traditional elegance, and the service they were accorded held the impressive deference normally reserved for the rich and famous.

'You come here often.' It was an observation, never a query, and his answering smile held a touch of cynicism.

'Whenever I am in Rome, yes,' he conceded, and she felt a tingle of pink colour her cheeks that he might have guessed her thoughts. 'The chef treats the preparation of food with practised artistry, hence the result is always a gastromic delight.'

'You are an obvious connoisseur,' she commented drily, and incurred his dark, slanting glance.

'Food, specifically, of course,' he drawled with hateful mockery.

'Naturally. Although I don't doubt such superiority extends to every sphere,' she offered sweetly, and caught the gleam of silent laughter in the depths of his eyes.

'Especially of women. Isn't that what you meant to imply?'

She met his gaze unflinchingly. 'Perhaps I find it difficult to believe you would accord entertaining the widow of a distant relative anything but a boring duty.'

Now he did laugh, a mocking, husky chuckle that hit an exposed nerve and made her feel vaguely uncertain.

'Boring, Emma? How could an enchanting auburn-haired young woman whose golden cat's eyes hide a multitude of emotions be regarded as anything other than intriguing?' An eyebrow lifted in quizzical query, and she was unable to suppress the tingle of electricity that filtered through her veins.

'Don't regard me as a challenge, Nick.' For some reason she felt like a butterfly caught in a trap, and unsure whether fate would be kind or cruel. Her eyes swept to meet his, widening measurably at his unwavering regard.

'Relax,' he bade silkily. 'I have no intention of harming so much as a hair on your beautiful head.'

If only she could believe him! He possessed an elemental charisma to which most women would be attracted, as a moth to flame, perhaps uncaring that such captivating appeal could lead to their own destruction.

'Have some wine,' he coaxed quietly, and she obediently lifted the fluted goblet to her lips and savoured its contents, glad of the slow warmth that crept soothingly through her body.

'Shall we order?' Nick inclined smoothly. 'I suggest *fettucini al funghi* as a starter, followed by breasts of chicken in a delicate honey and almond sauce. I prefer salad, but there is a choice of hot vegetables available.'

It was at least an escape to pretend an interest in the menu, and despite a fondness for mushroom sauce with pasta she elected to settle for spaghetti *marinara* with a salad to follow.

If he perceived her selection as a small act of defiance he made no comment, and merely sipped his wine, while

Emma let her gaze skim round the room with seeming fascination.

'Annalisa has persuaded me to coach her at tennis tomorrow while you are out with Rosa, followed by a swim in the pool.'

His lazy smile was warm and reached his eyes, and she said with total sincerity, 'Annalisa is a delightful child.'

'Yes. We are very close.'

The pasta was delicious, and she forked it into her mouth with practised ease. She was no stranger to Italian-style food, for Marc's mother was an excellent cook and Emma had shared Sunday dinner with Marc and his parents for almost as long as she could remember.

'*Caro!* How wonderful to see you.'

Emma turned slightly and caught sight of a stunning brunette who looked as if she'd just stepped out from between the pages of *Vogue*. Tall and superbly slender, her dress was a Dior original. Diamonds studded each earlobe, a matching choker graced her neck, and her classical features portrayed a flawless skin exquisitely adorned with skilfully applied make-up. Perfume, easily identifiable as Dior's *Poison*, exuded from her body in a soft, wafting cloud.

It was obvious she exulted in being the focus of attention. Also apparent was her adoration of Nick, for her eyes swept over him with thinly veiled hunger before swinging back to the man at her side.

Emma let her gaze drift as Nick stood to his feet and performed introductions with sophisticated ease.

'Danielle, my cousin Vincenzo. Emma Martinero.'

Danielle Fabrese. Emma wondered why visual recognition of the internationally famous model hadn't been synonymous, then it registered. The hairstyle. Previously shoulder-length and worn in a contrived windblown look, the model's tresses were now much shorter and cut to give her delicately boned face an elfin appearance.

'You have no objection if we join you?' The query was delivered with deliberate coquetry and gave Nick little opportunity to refuse as Danielle instructed a hovering and obviously enamoured waiter to increase the seating arrangements by two.

'Vince, order more wine, *piacere*,' the model implored with a faint, pouting smile. 'I am thirsty.'

'Perrier?' His teeth gleamed white. 'I refuse to be the subject of your wrath if a glass or two of wine tips the scales against you tomorrow.'

There was a family resemblance between the two men, slight but evident none the less, Emma perceived. However, Vince was younger by a few years, and lacked four or five inches of his cousin's height.

There was something vaguely amusing in being an innocent observer, Emma conceded as the meal progressed. Nick portrayed smooth-spoken urbanity without any effort at all, while appearing seemingly detached from the effect of Danielle's scintillating charm. He gave the appearance of being fascinated, but the keenest eye could detect that the attraction was merely superficial, and Emma couldn't help but wonder why. The model had it all; beauty, personality, fame. She could have any man she wanted with the merest flick of her exquisitely curled eyelashes. Except, maybe, Nick Castelli. Perhaps she *had* had him, Emma decided, for it didn't take much perception to read the sexual tension evident in the other woman's manner.

Whatever the reason, it seemed one-sided, and Emma felt a pang of pity. To be rejected by a man must be hell, especially someone like Nick Castelli. Perhaps that was why Danielle monopolised the conversation with witty anecdotes, and deliberately indulged in according Vince a number of adoring glances in the hope that Nick might be swayed towards jealousy.

A faint grimace flitted momentarily across Emma's features. Somehow she couldn't imagine Nick being the jealous type. He possessed sufficient nous to enable him to hold any woman he chose to pursue, and he was enough of a chauvinist to insist on being the hunter rather than the hunted.

'Martinero. The name is Italian,' Danielle declared with a careless gesture of her exquisitely manicured hand. 'But you are not, I think?'

Emma unconsciously stiffened, aware of a certain malevolence evident in the model's polite query. She caught the swift, spearing glance the brunette accorded to the ring adorning her left hand and was aware of the speculative interest it aroused.

'My husband was Australian-born of Italian parents,' Emma explained quietly.

'*Was?*' Danielle repeated with delicate emphasis.

'Yes.' She met the other girl's glittery gaze with remarkable steadiness, considering the discordant state of her nerves. 'Marc was killed in a car accident last year.'

There was an imperceptible silence, followed by an audible breathy sigh. 'Ah, I see. How sad for you.'

She didn't look in the least sad, Emma decided disparagingly.

'How kind of Nick to take pity on you.' The smile was fixed, curving her luscious mouth into a mere facsimile. 'I presume you are holidaying in Italy?'

'Emma is Rosa's and Enzo's granddaughter-in-law,' Nick revealed indolently, and Danielle's eyes hardened with instant comprehension.

'Then you are both staying at the villa.'

The air crackled with latent animosity, and Emma's eyes widened slightly as Nick drawled, 'Yes. You are aware Annalisa and I spend each summer vacation with Rosa and Enzo.'

'So—convenient, Emma, for you to have timed your visit to coincide with that of Nick's,' Danielle shifted her attention with a swift flick of her immaculately mascara-brushed lashes. 'I can vouch he is an attentive and amusing companion.' For a brief second the lashes swept upward and her eyes fixed Emma with a venomous glare, then it was masked as she centred her attention on her companion. 'Vince, we must call on Nick while he is at the Martinero villa. You are related, after all. How long are you staying, Emma?'

'Three weeks altogether.' It was on the tip of her tongue to explain she had been barely aware of Nick Castelli's existence until last week, and that if she had known Rosa and Enzo were entertaining guests, she would never have come to Italy.

'Would you care to dance with me, Emma?'

She turned slightly and glimpsed Nick's faintly hooded gaze. The slightly cynical edge to his tone brought a defiant sparkle to her eyes, and she was sorely tempted to refuse.

If they had been alone, she would have had no

hesitation, and his lips twisted fractionally in recognition of her indecision. Damn him, he knew she had little choice but to agree. To do otherwise would only play into Danielle's hands, and Emma was darned if she'd give the model that satisfaction.

The restaurant wasn't large, and the floorspace allocated for dancing could only be described as inadequate.

Perhaps she should have been prepared for the inevitability of physical contact, the strangeness of being in another man's arms. Dancing hadn't been one of Marc's favoured pursuits, and she felt awkward, ill at ease, and all too aware that being held by Nick Castelli was a highly evocative experience, despite his conventional hold. Some mystical, illusory chemistry had to be responsible for the tingling warmth that sprang to life and began pulsing through her veins.

'Relax,' he bade quietly, but it was easier said than done, and when the music quickened in tempo she moved backwards, out of his grasp, her features pale.

'I think I'd like to go——' She almost said 'home', except home was several thousand kilometres distant, on the other side of the world. 'To the villa. If you don't mind.' She added the last few words as an afterthought, and missed his narrowed gaze.

'Soon. An early escape will be seen to be precisely that, and I am damned if I will allow Danielle to win a slight advantage and use it against you.'

'Should I take that as a compliment?'

'You are fathoms out of your depth, *cara*,' he drawled. 'Why not appear to be enjoying each other's company?'

'And dance?' Her nerves seemed to be shredding into a

thousand threads, and her eyes mirrored an anguish that went right down to the depths of her soul.

'Would it be such a hardship?'

She caught his smile as he gently pulled her back into his arms. His hold was possessive, almost intimate, and she attempted to move back without success.

'Tell me,' she ventured evenly, lifting her head to look at him, then she immediately wished she hadn't for his face was far too close. Another inch, and her lips would brush his. 'Is this necessary?'

A faint gleam of amusement entered his eyes, and she could cheerfully have hit him. 'I won't be used,' she declared tightly.

She felt him stiffen, then he murmured with deceptive calm, 'You imagine I am deliberately attempting to establish you as my latest—conquest, shall we say?'

She had the oddest feeling he'd like to shake her until she begged for mercy, and a tiny shiver shook her slim frame.

'Thus making it painfully clear to Danielle that my interest lies elsewhere, and she should give up the foolish notion of pursuing me,' he inclined with dangerous softness. 'Is that what you think?'

'The possibility did occur.'

His teeth gleamed white in the subdued lighting, and she suppressed the urge to slap the wry amusement from his face.

'Danielle has a burning ambition to lure me into her manipulative net, and attempting to ensnare me has become something of an unenviable obsession.' His voice assumed mocking cynicism. 'The ironic part of it all is that if she succeeded the excitement would end, and I would be discarded without further thought.'

'I'm filled with compassion,' Emma remarked drily, and a soft, husky laugh emerged from his throat.

'Really?' he derided quietly.

She threw him a dark glance as she corrected sweetly, 'For Danielle. All that time wasted on a man who couldn't care less.'

'You make me sound like an inveterate rake.'

'And you're not?'

'There is one woman for whom I care very much.'

Her heart gave an imperceptible jolt, then steadied and resumed its normal beat. 'If she has an ounce of sense,' she declared lightly, 'she'll keep you dangling on a string to the very end.'

One eyebrow quirked in silent amusement, and Emma reiterated without humour, 'I don't imagine you've reached your thirties without being aware of the devastating effect you have on the female sex.'

'You being the exception, hmm?'

'I'm not interested in forming a liaison with any man.'

'Would you deny yourself another man's love—children?' His breath stirred her hair and she gave a sudden start as his lips brushed against her temple.

He sounded serious—too serious, and the breath caught in her throat as she endeavoured to control the way her pulse leapt out of control and began to thud visibly in the hollow at the base of her neck. He was treading dangerous ground, and she lifted her head and met his dark gaze. Not only met it, but she managed to hold it long enough to see the faint narrowing evident.

'Shall we go back and join Danielle and Vince?'

If looks could kill, she would be dead, Emma decided

when they reached the table, for Danielle's glittery gaze was full of thin veiled animosity.

'Really, Nick,' the model remonstrated in a soft, purring voice. 'You cannot be permitted to monopolise Signora Martinero in such a manner.'

'Emma is a valued guest,' Nick drawled silkily, and Emma took the utmost pleasure in turning slightly towards him as she offered a deliberately sweet smile.

'As a long-standing friend, Danielle has every right to feel neglected.'

It was impossible to read anything from his expression, apart from an initial flaring of something indefinable in the depths of his eyes, and she watched in mesmerised fascination as he reached out and caught hold of her hand.

'If you will excuse us?' He let his gaze encompass Danielle and Vince, and without waiting for their response he collected Emma's wrap.

For a moment she was tempted to resist, just for the sheer hell of it, then common sense overrode obstinacy as she made her farewell while Nick settled the bill.

'There is no need for you to take the role of my companion so seriously,' she declared as they reached the pavement. 'I won't be held responsible for inhibiting your social life.'

'Hasn't it occurred to you that I might prefer your company?'

She shot him a searching glance. 'Why?'

'Why not?' Nick parried blandly, taking hold of her arm as they began strolling along the *piazza* in search of a taxi.

'We rarely agree on anything.'

'Perhaps I see you as a refreshing change from most women of my acquaintance.'

'Who elect to hang on to your every word,' Emma opined drily, and heard his faint chuckle.

'Their motive is transparent at best.'

She nodded in mute agreement. 'Ah, yes! You must be quite a catch.'

'Don't be facetious,' he chided musingly. 'It doesn't suit you.'

'Why deny the truth?' Some demoniacal imp was urging her on, when every sane cell in her body cautioned she should desist. 'You're the embodiment of every quality attributed to the Italian male.' She subjected his lengthy frame to a deliberate, assessing appraisal. 'Tall, attractive. Attentive, pleasant, and eminently successful.' She pretended contemplation. 'There's a touch of arrogance apparent and a trend towards chauvinism, but aside from that I guess there's not much to detract from the image.'

'It's as well I don't beat young women or children,' Nick drawled with hateful cynicism, and she affected a stunning smile.

'Why, Nick,' she chastised softly, 'I could never attribute you with an act of violence.'

'Whereas you, sweet Emma, seem hellbent on treading a path towards provoking it.'

'Is that a threat?'

'The choice of interpretation is entirely yours.'

What on earth was the matter with her? It was as if she'd taken a stick and was intent on prodding a sleeping tiger. To what end? His retribution would be swift and deadly, and inevitably cause her pain of a kind she'd be wise to avoid.

She lapsed into silence, and was grateful when he successfully hailed a passing taxi. Maintaining silence, she stared beyond the windscreen and emerged when they reached the parked Ferrari.

Within minutes she slid into the passenger seat and watched with idle fascination as he fired the engine prior to sending the sleek vehicle into the flow of late-evening traffic.

His movements were smooth and sure, and Emma felt the soft hammering of her pulse in sheer reaction to his close proximity. He possessed a potent animalistic sense of power that succeeded in making her feel unaccountably cross and at odds with herself—worse, in the knowledge that some dark, swirling emotion was beginning to take root that had no basis in her existence. At least, not one of which she wanted any part. Impossible to define precisely what it was that bothered her. An expression, the intensity of his gaze; the sureness with which he was invading her life—even contriving to fashion it to his own advantage.

His daughter was a charming child, so earnest and caring, and whose affection for a remote Australian relative-by-marriage was daily becoming increasingly more obvious. In a way it wasn't fair to kindle such fondness, yet to discourage it was beyond Emma's capability.

'You're very quiet.'

She turned slowly to look at him in the darkness of the car's interior, and glimpsed the strong angles and planes of his profile in the reflection of light from a passing car.

'I thought you'd prefer to give illuminating conversation a miss and concentrate on driving.'

'How considerate,' he mocked softly. 'I was convinced you had chosen to disregard me.'

'Not at all,' she disclaimed, and missed the faint gleam in his eyes as she returned her attention to the passing night-time scenery.

Her eyelids began to feel heavy, and she wasn't aware she had slipped into a fitful doze until she felt a hand on her shoulder.

'Emma.'

She opened her eyes, and nothing looked familiar. 'Where are we?'

'The Villa d'Este,' Nick informed. 'A spectacular vista at night with the fountains lit—definitely a sight worth seeing.' He leaned across and unlatched her door. 'Come, we will walk through the gardens.'

His arm brushed the curve of her breast, and she was powerless to still the frisson of fear that began somewhere deep inside and intensified at his accidental touch.

Without a word she slipped out from the car and stood waiting as he crossed to her side.

'Five hundred fountains,' Nick revealed quietly. 'Aren't they magnificent?'

It was a magical fairyland with cascading water creating a multitude of pulsating dance sequences that varied and delighted with every movement.

'They're beautiful,' Emma breathed, spellbound. Her eyes were alive, her lips parted in receptive pleasure.

'Yes.'

Something in the tone of his voice alerted her attention, and she turned towards him in seeming slow motion as his hands settled on her shoulders.

'Please—don't,' she whispered as he impelled her forward, and at once the butterflies in her stomach began an erratic tattoo, making her frighteningly aware of the electric awareness between them.

Emma felt herself begin to tremble, and when she attempted to extricate herself from the enforced intimacy of his arms he lowered his head and touched his lips briefly against her temple.

'Nick——' She didn't care if she beseeched him, she was even prepared to beg—anything, for if he kissed her, nothing would ever be the same again.

The appeal was useless, and a further protest became lost as his mouth slid down to cover hers in a kiss that was tantalising, tender, yet with a hint of controlled passion and fleetingly brief.

To her utter chagrin it left her feeling vaguely bereft and wanting more. Then reaction set in, and with it came anger. 'How dare you!'

Nick was silent for several seconds, then he slowly shook his head. 'Oh, I dare, Emma,' he mocked gently.

'Let me go,' she whispered furiously.

'Really, *cara*,' he reproved in a hateful drawl, 'I fail to comprehend a reason for such anger.'

'Next you'll tell me your intentions are strictly honourable, I suppose?' She was so consumed with antipathy that her whole body was beginning to shake with it.

'Are you so sure they are not?'

Her eyes widened, dilating with confusion and, conscious of the painful thudding of her heart, she forced herself to breathe slowly in an effort to gain some measure of control.

'If this is a game,' she indicated unsteadily, 'I don't want to play.'

'Afraid I might win?'

'After which I go my way, you go yours, and thanks for the memory?' she spat out with unaccustomed bitterness. The thought of attempting further conversation with him tonight was almost more than she could bear, and she desperately needed to get away from him.

'Please take me back to the villa.'

'So you can be alone, to cry?' His eyes were dark, their expression unfathomable. 'All the tears in the world won't bring Marc back.'

The stark cruelty of his words brought a shocked gasp from her lips. 'How dare you speak to me like that?' she whispered, her face ashen.

'Someone should.'

Resentment began to rise to the surface at his apparent callousness, and she momentarily closed her eyes in an attempt to regain her composure.

'And you've elected yourself, I suppose?'

He regarded her silently for what seemed an age, then the edge of his mouth twisted into a sardonic smile. 'I consider I have a vested interest.'

Helpless anger flared, and her eyes assumed a golden brilliance as she swept his broad frame with a wrathful, encompassing glare. 'Oh? What comes next?' She tipped her head back to meet his impenetrable scrutiny. 'Some misguided homily about wanting to *help* me?'

He looked at her in silence and, defeated, she let her lashes slowly flicker down to blot out his forceful image.

Then her eyes flew wide as his hands cupped her face,

and surprise kept her transfixed as his head lowered until his mouth was on hers, brushing the outline of her lips in a slow, evocative movement that made her gasp.

She stood still, shocked into immobility as his kiss became warm and probing, his touch disruptively sensual as he brought her close against him, holding her fast without any effort at all. Then, with unhurried ease, he sought the soft, inner sweetness of her mouth.

A silent moan rose in her throat, then died, as he savoured the inner recesses with an infinite degree of sensuality, and when she attempted to close her teeth he caught hold of her lower lip and gently pulled it between his own.

Outraged indignation rose to the fore, and without thought she relaxed her jaw, only to groan impotently at her own folly as his mouth moved on hers, effecting a deliberately flagrant exploration; teasing, tantalising in a manner that promised much but delivered little, pacing with unlimited patience in an attempt to evoke her initial response.

She wouldn't kiss him back, she *wouldn't*! Yet slowly her resolve began to dissipate, and just as she thought she could stand it no longer he lifted his head and she stood immobile, her face devoid of colour and her eyes wide, deep pools mirroring pain and a degree of self-humiliation.

Without a word he lifted a hand and trailed his fingers gently down her cheek, then moved to trace the curve of her lower lip. 'Don't look like that,' he berated softly.

Emma wasn't able to utter a sound, and tears welled in her eyes, shimmering, then spilled over to run slowly down in twin rivulets to rest against the corners of her mouth.

'You sweet fool,' Nick cursed huskily, his eyes dark and unfathomable as he witnessed her desolation.

She felt infinitely fragile, vulnerable, and possessed of a strange complexity of sensibilities that had no part of her past.

'I'd like you to take me home.' Was that her voice? It sounded so bleak and forlorn.

Without a word he took hold of her arm and led the way back to the car.

They seemed to reach the villa in a very short time, and immediately the car slid to a halt inside the garage she slipped out and stood waiting while he locked up.

Indoors, she preceded him to the base of the curving staircase. Before she could ascend he reached out and caught hold of her arm and pulled her close.

She could feel his intent scrutiny, and was overcome with an inexplicable apprehension. It was almost as if he was deliberately adopting an urbane façade in an attempt to put her at ease, and she felt decidely wary. One false word or move and she'd be catapulted into an explosive situation.

'Don't——'

Her remonstrance was lost as his mouth closed over hers in a brief, passionate kiss, then she was free.

'Goodnight, *cara*.'

Without a backward glance he turned and moved up the stairs, and Emma watched his broad back disappear with a composite of shock and indignation. How dared he kiss her like that! Dear lord, she couldn't remember being so consumed with anger.

Something deep within seemed to be urging her towards a confrontation, tempting her to taunt in a manner that was the antithesis of her nature. She'd never lost her temper with Marc, nor felt the need to offer a differing opinion, let alone argue. Yet with Nick Castelli she experienced a whole gamut of emotions, the least desirable of all being a growing awareness of her own sensuality. Perhaps that was why she disliked him so much, she reflected, as she made her way to the sanctuary of her room.

CHAPTER FIVE

ROSA proved to be an amusing companion, informative and seemingly untiring as she strolled with Emma through the city's streets, frequenting several boutiques where a number of garments took their eye and a selected few were purchased.

Giorgio Armani had created a delightful range, and Emma gazed enviously at a silk-beaded gown by Karl Lagerfeld, seriously tempted, although after much thought she reluctantly decided against it. From a fashion viewpoint, Lagerfeld's theme was body-hugging and only for the very slender figure.

'What it is to be young,' Rosa murmured with a warm smile as they viewed a further selection. 'So many of the designs appear so extreme.'

'I'd hate to be a buyer,' Emma responded quietly. 'Working a season ahead, gauging consumer appeal and taking responsibility for such a huge financial outlay.' A faint smile curved her generous mouth. 'After all, there's no fashion if a projected line doesn't catch on, and viewing various designer collections is accorded such glamour it would be difficult not to be swayed at the time.'

'You enjoy your job, don't you?'

'Yes,' Emma accorded simply. 'Co-ordinating accessories with a garment can be tremendously inspiring. I like to study the client—her mannerisms, her choice of make-up and hairstyle, and most important of all, the image she wants to project. I assemble the basics, shoes, belts, even tights. Then I move on to jewellery, preferring to view her own before suggesting a new purchase.' A faint, mischievous smile lightened her features. 'Although few clients object to spending their husband's money!'

'Especially if the clientele are wealthy,' Rosa declared, and Emma's smile widened, then assumed a certain wryness.

'Yes. Some will simply buy a *name* label just for the sake of being able to claim ownership, regardless of whether or not it suits them.'

'Cynical, but all too accurate,' Rosa agreed. 'One sees the result on frequent occasions, and shudders at their appalling lack of taste.'

They were carrying a number of assorted packages in various carrier-bags which were beginning to prove cumbersome.

'Shall we leave?' Rosa suggested as they completed yet another purchase from a particularly exclusive boutique. 'By the time Carlo attempts to brave the traffic, it will be at least eight before we reach the villa.'

'I think so. We've done very well.'

Rosa turned to the manageress and requested the use of her telephone to summon Carlo with the car, and they waited patiently until the large silver sedan slid in to the kerb, then they seated themselves in the cool, air-conditioned interior while the chauffeur deftly stowed their purchases into the capacious boot.

'What a lovely day it's been,' the older woman enthused with genuine warmth as the car purred its way out of the city. 'I adore your new ensemble. You must wear it to the theatre tonight.' She placed a hand over one of Emma's and patted it gently. 'So very fortunate a colleague of Enzo's gave us two spare tickets, although the poor man was not to know Enzo and I had already seen the play.'

'Very fortunate,' Emma concurred, almost resigned at having been manoeuvred into an evening at the theatre with Nick. Circumstances seemed to contrive against her where he was concerned, and she entertained no doubts that he utilised every available one to his own advantage.

The tranquility of the villa after the city's bustling streets acted like a soothing balm, and a shower did wonders to restore Emma's energy.

Electing to wear the new pale lemon-yellow skirt and matching top Emma added a silver belt to her waist and fastened a wide silver bracelet over her wrist. Make-up came next, and she applied eyeshadow and mascara with skilful ease, then added blusher and coloured her lips with a soft, clear pink.

Emerging downstairs she entered the lounge to find Nick deep in conversation with Enzo.

Impeccable tailoring merely accentuated his tautly muscled frame, and she noted the proud angle of his head, the strength apparent in the powerful set of his shoulders.

Her pulse leapt, then quickened as a thousand tiny nerve-endings surged into pulsating life, and she fought off the treacherous ache that began somewhere in the region of her stomach. It was maddening the way her body was reacting, she decided dispassionately as she moved further into the room.

At that moment he turned, and she was held an

unwilling prisoner by the sudden brilliance in his eyes, the latent passion, and she felt immeasurably afraid.

'Emma, my dear,' Enzo greeted her effusively. 'Do have a drink. What can I get you?

'A mineral water, please,' she requested, offering him a gentle smile before glancing towards Nick, whose dark eyes pinned hers, their gleaming depths alive with cynical amusement.

'The need for a clear head, Emma?'

She directed him a quick glance that was remarkably steady. 'Not at all.'

'Here you are,' Enzo proffered a slim crystal goblet filled with clear, sparkling liquid. '*Salute*,' he bade genially, watching as she sipped the refreshing mineral water. 'I gather you enjoyed your day exploring the various fashion houses with Rosa?'

'Yes,' Emma declared sincerely. 'The clothes are fabulous.'

'And what of tonight, Emma?' Nick parried smoothly. 'Are you looking forward to my company with equal pleasure?'

'But of course,' she responded evenly. 'I'm quite sure you can be guaranteed to entertain me with gentlemanly decorum.' Her sweet smile looked utterly genuine, and from the corner of her eyes she glimpsed Enzo's benevolent observance of their exchange.

'Emma, Nick—please excuse the delay in joining you,' Rosa offered apologetically as she moved towards them. 'A telephone call. Not important, but one which proved difficult to terminate. *Caro*,' she murmured gratefully as Enzo placed a glass of wine in her hand. 'Where is Annalisa?'

'Asleep,' Nick revealed with a slow smile. 'We played several games of tennis, followed by more than an hour in the pool. Then we took a picnic lunch and drove until my daughter discovered a grassy slope deemed suitably picturesque on which to spread a blanket and eat our simple fare.' His shoulders lifted in a negligible shrug as he slanted them each a musing glance. 'The combination of sunshine, exercise and food, without the benefit of an afternoon siesta, took their toll, I'm afraid.'

'Poor *piccina*,' Rosa sympathised warmly.

'If you will excuse us, we will leave, Nick intimated, placing his empty tumbler down on to a nearby table.

'Enjoy yourselves,' said Rosa with a gentle smile. 'We will look forward to seeing you both at breakfast.'

Emma permitted Nick to lead her out to where the Ferrari was parked, and she slid into the passenger seat and fastened the safety-belt with quick sure movements, aware of a sense of misgiving at spending several hours in his company.

A dozen times in as many minutes she summoned the words to begin some meaningless conversational gambit, then she discarded them as being completely inane.

'Don't look so serious. The play has received good reviews. I'm sure you'll enjoy it.'

'Good heavens,' Emma protested mildly, 'I'm not difficult to please.'

Nick's glance was swift and infinitely mocking. 'Indeed?'

A faint tinge of colour rose to her cheeks at his implication, and the look she flung him would have felled a lesser man. 'If I remain in your presence for much longer I'm liable to *hit* you!'

'You rise to the bait so beautifully,' Nick declared. 'Like a miniature virago.'

'Be careful I don't decide to erupt!' She was so angry the emotion seemed to consume her, and its magnitude was quite frightening.

'I am sure I can handle such an event—and its aftermath,' Nick declared silkily, leaving her in little doubt as to how he would deal with it.

She shivered as icy fingers scudded stealthily down her spine, for the mere thought of being subdued by him shook her composure and tore it to shreds. Faced with imagining Nick in the role of lover made her sick with apprehension. He was no insecure beginner, unsure and unaware how to please.

'Do you derive satisfaction from taunting me?' Her voice sounded alien to her ears, and almost afraid.

He shot her a quick, discerning glance, then stifled a savage oath. 'What do you think I intend, for the love of God?'

'I don't know—I don't care,' Emma flung incautiously as she drew a shaky breath. 'I'm tired of being manipulated—by *everyone*.'

'Me, especially.'

'Yes, damn you!' Stupid, angry tears welled up and teetered precariously, ready to spill.

'I could shake you, do you know that?' Nick threatened with dangerous softness, and she retaliated swiftly, 'Why don't you? You've done everything else.'

There was a mesmeric silence, intensifying until she became conscious of every breath she took.

'On the contrary, I haven't put a hand out of place.'

'I wouldn't let you!'

'My dear Emma,' he drawled silkily. 'Do you really think you could stop me?'

'I'd have a damn good try!'

His expression lightened fractionally, and a glint of cynical amusement lit his darkened gaze. 'Yes, I do believe you would.'

'And don't call me your *dear* Emma,' she snapped furiously.

'Why, *cara*?' The cynicism became vaguely mocking. 'Does it bother you so much?'

'I'll never be your—*anything*,' she assured emotionally.

'We have arrived,' Nick drawled, and Emma realised with a start of surprise that the car was stationary.

'Shall we aim for disarmed neutrality?'

'I doubt that's possible,' she muttered, unable to believe they could spend an hour without being at cross-purposes—let alone several.

Nick slid out from behind the wheel, locked his door, then he crossed round to her side of the car. Taking her elbow, he led the way towards a sprawling *piazza*.

'Nevertheless, we shall try, hmm?'

They walked several blocks in companionable silence, and gradually Emma began to relax, dismissing most of her former anxiety as rational logic rose to the surface. Maybe she was over-reacting, having become too aware of her own vulnerability.

Having gained the theatre foyer they were led to a small table with an excellent view of the stage, and in a moment of recklessness Emma ordered a Galliano cocktail, then when it came she sipped it and was dismayed at its potency.

'Have you always lived with your parents?'

She almost choked at the unexpectedness of his query, and took several seconds to form her reply. 'Yes. Apart from the week I was married to Marc.'

Nick's eyes narrowed thoughtfully, and his voice was deceptively bland as he bade, 'Tell me about him.'

Emma had the greatest difficulty in swallowing the lump in her throat, and her voice held a trace of bitterness. 'I'm sure Rosa has told you everything you want to know.'

'Not the things I want to hear.'

She forced her eyes to remain steady beneath his intent gaze, hating him for placing her in such an invidious position. What could she say? Why *should* she say anything?

Nick was silent for what seemed an age, then he ventured with soft deliberation. 'You have an untouched quality—almost as if the heights and depths of passionate ecstasy still remain an elusive mystery.'

A cold anger began to burn inside her, and she threw him a baleful glare. 'Are you implying that I didn't love Marc?'

His hard, intent stare played havoc with her equilibrium. 'Love takes many forms.'

'And you're an expert, of course.' Her scepticism was clearly evident, and his mouth moved to form a sardonic smile.

'My experience has to be considerably more vast than yours.'

'I wouldn't doubt it!' The look she flung him conveyed disparagement, and his answering chuckle came out low and husky, and full of indolent humour.

'Has anyone told you how beautiful you are when you're angry?'

'I've never been sufficiently incensed for anyone to tell me,' she hissed furiously.

'The play is about to begin,' he declared urbanely, and Emma was reduced to impotent silence as the lights dimmed and the music heralded the onset of the evening's performance.

On reflection the play was a good one, an innovative slant on an old classic, and perhaps it was as well she required total concentration to comprehend the fast-paced Italian dialogue, for it meant she could temporarily forget the forceful man at her side.

'Would you like to visit a nearby bar for an espresso coffee or cappuccino?' Nick queried as they emerged from the theatre a few hours later.

The thought of spending a further hour in his company merely flared her nerve-endings into frightening life. 'I'm rather tired,' she evinced evenly, directing her attention to the vicinity of his black bow-tie. 'And it will be an hour before we reach the villa.'

'Then we will go home.'

His voice was bland, but Emma wasn't deceived by his amenability for a minute.

Once seated in the car she leaned her head against the cushioned head-rest and watched as Nick crossed round and slid in behind the wheel, then he fired the engine and eased the powerful vehicle into the stream of traffic.

He made no effort to converse, and she concentrated her attention on the passing night scene, fascinated by the bright splashes of neon above lit shop windows, the evidence of people strolling the pavements, the number of *ristorantes* with tables and chairs placed outside for patrons to sit at in relaxed enjoyment.

After a while she closed her eyes, lulled by the smooth purr of the engine and the lateness of the hour.

Emma woke with a start, unsure for a brief second what had disturbed her and equally unsure where she was. Then reality surfaced, and she became aware the Ferrari was stationary inside the garage. Was it a figment of her imagination, or had something brushed her temple?

Of their own volition her lashes swept upward and she met Nick's inimical gaze. Light reflected from the ceiling filtered into the car's interior and lent angles to his strong features, making it difficult to judge anything from his expression.

A tiny pulse quickened at the base of her throat and began to hammer in palpable confusion as he made no move to vacate his seat, and she wanted to run as fast as she could, yet *stay*. As crazy as it seemed, she wanted, *needed* to feel the strength of his arms, the touch of his mouth on hers, to be swept high on a tide of sensation that would ease the deep, aching void within.

It would take only the slightest gesture on her part, and there would be no turning back. She could see it in his eyes, sense it in the coiled tenseness of his body, the intent watchfulness apparent.

Even as she hesitated, a feeling of self-disgust washed over her, and she reached for the door handle, then slipped out from the car to stand waiting as he secured the garage.

Tension filled the air until it assumed a highly volatile quality, and her stomach muscles clenched in painful reaction as he crossed to her side.

A quick glance was all that was needed to witness Nick's narrowed scrutiny and the latent anger evident, and Emma felt a surge of blazing rage at her own stupidity in permitting him to get beneath her skin. The private battle she'd been waging for days against recognition of her emotions rose damnably to the surface, bringing guilt and self-loathing to a degree where she wanted to lash out at the one person responsible—hurt him as much as she was hurting.

'Leave me alone!' The words emerged as an anguished whisper the instant he caught hold of her elbow, and he swore briefly, explicitly, as his gaze raked her slender frame. 'I'm not a child in need of a restraining hand!'

'I was merely offering gentlemanly assistance,' Nick drawled, and her answering laugh came out sounding slightly off-key.

'Is that what you call it? Why, then, do I feel positively *shackled*?'

All of a sudden his presence was a definite threat in the semi-darkness, and she was supremely conscious of their surroundings, the dimly lit path leading through the garden and the lateness of the hour.

'Were you such a shrew with Marc?'

The query threw her off balance, and she looked at him with pain-filled eyes. 'No,' she denied unsteadily. 'We never argued.'

One eyebrow rose in sardonic cynicism. 'My dear Emma, *never*?' His eyes gleamed darkly with latent amusement. 'No outbursts that were healed with the sweetness of making up?'

'What would you have me do? Invent some arguments

just for your satisfaction?' she vented, endeavouring to control her temper. 'Marc was kind and thoughtful, and willing to do anything to please.'

He regarded her solemnly for several long seconds, then he remarked quietly, 'You argue with me.'

'Because you rub me up the wrong way!' she cried, sorely tried.

'Have you given a thought to *why*?'

'*Yes*, damn you!'

'And you don't like it,' he drawled imperturbably, his eyes watchfully intent.

'You're damned right, I don't!' Her anger had whipped itself into such a fine fury that her eyes sparkled with brilliant fire, making them appear like crystallised topaz.

'Such vehemence,' Nick mocked as he conducted a slow, encompassing appraisal, lingering on the agitated pulse-beat at the base of her throat, the deepness of her eyes and their dilation, the soft, trembling mouth. He lifted a hand and let his fingers trail down her left cheek. 'Why not take it one day at a time,' he suggested tolerantly, 'without attempting to analyse and pin down every provoking emotion?'

Her chin lifted fractionally. 'Is a degree in psychology one of your attributes?'

'What a delightful mixture you are,' he accorded musingly 'One minute a termagant, the next a polite child.'

Resentment flared, sharpening her tongue. 'You bring out the worst in me,' she retorted, and became incensed when he laughed.

Without thought her hand flew in a swift arc towards

his face, and the resounding slap sounded loud in the silence of the garden.

There was a brief glimpse of terrible anger in his eyes, and for a few timeless seconds she thought he meant to strike her back.

Shock kept her immobile, and as the consequences of her actions slowly penetrated her brain she became filled with a terrible sense of shame. Never in her life had she been so moved to anger, nor had there been a moment when her normally sunny nature digressed to such an extent she'd felt impelled to hit anyone.

An apology, *any* words she could utter in excuse seemed pointless, yet convention demanded she extend them.

'I'm sorry.'

'No, you're not,' Nick opined drily, and she raised startled eyes to meet his hooded expression.

A muscle tensed along his powerful jaw, and she suddenly felt as if she was about to tread on broken glass. One false move and she would be consumed with pain. Looking at him, there was no doubt as to what form it would take.

'Please—don't,' she implored shakily, held motionless in mesmerised fascination as he leant out a hand and caught hold of her chin.

Another slid beneath the swathe of her hair to capture her nape, and her lips parted in silent protest, her eyes widening into huge pools, mirroring despair as his head lowered down to hers.

A silent moan became locked in her throat as her lips were taken, *possessed*, in a manner that was punishingly cruel, and he plundered the sweet softness of her mouth in a kiss that became a total invasion of her senses. Her jaw ached, and her tongue felt numb and swollen as he exacted retribution. Just as she thought she could stand no more, he tore his mouth away in a gesture of self-disgust.

Emma almost swayed at the sudden movement, and she clutched for the only solid entity within reach to prevent herself from falling; then realisation of the strong, muscled arms beneath her hands made her lift them away as if they'd been scorched by flame.

Her eyes seemed locked with his, their expression trapped and filled with pain, and her lips began to tremble, their movement totally beyond her control.

Without conscious thought she lifted unsteady fingers to her mouth.

A husky string of epithets assailed her ears, and she cried out as hard hands drew her close, their grip bruising the delicate bones of her shoulders as his head bent towards hers, and she closed her eyes against a further onslaught, her hands fluttering uselessly to her side as his lips brushed against her temple, then slid across first one eyelid, then the other before trailing down to rest at the edge of her mouth.

His touch was curiously gentle as he traced the swollen outline with evocative slowness, savouring the faint saltiness before dispensing it with his tongue, then with infinite care he teased her lower lip apart and she gave an incoherent groan at such flagrant seduction.

A slow warmth entered her veins as his lips travelled down the pulsing cord at the edge of her neck to begin an erotic discovery of the hollows beneath her throat, and it was only when he moved lower towards the gentle swell of her breasts that reason surfaced and with it a stark horror at what she might be inviting.

Even as she struggled, he raised his head, and Emma stood frozen, almost afraid to move. She began to tremble as she instinctively crossed her arms across her breasts, hugging them tightly in an effort to still the deep shudders that shook her slim frame.

'Why do you look at me as if I intend rape, or worse?' A muscle tautened along the edge of his jaw, and his eyes darkened with smouldering bleakness. '*Cristo!*' His voice held a dangerous softness that sent icy shivers scudding down her spine, and she was powerless to resist the pressure of his hand as he grasped hold of her chin and forced her to look at him. 'I won't deny a need to have you in my bed,' he stated with brutal frankness. 'But when it happens it will be *me* you want, *my* possession you crave.' He paused deliberately, the leashed savagery in his voice flicking over her with the stinging rawness of a whip. 'Not someone to act as a shadowy substitute for Marc.'

To her consternation her mouth began to tremble and silly, ignominious tears welled in her eyes, distorting her vision. As if from a distance she heard his harsh curse, then gentle hands pulled her into his arms and cradled her head into the curve of his shoulder.

In the darkness his features appeared carved into an expressionless mask.

'It wasn't my intention to punish you. Myself, perhaps,' he mused wryly, letting his lips tease the delicately scented curls above her forehead before putting her at arm's length. 'Come, let us go inside.'

There wasn't a single thing she could think of to say in

response, and without a word she preceded him indoors, through to the wide, curving staircase that led to the upper floor.

Emma didn't falter, uncaring whether he followed her or not, and on reaching her bedroom she closed the door behind her then crossed to subside weakly on to the bed.

Dear God! Never in her life had she evoked such leashed violence. It was almost as if some diabolical force was intent on arranging a clash so horrendous she began to wonder if it wasn't born out of Hell.

CHAPTER SIX

EMMA studiously ignored Nick over the next few days, pleading the need for a rest from sightseeing, and expressing a desire to relax at the villa itself in order to spend more time with Rosa.

The gardens were alive with a variety of flowers and shrubs creating a riot of glorious colour, and Emma busied herself filling the numerous vases in the spacious foyer, the *sala* and the *salone* with freshly cut blooms.

There was a guest list to compile, Rosa told her, for the party she and Enzo intended giving on Saturday evening, and a menu to be selected.

Together they talked, reminiscing over the elderly couple's annual visits to Australia, the good times they'd all shared. And Marc. If Rosa suspected Emma's friendship with Nick was becoming more than platonic she sagely kept her own counsel, and Emma avoided even mentioning his name.

Each morning Nick retired with Enzo into the study to explore the intricacies of the financial world and, as Rosa laughingly indicated, to test each other's mental skill.

Annalisa busied herself writing letters to friends and her favourite boarding-school tutor, Sister Margherita, played tennis with her father and, on occasion, Emma, and sought to improve her butterfly stroke in the swimming pool.

During the evenings they watched television or played

a friendly game of cards, then relaxed over coffee before retiring to bed.

A drive through the Alban Hills was arranged for Friday, and Emma rose early, then showered. She selected a cool white jumpsuit with the trouser cuffs rolled several inches above her ankles, a deep aquamarine belt at her waist and matching sandals, then she applied sunscreen cream and covered it with minimum make-up. The result was one of casual elegance and, satisfied with her appearance, she made her way downstairs to the *sala* where she helped herself to fresh criossants and plum conserve.

Nick entered the room just as she was finishing her coffee, and she felt the tension begin to manifest itself inside her stomach, tightening her nerves into a painful knot.

It was useless to curse and rage against fate; equally impossible at the eleventh hour to invent a plausible excuse and opt out.

His presence created havoc and, attired in casual, dark blue cotton trousers teamed with a matching short-sleeved shirt, he excuded dangerous masculinity from every nerve and fibre.

'Good morning.' His voice was a soft drawl, and dark eyes lanced hers, narrowing faintly as he glimpsed the defensiveness apparent. Then he crossed to the table with indolent grace and folded his lengthy frame into a nearby chair.

At once her pulse-beat began hammering in chaotic confusion, and she strove valiantly to maintain her composure as she returned his greeting.

'Are you waiting for me?'

'There is no immediate hurry,' Nick told her with a

negligible shrug. He appeared to study her, his gaze thoughtful and far too shrewd for her peace of mind. 'Annalisa will be down any minute, then we'll leave.' One eyebrow slanted in musing mockery. 'Do you want more coffee?'

Her eyes flashed golden sparks, then became veiled as she deliberately lowered her lashes. 'Is that a polite reminder to suggest you join me?'

'Do you imagine I need an invitation?'

A frisson of inexplicable apprehension feathered its way through her body at the unwarranted implication, and she declined to answer.

At that moment the door opened and Rosa entered the room. 'Good morning, Emma. Nick.' Her gaze moved from the slim auburn-haired girl to her nephew, sensing the electric tension apparent and choosing to ignore it. 'I trust you both slept well?'

'Yes, thank you,' Emma responded with undue politeness. A downright lie, but it was hardly to her advantage to admit the truth. Summoning a smile, she excused herself lightly. 'I'll just put the finishing touches to my make-up and collect my bag. I won't be long.'

If she'd had a choice she would have elected to sit next to Annalisa in the rear of the car, but any thoughts she might have entertained in that direction were quelled in an instant by the implacability evident in Nick's expression as he held open the front passenger door and saw her into her seat.

The sky was a clear azure, and at this early hour the sun's heat had yet to reveal its intense beat. Beneath Nick's drawling commentary they explored the charming Alban Hill towns where vineyards on the slopes above Lake Albano and Lake Nemi were purported to produce most of the white wine consumed in Rome.

'Marino, Rocca de Papa and Frascati are famous for their grape-harvest festivals in the autumn,' Nick relayed, and Emma gazed at the neat rows of vines with their plump grapes almost ready for picking. There were white and pink splashed houses, some fresh-painted and others which bore an aged sienna hue.

All told, it was an artist's dream, and one which she couldn't help but admire. 'It's beautiful,' she stated simply, unwilling to accord the exotic, but startlingly rustic scenery with extravagant superlatives.

'The lakes are splendid,' Nick murmured gently, sparing her a warm, musing glance. 'We will stop further on and visit one of the vineyards where it is possible to sample wine direct from the barrel.'

There was an element of shared intimacy, something that went beyond apparent friendliness. The man projected an aura of quiet strength and indomitable will; a lethal mixture of silk and steel from which escape was becoming increasingly more difficult.

Maybe she should just give in and allow him to lead her in whichever direction he chose, without thought for anything other than *now*.

Yet something held her back, some intrinsic element of integrity that baulked at acting in such a capricious fashion, even in today's era, where selective promiscuity was the norm. And deep down she was afraid. Afraid the dreams and esteem interwoven with her memory of Marc might crumble into obscurity beneath the sensuality and sexual expertise of the man who wanted to usurp his place.

With determined effort Emma dragged her mind back to the present and concentrated her attention on the scene beyond the windscreen. The views were breathtaking, with wooded hills providing a startling contrast with the deep blue of the lakes. It was a glorious vista of vivid colour, and she gave a small gasp of surprise when Nick pointed out a ruined castle and acquiesced with indulgence when Annalisa begged if they could stop so she could explore it.

'Of course.' He brought the car to a halt and slid out from behind the wheel, then crossed round to open the passenger door.

The ruins were a mixture of rubble and outer walls, with some evidence of apportioned rooms. There was a feeling of unreality walking the same ground that emperors and soldiers had trod several centuries before. If one closed one's eyes it was almost possible to imagine the clanking of swords and the rollicking laughter of the Sybarites.

Back in the car, Nick drove for several kilometres, then stopped within sight of Lake Albano so they could have a picnic lunch.

Annalisa helped spread the checked cloth on the grassy bank beneath the spreading branches of a shady tree, then chattered innocuously as Nick extracted the hamper from the boot and deposited it within easy reach.

'Lovely!' the young girl exclaimed as she began unpacking an assortment of covered containers. 'Maria has packed chicken and ham, two kinds of salad, some fruit and lots of fresh-baked crusty bread rolls.'

'And wine,' Nick smiled, retrieving a bottle from its cooled container. He selected three glasses and filled one with lemonade for his daughter, then poured wine into the remaining two, handing one to Emma before lifting his own in a silent salute.

'What will you have, Emma?' Annalisa asked as she busied herself with plates and cutlery.

'I'll help you.'

Dividing the food, she passed one plate to Nick, another to Annalisa, then placed a small selection on to her own.

'Isn't this *nice*?' Annalisa grinned engagingly as she bit into her chicken leg. 'What are you going to wear for the party, Emma?' Her eyes became round with intense interest. 'Zia Rosa and Zio Enzo always have grand parties. The ladies wear masses of jewellery and try to outdo each other. And very important people come. Don't they, *Papa*?'

'Indeed they do, *piccina*,' Nick agreed gently. 'Zio Enzo is a very clever financial entepreneur who maintains an active interest in several business ventures.'

'Just like you,' his daughter agreed solemnly. She finished her chicken and filled a split roll with slices of ham, then munched it appreciatively before washing it all down with lemonade. 'I think,' she declared, standing to her feet with graceful agility, 'I will go and pick some flowers to take back to Zia Rosa.'

'They may not stay fresh for long inside the car,' Nick warned, only to recieve a blithe smile in return.

'But water will revive them, and besides, Zia won't mind. It is the thought that counts.'

Emma lifted her glass and sipped its contents, unsure whether Annalisa had deliberately contrived an excuse in order to leave the two adults on their own.

'More chicken?'

She glanced up and met Nick's gleaming gaze. 'No, thanks.'

'Wine?'

Shaking her head in silent negation she placed her empty plate down on to the checked cloth and selected a paper napkin to wipe her fingers.

Sitting so close, she could see the tiny lines fanning out from the edge of his eyes, sense their clear, unwavering regard for an infinitesimal second before she lowered her eyes to the deep grooves slashing each cheek. She hadn't meant to look at his mouth, but her eyes were drawn to the sensual curve of their own volition. Her pulse tripped its beat and gathered speed until she could feel it pounding at the base of her throat.

'I think I'll go and help Annalisa,' she declared unevenly, and he looked at her with a steady regard, holding her gaze for what seemed an age.

'Do I pose such a threat that you must run away?'

His words jolted her composure, and in the need to retain it she blurted out, 'Threat?' Her voice sounded husky and strangely vulnerable. 'You'd have to be impossibly arrogant to suppose that.'

'*Impossibly*, Emma?'

A prickle of apprehension slithered icily down to the base of her spine, warning her to desist before she found herself engaged in a verbal battle. He had the most damnable way of deploying words, calculated without doubt to pull her off balance.

'I'm in no position to judge,' she returned evenly, determined not to give him the satisfaction of rousing her to anger.

'Would you like to be?'

Even as she registered the implication of his words, a silent, screaming refusal roared through her brain, almost deafening in its volume. 'No.'

His soft laughter sent a multitude of sensations

spiralling through her body, and before she had a chance to move he reached forward and brushed his lips against her cheek; then his mouth fastened over hers in a kiss that was brief and punishingly hard.

'That wasn't fair,' she accused him shakily, silently hating him. She almost died when his head descended once more, although this time there was a wealth of seduction in his touch, a gentleness that was bewitchingly sensual as his lips caressed hers, settling with unerring ease over their delicate curves, savouring, tasting in a manner that made her gasp with outraged indignation.

Too late she realised her mistake, for his mouth became demanding, possessive as he invaded the soft inner sweetness to create a ravishment of her senses.

Slowly, he began a deliberately flagrant exploration before slipping to nuzzle the delicate hollows at the base of her throat. Next, he trailed the pulsing cord at the edge of her neck up to her earlobe before slipping across to reclaim her mouth.

Emma was melting inside, warmth slowly encompassing her body, sending the blood coursing through her veins until her whole being was consumed by a deep, throbbing awareness. She dimly registered Nick's quick, indrawn breath before his mouth hardened, its pressure becoming relentless as he plundered at will, introducing her to a degree of sensual mastery she hadn't dreamed existed.

Emma became conscious of an almost mindless ecstasy that combined a beautiful melding of sheer sensation with elusive alchemy, and she experienced a terrible sense of loss as he gently disentangled her arms and released her.

She could only look at him as gentle fingers lifted her

chin, and her lashes swiftly lowered as he traced the outline of her trembling mouth. Pride alone was responsible for the way she slowly let her lashes sweep upwards to focus on a point slightly beneath his eyes.

'That shouldn't have happened.'

'Why ever not?' Nick queried gently. 'We shared a few kisses, that was all.'

All? If his kisses affected her so tumultuously, how could she cope with his lovemaking? She felt helplessly out of her depth, unable and unwilling to say anything that would highlight the complex state of her emotions. At last, when the silence between them seemed to have stretched into an eternity, she rose slowly to her feet and began tidying their picnic things back into the hamper.

Nick helped her, and by the time everything was stowed in the boot Annalisa had returned carrying an armful of flowers which were reverently placed in damp newspaper in the boot.

They headed north for a number of kilometres to a nearby village where Nick indicated they would stop to sample wine in one of the many vineyards dotted across the meandering hillside.

'A small family establishment which has been handed down from generation to generation,' he explained as he drew the car into the courtyard and brought it to a halt in front of an aged stone house. 'Their claim to fame is an excellent vintage dry white, the fermentation process being a closely guarded secret known only to selected family members,' he revealed as they walked towards the cellars.

They were welcomed with enthusiastic conviviality, and Emma accepted a glass of wine and sipped it tentatively, surprised to find the bouquet was exceptional, the taste sharp to her relatively untutored palate.

'Excellent,' Nick declared, letting his gaze sweep towards Emma. 'Don't you think so?'

'Yes.' Even so, she couldn't finish it, and after a few minutes he took the glass from her hand and with a gesture that was vaguely intimate he lifted it to his lips and drained the contents in one long swallow.

She looked at him in surprise, glimpsing the warmth apparent in the depths of his eyes, and she was unable to prevent the agonising shaft of sensation that slowly unfurled inside her stomach. Then Annalisa drew her attention to the huge barrels of wine lined up against one wall, and she dragged her thoughts away from the compelling man at her side.

It was almost seven o'clock when they returned to the villa, and after sharing a cool drink in the *salone*, during which Annalisa imparted a résumé of their day for Rosa's benefit, Emma excused herself and made her way upstairs to shower and change before dinner.

Rosa and Enzo's party promised to be a glittering formal affair, and Emma dressed with care.

The dress she'd elected to wear was a deep cobalt-blue silk with draped bodice, delicate straps and a softly draped skirt that flowed with every movement she made. Slim-heeled shoes completed the outfit, and she viewed her mirrored reflection with detached satisfaction before selecting a diamond and sapphire pendant and matching earstuds from her jewellery case; then she clipped on a bracelet that had formed part of her wedding gift from Marc.

There were only the final touches of her make-up to attend to, and she chose to highlight her eyes with a careful blending of shadow and mascara, then added a thin film of gloss over her lipstick. Givenchy's *L'Interdit* was her favourite perfume, and she sprayed the atomiser generously over the valley between her breasts, at her nape, the hollows at the base of her throat, her wrists and ankles before giving her appearance one final scrutiny in the cheval-glass mirror.

A slim, attractive-looking young woman gazed solemnly back, and Emma smiled, pleased with her total look. She was armed and ready to do battle with the indomitable Nick Castelli, and any other male guests who might attempt to indulge in a harmless flirtation!

A slight mirthless laugh escaped her lips. There was nothing *harmless* about Nick. His resolve to infiltrate her emotions was nothing less than daunting, and it took every ounce of courage to turn and walk calmly down the stairs.

'Ah, there you are,' Annalisa declared with delight as Emma entered the *salone*, and her warm, hazel eyes glowed with genuine admiration. 'You look beautiful. Doesn't she, *Papa*?'

'Indeed she does,' Nick agreed appreciatively, and Emma met his dark, enigmatic gaze with equanimity.

'Thank you,' she returned gracefully. The sight of him attired in a dark, formal evening suit did strange things to her equilibrium, and she accepted the glass of wine Enzo proffered, sipping its contents in the vain hope that alcohol might restore some sense of calm.

There had to be some sane, logical reason for the way he affected her, surely? Perhaps it was quite normal to wonder what it would be like to sleep with another man? To be able to compare . . . No! Her mind screeched to a shuddering halt at such a wayward train of thought. Oh

God, what was happening to her? Instead of getting better, it was becoming worse with every passing day. If she didn't leave Italy soon, she'd go completely mad!

'Emma! How lovely you look!'

She turned slightly and a generous smile curved her lips. 'Thank you, Rosa. Is there anything I can do to help?'

'No, *cara*,' the older woman responded warmly. 'However, there are a few friends who are waiting for an introduction. Will you come and meet them?'

Two hours and two glasses of wine later Emma was convinced her face had assumed a masklike quality from projecting polite congeniality to a number of people it was unlikely she'd ever see again after tonight.

There were approximately fifty guests mingling in the luxuriously appointed *salone*, and she registered the lilt of subdued chatter at the same moment she caught sight of a familiar dark head apparently engaged in conversation with, of all people, Danielle Fabrese.

Emma's stomach performed a painful somersault, then settled down to a dull ache as her already tautened nerves stretched to breaking point. Somehow she doubted Danielle had been invited on her own account. It was far more likely the model had ingratiated herself as a partner to one of Rosa and Enzo's bona fide guests.

At that moment Nick glanced up and Emma met his intent gaze with a slight lift of her chin and a hint of coolness in the depths of her gold eyes.

'Emma. Let me fetch you another drink.'

She turned towards the owner of that friendly voice and gave Vince such a stunning smile he looked visibly taken aback for an instant. Then his teeth gleamed and a silent laugh parted his lips.

'Ah, I see,' he mocked lightly. 'You want to use me as a foil to get back at Nick!'

'Not at all,' she disclaimed quietly. 'You're a very pleasant young man whose company I happen to enjoy.'

'And Danielle, deep in conversation with Nick, has nothing to do with it?'

'No,' she said firmly, willing it to be true as she attempted to ignore a tiny gremlin who suddenly materialised inside her head and whispered 'Liar!' in a deliberate taunt.

A waiter paused discreetly, and Vince took two glasses from the tray, one of which he offered Emma.

'Hmm, gorgeous,' he murmured softly. 'Your perfume alone could drive a man wild.'

It was impossible not to laugh at such blatant flattery, and a winsome smile curved Emma's generous mouth. 'Careful,' she cautioned. 'I might take you seriously.'

'I should be so fortunate.'

'What of Danielle?' she reminded him, wrinkling her nose at him in silent admonition, and caught his faint grimace.

'A pretty playmate, nothing more, who shamelessly uses me in an effort to get close to my inestimable cousin.' His smile broadened as he glimpsed her expression. 'I have no illusions about Danielle,' he continued wryly, 'whereas you, Emma, are a sweet young woman. Nick thinks so, too, and Annalisa already adores you.'

'Your cousin has been very helpful,' she answered carefully. 'I've appreciated the time he has spared me.'

'And you are just "good friends", hmm?' Vince mocked.

Anyone further removed from *friend* was difficult to imagine, yet she was loath to pursue the subject. 'I don't think I have to answer that.'

'Ah, astute,' he concluded sardonically, sparing her a whimsical smile. 'Astute enough, I wonder, to realise that Nick has a reputation for getting what he wants? And——' he paused with soft deliberation, then added, 'my guess favours *you*, sweet Emma.'

Her heart gave a sudden lurch, then settled back to its normal pattern as she endeavoured a semblance of tranquillity in the face of Vince's revelation.

'If the studied ease with which Nick has been regarding us for the past five minutes is any indication, you don't stand a chance in hell of escaping him.'

She met his gaze inflinchingly. 'He doesn't own me.'

'Not yet,' he corrected softly.

'Not ever!'

'Such vehemence,' he chided musingly. 'I am almost inclined to think you protest too much.'

'You're wrong,' Emma assured quickly, tempering her words with a smile.

Vince reminded her so much of Marc, and she experienced a strange, inexplicable pang of sadness, intermingled with the knowledge that soon she would have to return to her memories, face again her parents, Marc's, and various friends. Say goodbye to the overpowering Nick Castelli, whose motives she failed to understand.

'Talk of the devil,' Vince murmured, and Emma turned slowly to see Nick weaving his way steadily towards them.

It was impossible to discern anything from his expression, and she offered him a slight smile as he reached her side.

'Would you prefer mineral water?' Nick enquired,

glancing at her barely touched wine.

'No, thank you,' she responded evenly, hating the faint tremor that ran through her body in reaction to his close promixity. His slight smile drew attention to his mouth, and remembering the way it felt to have him kiss her brought a rush of colour to her cheeks.

'Something to eat?'

She bore his probing scrutiny equably, and gave a negative shake of her head. 'Maybe later.'

The depths of his eyes assumed a degree of lazy tolerance. 'You wouldn't by any chance have decided to be perverse and deliberately oppose me?'

'What makes you think that?'

His gaze narrowed and assumed an inscrutability, a watchfulness that was somehow worse than any partronising amusement.

'Perhaps you resented me talking to Danielle and decided to reciprocate by flirting with Vince?'

Her chin lifted fractionally at the unfairness of such a supposition, and she directed him a cool glare. 'I did *not* flirt! Besides, Vince is uncomplicated, and nice.'

'While I am not.'

What could she say? Anything would be equally damning, so she chose silence for what seemed for ever before saying slowly, 'I'm very grateful to you for making my stay in Rome so interesting.'

'Very politely spoken,' he declared cynically.

'You doubt my sincerity?'

'No.'

'*Papa*, have you told Emma yet?'

The sound of Annalisa's voice brought some semblance of normality to their conversation, and Emma moved slightly to allow Annalisa to join them.

'I am so looking forward to driving to Naples next week,' the young girl enthused, clearly excited at the prospect. 'Emma will adore it, won't she, *Papa*?' She turned towards Emma and caught hold of her hand. 'They say "see Naples and die". The scenery is magnificent, and as for Capri—I love it there.'

Somehow Emma managed to school her features and offer a pleasant comment, wondering if there was any chance she could invent some excuse and not go.

'I haven't had the opportunity to discuss it with Emma yet, *piccina*. She may have other plans.'

The disappointment on his daughter's face was plainly evident as she looked at Emma. 'But you *must* come with us! It won't be the same if you don't.'

Diplomacy was the only way to deal with the situation, and Emma gently squeezed Annalisa's hand. 'Can I think about it and let your father know?'

'Yes, of course.'

Emma felt her heart turn over at the girl's quiet resignation, and she almost relented and said she would accept. Dammit, why did she feel so—wretched? The choice to refuse should be hers without the need for guilt at doing so.

'Will you excuse me for a few minutes?' She put her glass down on a nearby table and made her way from the *salone* with the intention of freshening her make-up.

The powder room placed at the guests' disposal was adjacent the foyer on the ground floor, and Emma was about to enter it when the door was opened from the inside and she came face to face with Danielle, who, instead of emerging, elected to retrace her steps.

'Perhaps I could re-touch my lipstick,' Danielle murmured with a false smile, and Emma mentally prepared herself for a verbal onslaught without the slightest doubt to whom it would pertain.

'Nice strategy, *cara*. Inveigling an invitation to the villa at the time when Nick is here with his daughter.' Her eyes were glittery and strangely avid, and Emma endeavoured to remain calm beneath the model's intent stare.

'I had no idea,' she assured Danielle evenly, crossing to the marble basin. Via mirrored reflection she glimpsed Danielle's expression and saw one eyebrow arch delicately in disbelief.

'Next you will tell me Rosa and Enzo neglected to inform you of Nick's existence.'

Emma lifted a hand to her hair and smoothed back a few stray curls, then she pretended to scrutinise her make-up. 'They probably did mention him at some time during their visits to Sydney, but I can't honestly remember.'

'And this holiday in Rome *now* is merely coincidence, and not specifically contrived to ensnare Nick——' A tinkling laugh full of bitterness emerged from her lips. '—who has to be much bigger fish than your sadly departed husband, surely?' Her eyes assumed a malevolent gleam as she thrust in for the verbal kill. 'So much better, when considering re-marriage, to keep it in the family? Especially when the lineage is affiliated to the rich and powerful Martinero dynasty.'

'I think this has gone far enough, don't you?' Emma managed quietly, sure that she couldn't cope with any futher disparaging invective. It had been bad enough listening to Vince's light, bantering innuendo without compouding it further.

'Nick Castelli is going to be mine,' Danielle declared

viciously. 'Do you understand?'

Emma looked at the model and tried to be objective. 'I understand, Danielle,' she said evenly. 'But do you? If you have known Nick for so long, why isn't he already yours?' She let her eyes sweep slowly over Danielle's superb figure. 'You are very beautiful, except,' she paused fractionally, then continued, 'in your heart, where it really matters. A fact which Nick has obviously recognised, wouldn't you say?'

For a moment Emma thought Danielle meant to launch a physical attack, and she braced herself in an attempt to ward off the sudden push that spun her back against the marble pedestal.

'*Bitch!*'

Danielle turned and swept from the room, and Emma was left to shakily gather herself sufficiently together in order to rejoin the other guests and attempt to pretend none of this had happened.

Something, she perceived several long minutes later, it would take considerable effort and no mean feat of acting ability to achieve.

CHAPTER SEVEN

'MAY I join you?'

Emma glanced up and met Vince's gleaming gaze as he leaned forward and bestowed a light kiss to Rosa's cheek.

'Lovely party, Zia Rosa,' he said gently.

'Thank you, Vince,' Rosa accepted warmly. 'Emma and I were discussing a visit to the galleries one day next week.'

'What a pity I must be in Milan until Sunday,' he declared with sincere regret. 'Otherwise it would give me pleasure to accompany you.'

The slight nagging ache at the back of her eyes had begun within ten minutes of the scene with Danielle, and had intensified over the past hour until it bore all the symptoms of a migraine. A regrettable legacy from last year's car accident, although admittedly they recurred with less frequency. A deep, throbbing sensation manifested itself at one temple and threatened to overwhelm her with pain, and she cursed beneath her breath. If she didn't swallow some tablets soon, she'd have little option but to take to her bed. Prescribed medication combined with half an hour's rest might alleviate the worst of it, and with luck her absence wouldn't even be noticed, she decided as she quietly informed Rosa of her intention.

'Oh, Emma, I am so sorry.' Rosa sympathised at once, her kindly features creased with concern. 'You do look very pale. Are you sure you will be all right?'

'Quite sure,' she declared, attempting a smile, except it didn't quite come off and merely ended up as a wobbly substitute. 'Don't worry, I'll be fine.' Excusing herself, she turned and threaded her way through the milling guests to the staircase, and once in her bedroom she stripped off her dress, slipped out of her shoes and donned a silk wrap. Then she extracted two tablets and washed them down with water before laying down on the bed.

The darkened room was bliss after the electric brightness of the *salone*, and Emma closed her eyes and willed the pain to subside.

What had triggered it off this time? she brooded wearily. Perhaps it was a culmination of several factors, not the least of which was Nick Castelli.

Dammit, she'd felt so *safe* with Marc, so sure, even in grief, of what her future would entail. She had a fascinating, fulfilling career, and there were numerous friends available whenever she needed a social partner. She didn't *need* an involvement with any man, much less one who resided on the opposite side of the world.

A slight sound alerted her attention and she slowly let her eyelids drift open to focus on a slight figure standing hesitantly beside the bed.

'Emma? Zia Rosa said I could come and see if you are feeling any better.'

'A little,' Emma responded cautiously.

'Is it very bad?' Annalisa whispered with concerned awe. 'I have never had a headache before.'

She couldn't help the faint smile that parted her lips. 'Pray that you never do. At least, nothing as dramatic as a migraine.'

'Can I get Maria to bring you some tea, or a cool drink?'

'A cup of tea would be lovely, *piccina*,' she declared, unconsciously using Nick's pet name for the young girl.

'It might help.' Annalisa ventured, and Emma lifted a hand in silent agreement.

'Thank you.'

Annalisa crept from the room, and Emma closed her eyes against the misting pain. Already she felt heavy and vaguely disorientated as the tablets began to take effect. If only she could sleep, even briefly. An hour would be sufficient, then she'd wake feeling considerably refreshed.

It was some time later that she became aware someone had entered the room, and she sensed rather than heard their passage towards the bed. Then there was a faint click as the bedside lamp sprang on, and she gave a faint murmur of distress at the sudden intrusion of light.

'Please—that hurts my eyes,' she protested, and gave a slight sigh of relief when it was switched off and the light in the adjoining bathroom provided a subdued and slightly removed illumination.

'Just put the cup on the pedestal. I'll drink it soon.'

'Unless you have a penchant for lukewarm tea, I would advise drinking it now,' a deep, all too familiar voice drawled.

Emma's eyes opened to centre on the man standing indolently near the bed.

'What are you doing here?' It wasn't really a query, merely a shocked acknowledgment of his presence in her bedroom.

'You're quite safe,' Nick murmured with deceptive

softness, and she felt the prick of futile tears at his implication.

I don't *feel* safe, she longed to scream at him.

'Rosa showed concern over your welfare,' he continued quietly. 'And Annalisa showed considerable alarm. I deemed it wise to check for myself.'

'I've already taken two tablets,' she managed wearily. 'So your solicitude, although—gratifying, is unnecessary.' A spasm of pain seemed to focus itself behind one eye, and she winced.

'You really do have a headache,' Nick declared with a brooding frown, and she felt every muscle in her body tense with reaction as he folded his length down on to the edge of the bed.

'What did you imagine?' she flung at him tiredly. 'That I invented the excuse solely to escape your diabolical presence?'

'The thought did occur.' Lifting a hand, he touched his fingers to her temple. 'There?'

Emma closed her eyes against the effect he was having on her, and she willed her pulse to steady from its sudden leaping beat as he began a gentle, soothing massage, using the tips of his fingers to probe out the pain and attempt to alleviate it.

There was an element of danger in permitting him to continue, for the seducing quality of his touch played havoc with her senses, making her all too aware of just how easy it would be to succumb. All she had to do was lift her arms and let her hands encircle his neck, pull his head down to hers and allow herself to be swept away on a tide of emotion.

'Is that any better?'

Emma slowly opened her eyes and almost died at the

intense awareness evident in his dark gaze. 'Yes. Thanks,' she added unsteadily, more as an afterthought than in gratitude. Her lashes swept down, veiling the bruised darkness in her eyes.

'Do you get these attacks often?'

His voice seemed to invade her body, and she shivered at its traitorous compliance.

'They have become less frequent,' she answered quietly. 'The doctor assures they will gradually fade altogether after the first year.'

'You suffered concussion at the time of the accident?'

'Yes.'

'Sit up and drink your tea,' Nick instructed gently, sliding an arm beneath her shoulders as he lifted her to lean back against the pillow.

Obediently she sipped from the cup, then when it was empty he replaced it down on to the pedestal.

'You resemble a lost little waif,' Nick remarked with a twisted smile. 'All eyes, pale skin, and infinitely fragile.'

'And you, Nick? What role do you play? That of my protector?'

Her eyes widened measurably when he leaned forward and lightly caressed her lips with his own. It was an evocative gesture, and one which left her aching for more.

'It would take an utter brute to be anything else.' A smile curved his wide mouth, and a gleam of amusement lit his eyes.

'I think you'd better go.' Was that her voice? She felt like a disembodied spectator, watching a scene unfold in which she had no living part.

'As soon as you have settled down for the night.' He moved the pillow back into its original position and straightened the sheet. 'Rosa gave me strict instructions that you were to stay where you are.'

She opened her mouth to protest, only to have him press his fingers fleetingly against her lips.

'No arguments. Where do you keep your nightgown?'

A strangled gasp emerged in outraged indignation. 'I'll change just as soon as you leave.'

'*Now*, Emma.' He was smiling, but there was an inflexible quality in his voice that commanded compliance. 'You should realise I am quite capable of carrying out the task myself, if you refuse.'

Stupid, mutinous tears brimmed to the surface and threatened to spill over and run down her cheeks.

'Sweet Mother of God, don't cry,' he berated huskily.

'I'm not. I just can't handle you any more.' One solitary tear escaped and trickled slowly down to rest at the edge of her mouth. 'At least, not tonight.'

Something darkened in the depths of those obsidian eyes for a brief second before vanishing beneath a mask of inscrutability. 'Will it make you feel better if I retreat into the hallway for the necessary few minutes it takes you to change?'

'I'm not a child you need to check up on,' she voiced, immeasurably hurt.

'Indulge me, *cara*.'

Without a further word he stood to his feet and vacated the room, and Emma gingerly slid off the bed, then reached beneath her pillow for the thin slither of nylon and lace that comprised her nightwear.

It took two minutes to slip out of her wrap and remove her slip and panties; a further three to don her nightgown and scrub her face free from any traces of make-up.

She emerged from the bathroom just as Nick re-entered the bedroom, and she stood still, frozen into immobility beneath his swift, raking appraisal.

'Get into bed,' he bade gently. 'Then I'll leave.'

Her eyes were held and captured by his, and she couldn't have looked away if her life had depended on it. The tenuous hold she had on her temper strengthened with every passing second, and her tawny eyes turned liquid gold in visible defiance at his high-handedness.

'Don't,' he warned in a voice that sounded vaguely like silk being cut by razor-sharp steel, 'even think about it.'

Without looking at him she crossed to the bed and slid in between the sheets. 'Satisfied?' It was a taunt she couldn't resist, and his eyes glittered with sardonic cynicism.

'No.'

For a brief, horrifying second she thought she'd pushed him too far, and she watched in mesmerised fascination as he crossed to the bed.

Bending low, he leaned forward and grazed his lips against her own. 'Sweet Emma, how lovely you are.' His smile was gentle, softening his rugged features and dispelling much of the compelling formidability apparent.

Stay with me, she wanted to beg. Supplant Marc's ghost with a living entity, and ease this terrible need. Yet even as the words whispered silently through her brain, her body began to recoil in rejection, and she shivered, hating her traitorous flesh for craving Nick's possession.

It was almost as if every sane, sensible thought had fled, the moral convictions she'd held in such high esteem dismissed as if they were of no consequence.

Like someone emerging from a dream, she became

aware of the warm sensuality of his fingers as they traced the outline of her mouth.

'Nick——' She broke off, her eyes huge golden pools as she silently implored him to leave.

'Shh, be quiet,' he remonstrated softly as he caressed her mouth with his own, tantalising with an evocative sensuality she found almost impossible to resist. Then he raised his head with obvious reluctance, and his eyes were warm with an infinite degree of intimacy as he got to his feet.

'Goodnight, Emma. Sleep well.'

She watched him cross the room and reach for the doorknob, then he was gone, and she released her breath slowly, hardly conscious that she'd been holding it. Oh, God! She closed her eyes against his forceful features, hating the turmoil he was able to evoke without any seeming effort at all.

No matter how hard she tried, she failed to bring Marc's image easily to mind. Another vied for supremacy, his strong, masculine features an arresting, primitive force that could not be easily cast to one side.

Emotions she'd never thought to experience rose damnably to the surface, demanding recognition. Passion, in its most dangerous form. Tormenting, torturing—a bittersweet agony of the flesh. Somehow she'd identified love as encompassing that volatile emotion. Now she knew they could be separate, without any linking connection.

If fate has been a tangible entity, she could have raged against it, she decided vengefully as she fought sleep and lost, slipping into a deep medication-induced somnolence that imprisoned her until well into the following morning.

Emma rose feeling refreshed, all traces of her headache gone, and she emerged downstairs to discover from Rosa that Nick was ensconced in Enzo's study prior to the imminent arrival of an associate from London, whose fleeting visit to Rome would require much of Nick's time over the next forty-eight hours.

It was a relief to be free of his disturbing presence, and when, the following morning, Rosa suggested they should spend the day shopping, Emma agreed with alacrity, for there were a few gifts she wanted to buy for her parents and friends. Together with Annalisa they set off early, in an attempt to beat the worst of the heat.

By the end of the day they were pleasantly weary and only too glad to slip into the waiting car and be driven back to the villa by Carlo.

Showered and rested they met in the *salone* for a relaxing aperitif before adjourning to the *sala* for dinner.

Nick was unable to join them, due, Enzo revealed almost apologetically, to a business appointment which would encompass dinner and most of the evening.

Emma wondered darkly if a feminine companion formed any part of his plans, and assured herself that she didn't care if his dinner was a bona fide business engagement or otherwise.

However, even imagining him sharing an intimate evening with another woman brought forth a gamut of unenviable feelings, not the least of which she was reluctant to admit as being jealousy.

To successfully alleviate the wayward trend of her thoughts she threw herself into a bright *divertissement* regarding the merits of several different designers, discovering some hours later, to her utter surprise, that they had progressed through dinner, partaken coffee, and were comfortably seated in the *salone* without her being aware of the passage of time.

'It's quite late,' Emma declared with a degree of disbelief as Rosa stood to her feet.

'Indeed it is, my dear. I think we should retire.' Her eyes kindled with affection as they took in Emma's slightly flushed features. 'Tomorrow you drive to Naples, and Nick will doubtless want to make an early start in the morning.'

Of course! She had temporarily put it to the back of her mind, although Annalisa had mentioned the trip several times during the day, ecstatic that Emma had agreed to accompany them, after all.

Together they walked towards the foyer and mounted the staircase, bade each other goodnight at its head, then they moved in opposite directions towards their own suites.

Emma undressed and slid into bed, to lie staring sightlessly at the room's darkness for what seemed hours before slipping into a restless doze from which she woke to discover that the luminous hands of her bedside clock pointed to the witching hour of midnight instead of nearly dawn, as she had hoped.

Damn! She'd never felt less like sleep in her life. Perhaps if she went down to the kitchen and heated some milk it might help. Without further thought she slid out of bed, pulled on a silk wrap, then made her way quietly downstairs.

The kitchen was large and equipped with every modern appliance available, and it took a few scant minutes to pour milk into a saucepan and heat it while she spooned sugar into a pottery mug. Filling it with milk, she carried it to a nearby table and sank into a chair.

Sipping the steaming contents with evident enjoyment she picked up a magazine and browsed through its pages, skimming over the captions until she discovered something of interest to read.

A slight sound alerted her attention and she turned slowly to see Nick standing a few feet distant.

'I can't imagine you to be waiting up for me?'

He sounded incredibly cynical, and she met his gleaming gaze steadily, despite the faint stirring of resentment deep within.

'I couldn't sleep,' she explained carefully. 'Can I get you anything?'

'*Grazie*, but no.' He lifted a hand and raked fingers through his hair, ruffling it into attractive disorder. 'I saw the light and thought it advisable to check.'

He looked tired, almost jaded, and Emma suppressed the impossible urge to smooth the tension from his forehead, loosen his tie and unbutton his shirt and bid him relax into a comfortable chair.

'How was your business dinner?'

'You sound like a wife,' he drawled, and she felt her heart constrict with pain.

Without a word she slid to her feet and crossed to the sink with her mug, then she moved towards the door.

'Emma.' He reached out and caught hold of her arm, halting her progress, and she pulled away from him, wincing slightly as the pressure increased with steel-like intensity.

'What do you want?'

'Would you believe—*you*?'

Her eyes glittered with brilliant golden fire as a

complexity of primitive emotions fought valiantly for control. 'Do you get a kick out of trying to wear down my resistance? Is that it?'

She shivered, despite the warm evening temperature, and just looking at him she was made frighteningly aware that the chemistry between them had somehow combined to form a perilous, combustible force.

In seeming slow motion she saw his head descend, then his mouth closed over hers in a kiss that made anything she had experienced before pale into insignificance. There was a wealth of seductive mastery in his touch, a sensuality that transcended mere feeling and scaled the heights.

Emma felt as if she was slowly drowning in a deep, translucent pool where sheer sensation ruled. Hardly aware of what she was doing, she let her arms creep up to clasp behind his neck as she unconsciously moved close against him.

His mouth coaxed hers, seeking a possession she was afraid to give, and his tongue became an erotic instrument in subtle persuasion as one hand held her nape, while the other slid up to cup one burgeoning breast, teasing its swollen peak into tantalising awareness.

It would be so easy to agree to sexual fulfilment, and for a moment she was almost tempted. Out of curiosity, a sheer need to discover if his sensual expertise extended to dispensing with her frigidity. Would this pulsing ache deep within dissipate and leave her feeling disappointed and somehow deprived? Or would it flare and explode into something glorious; be equally an orgasmic attuning of the flesh as well as of the mind?

A feeling of self-loathing rose to the fore, and with it

came guilt and a sense of disloyalty. How could she think like this, let alone consider . . .

With a whimper of distress she pulled away from him, shaken by the depth of her arousal and the ease with which he was able to achieve it.

Slowly she lifted her eyes to his, glimpsing little more than a keen scrutiny in his expression.

'I shall have to plead temporary insanity,' she said at last. 'Anything else would be impossible.'

A muscle tautened along his jaw, making his features appear harsh and forbidding. 'Would it?' His wry smile was not in the least kind, and her lips pursed slightly, then began to tremble at the thought of his ability to look into her soul.

'I'm going back to bed,' she declared, wanting only to get away from him.

'What a shame you insist it must be alone.'

'Would you believe I prefer it that way?'

'No,' said Nick with dangerous softness. 'Not if the way you react to me is any indication.'

Such a damning accusation was almost her undoing, and she felt a flood of colour heat her cheeks; then they went white, almost ashen. 'I hate you,' she breathed bitterly. 'My God, you can't know how much!'

Without a further word she stepped round him and made her way upstairs to her room, uncaring whether he followed or not.

CHAPTER EIGHT

THE panoramic vista of Naples, its beautiful, picturesque bay with the Isles of Ischia and Capri at its entrance, was a scenic delight. Vineyards and citrus groves dotted the hillside on the Bay's eastern shore, and the many houses with their multi-coloured roof-tiles, dulled and aged by the years, provided a pleasant contrast.

Emma had elected to wear a light cotton skirt with a blouse in spearmint green. The shade suited her colouring and looked both cool and fresh. Nick had stipulated casual attire, and he looked incredibly fit and virile in cream cotton Levis and a matching short-sleeved shirt. Annalisa chattered virtually non-stop during the drive down, and Emma was grateful for the young girl's presence. It made it easier to project a façade of normality; temporarily to forget what had transpired the previous evening.

From Sorrento they boarded the hydrofoil out to Capri, the fabled green isle of the Parthenopean Gulf, where they stopped at the Blue Grotto. The limestone sea cave was truly spectacular, with water reflections casting an eerily beautiful iridescence, a translucence that resembled a rare silk-encased jewel.

After a late lunch, eaten at one of Sorrento's colourful restaurants, Nick headed the Ferrari along the rugged coast road. Negotiating the twisting hairpin bends of Amalfi Drive took all his concentration, and Emma was unable to dampen her acute apprehension at the dramatically steep hillsides of the magnificent ravine which plunged down to the sea.

It was impossible not to be alarmed, and seated closest to the perilous drop made it all the worse. Perhaps if she closed her eyes . . . Damn! Assuring herself that Nick was an expert driver did little to aid her rapidly shredding nerves! Positano, with its pink, white and yellow houses perched precipitously against the perpendicular hillsides, was a revelation, and masses of bougainvillaea provided a colourful splash in contrast to the wide expanse of aquamarine sea.

By the time they reached Amalfi, Emma was a quivering wreck, and she viewed Nick's suggestion to stop for refreshments with immense relief.

'Can we have pizza, *Papa*?'

'Of course, if that is what you want.' He paused at a junction, then drove until he was able to park close to a *ristorante*. 'This should do.' He turned slightly and smiled, and Emma summoned every ounce of acting ability in an effort to appear relaxed.

'Wasn't that exciting?' Annalisa demanded as she slipped out from the car. 'I loved all the olive and lemon groves and the scent of orange blossom, the steep hills and all the twists and bends in the road. Didn't you, Emma?'

How could she say no, when the scenery was exquisite? Or spoil the young girl's pleasure by explaining that since being involved in a car accident a year ago she had developed a morbid fear of travelling as a passenger in *any* vehicle, no matter how competent the driver? It was a natural fear, her doctor had assured her, that would gradually lessen with time.

'It was beautiful,' she agreed, and started visibly when Nick caught hold of her elbow.

His eyes narrowed, and she bore his intent scrutiny with equanimity. 'You have become very pale. Are you feeling unwell?'

Oh, lord, Emma deplored silently. She'd have to get a grip on herself. 'I'm fine,' she assured him steadily, summoning a faint smile as she diverted her attention to Annalisa. 'Thirsty for something long and cool. Aren't you?'

'*Yes,*' the young girl enthused with an impish grin. 'In a tall glass, and *icy!*' She looked up at her father. 'Can we sit outside, *Papa*? I think watching people is fun, don't you?'

'I can see I am outnumbered,' Nick declared with mock resignation as he led them to an unoccupied table. Then, when they were comfortably seated, he sought their opinion on which type of pizza they should order.

'Seafood, with lots of cheese, capsicum and *everything,*' his daughter announced ravenously. 'Do say you like seafood, Emma,' she went on to implore. 'We love it, don't we, *Papa*?'

Nick let his gaze rest with affection on his daughter's shining head, then shifted a gleaming glance to Emma. 'Don't be unduly influenced,' he drawled musingly. 'It is possible to order pizza in a variety of sizes. You must have what you want.'

'Seafood will be fine. It's a favourite of mine.'

'We never have pizza at school, and Teresa refuses to make it for me more than once when I am home,' Annalisa declared.

'My housekeeper,' Nick explained drolly, 'is a woman who considers her culinary talents exceed the demands of pizza.'

'That is why *Papa* indulges me during the holidays,' Annalisa enlightened, throwing her father a beauteous smile, to which he responded with a gentle brush of his fingers to her cheek.

Emma felt something tighten with pain deep within that was difficult to explain. A sense of loss; envy, perhaps, of the genuine loving and caring that father and daughter shared. They represented a complete unit that was seemingly without need of a wife and mother. Why not, when there were a string of attractive women waiting discreetly in the wings to satisfy Nick's sexual appetite, and Annalisa was adequately cared for between Silvana, boarding school and her father? Emma knew she would be sad to relinquish their friendship when she left Italy. Sharing their company had proved a welcome salve to her own wounds, yet it had succeeded in opening the deepest and most hurtful of them all; the recognition that love possessed many facets, of which Marc had commanded only one.

The startling clarity of this discovery should have caused surprise. Instead, she was filled with a sense of release, almost freedom.

'Emma? I thought you were thirsty.'

For one split second she felt completely disorientated as she dragged her mind back from the past, and she proffered an apologetic smile across the table. 'I'm sorry, I was miles away.' She included Nick by sweeping a glance in his direction, then felt her eyes widen beneath his steady gaze, aware to her considerable chagrin that he knew just where her thoughts had been centred and their ultimate conclusion.

Dear lord in heaven—was she so transparent? It wasn't fair that he possessed the ability to read her mind, when *his* was a mystery. She knew he regarded her with affection, but affection affiliated to *what*? Was she simply a pretty diversion to fill his holiday, a companion for his daughter on their numerous excursions? If that were true, why had he kissed her with such dreamy sweetness and wrought havoc to her tender emotions? She frequently swung like a pendulum between agony and ecstasy, stricken by an angry helplessness at her awakening desire, yet rendered intensely vulnerable by her own fragility where he was concerned.

A decision to confirm her return flight to Sydney strengthened her resolve to leave Rome at the soonest opportunity, otherwise she was seriously in danger of losing the tenuous hold she had on her own sanity. To stay any longer was cruel, not only to herself, but to Annalisa, for there was little doubt that the young girl had become very fond of her Australian relative.

The arrival of a waiter with their order proved a welcome distraction, and Emma picked up a wedge of deliciously aromatic pizza and bit into it with relish, laughing when she was urged by Annalisa to take another piece.

It was half an hour before they made their way back to the car, contentedly replete, and ready for the last leg of coastal road to Salerno where they would pick up the autostrada direct to Rome.

Small villages dotted the landscape, charming, and so quiet they could have belonged to a former century, Emma decided as the Ferrari purred along the smooth ribbon of winding bitumen. Some of the houses bore the evidence of time, heightened by vivid splashes of colour portrayed by flowering plants in innumerable clay pots. It was too late to see young children at play, but there were fishing vessels anchored in one of the bays and yards of netting spread wide to dry.

Perhaps it was the food, or the numerous hours of travel, but Emma felt her eyelids begin to droop as weariness descended. Annalisa had become strangely quiet, and a glance towards the rear seat ascertained the young girl had fallen asleep.

It would be wonderful to give in to the weight of somnolence, and doze. Dared she? Nick wouldn't mind, in fact, he'd probably appreciate being able to concentrate solely on driving instead of keeping up a commentary on passing points of interest.

Gently lowering her lashes, she allowed herself a masked peep at his profile, admiring the strength in repose, a relaxation she could never hope to emulate. He looked totally in control, his movements at the wheel merely an extension of the vehicle as he negotiated the road.

Emma sensed his sudden alertness an instant before the vehicle braked, then swerved sharply to the right. It happened so quickly there was no time to prepare for the sickening thud as the Ferrari lurched into a concrete post.

A variety of sounds reverberated inside her head all at once; Annalisa's shocked cry, Nick's muffled oath, the horrendous screech of car brakes.

'Emma? Annalisa? Are you hurt?'

Nick's voice penetrated her stunned brain, and she added her own assurance to that of his daughter. The impact had left her more shaken than anything, and she bore his swift, analytical scrutiny in silence before he turned to check Annalisa.

Emma was aware that he had slipped out from behind the wheel, and she heard his deep voice, clipped and chillingly quiet, amid a stream of voluble Italian. She could see two pretty girls and two brash young men standing beside an expensive sports car. On their way to a party, and the driver presumably out to impress his passengers with a burst of speed round a hairpin bend.

'I was asleep,' Annalisa professed, her eyes wide with a mixture of shock and excitement, and Emma fought down the feeling of nausea that threatened to engulf her by taking several deep breaths in an effort to restore calm to her shattered nerves. 'Are you all right, Emma? You look white.'

She lifted a hand and ran shaky fingers through her hair. 'I'm fine, really.' Somehow she had to dampen this terrible sense of fear, precipitating memories of another accident, thus providing a terrifying feeling of *déjà vu*. Haunting and all too vivid was the crash scene in which Marc had been killed, and for a few petrifying minutes she was back there, reliving every painful detail in her mind.

It seemed an age before Nick returned to the car, time which she'd filled by recounting the day's events with Annalisa; and gradually the enormity of what could have been had begun to fade.

'I'll call the police, then arrange for a tow-truck,' Nick announced as he slid behind the wheel, and reached for the mobile telephone set into the centre console.

'Won't we be able to drive back to Rome, *Papa*?'

'Not tonight, *piccina*.' He pressed the final digit, then spoke into the receiver as he relayed the relevant information.

Why hadn't it occurred to her that they would be unable to continue their journey? Emma queried silently. Damage to the Ferrari precluded travelling so much as one kilometre, let alone a few hundred!

With smooth efficiency Nick arranged for the car to be towed to a garage in the nearby village of Vietri Mare, then he organised accommodation, rang Rosa to inform her of their delay, and finally, what was to prove the highlight of the evening for Annalisa—a lift into Vietri Mare in the police car when all the details had been completed.

The *pensione* was small, and the suite they were given immaculately neat and clean. Situated on the second floor it comprised two bedrooms, each of which led off from a central lounge. There was a functional bathroom and facilities to make tea or coffee. Breakfast, Nick told them, would be served in their suite at eight the following morning.

'We will have to sleep in our underwear,' Annalisa declared, apparently delighted by the novelty of it all, and she burst into undisguised laughter at her father's wry smile.

'Fortunately the *signora* who runs this humble establishment prepares for any emergency. She has been able to supply an assortment of toiletries, and extra towels. I am sure we'll manage.'

Emma managed a faint smile. 'How extensive is the Ferrari's damage?'

'It requires some basic repair work to make it roadworthy.' He raked a hand through his hair. 'I'll get the panel work done once we get back to Rome.'

'Will it take long, *Papa*?'

'Much depends on whether the local Ferrari agent has the necessary parts,' Nick declared. 'If not, he will have to send to Salerno.' He effected an imperceptible shrug. 'With luck, we should be able to leave late tomorrow.'

'Otherwise we get to stay another night,' Annalisa

stated solemnly. 'We might have to buy more clothes.' An irrepressible grin appeared, and her eyes sparkled mischievously. 'I will have an adventure to tell everyone when I get back to school. What fun!'

Emma privately thought she could do without just such an adventure! What it was to have the uncomplicated vision of the young, she decided with envy. Annalisa was extremely fortunate in having a father with sufficient power and wealth at his command to ensure maximum service was accomplished in the swiftest possible time.

It was quite late, well after eleven o'clock, and she glimpsed Annalisa's stifled yawn and offered a sympathetic smile. 'It's been a long day,' she pointed out gently. 'Do you want to go to bed?'

The young girl appeared a trifle reluctant, then she relented with a rueful grin. 'I think so.' Her eyes brightened considerably. 'You will share with me, won't you, Emma?' She looked askance at her father. 'You don't mind, do you, *Papa*?'

'Not unless Emma would prefer a room to herself,' Nick stipulated, and Emma felt her heart lurch, then begin a rapid beat as his gaze rested overlong on her slightly flustered features.

There was faint mockery evident in those dark depths that upset her composure and did strange things to her breathing. With considerable effort she dragged her eyes away from his and turned towards Annalisa. 'I don't mind sharing with you,' she said quietly. 'I'm feeling tired, too. Shall we both say goodnight to your father now?'

'Yes. We can talk for a while, can't we? Like sisters do,' the young girl declared happily, and reaching out she caught hold of Emma's hand, then she stretched up and planted a generous kiss to her father's cheek.

'Goodnight, *piccina*. Sleep well,' Nick bade, lifting his head.

'Do you want to kiss Emma, too, *Papa*?'

Innocence, or calculated guile? Emma pondered in a haze of embarrassment as she deliberately kept her eyes fixed on the hollow at the base of his throat, and she prayed fervently he would dismiss bestowing such a gesture.

'Why not?'

She heard his smooth query, then she stood completely still as he leant forward and kissed her softly parted mouth with considerable thoroughness.

'Goodnight, Emma.'

It took every ounce of will-power to retain a hold on her temper. How dared he subject her to such a display in front of Annalisa? Expose her to something that could so easily be misconstrued?

Emma didn't deign to look at him, and without a further word she turned and made her way with Annalisa to the bedroom they had elected to occupy for the night.

'Are you cross with me because I asked *Papa* to kiss you?' the young girl queried hesitantly as soon as the door closed behind them.

Emma was about to say *yes*, when she caught sight of the wretched uncertainty mirrored in Annalisa's expression, and she softened her rebuke with a slight smile. 'Not really.' With your father, she added silently, for taking unfair advantage of the situation.

'You do like him, don't you?'

What could she say? *Any* answer at all was potentially dangerous.

'I've enjoyed sharing his company with you,' she said carefully.

'Do you think you would like to—live in Italy?'

Oh lord, this was getting worse by the minute! She could see the wistful hope in Annalisa's hazel eyes, a fervent, childish wish to play matchmaker to two adults, one of whom she adored and wanted more than anything to provide her with a mother.

'My home is in Australia,' she answered gently. 'I have parents who would miss me dreadfully if I moved away.'

Annalisa was silent for several minutes, then her eyes misted with unshed tears. 'You think I am being silly, don't you?'

'Sweetheart, *no*! Never silly,' she answered swiftly, and she gathered the young girl's slight figure close against her own, feeling her throat constrict as small arms curled round her waist.

'I like you so much,' Annalisa vowed with muffled fervour. 'I wish you could stay for ever.'

'My boss would give me the sack,' Emma joked in an attempt at lightness. 'Then what would I do?'

'*Papa* could find you a job. I know he could.'

She felt the faint tremor that shook Annalisa's body, and she cursed Nick afresh for being instrument in fostering a young child's romantic dreams.

'We've had a lovely time together, haven't we?' she queried gently.

'Just like a real family.'

'We all indulge in pretend games, Annalisa,' she began quietly, stroking the silky hair with soothing movements. 'Even adults. Sadly, it isn't always possible to change make-believe into reality.'

'But I want it so badly.'

'I'm sure your father does everything he can to see that you are well cared for and content.' She took hold of Annalisa's chin and lifted it a little. 'Would you want him to be unhappy? He must have loved your mother very much—perhaps too much to think of allowing anyone to take her place.'

'I never knew her,' Annalisa owned wretchedly, and Emma's heart tightened painfully, feeling the young girl's hurt as if it were her own.

'The photographs you showed me of her were lovely. She was very beautiful.' A lump rose up in her throat as the celluloid vision of a laughing attractive young woman sprang readily to mind. Anna Castelli had held the world in her hands by virtue of being Nick Castelli's wife. Her eyes had glowed with it, and Emma experienced a shaft of pure, unadulterated jealousy slice through to her very soul. 'Just as you will be in a few short years,' she added unsteadily.

'Do you think so?' Annalisa queried doubtfully. 'Do I really look like my mother?'

'Really,' Emma declared softly. 'Now, shall we undress and get into bed? You use the bathroom first, while I turn down the covers, then I'll have a shower.'

Within minutes of slipping between the sheets Annalisa was asleep, her measured breathing indicative of a swift passage into blissful slumber. Not so Emma, who found it increasingly impossible to fall asleep. Even counting sheep didn't help, nor did any one of several relaxing techniques. In the end she simply gave up and resigned herself to laying awake until sheer weariness provided its own release.

Somehow she must have dozed without being aware of it, for she came sharply awake, still in the grip of a fearful nightmare, where it was dark and damp and the sound of her own screams mingled with those of several wailing sirens. She was in the car, and she was hurting, and there was a male body slumped grotesquely over the wheel beside her.

It was so vivid, so *real*, she could smell the spilt petrol, hear the voices of the men who dragged her clear, then the terrifying *whoosh* as the car ignited into flames.

God, oh dear God, *no*! Silent tears trickled down her cheeks unchecked as she stared sightlessly into the darkness.

It's all right, a tiny voice soothed, *it's all right*, it's just a bad dream. It's over, you're here, safe and alive. Just breathe deeply. But Marc is dead, she longed to scream.

Except she didn't, and gradually reality overtook the insanity of re-lived memory.

With shaking movements she brushed the wetness from her face, then she lay still, recalling all the pleasant events in her life with cold-hearted determination.

CHAPTER NINE

An hour later Emma was still staring at the ceiling, and the faint niggle at each temple had become a throbbing headache. A silent curse whispered in the darkness of the room. Now there was no hope of sleep, only the promise of enervating pain unless she took something to alleviate it. There were some tablets in her bag, and gingerly she slid out of bed and quietly wound one of the huge bathtowels sarong-wise round her body.

Sleeping *au naturel* wasn't something she normally indulged in, but there was little choice if she wanted to don fresh underwear in the morning. The light, wispy nylon would dry in a few hours, spread over a towel in her room, and she felt their slight dampness now, then shook her head. What did it matter? She was adequately covered, and besides, Nick was behind a closed door on the opposite side of the lounge. It would take only a few minutes to get some water from the bathroom and wash down two tablets.

Extracting the strip of foil from her bag, she quietly made her way from the room and crossed the lounge to the bathroom. Once there she switched on the light, then turned the faucet and half filled a glass with water.

She had just replaced it on the pedestal beside the white porcelain basin when she felt the hairs prickle at the back of her neck, and she moved her head in seemingly slow motion, half fearful whether some sixth sense had alerted her to the presence of another human or whether it was a figment of her imagination.

The last person she expected to see was Nick. No, she corrected dazedly—he was the last person she'd hoped to see.

'Unable to sleep?'

His voice was quiet, and she blinked, finding it difficult to focus on his features, for razing pain had seeped behind her eyes.

'I'm sorry if I disturbed you.' Her hand fluttered to the tucked edge of her towel, supremely conscious of her attire.

He moved further forward into the light, and she saw he too wore a towel, although his was knotted carelessly at his waist and reached his knees. The result was an expanse of muscular chest whorled with dark hair, broad shoulders, and an overall portrayal of silent, deadly strength.

'I was still awake.' He gave an imperceptible shrug as he shortened the distance between them. 'What is it? A headache?'

'Yes.' Her monosyllabic answer was scarcely more than a whisper, and she glimpsed his slight frown, the faint narrowing of his eyes, then her chin was taken between firm fingers and lifted so that she had little option but to bear his scrutiny.

'Where?' He gently probed one temple, then the other. 'There?'

'Yes,' she whispered, incapable of uttering another word, and of their own volition each eyelid drifted down in unison, hiding the pain and anguish from his view.

'What did you take? Prescribed medication?'

The action of his fingers was incredibly soothing, a tactile massage she could have borne indefinitely.

'Emma?'

She wanted to lay her head into the curve of his shoulder and absorb his strength, pretend for a short space of time that she was infinitely precious and possessed the right to expect his comfort.

'*Cara*——'

It was the endearment that did it, the careless affectionate inflection in his voice. Her eyes pricked with hot hears, then welled and spilled to trickle in slow twin rivulets down to her chin.

'Sweet Mother of God,' he muttered huskily. 'I was desperately afraid tonight's accident might revive that ill-fated crash.'

She didn't care any more, she just wanted solace to expiate a haunting memory, and she offered no resistance as he drew her into his arms.

It was like coming home: to warmth, security, and something much, much more. She could feel the faint stir of his breath against her hair, the steady thud of his heartbeat beneath her cheek.

With a featherlight touch Nick brushed his lips across one exposed temple, then trailed down to the sensitive cord at the edge of her neck. He created a slow, leisurely path along a pulsing hollow, caressing it with his tongue, teasing the delicate pulse that began to quicken beneath his touch, urging the beat to a thudding crescendo before lifting her head so that he could possess her mouth.

Slowly, with incredible sensitivity, he sought a response she was desperately afraid to give. There was a wealth of seduction in his touch that was impossible to ignore, and she gave a silent gasp as he caught hold of her lower lip between his teeth, nibbling at the full curve as he traced its outline with the tip of his tongue.

It was hopelessly erotic, transcending mere pleasure, and she moved restlessly in his arms, unconsciously wanting more.

A slow ache began in the region of her stomach, spreading in an ever-increasing circle, until her entire body seemed to radiate with passionate desire.

Emma closed her eyes, drowning in sheer sensation as his lips moved down to the edge of her towel, which somehow no longer provided any restriction. She cried out as his mouth took possession of one roseate peak, rolling it gently with his tongue before catching it between his teeth and applying sufficient pressure to place her on a knife-edge between intense pleasure and the threat of pain.

Somehow she seemed to be floating, transported high on to a sensual plateau from which she never wanted to descend, and it wasn't until she felt the soft cotton sheets beneath her back that she realised they were no longer in the lounge.

A subtle glow from a dimmed bedside lamp provided the room's only illumination, and was sufficient for her to be aware that she no longer wore the towel. Nor did Nick, his splendid, tautly muscled body a potent force, and her eyes dilated with a mixture of shock, anguish and pain, then became luminous as she silently begged fulfilment—too caught up with an aching physical need to struggle with her conscience.

Afterwards she would fight self-inflicted recriminations, undoubtedly hate herself for not rising up out of this illusory torpor which appeared responsible for weighting her limbs and keeping her enmeshed within a sensual web so powerful that only total satiation could provide its release.

Nick's mouth closed over hers, caressing, teasing, promising; yet just as she thought he'd deepen the kiss, his lips softened to brush a tantalising, evocative path over the curve of her mouth, until with a groan she lifted her hands and encircled his neck, tangling her fingers in the thick hair at his nape to hold fast his head.

Her body moved against his, unconsciously inviting his possession. Deliberately releasing her arms, he began a shameless exploration of the soft hollows at the base of her throat before moving lower to savour the delicate curves of one breast with its sensitised, hardened peak, then traced a path to its twin.

Slowly, with sensuous ease, his lips edged down over her ribcage, seeking the soft indentation of her navel before trailing lower.

Her shocked protest brought no respite, and she was powerless to still the restless movements of her limbs as they threshed impotently against the promised ecstasy of his touch; wanting, craving for him to continue, yet too caught up with untutored inhibitions to allow him licence to what he sought.

His mouth lifted to graze across her hip before tracing a path over her stomach to caress the curve of her waist, moving higher until his lips claimed hers in a deep, drugging kiss that wiped out any uncertainty.

A treacherous hunger clamoured assuagement, and soft whimpering sounds emerged from her throat as she begged his possession, crying out as his head lowered once more to discover her ultimate feminine core.

With deliberate eroticism he introduced her to an experience so fraught with sensual ecstasy she was unable to control its tide as it washed through her body, each successive wave seeming to lift her higher on to yet another sensory plateau.

Just as she thought she'd scaled the heights, he began to feather light kisses in a steady upward trail to her breasts, and her body arched of its own volition as he bestowed each a lingering caress, then leapt with hunger as he lowered his body over hers and effected one sure thrust.

She cried out as he began a slow, gentle pacing, withholding his pleasure until her body was in perfect accord with his own, then he guided her toward a euphoric vortex of emotion.

Afterwards she lay spent, consumed with a sweet-lethargy that made the simplest movement an effort. Even *thinking* about what had transpired between them brought a resurgence of languorous warmth, and her eyes flew wide open as Nick trailed gentle fingers across her cheek, then smoothed the thick auburn curls from her temple.

Don't say anything, she implored silently. Don't spoil something so beautiful, I'll probably never again know its equal.

His lips moved to her shoulder, caressing the delicate curves and hollows, before wandering with tactile sensuality to tease the lobe of her ear, taking it between his teeth then releasing it as he lifted a hand to her chin and forced her to meet his gaze.

Emma let her lashes sweep down, protectively veiling her eyes, knowing the deep, slumbrous passion evident in their depths would reveal with startling clarity the extent of her emotions.

She could feel his breath warm on her face as he leant forward and covered her lips with his own, softly, with a tenderness that made her want to cry. Then she gave an incredulous gasp as he caught hold of her hand and gently slid off Marc's wedding band and slipped it on to the third finger of her right hand.

Without a word he lifted her left hand to his lips, brushing them against the pale, exposed strip of skin, and her eyes dilated with dawning anguish.

Remorse, shame, flowed through her body, all-consuming as it mingled with guilt and a number of other equally untenable feelings.

'Let go of the past, *cara*.'

'I can't.' It was a cry from the heart, and she strove hard to regain her composure, hating herself, and *Nick*, with an intensity that was frightening.

'You can,' he insisted quietly, and her breathing became ragged as her eyes filled with distress.

'You're asking too much!' Emma whispered emotionally, wrenching against the hands that held her as she fought to be free. Except Nick wouldn't let her go, and she began to struggle in earnest, hating the ease with which he was able to reduce her wildly threshing form to impotent helplessness.

His arms were like bands of steel, moulding her against his body as if he intended for her to absorb some of his strength, and after a while she became less rigid, her agitation decreasing as her breathing began to quieten.

Slowly, with gradual perceptiveness, she became aware of the soothing movement of his hand as he traced a gentle path down the length of her spine, across her shoulders, then slid to her nape as his fingers began a tactile massage of the tense cores at the base of her scalp.

His head moved slightly, and she felt his lips brush her forehead, then rest against one throbbing temple, caressing it with sensitivity for what seemed an age.

With infinite gentleness he trailed his lips down to the

edge of her jaw, then slipped lower to the delicate hollows at the base of her neck, tasting the sweet indentations with unhurried ease.

'Please,' she begged brokenly as a traitorous warmth began to unfurl itself and steal treacherously through her veins. She felt herself tremble, and tears welled up behind her eyes until they became large pools of shimmering gold. 'Don't. I couldn't bear it.'

His lips grazed the length of her throat, and she felt, sensed, his murmured endearment as they settled on the edge of her mouth to tease the fullness of her lower lip before beginning a gentle probing exploration of the soft moistness within.

Nothing seemed to matter except the hungry desire spiralling through her body, encompassing and all-consuming until she became a willing supplicant, *his* to command in any way he chose.

'Stay with me.' His voice was deep and husky, his gaze gleaming with passionate intensity, yet there was a stillness about him, almost as if he was waiting for her willing complicance.

Comprehension brought forth a gamut of emotions, and she dared not look at him, or she'd be swept away by a complexity of sensations too diverse to analyse.

'No,' she refused with a strangled gasp, and her eyes dilated with sheer torment as she stammered quickly, 'What you're asking—isn't fair. Annalisa——' Her voice trailed off, then returned in agonised indecision. 'How can I?' She was almost shaking with reaction, becoming aware of her nakedness, his. She looked wildly for something to cover herself, and grabbed hold of a nearby towel and wound it sarong-wise round her body. 'Please,' she implored, 'don't you see that it isn't possible?'

His gaze was carefully inscrutable, his fingers gentle as they brushed lightly across her cheek. 'I can't persuade you to change your mind?'

All too easily, she declared silently as she shook her head in mute negation. 'I must go.' It became imperative to leave now, if she was to retain a shred of sanity, and she almost ran towards the door in her hurry to get away.

'Emma.'

There was something in his voice that brought her to a standstill, and she let go of the doorknob and slowly turned back to face him.

'Thank you,' he said gently.

How could she respond to that? Reciprocate and assure him he was the most sensitive man she'd ever had the pleasure to know? Her limited experience with men precluded the necessary *savoir-faire* to utter even a simple acknowledgment, and she dragged her eyes away from the paganistic splendour he represented and moved quickly from the room.

In the bathroom she quietly closed the door behind her and stepped beneath the shower, then she soaped every square inch of skin until it glowed before she rinsed off the suds and emerged to towel herself dry.

A quick glance in the mirror drew forth a startled gasp, and her eyes widened in disbelief that the reflected mirror-image was herself. Why, she looked positively *ethereal*! Her mouth was soft and slightly swollen, and her eyes ... They bore a dreamy expression, their depths secretive and gleaming with the intense satisfaction of sexual satiation. Anyone seeing her now would be in no doubt as to how she'd spent the previous few hours. All the evidence was there, and she closed her eyes in self-remorse, fearful that life would never again be the same.

Don't think, she bade herself silently as she wound the towel around her slim curves and switched off the light.

Within seconds she slid between the sheets of the bed in the room she shared with Annalisa, and she endeavoured to cull sleep in the hope it would provide a blissful oblivion from the numerous condemnations invading her brain.

Perhaps a guardian angel looked down with beneficence, for it seemed only minutes before her eyelids fluttered closed, and she woke to the sound of Annalisa's bright voice mingling with that of Nick's deeper tones just outside the bedroom door.

'Shall we wake Emma, do you think, *Papa*? Breakfast is ready, and it will get cold.'

'Just a little longer, *piccina*, hmm? We can always order more later.'

Without thought Emma threw back the covers and slid to her feet. Gathering up her clothes, she quickly donned bra and panties, then stepped into her half-slip and pulled on her skirt and blouse. Her hair, she groaned silently. What on earth could she do to restore it to some kind of order? The small brush she carried in her bag was totally inadequate for anything more than the briefest tidying of her tumbled tresses. At least the village shops would open this morning and she could buy the necessary requisites!

With a nervous gesture she smoothed the belt at her waist and fingered the top button on her blouse, then she took a deep breath and crossed to the door.

'Good morning.' The words sounded overbright and false, even to her own ears and, while she offered Annalisa a warm smile, she let her gaze skim towards Nick without meeting his eyes. She couldn't. After last night, it took all her courage to face him.

'Emma, you were fast asleep when I woke!' Annalisa cried as she closed the space between them. 'Come and eat breakfast. There's cereal and fruit, toast, coffee. Or you can have eggs, with *prosciutto* or salami.'

'Toast and coffee will be fine,' she said quickly, and privately thought she'd be fortunate if she ate anything at all.

'I trust you slept well?' Nick queried, and Emma aimed a quick smile in the direction of his right shoulder.

'Yes, thank you,' she responded evenly. He knew precisely how she'd spent a few hours of the night, none of which had been occupied with *sleeping*!

'Shall I pour you some coffee, Emma?' Annalisa asked solicitously, wielding the silver pot with ease as she filled her father's cup.

'Please. I'd love some.'

It was like playing a game, Emma determined with detachment. Nick's smile was as warm and friendly as it had ever been, his manner that of a man relaxed and totally at ease. Beneath the fringe of her lowered lashes she had the opportunity to view him unobserved—or so she thought until she incurred a gleaming glance full of passionate intensity, and something else she was unwilling to define.

Thank heavens for Annalisa's presence, otherwise she wouldn't be sitting across the table sharing something as mundane as breakfast. The promise of precisely *where* she would be was reflected momentarily in his eyes, and a shaft of exquisite pleasure rose from deep within, spiralling rapidly until it encompassed her entire body.

It was maddening to feel so—*possessed*, she decided shakily, aware that her breathing had quickened considerably and there was a painful lump in her throat.

Consequently it was a relief to escape the confines of their suite and wander through the village. The Ferrari looked sadly the worse for its encounter with a post, and Nick was able to find out that the car would be ready early that evening.

For the remainder of the morning they browsed among the village shops, lunched at a seaside *bistro*, then returned to the *pensione* to observe siesta and escape the heat.

After a shower and a light meal Nick left to collect the car, and it was almost seven when they reached Salerno and joined the *autostrada* leading back to Rome.

It was late when Nick brought the car to a halt outside the villa. Annalisa had lapsed into a fitful doze during the latter part of the drive, and Emma, ever conscious of Nick's immediate presence, took the easy way out and simply closed her eyes and leaned her head back against the cushioned head-rest. It precluded the need for conversation, and quite frankly she couldn't think of a thing to say to him. Her own thoughts were damning, her sense of self-recrimination increasing with every passing hour until her mind seemed filled with jagged sequences that taunted with kaleidoscopic confusion.

'We have to talk.'

Emma lifted her head slowly and turned towards the owner of that deep, slightly accented voice.

'Whatever for?' she managed calmly, and glimpsed the slight hardening of his expression in the reflection of light illuminating the sheltered portico.

'Don't freeze me out, Emma,' Nick warned quietly, and she bit back a swift retort as Annalisa stirred into wakefulness and asked if they'd arrived home.

'Yes, we have,' her father imparted, shooting Emma a wry glance before shifting his attention to his daughter. 'And here is Zia Rosa to welcome us.'

Emma reached for the door-handle and slipped out from the car, whereupon she was immediately enveloped in an affectionate embrace, and there was very little need for her to say anything at all in light of Annalisa's excited recounting and Nick's affirmation of the facts.

'Maria will bring some refreshments,' Rosa insisted as she urged them towards the *salone*. 'You must be hungry.'

'I'm thirsty,' Annalisa pronounced. '*Papa* drove straight through without stopping.'

'After feeding you an early dinner,' Nick pointed out teasingly, and she burst into delicious laughter.

'Marinaded baby octupus! Emma was not impressed.'

'There were other selections on the menu,' he chided good-naturedly as he greeted Enzo and accepted a glass of white wine.

'Emma? What will you have?'

Wine would undoubtedly go to her head, and she needed clarity of mind if she was to bear Nick's presence with any equanimity. 'Soda water will be fine,' she acquiesced, and met Enzo's faintly raised eyebrow with a slight smile. If only she could escape to her room, yet to do so too soon would be tantamount to an admission of sorts. It was bad enough that Nick could see through her pretence. To allow Rosa and Enzo to discern any subtle change in her relationship with their nephew would be more than she could bear.

So she stayed where she was, listening as Rosa relayed a message for Nick that had come through from his office in Milan late the previous afternoon, then contained a mixture of disappointment and swift calculation when he returned from making the call to announce that he would have to absent himself for a few days.

'It cannot wait, unfortunately. An important associate has arrived unexpectedly from France, and he refuses to deal with anyone else.' One eyebrow rose in a semblance of wry resignation. 'No amount of appeasement will satisfy, despite the fact there are two men on hand more than capable of coping with him.' He shot Rosa a conciliatory smile. 'I've booked an early-morning flight. I hope you don't mind?'

'Of course not,' Rosa determined at once. 'Annalisa must stay with us.' She lifted a hand as Nick would have intervened. 'No, I insist. You have been so kind to Emma while she has been here. Now it is my turn. Together with Annalisa, we will explore the boutiques. Something, I have learned,' she continued with a wicked twinkle, 'men prefer to avoid.'

'I could easily contact Silvana and have her take care of Annalisa for the time I will be away.'

'Oh no, *Papa*,' his daughter implored. 'I would much prefer to stay here at the villa with Zia Rosa and Emma. It will be such fun, I will hardly have time to miss you.'

Nick's teeth showed white as he bit back his laughter, but his eyes were sober as he directed Emma a piercing glance, taunting silently if *she* would miss him.

She caught his crystalline gaze and a faint line of colour ran fleetingly along her cheekbones, betraying the strength of her emotions. She felt bewitched and tormented by a memory that would live with her for ever—solitary, beautiful, and never to be repeated. Tomorrow she would ring the airport and book the first plane bound for Sydney.

'It's late, *piccina*,' Nick directed gently. 'More than time you went upstairs to bed, hmm?'

The young girl looked at him earnestly. 'Will you be gone before I wake in the morning?'

'Probably,' he concurred musingly. 'I must leave the villa before six.'

'Then I'll say goodbye now.' She crossed to where he sat and twined her arms around his neck. 'Take care, *Papa*. Hurry back.'

'Indeed I shall,' he assured her, returning her kiss.

It seemed a good opportunity for Emma to make good her escape, and she rose to her feet, indicating her intention to retire.

'I'll come with you,' Nick declared, unwinding his lengthy frame from the chair. 'It's been a long day, and I have to make an early start.'

She suffered his light clasp at her elbow, only because it was impossible to wrench away. He must have sensed her disquiet, for his fingers tightened with iron-like intensity, and she stood helplessly still as Annalisa bade them goodnight and ran lightly ahead up the stairs.

'Would you prefer your bedroom, or mine?' Nick asked quietly, and silently mocked her as she broke into soft-voiced fury.

'Neither!'

'Such vehemence,' he said gently. 'When only last night you——'

'Last night was a mistake!' she cried wretchedly.

'I refuse to believe you mean that.'

Oh lord, she was falling deeper into the mire with every word she uttered! 'I'd like to go to bed,' she insisted, meeting his gaze with effort, and his eyes darkened fractionally, then lightened as they assumed a musing gleam.

'No moonlight stroll through the garden?'

'I really am tired.' Perhaps she sounded weary, for he led her upstairs to her room and before she could protest he followed her inside.

'Nick—don't. *Please.*' If he touched her, she'd break into a thousand pieces.

'Poor little girl, you sound terribly fragile in mind and spirit. Perhaps I will let you escape, after all—until I get back from Milan.' He lifted a hand and smoothed gentle fingers along the length of her jaw. 'Goodnight, *cara.*'

She closed her eyes as he brushed his lips lightly across her own, and she could have wept from the need to reach up and kiss him back.

'I'll ring tomorrow evening, about ten,' he said huskily, then he turned and left the room without so much as a backward glance.

CHAPTER TEN

'EMMA! *Darling*—over here.'

Through a sea of faces Emma caught sight of her parents and within seconds she was embraced and hugged, laughingly, lovingly besieged by countless questions. Her father took charge of her luggage, hefting the suitcases with ease, and together they made their way out to the airport car park.

It was cool, the skies bleak and heavy with imminent rain, and Emma shivered. After experiencing several weeks of Northern hemispheric sunshine, Sydney's winter temperatures seemed positively icy.

'You look so well,' Mrs Templeton enthused, her face wreathed with warm affection. 'And your tan! I'm dying to hear all about your trip.' She tucked her arm through that of her daughter's and gave it a firm squeeze. 'Postcards and letters are fine, but nothing compares with first-hand news.'

Amazing, Emma decided ruefully, that they failed to detect the misery through her outwardly cheerful façade. Inside she was breaking into a hundred tiny pieces, glad yet sad to be back home, although her emotions were in such a state of turmoil she seemed to be functioning by some form of automatic remote control.

Leaving Italy had involved subtle subterfuge, and saying goodbye to Rosa and Enzo had been the hardest part of all, not to mention Annalisa of whom she had become inordinately fond. However, there was no power on earth that could have persuaded her to stay and await Nick's return from Milan—two, three days hence.

A tiny bubble of hysterical laughter rose in her throat. They never had got around to talking. Even thinking about those fateful hours in his room brought pulsing heat vibrating through her veins until her whole body seemed to throb, aching even now with a damnable craving for his possession. It was sickening, and she didn't know who to hate more—Nick, or her own traitorous flesh.

'Two suitcases, when you left with only one. Did the airline charge you excess baggage?'

Emma forced her attention back to the present at the sound of her father's voice, and she even managed a light laugh as she slid into the rear seat of her parents' Daimler. 'I smiled sweetly,' she ventured with a deprecatory smile. 'And they let me through. Who could resist a shopping spree in Rome?'

'We'll have a lovely day together tomorrow sorting it all out,' her mother declared with all the contented happiness of a clucky hen having gathered its solitary chick beneath her protective wing.

'I thought I might go in to work,' Emma broached tentatively, and received an immediate remonstrative response.

'So soon? Surely you could leave it until Monday?'

She could, very easily. Except the thought of remaining idle at home for more than a few days was impossible. If she wanted to retain a shred of sanity, she needed to immerse herself in work.

'Just for a few hours,' she declared, compromising in

part. 'To drop off my sketches, so that Roberto can sort through them over the weekend.'

A month from now her holiday would be a pleasant memory and she would be able to relegate her encounter with Nick Castelli to its rightful place—that of a transitory romance which had no lasting importance in her life.

Except it didn't work that way. Instead of getting better with each passing day, it only became worse. She ate barely at all, and slept even less. Nick's forceful image was a vivid, haunting entity, ever present, filling her thoughts to such an extent that dispelling it became an impossibility. He was *there*, his deeply etched features imprinted in her mind, taunting and infinitely disturbing. The days were bad enough, but the nights were totally unbearable. Remembering her wanton response, the way she had actively craved his possession made her want to die with remorse and shame. Nick's musing observation that she was seemingly untouched by the heights and depths of passionate intensity was true, for Marc's lovemaking had never explored the realms of tactile sensuality to such an extent that she'd become utterly mindless, incapable of rational thought in an attempt to please as she was being pleasured, permitting liberties her untutored flesh hadn't known existed.

Flinging herself into a social whirl with numerous friends did no good at all, except to remove her presence from the house and the increasingly concerned eye of her parents.

Two weeks—no word, no letter, not even a phone call.

What did you expect? Emma demanded with unaccustomed scepticism. Nothing—*nothing*.

The words seemed to echo and re-echo in open mockery, and with a gesture of impotent despair she crossed to the dressing-table and began applying make-up in an effort to add some colour to her pale features. Attending church each Sunday with her parents was a lifelong habit, and she viewed her mirrored reflection with something akin to critical cynicism, seeing the faint—almost bruising—smudges beneath her eyes, the lack of sparkling warmth in their depths whenever she smiled. Anyone with a modicum of perception must see there was something wrong, and a derisive grimace momentarily clouded her features.

When would this agonising longing diminish and become less than an unbearable, aching need?

Lust, she dismissed hollowly. It couldn't be anything else—*could it*? Oh, dear lord, *no*—not *love*! It wasn't possible to love two men. Yet the degree of passion, the sheer magical ecstasy Nick had been able to evoke went beyond mere desire.

Shock stilled her fingers, and she gazed sightlessly ahead, riveted by her own revelation. Like a jigsaw, all the pieces began to fall slowly into place.

Nick's forceful features came to mind with startling clarity, and she closed her eyes against an awakening knowledge. Up until now she hadn't been willing to define her emotions, much less accept that love might be any part of them.

Unconsciously she sought Marc's wedding band where it still rested on the third finger of her right hand, letting her eyes sweep to the framed photograph placed within touching distance, depicting the features of a laughing young man captured on celluloid.

Of its own volition her hand reached out and she slowly traced the familiar face with a gentle finger. A pair of gleaming eyes looked back at her, so alive; his hair bore a gloss, an illusion of photographic artistry, and his mouth was parted in a carefree smile.

It was strange, she discovered with a sense of wonder, but looking at his image no longer brought the onset of pain. Just sweet regret for the loss of a very dear friend.

Almost silently she opened a drawer and withdrew a large photograph album, then she crossed to sit on the bed, opened the embossed cover, and began to leaf through the pages slowly, aware of so many memories, such a wealth of happiness, affection; love in its gentlest form, sharing, caring that encompassed every facet of their togetherness.

It seemed an age before she reached the final page, then she stood to her feet and replaced the album back into the drawer where it belonged. Somehow the action seemed symbolic with the closing of a chapter in her life.

'Emma?'

The sound of her mother's voice intruded, and she turned, summoning a smile.

'We'll be late, darling. It's almost eleven, now,' Mrs Templeton advised with a faintly anxious frown.

'I'm ready,' Emma assured as she caught up her coat from the bed and shrugged it on before collecting her shoulder-bag.

It was after midday when they arrived home, and once indoors Emma changed into designer jeans and a loose-fitting multi-coloured knitted jumper, then she made her way towards the kitchen to help prepare lunch.

Just as she was placing a casserole into the microwave

the doorbell pealed, its melodic chimes sounding inordinately loud.

'I'll get it,' Emma called, aware that her father was comfortably ensconced in the library studying the Sunday papers and her mother was in the midst of setting the table.

Who could be visiting at this hour? And on a cold day with rain lashing the house in noisy gusts that rattled the windowpanes and shook the roof struts? Two hours previously it had been fine, a false preliminary to southern hemispheric spring, sharp and cool with wind whipping through the tree branches and buffeting all that stood in its path.

Emma reached the front door and opened it, a ready smile poised in greeting, then she froze, shocked into immobility as she recognised the man standing on the sheltered porch.

Nick stood comfortably at ease, his tall frame filling the aperture, and her heart gave a sickening lurch.

Leashed strength was apparent in his stance, an almost animalistic sense of power, and his dark brown eyes bore an expression of deliberate inscrutability as they met hers, forcing her to hold his gaze before subjecting her to a swift, analytical appraisal.

'Emma.' The faintly inflected drawl held wary cynicism, and a dozen questions rushed to the fore, demanding answer, but only two rose to the surface.

What are you doing here? Why have you come? Except neither found voice, and she wondered hysterically if she was in the grip of some nerve-racking form of paralysis.

'Aren't you going to ask me in?'

No! The emphatic denial screamed in immediate

response, and for a few horrifying seconds she thought the sound had actually escaped her throat. Raw, aching pain clenched in her stomach, and for one heart-stopping second she considered shutting the door in his face, sure that his image was nothing more than a cruel quirk of her own damnable imagination.

Confusion reigned as a multitude of conflicting thoughts raced without coherence through her brain, and she knew with chilling certainty that there could be no escape.

It was there in his eyes, a seemingly calm inflexibility combined with indomitable will—almost as if he was issuing a silent threat.

'Who is it, darling?'

Oh lord, her mother, half-way down the hall, and certainly within hearing distance.

'Emma?' Mrs Templeton came to a faltering halt within touching distance, her pleasant features schooled into polite enquiry as they caught sight of the tall, casual but elegantly dressed man standing in her doorway. 'Is something wrong?'

With skilled adroitness Nick introduced himself, explained both his recent arrival and his connection with the Martinero family, by which time Mrs Templeton had ushered him inside and divested him of his coat, while Emma stood unable to utter so much as a word, hearing with sickening clarity the invitation her mother extended him to join them for lunch.

The next few minutes held all the connotations of a comic farce as her father was summoned from the library, and somehow Emma found herself seated in the lounge with a drink in her hand.

'Do sit down, my dear fellow,' Mr Templeton insisted heartily. 'Let me get you something to drink. Wine? Or would you prefer something stronger?'

Emma took an appreciative sip of wine from the goblet, glad of an excuse to occupy her hands as Nick accepted whisky and soda and then lowered his length into a chair directly opposite her own.

Attired in dark hip-hugging trousers, an equally dark shirt beneath a black V-necked jumper, he looked vaguely satanical and as much of a threat to her equilibrium as he had been within the first week of her meeting him.

The need to say something forced a polite query from her lips. 'When did you arrive?'

His eyes held hers with unwavering scrutiny, and the seconds seemed interminably long before he informed her, with damning imperturbability, 'Yesterday.'

Yesterday? He'd been here for more than twenty-four hours, and she hadn't known? Surely some instinctive defence mechanism should have warned her? Yesterday she'd calmly driven into the city, put in two extra hours at work assembling co-ordinates for an important client, eaten, slept, all the while ignorant and unaware that he was *here?* It didn't seem possible.

'I presume you've come on business?'

His gaze was bleak, dark with an indefinable quality she was unable to penetrate. 'No.'

Emma's heart gave a jolt, then began to thud loudly against her ribs. The sound seemed to reach her ears, momentarily filling them, and she was conscious of the rapid pulse-beat at the base of her throat—so much so, that she lifted a defensive hand to shield it from view.

'How long are you staying?' Was that her voice? So polite, *calm*, when inside she was a mass of conflicting emotions.

'As long as it takes.'

To do what? she longed to scream.

After what seemed an age, Mrs Templeton announced lunch was ready, and seated across the table from him Emma attempted to do some justice to the excellent casserole.

Nick, damn him, ate with evident enjoyment, and gave every indication of being totally at ease. Emma's parents, while seemingly benevolent hosts, couldn't help but be aware of the electric tension generated between their daughter and their guest, and were doubtless curious as to the reason why.

To say her parents were intrigued by Nick Castelli's presence was an understatement, and all through lunch Emma could sense their veiled evaluation of him.

His visit here *now* was the antithesis of coincidence, and her mind seethed with a multitude of possibilities—none of which provided a satisfactory answer.

All her senses seemed to have developed a heightened awareness, and she was acutely concious of him, the muscular tautness of his countenance, the breadth of his shoulders. It was crazy, but she wanted to reach out and touch him, feel the strength of him beneath her hands, his mouth on hers as he transported her high on to an illusory, elusive plateau where sheer sensation surpassed all rational thought.

The knowledge lent a haunting quality to her finely moulded features, a faint breathlessness to her voice as the meal progressed, and it irked her unbearably that he knew. Not only *knew*, but he seemed to be silently taunting her with her own perceptiveness.

'Could you spare Emma for a few hours?' he enquired with studied indolence, daring her to refuse as he added quietly, 'Sightseeing is infinitely more pleasurable in the company of someone familiar with this beautiful city.'

'Of course Emma must go with you,' Mrs Templeton declared at once. 'Rosa and Enzo mentioned how kind you were to Emma when she stayed with them in Rome. It's the very least she can do in return.'

Oh, he was far too shrewd for his own good, Emma seethed in frustrated silence. Couldn't her parents see that he had deliberately contrived to get her alone?

'Fetch your coat, darling. It will be cold outside,' her mother bade, unaware that Emma was already cold, shivering with an unspecified fear that had as its base the agony of Nick's unknown intention once they left the sanctuary of her home.

One thing was remarkably clear, she decided darkly. *Sightseeing* was the last item on his agenda.

'You must stay for dinner. I could ask Marc's parents to join us. After all, his father is your cousin. Have you never met?'

Don't, Emma almost cried out. It would be akin to setting a cat among the pigeons. Worse, for Nick Castelli was no ordinary cat—his affiliation to the feline family went beyond the domestic variety.

'When we were young, yes,' Nick concurred with a faint smile. 'Although I was barely in my teens when Bruno emigrated to Australia.'

'Then that's settled,' Mrs Templeton beamed, pleased with the prospect of what she envisaged would be a family reunion. 'I'll ring them at once. Shall we say six-thirty?'

'Thank you,' Nick responded gently. 'You're very kind.'

Kind? Emma didn't doubt the motive behind her mother's invitation. It was Nick's purpose that was highly suspect. And what was there to gain by causing Lena and Bruno Martinero the added pain of witnessing their son's widow in the company of another man?

Somehow Emma made it to the car, and once seated she waited only until they were mobile before accusing furiously, 'You did that on purpose, didn't you?'

The car reached the end of the street, then eased into the main stream of traffic heading towards the city.

She could feel herself begin to shake, both outwardly and inwardly, and she hugged her arms in an effort towards control, fixing her gaze beyond the windscreen and watching with mesmerised detachment the spots of rain that began to dot the plated glass. Within seconds they grew and spread as the elements lashed the car with windswept fury, restricting visibility to a minimum.

'Where are you taking me?' Even as she asked the question, she realised with startling clarity that he had only one destination in mind, and fear knotted her stomach into a painful ball. 'Damn you, Nick! *Damn you!*'

A muscle tensed along the edge of his jaw, and his eyes glittered with latent anger. 'Have a care, Emma. I'm not entirely familiar with this vehicle, or the precise route into the city.'

'Where in the city, exactly?'

'Adjacent Hyde Park.'

She directed him with cool civility and the minimum

of words, and it wasn't until he slid the car to a halt in the
entrance of an impressive hotel that she gave vent to her
anger.

'If you think I'm getting out of this car, you're
mistaken!'

'Brave words, *cara*,' he drawled with hateful cynicism.
'But you don't have a say in the matter.' Sliding out from
behind the wheel he crossed to her side and opened her
door, then leant forward and unfastened her seat-belt.

Emma became aware of the porter hovering discreetly
nearby, together with a uniformed attendant who
accepted the keys Nick handed him with polite
deference.

'Emma.' His voice held an invincible quality that
threatened retribution, but she was damned if she'd
meekly comply.

'Give me one valid reason *why*,' she sallied with
unaccustomed stubbornness, and saw his expression
harden into a compelling mask.

'You're coming with me, one way or another—so
choose, Emma,' he declared with bleak implacability.
'On your feet—or hoisted over my shoulder.' He paused
fractionally, then continued with deadly softness, 'I find
it difficult to believe you'd appreciate causing a
spectacle.'

She looked at him in silence for several seconds,
waging a mutinous war against his high-handedness.
However, capitulation seemed the only advisable course
if she was to retain a shred of dignity, and without a word
she slipped out from the passenger seat.

His hand closed round her arm with a steely grasp, and
she gritted her teeth together against his strength.

'You're hurting me.'

'Believe me, I'm showing remarkable restraint.'

They traversed the deep-piled carpeted foyer towards the elevator, and the doors whispered open within seconds of Nick pressing the call-button.

Inside, and mercifully alone in the confines of the electronic carriage, she turned to face him.

'What do you want from me?' It was a cry from the heart, and his features tautened until they resembled hewn stone.

'The truth.'

CHAPTER ELEVEN

'WHAT *is* the truth, Nick?' Raw cynicism edged Emma's voice, lending it a mockery she'd never thought to possess.

The elevator slid to a halt and they emerged into an empty corridor. Nick indicated a door to the right, and when they reached it he produced a key, inserted it into the lock, then gently pushed her inside.

It was a suite, Emma discovered with a quick glance, and one commanding a top-of-the-range tariff, for the furnishings looked expensive and from this height there had to be a spectacular view over the harbour.

'Would you like a drink?'

Something seemed to snap inside her, and a burst of hysterical laughter emerged from her lips. 'Oh, by all means, let's observe the conventions.'

He crossed the lounge to a small bar-fridge and extracted two glasses into which he poured what appeared to be a fairly potent mixture of spirits before placing one glass into her nerveless hand.

'*Salute.*'

She took a generous sip and endeavoured not to cough as the fiery liquid hit the back of her throat. It tasted horrible, but it had the desired effect, for within seconds a delicious warmth invaded her veins, and she no longer felt quite so on edge.

'Now,' Nick began silkily. 'Suppose you explain why you fled so swiftly from the villa, and Rome.'

His voice was deceptively quiet, but his eyes were

dark, gleaming depths of inimical anger, and she began to shake, the tremors of her body seemingly beyond her control as she opted for flippancy. Anything else was madness.

'You don't mess around with the niceties, do you? Just aim for the jugular.'

She watched in mesmerised fascination as he replaced his glass on a nearby table, and there was everything predatory about his movements as he shortened the distance between them.

'I could easily have killed you when I telephoned the villa and discovered from my unusually flustered aunt that you had two hours previously boarded a flight out of Rome.' His voice hardened with frightening intensity. 'I returned at once, to find Annalisa distraught and confused. She quite wrongly attributed some of the blame for your exit on to her own head, imagining that you didn't want either of us and had consequently fled to avoid further embarrassment.'

Emma closed her eyes, then slowly opened them to find he was within touching distance, and she fixed her attention on the V of his jumper, unwilling to meet his gaze.

'I didn't mean for Annalisa to be hurt.' The words came out in a ragged flow of remorse.

'She wouldn't have been, if you had stayed,' Nick went on with pitiless disregard. His eyes darkened until they resembled polished onyx, glittery with unabated anger.

Emma took a backwards step as she glimpsed the icy rage apparent, and her eyes widened as he caught hold of her shoulders and dragged her close.

Even as his head lowered she twisted her own in a desperate attempt to avoid the forceful pressure of his mouth, and she gave an anguished groan as her lips were crushed with bruising insistence, his touch hard and merciless, almost cruel, as he sought the sweet inner moistness she fought so hard to deny him.

A shudder shook her slender frame, an almost convulsive reaction to the traitorous kindling of desire that swept like flame through her body, consuming all her inhibitions with galling swiftness.

Sheer perversity kept her mouth tightly closed, and it was only when his hand slid to capture her nape, his fingers tightening ruthlessly in the riot of curls there, pulling the tender roots, that she gasped against the excruciating pain. Then she almost cried as he gained entry, filling her mouth and plundering its depths with such utter devastation that it became nothing less than a total ravishment of her senses.

Nothing, *nothing* could be worse than this, she agonised mindlessly as she silently willed him to stop for fear she might slip into an engulfing, threatening void.

Then suddenly she was free, thrust roughly away, and she dimly registered his husky, almost guttural exclamation of self-disgust a few brief seconds before he pulled her back into his arms, burying her head into the curve of his shoulder, and she felt his lips drift softly against her temple.

'Forgive me,' he murmured gently. Fingers that seemed oddly shaky slid through her hair, and she felt a tremor run through his powerful body, heard the rapid thud of his heartbeat beneath her cheek racing almost as fast as her own; then his mouth travelled slowly to seek the sensitive curve of her neck, brushing the deep pulsing cord before lifting his hands to cup her face.

Emma closed her eyes against his dark, chiselled profile, and her mouth began to tremble of its own volition as his lips trailed over her cheekbones, the delicate length of her nose, then each closed eye in turn before claiming her mouth.

This time there was only gentleness in his touch, an incredible tenderness that was almost a benediction, as he traced the bruised outline with his tongue before sliding up to caress an earlobe, taking it gently between his teeth, and she could almost sense his smile as he murmured teasingly, '*Cara . . . Bellissima.* Or perhaps you would prefer *amante—inamorata?*'

Lover. Even thinking about those hours she'd spent in his arms brought a fresh flood of ignoble colour to her cheeks. Her voice seemed locked in her throat, unable to emerge, and after a few miserable seconds she let her lashes sweep slowly down, veiling their expressive depths.

'Emma?'

She not only couldn't speak, she couldn't bear to look at him.

'*Dio,*' Nick groaned emotively. 'How can you be so *blind?*' He shook her gently, and she felt his hands slip up to cradle her face. 'Look at me.'

Her eyelids quivered, then slowly flickered upwards in obedience, and she glimpsed the wealth of emotion apparent, the sheer depth of feeling that was solely for her.

'The past two weeks have been hell.' He lifted a hand and raked weary fingers through his hair, ruffling it into attractive disorder, and Emma glimpsed the tension etching his features, the bleakness evident in his eyes.

'I picked up the telephone at least once every night. There were so many words I wanted to say—simple, yet desperately important words, like—*I love you.* Instead, I was swayed by a pair of haunting gold eyes which alternately begged and pleaded with me, and I replaced the receiver before the call could connect.'

She wasn't capable of uttering so much as a word, and she watched with captivating fascination as Nick lifted a hand and brushed gentle fingers across her cheek, then along the edge of her chin, tilting it as he forced her to retain his gaze.

'I knew you needed time away from me, time in which to be able to evaluate your own feelings and gain some kind of perspective. I was sure of my emotions. Sure of yours.' A faint smile lifted the edges of his mouth, then twisted with a degree of cynicism. 'Does that sound presumptuous? God knows, I've suffered the tortures of the damned—wanting, needing you.' His expression became infinitely serious as he caressed the fine bones of her face. 'I want to be in your life, part of your future. I *know* I want you as my wife.' He paused, his eyes becoming deeply intent, and his hands slid down to her shoulders, his thumbs creating havoc as they moved absently back and forth along the delicate hollows at the edge of her collarbone. 'I want to kiss you until there isn't a vestige of doubt in your mind as to who I am. Hold you, *love* you. Never let you go.'

A shaft of exquisite longing began to unfurl deep inside her, radiating slowly until it encompassed her whole body.

'Marc——'

She lifted a hand and placed her fingers against his lips, silently begging him to listen, to understand what she had to say.

'Marc was——' she faltered slightly, searching for the right words. 'My very dear friend. It never occurred to either of us to question the quality of our emotions; we simply accepted our shared togetherness, the happiness we had, our mutual enjoyment of each other, and thought it was love.' Her mouth trembled a little, and her voice shook. 'Perhaps that's why I hated you so much,' she revealed with a trace of sadness. 'For showing me the difference.' Her eyes became wide and clear, almost luminous as she held his gaze. 'It made me afraid. Not only of you, but of myself.' Her fingers wavered as she felt his lips move, and she shook her head in silent negation.

'I imagined the warmth I shared with Marc was all there was to—sexual pleasure. Sensual ecstasy was something I believed to exist only in the imaginative female mind.' Her eyes roved over his features, seeing the rugged strength apparent, the depth of emotion evident, and gathered sufficient courage to continue.

'After that—night, with you, I felt like a traitor. To Marc, to myself.' A slightly hollow laugh emerged from her throat in a gesture of self-deprecation. 'I was filled with guilt in every conceivable form. And shock. Disbelief. All of those emotions. What was worse was being made painfully aware of a deep, abiding passion that daily became more impossible to ignore.'

Emma felt his mouth open beneath her fingers as he gently caressed each one in turn, then he removed her hand to thread his fingers through her own.

'So you ran away,' Nick declared softly, and she shivered beneath the latent sensuality evident in his eyes.

'I couldn't stay.'

'If I'd followed my baser instincts, I would have taken you to Milan with me and kept you chained to my side day and night,' he revealed with brooding, almost wry amusement. 'For most of that first week at the villa I had to content myself with being the ideal companion, convinced you preferred Annalisa's company to that of my own.' He slanted her a teasing smile. 'The only thing that gave me some hope was evidence of your increasing awareness of me, although I began to wonder if I would ever break through the silken threads of your self-made cocoon, and I was torn between using tender loving care and brute force. Fearful that if I lost control, I would merely succeed in frightening you with the strength of my desire. And you, my sweet Emma, were preoccupied with fighting your own inner battles. The result of which was a number of volatile clashes.'

His eyes darkened measurably for a few long seconds, then became vaguely rueful as he leaned his head down and bestowed a long, lingering kiss to her softly parted lips, deepening the caress with an evocative skill that stirred her senses and dispelled any lingering doubt.

Slowly she lifted her arms, linking her hands together behind his neck as she gave herself up to the elusive alchemy of his touch, and it was a long time before he slowly lifted his head.

Emma stood enraptured and totally bemused as he slid his hands from her waist up to close over her shoulders, helpless beneath an emotive maelstrom from which she never wanted to emerge.

'When will you marry me?'

She began to smile, a mischievous sparkle lightening her eyes to a brilliant shade of topaz. 'I wasn't aware I had been asked.'

She was lightly shaken for her temerity. 'Sweet fool,' Nick growled huskily. 'There can be no doubt that you *will*.'

Her expression sobered a little, her gaze becoming remarkably steady as she met the dark intensity apparent in his own, the latent passion evident, and she was aware of a matching aching need, a longing so tumultuous it was almost impossible to contain.

'A few months——'

'Next week,' he insisted with quiet certainty. 'I refuse to wait any longer.'

'You're joking!' The words left her lips in an incredulous gasp, and he shook his head, chiding gently,

'Don't make unnecessary obstacles, *cara*. Your need to be with me is almost equal to my own.'

'But we can't get married so soon' Emma declared shakily, her mind racing with a multitude of complexities.

'*Yes*. Believe it.'

She seemed momentarily lost for words, and he offered quietly, 'I want you with me, by my side every day and in my bed all night long.' His hands slid up to caress her face before slipping to cradle her head. 'To wake in the morning and see you there, *know* you are mine.' His voice was a soothing, slightly inflected drawl that carried the weight of his conviction. 'Could you live in Italy, do you think?'

It didn't matter where, as long as he was there, and she said so, her heart in her eyes. 'Yes. Milan—anywhere. Being together is all that matters.'

'*Grazie*,' Nick said gently. 'Annalisa will be ecstatic.'

'I will have to tell——'

'Your parents, Marc's,' he intervened quietly, 'will approve and agree when presented with a *fait accompli*. Be delighted for your future happiness with a man who regards you as the reason for his existence.' He paused, his eyes softening as he caught sight of her bemused confusion. 'There will be no difficulties, I promise.'

And there weren't. It was exactly as Nick had predicted, and Emma floated through the ensuing week on a euphoric cloud, finding it incredibly easy to fall in with every arrangement that was made.

The simple ceremony at the register office was quiet, with immediate family present, and afterwards there were only the closest of friends invited to a buffet dinner held in the privacy of her parents' home.

Hamilton Island, part of the Whitsunday group of islands in tropical North Queensland, had been chosen for a few days' holiday prior to their departure from Sydney for Rome. One of the more recently developed tourist resorts, Hamilton Island was advertised as an idyllic paradise, and it was exactly that.

Emma surveyed their luxurious unit with its panoramic view over the wide, sweeping pool to the sparkling blue ocean, then she turned back towards the man at her side.

'It's beautiful, so peaceful. Almost heaven,' she declared quietly.

'Almost, *amante*?' Nick teased huskily, pulling her close, and she looked up at him glimpsing the faint edge of tension beneath the surface, a waiting expectancy that was carefully hidden, yet there none the less.

Slowly, and with infinite care, she lifted her arms and linked them together at his nape.

'I love you,' she vowed simply. 'With everything I have to give—for as long as I live.'

His eyes flared with naked desire, then became dark with a deep, slumbrous warmth as he lowered his head down to hers, and she opened her mouth generously beneath the incredible gentleness of his own, glorying in his passivity as she initiated the kiss, exploring in a manner she would never have dreamt of doing in the past.

Fire swept through her veins, delicious and intoxicating, and she moved closer against him, exultant as she caught the faint, almost imperceptible catch in his breath before his mouth hardened, possessing hers with hunger and raw, aching need.

It was a long time before he reluctantly lifted his head, and the wealth of passionate intensity evident brought a faint tinge of delicate pink to her cheeks.

His smile was blatantly sensuous, the depths of his eyes filled with lazy amusement.

'What would you suggest, Emma Castelli?' he drawled softly. 'A stroll along the beach, a swim in the pool?'

She tilted her head to one side, contriving to give each suggestion some thought. 'You choose,' she offered demurely, and a soft, husky laugh left his throat.

'Such compliance.'

The temptation to tease him was irresistible. 'Perhaps we could explore the complex——'

'Witch! The only exploration I want to conduct is of *you*.' He trailed idle, almost chiding fingers along the edge of her jaw, then traced the outline of her mouth, his forefinger moving back and forth across the soft fullness of her lower lip in a gentle, caressing gesture.

An exquisite melting sensation consumed Emma's body, rendering her malleable, totally *his*.

'Do you need an invitation?' she whispered, becoming lost in the wealth of passion evident in his gaze, and without a word he swept an arm beneath her knees and lifted her into his arms, then he walked slowly towards the bedroom.

'I was way out of my league right from the beginning.'

'You should have stayed and fought the battle.' Stefano sounded impossibly cynical, and it rankled unbearably.

'I tried, but your concept of marriage was different from mine.'

'You're so sure of that?'

A lump rose unbidden in Carly's throat, and a great weariness settled down on to her shoulders, making her feel suddenly tired.

Helen Bianchin was born in New Zealand and travelled to Australia before marrying her Italian-born husband. After three years they returned to New Zealand with their daughter, had two sons, then resettled in Australia. Encouraged by friends to recount anecdotes of her years as a farmer's wife living in an Italian community, Helen began writing and her first novel was published in 1975. An animal lover, she says her terrier and Persian cat regard her study as much theirs as hers.

Passion's Mistress

HELEN BIANCHIN

Harlequin Mills & Boon
SYDNEY ❀ AUCKLAND ❀ MANILA
LONDON ❀ TORONTO ❀ NEW YORK
PARIS ❀ AMSTERDAM ❀ HAMBURG ❀ MILAN
STOCKHOLM ❀ MADRID ❀ ATHENS ❀ BUDAPEST
WARSAW ❀ SOFIA ❀ PRAGUE ❀ TOKYO ❀ ISTANBUL

First Published 1994
This Edition 1998
ISBN 0 733 51143 0

Published by
Harlequin Mills & Boon
3 Gibbes Street
Chatswood, NSW 2067
Australia

HARLEQUIN MILLS & BOON and the Rose Device are trademarks used under
license and registered in Australia, New Zealand, Philippines, United States
Patent & Trademark Office and in other countries.

Printed and bound in Australia by
McPherson's Printing Group

CHAPTER ONE

IT WAS one of those beautiful southern hemispheric summer evenings with a soft balmy breeze drifting in from the sea.

An evening more suited to casual entertainment outdoors than a formal gathering, Carly mused as she stepped into a classically designed black gown and slid the zip in place. Beautifully cut, the style emphasised her slim curves and provided a perfect foil for her fine-textured skin.

A quick glance in the mirror revealed an attractive young woman of average height, whose natural attributes were enhanced by a glorious riot of auburn-streaked dark brown curls cascading halfway down her back.

The contrast was dramatic and far removed from the elegant chignon and classically tailored clothes she chose to wear to the office.

Indecision momentarily clouded her expression as she viewed her pale, delicately boned features. *Too* pale, she decided, and in a moment of utter recklessness she applied more blusher, then added another touch of eyeshadow to give extra emphasis to her eyes.

There, that would have to do, she decided as she viewed her image with critical appraisal, reflecting a trifle wryly that it was ages since she'd attended a social function—although tonight's soirée was entirely business, arranged for the express purpose of affording a valuable new client introduction to key personnel, and only her employer's insistence had been instrumental in persuading her to join other staff members at his house.

'All done,' she said lightly as she turned towards the small pyjama-clad girl sitting cross-legged on the bed: a beautiful child whose fragility tore at Carly's maternal heartstrings and caused her to curse silently the implicit necessity to attend to-night's party.

'You look pretty.' The voice held wistful admiration, and a wealth of unreserved love shone from wide, expressive dark eyes.

'Thank you,' Carly accepted gently as she leant forward and trailed slightly shaky fingers down the length of her daughter's dark, silky curls.

Tomorrow the waiting would be over. In a way, it would be a relief to know the medical reason why Ann-Marie's health had become so precarious in the past few months. The round of referrals from general practitioner to paediatrician, to one specialist and then another, the seemingly endless number of tests and X-rays had proven emotionally and financially draining.

If Ann-Marie required the skills of a surgeon and private hospital care...

Silent anguish gnawed at her stomach, then with a concentrated effort Carly dampened her anxiety and forced her wide, mobile mouth into a warm smile as she clasped Ann-Marie's hand in her own.

'Sarah has the telephone number if she needs to contact me,' she relayed gently as she led the way towards the lounge.

Leaving Ann-Marie, even with someone as competent as Sarah, was a tremendous wrench. Especially tonight, when apprehension heightened her sense of guilt and warred violently with any need for divided loyalty. Yet her work was important, the money earned essential. Critical, she added silently.

Besides, Ann-Marie couldn't be in better hands than with Sarah, who, as a nursing sister at the Royal Children's Hospital, was well qualified to cope with any untoward eventuality.

'The dress is perfect.'

Carly smiled in silent acknowledgement of the warmly voiced compliment. 'It's kind of you to lend it to me.'

The attractive blonde rose from the sofa with unselfconscious grace. 'Your hair looks great. You should wear it like that more often.'

'Yes,' Ann-Marie agreed, and, tilting her head to one side, she viewed her mother with the solemn simplicity of the very young. 'It makes you look different.'

'Sophisticated,' Sarah added with a teasing laugh as she collected a book from the coffee-table. It was a popular children's story, with beautiful illustrations. 'Ann-Marie and I have some serious reading to do.'

Carly blessed Sarah's intuitive ability to distract Ann-Marie's attention—and her own, if only momentarily.

Their friendship went back seven years to the day they'd moved into neighbouring apartments—each fleeing her own home town for differing reasons, and each desperate for a new beginning.

'I won't be away any longer than I have to,' she assured quietly, then she gave Ann-Marie a hug, and quickly left.

In the lobby, Carly crossed to the lift and stabbed the call-button, hearing an answering electronic hum as the lift rose swiftly to the third floor, then just as swiftly transported her down to the basement.

The apartment block comprised three levels, and was one of several lining the northern suburban street, sharing a uniformity of pale brick, tiled roof, and basement car park, the only visual difference being a variation in the grassed verges and gardens, dependent on the generosity of any caring tenant who possessed both the time and inclination to beautify his or her immediate environment.

Carly unlocked her sedan, slid in behind the wheel and urged the aged Ford on to street level, taking the main arterial route leading into the city. It was almost seven-thirty, and unless there were any delays with traffic she should arrive at the requested time.

Clive Mathorpe owned an exclusive harbourside residence in Rose Bay, and a slight frown creased her forehead as she attempted to recall a previous occasion when her employer had organised a social event in his home for the benefit of a client—even the directorial scion of a vast entrepreneurial empire.

Acquiring Consolidated Enterprises had been quite a *coup*, for Mathorpe and Partners bore neither the size nor standing of any one of the three instantly recognisable internationally affiliated accounting firms.

Carly's speculation faded as she caught a glimpse of towering multi-level concrete and glass spires vying for supremacy in a city skyline, followed within minutes by an uninterrupted view of the unique architectural masterpiece of the Opera House.

It was a familiar scene she'd come to appreciate, for it was here in this city that she had developed a sense of self-achievement, together with an inner satisfaction at having strived hard against difficult odds and won. Not handsomely, she admitted a trifle wryly, aware of the leasing fee on her apartment and the loan on her car.

Negotiating inner-city evening traffic demanded total concentration, and Carly gave a silent sigh of relief when she reached Rose Bay.

Locating her employer's address presented no problem, and she slid the car to a halt outside an imposing set of wrought-iron gates.

Minutes later she took a curving path towards the main entrance, and within seconds of pressing the doorbell she was greeted by name and ushered indoors.

It was crazy suddenly to be stricken with an attack of nerves; mad to consider herself a social alien among people she knew and worked with.

Soft muted music vied with the chatter of variously toned voices, and Carly cast the large lounge and its occupants an idle sweeping glance. Without exception the men all wore black dinner-suits, white silk shirts and black bow-ties, while the women had each chosen stylish gowns in a concerted effort to impress.

Within minutes she was offered a drink, and she managed a slight smile as Bradley Williamson moved to her side. He was a pleasant man in his early thirties and considered to be one of Mathorpe and Partners' rising young executives.

His roving appraisal was brief, and his eyes assumed an appreciative sparkle as he met her steady gaze. 'Carly, you look sensational.'

'Bradley,' she acknowledged, then queried idly, 'Has Clive's honoured guest arrived yet?'

His voice took on an unaccustomed dryness. 'You're hoping he'll appear soon and let you off the figurative hook.'

It was a statement she didn't refute. 'Maybe he won't come,' she proffered absently, and caught Bradley's negative shake of the head.

'Doubtful. Mathorpe revealed that the director favours a personal touch in all his business dealings. "Involvement on every level" were his exact words.'

'Which explains why the company has achieved such success.'

Bradley spared her a quizzical smile that broadened his pleasant features into moderate attractiveness. 'Been doing your homework?'

Her answering response was without guile. 'Of course.' Figures, projections, past successes had been readily available. Yet mystery surrounded Consolidated Enterprises' top man, inviting intense speculation with regard to his identity.

'Such dedication,' he teased. 'The way you're heading, you'll be the first woman partner in the firm.'

'I very much doubt it.'

His interest quickened. 'You can't possibly be considering resigning in favour of working elsewhere.'

'No,' Carly disclaimed. 'I merely expressed the observation that Clive Mathorpe has tunnel vision, and, while an accountant of the feminine gender is quite acceptable in the workforce, taking one on as a partner is beyond his personal inclination.' A faint smile tugged the corners of her generously moulded mouth. 'Besides, I'm comfortable with things as they are.'

He absorbed her words and effected a philosophical shrug. 'Can I get you another drink?'

'Thank you. Something long, cool and mildly alcoholic.' She smiled at his expression, then added teasingly, 'Surprise me.'

Carly watched Bradley's departing back with an odd feeling of restlessness, aware of a time when her slightest need had been anticipated with unerring accuracy, almost as if the man in her life possessed an ability to see beyond the windows of her mind right to the very depths of her soul. Those were the days of love and laughter, when life itself had seemed as exotic and ebullient as the bubbles set free in a flute of the finest champagne.

Entrapped by introspection, Carly fought against the emergence of a vision so vivid, so shockingly compelling, that it was almost as if the image had manifested itself into reality.

Seven years hadn't dimmed her memory by the slightest degree. If anything the passage of those years had only served to magnify the qualities of a man she doubted she would ever be able to forget.

Their attraction had been instantaneous, a combustible force fired by electric fusion, and everything, everyone, from that moment on, had faded into insignificance. At twenty, she hadn't stood a chance against his devastating sexual alchemy, and within weeks he'd slipped a brilliant diamond on to her finger, charmed her widowed mother into planning an early wedding, and succeeded in sweeping Carly into the depths of passionate oblivion.

For the first three months of her marriage she had been blissfully, heavenly happy. Then the demands of her husband's business interests had begun to intrude into their personal life. Initially she hadn't queried the few occasions he rang to cancel dinner; nor had she thought to doubt that his overnight business trips were anything other than legitimate. Their reunions had always been filled with such a degree of sexual urgency that it never occurred to her that there could be anyone else.

Yet the rumours had begun, persistently connecting her husband with Angelica Agnelli. The two families had been linked together in various business interests for more than a generation, and Angelica, with qualifications in business management to her credit, held a seat on the board of directors of numerous companies.

Tall, slim, *soignée*, Angelica was the visual image of an assertive, high-powered businesswoman with her eye firmly set on the main chance. And that had included the man at the top of the directorial board. The fact that he had been legally and morally unavailable was considered of little or no consequence, his wife merely a minor obstacle that could easily be dismissed.

Carly's husband was possessed of an entrepreneurial flair that was the envy of his contemporaries, and his generosity to numerous charities was well known, thus ensuring his presence at prominent social events in and around Perth.

Carly reflected bitterly that it hadn't taken long for the gossip to take seed and germinate. Nor for the arguments to begin, and to continue unresolved until ultimately a devastating confrontation had finally supplied the will for her to escape.

Throughout her flight east she had been besieged by the machinations of her own imagination as it provided a litany of possible scenarios, and during those first few weeks in Sydney she'd lived on a knife-edge of nervous tension, fearful that her whereabouts might be discovered.

The bitter irony of having figuratively burned her bridges soon had become apparent with the knowledge she was pregnant.

The solution was something she'd chosen to face alone, and even in the depths of her own dilemma it had never occurred to her to consider abortion as the easy way out. Nor in those first few months of her pregnancy had she enlightened her widowed mother, and afterwards it was too late when emergency surgery resulted in her mother's death.

That initial year after Ann-Marie's birth had been difficult, caring for a child while juggling study and attempting a career. However, she'd managed...thanks to a private day-care centre and Sarah's help.

It was a source of pride that not only had she achieved success in her chosen field of accountancy, she'd also added a string of qualifications to her name that had earned respect from her peers.

'Sorry I took so long.'

Carly was brought sharply back to the present at the sound of Bradley's voice, and her lashes swept down to form a protective veil as she struggled to shut out the past.

'Your drink. I hope you like it.'

She accepted the glass with a slight smile, and murmured her thanks.

It was relief when several minutes later one of the firm's partners joined them and the conversation shifted entirely to business. A recent change in tax legislation had come into effect, and Carly entered into a lengthy debate with both men over the far-reaching implications on various of their clients' affairs.

Carly became so involved that at first she didn't notice a change in the background noise until a slight touch on her arm alerted her to examine the source of everyone's attention.

Clive Mathorpe's bulky frame was instantly recognisable. The man at his side stood at ease, his height and breadth a commanding entity. Even from this distance there was sufficient familiarity evident to send her heart thudding into an accelerated beat.

A dozen times over the past seven years she'd been shocked into immobility by the sight of a tall, broad-framed, dark-haired man, only to collapse with relief on discovering that the likeness was merely superficial.

Now, Carly stood perfectly still as logic vied with the possibility of coincidental chance, and even as she dismissed the latter there was a subtle shift in his stance so that his profile was revealed, eliminating any doubt as to his identity.

For one horrifying second Carly sensed the dark void of oblivion welling up and threatening to engulf her.

She couldn't, *dared not* faint. The humiliation would be too incredible and totally beyond conceivable explanation.

With conscious effort she willed herself to breathe slowly, deeply, in an attempt to retain some measure of composure as every single nerve-end went into a state of wild panic.

Stefano Alessi. Australian-born of Italian parents, he was a proven successor to his father's financial empire and a noted entrepreneur, having gained accolades and enjoyed essential prestige among his peers. In his late thirties, he was known to head vast multinational corporations, and owned residences in several European cities.

It was seven years since she'd last seen him. Seven years in which she'd endeavoured to forget the cataclysmic effect he'd had on her life.

Even now he had the power to liquefy her bones, and she watched with a sense of dreaded fascination as he glanced with seeming casualness round the room, almost as if an acutely developed sixth sense had somehow alerted him to her presence.

Carly mentally steeled herself for the moment of recognition, mesmerised by the sheer physical force of the man who had nurtured her innocent emotions and stoked them into a raging fire.

His facial features were just as dynamically arresting as she remembered, distinctive by their assemblage of broad-sculpted bone-structure, his wide-spaced, piercing grey eyes able to assess, dissect and categorise with definitive accuracy.

Dark brown, almost black hair moulded his head with well-groomed perfection, and he looked older—*harder*, she perceived, aware of the indomitable air of power evident that set him aside from every other man in the room.

She shivered, hating the way her body reacted to his presence, and there was nothing she could do to prevent the blood coursing through her veins as it brought all her senses tingling into vibrant life. Even her skin betrayed her, the soft surface hairs rising in silent recognition, attuned to a memory so intense, so incredibly acute, that she felt it must be clearly apparent to anyone who happened to look at her.

In seeming slow motion he captured her gaze, and the breath caught in her throat as his eyes clashed with hers for an infinitesimal second, searing with laser precision through every protective barrier to her soul, only to withdraw and continue an encompassing appraisal of the room's occupants.

'Our guest of honour is an attractive man, don't you think?'

Carly heard Bradley's voice as if from an immense distance, and she attempted a non-committal rejoinder that choked in her throat.

'I doubt there's a woman present who isn't wondering if he performs as well in the bedroom as he does in the boardroom,' he assessed with wry amusement.

All Carly wanted to do was escape the room, the house. Yet even as she gathered her scattered wits together she experienced a distinct feeling of dread with the knowledge that any form of retreat was impossible.

It became immediately apparent that Clive Mathorpe intended to effect an introduction to key personnel, and every passing second assumed the magnitude of several minutes as the two men moved slowly round the room.

Consequently, she was almost at screaming point when Clive Mathorpe eventually reached her side.

'Bradley Williamson, one of my junior partners.'

The lines fanning out from Clive Mathorpe's astute blue eyes deepened in silent appreciation of Carly's fashion departure from studious employee. 'Carly Taylor, an extremely efficient young woman who gives one hundred per cent to anything she undertakes.' He paused, then added with a degree of reverent emphasis, 'Stefano Alessi.'

It was a name which had gained much notice in the business section of a variety of newspapers over the past few months. Twice his photograph had been emblazoned in the tabloid Press accompanied by a journalistic report lauding the cementing of yet another lucrative deal. Even in the starkness of black and white newsprint, his portrayed persona had emanated an electrifying magnetism that Carly found difficult to dispel.

She held little doubt that the passage of seven years had seen a marked escalation of his investment portfolio. On a personal level, she couldn't help wondering whether Angelica Agnelli was still sharing his bed.

An ache started up in the region of her heart with a physicality so intense it became a tangible pain. Even now she could still hurt, and she drew on all her reserves of strength to present a cool, unaffected façade.

Cool grey eyes deliberately raked her slender frame, pausing imperceptibly on the slight fullness of her breasts before lifting to linger briefly on the generous curve of her mouth.

It was worse, much worse, than if he'd actually touched her. Equally mortifying was her body's instant recognition of the effect he had on all its sensual pleasure spots, and there was nothing she could do to still the betraying pulse at the edge of her throat as it quickened into a palpably visible beat.

Rage flared deep within, licking every nerve-fibre until it threatened to engulf her in overwhelming flame. How *dared* he subject her to such a sexist scrutiny? Almost as if she was an available conquest he was affording due contemplation.

Then his eyes met hers, and she almost died at the ruthlessness apparent, aware that his slight smile was a mere facsimile as he inclined his head in greeting.

'Miss Taylor.' His voice was a barely inflected drawl, each word given an imperceptible mocking emphasis.

'Mr Alessi,' Carly managed in polite response, although there was nothing she could do about the erratic beat of her heart in reaction to his proximity.

Something flared deep within her, a stirring that was entirely sexual—unwarranted and totally unwanted, yet there none the less—and it said much for her acquired measure of control that she managed to return his gaze with apparent equanimity.

His eyes darkened measurably, then without a further word he moved the necessary few steps to greet the next employee awaiting introduction.

Carly's mind reeled as several conflicting emotions warred in silent turmoil. Was his presence here tonight sheer coincidence, or did he have an ulterior motive?

She'd covered her tracks so well. She had even consulted a solicitor within days of arrival in Sydney, instructing that a letter be dispatched requesting any formalities to be handled by their individual legal representatives.

In seven years there had been no contact whatsoever.

It seemed incredibly ironic that Stefano should reappear at a time when she'd been forced to accept that he was the last ace in her pack should she have to raise more money for Ann-Marie's medical expenses.

Where her daughter's well-being was concerned there was no contest. Even it if meant sublimating her own personal reservations, and effecting a confrontation. His power and accumulated wealth could move figurative mountains, and if it was necessary she wouldn't hesitate to beg.

Carly caught the lower edge of her lip between two sharp teeth, then winced in silent pain as she unconsciously drew blood.

The desire to make some excuse and leave was strong. Yet only cowards cut and ran. This time she had to stay, even if the effort almost killed her.

Carly found each minute dragged interminably, and more than once her eyes strayed across the room to where Stefano Alessi stood conversing with Clive Mathorpe and two senior partners.

In his presence, all other men faded into insignificance. There was an exigent force apparent, which, combined with power and sexual magnetism, drew the attention of women like bees to a honeypot.

It was doubtful there was one female present whose pulse hadn't quickened at the sight of him, or whose imagination wasn't stirred by the thought of being able to captivate his interest.

Carly waited ten minutes after Stefano left before she crossed the room to exchange a few polite pleasantries with Clive Mathorpe and his wife, then she slipped quietly from the house and walked quickly down the driveway to her car.

Safely behind the wheel, she activated the ignition and eased the car forward. A quick glance at the illuminated dashboard revealed it was nine-thirty. One hour, she reflected with disbelief. For some reason it had seemed half a lifetime.

Stefano Alessi's disturbing image rose up to taunt her, and she shivered despite the evening's warmth. He represented everything she had come to loathe in a man.

For one brief milli-second she closed her eyes, then opened them to issue a silent prayer that fate wouldn't be so unkind as to throw her beneath his path again.

It was a relief to reach the sanctuary of her apartment building, and after garaging the car she rode the lift to the third floor.

'Hi,' Sarah greeted quietly as Carly entered the lounge. 'Ann-Marie's fine. How was the evening?'

I met Ann-Marie's father, she longed to confide.

Yet the words stayed locked in her throat, and she managed to relay an informative account as they shared coffee together, then when Sarah left she checked Ann-Marie before entering her own bedroom, where she mechanically removed her make-up and undressed ready for bed.

Sleep had never seemed more distant, and she tossed restlessly from one side to the other in a bid to dispel a flood of returning memories.

Haunting, invasive, they refused to be denied as one by one she began to recall the angry words she'd exchanged in bitter argument with a man she'd chosen to condemn.

CHAPTER TWO

CARLY slept badly, haunted by numerous dream sequences that tore at her subconscious mind with such vivid clarity that she woke shaking, shattered by their stark reality.

A warning, perhaps? Or simply the manifestation of a fear so real that it threatened to consume her?

Tossing aside the covers, she resolutely went through the motions entailed in her early morning weekday routine, listening to Ann-Marie's excited chatter over breakfast as she recounted events from the previous evening.

When pressed to reveal just how *her* evening had turned out, Carly brushed it off lightly with a smile and a brief but satisfactory description.

It was eight-thirty when Carly deposited Ann-Marie outside the school gates, and almost nine when she entered the reception area of Mathorpe and Partners.

There were several files on her desk demanding attention, and she worked steadily, methodically checking figures with determined dedication until mid-morning when she reached for the phone and punched out a series of digits.

The specialist's receptionist was extremely polite, but firm. Ann-Marie's results could not be given over the phone. An appointment had been set aside this afternoon for four o'clock.

It sounded ominous, and Carly's voice shook as she confirmed the time.

The remainder of the day was a blur as anxiety played havoc with her nervous system, and in the specialist's consulting-rooms it was all she could do to contain it.

Consequently, it was almost an anticlimax when she was shown into his office, and as soon as she was comfortably seated he leaned back in his chair, his expression mirroring a degree of sympathetic understanding.

'Ann-Marie has a tumour derived from the supporting tissue of the nerve-cells,' he informed her quietly. 'The astrocytoma varies widely in malignancy and rate of growth. Surgery is essential, and I recommend it be carried out as soon as possible.'

Carly's features froze with shock at the professionally spoken words, and her mind immediately went into overdrive with a host of implications, the foremost of which was *money*.

'I can refer you to a neuro-surgeon, someone I consider to be the best in his field.' His practised pause held a silent query. 'I'll have my nurse arrange an appointment, shall I?'

The public hospital system was excellent, but the waiting list for elective surgery was long. Too long to gamble with her daughter's life. Carly didn't hesitate. 'Please.'

It took only minutes for the appointment to be confirmed; a few more to exchange pleasantries before the receptionist ushered Carly from his rooms.

She walked in a daze to her car, then slid in behind the wheel. A sick feeling of despair welled up inside as innate fear overruled rational thought, for no matter how hard she tried it was impossible to dispel the terrible image of Ann-Marie lying still and helpless in an operating theatre, her life reliant on the skill of a surgeon's scalpel.

It will be all right, Carly determined as she switched on the ignition, then eased her car on to the street. One way or another, she'd make sure of it.

The flow of traffic was swift, and on a few occasions it took two light changes to clear an intersection. Taxis were in demand, their drivers competent as they manoeuvred their vehicles from one lane to another, ready to take the first opportunity ahead of city commuters.

The cars in front began to slow, and Carly eased her sedan to a halt. Almost absently her gaze shifted slightly to the right, drawn as if by some elusive magnet to a top-of-the-range black Mercedes that had pulled up beside her in the adjacent lane.

Her eyes grazed towards the driver in idle, almost speculative curiosity, only to have them widen in dawning horror as she recognised the sculpted male features of none other than Stefano Alessi behind the wheel.

Her initial reaction was to look away, except she hesitated too long, and in seeming slow motion she saw him turn towards her.

With a sense of fatalism she saw his strong features harden, and she almost died beneath the intensity of his gaze.

Then a horn blast provided a startling intrusion, and Carly forced her attention to the slow-moving traffic directly ahead. In her hurry she crashed the gears and let the clutch out too quickly for her aged sedan's liking, causing it to stall in retaliatory protest.

Damn. The curse fell silently from her lips, and she twisted the ignition key, offering soothing words in the hope that the engine would fire.

An audible protest sounded from immediately behind, quickly followed by another, then a surge of power shook the small sedan and she eased it forward, picking up speed as she joined the river of cars vacating the city.

It wasn't until she'd cleared the intersection that she realised how tight a grip she retained on the wheel. A light film of moisture beaded her upper lip in visible evidence of her inner tension, and she forced herself to relax, angry that the mere sight of a man she professed to hate could affect her so deeply.

It took almost an hour to reach Manly, yet it felt as if she'd been battling traffic for twice that long by the time she garaged the car.

Upstairs, Sarah opened the door, her eyes softening with concern at the sight of Carly's pale features.

'Sarah helped me draw some pictures.'

Carly leant forward and hugged her daughter close. Her eyes were suspiciously damp as Ann-Marie's small arms fastened round her neck in loving reciprocation.

'I'll make coffee,' Sarah suggested, and Carly shot her friend a regretful smile.

'I can't stay.' Her eyes assumed a haunting vulnerability. 'I'll ring you.' She paused, then attempted a shaky smile. 'After eight?'

Entering her own apartment, Carly moved through to the kitchen and prepared their evening meal, then when the dishes had been dealt with she organised Ann-Marie's bath, made the little girl a hot milky drink, then tucked her into bed.

It was early, and she crossed to the phone to dial directory service, praying they could supply the number she needed.

Minutes later she learned there was no listing for Stefano Alessi, and the only number available was ex-directory. *Damn.*

Carly queried Consolidated Enterprises, and was given two numbers, neither of which responded at this hour of the night. There was no after-hours number listed, nor anything connected to a mobile net.

Carly cursed softly beneath her breath. She had no recourse but to wait until tomorrow. Unless she rang Clive Mathorpe at home and asked for his coveted client's private telephone number.

Even as the thought occurred, it was instantly dismissed. What could she offer as the reason for such an unorthodox request? Her esteemed boss would probably suffer an instant apoplectic attack if she were to say, 'Oh, by the way, Clive, I forgot to mention that Stefano Alessi is my estranged husband.'

Tomorrow, she determined with grim purpose. Even if she had to utilise devious means to obtain her objective.

A leisurely shower did little to soothe her fractured nerves, nor did an attempt to view television.

Long after she'd switched off the bedside lamp Stefano's image rose to taunt her, and even in dreams he refused to disappear, her subconscious mind forcing recognition of his existence, so that in consequence she spent another restless night fighting off several demons in numerous guises.

The next morning Carly dropped Ann-Marie at school then drove into the city, and on reaching her office she quietly closed her door so that she could make the necessary phone call in private.

It was crazy, but her nerves felt as if they were shredding to pieces as she waited for the call to connect, and only Ann-Marie's plight provided the courage needed to overcome the instinctive desire to replace the receiver.

Several minutes later, however, she had to concede that Stefano was virtually inaccessible to anyone but a chosen few. The majority were requested to supply verbal credentials and leave a contact telephone number.

The thought of waiting all day for him to return the call, even supposing he chose to, brought her out in a cold sweat. There was only one method left open to her whereby she retained some small measure of power, and she used it mercilessly.

'Stefano Alessi,' she directed coolly as soon as the receptionist answered, and, hardly giving the girl a chance to draw breath, she informed her, 'Tell his secretary his wife is on the line.' That should bring some response.

It did, and Carly derived some satisfaction from the girl's barely audible surprise. Within seconds the call was transferred, and another female voice requested verification.

Stefano's personal staff were hand-picked to handle any eventuality with unruffled calm—and even a call from someone purporting to be the director's wife failed to faze his secretary in the slightest.

'Mr Alessi isn't in the office. Can I have him call you?'

Damn. She could hardly ask for his mobile number, for it would automatically be assumed that she already had it. 'What time do you expect him in?'

'This afternoon. He has an appointment at three, followed by another at four.'

Assertiveness was the key, and Carly didn't hesitate. 'Thank you. I'll be there at four-thirty.' She hung up, then quickly made two further calls— one to Sarah asking if she could collect Ann-Marie from school, and another to Ann-Marie's teacher confirming the change in routine.

The day loomed ahead, once again without benefit of a lunch-hour, and Carly worked diligently in an effort to recoup lost time.

At precisely four-fifteen Carly entered the lobby of a towering glass-faced edifice housing the offices of Consolidated Enterprises, stabbed the call-button to summon one of four lifts, then when it arrived stepped into the cubicle and pressed the designated disk.

The nerves she had striven to keep at bay surfaced with painful intensity, and she mentally steeled herself for the moment she had to walk into Reception and identify herself.

By now Stefano's secretary would have informed him of her call. What if he refused to see her?

Positive, think *positive*, an inner voice urged.

The lift paused, the doors opened, and Carly had little option but to step into the luxuriously appointed foyer.

Reception lay through a set of wide glass doors, and, acting a part, she stepped forward and gave her name. Her eyes were clear and level, and her smile projected just the right degree of assurance.

The receptionist's reaction was polite, her greeting civil, and it was impossible for Carly to tell anything from her expression as she lifted a handset and spoke quietly into the receiver.

'Mr Alessi is still in conference,' the receptionist relayed. 'His secretary will escort you to his private lounge where you can wait in comfort.'

At least she'd passed the first stage, Carly sighed with silent relief as she followed an elegantly attired woman to a room whose interior design employed a mix of soft creams, beige and camel, offset by opulently cushioned sofas in plush chocolate-brown.

There were several current glossy magazines to attract her interest, an excellent view of the inner city if she chose to observe it through the wide expanse of plate-glass window. Even television, if she were so inclined, and a well-stocked drinks cabinet, which Carly found tempting—except that even the mildest measure of alcohol on an empty stomach would probably have the opposite effect on her nerves.

Coffee would be wonderful, and her hand hovered over the telephone console, only to return seconds later to her side. What if the connection went straight through to Stefano's office, instead of to his secretary?

Minutes passed, and she began to wonder if he wasn't playing some diabolical game.

Dear lord, he must know how difficult it was for her to approach him. Surely she'd suffered enough, without this latest insult?

The thought of seeing him again, alone, without benefit of others present to diffuse the devastating effect on her senses, made her feel ill.

Her stomach began to clench in painful spasms, and a cold sweat broke over her skin.

What was taking him so long? A quick glance at her watch determined that ten minutes had passed. How much longer before he deigned to make an appearance?

At that precise moment the door opened, and Carly's eyes flew to the tall masculine frame outlined in the aperture.

Unbidden, she rose to her feet, and her heart gave a sudden jolt, disturbed beyond measure by the lick of flame that swept through her veins. It was mad, utterly crazy that he could still have this effect, and she forced herself to breathe slowly in an attempt to slow the rapid beat of her pulse.

Attired in a dark grey business suit, blue silk shirt and tie, he appeared even more formidable than she'd expected, his height an intimidating factor as he entered the room.

The door closed behind him with a faint decisive snap, and for one electrifying second she felt trapped. Imprisoned, she amended, verging towards silent hysteria as her eyes lifted towards his in a gesture of contrived courage.

His harshly assembled features bore an inscrutability that was disquieting, and she viewed him warily as he crossed to stand within touching distance.

He embodied a dramatic mesh of blatant masculinity and elemental ruthlessness, his stance that of a superior jungle cat about to stalk a vulnerable prey, assessing the moment he would choose to pounce and kill.

Dammit, she derided silently. She was being too fanciful for words! A tiny voice taunted that he had no need for violence when he possessed the ability verbally to reduce even the most worthy opponent to a state of mute insecurity in seconds.

The silence between them was so acute that Carly was almost afraid to breathe, and she became intensely conscious of the measured rise and fall of her breasts, the painful beat of her heart as it seemed to leap through her ribcage. Her eyes widened fractionally as he thrust a hand into his trouser pocket with an indolent gesture, and she tilted her head, forcing herself to retain his gaze.

'Shall we dispense with polite inanities and go straight to the reason why you're here?' Stefano queried hardily.

There was an element of tensile steel beneath the sophisticated veneer, a sense of purpose that was daunting. She was aware of an elevated nervous tension, and it took every ounce of courage to speak calmly. 'I wasn't sure you'd see me.'

The eyes that speared hers were deliberately cool, and an icy chill feathered across the surface of her skin.

'Curiosity, perhaps?' His voice was a hateful drawl, and her eyes gleamed with latent anger, their depths flecked with tawny gold.

She wanted to *hit* him, to disturb his tightly held control. Yet such an action was impossible, for she couldn't afford to indulge in a display of temper. She needed him—or, more importantly, Ann-Marie needed the sort of help his money could bring.

'Coffee?'

She was tempted to refuse, and for a moment she almost did, then she inclined her head in silent acquiescence. 'Please.'

Dark grey eyes raked her slim form, then returned to stab her pale features with relentless scrutiny. Without a word he crossed to the telephone console and lifted the handset, then issued a request for coffee and sandwiches before turning back to face her.

His expression became chillingly cynical, assuming an inscrutability that reflected inflexible strength of will. 'How much, Carly?'

Her head lifted of its own volition, her eyes wide and clear as she fought to utter a civil response.

One eyebrow slanted in a gesture of deliberate mockery. 'I gather that is why you're here?'

She had already calculated the cost and added a fraction more in case of emergency. Now she doubled it. 'Twenty thousand dollars.'

He directed her a swift calculated appraisal, and when he spoke his voice was dangerously soft. 'That's expensive elective surgery.'

Carly's eyes widened into huge pools of incredulity as comprehension dawned, and for one brief second her eyes filled with incredible pain. Then a surge of anger rose to the surface, palpable, inimical, and beyond control.

Without conscious thought she reached for the nearest object at hand, uncaring of the injury she could inflict or any damage she might cause.

Stefano shifted slightly, and the rock-crystal ashtray missed its target by inches and crashed into a framed print positioned on the wall directly behind his shoulder.

The sound was explosive, and in seeming slow motion Carly saw the glass shatter, the framed print spring from its fixed hook and fall to the carpet. The ashtray followed its path, intact, to bounce and roll drunkenly to a halt in the centre of the room.

Time became a suspended entity, the silence so intense that she could hear the ragged measure of her breathing and feel the pounding beat of her heart.

She didn't move, *couldn't*, for the muscles activating each limb appeared suspended and beyond any direction from her brain.

It was impossible to gauge his reaction, for the only visible sign of anger apparent was revealed in the hard line of his jaw, the icy chill evident in the storm-grey darkness of his eyes.

The strident ring of the phone made her jump, its shrill sound diffusing the electric tension, and Carly watched in mesmerised fascination as Stefano crossed to the console and picked up the handset.

He listened for a few seconds, then spoke reassuringly to whoever was on the other end of the line.

More than anything, she wanted to storm out of the room, the building, *his life*. Yet she couldn't. Not yet.

Stefano slowly replaced the receiver, then he straightened, his expression an inscrutable mask.

'So,' he intoned silkily. 'Am I to assume from that emotive reaction that you aren't carrying the seed of another man's child, and are therefore not in need of an abortion?'

I carried yours, she longed to cry out. With determined effort she attempted to gather together the threads of her shattered nerves. 'Don't presume to judge me by the numerous women you bed,' she retorted in an oddly taut voice.

His eyes darkened until they resembled shards of obsidian slate. 'You have no foundation on which to base such an accusation.'

Carly closed her eyes, then slowly opened them again. 'It goes beyond my credulity to imagine you've remained celibate for seven years.' *As I have*, she added silently.

'You're here to put me on trial for supposed sexual misdemeanours during the years of our enforced separation?'

His voice was a hatefully musing drawl that made her palms itch with the need to resort to a display of physical anger.

'If you could sleep with Angelica during our marriage, I can't even *begin* to imagine what you might have done after I left!' Carly hurled with the pent-up bitterness of *years*.

There was a curious bleakness apparent, then his features assumed an expressionless mask as he cast his watch a deliberate glance. 'State your case, Carly,' he inclined with chilling disregard. 'In nine minutes I have an appointment with a valued colleague.'

It was hardly propitious to her cause continually to thwart him, and her chin tilted fractionally as she held his gaze. 'I already thought I had.'

'Knowing how much you despise me,' Stefano drawled softly, 'I can only be intrigued by the degree of desperation that forces you to confront me with a request for money.'

Her eyes were remarkably steady, and she did her best to keep the intense emotion from her voice. 'Someone I care for very much needs an operation,' she said quietly. It was true, even if it was truth by partial omission. 'Specialist care, a private hospital.'

One eyebrow lifted with mocking cynicism. 'A man?'

She curled her fingers into a tight ball and thrust her hands behind her back. 'No,' she denied in a curiously flat voice.

'Then who, Carly?' he queried silkily. His eyes raked hers, compelling, inexorable, and inescapable.

'A child.'

'Am I permitted to know *whose* child?'

He wouldn't give in until she presented him with all the details, and she suddenly hated him, with an intensity that was vaguely shocking, for all the pain, the anger and the futility, for having dared, herself, to love him unreservedly, only to have that love thrown back in her face.

Seven years ago she'd hurled one accusation after another at the man who had steadfastly refused to confirm, deny or explain his actions. As a result, she'd frequently given vent to angry recrimination which rarely succeeded in provoking his retaliation.

Except once. Then he'd castigated her as the child he considered her to be, and when she'd hit him he'd unceremoniously hauled her back into their bed and subjected her to a lesson she was never likely to forget.

The following morning she'd packed a bag, and driven steadily east until hunger and exhaustion had forced her to stop. Then she'd rung her mother, offered the briefest of explanations and assured her she'd be in touch.

That had been the last personal contact she'd had with the man she had married. Until now.

'My daughter,' she enlightened starkly, and watched his features reassemble, the broad facial bones seeming more pronounced, the jaw clearly defined beneath the taut musculature bonding fibre to bone. The composite picture portrayed a harsh ruthlessness she found infinitely frightening.

'I suggest,' he began in a voice pitched so low that it sounded like silk being razed by steel, 'you contact the child's father.'

Carly visibly shivered. His icy anger was almost a tangible entity, cooling the room, and there was a finality in his words, an inexorability she knew she'd never be able to circumvent unless she told the absolute truth—*now*.

'Ann-Marie was born exactly seven months and three weeks after I left Perth.' There were papers in her bag. A birth certificate, blood-group records—hers, Ann-Marie's, a copy of *his*. Photos. Several of them, showing Ann-Marie as a babe in arms, a toddler, then on each consecutive birthday, all showing an acute similarity to the man who had fathered her: the same colouring, dark, thick, silky hair, and grey eyes.

Carly retrieved them, thrusting one after the other into Stefano's hands as irrefutable proof. 'She's your daughter, Stefano. *Yours*.'

The atmosphere in the lounge was so highly charged that Carly almost expected it to ignite into incendiary flame.

His expression was impossible to read, and as the seconds dragged silently by she felt like screaming—anything to get some reaction.

'Tell me,' Stefano began in a voice that was satin-smooth and dangerous, 'was I to be forever kept in ignorance of her existence?'

Oh, dear lord, how could she answer that? Should she even dare, when she wasn't sure of the answer herself? 'Maybe when she was older I would have offered her the opportunity to get in touch with you,' she admitted with hesitant honesty.

'*Grazie*.' His voice was as chilling as an ice floe in an arctic wasteland. 'And how, precisely, did you intend to achieve that? By having her turn up on my doorstep, ten, fifteen years from now, with a briefly penned note of explanation in her hand?'

He was furiously angry; the whiplash of his words tore at her defences, ripping them to shreds. 'Damn you,' he swore softly. 'Damn you to hell.'

He looked capable of anything, and she took an involuntary step backwards from the sheer force-field of his rage. 'Right at this moment, it would give me the utmost pleasure to wring your slender neck.' He appeared to rein in his temper with visible effort. 'What surgical procedure?' he demanded grimly. 'What's wrong with her?'

With a voice that shook slightly she relayed the details, watching with detached fascination as he scrawled a series of letters and numbers with firm, swift strokes on to a notepad.

'*Your* address and telephone number.' The underlying threat of anger was almost a palpable force. She could sense it, almost *feel* its intensity, and she felt impossibly afraid.

It took considerable effort to maintain an aura of calm, but she managed it. 'Your assurance that Ann-Marie's medical expenses will be met is all that's necessary.'

His eyes caught hers and held them captive, and she shivered at the ruthlessness apparent in their depths. 'You can't believe I'll hand over a cheque and let you walk out of here?' he said with deadly softness, and a cold hand suddenly clutched at her heart and squeezed hard.

'I'll make every attempt to pay you back,' Carly ventured stiffly, and saw his eyes harden.

'I intend that you shall.' His voice was velvet-encased steel, and caused the blood in her veins to chill.

A knock at the door provided an unexpected intrusion, and Carly cast him a startled glance as his secretary entered the room and placed a laden tray down on to the coffee-table. It said much for the secretary's demeanour that she gave no visible indication of having seen the deposed picture frame or the glass that lay scattered on the carpet.

Carly watched the woman's movements as she poured aromatic coffee from a steaming pot into two cups and removed clear plastic film from a plate of delectable sandwiches.

'Contact Bryan Thorpe, Renate,' Stefano instructed smoothly. 'Extend my apologies and reschedule our meeting for Monday.'

Renate didn't blink. 'Yes, of course.' She straightened from her task, her smile practised and polite as she turned and left the room.

Carly eyed the sandwiches with longing, aware that the last meal she'd eaten was breakfast. The coffee was tempting, and she lifted the cup to her lips with both hands, took a savouring sip, then shakily replaced it down on to the saucer.

The need to escape this room was almost as imperative as her desire to escape the man who occupied it, for despite her resolve his presence had an alarming effect on her equilibrium, stirring alive an entire gamut of emotions, the foremost of which was fear. The feeling was so intense that all her senses seemed elevated, heightened to a degree where she felt her entire body was a finely tuned instrument awaiting the maestro's touch. Which was crazy—*insane*.

'There's no need to cancel your appointment,' she told him with more courage than she felt, and she collected her bag and slid the strap over one shoulder in a silent indication of her intention to leave.

'Where do you think you're going?' Stefano said in a deadly soft voice, and she looked at him carefully, aware of the aura of strength, the indomitable power apparent, and experienced a stirring of alarm.

'Home.'

'I intend to see her.'

The words threw her off balance, and she went suddenly still. 'No,' she denied, stricken by the image of father and daughter meeting for the first time, the effect it would have on Ann-Marie. 'I don't want the disruption your presence will have on her life,' she offered shakily.

'Or yours,' he declared with uncanny perception. His eyes were hard, his expression inexorable. 'Yet you must have known that once I was aware of the facts there could be no way I'd allow you to escape unscathed?'

A shiver shook her slim frame; she was all too aware that she was dealing with a man whose power was both extensive and far-reaching. Only a fool would underestimate him, and right now he looked as if he'd like to shake her until she begged for mercy.

'There is nothing you can do to prevent me from walking out of here,' she said stiltedly.

'I want my daughter, Carly,' he declared in a voice that was implacable, emotionless, and totally without pity. 'Either we effect a reconciliation and resume our marriage, or I'll seek legal custody through court action. The decision is yours.'

A well of anger rose to the surface at his temerity. 'You have no right,' Carly retaliated fiercely. 'No——'

'You have until tomorrow to make up your mind.' He stroked a series of digits on to paper, tore it from its block, and handed it to her. 'You can reach me on this number.'

'Blackmail is a criminal offence!'

'I have stated my intention and given you a choice,' he said hardly, and her eyes glittered with rage.

'I refuse to consider a mockery of a marriage, with a husband who divides his time between a wife and a mistress!'

His eyes narrowed, and Carly met his gaze with fearless disregard. 'Don't bother attempting to deny it,' she advised with deep-seated bitterness. 'There was a succession of so-called friends and social acquaintances who took delight in ensuring I heard the latest gossip. One, in particular, had access to a Press-clipping service, and never failed to ensure that I received conclusive proof of your infidelity.'

'Your obsession with innuendo and supposition hasn't diminished,' Stefano dismissed with deadly softness.

'Nor has my hatred of you!'

His smile was a mere facsimile, and she was held immobile by the dangerous glitter in his eyes, the peculiar stillness of his stance. 'It says something for your maternal devotion that you managed to overcome it sufficiently to confront me.'

Angry, futile tears diminished her vision, and she blinked furiously to dispel them. 'Only because there was no other option!'

Without a word she turned and walked to the door, uncaring whether he attempted to stop her or not.

He didn't move, and she walked down the carpeted hallway to Reception, her head held high, pride forcing a faint smile as she inclined a slight nod to the girl manning the switchboard before sweeping out to the foyer.

A lift arrived within seconds of being summoned, and it wasn't until she reached ground level that reaction began to set in.

CHAPTER THREE

It took an hour for Carly to reach Manly, and she uttered a silent prayer of thanks to whoever watched over her as she traversed the car-choked arterial roads leading north from the city. Concentration was essential, and her own was in such a state of serious disarray that it was a minor miracle her sedan survived the drive intact.

Sarah answered the door at once, and Carly cast her a grateful glance as she entered her friend's apartment.

'Thanks for collecting Ann-Marie. I got held up, and the traffic slowed to a complete halt in places.'

'Sarah read me a story, and we watched television. I've already had my bath,' Ann-Marie informed her as she ran into her mother's outstretched arms.

Carly hugged the small body close, and felt the onset of emotion-packed tears. For more than six years she'd fought tooth and nail to support them both without any outside financial assistance. Soon that would change, and she wasn't sure she'd ever be ready for the upheaval Stefano Alessi would cause in their lives.

'Would you like some coffee?' Sarah queried. 'I'll put the kettle on.'

Carly shot her friend a distracted smile. 'Why not come over and share our meal?' It was the least she could do, and besides, it would be lovely to have company. Then she would have less time alone in which to think.

Sarah looked suitably regretful. 'I'd love to, but I'm going out tonight.'

Carly glimpsed the indecision apparent, the pensive brooding evident in Sarah's lovely blue eyes.

'I take it this isn't the usual casual meal shared with a female friend?' she queried slowly. 'Who's the lucky man?'

'A doctor who performed emergency surgery several months ago while I was on night duty. He's recently moved south from Cairns. We ran into each other a few days later, in the supermarket of all places, and we chatted. Then I saw him again at the hospital.' She paused, and effected a faint shrugging gesture. 'He's . . .' She paused, searching for the right words. 'Easy to talk to, I guess. Last week he asked me out to dinner.' Her eyes clouded, then deepened to cerulean blue. 'I said yes at the time, but now I'm not so sure.'

Aware that Sarah's disastrous first marriage and subsequent messy divorce had left her with a strong dislike and distrust of men, almost to the point where she refused to have anything to do with them other than in a professional capacity, Carly could only wonder at the man who had managed to break through her friend's defences.

'I'm delighted for you,' she declared with genuine sincerity.

'I'm terrified for me,' Sarah acknowledged wryly as she filled both mugs with boiling water.

The aroma of instant coffee was no substitute for the real thing, but the hot, sweet brew had a necessary reviving effect and Carly sipped the contents of her mug with appreciative satisfaction.

'What time is he picking you up?'

'Seven.' An entire gamut of emotions chased fleetingly across Sarah's attractive features. 'I'm going to ring him and cancel.'

If he was at all intuitive, he would have deliberately left his answering machine off with just this possibility in mind, Carly reflected as Sarah crossed to the telephone and punched out the requisite digits, only to listen and replace the receiver.

'Damn. Now what am I going to do?'

Carly viewed her with twinkling solemnity. 'Go out with him.'

'I can't. I'm nuts,' Sarah wailed. '*Nuts*.' Her expression assumed a sudden fierceness. 'If the situation were reversed, would *you* go out with another man?'

Her heart lurched, then settled into an accelerated beat in the knowledge that she would soon be inextricably involved with someone she'd sworn never to have anything to do with again, coerced by a set of circumstances that denied any freedom of choice. Yet her academic mind demanded independent legal verification of Stefano's threat of custody, even as logic reasoned that in a court of law the odds would be heavily stacked against Stefano being denied access to his daughter. Tomorrow was Saturday, but there was a friend she could contact outside office hours who would relay the vital information she needed.

'Carly?'

She proffered a faint smile in silent apology and shook her head. 'Not all men are made from the same mould as our respective first husbands,' she managed, evading Sarah's close scrutiny as she lifted the mug to her lips and sipped from it.

'When he arrives, I'll tell him I've changed my mind,' Sarah declared, and, placing a light hand on Carly's arm, she queried softly, 'Are you OK?'

There was no time for confidences, and Carly wasn't sure she was ready to share Stefano's ultimatum with anyone. 'I'm fine,' she assured quietly as she deliberately forced a slight smile. 'Let me give Ann-Marie dinner, then I'll come and help with your hair.'

Sarah shot her a dark musing glance. 'He's seen me in denim shorts, a T-shirt, trainers, and no make-up.' Her expression became faintly speculative as she took in the paleness of Carly's features, the edge of tension apparent. 'Give me twenty minutes to shower and change.'

Once in her own apartment, it took only a few minutes to heat the casserole she'd prepared the previous evening, and although Ann-Marie ate well Carly mechanically forked small portions from her plate with little real appetite.

Afterwards Ann-Marie proved an interested spectator as Carly used hot rollers to good effect on Sarah's hair.

'Why do I feel as nervous as a teenager about to go on a first date?' Sarah queried with wry disbelief. 'No, don't answer that.'

'All done,' Carly announced minutes later as she stepped back a pace to view the style she'd effected with critical favour. 'You look really great,' she assured her gently, her eyes softening with genuine feeling for her friend's state of panic. 'Are you going to tell me his name?' she prompted with a faintly teasing smile.

'James Hensley,' Sarah revealed. 'Surgeon, late thirties, widower, one son. He's slightly aloof and distinguished, yet warm and easy to talk to, if that makes sense.' Indecision, doubt and anxiety clouded her attractive features. A deprecatory laugh merged with an audible groan of despair. 'Why am I doing this to myself? I don't *need* the emotional aggravation!'

The intercom buzzed, and Carly reached out and caught hold of Ann-Marie's hand. 'Have a really fantastic time,' she bade Sarah gently. 'We'll let ourselves out.'

It was after eight before Ann-Marie fell asleep, and Carly gently closed the storybook, then gazed at her daughter's classic features in repose. She looked so small, so fragile. Far too young to have to undergo extensive surgery. Her beautiful hair——

A lump rose in Carly's throat, a painful constriction she had difficulty in swallowing. It wasn't fair. *Life* wasn't fair. Dammit, she wouldn't cry. Tears were for the weak, and she had to be strong. For both of them. At least her daughter would have the best medical attention money could buy, she consoled herself fiercely.

Carly remained seated in the chair beside Ann-Marie's bed for a long time before she stirred herself sufficiently to leave the room, and after carefully closing the door she crossed the lounge to the phone.

Twenty minutes later she slowly replaced the receiver. With a sinking heart she attempted to come to terms with the fact that any claim for custody by Stefano could succeed. Sole custody was not a consideration unless he could prove indisputably that Carly was an unfit mother. However, he could insist on joint custody—alternate weekends, half of each school holiday—and be granted any reasonable request for access.

On that premise, Carly was sufficiently intelligent to be aware of what would happen if she contested his claim in a court of law, or what emphasis his lawyer would place on her decision to leave Stefano in ignorance of Ann-Marie's existence.

She closed her eyes, almost able to hear the damning words uttered with appropriate dramatic inflexion. The moral issue would be played out with stunning effect. With the added weight of Stefano's wealth, she wouldn't stand a chance of him being refused custody.

Without conscious thought she sank into a nearby chair in despair. Dear God, she agonised shakily. How could she do that to her daughter? Ann-Marie would be pulled and pushed between two people who no longer had anything in common, torn by divided loyalties, and unsure whether either parent's affection was motivated by genuine love or a desire to hurt the other.

In years to come Ann-Marie would understand and comprehend the truth of her parents' relationship. But what damage would be done between now and then? It didn't bear thinking about.

There was really no choice. None at all.

Impossibly restless, she flung herself into completing a punishing few hours of housework, followed by a stint of ironing. At least it provided an outlet for her nervous tension, and she tumbled wearily into bed to toss and turn far into the early hours of the morning.

'You look—terrible,' Sarah declared with concern as Carly answered the door shortly after eleven. 'Is Ann-Marie OK?'

'She's fine,' Carly responded with a faint smile, then winced at the increasing pain in her head. 'She's dressing her doll in the bedroom and deciding what she should wear to Susy's party this afternoon. Come on in, we'll have some coffee.'

'I'll make the coffee, *and* get you something for that headache,' Sarah insisted, suiting words to action with such admirable efficiency that Carly found herself seated at the dining-room table nursing a hot cup of delicious brew.

'Now, tell me what's wrong.'

Carly effected a faint shrugging gesture. 'I must be feeling my age,' she qualified with a faint smile. 'One late night through the week, and it takes me the next two to get over it.'

'OK,' Sarah accepted. 'So you don't want to talk. Now take these tablets.'

'Yes, Sister.'

'Don't be sassy with me, young woman. It won't work,' Sarah added with mock-severity.

'How was your date with James?' Carly queried in an attempt to divert the conversation away from herself.

'We had dinner, we talked, then he delivered me home.' Sarah lifted her shoulders in a non-committal gesture. 'It was all right, I guess.'

'That's it?' Carly looked slightly incredulous. '*All right* wraps it up?'

'OK, so he was the perfect gentleman.' Sarah's expression became pensive. 'I was surprised, that's all.'

James was beginning to sound more astute by the minute.

'He's asked me out to dinner next Saturday evening,' Sarah informed her quietly, and Carly applauded his perception in taking things slowly.

'He sounds nice.'

'I get the feeling he's streets ahead of me,' Sarah owned. 'Almost as if he knows what I'm thinking and how I'll react. It's—uncanny.'

Carly sipped her coffee and attempted to ignore her headache. It would take at least ten minutes before the pain began to ease, maybe another ten before it retreated to a dull heaviness that would only be alleviated by rest. After she dropped Ann-Marie at Susy's house, she'd come back and rest for an hour.

Sarah left a short while later, and Carly headed for a long leisurely shower, choosing to slip into tailored cotton trousers and a sleeveless top in eau-de-Nil silk. The pale colour looked cool and refreshing, and accentuated the deep auburn highlights of her hair and the clear honey of her skin.

Lunch was a light meal, for Ann-Marie was too excited to eat much in view of all the prospective fare available at Susy's party.

'Ready, darling?'

Ann-Marie's small features creased into an expression of excited anticipation, and Carly felt a tug on her heartstrings.

'Checklist time,' she bade lightly with a smile. 'Handkerchief? No last-minute need to visit the bathroom?'

'Yes,' Ann-Marie answered, retrieving a white linen square from the pocket of her dress. 'And I just did. Can we go now?'

'After you,' Carly grinned, sweeping her arm in the direction of the front door.

The drive was a relatively short one, for Susy lived in a neighbouring suburb, and in no time at all Carly brought the car to a halt behind a neat row of several parked cars.

'We're cutting the cake at three,' Susy's mother bade with an expressive smile. 'And I'm planning a reviving afternoon tea for the mothers at three-thirty while Susy opens her presents. I'd love you to be here if you can.'

Carly accepted the invitation, wished Susy 'Happy Birthday', then bent down to kiss Ann-Marie goodbye.

On returning home she garaged the car in its allotted space, sparing its slightly dusty paintwork a faint grimace as she closed and locked the door. Perhaps she could leave early and detour via a carwash.

The apartment seemed strangely empty, and she drifted into the kitchen to retrieve a cool drink from the refrigerator.

The buzz of the doorbell sounded loud in the silence of the apartment, and Carly frowned in momentary perplexity as she crossed the lounge. Sarah?

Instead, a tall, broad-shouldered, disturbingly familiar male frame filled the doorway.

The few seconds between recognition and comprehension seemed uncommonly long as she registered his dominating presence.

'What are you doing here?'

'Whatever happened to *hello*?' Stefano drawled, and his dry mocking tones sent an icy shiver down the length of her spine.

Her eyes sparked with visible anger, dark depths of sheer mahogany, and it irked her unbearably that she'd discarded her heeled sandals on entering the apartment, for it put her at a distinct disadvantage.

Impossibly tall, he towered head and shoulders above her, his impeccably tailored suit seeming incredibly formal on a day that was usually given to informality and relaxation.

Three nights ago his presence had shocked and dismayed her. Yesterday, she'd been momentarily numbed, grateful for the impartiality of his office. Now, there was no visible shield, no barrier, and she felt inordinately wary.

'Aren't you going to ask me in?'

He projected a dramatic mesh of elemental ruthlessness and primitive power, an intrinsic physical magnetism that teased her senses and rendered them intensely vulnerable.

Her chin lifted fractionally, her eyes locking with his, and she caught the lurking cynicism evident, almost as if he guessed the path her thoughts had taken and was silently amused by their passage.

'What if I refuse?' Brave words, given his sheer strength and indomitable will.

'Would you prefer an amicable discussion, or have me channel everything through my lawyers?'

His voice was deadly quiet, and she felt the cold clutch of fear.

'This isn't a convenient time.' She was mad, *insane* to thwart him continually, yet she was damned if she'd meekly stand aside and allow him entry into the privacy of her apartment.

His expression hardened, the assemblage of muscle and bone tautening into a chilling mask depicting controlled anger. 'You've just returned from delivering our daughter to a birthday party. How long before you need to collect her? An hour? Two?'

Sheer rage rushed to the surface, destroying any semblance of restraint. 'You've had me watched— *followed*?' Words momentarily failed her. 'You *bastard*,' she flung at last, sorely tempted to slam the door in his face, yet even as the thought occurred to her she negated the action as not only foolish but extremely dangerous.

For one infinitesimal second his eyes leapt with icy anger, then sharpened and became infinitely compelling as he raked her slender frame.

A shivery sensation feathered its way down the length of her spine as she fought against the intrinsic pull of his innate sexuality, and of its own volition her body seemed to flare into life as if ignited by some hidden combustible flame.

Seven years ago she'd gone willingly into his arms, his bed, and tasted every sensual delight in a sexual discovery that had set her on fire, enraptured by an ecstasy so acute that it hadn't seemed possible such pleasure existed. A passionate lover, he'd teasingly dispensed with each and every one of her inhibitions, and taught her to become so in tune with her own sensual being that each time they made love it was a total conflagration of the senses.

To deny him access to her apartment would gain absolutely nothing, and, drawing in a deep breath, she gathered her scattered emotions together as she aimed for contrived politeness.

'Please,' Carly indicated as she gestured towards two sofas and a chair in the small lounge. 'Sit down.'

Stefano chose to ignore the directive, and moved slowly across the room to examine a large frame containing a montage of small snapshots showing Ann-Marie in various stages of development from birth to as recently as a month ago.

A palpable silence filled the room until it enveloped everything. A silence so incredibly damning that it was almost tangible.

At long last he turned towards her, his eyes so remarkably dark that it was impossible to discern anything from his expression. 'Why did you choose not to tell me you were pregnant?' he began with deceptive softness.

Her throat felt impossibly dry, and so constricted that she doubted if her larynx could cope with emitting so much as a sound. 'If I had, you would have hauled me back to Perth,' she said at last.

'Indeed,' Stefano agreed. 'And I wouldn't now brand you a thief for stealing from me the first six years of my daughter's life.'

'If you'd had sufficient respect for our marriage, I wouldn't have felt compelled to leave,' she managed carefully. There was an inherent integrity apparent, a strength that came from deep within.

'And rehashing the past has no relevance to Ann-Marie's future.'

She could feel his anger emanating through the pores of his skin, and all her fine body hairs rose in protective self-defence. He could have shaken her to within an inch of her life, and taken extreme pleasure in her pain. It was there in his eyes, the tautly bunched muscles as he held himself rigidly in control. The promise of retribution was thinly veiled, and she felt immeasurably afraid, aware that such punishment would be swift and without warning—an utter devastation. But not yet, she reasoned shakily. A superb tactician, he would derive infinite satisfaction from playing out her fear.

'You've reached a decision?'

Her heart stopped, then clamoured into a thudding beat. 'Yes.' One look at his hard, obdurate features was sufficient to ascertain his inflexibility.

'Must I draw it from you like blood from stone?' he pursued, his voice assuming a deadly softness, and her eyes flared with resentment.

'I won't allow Ann-Marie to be a metaphorical bone we fight over in a lawcourt,' she said hardily. 'Nor will I put her through the emotional trauma of being bandied back and forth between two parents.' Her head lifted slightly and her chin tilted with determination. 'However, I have one condition.'

One eyebrow slanted in silent cynicism. 'And what is that?'

'You give up your women friends.'

He looked at her for what seemed an age, and she was conscious of an elevated nervous tension as the silence between them stretched to an unbearable length.

'Could you be more specific?'

'Lovers,' she said tightly, hating him.

'Does that mean you are prepared to accommodate me in bed?' he pursued with deadly softness.

Her heart stopped, then clamoured into a thudding beat at the memory his words evoked, and the nights when she'd behaved like a mindless wanton in his passionate embrace. With concentrated effort she managed to keep her gaze steady. 'No, it doesn't, damn you!'

Stefano remained silent, his eyes watchful as he witnessed the fleeting change of her emotions, then after a measurable silence he ventured silkily, 'You expect me to remain celibate?'

Of its own volition, her hand lifted to her hair and eased a stray tendril behind on ear, the gesture unconscious and betraying her inner nervousness. 'I'll live in the same house,' she declared quietly. 'I'll play at being your social hostess. For Ann-Marie's sake, I'll pretend everything between us is fine.' Her eyes were wide, clear, and filled with resolution. 'But I refuse to share your bed.'

The edge of his mouth lifted in a gesture of musing mockery. 'I shall insist you share the same room.'

'Why?' Carly demanded baldly.

His eyes speared hers, their depths hard and inflexible. 'Because I choose never to lose.'

'Our marriage meant nothing to you!'

'You think not?' Stefano countered with unmatched cynicism. 'I retain a clear memory of your...' He paused imperceptibly, then added mockingly, 'Contentment.'

'You gave me beautiful things, put me in a beautiful home, took me out to beautiful parties where beautiful people mingled and made out they were friends.' She felt incredibly sad. 'Except nothing was beautiful. Not really. I was a new playmate, someone you could show off when the occasion demanded.' Her eyes clouded, and her lashes fluttered down to form a protective veil. 'I was too young, too naïve, and I didn't know the rules.'

His expression hardened, and only a fool would choose to disregard the element of tensile steel beneath his sophisticated veneer, for apparent was a sense of purpose, a formidability that was infinitely daunting.

'And now you do?' he taunted silkily.

Her eyes were remarkably clear and steady, her resolve derived from an inner strength she would never allow him to destroy. 'I care for my daughter more than life itself,' she vowed quietly. 'Her health and well-being take precedence over anything you can throw at me.'

His eyes reflected an indomitable strength of will, and, unless she was mistaken, a chilling degree of silent rage.

Self-preservation was a prime motivation, yet right at this instant she felt as vulnerable as a cornered vixen. 'I insist on continuing with my career—even if it's only on a part-time basis.'

He didn't display any emotion whatsoever, and she shivered, aware of the force she was dealing with.

'You'll take an extended leave of absence, effective almost immediately, until Ann-Marie has recovered fully from surgery and is able to return to school.'

An angry flush crept over her cheeks as she fought to remain calm beneath his deliberate appraisal. 'It never entered my head to do otherwise,' she retaliated, determined to press home every point in her intention to set a personal precedent. 'However, I studied very hard to achieve my present position, and I have no intention of giving it up.'

'I'm sure Clive Mathorpe will be amenable to your working a reduced number of hours consistent with the time Ann-Marie spends at school.'

Cool, damning words, but carrying a weight she found impossible to ignore. She felt drained, emotionally and physically, and she needed to be alone.

'Will you please leave?'

'When do you collect Ann-Marie from the party?'

Carly's eyes flew to her watch, confirming with immeasurable relief that it was only minutes past three.

'Soon,' she acknowledged. 'I told Susy's mother I'd join her and the other mothers for afternoon tea.'

'In that case, I'll drive you there.'

A surge of anger rose to the surface, colouring her cheeks and sharpening her features. 'Damn you,' she cursed fiercely. 'I won't introduce you to Ann-Marie in one breath and reveal you're her father in the next!'

'Putting off the inevitable won't achieve anything,' Stefano stated in a voice that was infinitely dangerous. 'Invite me to dinner tonight.'

She closed her eyes, then slowly opened them again. 'Can't it wait a few days?'

'I've spoken to the specialist and arranged an appointment with the neurosurgeon for Tuesday. It's highly possible she'll undergo surgery within a week.' His gaze seemed incredibly dark as his features assumed a harsh, implacable mask. 'It's imperative that you're both established in my home as soon as possible. Emotional stability is crucial to her recuperation.'

'When she's fully recovered is soon enough,' Carly cried, hating the way he was taking charge.

'Tomorrow,' he informed her with diabolical insistence.

'No,' she denied at once. 'It will only cause her anxiety and add to the trauma of hospitalisation and surgery.'

'Use whatever guise you choose,' he insisted softly. 'But do it, Carly. Ann-Marie will soon accept I have a rightful place in her life—as she has in mine.'

A holiday, a brief stay, was the only tenable explanation, she decided, aware that Ann-Marie would probably view the proposal as something of an adventure.

'I'll be back at five,' he declared hardly. 'And I'll bring dinner. All you'll have to do is serve it.' His gaze seared her soul. 'Don't even think about running away, Carly,' he warned softly. 'This time, I'll search until I find you, and afterwards you'll wish you were dead.'

She stood transfixed as he turned and walked to the door, then quietly left the apartment.

It took ten minutes for her to regain some measure of composure, a further five before she took the lift down to the underground car park.

To sit with several other young mothers sipping tea and sharing party fare proved an anticlimax, and Carly felt as if she was operating on automatic pilot while her brain whirled off on a tangent.

She smiled a lot, and she even managed to laugh with apparent spontaneity at an amusingly told anecdote. Inside, she was a mess, conscious with every passing minute, each glance at Ann-Marie, of the impact Stefano would have on their lives. Especially her own.

The most pressing problem was finding the right words that would prevent Ann-Marie from forming any prejudice, one way or the other, about her mother's actions. Children were incredibly curious, and Ann-Marie was no exception.

For the following half-hour Carly watched Susy unwrap her presents, unable afterwards to remember more than a few, then, when the birthday cake was cut, she helped distribute the pieces.

Soon it was time to leave, and in the car she tussled with her conscience, agonising over how she should explain Stefano and their reconciliation, aware that the little girl was too excited after the party to really absorb much of what her mother had to say.

While driving a car in traffic was hardly the time or place, and as soon as they entered the apartment she plugged in the kettle, made herself a cup of strong tea, then settled down beside Ann-Marie on the sofa.

'Someone very special is going to have dinner with us tonight,' Carly began quietly, aware that she had her daughter's undivided attention by the bright curiosity evident in a pair of grey eyes that were identical to Stefano's.

'Sarah?'

'No, darling.' She hesitated slightly, then offered quietly, 'Your father.'

Ann-Marie's eyes widened measurably and her expression assumed a solemnity beyond her tender years. 'You said my father lived a long, long way away, and you left him before he knew about me.' The eyes grew even larger. 'Why didn't you want to tell him?'

Oh, dear lord. Out of the mouths of babes! 'Because we had an argument,' Carly answered honestly. 'And we said things we didn't mean.' An extension of the truth, for *she* had said them—Stefano hadn't uttered a single word in his defence.

'How did he find out about me?' Ann-Marie queried slowly.

'Your father moved to Sydney several months ago,' Carly said quietly, watching the expressive play of emotions evident. 'I've been in touch with him.'

'Why?'

If only there were a simple answer! 'I thought it was time he knew about you.'

Ann-Marie's gaze didn't waver, and it seemed an age before she spoke. 'And you don't not like him any more?'

She hid a sad smile at Ann-Marie's phraseology, and prayed the good lord would forgive her for the fabrication. 'No.'

'Now he wants to meet me,' Ann-Marie said with childish intuition, and Carly nodded her head in silent agreement, then endorsed,

'Yes, he does. Very much.'

'Is he angry with you for not telling him about me?'

'A little,' she admitted gently.

Ann-Marie's expression became comically fierce, and her chin jutted forward. 'If he's nasty to you, I'll hit him.'

The mental picture of a delicate, curly-haired six-year-old lashing out at a six-feet-plus male frame brought a slight smile to Carly's lips. 'That would be very rude, don't you think? Especially when he's a very kind man.' Not to her, never to her. However, she had no doubt he would be kind to his daughter.

'Does he want us to live together and be a family?'

Her answer had to be direct and without hesitation. 'Yes,' she said simply.

'Do *you* want us to live with him?' Ann-Marie persisted, and Carly felt as if she was caught in a trap with no way out.

'Yes.' Two untruths in the space of two minutes. If she wasn't careful, it could become a habit. 'Let's go and freshen up, shall we? He'll be here soon.'

'What do I call him?' Ann-Marie asked several minutes later as she stood quietly while Carly tidied her hair and redid her ribbons.

Carly had a terrible feeling the questions could only get worse! 'What would you like to call him?'

Ann-Marie appeared to deliberate, her eyes pensive as a slight frown creased her small brow. 'Daddy, I guess.' Her eyes moved to meet those of her mother in the mirror. 'Will I like him?'

She forced her mouth to widen into a warm smile, then she bent down to brush her lips against her daughter's temple. 'I'm sure that once you get to know him you'll like him very much,' she assured her quietly.

Ann-Marie looked at her mother's mirrored reflection and queried with puzzlement, 'Aren't you going to put some lipstick on?'

Carly didn't feel inclined to do anything to enhance her appearance, although she reached automatically for a slim plastic tube and outlined her mouth in clear red.

The sound of the doorbell heralded Stefano's arrival, and, catching hold of Ann-Marie's hand, she summoned a bright smile. 'Shall we answer that?'

I don't want to do this, a voice screamed silently from within, aware that the moment she opened the door her life would change irrevocably.

Carly schooled her features into an expression of welcome, and although she registered his physical presence she felt akin to a disembodied spectator.

Except that this was no nightmarish dream. Stefano Alessi represented reality, and she issued a greeting, aware that he had exchanged the formal business suit worn a few hours earlier for casual dark trousers and an open-necked shirt.

Carly barely hid a gasp of surprise as he reached out and threaded his fingers through hers, tightening them imperceptibly as she attempted to pull away from his grasp.

She registered a silent protest by digging the tips of her nails into hard bone and sinew. Not that it did any good, for he didn't even blink, and she watched in silence as his mouth curved into a warm smile.

Supremely conscious of Ann-Marie's intent gaze, she managed to return it, and she glimpsed the faint narrowing of his eyes, the silent warning evident an instant before they swept down to encompass his daughter.

'Hello, Ann-Marie.'

He made no attempt to touch her, and Ann-Marie looked at him solemnly for several long seconds, her eyes round and unwavering before they shifted to her mother, then back again to the man at her side.

'Hello,' she answered politely.

Carly felt as if her heart would tear in two, and she held her breath, supremely conscious of the man and the child, one so much a part of the other, both aware of their connection, yet each unsure quite how to proceed.

In a strange way, it allowed her to see a different side of the man, a hint of vulnerability evident that she doubted anyone else had ever witnessed. It surprised her, and made her wonder for one very brief minute how different things might have been if she'd stayed in the marriage, and if he would have given up Angelica Agnelli and assumed the role of devoted father.

A knife twisted deep within her, and the pain became intense at the thought of Stefano taking delight in all the changing facets of her pregnancy,

the miracle of the birth itself, and the shared joy
of their new-born child.

She'd denied him that, had felt justified in doing
so, and if it hadn't been for Ann-Marie's illness she
doubted that she'd ever have allowed him to become
aware of his daughter's existence.

His fingers tightened around her own, almost as
if he could read her thoughts, and she summoned
the effort to move into the lounge, indicating one
of two chairs.

'Please, take a seat.' Her voice sounded strange,
not her own at all, and she extricated her hand from
his, aware that it was only because he allowed her
to do so.

'I hope you like chicken,' Stefano said, holding
out a large carrier bag suitably emblazoned with an
exclusive delicatessen logo. 'There's a variety of
salads, some fresh bread rolls, cheese. And a bottle
of wine.'

'Thank you,' Carly acknowledged with contrived warmth, and preceded him into the kitchen.

They ate at six, and Carly was aware of an inner
tension that almost totally destroyed her appetite.
There was no lull in conversation, and although
Ann-Marie displayed initial reservation it wasn't
long before she was chatting happily about school,
her friends, Sarah, and how much she'd love to own
a dog.

'I have a dog,' Stefano revealed, and Carly stifled
a mental groan in the knowledge that he had just
won a massive slice of Ann-Marie's interest, for the
'no animals allowed' rule enforced by the apartment
managers ensured that tenants couldn't have pets.

Ann-Marie could barely hide her excitement. 'What sort of dog?'

Carly waited with bated breath, and had her worst fears confirmed with Stefano enlightened her. 'A Dobermann pinscher.'

'Mummy said that one day when we live in a house we can have a poodle.'

Stefano cast Carly a musing glance at her choice before turning his attention back to his daughter. 'In that case, we'll have to see about getting you one.'

It was bribery, pure and simple, and Carly hated him for it.

By the time Ann-Marie was settled happily in bed and asleep, it was clear that Stefano had succeeded in winning a place in his daughter's affections.

'I have to congratulate you,' Carly said quietly as she handed him some freshly made coffee. Then she crossed the small lounge and selected a chair as far distant from his as possible.

His gaze was startlingly level. 'On developing an empathy with my daughter?'

She met his eyes and held their gaze with all the force of her maternal instincts. 'If you do anything to hurt her—*ever*,' she emphasised softly, 'I'll kill you.'

He didn't speak for several long seconds, and Carly felt close to screaming point. 'You wanted for her to hate me?'

'*No*. No,' she repeated shakily, knowing that it wasn't true.

'Yet you decry the speed with which she has gifted me a measure of her affection,' Stefano pursued.

She refused to admit it, and stirred her coffee instead, wanting only for the evening to end so that she could be free of his disturbing presence.

'Gaining her trust won't be achieved overnight,' he discounted drily, adding, 'And love has to be earned.'

'Why agree to gift her a poodle?'

'I said *we* would have to see about getting her one,' he responded evenly, and she instantly flared,

'A Dobermann and a poodle both on the same property?'

'Prince is a well-trained guard dog who is exceptionally obedient. I doubt there will be a problem.'

'And it matters little to you that I might have a problem moving into your home?'

His eyes were hard, with no hint of any softness. 'I'm sure you'll manage to overcome it.'

Suddenly she'd had enough, and she replaced her cup down on the coffee-table, then rose to her feet. 'I'm tired and I'd like you to leave.'

He followed her movements with a lithe indolence, then covered the distance to the front door. 'Be packed and ready at midday. I'll collect you.'

She wanted to hit him, and she lifted her hand, only to have it caught in a merciless grip.

'Don't even think about it,' Stefano warned silkily. 'This time I won't be so generous.'

There could be little doubt about the veiled threat, and she looked at him in helpless anger, wanting so much to strike out in temper, yet forced to contain it out of consideration to a sleeping child who, should she wake and perchance witness such a scene, would be both puzzled and frightened, and unable to comprehend the cause.

Stefano released her hand, then he opened the door and moved out into the foyer without so much as a backward glance.

CHAPTER FOUR

CARLY experienced a sense of acute nervousness as she caught sight of Stefano's imposing double-storeyed French-château-style home. Situated in the exclusive suburb of Clontarf and constructed of grey stone, it sat well back from the road in beautifully kept grounds.

A spreading jacaranda tree in full bloom with its carpet of lilac flowers provided a fitting backdrop to an assortment of precision-clipped shrubs, and symmetrical borders filled with a variety of colourful flowers that were predominantly red, pink, white and yellow.

Dear lord, what had she *done*? The enormity of it all settled like a tremendous weight on her slim shoulders. In the space of fifteen hours she had packed, cleaned the apartment, notified the leasing agent, and confided in Sarah. *And* tossed and turned for the short time she'd permitted herself to sleep. Now she had to face reality.

The car drew to a halt adjacent to the main entrance, and no sooner had Stefano slid out from behind the wheel than a short, well-built man of middle years emerged from the house to retrieve several suitcases from the capacious boot.

'Joe Bardini,' Stefano told them as Carly and Ann-Marie slid from the car. 'Joe and his wife Sylvana look after the house and grounds.'

The man's smile was warm, and his voice when he spoke held the barest trace of an Italian accent. 'Sylvana is in the kitchen preparing lunch. I will tell her you have arrived.'

Some of Carly's tension transmitted itself to her daughter, for Ann-Marie's fingers tightened measurably within her own as Stefano led the way indoors.

The foyer was spacious, with cream-streaked marble tiles and delicate archways either side of a magnificent double staircase leading to the upper floor. The focal point was a beautiful crystal chandelier, spectacular in design by day. Carly could only wonder at its luminescence by night.

'Would you prefer to explore the house before or after lunch?'

'Can we now?' Ann-Marie begged before Carly had a chance to utter so much as a word, and Stefano cast his daughter a musing glance.

'Why not? Shall we begin upstairs?'

'Yes, please.'

They ascended one side of the curving staircase, and on reaching the upper floor he directed them left to two guest rooms and a delightful bedroom suite with a connecting bathroom.

'Is this where I'm going to sleep?' Ann-Marie asked as she looked at the softly toned bedcovers.

'Do you like it?' Stefano asked gently, and she nodded.

'It's very pretty. Can Sarah come visit sometimes?'

'Of course,' he answered solemnly.

'Sarah lives in the apartment next door,' Ann-Marie explained carefully. 'She is our very best friend.'

To the right of the central staircase Stefano opened a door leading into the main suite, and Carly's eyes flew to two queensize beds separated by a double pedestal. A spacious *en suite* was visible, and there was an adjoining sitting-room complete with soft leather chairs, a television console, and escritoire.

'We'll use this suite,' Stefano indicated, and Carly refrained from comment, choosing instead to shoot him a telling glance as she preceded him to the head of the stairs.

If he thought she'd share the same bedroom with him, he had another think coming!

Once downstairs he led them into a formal lounge containing items of delicate antique furniture, deep-seated sofas and single chairs, employing a visually pleasing mix of cream, beige and soft sage-green. Oil-paintings graced the walls, a sparkling crystal chandelier hung suspended from a beautiful fili-gree-plastered ceiling, and wide floor-to-ceiling sliding glass doors opened out on to a covered terrace.

Even at a glance it was possible to see the blue-tiled swimming-pool beyond the terrace, and catch a glimpse of the magnificent view out over the harbour.

The formal dining-room was equally impressive, and his study held an awesome arsenal of high-tech equipment as well as a large mahogany desk, and wall-to-wall bookshelves.

The southern wing comprised an informal family room, dining-room and an enormous kitchen any chef would kill for.

A pleasantly plump middle-aged woman turned as they entered, and her kindly face creased into a warm welcoming smile as Stefano effected introductions.

'Lunch will be ready in ten minutes,' Sylvana declared.

'Is Prince outside? Can I see him?' Ann-Marie asked, and she made no objection when Stefano reached forward and caught hold of her hand.

'Come and be properly introduced.'

The dog was huge, and looked incredibly fearsome, yet beneath Stefano's guidance he became a docile lamb, his eyes large and soulful, his whimpering enthusiasm as close to canine communication as it was possible to get.

'After lunch we'll take him for a walk round the grounds, and you can watch him go through his paces.'

Lunch was served in the informal dining-room, and Ann-Marie did justice to the tender roast chicken with accompanying vegetables, as well as the delicious crème caramel dessert.

The excellent glass of white wine Carly sipped through lunch helped soothe her fractured nerves, and afterwards she walked quietly with Ann-Marie as Stefano led the Dobermann through a series of commands.

It was very warm outdoors, and Carly glimpsed a few tell-tale signs of her daughter's tiredness. The symptoms of her condition could descend with little warning, and it was essential that her reserves of strength were not overtaxed.

'Shall we go upstairs?' Carly suggested, catching hold of Ann-Marie's hand. 'You can lie down while I unpack your clothes.'

Stefano shot her a quick glance, his expression pensive as Ann-Marie stumbled slightly.

'Can I see Prince again before dinner?'

'Of course. You can watch Joe feed him.'

Carly lifted her into her arms, and Ann-Marie nestled her head into the curve of her mother's shoulder, her small hands lifting to link together around Carly's neck.

'Let me take her,' Stefano bade quietly, and Carly made to demure, barely able to control her surprise as Ann-Marie allowed Stefano to transfer her into his arms without protest.

Ann-Marie fought against encroaching lassitude as they made their way indoors, and by the time Stefano deposited her gently down on to the bed she was asleep.

His eyes were dark and slightly hooded as he watched Carly deftly remove the little girl's shoes then draw up a light cover before crossing to the window to close the curtains.

'She just needs to rest,' she said quietly. 'She'll be all right in an hour or two.'

Carly turned and walked from the room, supremely conscious of a distinct prickling sensation feathering her spine as he followed close behind.

It was damnable to be so aware of him, and in the hallway she quickened her step towards the main suite. 'I'll begin unpacking.' Her voice sounded incredibly stilted and polite, almost dismissing, for he had the power to ruffle her composure more than she was prepared to admit.

Their combined luggage was stacked neatly on the floor, and her eyes swept the room, hating the invidious position in which she'd been placed and the man who deliberately sought to put her there.

'Afraid, Carly?' a deep voice drawled from behind, and she turned slowly to face him, her eyes steady.

'You intend me to be,' she said with hesitation, aware of an inner resentment. 'This is part of a diabolical game, isn't it?' she flared, on a verbal rollercoaster. 'Separate beds, but having to share the same room. An *en suite* with no lock, ensuring you can invade my privacy any time you choose.' A degree of bitterness made itself apparent. 'And you will choose, won't you, Stefano? Just for the hell of it.' Her eyes darkened measurably, the gold flecks appearing like chips of topaz against brown velvet. 'Don't ever mistake your bed for mine,' she warned with deadly softness. 'I'd mark you for life.'

His gaze raked hers, harsh and unrelenting. 'Be grateful I've allowed you a separate bed,' he drawled smoothly. 'It wasn't my original intention.'

Her heart lurched, then missed a beat as sensation unfurled deep within her, the pain so acute that she almost gasped at its intensity. For one horrifying moment she held a clear vision of their bodies locked in lovemaking, aware that if he chose to take her now it would be a violation motivated by revenge.

Her eyes grew large, expressing a mixture of shock and anger, yet she refused to be subjugated to him in any way. 'Rape, even between husband

and wife,' she reminded stiltedly, 'is a criminal offence.'

Something flickered in the depths of his eyes, then it was successfully masked. 'You know me well enough to understand that rape would never be a consideration.'

No, she thought shakily. He was too skilled a lover to harm his partner with any form of physical pain. His revenge would be infinitely more subtle.

As it had been on one previous occasion, when she'd driven him to anger with a heated accusation she'd refused to retract or explain, and he had simply hauled her unceremoniously over his shoulder and carried her into the bedroom where he had conducted a deliberate leisurely assault on her senses until she was on fire with a desire so intense that she had possessed no reason, no sanity, only base animal need and a wild driven hunger for the release that only he could give. Except that he had taken pleasure in making her wait until she was reduced to begging unashamedly like a craven wanton caught in the throes of some primeval force, and then, only then, had he taken her with a merciless mastery that knew no bounds in a totally erotic plundering of her senses. With no energy left to move, she'd drifted into sleep, only to waken in the early morning hours, where self-loathing had surfaced, and a degree of shame. It had been the catalyst that had motivated her to leave.

Carly shivered suddenly, hating him more than she thought it was possible to hate anyone, and she watched in silence as he crossed to a concealed wall-safe, activated the mechanism, then removed a small jeweller's box before covering the distance between with calm, leisurely steps.

'Your rings,' Stefano declared, extracting the exquisite square-cut diamond with its baguette-cut diamond mounting, and its matching band.

Surprise momentarily widened her eyes as she recalled tearing both from her finger in a fit of angry rage. 'You kept them?'

His gaze was remarkably steady. 'What did you expect me to do with them?'

She was lost for words, her mobile features hauntingly expressive for a few seconds before she schooled them into restrained reserve, unable in the few ensuing seconds to make any protest as he took hold of her left hand and slid both rings in place.

Of their own volition her fingers sought the large stone, twisting it back and forth in a gesture that betrayed an inner nervousness.

His proximity disturbed her more than she was prepared to admit, and she was aware of a watchful quality in his stance, an intentness so overpowering that she felt almost afraid.

Her whole body stirred, caught up in a web of sensuality so acute that it seemed as if every vein, every nerve cell in her body flamed in electrifying recognition of *his*, which was totally opposite to the dictates of her brain.

To continue standing here like this was madness, and without a further word she turned away from him, crossing to her luggage to begin the chore of unpacking.

Carly's movements were steady and unhurried as she placed clothes on hangers in a capacious walk-in wardrobe, and she was aware of the instant he turned and left the room.

Dinner was a simple meal comprising minestrone followed by pasta, and afterwards Sylvana served coffee in the informal lounge.

Settling Ann-Marie to bed was achieved without fuss, and Stefano willingly agreed to his daughter's request to listen to a bedtime story.

A novelty, Carly assured herself as she chose the opposite side of Ann-Marie's bed, conscious that she was the focus of two pair of eyes—one pair loving and direct, the other musing and faintly speculative.

Forget he's there, a tiny voice prompted as she picked up the book and began to read. Who do you think you're kidding? another derided.

Somehow Carly managed to inject her voice with its customary warmth and enthusiasm, and she had almost finished when Ann-Marie's eyes fluttered down.

Minutes later Stefano rose quietly to his feet and waited at the door for Carly to precede him from the room.

'Does she usually wake in the night?' he queried as they neared the head of the stairs, and Carly shook her head.

'Very rarely.' She was a nervous wreck, she had a headache, and all she wanted to do was have a long leisurely shower, then slip into bed. She said as much, adding, 'I'll drop Ann-Marie at school in the morning, then go into the office for a few hours.'

'Clive Mathorpe isn't expecting you,' Stefano drawled, and she felt a *frisson* of alarm at his long hard glance. 'I've already enlightened him that his highly regarded Carly Taylor is Carly Taylor *Alessi*.'

Anger surged to the surface at his high-handedness. 'How dare you?' she vented in softly voiced fury. 'I am quite capable of telling him myself!'

'As my wife, there's no necessity for you to work. Your first priority lies with Ann-Marie.' The velvet smoothness in his voice should have been sufficient warning, but she was too stubborn to take any heed.

'I agree,' she conceded, determined to win points against him. 'However, as she'll be at school from eight forty-five until two-thirty, I don't see why I shouldn't spend those hours delegating work to whoever will take my place over the next few weeks.'

'I'll allow you tomorrow,' Stefano agreed hardly. 'But that's all.'

'Don't begin dictating what I can and can't do!' Carly said fiercely. She felt defensive, and very, very angry. 'And don't you *dare* imply that I'm an irresponsible mother! What sort of father will *you* be?' she demanded. 'It isn't nearly enough to provide a child with a beautiful home and numerous possessions. The novelty soon wears off when you can't be present at the school fête, or attend the end-of-year play.' Her eyes flashed with fiery topaz as her anger deepened. 'What happens next week, the week after that, and all the long months ahead?' she queried fiercely. 'You'll be too busy jetting off to God knows where, cementing yet another multi-million-dollar deal. When you *are* home, you'll probably leave in the morning before she wakes, and return long after she's given up any hope of catching a glimpse of you. How am I going to explain that your liaison with fatherhood will be conducted by remote control?'

His eyes were dark and unfathomable, and she was aware of a degree of anger apparent. 'Why are you so sure it will be?'

'Because you lead such a high-profile existence,' she flung in cautiously. 'It can't be any other way, damn you!'

He looked at her in silence for what seemed an age, and it was all she could do to hold his gaze. Yet she wouldn't subvert her own beliefs in deference to a man whose credo was different from her own.

'Tell me, are you staging a fight as a matter of principle, or merely as an attempt to vent some of your rage?'

'Both!'

'With any clear thought to the consequences?' Stefano pursued, his eyes never leaving hers for a second.

'Don't you dare threaten me!'

One dark eyebrow rose in cynical query. 'If you imagine I'll take any invective you choose to throw in my direction without retaliation, you're mistaken,' he warned silkily.

Carly felt as if she was on a rollercoaster leading all the way down to hell. 'I'm damned if I'll play happy families at a flick of your fingers!'

'I doubt you'll do or say anything to upset Ann-Marie.'

He was right. She wouldn't. Yet she desperately wanted to hit out at him for invading her life and turning it upside-down.

'Do you enjoy the power it gives you to use my daughter as an excuse to blackmail me?'

'Are you making an allegation?' Stefano countered in a voice that would have quelled an adversary.

For a few fateful seconds they seemed locked in silent battle, and she felt as if she was shattering into a thousand pieces. 'It's the truth!'

He stood regarding her in silence, his eyes darkly inscrutable, yet there was an air of leashed anger apparent, a sense of control that was almost frightening.

'Quit while you're ahead, Carly.'

She felt the need to be free of him, and preferably alone. For a few hours at least. 'I'm going to take a shower and watch television for a while.'

One eyebrow rose fractionally. 'A desire for solitude?'

'I'm off duty,' she declared, uncaring of his reaction.

'Careful with your claws, my little cat,' Stefano warned softly. 'Or I may choose to unsheathe my own.'

There was nothing she could add, so she didn't even try. Instead, she turned and walked towards their suite, and once inside she carefully closed the door.

He didn't follow, and she moved into the *en suite* and shed her clothes, then took a long shower, and, towelled dry, she pulled on a thin cotton shift and emerged into the bedroom, to stand hesitantly, unsure which of the two beds she should occupy.

Dammit, she swore softly. With her luck, she'd choose the wrong one, and then Stefano would be cynically amused by her mistake.

There was only one solution, and she caught up a towelling robe and slid it on, then walked through to the sitting-room, activated the television, and sank into a comfortable chair.

If necessary, she determined vengefully, she'd sleep here, rather than slip into the wrong bed!

Sunday evening television offered the choice of three movies, an intellectual book review, or a play spoken entirely in Hungarian. A karate-kickboxer epic wasn't her preferred viewing, nor was a terminator blockbuster, and she wasn't in the mood for a chilling thriller. After switching channels several times, she simply selected one for the sake of it and allowed her attention to wander.

At some stage she must have dozed, for she was aware of a strange sense of weightlessness, a desire to sink more comfortably into arms that seemed terribly familiar.

A small sigh escaped her lips, and she burrowed her face into the curve of a hard, muscular shoulder, then lifted her hands to encircle a male neck.

It felt so good, so *right*, and she murmured her appreciation. Her lips touched against warm skin, moving involuntarily as they savoured a texture and scent her subconscious recognised—not only recognised, but delighted in the discovery.

Except that she wanted more, and the tip of her tongue ventured out in a tentative exploratory tasting, edging up a deeply pulsing cord in search of a mouth she instinctively knew could bestow pleasure.

Then the barriers between unconsciousness and awareness began to disperse, bringing a horrifying knowledge that, although the arms that held her belonged to the right man, it was the wrong time, the wrong room, and her dream-like state owed nothing to the reality!

For a moment her eyes retained a warm luminescence, a musing witchery, then they clouded with pain before being hidden by two thickly lashed veils as she struggled to be free of him.

'Put me down!'

'I was about to,' Stefano drawled as he placed her between fragrantly clean sheets, and her lashes swept up to reveal intense anger.

His touch was impersonal, yet she felt as if she was on fire, with every separate nerve-end quivering into vibrant life, each individual skin-cell an ambivalent entity craving his touch.

Carly snatched the top sheet and pulled it up to her chin in a defensive gesture. 'Get away from me!'

His eyes speared hers, darkly mesmeric as she forced herself not to look away.

'You're as nervous as a kitten,' he drawled musingly. 'Why, when we've known each other in the most intimate sense?'

Reaching out, he brushed gentle fingers down the length of her cheek to the edge of her mouth, then traced the curving contour with a stray forefinger. 'What are you afraid of, *cara*?'

'Nothing,' Carly responded carefully. 'Absolutely nothing at all.'

Liar, she derided silently. No matter how hard she tried she was unable to still the fast-beating pulse that hummed through her veins, seducing every nerve and fibre until she felt incredibly *alive*.

His smile was wholly cynical, and his eyes held a gleam of mockery as they conducted a deliberately slow appraisal of her expressive features, lingering over-long on the visible pulsebeat at the base of her throat before travelling up to meet her gaze.

'Goodnight, Carly,' he bade her lazily. 'Sleep well.'

She mutinously refused to comment, and she watched as he turned and walked from the room. Damn him, she cursed silently. She *wouldn't* sleep in this bed, this room!

Anger fuelled her resolve, and she flung aside the covers, grabbed hold of her robe, then retreated quietly to an empty suite near by.

It held a double bed—made up in readiness, she discovered—and she slid beneath the covers, then switched off the bedside lamp.

Quite what Stefano's reaction would be when he found her missing wasn't something she gave much thought to for a while. She was too consumed with numerous vengeful machinations, all designed to cause him harm.

By the time she focused on what he might do, she was drifting off to sleep, too comfortable and too tired to care.

At some stage during the night she came sharply awake as a light snapped on, and she blinked against its brightness, disorientated by her surroundings for one brief second before realisation dawned. Except that by then it was too late to do anything but struggle as hard hands lifted her unceremoniously to her feet.

The face above her own was set in frightening lines, jaw clenched, mouth compressed into a savagely thin line, and eyes as dark as obsidian slate burning with controlled anger.

'You can walk,' Stefano drawled with dangerous softness. 'Or I can carry you.' His eyes hardened with chilling intensity, and Carly felt immensely afraid. 'The choice is yours.'

He resembled a dark brooding force—lethal, she acknowledged shakily, noting a leashed quality in his stance that boded ill should she dare consider rebellion.

'I won't share the same bedroom with you,' she ventured with a brave attempt at defiance, and saw his eyes narrow for an instant before they began a deliberately slow raking appraisal of her slim curves.

It was terrifying, for her skin flamed as if he'd actually trailed his fingers along the same path, and her eyes filled with futile rage. Her fingers curled into her palms, the knuckles showing white as she restrained herself from lashing out at him.

'We agreed to a reconciliation,' he reminded her with icy detachment. 'For Ann-Marie's benefit.' His dark gaze seared hers, then struck at her heart. 'I think we each realise our daughter is sufficiently intelligent to know that happily reconciled parents don't maintain separate bedrooms.' He knew just how to twist the knife, and he did it without hesitation. 'Are you prepared for the questions she'll pose?'

Carly's slim form shook with anger, and her eyes blazed with it as she held his gaze. 'If you so much as touch me,' she warned as she collected her wrap and slipped it on, 'I'll fight you all the way down to hell.'

It took only seconds to reach the master suite, and only a few more to discard her wrap and slip into one of the two beds dominating the large room. With determination she turned on to her side and closed her eyes, uncaring whether he followed her or not.

She heard him enter the room and the soft decisive snap as the door closed, followed by the faint rustle of clothes being discarded, then the room was plunged into darkness, and she lay still, her body tense, until sheer exhaustion triumphed and she fell asleep.

Monday rapidly shaped up to be one of those days where Murphy's Law prevailed, Carly decided grimly, for whatever could go wrong did, from a ladder in her tights to a traffic jam *en route* to the city.

On reaching the office, there appeared to be little improvement. She didn't even manage coffee mid-morning, and lunch was a salad sandwich she sent out for and washed down quickly with apple juice as she checked and double-checked details required urgently for an eminent client.

Given normal circumstances she excelled under pressure, regarding it as a challenge rather than nerve-destroying, and it was with mixed feelings that she tidied her desk, took leave of her colleagues and drove to collect Ann-Marie from school.

They arrived at Stefano's elegant mansion—Carly refused to call it home—shortly after three to find a silver-grey BMW standing in the driveway.

'For you,' Joe Bardini informed Carly as he emerged from the house to greet them. 'Mr Alessi had it delivered this morning.'

Had he, indeed! 'It's very nice, Joe,' she accorded quietly, and she veiled her eyes so that he wouldn't see the anger evident.

'Mr Alessi suggested you might like to take it for a test drive.'

She managed a warm smile, and indicated her briefcase. 'I think I'll get changed first.'

'It's really hot,' Ann-Marie declared as she followed Carly indoors. 'Can we go for a swim?'

Ten minutes later they were laughing and splashing together in the shallow end of the pool, and after half an hour Carly persuaded her daughter to emerge on the pretext of having a cool drink.

'Look,' Ann-Marie alerted her from the pool's edge. 'Daddy's home.' The name slid so easily, so naturally off the little girl's tongue, with no hesitation or reservation whatsoever, and Carly felt her stomach clench with pain.

She was suddenly supremely conscious of the simply styled maillot, and, although it was perfectly respectable when dry, wet, it clung lovingly to soft curves. Much too lovingly, she saw with dismay, conscious of the way it hugged her breasts.

Slowly she turned to face him, a faint false smile pulling at the edges of her mouth as she wound a towel around Ann-Marie's small frame, then she quickly reached for another, draping it over one shoulder in the hope that it would provide some sort of temporary cover.

Her action amused him, and she met his gaze with equanimity, heighteningly aware of his studied appraisal and her own damning reaction.

It was difficult to keep the smile in place, but she managed—just. If she'd been alone she would have slapped his face.

It was perhaps as well that he turned his attention to his daughter, whose wide, solemn eyes switched from one parent to the other as she assessed his show of affection and her mother's reaction.

Consequently Carly presented a relaxed façade, deliberately injecting some warmth as she enquired as to his day, and commented on his early return.

'I thought we might drive out to one of the beaches for a barbecue,' Stefano suggested, and was immediately rewarded with Ann-Marie's enthusiastic response.

'Can we go in the new car?'

His answering smile was her reward. 'I don't see why not.'

There was no way Carly could demur, and with a few words and a fixed smile she directed her daughter upstairs to shower and change.

It was after five when Stefano drove the BMW out of the driveway and headed towards one of the northern beaches, where he played chef, cooking steak and sausages to perfection while Carly busied herself setting out a variety of salads, sliced a freshly baked French breadstick, and enjoyed a light wine spritzer.

The air was fresh and clean, slightly tangy with the smell of the sea. A faint warm breeze drifted in from the ocean, teasing the length of her hair, and she gazed out to the horizon, seeing deep blue merge with clear azure, aware in that moment of a profound feeling of awe for the magnitude and greatness of nature. There was a sense of time-lessness, almost an awareness that life was ex-tremely tenuous, gifted by some powerful deity, and that each day, each hour, should be seized for the enjoyment of its beauty.

Tears welled at the backs of her eyes and threatened to spill. Dear God, what would she do if anything happened to Ann-Marie? How could she cope?

'Mummy, what's wrong?'

Carly caught her scattered thoughts together and summoned a smile. 'I'm admiring the view,' she explained, and, reaching down, she lifted Ann-Marie into her arms and directed her attention out over the ocean. 'Look, isn't that a ship in the distance?'

They ate sausages tasting faintly of smoke, tender steak, and the two adults washed it all down with a light fruity wine, then they packed everything back into the boot of the car and walked along the foreshore.

Ann-Marie chattered happily, pausing every now and then to inspect and collect seashells, which she presented for Carly's inspection, then when she grew tired Stefano lifted her high to sit astride his shoulders, and they made their way slowly back to the car.

A gentle breeze tugged at Carly's long cotton skirt and teased the length of her hair. The sun's warmth was beginning to cool as the giant orb sank lower in the sky, its colour flaring brilliantly as it changed from yellow to gold to orange, then to a deep rose before sinking below the horizon. The keening seagulls quietened, and took their last sweeping flight before seeking shelter for the night.

There was a sense of peace and tranquillity, almost a feeling of harmony with the man walking at her side, and for a moment she wondered if their marriage could have worked... Then she dismissed it in the knowledge that there were too many 'if only's. There was only *now*.

'You take the wheel,' Stefano instructed as they reached the car, and Carly shook her head, unwilling to familiarise herself with a new vehicle while he sat in the passenger seat. 'I insist,' he added quietly, and in Ann-Marie's presence she had little option but to accede.

It was almost nine when they arrived home, and Ann-Marie was so tired that she fell asleep almost as soon as her head touched the pillow.

CHAPTER FIVE

'COFFEE?' Stefano queried as they descended the staircase, and Carly nodded her head in silent acquiescence.

In the kitchen she filled the percolator with water, selected a fresh filter, spooned in a measure of freshly ground coffee-beans, then activated the machine before reaching for two cups and saucers, sugar.

'From now on, use the BMW.'

Resentment flared in his mocking command. 'There's nothing wrong with my car,' she retaliated at once. 'It's roadworthy and reliable.'

His gaze trapped hers and she felt every single hair on her body prickle with inexplicable foreboding. 'When was it last fully serviced?'

Too long ago, Carly admitted silently, all too aware that over the past few months all her money had gone on expensive medical bills.

'You don't like the BMW?' Stefano queried with deceptive mildness, and she summoned a false smile.

'I presume it's the "in" vehicle that wives of wealthy corporate directors are driving this year.'

His eyes narrowed fractionally, and the edges of his mouth curved with cynicism. 'That wasn't the reason I chose it.'

'No?' Her faint smile was tinged with mockery. 'It does, however, fit the required image.'

'And what is that, Carly?' Stefano pursued with dangerous softness.

'You're a very successful man,' she returned solemnly, 'who has to be seen to surround himself with the trappings of success.' She lifted an expressive hand and effected an encompassing gesture. 'This house, the cars. Even the women who grace a part of your life.'

His eyes locked with hers, and she suppressed a faint shivery sensation at the dark implacability evident.

'You know nothing of the women in my life.'

It was like a knife twisting deep inside her heart, and she fought visibly to contain the pain. She even managed to dredge up a smile as his eyes seared hers, dark, brooding, and infinitely hard.

Carly felt as if she couldn't breathe, and the beat of her heart seemed to thud right through her chest, fast-paced and deafening in its intensity. She wanted to escape—from the room, the man, the *house*. Except that she had to stay. For a while, at least. Until Ann-Marie was fully recovered. Then ...

'The coffee is ready.'

His voice intruded, and she turned blindly towards the coffee-machine. Dear God, she doubted her ability to walk the few paces necessary and calmly pour the brew into cups, let alone drink from one. She'd probably scald her mouth, or drop the cup. Maybe both.

'I no longer feel like any,' she managed in a voice that sounded indistinct and far removed from her own.

'Add a dash of brandy, and cream,' Stefano ordered steadily. 'It will help you sleep.'

She opened her mouth to respond, only to have him pursue with dangerous softness, 'Don't argue.'

'I'm not arguing!'

'Then stop wasting energy on being so stubbornly determined to oppose me.'

'You must know how much I hate being here,' she flung with restrained anger. She was so infuriated that it took every ounce of control not to lash out at him.

'Almost as much as you hate me,' Stefano drawled imperturbably as he moved to pour the coffee, then he added brandy and cream to both cups.

'You have no intention of making things easy for me, do you?' Carly demanded bitterly.

His eyes assumed a chilling bleakness, his features assembling into a hard, inflexible mask. 'You're treading a mental tightrope.' He lifted a hand and caught hold of her chin, his fingers firm and faintly cruel. 'And I'm in no mood to play verbal games.'

'Then stop treating me like a fractious child.' It was a cry from within, heartfelt, and more revealing than she intended.

'Start behaving like a woman and I'll respond accordingly,' he said hardly, and flecks of fiery topaz lightened the darkness of her eyes.

'Close my mind and open my legs?' Rage bubbled to the surface and erupted without thought to the consequence. 'Sorry, Stefano. I'm not that desperate.'

For a moment she thought he meant to strike her, and she was powerless to escape him as hard hands curled round her arms and pulled her close.

'This time,' he ground out grimly, 'you push me too far.'

He possessed sufficient strength to do her grievous bodily harm, yet she stood defiant, unwilling to retract or apologise for so much as a single word.

With slow deliberation he caught both her hands together, then slid one hand beneath her head, tilting it as he impelled her forward, then his mouth was on hers, hard and possessively demanding.

A silent scream rose and died in her throat, and she began to struggle, hating him with all her heart as he exerted sufficient pressure to force open her mouth, then his tongue became a pillaging destructive force that had her silently begging him to stop.

His stance altered, and one hand splayed down over the gentle swell of her bottom, pressing her close in against him so that the heat of his arousal was a potent virile force that was impossible to ignore.

The invasion of her mouth didn't lessen, and she felt absorbed, overwhelmed, *possessed* by a man who would refuse anything other than her complete capitulation.

Something snapped inside her, swamping her with anger and a need for retribution. She began to struggle more fiercely, managing to free one hand, which she balled into a fist to flail against his back. She clenched her jaw against the considerable force of his, and gained a minor victory when she managed to capture his tongue with her teeth.

Not enough to inflict any damage, but sufficient to cause him to still fractionally, then he was free, but only momentarily, for he lifted her effortlessly over one shoulder and strode from the room.

'You bastard,' Carly hissed vehemently as she pummelled her fists against the hard muscles of his back. 'Put me down, damn you!'

She fought so hard that she lost all sense of direction, and it wasn't until he began to ascend the central staircase that she began to feel afraid. Her struggles intensified, without success, and several seconds later she heard the solid clunking sound of the bedroom door as it closed behind them, then without ceremony she was lowered down to her feet.

Defiance blazed from her expressive features as she met his hardened gaze, and despite their compelling intensity she refused to bow down to fear. Her mouth felt violated, her tongue sore, the delicate tissues grazed and swollen. Even her throat ached, and her jaw.

'If it weren't for Ann-Marie . . .' She trailed to a halt, too incensed to continue.

'Precisely,' Stefano agreed succinctly. His implication was intentional, and she burst into voluble speech.

'You're so damned *ruthless*,' Carly accused vengefully. 'You dominate everything, *everyone*. I can't wait to be free of you.'

He went completely still, and she was vividly reminded of a superb jungle animal she'd viewed on a television documentary; of the encapsulated moment when every muscle in his body had tensed prior to the fatal spring that captured and annihilated his prey. Stefano looked just as dangerous, portraying the same degree of leashed violence.

'You believe our reconciliation to be temporary?' he queried in a voice that sounded like the finest silk being torn asunder.

She drew in a deep breath, then slowly released it. 'When Ann-Marie is completely recovered, I intend to file for divorce.'

His eyes lanced hers, killing in their intensity. 'You honestly believe I'd allow you to attempt to take her away from me?'

'Dear lord in heaven,' Carly breathed shakily. 'Who do you think you are? *God*?'

He was silent for so long that she thought he didn't mean to answer, then he drawled with deliberate softness, 'I have the power to hound you through every lawcourt in the country for whatever reason I choose to nominate.'

She felt sickened, and *raw* with immeasurable pain. 'Are you so bent on revenge that you'd punish yourself as well as me?'

His eyes raked her slim frame. 'Punish? Aren't you being overly fanciful?'

'Angelica Agnelli. I imagine she still——' She paused fractionally, then continued with deliberate emphasis, '*Liaises* with you?'

His voice was tensile steel, and just as dangerous. 'In a professional capacity—yes.'

'And is she still based in Perth?' Carly pursued unrepentantly. 'Or has she also moved to Sydney?'

'Sydney.'

'I see,' she said dully, and wondered at her own stupidity in querying if the relationship between Stefano and Angelica still existed. It hadn't ceased and probably never would.

'Do you?' Stefano queried, and she smiled with infinite sadness, all the fight in her suddenly gone.

'Oh, yes,' she assented wearily. 'I was way out of my league right from the beginning.'

'You should have stayed and fought the battle.' He sounded impossibly cynical, and it rankled unbearably.

'I tried.' Dear lord, how she'd tried. But one battle didn't win the war, as she had discovered to her cost. Carly tilted her head at a proud angle. 'Being figuratively savaged by a female predator held no appeal. I much preferred to retreat with dignity.' Her eyes were remarkably clear. 'Besides, it's impossible to lose what you never had.'

'I willingly slid a ring on your finger, and pledged my devotion.' His voice held a soft drawling quality that sent shivers scudding down the length of her spine. 'Was your faith in me so lacking that there was no room for trust?'

The entire conversation had undergone a remarkable change, and she wasn't comfortable with its passage. 'That was a long time ago,' she responded slowly, aware of the tug at her heartstrings, the ecstasy as much as the agony of having loved him. 'Your concept of marriage was different from mine.'

'You're so sure of that?'

A lump rose unbidden in her throat—she doubted her voice could surmount it—and a great weariness settled down on to her young shoulders, making her feel suddenly tired.

'If you don't mind, I'd like to shower and go to bed.'

'Enjoy your solitude, *cara*,' Stefano told her with soft mockery. 'I have a few international calls to make.' His expression was veiled, making it impossible to detect his mood, and she watched as he walked to the door, then he turned towards her.

'Incidentally, I've located a reputable breeder who will deliver Ann-Marie's poodle late tomorrow afternoon.' He paused, a faint smile tugging his lips at her surprise. 'A house-trained young female, black, with impeccable manners, who answers to Françoise. I'll see that I'm home to ensure she has a proper introduction to Prince.'

He opened the door, then closed it quietly behind him before Carly had a chance to say so much as a word.

He was an enigma, she decided as she became caught up in a maelstrom of contrary emotions. There was a sense of unresolved hostility, an inner need that bordered on obsession, to get beneath his skin and test the strength of his anger.

Or his passion, her subconscious mind taunted mercilessly. Wasn't that what she really wanted?

No. The silent scream rose in her throat, threatening, agonising in its intensity, and she gazed sightlessly around the room for several seconds as she attempted to focus on something—anything—that would rationalise her feelings.

All she could see were the two pieces of furniture that totally dominated the large room. Two queensize beds, each expensively quilted in delicately muted matching colours that complemented the suite's elegant furnishings.

A leisurely shower would surely ease some of her emotional tension, she rationalised as she stripped off her outer clothes, wound the length of her hair into a knot atop her head, and stepped beneath the therapeutic warm spray.

Ten minutes later she stood before the mirror clad in a towelling robe, her hair brushed and confined into a single braid. Her features were too pale, she decided, and with a slight shrug she transferred her gaze to the opulence of her surroundings.

It provided an all too vivid reminder of another house, in another city, and another time. Then, she'd followed her heart, so totally enthralled with the man she had married that every hour apart from him was an agonising torment.

In those days she'd behaved like a love-crazed fool, she reflected a trifle grimly. So young, so incredibly naïve, *aching* all day for the evening hours she could spend in his arms.

Beautiful, soul-shaking hours filled with a love-making so incredibly passionate that she would often wake trembling at the thought that she might lose him and have it end.

Carly studied her reflection, seeing the subtle changes seven years had wrought. Her eyes lacked the luminescent lustre of love, and held an elusive quality that bore evidence of a maturity gained from the responsibility of caring emotionally and financially for herself and her child. Any hint of naïveté had long since departed, and there was an inherent strength apparent, an inner determination to succeed. There was also pain, buried so deep within her that she rarely allowed it to emerge.

Now she had to fight against the memories that rose hauntingly to the surface, each one a separate entity jealously guarded like a rare and precious jewel.

If she closed her eyes she could almost imagine that seven years had never passed, that any moment Stefano would step behind her and slowly, erotically tease her tender nape with a trail of lingering kisses, then gently slide the robe from her shoulders, and extend the physical sense of touching that had begun hours before over dinner with the veiled promise of passion in the depths of those dark eyes. The shared flute of wine; a morsel of food proffered from his plate; the deliberate lingering over coffee and liqueurs, almost as if they were delaying the moment when they'd rise leisurely to their feet and go upstairs to bed.

Even then, they'd rarely hurried, and only once could she recall him being so swept away that he'd lost control, kissing her with such savage hunger that she'd responded in kind, evincing no protest as he'd swiftly slaked his desire. Afterwards he'd enfolded her close in his arms, then he'd made love to her with such exquisite gentleness that she'd been unable to still the soft flow of silent tears.

Carly blinked, then shook her head faintly in an effort to clear away any further treacherous recollection from the past. Yet it wouldn't quite submerge, and she gazed sightlessly into the mirror as she pondered what Stefano's reaction had been when he'd discovered she'd left him.

Good grief! What are you? she demanded of her reflected image. A masochist? He didn't choose to instigate a search to discover your whereabouts, and in all probability he was pleased to be relieved of

a neurotic young wife who warred with him over
his indiscretions.

Damn. The silent curse whispered past her lips,
and with a gesture of disgust she turned off the
light and moved into the bedroom.

There was no purpose to damaging introspection, she resolved as she slid into bed. She was
an adult, and, if he could handle spending the night
hours lying in another bed in the same room, then
so could she.

The challenge was to fall asleep *before* he entered
the bedroom, rather than afterwards, and despite
feeling tired it proved impossible to slip into a state
of somnolent oblivion.

How long she lay awake she had no idea, but it
seemed *hours* before she heard the faint click of the
bedroom door as it unlatched, followed by another
as it was quietly closed.

Every nerve-end tautened to its furthest limit as
she heard the indistinct sound of clothing being
discarded, and she unconsciously held her breath
as she visualised each and every one of his movements, her memory of his tightly muscled naked
frame intensely vivid from the breadth of shoulder
to his slim waist, the whorls of dark hair on his
chest that arrowed down to his navel before feathering in a delicate line to a flaring montage at the
junction of his loins. Firm-muscled buttocks, lean
hips, and an enviable length of strong muscled legs.
Beautiful smooth skin, a warm shield for the blood
that pulsed through his veins and entwined with
honed muscle and sinew.

It was a body she had come to know as intimately as her own as he had tutored her where to

touch, when to brush feather-light strokes that had made him catch his breath, and how the touch of her lips, her tongue, could drive him almost beyond the edge of sensual sanity.

But it had been little in comparison to the response he was able to evoke in her, for all her senses had leapt with fire at his slightest touch, and she had become a willing wanton in his arms, encouraging everything he chose to give, like a wild untamed being in the throes of unbelievable ecstasy. Abandoned, exultant—passion's mistress.

Carly closed her eyes, tight, then slowly opened them again. Dear lord, she must have been insane to imagine she could share this room with him and remain unaffected by his presence.

Was this some form of diabolical revenge he'd deliberately chosen? Did he really intend to *sleep*?

The acute awareness was still there, a haunting pleasurable ache that fired all her senses and ate into her soul. In the past seven years there hadn't been a night when she didn't think of him, and many a time she'd woken shaking at the intensity of her dreaming, almost afraid in those few seconds of regained consciousness that she had somehow regressed into the past. Then she would look at the empty pillow beside her and realise it had all been a relayed figment of her overstimulated imagination.

Several feet separated each bed, yet the distance could have been a yawning chasm ten times that magnitude. Carly heard the almost undetectable sound of the mattress depressing with Stefano's weight as he slid in between the sheets, followed by the slowly decreasing rhythm of his breathing as it steadied into a deep, regular beat denoting total relaxation.

It seemed unbelievable that he could summon sleep so easily, and a seed of anger took root and began to germinate deep within her, feeding on frustration, pain and a gamut of emotions too numerous to delineate.

Rational thought disappeared as her febrile brain pondered the quality of his lovemaking, and whether it would be any different now from what it had been seven years ago.

In that moment she realised how much she was at his mercy, and that the essence of Stefano Alessi the man *now* was inevitably different from the lover she had once known.

At some stage she must have fallen into a blissful state of oblivion, for she gradually drifted into wakefulness through various layers of consciousness, aware initially in those few seconds before comprehension dawned that something was different. Then her lashes slowly flickered open, and she saw why.

In sleep she had turned to lie facing the bed opposite her own, and her eyes widened as she encountered Stefano's steady gaze. Reclining on his side, head propped in one hand, he regarded her with unsmiling appraisal.

Carly's first instinct was to leap out from the bed, and perhaps something in her expression gave her intention away, for one of his eyebrows arched in silent musing cynicism.

The gesture acted as a challenge, and she forced herself to remain where she was. 'What's the time?' she asked with deliberate sleepiness, as if this were just another morning in a series of mornings she woke to find herself sharing a room.

'Early. Not long after six.' His eyes slid lazily down to her mouth, then slipped lower to pause deliberately on the soft swell of her breast. 'No need to rush into starting the day.'

Carly's fingers reached automatically for the edge of the sheet and pulled it higher, aware of a tell-tale warmth tingeing her cheeks, and her eyes instantly sparked with fire. 'If you think I'm going to indulge in an exchange of pleasantries, you're mistaken!'

'Define *pleasantries*,' Stefano drawled, and she froze, her eyes widening into huge pools of uncertainty in features that had suddenly become pale. There wasn't a shred of softness in his voice, and she was frighteningly aware of her own vulnerability in the face of his superior strength.

'Afraid, Carly?'

'Of a display of raging male hormones?' she managed with a calmness she was far from feeling. He looked dangerous, like a sleek panther contemplating a helpless prey, and it was impossible not to feel apprehensive.

Her lashes flicked wide as his gaze travelled to the base of her throat, then his eyes captured hers with an indolent intensity, and she dredged up all her resources in an attempt to portray some measure of ease.

'Is that all you imagine it will be?' he queried silkily.

'Sex simply to satisfy a base animal need?'

'Cynicism doesn't suit you,' he said in a voice that was deadly soft.

'I've learnt to survive,' she returned with innate dignity. 'Without benefit of anyone other than myself.'

Stefano looked at her for what seemed an age, his gaze dark and inscrutable. 'Until now.'

'Payback time, Stefano?' She forced herself to study him, noting the almost indecently broad shoulders, the firm, sculptured features that embodied an inherent strength of will. 'Are you implying I should slip into your bed and allow you to score the first instalment?'

'With you playing the role of reluctant martyr?' He paused, and his voice hardened slightly. 'I think not, my little cat. I don't feel inclined to give you that satisfaction.'

Her stomach lurched, then appeared to settle. It was only a game, a by-play of words designed to attack her composure. Well, she would prove she was a worthy opponent.

'What a relief to know I don't have to fake it,' she told him sweetly. 'Is there anything else you'd like to discuss before I hit the shower?'

There was lurking humour evident in those dark eyes, and a measure of respect. 'Last week I extended an invitation to Charles and his wife to dine here this evening. They flew in from the States yesterday.'

The thought of having to act the part of gracious hostess in his home, while appearing capable and serene, was a hurdle she wasn't sure she was ready to surmount—yet. However, Charles Winslow the Third was a valued colleague, who, the last time she'd dined in his presence, had been in the throes of divorcing one wife in favour of wedding another.

'What time had you planned for them to arrive?' she queried cautiously, unwilling to commit herself.

'Eight. Sylvana will prepare and serve the meal.'

She had to ask. 'Are they the only guests?'

'Charles's daughter, Georgeanne.'

Seven years ago Georgeanne had been a precocious teenager. Time could only have turned her into a stunning beauty. 'Another conquest, Stefano?' she queried with musing mockery.

'I don't consciously set out to charm every female I come into contact with,' he drawled, and she gave a soundless laugh.

'You don't have to. Your potent brand of sexual chemistry does it for you.'

'An admission, Carly?'

'A statement from one who has sampled a dose and escaped unscathed,' she corrected gravely, and glimpsed the faint edge of humour curve his generous mouth.

'And tonight?'

She looked at him carefully. 'What if I refuse?'

'Out of sheer perversity, or a disinclination to mix and mingle socially?'

'Oh, *both*,' she disclaimed drily. 'I just love the idea of being a subject of conjecture and gossip.'

'Charles is a very good friend of long standing,' Stefano reminded her.

'In that case, I'll endeavour to shine as your hostess,' Carly conceded. 'What of *my* friends?' she pursued.

'Sarah?'

'Yes.' And James. She would mention it when she phoned Sarah this afternoon.

'Feel free to issue an invitation whenever you please.'

Stefano watched with indolent amusement as she slid from the bed, slipped her arms into a towelling wrap, then escaped to the adjoining *en suite*.

Breakfast was a shared meal eaten out on the terrace, after which Stefano withdrew upstairs only to re-emerge ten minutes later, immaculately attired in a dark business suit.

He looked every inch the directorial businessman that he was, and arrestingly physical in a way that set Carly's pulse racing in an accelerated beat. She watched with detached interest as he crossed to the table and brushed gentle fingers to Ann-Marie's cheek.

Somehow she managed to force her features into a stunning smile when his gaze assumed musing indolence as it rested on her mobile mouth.

'Bye. Don't work too hard.' The words sounded light and faintly teasing, but there was nothing light in the glance she spared him beneath dark-fringed lashes.

Minutes later there was the muted sound of a car engine as the Mercedes traversed the long curving driveway.

Ann-Marie's appointment with the neuro-surgeon was at ten, and afterwards Carly drove home in a state of suspended shock as she attempted to absorb Ann-Marie's proposed admission into hospital the following day, with surgery scheduled for late Wednesday afternoon.

So *soon*, she agonised, in no doubt that Stefano's influence had added sufficient weight to the surgeon's decision to operate without delay.

It was impossible not to suffer through an entire gamut of emotions, not the least of which was very real fear. Even the neuro-surgeon's assurance that the success-rate for such operations was high did little to alleviate her anxiety.

Stefano arrived home shortly after four, and half an hour later the breeder delivered Françoise—a small, intelligent bundle of black curls who proved to be love on four legs.

The delightful pup took an instant liking to the hulking Prince, who in turn was initially tolerant, then displayed an amusing mixture of bewitchment and bewilderment as Françoise divided her attention equally between him and her new mistress.

There was a new kennel, an inside sleeping-box, leads, a collar, a few soft toys, and feeding bowls.

Ann-Marie looked as if she'd been given the world, and Carly experienced reluctant gratitude for Stefano's timing.

'Thank you,' she said quietly as they emerged from their daughter's bedroom, having settled an ecstatically happy little girl to sleep. Françoise was equally settled in her sleeping-box beside Ann-Marie's bed.

His smile was warm, genuine, she perceived with a slight start of surprise, for there was no evidence of his usual mockery.

'She has waited long enough to enjoy the company of a much wanted pet.'

Carly felt a pang of remorse for the years spent living in rented accommodation which had excluded the ownership of animals. It seemed another peg in the victory stakes for Stefano—a silent comparison of provision. His against hers.

'We have fifteen minutes before Charles is due to arrive,' Stefano intimated as they reached their suite. 'Can you be ready in time?'

She was, with a few seconds to spare, looking attractive in a slim-fitting dress in vivid tones of peacock-green and -blue. Her hair was confined in a simple knot, her make-up understated with practised emphasis on her eyes... Eyes which met his and held them unflinchingly as she preceded him from the room.

CHAPTER SIX

CHARLES WINSLOW THE THIRD was a friendly, gregarious gentleman whose daughter was of a similar age to his second wife.

If appearances were anything to go by, each young woman had worked hard to outdo the other in the fashion stakes, for each wore a designer label that resembled creations by Dior and Ungaro.

Carly felt her own dress paled by comparison, for although the classic style was elegant it was hardly new.

Within seconds of entering the lounge Charles took hold of Carly's hand and raised it, Southern-style, to his lips.

'I'm delighted the two of you are together again,' he intoned solemnly. 'You're too beautiful to remain unattached, and Stefano was a fool to let you escape.'

Carly caught Stefano's faintly lifted eyebrow and was unable to prevent the slight quiver at the edge of her mouth. Without blinking an eyelid, she sent Charles her most dazzling smile. 'Charles,' she greeted with equal solemnity. 'You haven't changed.'

His faintly wolfish smile was no mean complement to his sparkling brown eyes. 'My wife tells me I become more irascible with every year, and Georgeanne only tags along because I pay her bills.'

'Ignore him,' Kathy-Lee advised with a light smile.

'Stefano...' Georgeanne purred, offering Carly a sharp assessing glance before focusing her attention on her father's business associate. 'It's wonderful to see you again.'

'Wonderful' was a pretty fine superlative to describe Charles's daughter, Carly mused, for the young woman was all grown up and pure feline.

Kathy-Lee, at least, opted to observe the conventions and set out to charm superficially while choosing to ignore the machinations of her stepdaughter. Which, Carly noted circumspectly, grew more bold with every passing hour. Perhaps it was merely a game, she perceived as they leisurely dispensed with one delectable course after another.

Whatever the reason, Carly refused to rise to the bait, and instead drew Charles into a lengthy and highly technical discourse on the intricacies of computer programming. As he owed much of his fortune to creating specialised programs, his knowledge was unequalled.

Stefano, to give him his due, did nothing to encourage Georgeanne's attention, but Carly detected an implied intimacy that hurt unbearably. It clouded her beautiful eyes, leaving them faintly pensive, and, although her smile flashed with necessary brilliance throughout the evening, her hands betrayed their nervousness on one occasion, incurring Stefano's narrowed glance as she swiftly averted spilling the contents of her wine glass.

Carly told herself she couldn't care less about her husband's past indiscretions, but deep within her resentment flared, and mingled with a certain degree of pain.

Outwardly, Stefano was the perfect host, his attention faultless, and only she knew that the implied intimacy of his smile merely depicted a contrived image for the benefit of their guests.

It was almost eleven when Charles indicated that they must leave.

'It's so early,' Georgeanne protested with a pretty pout. 'I thought we might go on to a nightclub.'

'Honey,' Charles chided with a slow sloping smile before directing Carly a wicked wink, 'I have no doubt Stefano and Carly have a different kind of socialising in mind.'

His daughter effected a faint moue, then sent Stefano a luscious smile. 'Don't be crude, Daddy. I'm sure Stefano has the stamina for both.'

Charles gave Kathy-Lee the sort of look that made Carly's toes curl before switching his attention to his daughter. 'It's no contest, darlin',' he drawled.

Georgeanne evinced her disappointment, then effected a light shrugging gesture. 'If you say so.' She moved a step closer to Stefano and placed scarlet-tipped nails against his jacket-encased arm. '*Ciao, caro.*' She reached up and brushed her lips against his cheek—only because he turned his head and she missed his mouth. Her smile was pure celluloid, and there was a faint malicious gleam as she turned towards Carly. 'You look—tired, sweetie.'

Without blinking, Carly met the other girl's sultry stare, and issued softly, 'Stefano doesn't allow me much time to sleep.'

Charles's eyes danced with ill-concealed humour.
'Give it up, Georgeanne.' With old-fashioned charm
he took hold of Carly's hand and squeezed it gently.
'You must be our guests for dinner before we fly
back to the States.'

Carly simply smiled, and walked at Stefano's side
to the foyer. Minutes later Charles, Kathy-Lee and
Georgeanne were seated in their hired car, and
almost as soon as the rear lights disappeared
through the gates Carly moved upstairs to check on
Ann-Marie and Françoise.

A tiny black head lifted from the sleeping-box to
regard her solemnly, then nestled back against the
blanket.

'I'll take her outside for a few minutes, then she
should be all right until morning.'

Carly turned slowly at the sound of Stefano's
voice, and she nodded in silent acquiescence. Ann-
Marie was lost in sleep, her features relaxed and
cherubic in the dull reflected glow of her night-light,
the covers in place, and her favourite doll and teddy
bear vying for affection on either side of her small
frame.

Carly felt the sudden prick of tears, and blinked
rapidly to dispel them. Her daughter was so small,
so dependent—so damned vulnerable.

She was hardly aware of Stefano's return, and it
took only seconds to settle the poodle comfortably
among its blankets.

Once inside their own suite, Carly stepped directly through to the bathroom and removed her
make-up with slightly shaking fingers. Her nerves
felt as if they were shredding into a thousand pieces,

and she needed a second attempt at replacing the lid on the jar of cleanser.

When she re-entered the bedroom Stefano was propped up in bed, stroking notes into a leather-bound book, and her stomach executed a series of flips at his breadth of shoulder, the hard-muscled chest with its liberal whorls of dark hair tapering down to a firm waist.

The pale-coloured sheet merely highlighted the natural olive colour of his skin, and as if sensing her appraisal he looked up and pinned her gaze, only to chuckle softly as she quickly averted her eyes.

'Shy, Carly?' he drawled, and she hated the faint flood of pink that warmed her cheeks as she moved towards her bed.

He possessed all the attributes of a superb jungle animal, resplendent, resting, yet totally focused on his prey.

An arrow of pain arched up from the centre of her being in the knowledge that seven years ago she would have laughed with him, tantalisingly slid the nightgown from her shoulders—if she'd even opted to wear one—and walked towards him, sure of his waiting arms, the rapture that would take them far into the night.

Now, she fingered the decorative frill on the pillowslip, and made a play of plumping the pillow, feeling oddly reluctant to skip into bed, yet longing for the relaxing effect of several hours' sleep.

'How delightful, *cara*,' Stefano teased mercilessly. 'You can still blush.'

Carly lifted her head and her eyes sparked with latent fire. 'If you wanted a playmate for the evening, you should have gone nightclubbing with Georgeanne.'

One eyebrow slanted in silent mockery. 'Why—when I have my very own playmate at home?'

Anger mingled with the fire, and produced a golden-flecked flame within the brilliant darkness of her gaze. 'Because I don't like playing games, and I particularly don't want to play them with *you*!'

'Georgeanne is——'

'I know perfectly well what Georgeanne is!' she vented quietly, hating his level gaze. She was angry, without any clear reason *why*.

'—the daughter of a very good friend of mine,' he continued as if she hadn't spoken, 'who delights in practising her feminine witchery.' His eyes hardened fractionally. 'Charles should have disciplined her precociousness at a young age.'

'Oh—*fiddlesticks*,' Carly responded, unwilling to agree with him. 'Georgeanne suffers from acute boredom, and views any attractive man as a contest. If he's married, that presents even more of a challenge.'

Stefano's eyes speared hers, and his expression assumed a lazy indolence. 'Jealous, *cara*?'

'Stop calling me that!'

'You're expending so much nervous energy,' he drawled imperturbably. 'You'll never be able to relax sufficiently to sleep.'

Without thinking she picked up the pillow and threw it at him, then gasped as he fielded it with one hand and moved with lightning speed to trap her before she had the chance to move. She wrenched her arm in an effort to be free of him, then she cried out as he tightened his grip and pulled her down on to the bed.

There wasn't a chance she could escape, yet to lie quiescent was impossible, and she flailed at him with her free arm, then groaned with despair as he caught it and held her immobile.

His mouth was inches above her own, and she just looked at him, unable to focus her gaze on anything except his strong, chiselled features and the darkness of his eyes.

Time became suspended as she lay still, mesmerised by the look of him, imprisoned in a spellbinding thrall of all her senses. This close, the warmth of his breath skimmed her mouth, and she could smell the faint musky tones of his aftershave, the clean body smell emanating from his skin, and the essential maleness that was his alone. An answering awareness unfurled deep within her, flaring into vibrant life as it coursed through her body with the intensity of flame.

She could see the knowledge of it reflected in his eyes, the waiting expectancy evident as every cell, every nerve-end flowered into a sexual bloom so vivid, so hauntingly warm that she caught his faint intake of breath an instant before his head slowly lowered to claim her mouth in a teasingly gentle kiss that was so incredibly evocative that she was powerless to still the faint prick of tears.

His lips trailed to the sensitive cord at the edge of her neck, nuzzling the sweet hollows, before continuing a slow descent to a highly sensitised nub peaking at her breast.

The anticipation was almost more than she could bear, and she murmured indistinctly, craving the exquisite pleasure of his touch, exulting when he took the tender peak into his mouth and began teasing it with the edge of his teeth.

A deep shooting pain arrowed through her body, and she slid her hands up over his shoulders in a tactile voyage of discovery until her fingers reached the dark curling hair at his nape.

An ache began at the junction of her thighs, and she arched her body against his in unbidden invitation, then she gave a pleasurable sigh as his fingers slid to caress the aroused orifice to a peak of exquisite pleasure, his movements deftly skilled, until nothing less than total possession was enough.

She became mindless, caught in the thrall of a passion so intense that she began to beg, pleading with him in wanton abandon, until with sure movements he plunged deep inside, stilling as she gasped at his level of penetration.

Then slowly he began to withdraw, only to repeat the initial thrust again and again, increasing in rapidity until her body caught hold of his rhythm and then paced it in unison until the momentum tipped them both over the edge into an explosion of ecstasy so tumultuous that she began to shake uncontrollably as the tremors radiated through her body, incandescent, shattering, primitive, the most primal of all the emotions, subsiding gradually to assume a piercing sweetness that stayed with her long after he curled her close in against him and his breathing steadied with her own into the slow, measured pattern of sleep.

* * *

Carly retained very little memory of the ensuing few days, for one seemed to run into the other as she spent all her waking hours at the hospital.

'I want to stay with her,' she said quietly to the sister on duty shortly after Ann-Marie was admitted.

'My dear, I understand your concern, but we've found a young child tends to become distraught if the mother rooms in with the child. It really is much more practical if you visit frequently for short periods. Quality time is much better than quantity. Besides,' she continued briskly, 'it allows the medical staff to do their job more efficiently.'

It made sense, but it didn't aid Carly's natural anxiety, for she had hardly slept the night prior to Ann-Marie's surgery, and was a nervous wreck all through the following day, choosing to sit in silent vigil well into the evening, despite being advised to go home and rest.

Stefano came and fetched her, his voice quietly insistent, and she was too mentally and emotionally exhausted to give more than a token protest as he led her out to the car. At home he heated milk, added a strong measure of brandy, and made sure she drank it all.

One day seemed to run into another without Carly having any clear recollection of each, for Ann-Marie was her entire focus from the time of waking until she fell wearily into bed at night.

From Intensive Care, Ann-Marie was released into a suite of her own, and designated a model patient as she began the slow path towards recuperation.

Carly, however, became increasingly tense, for there were still tests to be run, and by the fifth evening she was powerless to prevent the silent flow of tears long after she'd crept into bed.

Reaction, she decided wearily, to all the tension, the anxiety, and insufficient sleep. Yet she couldn't stop, and after a while she slid soundlessly to her feet, gathered up a wrap and walked silently down the hall.

Ann-Marie's bedroom door was closed, and she opened it, her breath catching as she saw the night-light burning and two bright button eyes as Françoise lifted her head to examine the intruder.

A lump rose in her throat as she crossed to the sleeping-box and scooped the curly-haired black bundle into her arms.

The poodle's nose was cool and damp, and Carly hugged her close. A small, wet pink tongue emerged to lick her cheek, then began to lap in earnest at the taste of salty tears. After several long minutes she restored the poodle into its sleeping-box, then slowly crossed to the window.

The curtains were closed, and she opened them fractionally, looking out at the moonlit grounds in detached contemplation.

The small shrubs appeared large with their looming shadows, and everything seemed so still, almost lifeless. Pin-pricks of electric light glittered across the harbour, merging with splashes of flashing neon advertisements gracing several city buildings. By night it resembled a tracery of fairy-lights, remote, yet symbolising activity and pulsing life.

She had no idea how long she remained motion-less, for there was no awareness of the passage of time, just a slide into introspection that took her back over six years to the day her daughter was born, and the joy, the tears and the laughter that had followed through a few childhood illnesses, the guilt of having to leave her in child care while she worked, Ann-Marie's first day at kindergarten, her first visit to the zoo, and the day she had started school. She was a quiet, obedient child, but with a mind of her own.

'Unable to sleep?' The query was quietly voiced, and Carly turned slowly to face the man standing in the aperture.

For an age she just looked at him, her eyes large and unblinking in a face that was pale and shadowed, then she turned back to the scene beyond the window. 'I wish it was all over and she was home,' she managed in an emotion-charged voice, and felt rather than heard him move to stand behind her.

'Likewise,' Stefano muttered in agreement.

No power on earth could speed up time, and she closed her eyes in an effort to gain some measure of inner strength. She had to be strong, she *had* to be, she resolved silently.

Hard, muscular arms slid around her waist from behind and pulled her gently back against a solid male frame.

For a moment she resisted, stiffening slightly, then she became prey to the protective shelter he offered, and she relaxed, allowing his strength to flow through her body.

It was like coming home, and the sadness of what they'd once shared, then lost, overwhelmed her. She closed her eyes tightly against the threat of tears, feeling them burn as she fought for control.

For all of a minute she managed to keep them at bay, then they squeezed through to spill in warm rivulets down each cheek to fall one after the other from her chin.

Firm hands slid up to her shoulders and turned her into his embrace, one hand slipping through the thickness of her hair while the other slid to anchor the base of her spine.

It felt so good, so right, so *safe*, and after a long time she slid her hands round his waist, linking them together behind his back.

The strong, measured beat of his heart sounded loud against her ear, and she rested against him for a long time, drawing comfort from his large frame, until at last she stirred and began to pull free of him.

Without a word he loosened his hold, and, slipping one arm about her waist, he led her back to their suite. Both beds bore evidence of their occupation, and she viewed each, feeling strangely loath to leave the sanctuary of his embrace, yet to go tacitly to his bed would reveal an unspoken willingness for something she was as yet unprepared to give.

For what seemed an age he stood in silence, watching the expressive play of emotions chase across her features, then he leant forward and brushed his lips against her cheek, trailing gently up to her temple before tracing slowly down to the edge of her mouth.

It was an evocative caress, his lips gently tracing her own with such a heightened degree of sensitivity, it was almost more than she could bear.

It would be so easy to allow him to continue, to follow a conflagrating path to total possession and its resultant euphoria. Except that it would only be a merging born out of sexual desire, not the meeting of two minds, two souls, the sharing of something so beautiful, so exquisite, that the senses coalesced and became one.

She went still, lowering her hands slowly down to her side, and Stefano lifted his head slightly, viewing the soft mouth, the faint smudges beneath her shimmering eyes, and his expression became watchful, intent, as she sought to swallow the sudden lump that had risen in her throat.

Carly wanted to cry out, yet no sound emerged, and she willed herself to breathe slowly, evenly, as he drew her down on to his bed and pulled her gently into the circle of his arms.

His quietly voiced, 'Sleep easy, *cara*,' sent goosebumps scudding in numerous directions to places they had no right to invade. She lay there, unable to make so much as a sound, and within minutes she became aware of the steady pattern of his breathing. Then slowly she began to relax, and gradually sheer emotional exhaustion provided a welcome escape into somnolence.

CHAPTER SEVEN

ANN-MARIE continued to improve with each passing day, and there was immense relief at the week's end to receive the neuro-surgeon's voiced confidence of a complete recovery. It balanced the shock of seeing the bandages removed for the first time, and evidence of a vivid surgical scar.

Carly was so elated on leaving the hospital that she decided against phoning Stefano, and opted to tell him the news in person. Consequently it was almost four when she entered the towering modern city block and rode the lift to Reception.

There was a sense of *déjà vu* on stepping into the luxuriously furnished foyer, although this time there was the advantage of needing no introduction. Carly entertained little doubt that an expurgated version of her previous visit had filtered through the office grapevine, and she kept her eyes steady with a friendly smile pinned in place as the receptionist rang through to Stefano's personal secretary.

Renate appeared almost immediately, her features schooled to express warmth and a degree of apologetic charm. 'Stefano is in conference with a colleague,' she enlightened Carly as she ushered her into his private lounge. 'I've let him know you're here, and he said he'll be with you in a matter of minutes.' The smile deepened. 'Can I get you a drink? Coffee? Tea? Something cool?'

'I'd like to use the rest-room first, if I may?'
Carly returned the woman's smile with one of her
own. 'And something cool would be great.'

As she was about to re-enter the lounge several
minutes later a door opened several feet in front of
her to reveal a tall, attractive brunette whose
stunning features were permanently etched in
Carly's mind.

Recognition was instantaneous, and Carly's
whole body went cold as she watched Angelica
Agnelli turn back to the man immediately behind
her and bestow on him a lingering kiss.

Carly felt as if the scene was momentarily frozen
in her brain, like the delayed shutter of a camera,
then the figures began to move, and she watched
as Stefano stood back a pace and let his hands fall
from Angelica's shoulders.

His expression held warm affection, and stabbed
at Carly's heart. At the same moment he lifted his
head, and Carly watched with a sort of detached
fascination as they each became aware of her
presence.

It was rather like viewing a play, she decided as
she glimpsed the darkness in Stefano's eyes an instant before he masked it, and she was prepared to
go on record that the dismay evident in Angelica's
expression was deliberate, for the faint smile of
contrition failed to reach her eyes.

'Carly,' Angelica greeted her with apparent
warmth. 'Stefano told me you were back.' Her expression pooled into one of apparent concern. 'How
is your daughter?'

The faint emphasis on 'your' wasn't missed, and
Carly marshalled innate dignity as a weapon in her

mythical arsenal. 'Ann-Marie is fine, thank you,' she responded steadily. Her eyes lifted to meet Stefano's slightly narrowed gaze, and she summoned a deliberately sweet smile. 'Renate is fetching me a cool drink. I'll wait in the lounge while you see Angelica out.' She placed imperceptible stress on the last word, then softened it with a studied smile as she turned towards the beautifully attired young woman whose *haute-couture* clothes hugged a perfect figure. 'Goodbye, Angelica. I'm sure we'll run into each other again.' Not if I see you first, she added silently as she turned into the private lounge.

With extreme care Carly closed the door behind her, then crossed towards the bar where an iced pitcher of orange juice stood beside a tall frosted glass.

Pouring herself a generous measure, she sipped at it abstractly and told herself she felt no pain. Dammit, she swore softly. There had to be subversive psychic elements at play somewhere in the vicinity, for each time she entered Stefano's private lounge she was moved to blinding rage.

However, *this* time she'd be calm. Another voluble, visible display of temper would have the staff labelling her a shrew. Yet she defied even the most placid woman not to be driven to anger when she was faced with evidence of her husband's *affaire de coeur*.

It was five minutes before Stefano joined her, and she turned quietly to face him as he entered the room. His expression was inscrutable, his eyes faintly hooded, and he made no attempt at any explanation.

He looked the epitome of a successful businessman, his three-piece suit dark and impeccably tailored, the pale blue shirt made of the finest silk, and his shoes hand-stitched imported leather.

She was reminded of the saying that 'clothes made the man'. Yet her indomitable husband could have worn torn cut-off jeans and a sweatshirt, and he'd still manage to project a devastating raw virility that had little to do with the physical look of him.

If his relationship with Angelica Agnelli continued to extend beyond that of friends, then anything Carly said would only fuel her own anger and lead inevitably to another confrontation.

Besides, she was twenty-seven, and no longer the naïve, trusting young girl who had believed in one true love. Reality was the knowledge that love didn't conquer all, nor did it always last forever.

'How was Ann-Marie this afternoon?'

Carly met his dark gaze with equanimity. 'Improving,' she informed him steadily. 'The specialist is confident she'll make a full recovery.'

His features relaxed into an expression of immense relief. '*Grazie a Dio*,' he breathed with immense gratitude.

'Obviously it would have been better if I'd phoned with the news.'

One eyebrow slanted above a pair of eyes that had become strangely watchful. 'Why *obviously*?'

'Business, pleasure and personal affairs are an incompatible mix,' she hinted with unaccustomed cynicism, and saw his eyes narrow.

'Angelica——'

'Don't even consider proffering the rather hackneyed explanation that she's merely an associate.' She lifted her chin, and her eyes were remarkably clear as they held his. 'I've heard it all before.'

'Angelica is a valued family friend,' he continued with hard inflexibility, and the gold flecks in her eyes flared with brilliant topaz as she refused to be intimidated in any way.

'*Valued* is a very tame description, Stefano,' Carly responded, wondering what devilish imp was pushing her in a direction she'd sworn not to tread.

'Perhaps you'd care to offer a more lucid alternative,' he drawled with dangerous silkiness, and she was powerless to prevent the surge of anger coursing through her body.

'She wants *you*,' she declared with quiet conviction. 'She always has. For a while I stood in her way. Now that I'm back . . .' She trailed off deliberately, then effected a slight shrug. 'If she can hurt me emotionally, she will.' The need to be free of him was paramount, and she turned to leave, only to have a detaining hand catch hold of her arm and pull her back to face him.

Any escape could only be temporary. It was there in his eyes, the latent anger a silent threat should she continue to thwart him.

'Let me go.' The words left her throat as his head lowered, and she turned slightly so that his lips grazed her cheek. Then she cried out as he slid his fingers through the thickness of her hair, and his mouth captured hers in a kiss that was nothing less than a total possession of her senses.

A muffled groan of entreaty choked in her throat as he brought her even closer against his hard, muscular frame, and when he finally lifted his head she stood quite still, bearing his silent scrutiny until every nerve stretched to its furthest limit.

His hands slid with seductive slowness to her waist, then cradled her ribcage, the pads of each thumb beginning an evocative circle over the hardening peaks of her breasts in a movement that was intensely erotic.

She had to stop him *now*, before she lost the will to move away. 'Sex in the office, Stefano? Whatever will Renate think?' she taunted softly. 'Or maybe she's accustomed to her boss's . . . discreet diversions?'

His eyes narrowed, and a muscle hardened at the edge of his jaw. 'Watch your foolish tongue.'

Carly laughed, a soft mocking sound that was the antithesis of anything related to humour. Gathering courage, she added with unaccustomed cynicism, 'I imagine many women shared your table as well as your bed in the last seven years.'

His eyes stilled for a second, then assumed a brooding mockery. 'You want me to supply a list, *cara*?'

For one heart-stopping moment she looked stricken. The thought of that long, superbly muscled body giving even one other woman the sort of sexual pleasure he gave her was sickening. To consider there had probably been *several* made her feel positively ill. Suddenly she'd had enough, and was in dire need of some breathing space—preferably as far away from her inimical husband as possible.

If she didn't leave soon, the ache behind her eyes would result in silent futile tears, and without a further word she turned and left the room.

Within minutes of reaching home she crossed to the phone and dialled Sarah's number. At the sound of her friend's voice she clutched hold of the receiver and sank down into a nearby chair for a long conversation that encompassed an exchange of news as well as providing a link to normality.

'You must bring James to dinner,' Carly insisted as Sarah exclaimed at the time. 'I'll check with Stefano and give you a call.'

'Lovely,' the other girl declared with enthusiasm. 'Give Ann-Marie a big hug from me, and tell her I'll visit tomorrow.'

Dinner was a strained meal, for Carly found it difficult to contribute much by way of conversation that didn't come out sounding horribly banal. In the end, she simply gave up, and pushed her food around the plate before discarding her cutlery to sip iced water from her glass.

Stefano, damn him, didn't appear a whit disturbed, and he did justice to the dishes Sylvana provided before finishing with fresh grapes, biscuits and cheese.

Carly sat in silence during the drive to hospital, unwilling to offer so much as a word in case it ended in a slanging match—or worse.

There was such a wealth of resentment at having witnessed the touching little departure scene between Angelica and Stefano that afternoon—and unabating anger. It almost eclipsed the joy of witnessing Ann-Marie's pleasure in their visit, and the expressive smile when Stefano presented her with yet another gift.

'I'm getting spoilt,' Ann-Marie concluded, hugging the beautifully dressed doll close to her small chest, and her eyes gleamed when her father leaned down to brush his lips against her cheek. 'Thank you, Daddy.'

The words held such poignancy that Carly had to blink fast against the threat of tears.

'My pleasure, *piccina*.'

'What's a *piccina*?'

'A special endearment for a special little girl,' he responded gently.

It was almost eight when the Mercedes pulled into the driveway leading to Stefano's elegant home, and once indoors Carly made her way through to the kitchen.

'Coffee?' It was a perfunctory query that incurred his narrowed gaze.

'Please.'

Her movements were automatic as she filled the percolator, selected a fresh filter, then spooned in a blend of ground coffee-beans.

'Would you prefer yours here, or in the lounge?'

'The lounge.'

Damn, that meant she'd have to share it with him, yet if she opted out he'd only be amused, and she refused to give him the satisfaction.

Five minutes later she placed cups and saucers, sugar and milk on to a tray and carried it through to the informal lounge. Placing his within easy reach, she selected a chair several feet distant from where he was seated.

'We've been invited out to dinner tomorrow evening,' Stefano informed her with indolent ease as he spooned in sugar and stirred the thick black liquid in his cup. 'Charles Winslow will be there with Kathy-Lee.' His eyes seared hers, darkly analytical in a manner that raised all her fine body hairs in a gesture of self-defence.

'And Georgeanne?' She arched a brow in deliberate query. 'I'm not sure I want to go.' The thought of standing at his side for several hours playing a part didn't figure very high in her order of preferred entertainment.

'Most of the men present will have their wives or partners in attendance,' he drawled, and she said sweetly,

'Why not invite Angelica? I'm sure she'd delight in the opportunity. Then you could have two women vying for your attention.'

One eyebrow slanted in quizzical mockery, although anything approaching humour was sadly lacking in his expression. 'I'll ignore that remark.'

A crazy imp prompted her to query, 'Good heavens, *why*? It's nothing less than the truth.'

His expression didn't alter. 'Watch your unwary tongue, *mi moglie*,' he cautioned in a deadly soft voice.

'Don't threaten me,' she responded swiftly, feeling the deep-rooted anger begin to surge to the surface.

'Warn,' he amended with quiet emphasis.

'There's a difference?'

His eyes lanced hers, silent and deadly in their intent. 'Give it up, Carly.'

'And concede defeat?'

'If you want to fight,' Stefano drawled with dangerous silkiness, 'I'm willing to oblige.' He paused deliberately, then continued, 'I doubt you'll enjoy the consequences.'

A shaft of exquisite pain arrowed through her body, although defiance was responsible for the angry tilt of her chin as she berated, 'I seem to remember you preferred your women warm and willing.'

'What makes you think you won't be, *cara*?' Stefano drawled, his expression veiled as pain clouded her beautiful eyes, rendering her features hauntingly vulnerable for a few heart-stopping seconds before the mask slipped into place.

She was treading dangerous waters, yet she was too incensed to desist. 'Did it never occur to you that my taste in men may have changed?'

'Have there been that many?' His voice sounded like finely tempered steel grazing satin, and she had the incredible desire to shock.

'Oh—*several*.'

Something leapt in the depth of his eyes, and she wanted to cry out a denial, yet the words remained locked in her throat.

What on earth was the matter with her in taunting him? Playing any kind of game with a man of Stefano's calibre was akin to prodding a sleeping jungle animal.

'I had a life during the past seven years, Stefano,' she flung, more angry than she'd care to admit. 'Didn't you?'

'Do you really want to pursue this topic?'

'Why?'

'Because it will have only one ending,' he warned with incredible silkiness, although his eyes were hard and obdurate, and there could be no doubt as to his meaning.

'Go to hell,' she whispered, hating him more at that precise moment than she'd thought it possible to hate anyone.

The need to get away from him was paramount, and, uncaring of his reaction, she turned and walked out of the room, out of the house, moving with a quick measured pace along the driveway to the electronically locked steel gates.

For the first time she damned Stefano's security measures as logic and sanity temporarily vanished in the face of a fierce, unbating anger.

The house, the grounds, were like an impenetrable fortress, necessary in today's age among the exceedingly wealthy in a bid to protect themselves, their family and their possessions.

She could return indoors, collect her keys and the necessary remote module to release the main gates, but even in anger sufficient common sense exerted itself to warn silently against walking the suburban streets alone after dark. And if she took her car, where would she go? It was too late for visiting, and Sarah, if she wasn't working, would probably be out with James.

Carly turned back towards the house and slowly retraced her steps. The air was warm, with the faintest breeze teasing a few stray tendrils of her hair, and she lifted her face slightly, looking deep into the indigo sky with its nebulous moon and sprinkling of stars.

Drawing in a deep breath, she released it slowly. A strange restlessness besieged her, and she felt the need for some form of exercise to help expel her pent-up emotions.

There was a pool in the rear of the grounds, and she instinctively took the path that skirted the southern side of the house.

Reflected light from several electric lamps strategically placed in the adjacent rockery garden lent the pool a shimmering translucence, and, without giving too much thought to ner actions, Carly stripped off her outer clothes and executed a neat dive into the pool's clear depths. Within seconds she was cleaving clean strokes through the cool water, silently counting as she completed each length. After twenty-five she rested for a few minutes, clearing the excess water from her face, her hair.

'Had enough?'

Carly lifted her head and looked at the tall figure standing close to the pool's edge. In the subdued light he loomed large, his height and breadth magnified by reflected shadows.

'Is there some reason why I shouldn't take advantage of the pool?'

'None whatsoever,' Stefano declared mockingly. 'Shall I help you out?' At his drawled query she raised a hand, then when he grasped it she tugged *hard*, experiencing a thrill of exultation as he lost his balance and was unable to prevent a headlong fall into the water.

Fear of retaliation lent wings to her limbs as she levered herself up on to the pool's edge, then, scooping up her clothes, she sped quickly into the house.

A faint bubble of laughter emerged from her throat as she entered the bedroom. She'd have given almost anything to glimpse the expression on his face!

Moving straight through to the adjoining bathroom, she turned on the shower, discarded her briefs and bra, then stepped beneath the warm, pulsing water.

Selecting shampoo, she massaged it through the length of her hair, then rinsed it off before reaching for the soap—and encountered a strong male hand.

'Is this what you're looking for?'

She went still with shock as fear unfurled in the region of her stomach. Slowly she pushed back the wet length of her hair, and a silent gasp parted her lips at the sight of him standing within touching distance, every last vestige of clothing removed from his powerful frame.

'Ready to cry wolf, Carly?'

No sooner had the soft taunt left his lips than she felt the soap sweep in a tantalisingly slow arc from the tip of her shoulder to the curve at her waist. She had to get out *now*. She tried, except that one hand closed over her arm, holding her still, while the other curved round her shoulder, and she was powerless to resist as he turned her round to face him.

'I'm sorry.' It was a half-hearted apology, and his answering smile was wholly cynical as his fingers trailed an evocative path over the surface of her skin, tracing the delicate line of her collarbone, then brushing lower to the dark aureole surrounding the tight bud of her left breast.

'Don't.' The single plea went unheeded, and her stomach quivered as his hand slid to caress her hip, the narrow indented waist, before traversing to cup the soft roundness of her bottom.

Without her being aware of it, he'd managed to manoeuvre her so that the jet of water streamed against his back, and she stood still, her eyes wide and luminous beneath his hooded gaze.

'Stefano——' she protested as he pulled her close against him. His arousal was a potent virile force, and she arched back, straining against the circle of his arms in an effort to put some distance between them.

'You can't do this,' she whispered in a broken voice.

Yet he could, very easily. He knew it, just as she did. All it would take was one long drugging open-mouthed kiss to destroy any vestige of her self-restraint.

One strong hand slid up to cup her nape, his thumb tilting the uppermost edge of her jaw, holding it fast as she attempted to twist her head away from him. Then his lips brushed hers, lightly at first, teasing, nibbling, tasting in a manner that was deliberately erotic, and left her aching with a terrible hunger, that longing for the satisfaction only he could give.

She resisted for what seemed a lifetime, but playing cool to Stefano's undoubted expertise wreaked havoc with her nervous system, and she gave a hollow groan of despair as he lifted her high up against him, parting her thighs so that she straddled his waist, then she cried out as he lowered his head and took one tender peak into his mouth, suckling with such flagrant eroticism that she clutched hold of his hair in an effort to have him desist.

Just when she thought she could stand it no longer, he transferred his attention and rendered a similar attention to its twin until she begged him to stop.

Then he slowly raised his head, his eyes incredibly dark as they speared hers, and she felt her lips tremble uncontrollably at the sense of purpose evident. Time became a suspended entity, and she couldn't have torn her gaze away if her life depended on it.

With a sense of impending fascination she watched in mesmerised silence as his mouth lowered down over her own, and she gave a silent gasp as he plundered the moist cavern at will, punishing, tantalising, until she gave the response he sought.

When at last he lifted his head she wanted to weep, and she just looked at him, her soft mouth quivering and faintly bruised as she blinked rapidly against the rush of warm tears.

As soon as his hands curved beneath her bottom she knew what he meant to do, and she swallowed convulsively.

His entry was slow, stretching silken tissues to their furthest limit as they gradually accepted his swollen length, and his eyes trapped hers, witnessing her every expression as he carefully traversed the tight, satiny tunnel leading to the central core of her femininity.

Her beautiful eyes widened measurably as his muscular shaft attained its pinnacle. The feeling of total enclosure was intense, and a slow warmth gradually flooded her being, radiating in a tumultuous tide until her whole body was consumed with it. The blood vessels swelled and became engorged, activating muscle spasms over which she had no control, and she unconsciously clenched her thighs, instinctively arching away from him as a pulsating rhythm took her towards fulfilment.

At the zenith, she threw back her head, gasping as he drew her close and feasted shamelessly at her breast, tossing her so close to the edge between pain and pleasure that the two became intermingled, and she cried out, caught in the sweet torture of sexual ecstasy.

Then his hands shifted to her hips, lifting her slightly as he began a slow, tantalising circular movement that sent her to the brink and beyond before he took his pleasure with deep driving thrusts that drew soft guttural cries of encouragement which she refused to recognise as her own.

Afterwards he held her close for what seemed an age, then he gently withdrew and lowered her carefully to her feet.

She stumbled slightly, and clutched hold of him, then she stood transfixed as he caught up the soap and slowly cleansed every inch of her body.

When he'd finished he held out the bar of soap and when she shook her head he placed it in her palm before covering it with his own and transferring it to his chest. His eyes never left hers as he carefully traversed every ridge, every muscle, until his ablutions were complete.

She ached, everywhere. Inside and out. And she stood quiescent as he gently towelled her dry, then transferred his attention to removing the moisture from his own body.

Carly felt totally enervated, and she was powerless to resist as he placed a thumb and forefinger beneath her chin. She wanted to cry, and there were tears shimmering, welling from the depth of her eyes. There was a deep sense of emotional loss for the passion of mind and spirit they'd once shared. For then it had been a joy, a total merging of all the senses, transcending everything she'd ever dreamed . . . and more.

Her lashes fluttered down, veiling her expression, and concealing the haunting vulnerability she knew to be evident.

Without a word he slid an arm beneath her knees and carried her through to the bedroom, sweeping back the covers on the bed before slipping with her beneath the sheets.

Carly craved the sweet oblivion of sleep, but it had never seemed more distant, and she provided little resistance as Stefano curved her close in against him. She felt his lips brush the top of her head, and the gentle caress of his hand as it stroked the length of her body before coming to rest on the soft silken curls at the junction between her thighs. His fingers made a light probing foray, and she stiffened as they encountered the slight ridge caused by endless sutures.

'You had a difficult birth with Ann-Marie?'

Carly closed her eyes, then opened them again. 'Yes,' she acknowledged quietly, and felt silent anger emanate through his powerful body as he swore softly, viciously, in his own language. There was no point informing him that her meagre savings hadn't allowed for the luxury of private care.

Nor, in the long silent minutes that slowly ticked by, could she assure him that the wonder of holding Ann-Marie in her arms for the first time swept aside the trauma of a painful birth.

Even now it was a vivid memory, and she stared sightlessly into the darkness as she recalled the joy and the tears associated with those initial few years as she'd struggled to support them both.

Carly became aware of the soft brush of his fingers against her skin, and felt the faint stirring deep within her as her body responded to his touch. She wanted to move away, but she was caught in a mystical mesmeric spell, and she gave a faint despairing moan as his lips sought the soft hollows at the base of her throat in an erotic savouring that sent the blood coursing through her veins like quicksilver.

Not content, he trailed a path to her breasts to begin an evocative tasting that made her arch against him, and she barely registered the faint guttural sounds that whispered into the night air as his mouth travelled lower, teasing, tantalising, until she was driven almost mad with need.

When he reached the most intimate crevice of all she cried out at the degree of pleasure he was able to arouse, until ecstasy transcended mere pleasure, and she begged, pleading with him to ease the ache deep within her. Yet he stilled her limbs, soothing her gently as he brought her to a climax so tumultuous that it was beyond any mortal description, then he took her in his arms and rolled

on to his back, carrying her with him so that she
straddled his hips, his mouth warm as he pulled her
head down to hers in a kiss so sweetly passionate
that she almost cried.

His mouth left hers and trailed to nuzzle the sweet
hollows at the base of her throat, then he shifted
his hands to her ribcage as he gently positioned her,
his eyes dark and intently watchful of the play of
emotions chasing across her expressive features as
she accepted his full length.

Carly felt a heady sense of power, and her eyes
widened slightly as she glimpsed the slumberous
passion evident in his dark eyes, the gleam of immense satisfaction, and knew the measure of his
control. Unconsciously she arched her body,
stretching like a playful young kitten, and revelled
at his immediate response.

'Careful, *cara*,' he bade teasingly. 'Or you may
get more than you bargained for.'

She moved against him with slow deliberation,
undulating her hips in a gentle erotic movement that
drew a warning growl, then his hands closed over
her lower waist, and she lost control as he set the
pace, taking her higher and higher until she cried
out and clung on to his arms in a bid to gain some
balance in an erotic ride that had no equal. At least,
not in her experience.

Slowly, gradually, his movements began to ease,
and then his hands slid to her hips, holding her still
as he gently stroked his length, almost withdrawing
before plunging with infinite slowness until she felt
a wondrous suffusing of heat that swelled, trig-
gering a miasma of sensation spiralling through her

body until every nerve-end seemed to radiate with exquisite sweetness.

He shuddered, his large body racked with emotion, and she looked at him with an incredible sense of wonder as he became caught in the throes of passion: man at his most vulnerable, adrift in a swirling vortex of sexual experience.

Then his breathing began to slow, and the madly beating pulse at his throat settled into a steady beat. His features softened and his eyes became luminescent for a few heart-stopping minutes, and just for a milli-second she glimpsed the heart of his soul.

Then his hands slid up to cup her breasts, caressing with such acute sensitivity that she caught her breath, and she made no demur as he gently drew her down to him, cradling her head against a muscled shoulder. His fingers trailed over her hair, while a hand slid with tactile softness down the length of her spine. She felt his lips brush across her forehead, then settle at her temple, soothing, until the shivery warm sensation gradually diminished and she was filled with a dull, pleasurable ache.

'I hurt you.' The words held a degree of regretful remorse, and she stirred faintly against him.

Tomorrow there would be an unaccustomed tenderness evident, but she didn't care, for it had nothing to do with physical pain, merely satiated pleasure in its most exhilarating extreme. She sought to reassure him, and moved her lips against his throat, then gently nipped a vulnerable hollow.

'You still want to play?' His voice reverberated against her mouth, and she felt rather than heard his soft husky laughter when she shook her head in silent negation.

'Then go to sleep, *cara bella*,' Stefano bade her gently.

And she did, drifting easily into dreamless oblivion, unaware that he carefully disengaged her and curled her into the curve of his body before reaching for the sheet to cover their nakedness.

CHAPTER EIGHT

CARLY put the final touches to her hair, then stood back and surveyed her reflection. The deep jacaranda-blue gown was classically styled, comprising a figure-hugging skirt and a camisole top with twin shoestring straps that emphasised her slim curves and pale honey-gold skin. Make-up was understated, with emphasis on her eyes, and a clear peach lipstick coloured her generous mouth. Her only jewellery was a slim gold chain at her neck and small gold hoops at her ears. With the length of her hair confined in an elaborate knot atop her head, she looked ... passable, she decided. Or at least able to feel sufficiently confident among guests at a dinner to be held in one of Stefano's business associate's home in nearby Seaforth.

'Stunning,' a deep voice drawled, and she turned slowly to see Stefano standing a few feet distant, looking the epitome of sophistication in an impeccably tailored dark suit, white silk shirt and dark silk tie.

Carly proffered a slight smile and let her eyes slide to a point just beyond his left shoulder. 'Thank you.' Turning, she collected a black beaded evening bag, slipped in a lipstick and compact, then drew in a deep breath as she preceded him from the room to the head of the staircase.

Several minutes later she was seated in the Mercedes as it purred down the driveway towards the street.

When they reached the hospital Ann-Marie was sitting up in bed, together with the doll Stefano had given her, a favoured book, and a teddy bear slightly the worse for wear from which she refused to be parted because, she assured her mother, he was as old as she was, and watched over her as she slept.

She looked, Carly decided with maternal love, as bright as a proverbial button, although there were still slight smudges beneath the beautiful dark eyes, and her skin was transparently pale—visible effects of the aftermath of extensive surgery, the specialist had assured.

Soon she would be able to come home. By the start of the new school year in February, she would be able to resume her classes. Except for the short curly hair, no one would ever know she'd undergone extensive neuro-surgery.

Stefano was wonderful with her, gently teasing, warm, ensuring that Ann-Marie's initial wariness was a thing of the past.

'You look tired, Mummy. Didn't you sleep well last night?'

The words brought a faint smile to Carly's lips. Out of the mouths of babes! 'I stayed up too late,' she relayed gently. 'And woke early.' Was woken up, she amended silently, and persuaded to share a spa-bath, then put back into bed and brought fresh orange juice, toast and coffee on a tray.

'You should rest, like me,' Ann-Marie advised with the ingenuousness of the very young, and Stefano lifted a hand to ruffle her curls.

'I shall ensure she does.'

It was eight when they left, and Carly turned slightly towards him as he eased the car on to the main road.

'How many people will be there tonight?' Her features assumed a faint pensive expression. 'Perhaps you should fill me in with a few background details of key associates.'

'Relax, Carly. This is mainly a social occasion.'

'Yet the men will inevitably gravitate together and discuss business,' she said a trifle drily, and incurred a long probing look as he paused through an intersection.

'Nervous?'

'Should I be?' she countered with remarkable steadiness, considering the faint fluttering of butterfly wings already apparent in her stomach.

'I have no doubt you'll cope admirably.'

She sat in silence during the drive, and glanced out of the window with interest as he turned the Mercedes into a suburban street bordered on each side by tall, wide-branched trees. Seconds later the car turned into a curved driveway lined with late-model cars.

The butterflies in her stomach set up an increasing beat as she slid out from the passenger seat and moved to his side, unprepared within seconds to have him thread his fingers through hers as they walked towards the main entrance. The pressure of his clasp was light, yet she had the distinct feeling he wouldn't allow her to pull free from him.

They were almost the last to arrive, and after a series of introductions Carly accepted a glass of mineral water and attempted to relax.

It wasn't a large group, sixteen at most, she decided as she cast a circumspect glance around the elegantly furnished lounge.

Stefano possessed a magnetic attraction that wasn't contrived, and Carly couldn't help but be aware of the attention he drew from most of the women present.

Seven years ago she'd lacked essential *savoir-faire* to cope with the socially élite among Stefano's fellow associates. Nervous and unsure of herself, she'd chosen to cling to his side and smile, whereas now she was well able to stand on her own feet. It had to make a difference in her ability to cope with his lifestyle.

Canapés and hors-d'oeuvres were proffered at intervals over the next half-hour, and it was almost nine when Charles and Kathy-Lee Winslow arrived with Georgeanne.

'We were held up,' Charles declared with droll humour as he steered his wife to where Carly stood at Stefano's side.

'By a taxi driver who decided to take advantage of the obvious fact we weren't residents, and drove us via a few scenic routes that lost us twenty minutes and gained him twenty extra dollars,' Georgeanne declared in explanation.

'Stop complaining,' Charles chastised with a broad smile. 'We enjoyed a pleasant ride, we're here, and I doubt anyone has missed us.'

'I need a drink,' his daughter vowed, her eyes settling deliberately on Stefano. 'Would you mind?'

The smile she bestowed was nothing short of total bewitchment. 'I'm thirsty.'

Not just for a drink, Carly surmised wryly, for Georgeanne's behaviour fell just short of being blatant, and she watched with faint bemusement as Stefano elicited Georgeanne's preference.

'Why, there's Angelica,' Charles's daughter announced, and her eyes flew towards Carly with a very good imitation of expressed concern. 'Oh, dear, how—awkward.'

This could, Carly decided, become one of those evenings where Murphy's Law prevailed, and she wondered what on earth she could have done to upset some mythical evil spirit who clearly felt impelled to provide her with such an emotional minefield.

With detached fascination she watched Angelica locate Stefano's tall frame at the bar, then cross leisurely to join him. She saw the beautiful brunette lift a manicured hand and touch his arm, saw him turn, and caught his smile in greeting. Angelica's expression was revealingly warm. *Loving*, Carly added, feeling as if she'd just been kicked in the stomach.

A confrontation was inevitable, and when they were seated for dinner Carly cursed the unkind hand of fate as she saw Georgeanne opposite at the large dining-table, with Angelica slightly to Georgeanne's right.

Wonderful, she groaned silently as she sipped a small quantity of white wine in the hope that it would provide a measure of necessary courage with which to get through the evening.

Their hosts provided a sumptuous meal comprising no fewer than five courses if one counted the fresh fruit and cheeseboard that followed dessert. The presentation of the food was impressive, and Carly dutifully forked morsels into her mouth without tasting a thing.

Conversation flowed, and she was aware of an increasing tension as she waited for the moment Angelica would unsheathe her claws.

'How is *your* daughter?'

Again, the faint emphasis didn't go unnoticed, and Carly turned slightly to meet the brunette's seemingly innocent gaze as she summoned a polite smile. 'Ann-Marie is improving steadily.' She aimed for a subtle emphasis of her own. '*We're* hopeful it won't be long before she's released from hospital.'

Angelica picked up her wine glass and fingered the long crystal stem with studied deliberation. 'Stefano appears to delight in playing the role of devoted *Papà*.'

Carly effected a negligible shrug. 'You, more than anyone, should appreciate that Italian men are renowned for their love of family.'

Carefully shaped eyebrows rose a fraction in unison with the faint moue of evinced surprise that was quickly camouflaged with a smile. 'Proud of their sons, protective of their daughters.'

Carly couldn't resist the dig. 'And their wives.'

'Well, of course.' The voice resembled a husky purr, infinitely feline. 'And their mistresses.' Her eyes assumed a warm intimacy that was deliberate. 'What female of any age could resist Stefano?'

Carly felt like screaming, but she forced her mouth to curve into a soft smile, and her beautiful

eyes assumed a misty expression that was deliberately contrived as she lifted her shoulders in a
helpless shrugging gesture that she tempered with
a light musing laugh. 'None, I imagine.'

Stefano, damn him, was seemingly engrossed in
conversation with Charles, and appeared oblivious
to the content of her conversation with Angelica.

What on earth did he imagine they had to discuss,
for heaven's sake? The weather? The state of the
nation?

It seemed forever before their host suggested adjourning to the lounge for coffee, and she felt
strangely vulnerable as the men gravitated together
on the pretext of sharing an after-dinner port while
the women sought comfortable chairs at the opposite end of the large room—with the exception
of Angelica, who stood at Stefano's side, a blatant
disparity among men, yet totally at ease with their
conversation. It was carrying feminism and equality
among the sexes a little too far, surely? Carly
couldn't help wondering if the men felt entirely
comfortable. Yet she knew Angelica didn't give a
fig what her male colleagues thought. Her main
motivation in joining the men was to clarify the
contrast between two women—herself and
Stefano's wife.

The difference was quite marked in every way,
from physical appearance to business qualifications. Seven years ago it had seemed important,
the chasm too wide for Carly to imagine she would
ever bridge. Except that in her own way she had,
for there was now a diploma, experience and added
qualifications in her field, as well as respect from
her peers. There wasn't a thing she needed to prove,

and if she so chose she could join Stefano's associates and discuss any topic relating to corporate accounting and tax legislation.

The coffee was liquid ambrosia, and Carly sipped it appreciatively, wondering just how long it would be before they left.

'You must visit when Stefano brings you to the states.'

Carly smiled, then thanked Charles's wife for the invitation. 'It's quite a few years since I was last there.'

'The house is large,' Kathy-Lee pursued. 'We'd be delighted if you'd stay. We love having guests.'

Carly could only admire Kathy-Lee for keeping pace with Charles's high-flying existence, *and* playing stepmother—a masterly feat in keeping the peace, for Charles adored his precocious daughter.

'I'll leave the decision to Stefano,' she said gently, indulging in inconsequential conversation for almost thirty minutes before Kathy-Lee had her cup refilled and was drawn by their hostess to join another guest who had professed an interest in Kathy-Lee's preoccupation with interior design.

Carly let her gaze wander round the room, settling on the broad frame of her husband as he stood idolently at ease and deep in conversation with two of his associates—one of whom was Angelica.

Carly forced herself to study them with impartial eyes—difficult when she wanted physically to tear Stefano and Angelica apart.

Angelica was a seductive temptress beneath the designer gown, leaning imperceptibly towards Stefano, her eyes, hands, *body* receptive to the man at her side, whereas Stefano stood totally at ease, his stance relaying relaxed confidence, an assurance that wasn't contrived. And, try as she might, Carly could find no visible sign of any implied intimacy—on his part.

Almost as if he was aware of her scrutiny, he turned slightly and met her gaze. For a moment everything else faded into obscurity, and she watched in bemused fascination as he excused himself and crossed the room to settle his length comfortably on the padded arm of her chair.

His proximity put her at an immediate disadvantage, for she was extremely aware of the clean smell of his clothes, the faint aroma of soap intermingling with his chosen aftershave, an exclusive mixture of spices combined with muted musk that seemed to heighten the essence of the man himself.

Within minutes his associates followed his actions in joining their wives, and Carly wasn't sure which she preferred . . . being alone with a clutch of curious women, or having to contend with Stefano's calculated attention.

'Almost ready to leave, *cara*?'

His voice was a soft caress, and if anyone was in any doubt as to his affection for his wife he lifted a hand and swept back a swath of curls that had fallen forward, letting his fingers rest far too long at the edge of her throat.

There was a degree of deliberation in his movement, almost as if he was attempting to set a precedent, and it made her unaccountably angry.

She wanted to move away, yet such an action was impossible, and it took all her acting ability to sit still as he brushed gentle fingers across her collarbone then slid them down her arm to thread through her own. The look in his eyes was explicitly seducing, and to any interested observer it was only too apparent that he couldn't wait to get her home and into bed.

Well, two could play at that game, and she gently dug the tips of her nails into the tendons of his hand, then pressed *hard*. 'Whenever you are,' she acquiesced lightly, casting him a soft winsome smile that was deceptively false. She would have liked to *kill* him, or at least render some measure of physical harm, yet in a room full of people she could only smile. As soon as they were alone, she'd verbally *slay* him.

He knew, for his eyes assumed a mocking gleam that hid latent amusement, almost in silent acceptance of an imminent battle.

With an indolent movement he rose to his feet, and Carly followed his actions, adding her appreciation with genuine politeness as they thanked their hosts and bade Charles and Kathy-Lee goodbye.

'So early, Stefano?' Angelica queried, effectively masking her displeasure.

'My wife is tired.'

It was nothing less than the truth, but she resented the implication.

Angelica's eyes narrowed, then assumed speculative amusement as she proffered Carly a commiserating smile. 'Can't stand the pace?'

'Quite the contrary,' Carly demurred sweetly. 'Stefano is merely providing a clichéd excuse.'

The resentment was simmering just beneath the surface of her control, and she contained it until the Mercedes had swept from the driveway.

'You enjoyed setting me among the pigeons, didn't you?' she demanded in a low, furious tone.

'Was it so bad?'

To be honest, it hadn't been. Yet she was loath to agree with him—on anything. 'On a scale of one to ten in the curiosity stakes, our reconciliation has to rate at least a nine,' she declared drily as he sent the opulent vehicle speeding smoothly through the darkened streets.

'You more than held your own, *cara*,' he said with drawled humour.

Inside she felt like screaming, aware that it would take several weeks before the speculative looks, the gossip abated and eventually died. In the meantime she had to run the gauntlet, and she felt uncommonly resentful.

'Nothing has changed,' Carly voiced with a trace of bitterness, and incurred his swift scrutiny.

'In what respect?'

'You have to be *kidding*,' she declared vengefully. 'Angelica would have liked to eat you alive.' She was so incensed that she wasn't aware of the passion evident in her voice, or the pain.

Turning her attention to the darkened city streets, she watched the numerous vehicles traversing the well-defined lanes with a detached fascination. The bright neon signs provided a brilliant splash of colour that vied with the red amber and green of traffic-lights controlling each intersection.

Transferring her attention beyond the windscreen, she looked sightlessly into the night, aware that Stefano handled the car with the skilled ease of long practice.

The same ease with which he handled a woman: knowledgeable, experienced, and always one step ahead. Just once she'd like to be able to best him, catch him off guard.

Yet even as the resentment festered she knew instinctively that he'd never allow her to win. A solitary battle, possibly, in their ongoing private war, as a musing concession to her feminine beliefs. But never the war itself.

It was twenty minutes before the Mercedes drew to a halt inside the garage, and Carly made her way upstairs to the main suite.

She was in the process of removing her make-up when Stefano entered the room, and her eyes assumed a faint wariness as she completed the task.

It required only a few steps to move into the bedroom, a few more to reach the bed. Yet she was loath to take them, knowing what awaited her once she slipped between the cool percale sheets.

Fool she derided silently. It's not as if you lack enjoyment in the marital bed.

The knowledge of her exultant abandon in Stefano's arms merely strengthened her resolve to provide delaying tactics, and she plucked the pins from the elaborate knot restraining her hair, only to catch hold of her brush and stroke it vigorously through the length of tumbled auburn-streaked curls.

It was mad to want more, insane to build an emotional wall between them. A tiny logical voice rationalised that she should be content. She had a beautiful home, and a husband whose business interests ensured they were among the denizens of the upper social echelon.

Many women were confined in marriages of mutual convenience, happy to bury themselves in active social existences as their husbands' hostesses, in return for the trappings of success: the jewellery, exotic luxury cars, trips abroad.

Carly knew she'd trade it all willingly to erase the past seven years, to go back magically in time to the days when *love* was an irrepressible joy.

Now it was an empty shell, their sexual coupling merely an expression of physical lust untouched by any emotion from the heart.

Perhaps she was too honest, with too much personal integrity to survive within the constraints of such a marriage. Yet she was trapped, impossibly bound to Stefano by Ann-Marie. To remove her daughter from her father and return to their former existence would cause emotional scarring of such magnitude that the end result would be worthless.

'If you continue much longer, you'll end up with a headache.'

Carly's hand stilled at the sound of that deep drawling voice, and she stood motionless as Stefano moved to stand behind her.

'I have nothing to say to you,' she managed in stilted tones, watching him warily.

He was close, much too close for her peace of mind, and all her fine body hairs quivered in anticipation of his touch.

'We seem to manage very well without words,' he said with a degree of irony, and she lashed out verbally at his implication.

'Sex isn't the answer to everything, damn you!'

Her eyes unconsciously met his in the mirror, large and impossibly dark as she took in the image her body projected against the backdrop of his own.

Without the benefit of shoes, the tip of her head was level with his throat, and his breadth of shoulder had a dwarfing effect, making her appear small and incredibly vulnerable.

'No?' he queried softly, and she was damningly aware of the subtle pull of her senses as she fought his irresistible magnetism.

Her gaze remained locked with his, their darkness magnifying as he slowly lifted a hand and swept a heavy swath of her hair aside, baring the edge of her neck. His head slowly lowered as his mouth sought the pulsing cord in that sensitive curve, and she was powerless to prevent the sweet spiralling sensation that coursed through her body at his touch.

Carly was conscious of his hands as they shifted to her shoulders, then slid slowly down her arms to rest at her waist, before slipping up to cup the swollen fullness of her breasts.

She wanted to close her eyes and pretend the seduction was real, and for a few minutes she succumbed to temptation.

His fingers created a tactile magic, sensitising the engorged peaks until she moved restlessly against him, craving more than this subtle pleasuring. A hollow groan whispered from her throat as his hands slid to her shoulders, slipping the thin straps of her nightgown down over her arms, so that the thin silk slithered in a heap at her feet.

He didn't move, and she slowly opened her eyes to focus reluctantly on their mirrored image, watching in mesmerised fascination as his hands slid round her waist and pressed her back against him.

Her eyes widened as she watched the effect he had on the texture of her skin, the tightening of her breasts, each tumescent peak aroused in anticipation of his possession.

It was almost as if he was forcing her to recognise something her conscious mind refused to acknowledge, and she gazed in mesmeric wonder as her body reacted to the light brush of his fingers as he trailed them across the curve of her waist, then slid to trace the soft mound of her stomach before allowing his fingers to splay into the soft curls protecting the central core of her femininity.

Of their own volition, her lower limbs swayed into the curve of his hand as they sought closer contact, and she was totally unprepared for the soft dreaminess evident in her eyes, the faint sheen on her parted lips.

She looked . . . incandescently bewitched, held in thrall by passionate desire, and in that moment she felt she hated him for making her see a side of herself she preferred to keep well-hidden. Especially from him.

Yet it was too late, and even as she arched away he turned her fully into his arms, his mouth successfully covering hers in a manner that left her no hope of uttering so much as a word.

Her initial struggle was merely a token gesture, as was her determination to prevent his open-mouthed kiss. Seconds later she cried out as one long arm curved down the length of her back in a seeking quest for the tell-tale dewing at the aroused nub of her femininity.

Every nerve in her body seemed acutely sensitised, the internal tissues still faintly bruised from the previous night's loving, so much so that she tensed involuntarily against his touch.

Without a word he placed an arm beneath her knees and lifted her high against his chest to carry her to his bed, sinking down on to the mattress in one fluid movement as he cradled her gently into the curve of his body.

His lips trailed a path to her mouth, soothing her slight protest, before tracing a path down her neck. Slowly, with infinite care, he traversed each pleasure pulse, anointing the tender peak of each breast with delicate eroticism.

Her stomach quivered in betrayal beneath the seductive passage of his mouth, and when he reached the junction between her thighs she gave a beseeching moan, an entreaty to end the consuming madness that flared through her body, igniting it with flame.

Carly consoled herself that nothing mattered except this wonderful slaking of sensual pleasure in a slow, gentle loving that touched her soul. But in her subconscious mind she knew she lied, and she drifted into sleep wondering if there could ever be a resolution between the dictates of her brain and the wayward path of her emotions.

CHAPTER NINE

'I HAVE to attend a meeting on the Central Coast,' Stefano declared as he rose from the breakfast table. 'I doubt I'll be home before seven.'

'Angelica is naturally one of the associates accompanying you.' It wasn't a question, and he shot her a dark encompassing glance.

'She is on the board of a number of family companies,' he informed coolly. 'And a dedicated businesswoman.'

'Very dedicated,' Carly mocked, and was unable to resist adding, 'Have fun.'

After he left she finished her coffee, then moved quickly upstairs to change into a white cotton button-through dress, slipped her feet into flat sandals, then collected the keys to the BMW, informed Sylvana she'd be home in the late afternoon, and drove into the city.

There were a few things she wanted to pick up for Ann-Marie, and she'd fill in time between hospital visits by browsing the shops in the hope of gaining some inspiration for Christmas gifts.

Carly returned home at five, and after a leisurely shower she changed into a cool sage-green silk shift, wound her hair up into a casually contrived knot, then went downstairs to check on dinner with Sylvana.

The portable television was on in the kitchen, and highlighted on the screen was an area of dense bush-covered gorge and a hovering rescue helicopter. The presenter's modulated voice was relaying information regarding a light plane crash just south of the Central Coast. There were no survivors, and names had not yet been released of the pilot and two passengers.

Carly went cold. It was as if her limbs were frozen, for she couldn't move, and she gazed sightlessly at the flashing screen without comprehending a single thing.

Then she began to shake, and she clutched her arms together in an effort to contain her trembling limbs.

It couldn't be the plane carrying Stefano and Angelica—*could it*? A silent agonised scream rose in her throat. Dear God—*no*.

The thought of his strong body lying broken and burned in dense undergrowth almost destroyed her. His image was a vivid entity, and she saw his strongly etched features, the dark gleaming eyes, almost as if he were in the same room.

The phone rang, but the sound barely registered, nor did Sylvana's voice as she answered the call, until it seemed to change in tone and Carly realised that Sylvana was attempting to gain her attention. 'Stefano rang to say he'll be home in twenty minutes.'

The words penetrated her brain, barely registering in those initial few seconds, then she turned slowly, her eyes impossibly large. 'What did you say?'

Sylvana repeated the message, then added in puzzlement, 'Are you all right?'

Carly inclined her head, then murmured something indistinguishable as her stomach began to churn, and she only just made it upstairs to the main suite before she was violently ill.

Afterwards she clenched her teeth, then she sluiced warm water over her face in an effort to dispel the chilled feeling that seemed to invade her bones.

Attempting to repair the ravages with make-up moved her to despair, for she looked incredibly vulnerable—*haunted*, she amended silently as she examined her mirrored image with critical deliberation.

How could you *love* someone you professed to hate? Yet an inner voice taunted that love and hate were intense emotions and closely entwined. Legend had it that they were inseparable.

Stefano's arrival home was afforded a restrained greeting. If she'd listened to her heart she would have flown into his arms and expressed a profound relief that he was alive. Yet then he couldn't fail to be aware of her true feelings, and that would never do.

Consequently dinner was strained, and Carly failed to do any justice to Sylvana's beautifully prepared food, and throughout the meal she was conscious of his veiled scrutiny, so much so that she felt close to screaming with angry vexation.

'Did it bother you that it might have been my body lying lifeless in some rocky gorge?'

The blood drained from her face at his drawled query, and she got to her feet, wanting only to get away from his ill-disguised mockery.

She hadn't moved more than two paces when hard hands closed over her shoulders, and she struggled in vain, hot, angry tears clouding her eyes as she fought to be free of him.

One hand slid to hold her nape fast, tilting her head, and her lashes swept down to form a protective veil, only to fly open as his mouth closed over hers in a hard open-mouthed kiss that was impossibly, erotically demanding.

It seemed to go on forever, and when it was over she lifted shaking fingers to her lips.

His eyes were dark with brooding savagery, their depths filled with latent passion and an emotion she didn't even attempt to define. Carly glanced past him and fixed her eyes on a distant wall in an attempt to regain her composure. If she looked at him she knew she'd disgrace herself with stupid ignominious tears.

'I rang through the instant we touched base,' he enlightened quietly. 'Our helicopter pilot sighted the crash, radioed for help, then circled the area until a rescue unit arrived.' He raised a hand and trailed gentle fingers along the edge of her cheek.

She lifted her shoulders in a faint shrugging gesture. Somehow she had to inject an element of normality, otherwise she was doomed. 'Would you like some coffee?'

A forefinger probed the softness of her swollen lower lip, then conducted a leisurely tracery of its outline. 'I'd like *you*,' Stefano drawled in mocking tones, and watched the expressive play of emotions chase each other across her mobile features.

'It's early,' she stalled, hating the way her body was reacting to the proximity of his.

'Since when did time have anything to do with making love?' His head lowered and he touched his mouth to the thudding pulse at the edge of her neck, then traced a path to her temple. His lips pressed closed one eyelid, then the other, and his hands shifted as he caught her up in his arms.

'What are you doing?' The cry was torn from her lips as he calmly strode from the room, and headed for the stairs.

'Taking you to bed,' Stefano declared in a husky undertone, 'in an attempt to remove the look of shadowed anguish lurking in your beautiful eyes.'

She struggled in helplessness against him, aware of an elemental quality that was infinitely awesome. No one man deserved so much power, or quite such a degree of latent sensuality.

'Must you be so—physical?' she protested as he entered their suite and closed the door.

He lowered her down to stand within the circle of his arms, and her limbs seemed weightless as he caught her close. Then he kissed her, slowly and with such evocative mastery that she didn't have the energy to voice any further protest as he carefully removed her clothes, then released the pins holding her hair before beginning on his own.

'Tell me to stop,' he murmured seconds before his mouth closed over hers, and the flame that burned deep within them flared into vibrant life, consuming them both in a passionate storm that lasted far into the night.

The following days settled into a relatively normal routine. The nights were something else as Carly fought a silent battle with herself and invariably lost.

Their lovemaking scaled hitherto unreached heights, transcending mere pleasure, and it was almost as if some inner song were demanding to be heard, yet the music was indistinct, the words just beyond her reach.

Introspection became an increasing trap in which she found herself caught, in the insidious recognition that *love* was inextricably interwoven with physical desire—which inevitably led to the agonising question of Angelica, and the degree of Stefano's personal involvement. Were they still on intimate terms? *Had they ever been*? Dear God, could she have been wrong all these years?

One day in particular she couldn't bear the tension any more, and she moved restlessly through the house, unsure how to fill the few hours until it was time to visit Ann-Marie.

Making a split-second decision, she changed clothes, stroked a clear gloss over her lips, then caught up her sunglasses and bag, and made her way down to the car, intent on spending a few more hours in the city looking for suitable Christmas gifts. She might even do lunch.

Two hours later Carly wasn't sure shopping was such a good idea. It was hot, there were crowds of people all intent on doing the same thing, and it took ages to be served. All she'd achieved was a bottle of Sarah's favourite French perfume, a book and an educational game for Ann-Marie, and nothing for Stefano. What did you buy a man who had everything? she queried with scepticism. Another silk tie? A silk shirt? Something as

mundane as *aftershave*, when she didn't even recognise what brand he preferred?

A glance at her watch revealed that it was after
one. Something to eat and a cool drink would
provide a welcome break, and ten minutes later she
was seated in a pleasant air-conditioned restaurant
eating a succulent chicken salad.

'Mind if I join you?'

Carly glanced up and endeavoured to contain her
surprise. Coincidence was a fine thing, and the
chance of choosing the same restaurant as Angelica
Agnelli had to run at a thousand to one. 'If you
must,' she responded with bare civility. The restaurant *was* crowded, after all, and short of being
rude there wasn't much she could do except accept
the situation with as much grace as possible.

'Shopping?' Angelica queried, arching an elegantly shaped eyebrow as she caught sight of the
brightly designed bags.

'Yes.' As if an explanation was needed, she
added, 'Christmas.'

'Stefano is caught up in a conference, so I came
on ahead.' She allowed the information to sink in,
then added with deadly timing, 'This is a charmingly secluded place, don't you agree?' For furtive
assignations. The implication was there for anyone
but the most obtuse, but just in case there was any
doubt she added smoothly, 'You don't normally
lunch here, do you?'

'No. I preferred to eat a packed lunch at my
desk,' Carly explained with considerable calm, and
tempered the words with a seemingly sweet smile.

Angelica deliberately allowed her eyes to widen.
'Rather clever of you to present Stefano with a child

conveniently the right age to be his own.' Her mouth curled fractionally. 'I almost advised him to insist on a DNA test.' She lifted a hand and appeared to study her immaculately manicured nails. 'But of course, I wouldn't presume to interfere in his...' She trailed off deliberately, then added with barbed innuendo, 'Private affairs.'

'You've obviously changed your strategy,' Carly returned with considerable fortitude, when inside she felt like screaming.

'Whatever do you mean?'

Carly had quite suddenly had enough. 'You had no such compunction about interfering in his private life seven years ago. You deliberately set out to destroy me. Like a fool, I ran.' Her eyes sparked gold-flecked fire that caused the other woman's expression to narrow. 'I realise your association with Stefano goes back a long time, but perhaps you should understand it was *he* who did the chasing in our relationship, and he who insisted on a reconciliation.' She drew in a deep breath, then released it slowly. 'Stefano has had seven years to instigate divorce proceedings.' Her voice assumed a quietly fierce intensity. 'I would suggest you ask yourself why he never did.'

'*Brava*,' a deep voice drawled quietly from behind, and Carly closed her eyes in vexation, only to open them again.

Stefano stood indolently at ease, his expression strangely watchful as he took in Carly's pale features. All of her pent-up emotion was visible in the expressive brilliance of her eyes, their gold-flecked depths ringed in black.

'Stefano.' Angelica's tone held a conciliatory purr, yet his eyes never moved from Carly's features.

'If you'll excuse me?' She had to get out of here before she erupted with volatile rage—with Angelica for being a bitch, and Stefano simply because he was *here*.

Rising to her feet, she collected her bag and assorted carriers. 'Enjoy your lunch.'

His hand closed on her arm, bringing her to a halt, and she just looked at him, then her lashes swept down in a bid to hide the pain that gnawed deep inside.

'Please. Let me go.' Her voice was softly pitched, yet filled with aching intensity, and there was nothing she could do to prevent the descent of his mouth or the brief, hard open-mouthed kiss he bestowed.

Then he released her, and it took all her reserve of strength to walk calmly from the restaurant.

By the time she reached the street her lips were quivering with pent-up emotion, and she fumbled for her sunglasses, glad of their protective lenses as they hid the well of tears that blurred her vision.

Tonight there would be no respite, for Sarah and James were coming to dinner. To present anything approaching a normal façade would take every ounce of acting ability, and Carly wished fervently for the day to be done, and the night.

Only a matter of weeks ago everything had seemed so uncomplicated. Ann-Marie and work had been the total focus of her life. Now she was in turmoil, her emotions as wild and uncontrollable as a storm-tossed sea.

At the hospital, Ann-Marie's exuberant greeting, the loving hug and beautiful smile acted to diffuse Carly's inner tension, and she listened to her daughter's excited chatter about a new patient who had been admitted that morning.

As Carly left the hospital and drove home she couldn't help wishing her life were clear-cut, and there were no tensions, no subtle game-playing that ate at the heartstrings and destroyed one's self-esteem.

Perhaps she should stop fighting this conflict within herself and just accept the status quo, be content with her existence as Stefano's wife, and condone the pleasure they shared each night. To hunger for anything more was madness.

After garaging the car, Carly consulted with Sylvana, made suitably appreciative comments, then opted to cool off with a leisurely swim in the pool.

Stefano arrived home as Carly was putting the finishing touches to her make-up, and she turned as he entered their suite, her expression deliberately bland as she registered his tall, dark-suited frame before lifting her head to meet his gaze.

His eyes were dark, probing hers, and after a fleeting glance her own skittered towards the vicinity of his left shoulder. The last thing she needed was a confrontation. Not with Sarah and James due within minutes.

'I'll go down and check with Sylvana,' Carly said evenly. 'I'll wait for you in the lounge.'

It was a relief to escape his presence, and she was grateful for Sarah's punctuality, immensely glad of her friend's warm personality.

The meal was a gourmet's delight, and although conversation flowed with ease Carly merely operated on automatic pilot as she forked food intermittently into her mouth, then toyed with the remainder on her plate.

She laughed, genuinely enjoying Sarah's anecdotes intermingled with those of James, but all the while she felt like a disembodied spectator.

It was almost ten when they rose from the table.

'I'll make the coffee,' Carly declared, and smiled when Sarah rose to her feet.

'I'll help you.'

Sylvana had set everything ready in the kitchen, so that all Carly had to do was percolate the coffee.

'How are things going——?' Carly broke off with a laugh in the realisation that Sarah was asking the same question simultaneously with her own. 'You go first,' she bade her, shooting her friend a smiling glance.

'Where shall I start?' Sarah returned with a grin as she crossed to the servery, and cast the stylish kitchen an appreciative glance. 'Lucky you,' she smiled without a trace of envy. 'All this, and Stefano, too.'

'Sarah...' Carly warned with a low growl, and Sarah grinned unrepentantly.

'James and Stefano seem to have a lot in common,' Sarah offered innocuously, her eyes sparkling as Carly shot her a speaking glance. 'James is nice,' she admitted quietly. 'I like him.'

'*And*?' Carly prompted.

'Sometimes I think I could get used to the idea of a relationship with him, then I'm not sure I want to make that sort of change to my life.' Her eyes sought Carly's, and her voice softened. 'How about you?'

'Ann-Marie is improving daily.'

'That wasn't what I asked,' Sarah admonished teasingly, and Carly's expression became faintly pensive.

'I seem to swing like a pendulum between resentment and acceptance.'

'You look . . .' Sarah paused, her eyes narrowing with thoughtful speculation. 'Pregnant. Are you?'

Carly opened her mouth to deny it, then closed it again as her mind rapidly calculated dates. Her eyes became an expressive host to a number of varying fleeting emotions.

'You have that certain look a woman possesses in the initial few weeks,' Sarah observed gently. 'A subtle tiredness as the body refocuses its energy. You had the same look the day we met moving into neighbouring apartments,' she added softly.

'It could be stress from juggling twice-daily hospital visits, marriage,' Carly offered in strangled tones as the implications of a possible pregnancy began to sink in. She *couldn't* be, surely? Yet the symptoms were all there, added to facts she'd been too busy to notice.

She lifted a shaking hand, then let it fall again, and for one heartfelt second her eyes filled with naked pain before she successfully masked their expression.

'The coffee is perking,' Sarah reminded gently, and Carly crossed to turn down the heat, then when it was ready she placed it on the tray.

The men were deep in conversation when Carly and Sarah re-entered the lounge, and if either detected that the girls' smiles were a little too bright they gave no sign.

It was almost eleven when Sarah indicated the need to leave, explaining, 'I'm due to go on duty tomorrow morning at seven.' She rose to her feet, thanked both Stefano and Carly for a delightful evening, and at the door she gave Carly a quick hug in farewell. 'Ring me when you can.'

Carly turned back towards the lobby the instant the car headlights disappeared down the drive, moving into the lounge to collect coffee-cups together prior to carrying them through to the kitchen.

'Leave them,' Stefano instructed as he saw what she was doing. 'Sylvana can take care of it in the morning.'

'It will only take a minute.' In the kitchen, she rinsed and stacked them in the dishwasher, then turned to find him leaning against the edge of the table, watching her with narrowed scrutiny.

She stood perfectly still, despite every nerve-end screaming at fever pitch, and her chin lifted fractionally as he took the necessary steps towards her.

'What now, Stefano?' Carly queried with a touch of defiance. 'A post-mortem on lunch?'

One eyebrow slanted in mocking query. 'What part of lunch would you particularly like to refer to?'

'I disliked being publicly labelled as your possession,' she insisted, stung by his cynicism.

'Yet you are,' he declared silkily. 'My feelings where you're concerned verge on the primitive.'

A tiny pulse quickened at the base of her throat, then began to hammer in palpable confusion as she absorbed the essence of his words. 'Is that meant to frighten me?'

Tension filled the air, lending a highly volatile quality that was impossible to ignore. 'Only if you choose to allow it,' he mocked, and she stood perfectly still as he conducted a slow, all-encompassing appraisal, lingering on the deepness of her eyes, and her soft, trembling mouth.

He lifted a hand to brush gentle fingers across her cheek, and she reared back as if from a lick of flame.

'Don't touch me.'

'Whyever not, *cara*?'

'Because that's where it starts and ends,' she asserted with a mixture of despair and wretchedness.

'You find my lovemaking so distasteful?'

His musing indulgence was the living end, and she lashed out at him with expressive anger. '*Lust*, damn you!' she corrected heatedly, so incensed that she balled both hands into fists and punched him, uncaring that she connected with the hard, muscular wall of his chest.

'Lust is a bartered commodity. What would you like me to give you?' His voice was a low-pitched drawl that cut right through to the heart. 'An item of jewellery, perhaps?'

For several long seconds she just looked at him, filled with an aching pain so acute that it took all her effort to breathe evenly. What was the use, she agonised silently, of aiming for something that didn't exist?

'In return for which I reward you in bed?' The words were out before she had time to give them much thought, and afterwards it was too late to retract them.

His dark brooding glance narrowed fractionally, then his mouth curved in mocking amusement. 'Ah, *cara*,' he taunted softly. 'You reward me so well.'

The need to get away from him, even temporarily, was paramount, and she turned towards the door, only to be brought to a halt as hard hands caught hold of each shoulder and spun her round.

Her eyes blazed with anger through a mist of tears as she tilted her head in silent apathy, hating him more at that precise moment than she thought it possible to hate anyone.

'Stop making fun of me! I won't have it, do you hear?' Angry, frustrated tears filled her eyes as he restrained her with galling ease, and she shook her head helplessly as he drew her inextricably close.

'*Don't*——' Carly begged, feeling the familiar pull of her senses. It would be so easy to succumb, simply to close her eyes and become transported by the special magic of their shared sexual alchemy.

'When have I ever made fun of you?' he teased gently, and she shivered slightly as one hand slid down over the soft roundness of her bottom, pressing her close against the unmistakable force of his arousal, while the other slid up to cup her nape.

'Every time I oppose you,' she began shakily, then, gathering the scattered threads of her courage, she continued with strengthened resolve. 'You resolve it by sweeping me off to bed.' Lifting her hands, she attempted to put some distance between them, only to fail miserably.

'Am I to be damned forever for finding you desirable?'

The thread of amusement in his voice hurt unbearably. 'I'm not a sex object you can use merely to satisfy a need for revenge.'

His eyes searched hers, dark and unfathomable as he held her immobile.

'Let me go, damn you!'

He looked at her in silence for what seemed an age, his eyes darkening until they resembled the deepest slate—hard and equally obdurate.

'Does it feel like revenge every time I take you in my arms?' he queried with dangerous silkiness.

It was heaven and the entire universe rolled into one, ecstasy at its zenith. She looked at him for what seemed an age, unable to utter so much as a word.

Dared she take the chance? All the pent-up anger, her so-called resentment, dissipated as if it had never existed.

'No,' Carly voiced quietly, and he shook her gently, sliding his hands from her shoulders up to cup her face.

'From the moment I first met you I wanted to lock you in a gilded prison and throw away the key. Except such a primitive action wouldn't have been condoned in this day and age.' His eyes were level, and she was unable to drag her own away from the darkness or the pain evident. 'You were a prime target ... young, and incredibly susceptible,' he enlightened her softly.

'If I had been able to get my hands on you during those first few weeks after you left Perth I think I would have strangled you,' he continued slowly.

'Your mother disavowed any knowledge of your whereabouts, and I soon realised you had no intention of contacting me.' His voice hardened measurably, and assumed a degree of cynicism. 'The letter dispatched from your solicitor merely confirmed it.'

He was silent for so long that she wondered if he intended to continue.

'A marriage has no foundation without trust, and as you professed to have lost your trust in me I let you go. Fully expecting,' he added with a trace of mockery, 'to be officially notified of an impending divorce.'

He hadn't been able to instigate such proceedings any more than she had. Her heart set up a quickened beat.

'Not long after shifting base to Sydney I attended an accounting seminar with a fellow associate at which Clive Mathorpe was a guest speaker. I was impressed. Sufficiently so to utilise his services.' He proffered a faint smile. 'Coincidence, *fate* perhaps, that Carly Taylor *Alessi* should be a respected member of his firm. The night I met you at Clive's home I was intrigued by your maturity and self-determination. And very much aware that the intense sexual magic we once shared was still in evidence.' His eyes held hers, and his voice was deliberate as he continued, 'For both of us.'

Carly looked at him carefully, seeing his innate strength, the power in evidence, and knew that she would never willingly want to be apart from him. It was always easy, with hindsight, to rationalise—to indulge in a series of 'what if's, and 'if only's. Maturity had taught her there could only be *now*.

'Angelica's ammunition was pretty powerful,' she offered quietly. 'I found it emotionally damaging at the time.'

There was a mesmeric silence, intensifying until she became conscious of every breath she took.

'I have known Angelica from birth,' Stefano revealed with deceptive mildness, and a muscle tensed along the edge of his jaw. 'Our affiliation owes itself to two sets of parents who immigrated to Australia more than forty years ago. They prospered in one business venture after another, achieving phenomenal success. So much so that hope was fostered that the only Alessi son might marry an Agnelli daughter and thus form a dynasty.' He paused fractionally, and searched her pale features, seeing the faint shadows evident beneath her eyes. 'It was a game I chose not to play,' he added gently.

Carly swallowed the lump that had suddenly risen in her throat. 'The way Angelica told it,' she informed him shakily, 'you were unofficially betrothed when you met me. If our engagement surprised her, our wedding threw her into a rage,' she continued, unwilling to expound too graphically on just how much she'd been hurt by a woman who refused to face reality. 'It appeared I was merely a temporary diversion, and there was little doubt she intended to be there to pick up the pieces.' She effected a deprecatory shrug that hid a measure of pain.

'Angelica,' Stefano declared hardly, 'possesses a vivid imagination. After today,' he grained out with chilling inflexibility, 'she has no doubt whom I love, or why.' His expression softened as he watched the expressive play of emotions chasing each other across her features. '*You*, Carly,' he elaborated gently. 'Always. Only you.'

Stefano shifted his hold, catching both her hands together in one of his, feeling her body quiver slightly as he traced a gentle pattern over the slim curve of her stomach before resting possessively at her trim waist. When his gaze met hers, she nearly died at the lambent warmth revealed in those dark depths.

'There is nothing else you want to tell me?'

Carly stood hesitantly unsure, and at the last moment courage failed her. Slowly she shook her head.

Tomorrow, she'd visit the doctor and undergo a pregnancy test. Then she'd tell him.

CHAPTER TEN

THE morning began the same as any other week day. Stefano rose early, swam several lengths of the pool, ate breakfast with his wife, then showered, dressed and left for the city.

At nine Carly checked with Sylvana, then changed into a smart lemon-yellow button-through linen dress, applied make-up with care, slid her feet into elegant shoes, and went downstairs to the car.

The pregnancy test was performed with ease, and pronounced positive. Carly drove on to the hospital in a state of suspended euphoria.

Ann-Marie looked really *well*, her eyes bright and shining as Carly walked into her room, and her beautiful hair was beginning to show signs of growth. A consultation with the specialist revealed that Ann-Marie could be discharged the following day.

Carly almost floated down the carpeted corridor, and on impulse she crossed to the pay-phone, checked the directory, slotted in coins and keyed in the appropriate series of digits, then relayed specific instructions to the voice on the other end of the phone.

A small secretive smile tugged the edges of her mouth as she drove into the city, and twenty minutes later she stood completing formalities in Reception at one of the inner city's most elegant hotels.

The lift whisked her with swift precision to the eleventh floor, and inside the luxurious suite she swiftly crossed the room, lifted the handset and dialled a memorised number.

She was mad, absolutely crazy, she derided as the line engaged after a number of electronic beeps. What if Stefano wasn't in the office? Worse, what if he was in an important meeting, and couldn't leave? she agonised as the number connected with his personal mobile net.

'Alessi.' His voice sounded brisk and impersonal, and her stomach flipped, then executed a number of painful somersaults.

'Stefano.'

'Carly. Is something wrong?'

'No——' *Hell*, she was faltering, stammering like a schoolgirl. Taking a deep breath, she clenched the receiver and forced herself to speak calmly. 'I'm fine.' Dammit, this was proving more difficult than she'd envisaged.

'Ann-Marie?'

'She's coming home tomorrow.' The joy in her voice was a palpable entity that was reciprocated in his.

Do it, *tell* him, a tiny voice prompted. 'I wanted to ring and say...' She hesitated slightly, then uttered the words with slow emphasis. '*I love you.*'

A few seconds of silence followed, then his voice sounded incredibly husky close to her ear. 'Where are you?'

'In a hotel room, in the city.'

His soft laughter sent spirals of sensation shooting through her body. 'Which hotel, *cara*?'

She named it. 'It's Sylvana's day to vacuum,' she explained a trifle breathlessly.

'Ensuring that total privacy is out of the question,' he drawled with a tinge of humour.

'Totally,' she agreed, and a tiny smile teased the edges of her mouth. 'Is this a terribly inconvenient time for you?'

'It wouldn't make any difference.'

Her heart leapt, then began thudding to a quickened beat. 'No?'

His husky chuckle did strange things to her equilibrium. 'I'll be with you in twenty minutes.'

Carly relayed the room number, then softly replaced the receiver.

Twenty minutes, she mused as she eased off her shoes. How could she fill them? Make a cup of coffee, perhaps, or select a chilled mineral water from the variety stocked in the bar-fridge.

Her eyes travelled idly round the large room, noting the customary prints, the wall-lights, before settling on the bed.

If she turned down the covers, it would look too blatant, and she didn't quite possess the courage to remove all her clothes. What if she opened the door to find a maid or steward on the other side? she thought wildly.

Damn. Waiting was agony, and she crossed to the sealed window and stood watching the traffic on the busy street below.

Everyone appeared to be hurrying, and when the southbound traffic ground to a halt a clutch of people surged across the road to the opposite side. The lights turned green, and the northbound traffic gathered momentum, moving in a seemingly endless river of vehicles until green changed to amber and then to red, when the process began all over again.

From this height everything seemed lilliputian, and she watched the cars, searching for the sleek lines of Stefano's top-of-the-range Mercedes, although the likelihood of catching sight of it when she wasn't even sure from which direction he'd be travelling seemed remote.

It was a beautiful day, she perceived idly. There was a cloudless sky of azure-blue, the sun filtering in shafts of brilliant light between the tall city buildings.

Time became a suspended entity, and it seemed an age before she heard the quiet double knock at the door.

Her stomach reacted at once, leaping almost into her throat, and she smoothed suddenly damp hands down the seams of her dress as she crossed the suite to open the door.

Stefano stood at ease, his tall frame filling the aperture, and she simply looked at him in silence. There was a vital, almost electric energy apparent, an inherent vitality that was compelling, and her pulse accelerated into a rapid beat.

A faint smile teased his generous mouth, and his eyes were so incredibly warm that she almost melted beneath their gaze.

'Do you intend to keep me standing here?'

Pale pink tinged her cheeks as she stood to one side. Fool, she berated herself silently, feeling about as composed as a lovestruck teenager as she followed him into the centre of the room.

When he turned she was within touching distance, yet he made no attempt to draw her into his arms.

'I gather there was a degree of urgency in the need to book in to a hotel room?'

There was no mistaking his soft teasing drawl, nor the expression evident in his eyes. It gave her the confidence to resort to humour.

The sparkle in the depths of her eyes flared into brilliant life, and she laughed softly. 'Tonight we're supposed to dine out with Sarah and James to celebrate Sarah's birthday. If it were anyone else, I wouldn't hesitate to cancel.' A devilish gleam emerged, dancing in the light of her smile. 'I did consider a confrontation in your office, but the thought of Renate or any one of the staff catching sight of their exalted boss deep in an erotic clinch might prove too embarrassing to be condoned.'

His lips twitched, then settled into a sensual curve. 'Erotic?'

'There's champagne in the bar-fridge,' Carly announced inconsequentially. 'Would you like some?'

'I'd like you to repeat what you said to me on the phone,' he commanded gently, and her eyes were remarkably clear as they held his.

'I love you. I always have,' she stressed.

'*Grazie amore.*' He reached out and pulled her close in against him. His lips brushed her forehead, then began a slow, tantalising trail down to the edge of her mouth.

'You're my life,' he said huskily. 'My love.'

There was such a wealth of emotion in his voice; she felt a delicious warmth begin deep within her as a thousand tiny nerve-endings leapt into pulsating life.

'So many wasted years,' she offered with deep regret. 'Nights,' she elaborated huskily. 'Dear heaven, I *missed* you.'

Her eyes widened as she glimpsed the expression in those dark depths mere inches above her own, then she gasped as his mouth moved to cover hers in a kiss that left her feeling shaken with a depth of emotion so intoxicating that it was as if she was soaring high on to a sensual pinnacle of such incredible magnitude that she felt weightless, and totally malleable.

'*Don't*,' Stefano chastised softly. 'We have today, and all the tomorrows. A lifetime.'

Her eyes were wondrously expressive as she lifted her hands and wound them round his neck. 'What time do you have to be back at the office?'

'I told Renate to reschedule the remainder of the day's appointments,' he revealed solemnly.

A delightfully bewitching smile lit her features, and her lips curved to form a teasing smile. 'We have until two, when I visit Ann-Marie in hospital.'

His hands slid down over her hips, and she gloried in the feel of him as he drew her close and brushed his lips close to her ear. 'We'll go together.' The tip of his tongue traced the sensitive whorls, and she shivered as sensation shafted through her body.

A soft laugh bubbled up from her throat to emerge as an exultant sound of delicious anticipation. 'Meantime, I have a few plans for the next few hours.' Leaning away from him, she murmured her pleasure as he loosened his hold so that she could slip the jacket from his shoulders.

His eyes gleamed with humour, and a wealth of latent passion. 'Do you, indeed?'

'Uh-huh.' Her fingers set to work on his tie, then the buttons of his shirt. The belt buckle came next, and she hesitated fractionally as she undid the fastener at his waist and freed the zip. 'Something wildly imaginative with champagne and strawberries.' A bubble of laughter emerged from her throat. 'It's rather decadent.'

His shoes followed, his socks, until all he wore was a pair of silk briefs.

'My turn, I think.'

With unhurried movements he removed every last vestige of her clothing, then he leaned down and tugged back the covers from the large bed before gently pulling her down to lie beside him.

His kiss melted her bones, and she gasped as his mouth began a treacherous path of discovery that encompassed every inch, every vulnerable hollow of her body.

By the time his lips returned to caress hers, there wasn't one coherent word she was capable of uttering, and she clung to him, eager, wanting, *needing* the sweet savagery of his lovemaking.

A long time afterwards she lay catching her breath as she attempted to control the waywardness of her emotions, then slowly she moved, affording him a similar pleasuring until he groaned and pulled her to lie on top of him.

'Minx,' he growled softly, curving a hand round her nape and urging her mouth down to his. 'Keep doing that, and I won't be answerable for the consequences.'

'Promises, promises,' Carly taunted gently as she initiated a kiss that he allowed her to control. Then she rose up and arched her back, stretching like a kitten that had just had its fill of cream.

The soft sigh of contentment changed to a faint gasp as he positioned her to accept his length, and now it was he who was in command, watching her fleeting emotions with musing indulgence as he led her towards a climactic orgasmic explosion that had her crying out his name as wave after wave of sensation exploded from deep within her feminine core, radiating to the furthest reaches of her body in an all-consuming pleasurable ache that gradually ebbed to a warm afterglow, lasting long after they'd shared a leisurely shower and slipped into the complimentary towelling robes.

'Hmm,' Carly murmured as Stefano came to stand behind her and drew her back into the circle of his arms. 'I'm hungry.' She felt his lips caress her nape, and she turned slightly towards him. 'For food, you insatiable man!'

'Do you want to dress and go down to the restaurant, or shall I order Room Service?'

She pretended to consider both options, then directed him a teasing smile. 'Room Service.' She was loath to share him with anyone, and although the time was fast approaching when they must dress and leave she wanted to delay it as long as possible. 'Besides,' she teased mercilessly, 'there's still the champagne.'

Choosing from the menu and placing their order took only minutes, and afterwards Stefano pulled her back into his arms and held her close.

She drew in a deep breath, then released it slowly. 'I've been giving some thought to going back to work next year.'

His eyes took on a new depth, then assumed a musing speculative gleam. 'What if I were to make you a better offer?'

'Such as?'

'Working from home, maintaining order with my paperwork, liaising with Renate?'

Carly pretended to consider his proposal, tilting her head to one side in silent contemplation.

'Flexible hours, harmonious working conditions, and intimate terms with the boss?' she teased.

'Very intimate terms,' he conceded with a sloping smile.

'I accept. Conditionally,' she added with attempted solemnity, and was unable to prevent the slight catch in her breath. 'I'm not sure of your stance on employing pregnant women.'

He didn't say anything for a few seconds, then he kissed her, so gently and with such reverence that it was all she could do not to cry.

'Thank you,' Stefano said simply, and she smiled a trifle tremulously.

'If this pregnancy follows the same pattern as it did with Ann-Marie,' she warned with musing reflection, 'I'll begin feeling nauseous within the next few weeks.' She wrinkled her nose at him in silent humour. 'How will you cope with a wife who has to leap out of bed and run to the bathroom every morning?'

'Ensure that you have whatever it is you need until such time as you feel you can face the day.'

Carly blinked rapidly, then offered shakily, 'Did I tell you how much I love you?'

Room Service delivered their lunch, but it was another hour before they ate the food. Afterwards they slowly dressed and made their way down to the car park.

'I'll follow you to the hospital,' Stefano said gently as he saw her seated behind the wheel of her car. 'Travel carefully, *cara*.'

'We really should stop meeting like this,' Carly declared with impish humour, and heard his husky laugh. Her smile widened into something so beautiful that he caught his breath. 'People might get the wrong idea,' she said with mock-solemnity.

'Indeed?'

'Indeed,' she concurred with a bewitching smile. 'I think we should limit it to special occasions.'

'Such as?'

She fastened her seatbelt, then fired the engine. 'Oh, I'm sure I'll think of something.' With a devilish grin, she engaged the gear, then eased the car out of its parking bay. '*Ciao, caro*.'

She felt deliciously wicked as she cleared the exit and slid into the flow of traffic. An exultant laugh emerged from her throat.

Anyone could be forgiven for thinking she was a mistress having an affair with a passionate lover. And she was. Except that the lover was her husband, and there was nothing illicit or furtive about their relationship.

Only mutual love and a shared bond that would last a lifetime.

'Did you *have* to be so——' she paused as words momentarily failed her '—proprietorial?' Lexi's fingers clenched until the knuckles showed white. 'You sat there so damned *calmly*, looking at me as if...' She trailed to a frustrated halt, loath to say what Georg had no compunction in voicing.

'I couldn't wait to get you home and into bed?' he completed in a drawling tone, adding with cynical mockery, 'Is it so surprising that I might want to?'

NO GENTLE SEDUCTION

BY

HELEN BIANCHIN

Harlequin Mills & Boon

SYDNEY ❀ AUCKLAND ❀ MANILA
LONDON ❀ TORONTO ❀ NEW YORK
PARIS ❀ AMSTERDAM ❀ HAMBURG ❀ MILAN
STOCKHOLM ❀ MADRID ❀ ATHENS ❀ BUDAPEST
WARSAW ❀ SOFIA ❀ PRAGUE ❀ TOKYO ❀ ISTANBUL

First Published 1991
This Edition 1998
ISBN 0 733 51143 0

Published by
Harlequin Mills & Boon
3 Gibbes Street
Chatswood, NSW 2067
Australia

HARLEQUIN MILLS & BOON and the Rose Device are trademarks used under
license and registered in Australia, New Zealand, Philippines, United States
Patent & Trademark Office and in other countries.

Printed and bound in Australia by
McPherson's Printing Group

CHAPTER ONE

HOT, humid southern hemispheric temperatures prevailed, shrouding Sydney's tall city buildings in a stultifying summer heat-haze capable of frazzling the most even temperament.

Traffic in all city-bound lanes had slowed to a standstill, and Lexi spared a quick glance at her watch as she waited for the queue of cars to begin moving again.

A faint frown furrowed her smooth brow, and her lacquered nails played out an abstracted tattoo against the steering-wheel as she pondered her brother's telephone call of the previous evening. The serious tone of David's voice had proved vaguely perturbing, and no amount of cajoling had persuaded him to reveal any information.

Lexi shifted gears as the lights changed and she sent the sports car forward with a muted growl from its superb engine.

The movement of air teased tendrils of dark auburn hair loose from its careless knot atop her head, and she lifted a hand to brush them back from her cheek. Designer sunglasses shaded golden hazel eyes, and her attractive fine-boned features drew several admiring glances as she made her way into the city.

A wry smile twisted the edges of her generous mouth in the knowledge that as much of the envious speculation was for the aerodynamic lines of her

brother's near-new red Ferrari 348 as it was for the
girl driving it. Wealth wasn't everything, she silently
derided, and natural good looks could prove a
handicap—something she'd discovered to her cost.

Such thoughts were detrimental, and she determinedly shut out the past by deliberately concentrating on negotiating the heavy inner-city traffic.

Ten minutes later a soft sigh of relief escaped her
lips as she turned into the car park beneath a
towering modern block housing her brother's suite
of offices. Using extreme care, she eased the red
sports car down two levels and brought it to a
smooth halt in its reserved parking bay.

Gathering up her bag, she slid to her feet just as
another car pulled into a nearby space, and her eyes
widened fractionally at the sight of an almost
identical Ferrari. The coincidence of two expensive
Italian sports cars parking within such close
proximity was highly improbable, and she watched
with detached interest as the driver emerged from
behind the wheel.

He was tall, she noticed idly, with an enviable
breadth of shoulder evident beneath the flawless
cut of his jacket, and he moved with the lithe ease
of inherent strength. His hair was dark and well-
groomed, and the broad-chiselled bone-structure
moulded his features into rugged attractiveness.

Features that were vaguely familiar, and yet even
as she searched her memory there was no spark of
recognition, no name she could retrieve that would
identify him.

As if sensing her scrutiny he lifted his head, and
she was unprepared for the dark probing gaze that

raked her slim curves in analytical appraisal before returning to settle overlong on the soft fullness of her mouth. Then his eyes travelled slowly up to focus on her startled expression.

She felt a surge of rage begin deep inside, and its threatened eruption brought a fiery sparkle to her beautiful eyes. How *dared* he subject her to such blatantly sexual assessment?

Impossibly angry, she turned towards the car, locked the door and activated the alarm, then she crossed to the lifts to jab the call-button with unnecessary force, silently willing any one of three lifts to descend and transport her to the fifteenth floor.

It irked her unbearably that she should still be waiting when he joined her, and she stood silently aloof until a faint hydraulic hiss heralded the arrival of a lift. As soon as as the doors slid open she stepped forward with easy grace into the electronic cubicle, pressed the appropriate digit on the illuminated panel, then stood back in silence, mentally distancing herself from the man's physical presence.

A faint prickle of apprehension feathered the surface of her skin, which was crazy, for he posed no threat. Yet she was frighteningly aware of his studied evaluation, and she hated the elusive alchemy that pulled at her senses. She was damned if she'd give him the satisfaction of returning his gaze. Who did he think he was, for heaven's sake?

A sobering inner voice silently derided that he knew precisely who he was, and without doubt his action was a deliberate attempt to ruffle her composure.

Somehow she expected him to voice any one of several differing phrases men inevitably used as an opening gambit with an attractive woman, and when he didn't the rage within only intensified, for it gave her no opportunity to deliver a scathing response.

It took only seconds to reach the fifteenth floor, but it felt like minutes, and so intense was her need to escape that she stepped from the lift the instant the doors slid open, unable to prevent the feeling that she was fleeing from a predatory animal.

A sensation that was as totally insane as it was out of perspective, she mentally chided as she entered the foyer of her brother's suite of legal offices.

'Good morning, Miss Harrison,' the receptionist greeted warmly. 'Mr Harrison said to go straight through.'

'Thanks,' Lexi proffered with a faint smile as she continued past the central desk and turned down a corridor leading to a large corner office which offered panoramic views of the city and inner harbour.

'David,' she greeted as the door closed behind her, accepting the affectionate brush of her brother's lips against her cheek before she subsided into a nearby chair. 'Thanks for organising my car into the repair shop. I've parked the red monster in its usual space.'

David's eyebrows rose in a gesture of feigned offence. '*Monster*, Lexi?'

A faint grin curved her generous mouth. 'Sorry,' she corrected, aware that the Ferrari represented an unaccustomed flamboyance in his otherwise staid existence as one of Sydney's leading barristers. 'Your magnificent motoring machine.'

As the son and daughter of one of Australia's most respected financial entrepreneurs, they had each achieved success in their own right, choosing to decline any assistance afforded them by virtue of their father's considerable wealth and position.

'Have you any plans for tonight?'

Her eyes widened slightly. 'I can't imagine you need to resort to your sister's company through lack of a suitable female partner.'

His glance was level and strangely watchful as he offered a light bantering response. 'Now that your decree absolute has been granted I thought we might celebrate by having dinner together.'

An entire gamut of emotions flitted in and out of her expressive eyes, and for a moment he glimpsed her pain before a wry, faintly cynical smile tugged the edges of her mouth.

Despite her reluctance, memories sharpened into startling focus. The dissolution of her marriage meant that she no longer bore any affiliation, legal or otherwise, to a man who had deliberately pursued her for the fame of her family name and the considerable fortune he imagined would be his to access at will as the husband of Jonathan Harrison's daughter.

Paul Ellis had epitomised every vulnerable young girl's dream and every caring parent's nightmare, Lexi reflected with grim hindsight. Within weeks of returning to Australia from a two-year working stint in Europe she met Paul at a party, and became instantly attracted to him. Blindly infatuated, she had discounted her father's caution, disregarded

David's advice, and married Paul three months later in a whirl of speculative publicity.

To Jonathan's credit he had concealed his concern and provided a wedding that had proved to be the social event of the year.

Mere days into a Caribbean honeymoon Lexi's dream of marital bliss had begun to fragment as Paul voiced a series of protests. The home her father had presented them with as a wedding gift was considered by Paul as too small for the sort of entertaining he had had in mind, and his disappointment in Jonathan's failure to appoint his son-in-law to the board of directors had been compounded when Lexi had refused to exert any influence in Paul's favour. His sudden enthusiasm for a child had raised doubts in Lexi's mind, and when she had elected to defer pregnancy for a year he'd lost his temper and the rift between them had become irreparable.

Paul, when faced with the *fait accompli* of legal separation, had filed claim for a huge financial settlement and threatened court proceedings if his demands were not met.

One of David's colleagues had conducted such superb legal representation that Paul's case was thrown out of court.

Concentrating on her modelling career, Lexi had declined her father's offer to occupy his prestigious Vaucluse mansion, opting instead to live alone in a beautifully furnished apartment at Darling Point overlooking the inner harbour.

At twenty-five she was considered to be one of Sydney's top models, and work provided a panacea that helped relegate Paul to the past.

The experience had left her with a cynical attitude towards men to such an extent that she chose not to date at all, preferring the company of Jonathan and David on the few occasions it became necessary for her to provide an escort.

Now Lexi met David's steady gaze with equanimity. 'That's the momentous news you wanted to discuss with me in person?'

He was silent for a few long seconds as he chose his words with care. 'Part of it.'

Her eyes widened fractionally at his hesitation.

'Paul has somehow discovered Jonathan is at present undertaking extremely delicate negotiations with a Japanese consortium to finance a proposed tourist resort on Queensland's Gold Coast,' he revealed slowly, and Lexi cast him a puzzled glance.

'In what context can Paul pose any threat?'

'He has made a demand for money.'

'Why?' she demanded at once.

David seemed to take an inordinate amount of time in answering. 'He is threatening to sell his story of the marriage break-up to the Press, detailing how he was discarded by the Harrison family without a cent.' His lips twisted. 'The fact that Paul deliberately set Jonathan's fortune in his sights and preyed upon your emotions is immaterial,' he informed cynically. 'The Press, at Paul's direction, will have a field-day. Especially when it can run a concurrent story of the extent of Jonathan's financial involvement in the Japanese deal.'

Lexi didn't need to be told just how Paul's supposed plight would be highlighted. Without doubt he would portray the injured party to the

hilt, invoking reader sympathy against the pluto-
cratic Harrison family. As long as there was some
basis of fact the truth was unimportant with some
tabloids, and the major criterion was saleable copy.

'But surely the Japanese consortium is astute
enough not to allow personalities to enter into any
business dealings?'

'Indeed,' he agreed drily. 'However, they will
acquire their tourist resort regardless of whether
Jonathan's company is the majority shareholder or
not. There are other viable companies which would
clutch at any straw in their struggle for power.'

Lexi didn't need to be enlightened as to her ex-
husband's duplicity. 'The price for his silence is a
financial settlement,' Lexi concluded, her eyes
hardening until they resembled dark topaz. 'A
settlement he was legally unable to obtain when we
separated.'

'Unfortunately it isn't that simple,' David
declared slowly. 'Jonathan is as yet unaware of
Paul's intention. With your help I intend to keep
it that way.'

Her eyes flashed with brilliant gold. 'Paul has no
scruples whatsoever, and I'm damned if I'll allow
you or Jonathan to pay Paul what amounts to
blackmail on my account. It would only be the
beginning, and you know it!'

David moved to stand beside the wide expanse
of plate-glass, his expression pensive and incredibly
solemn as he appeared to admire the view. After
what seemed an age he turned towards her and
thrust hands into his trouser pockets.

'The Japanese deal is important to Jonathan.' He
effected a negligible shrug. 'But its failure or success

is immaterial in the long term. There are other deals, other opportunities. However, in this particular issue the element of timing is crucial, and with Jonathan's health at stake I'll do anything in my power to prevent him from suffering any unnecessary stress.'

A painful hand clutched at her heart, and her voice became husky with concern. 'What's wrong with Jonathan?' Her eyes clung to his. 'Why haven't you told me?'

'Because there was no point until all the tests were conclusive,' David said gently. 'His only option is a triple bypass, and surgery is scheduled for the beginning of January. Timed,' he added wryly, 'at Jonathan's insistence, to coincide with the anticipated conclusion of the Japanese negotiations. In the meantime it's essential he leads a quiet life with minimum stress.' He drew a deep breath as he surveyed her pale, stricken features. 'I hardly need to tell you what effect Paul's threatened publicity will have on Jonathan if we're unable to prevent it from erupting prior to surgery.'

The fact that her indomitable human dynamo of a father was victim of a heart disease was more than she could bear. 'It's that serious?'

David reached out and caught hold of her hand. 'You must know he'll have the best surgeon,' he reassured gently. 'And such operations are now considered routine.'

Lexi could only look at him blankly, her mind filling with conflicting images and an unassailable anger that anything Paul attempted might damage her father's health. 'What possible solution have you come up with?' she managed at last.

David seemed to take his time, then offered quietly, 'Paul's adverse publicity attempt will look extremely foolish if you were already heavily involved, even engaged, to a man who is sufficiently wealthy to finance the necessary fifty-one-per-cent stake. A man who could present the role of adoring fiancé with conviction.' Seeing her silent scepticism, he lifted his hand in a dismissive gesture as he sought to assure. 'With careful orchestration and the right publicity we could ensure that any demands Paul sought were seen to be merely a case of sour grapes.'

'Since I'm not romantically involved with anyone, just *who* do you propose to link me with?' she queried with deceptive calm, then said with categoric certainty, 'It won't work.'

'It has to work,' David insisted. 'I can provide sufficient delaying tactics for a week or two on the premise of considering Paul's demands.'

'And the man, David? Just who is this paragon who will give his time to act out a charade?' A faint bitterness crept into her voice. 'And what's *his* price?'

'Georg Nicolaos,' he revealed slowly. 'And there is no price.'

'I find that difficult to believe,' she replied with scepticism. 'Everything has a price.'

'Jonathan's association with the Nicolaos family is well known. He has entered into several joint financial ventures with Alex and Georg Nicolaos in the past. It will come as no surprise if, now that your divorce from Paul is final, Georg Nicolaos is seen escorting you to a variety of functions during the run-down to the festive season.' A faint smile tugged the corners of his mouth. 'It will be alleged in the gossip columns that you and Georg have enjoyed a clandestine relationship for some time, and now that you're legally free Georg is losing no time in staking his claim.'

'Are Alex and Georg Nicolaos involved in this particular venture?'

'Yes.'

'And what if Paul suspects it's merely a smokescreen?'

'I will utilise all my legal ability to persuade him we're more likely to take a magnanimous view of his demands now you're considering marriage with Georg. I can gain time with negotiations by insisting that Paul sign a document indicating he has no further financial claim on acceptance of an agreed amount.'

She gave him a look of scandalised disbelief. 'So you *do* intend to pay him?'

'A token sum, commensurate with the length of time he was married to you.' His good-looking features hardened into a mask of distaste. 'Added to the car and furniture he spirited out of the house within hours of your leaving him, the total value will be more than generous under the circumstances.' His expression gentled. 'Four weeks, Lexi—five at the most. Surely it's not too much to ask?'

She hesitated, unwilling to voice her own reluctance for fear it would sound ungrateful in light of the caring support her father and brother had each given her during the past two years. 'I can hardly refuse, can I?' she said at last, and glimpsed the relieved satisfaction in his eyes.

'In that case, I'll contact Georg and arrange for him to meet us this evening.'

So soon? Yet logic demanded there was no reason for delay.

Almost as if he sensed her reserve, he gave her hand a reassuring squeeze. 'I'll call for you at six-thirty.'

She possessed a wardrobe filled with designer clothes, and she mentally reviewed them in an attempt to make an appropriate selection. 'I imagine you require me to present a dazzling image?'

'You look fantastic in anything.'

'Now that's what I call brotherly love,' Lexi accepted with a contrived smile. Sparing her watch a quick glance, she rose to her feet and delved into her bag to extract a set of keys which she pressed into his hand. 'Thanks for the loan of the Ferrari.'

David tossed them down on to his desk and reached into a nearby drawer. 'Here's yours. It's parked on level three, close to the lifts.'

'Give me the bill,' she insisted, 'and I'll write you a cheque.'

He made no demur and merely extracted the itemised account, watching as she wrote in the amount and attached her signature with unaffected flair.

Collecting her keys, she made her way towards the door. 'I have a modelling assignment at eleven. Jacques will have a fit if I'm late.'

The Mercedes sports car purred to life at the first turn of the key, and Lexi exited the car park, then headed towards the eastern suburbs.

The address she'd been given was for a restaurant venue in Double Bay whose patron had generously donated to charity the cost of providing food for the seventy ticket-paying guests.

It was, Jacques assured, a long-standing annual event for which the particular charity involved was dependently grateful.

Parking was achieved with ease, and Lexi locked up, activating the car alarm before walking towards the main street.

She located the discreet restaurant display-board without difficulty, and traversed a wide curving staircase to the main entrance, where an elegantly gowned hostess greeted and directed her to a make-shift changing-room.

'Lexi, you're late,' a harassed voice announced the instant she entered the small room, and she checked her watch with a faintly raised eyebrow.

'By less than a minute,' she protested as she deftly began discarding her outer clothes. 'The fashion parade isn't due to begin for another half-hour.'

'Time which must be spent perfecting the hair and make-up, *oui*?'

The models were due to take to the catwalk at precisely eleven-thirty, displaying a variety of exclusive labels for an hour, after which lunch would be served, followed by customary speeches and the giving of a few token awards.

Thank heaven today's modelling assignment was being held indoors in air-conditioned comfort, Lexi consoled herself more than an hour later as she hurriedly discarded an elegantly tailored suit and reached for a superb evening gown, the final selection in a superb fashion range.

Yesterday had involved a beach, searing sun, hot sand, and a gathering of ogling, wolf-whistling young men intent on upsetting her composure.

Modelling was hard work, and often the antithesis of its projected glamorous image, Lexi mused as she took her cue and moved out on to the small makeshift stage. Her hazel-gold eyes were wide and clear, and she portrayed graceful dignity as she took to the catwalk, pausing momentarily as she executed a series of choreographed movements; then she returned to the stage to effect one final turn before slipping through the curtain to backstage.

'The restaurateur has set a table aside for those of you who wish to eat,' Jacques informed them as he carefully slid the last garment into its protective cover. 'Of course, there is no obligation to stay.'

The three other models opted to remain, while Lexi shook her head in silent negation. 'I can't. I have a dental appointment in half an hour.'

He gave a typical Gallic shrug. 'Tomorrow at three, Lexi,' he reminded her, and she nodded in acquiescence as she cast her reflection a quick glance before collecting her bag.

'I must fly, or I'll be late.'

Slipping out of the changing-room, Lexi quickly manoeuvred her way between tables, inadvertently bumping into a solid masculine frame which seemed to appear out of nowhere.

Her hand clutched his arm in an instinctive attempt to steady herself, and a faint smile parted her lips accompanied by a few words in murmured apology.

Words that froze in the back of her throat as she recognised the man with whom she'd shared a lift only a few hours earlier.

This close she could see the fine lines fanning out from the corners of his eyes, the deep groove slashing each cheek.

He possessed an animalistic sense of power, as well as an indefinable sensual quality that was infinitely dangerous to any sensible woman's peace of mind.

There was a degree of mocking amusement evident in the depths of his gaze, and Lexi became aware that she was still clutching his arm.

She snatched her hand away as if burned by fire, and her eyes flared to a brilliant gold as she regained the power of speech. 'I'm sorry. Excuse me,' she added in a huskily spoken afterthought as she made to move past him.

'You are not staying?'

His drawled query held the faintest accent, and the sound of it sent a tiny shiver of alarm scudding down the length of her spine.

'No.'

His gaze was steady, his brown eyes dark, inscrutable depths in which it would be all too easy to become lost, and there could be no doubt that he possessed sufficient sensual expertise to melt the hardest heart.

But not hers, she assured herself silently. Definitely not hers. She'd travelled that particular road before, and there was no way she intended being hurt again. By *any* man.

He made no comment, and merely inclined his head in silent mocking acceptance of her decision.

The desperate need to get away from him surprised her, and she lifted a hand to push back the length of her hair in a gesture that was born from nervous tension.

A fact that was unsettling, given her exclusive schooling, she acknowledged as she made her way towards the foyer. And after her disastrously short marriage to Paul she had managed to acquire a protective façade she considered virtually impregnable.

It was after five when Lexi entered her luxurious Darling Point apartment, and her arms were laden with an assortment of brightly coloured carrier-bags that held Christmas gifts for Jonathan and David, as well as an exquisite new perfume she'd bought for herself.

With a sigh of relief she closed the door behind her, eased off her shoes, then carried her purchases through to the spare bedroom. From there she made her way into the kitchen and poured herself a long cool drink of orange juice, then she drifted into the lounge and sank into one of several soft leather chairs.

It had been an unsettling day, fraught with surprises, and she needed ten minutes in which to relax and *think*.

Blind dating—if dining with Georg Nicolaos could be termed that—was something in which she'd never indulged, and she was reluctant to begin, even given such an essentially worthy cause.

Any choice she might have in the matter was a mere fallacy, for there *was* no choice, she decided wryly. Somehow she had to endure being in the constant company of a man she'd never met for the next five weeks; to smile and laugh, and generally give the impression that she was relieved and delighted that their romance, which had supposedly been kept under wraps for months, was now out in the open.

Without doubt it would tax her acting ability to the limit.

With a sigh of resignation she stretched her arms above her head and flexed her shoulders, then rose to her feet and made her way into the bedroom, where she stripped, and took a shower in the adjoining *en suite* bathroom.

Lexi was ready a few minutes before six-thirty, her long hair confined into a knot atop her head from which she deliberately teased free a few soft-curling tendrils. Make-up was deliberately under-stated, with the accent on subtle shadings of eyeshadow, a touch of blusher, and soft clear rose colouring her lips. The gown she'd chosen was black with a cleverly designed ruched bodice and figure-hugging skirt. It came with a stole which she casually draped across her shoulders, and her feet were encased in black Jourdan slender-heeled shoes.

'Beautiful,' David complimented warmly when she opened the door at his summons.

'Thanks,' she accepted without guile as she preceded him into the lounge. 'Would you like a drink?'

'I told Georg we'd meet him at seven.'

Lexi cast him a quick glance before collecting her evening-bag from a nearby mahogany table. 'In that case, I guess we'd better not keep him waiting.'

Double Bay was a popular 'in' place to eat, hosting a variety of exclusive restaurants, and it wasn't until David led her to a familiar flight of stairs that she realised their destination.

'I was here this morning on a modelling assignment.'

'Really? Georg is known to favour a few worthy charity organisations.'

A brief flicker of surprise lit her features. 'Georg Nicolaos owns the restaurant?'

'It belongs to the Nicolaos family,' David corrected. 'Georg assumed a personal interest in it after the death of his father. If you remember, Alex and I attended university together.'

A darkly handsome figure sprang to mind, formidable and intensely Greek. 'I seem to recollect hearing Alex had married.' A faint gleam sparkled in the depths of her eyes. 'His wife has my sympathy.'

'Dear lord, *why*?'

Lexi gave a husky laugh. 'Oh, for heaven's sake, David! Alex is one of the most frighteningly sexy men I've met. The woman who managed to snare him must be quite something.'

'Samantha is charming,' David allowed, before giving his name to the hostess at the desk.

'Ah, yes, Mr Harrison.' Her smile was practised, bright, and deferential. 'Mr Nicolaos has instructed me to let him know the moment you arrive. If you'd care to follow me, I'll direct you to your table. Mr Nicolaos will join you shortly.'

'You seem to be very much in favour,' Lexi teased minutes after they had taken their seats, and David effected a self-deprecatory shrug.

'I've known the family a long time. Alex waited tables between college and university semesters in

NO GENTLE SEDUCTION 23

the days when his father headed the restaurant. As did Georg and Anna.'

'I find it strange that, although I've met Alex on a number of occasions over the years, I have yet to meet his brother.'

David leaned well back in his chair, a habit he unconsciously adopted whenever he was about to choose his words with care. Lexi wondered if he was aware of it, and why he should do so now.

'Perhaps because Alex chooses to adopt a stand on certain political issues, and enjoys a prominent social existence.'

'And Georg doesn't?' she queried idly.

'Not to the same degree.'

Her eyelids flicked wide. 'Why? Is he a recluse? Or does he not enjoy the company of women?'

David's gleaming humour was somehow directed to a point somewhere beyond her left shoulder.

'On the contrary,' a deep slightly accented, vaguely familiar voice interjected in a silky drawl. 'I very much enjoy the opposite sex.'

Lexi turned slowly to find her worst fears were confirmed, and a silent scream of rejection rose against the irony of fate that Georg Nicolaos and the driver of the red Ferrari were one and same.

CHAPTER TWO

LEXI'S eyes flared briefly in silent resentment as David effected an introduction.

'Mr Nicolaos,' Lexi acknowledged, hating the way her stomach began to knot in sheer reaction to his presence.

'*Georg*, please,' he insisted, holding her gaze a few seconds longer than was necessary before switching his attention to the man seated opposite. 'David.'

A waiter appeared the instant Georg folded his lengthy frame into a chair, and he hovered with intent solicitude as his employer enquired about his guests' choice of wine while Lexi sat stiffly upright as every last nerve-ending tingled alive in silent antipathy.

Not even in her wildest imagination had she envisaged being placed in the invidious position of having to act out a charade with someone of Georg Nicolaos's calibre.

Part of her demanded an escape *now*, while she still had the courage to do so. Except that she was impossibly bound to remain, and she viewed him surreptitiously under the guise of perusing the menu.

In his late thirties, he managed without effort to portray a dramatic mesh of blatant masculinity and elemental ruthlessness—a facet that was obviously a family trait, she decided uncharitably, recalling Alex's formidable features.

The menu was extensive, and she opted for a chicken consommé, followed it with a salad, and waived dessert in favour of the cheeseboard.

'I can't persuade you to sample even one dish from our selection of Greek cuisine?'

Lexi met Georg's dark gaze, and was unable to read anything from his expression. His faint smile held a degree of warmth and was doubtless aimed to put her at ease. Yet beneath the façade she detected a lurking cynicism, and it rankled.

Her eyes held his with deliberately cool regard. 'Thank you, but no,' she refused quietly.

'Another occasion, perhaps?'

She wanted to tell him that there would be no other occasion, but the reality of the next few weeks emerged with vivid clarity.

Lifting her glass to her lips, she savoured its excellent contents, then set it down on to the table, unconsciously tracing the patterned cloth with the tip of her elegantly shaped nail.

Mockery appeared to be her only defence, and she utilised it mercilessly. 'Do we each bring out our figurative engagement books, and consult?'

A gleam of humour sharpened his dark eyes. 'You have your engagement book with you?'

It was crazy to feel so vulnerable, yet she was supremely conscious of every single breath, and it wasn't a sensation she enjoyed.

'Like the advertisement for a well-known credit card,' she responded, 'I never leave home without it.'

'For tomorrow night,' Georg drawled, 'I have tickets for the opera.'

Lexi shook her head. 'I have a photographic modelling session tomorrow afternoon.'

'Which is due to finish—when?'

She effected a faint shrug. 'Five, six,' she hazarded. 'Maybe later. Peter is a perfectionist. He'll take as many shots as he needs to capture precisely the right image.'

'Dinner is obviously out. I'll collect you at seven-thirty.'

She regarded him coolly. 'I could have made other plans.' She heard David's audible intake of breath and registered his protest before he had the opportunity to voice the words.

'Lexi——'

'Perhaps you could check?' Georg interceded in a deep, faintly accented drawl, and an icy chill feathered across the surface of her skin.

Lexi knew she was behaving badly, yet she was unable to prevent herself from searching for her pocket diary and riffling through its pages until she reached the appropriate one. 'Drinks with Elaine, seven o'clock,' she read out, then spared him an apparently regretful glance. 'Sorry. Not the opera.' A shaft of remorse prompted her to offer a slight smile. 'Unless I miss the first act and join you during the second?'

'Alternatively, we could both miss the first act,' Georg declared silkily.

It was a clash of wills, and she was determined to win. 'I wouldn't dream of allowing you to make such a concession. If you let me have the ticket I'll meet you there.'

'Surely you could cancel Elaine?' David intervened, shooting her a cautionary look that ordinarily she would have heeded.

'Arrangements were made weeks ago for a number of friends to meet for a few pre-Christmas drinks,' she explained. 'If I opt out she'll be hurt. Besides,' she qualified, unable to prevent a faint tinge of bitterness entering her voice, 'once my supposed romance with Georg hits the gossip columns there will be no peace at all. At least permit me another day of relative freedom.'

'I should remind you that Georg is under no obligation whatsoever,' David declared heavily.

'Perhaps not,' she tempered sweetly. 'Although, business-wise, I doubt if either Alex or Georg wants this particular deal to fall through. Therefore, Georg *does* have an interest. Am I not right?' She spared her brother a winsome smile before switching her attention to his companion. 'Unless, of course, he's bored with life and not averse to a little subterfuge by way of adventure. Is that the reason you've agreed to act as a mythical knight in shining armour, Georg?' She deliberately gave his name its correct phonetic pronunciation, so that it fell from her lips as 'Jorj'.

His eyes swept her features in raking assessment, then locked with hers for a brief instant before assuming an expression of bland inscrutability. 'My life is far from boring,' he acknowledged with velvet-smoothness, although only a fool would have failed to perceive the steel evident.

'Yet you are willing to reorganise your social life to the extent of putting it entirely on hold for a month.' She let her eyes travel at will over each and every one of his visible features in an appraisal that was meant to diffuse the sheer overwhelming presence of the man. 'Your current—er—companion,' she accorded with delicate emphasis, 'must be extremely understanding.'

Georg regarded her steadily until she almost felt impelled to wrench her gaze away from those fathomless dark eyes, then his eyelids lowered slightly, successfully masking his expression as he proffered a faintly mocking smile.

'You're a very attractive young woman,' he drawled. 'Being your escort for a few weeks in an attempt to perpetrate an illusion will provide no hardship at all.'

It was as well the waiter arrived at that precise moment with their starter, and Lexi spooned the excellent chicken consommé with little appetite, and merely picked at her salad.

The wine helped soothe her nerves, although she refused to allow her glass to be refilled and opted for chilled water throughout the remainder of the meal.

It was almost ten when David indicated that they should leave, and Lexi experienced considerable relief that the evening was almost over.

'Your ticket for the opera,' Georg indicated as he withdrew a slim envelope from his jacket pocket and handed it to her.

She took care that their fingers didn't touch, aware from the faint gleam of amusement evident that he *knew*. 'I'm not sure what time I'll get there,' she ventured, determined not to rush away from Elaine's party before she was ready.

'Try to make it before the final act,' he advised in a cynical drawl. 'And take a taxi,' he added. 'We'll go on to a night-club afterwards.'

Her lashes swept up as she cast him a cool glance. 'Is that necessary?'

'It is if we're to be seen together, photographed and captioned in the gossip columns.' His smile was totally without humour. 'Our supposed "romance" won't have much credence if we depart in separate vehicles.'

She felt her stomach give a sickening lurch at the reality of what she was about to undertake. Yet any visible sign of apprehension was unthinkable, and she tilted her chin fractionally as she proffered a brilliant smile. 'I'll endeavour to dazzle.'

'You appear to do that without effort,' Georg accorded drily as he rose to his feet, and Lexi followed suit, collecting her evening-bag as he escorted them both to the lobby.

'Really, Lexi,' David chastised her the instant they were out of earshot. 'You were incredibly rude——'

'I know everything you're going to say,' she intercepted a trifle wearily, glad that they had reached the street. 'Treat it as a temporary aberration.' Her voice assumed an unaccustomed asperity. 'I just hate the degree of my own involvement in this ill-fated scheme.' Especially with someone like Georg Nicolaos, a tiny voice taunted.

David shot her a perceptive look. 'Georg is unlikely to proposition you, if that's your concern.'

Oh, *David*, she longed to deride him. If only you knew how emotionally insecure I feel—how afraid

I am to get close to *any* man, even if it's only to participate in an inglorious charade!

Yet she said nothing, and merely walked at his side to the car, opting to remain pensively silent as he drove her the short distance to her apartment block.

'Ring me at the office on Wednesday. Jonathan mentioned something about our both joining him at home for dinner.' His kindly eyes pierced hers in the dim interior of the car. 'Georg will make a welcome guest. Invite him along.'

She was caught in a trap, and already she could feel the first tinge of pain. 'I'll mention it,' she compromised, slipping easily from the low-slung vehicle the instant it pulled to a halt. 'Goodnight.'

'Darling, *must* you?'

The words appeared to be sincere, but in reality masked boredom and lack of interest, and Lexi wondered why she'd stayed at Elaine's party for so long.

Sheer perversity, born from a desire to tread the edge of Georg Nicolaos's self-control; something that was akin to total madness, she decided as she declared that she really *must* leave.

'I'll just say goodnight to Elaine,' she murmured, then drifted towards a group of three women deep in animated conversation near the door.

Kisses, a few shared hugs, the exchanged avowals to enjoy a really great 'Chrissie', then Lexi managed to slip away.

The taxi she'd ordered was parked outside, waiting, and the driver merely shrugged in complacent resignation as she directed him to the Opera House.

Lexi checked the ticket—something she hadn't bothered to do until now—and saw that the reservation was for *Madame Butterfly*.

The torturous and incredibly sad aspects of love, no matter how beautifully enacted, could hardly be her favoured selection. Yet a quirk of sardonic irony permitted her to see humour in the unwanted parable. The question that sprang immediatcly to mind was whether Georg Nicolaos's choice was deliberate or merely happenstance.

Some thirty minutes later Lexi was led unobtrusively to a section which comprised some of the best seats in the house, and with a murmured apology she moved along the aisle and sank down into the reserved space.

Her hand was captured almost at once, and she instinctively pulled against the strength of Georg's fingers as he threaded them through her own.

'Seated behind us, to your left, is Anaïs Pembleton,' he cautioned softly as he leaned closer, and she closed her eyes in frustration that one of the city's leading matrons should have chosen tonight of all nights to visit the opera. Worse, that the society doyenne should be seated in the immediate vicinity. Sharp-eyed and acid-tongued, Anaïs Pembleton had a nose for gossip to the extent that she was accorded the status of the uncrowned queen of the gossip-mongers. Lexi hardly needed Georg to remind her to behave.

'How . . . opportune,' she murmured, hating his close proximity, the faint helplessness at having her hand enclosed within his own, and the sheer animal magnetism he managed to exude without any seeming effort.

'Try to smile,' he drawled, and she could sense his cynical amusement. 'The curtain is about to fall.'

A minute was all she had to prepare herself, and for one brief second her eyes felt incredibly large, their poignant depths strangely dry as she fought to quell the faint trembling of her lips.

'Would you prefer to remain seated?'

He was quite devastating when he deliberately set out to charm and she endeavoured to match the warmth reflected in his smile. 'Could we mingle in the foyer?' At least then she could move around, and there was always the chance she might meet an acquaintance, thus providing an opportunity to focus her attention on someone other than *him*.

Georg rose to his feet without a word, leading her through a throng of fashionably attired men and women.

Lexi had chosen to wear a formal gown of rich red velvet, its body-hugging lines emphasising her soft feminine curves. A wrap in matching velvet added undeniable elegance, and she'd utilised two side-combs to sweep the hair back from her face. Her only jewellery was a diamond pendant on a slim gold chain, and matching ear-studs.

'A drink?' he queried as they reached the foyer.

'Lime and soda, with a dash of bitters.'

'Ice?'

'Please,' she acceded, watching as a waiter appeared at their side as if by magic.

Georg Nicolaos emanated an infinite degree of power of a kind that commanded instant attention.

Yet there was no arrogance apparent, just a compelling omnipotence that scorned all forms of weakness.

It was little wonder that women were held enthralled by him, she perceived wryly. Even if he wasn't extraordinarily wealthy, he would still manage to snare most feminine hearts.

He smiled, and deep grooves slashed his cheeks. 'How was the party?'

She looked at him carefully, analysing the broad-sculptured bone-structure, the steady wide-spaced dark eyes. 'Fine.' A faint moue appeared momentarily, then it was gone, and she effected a slight shrug. 'Am I now supposed to enquire about your day?'

'Are you in the least interested?' he queried, watching as she lifted her glass and took a small sip.

'I know very little about you,' Lexi ventured, and her eyes flared as he reached out and threaded his fingers through her own. Her initial instinct to pull free was thwarted, and she retaliated with a surreptitious dig from her long hard nails.

'Why, Georg,' a breathy feminine voice intruded, 'how wonderful to see you! Are you going on to the club afterwards?'

Lexi turned slowly and met a vision of brunette perfection attired in black silk that shrieked an exclusive designer label only the favoured few could afford.

'Louise,' he acknowledged, then performed an introduction.

'Your face is familiar, yet I'm sure we've never met,' the brunette declared with a faint frown.

'Lexi is a model,' Georg revealed smoothly, clasping Lexi's hand even more firmly within his own.

The gesture didn't go unnoticed, and Lexi caught the sharpness apparent in Louise's beautiful blue eyes before the expression was carefully masked.

'Harrison. Are you any relation to Jonathan Harrison?'

There was no point in denying the truth. 'His daughter.'

There was instant, inevitable knowledge evident in the other girl's exquisite features. 'Of course. Now I remember. Your marriage and divorce achieved notoriety in the Press.'

During the past two years Lexi had encountered several occasions such as this one, and had become accustomed to dealing with them. Pride lifted her chin, and her lashes swept down to form a partial protective veil. 'At the time it was a seven-day wonder,' she allowed with quiet dignity.

'A sensation,' Louise corrected with sweet emphasis. 'No sooner was the honeymoon over than so was the marriage.' There was a delicate pause as she waited for Lexi's comment, and when none was forthcoming a glitter of malice appeared briefly before it was quickly masked. 'I imagine it was a difficult time for you.'

Lexi felt she owed no one an explanation, and any comment was superfluous.

'Finish your drink, darling,' Georg drawled, 'and we'll return to our seats.'

Lexi heard the cool bland words, yet they barely registered. *'Darling'*?

'You'll excuse us, Louise?'

Lexi's glass was taken from her hand, and beneath her startled gaze she watched as he calmly placed it, only half-empty, down on to a nearby tray.

Within seconds she found herself being drawn towards the auditorium.

'Do you mind unshackling me?' she demanded in a vicious undertone.

'Behave,' Georg adjured quietly. 'If you continue to struggle you'll only hurt yourself.'

'Damn you, let me go! I'm not a child in need of a restraining hand!'

It was a relief to reach their seats, and she was glad of the subdued lighting. It hid the faint angry flush that lay along her cheekbones and the glittering sparkle in the depths of her eyes.

A furtive but strong tug of her hand did no good at all, and the breath stilled in her throat as she felt the slight pressure of his thumb caressing the fast-pulsing veins at her wrist.

She turned towards him, only to find he had leaned sideways and his face was mere inches from her own.

'Have you no shame?' Lexi hissed, incensed almost beyond words as she saw his attention deliberately centre on the fullness of her mouth.

Slowly his eyes travelled up to meet her own, and she had to restrain herself from hitting him at the glimpse of mocking amusement apparent in their depths.

'None whatsoever.'

It was as well that the house lights dimmed then as the curtain rose for the third and final act, she decided vengefully. Otherwise she would have been tempted to slap his hateful face!

The dramatic conclusion to Cio-cio-san's tragic romance with an American naval officer was splendidly performed, and the depth and agonising pathos portrayed brought a lump to Lexi's throat as she was held enraptured by the sheer magical spell of the Japanese girl's emotional trauma.

Lexi was unable to prevent thoughts of her own disenchantment with Paul, the loss of trust, the deliberate deception, and her eyes began to ache as she sought to suppress the tell-tale shimmer of tears.

Dear heaven, what was the matter with her? Why tonight, of all night, did she have to fall prey to such maudlin emotions?

Because, an inner voice taunted, you've been thrust into a damnable situation where you're forced to conform to a set of circumstances with a man whose sense of purpose is nothing less than daunting.

Members of the Press were waiting in the foyer to photograph the more famous of the opera devotees, and any hope Lexi held for being able to slip away undetected died even before it was born as camera lenses were thrust in her face and a hard-voiced journalist asked a host of probing questions.

Georg handled it all with urbane charm, and Lexi had merely to smile. At last they were free, and she moved quickly at Georg's side as he led her through a side-door and down into the car park.

It wasn't until they were in the car that she began to relax, although her relief was short-lived as she realised that the Ferrari was heading towards the city.

'I'd prefer to go home, if you don't mind.'

He turned his head slightly and spared her a brief, inflexible glance, then concentrated on negotiating the traffic. 'Half an hour at the club will provide the opportunity for more publicity.' His voice assumed a silky drawl. 'I think you'll agree that's the main objective?'

'I would have thought the news hounds would be satisfied with our appearance at the opera,' she offered with a touch of cynicism, becoming impossibly angry when he offered no comment.

She maintained an icy silence until Georg brought the car to a halt in a city car park, and she slid out from the passenger seat, then closed the door with a firm clunk before flicking him a cool aloof glance.

'Thirty minutes,' she vouchsafed. 'Any longer and I'll call a taxi.'

He could annihilate her in a second. It was there in his eyes, the firm set of his mouth, and Lexi wondered at her own temerity in acting like a spoilt bitch.

'We either do this properly, or we won't do it at all,' Georg stated with chilling cynicism.

The desire to rage against his implacability was paramount, and her eyes warred openly with his, longing to consign him to hell. Never could she remember feeling so intensely angry; not even with Paul.

Without a word she moved away from the car and began walking towards the flight of stairs leading up to the carpeted lobby.

It wasn't surrender—more a case of restrained capitulation, she assured herself, supremely conscious of several patrons waiting for a lift to transport them to the trendy night-club situated on the top floor of the building.

The venue was crowded, attesting to its popularity, and intent on playing host to a plethora of 'beautiful' people who were more interested in being 'seen' as they flitted from table to table in the pursuit of compliments regarding their designer-label clothes and the success of their latest business dealings.

'What would you like to drink?'

Lexi's eyes flashed with a mixture of resentment and silent antipathy for one brief second before long thick lashes swept down to form a protective veil. 'Do I look as if I need one?'

'You look,' Georg drawled in a silky undertone, 'as if you've been thrown into a den of lions.'

He was too perceptive by far! The music was loud, the band excellent, and she let her gaze rove round the room, recognising at least half a dozen familiar faces.

'Georg, you decided to come. Louise said you would, but I hardly dared believed her.'

Lexi turned slightly to encounter an exquisite blonde whose appearance was as sexually blatant as her voice.

'Brigitte,' he acknowledged in an amused drawl. With casual ease he curved a possessive arm around Lexi's waist as he effected an introduction, and it took considerable effort on her part to proffer a brilliant smile.

'Are there any women you *don't* know?' she queried the instant Brigitte moved out of earshot.

'Shall we attempt the dance-floor?'

Oh, he was the very limit! 'Do I have any choice?'

Without a word he drew her towards the centre of the room, and she instinctively stiffened as he caught her close.

His hold was hardly conventional, and she wanted to tear herself away. *Pretend,* an inner voice chided. In all probability he no more wants to dance with you than you do with him! So just close your eyes, and follow his lead.

Except that it wasn't that simple. The cool crisp smell of his cologne mingled with the slight muskiness emanating from his skin, stirring alive an elusive chemistry that made her want to move even closer within his grasp.

It was almost as if she were in the grip of some magnetic force, and she gave an imperceptible start as she felt the brush of his lips against her temple.

Her eyes flew wide open, and for one brief second those brilliant depths mirrored a mixture of pain and outrage before assuming an opaqueness that shuttered the windows to her soul.

It was totally insane, but she felt as if somehow with subtle manipulation Georg Nicolaos had assumed control of her life, and it rankled unbearably.

Sheer will-power helped her survive the next half-hour as they alternately drifted round the dance-floor and paused to converse with fellow guests.

Lexi even managed to smile as they bade good-night to a few of Georg's acquaintances, and she suffered his arm at her waist as they traversed the lobby, rode the lift and ultimately reached the car.

Safely seated inside, she simply maintained an icy silence as he fired the engine and sent the car purring towards street level.

Traffic was moderately light, and she stared sightlessly out of the windscreen as he headed for Darling Point.

Lexi reached for the door-handle the instant the Ferrari slid to a halt outside the entrance to her apartment block, and she cast Georg a look of disbelief as he switched off the ignition and calmly stepped out of the car.

'Where do you think you're going?'

'Escorting you safely indoors, where you'll make me some coffee, which will take at least half an hour to consume.'

'The hell I will!' She was so furious she could have hit him, and she wrenched her arm in a fruitless attempt to be free of him. 'I'm tired, and I want to go to bed. I have an early-morning photographic shoot, and I need to look good!'

He was leading her inexorably towards the entrance. What was more, he'd calmly retrieved her security-coded card and a set of keys from her hand. Before she could voice any further protest they were indoors and heading towards the lift-shaft.

'A car tailed us all the way here,' Georg informed her silkily. 'Without doubt an enthusiastic journalist from one of the less salubrious tabloids.' He jabbed the call-button and the doors immediately slid open. 'We've brought a supposedly clandestine affair out into the open, and it will seem contradictory if I merely drop you off and drive away, don't you think?'

Safely inside the cubicle, she let loose some of her rage. 'I could have a headache!'

His hard, rough-chiselled features assumed mocking cynicism. 'Have you?'

'You, David—this whole wretched farce gives me a headache!' Lexi retorted waspishly.

The lift came to a halt, and she stepped quickly out and headed towards the furthest of two doors situated to the left.

Georg was there before her, the key in the lock, and she turned to face him as soon as the door closed shut.

All the pent-up fury erupted with potent force, and, unbiddcn, her hand snaked towards his face, the small explosion of sound seeming to rebound in the silence of the room.

His eyes gleamed with glittery anger, and for one horrifying second she thought he meant to strike her back.

He stood curiously still, in perfect control, yet Lexi only barely managed to suppress an involuntary shiver. Never in her life had she felt so threatened, and she unconsciously held her breath, her eyes wide and unblinking as she stood transfixed in mesmeric horror.

'Does that make you feel better?' Georg drawled with dangerous softness. He conducted a slow, deliberate appraisal of each and every one of her physical attributes, and she almost died at the expression in those dark eyes as they returned to meet her own, reflecting a savage ruthlessness that made her want to turn and run.

'Be warned,' he cautioned with icy remoteness. 'I will not be your whipping boy.' His eyes speared hers, activating an angry defiance deep within, turning her golden-hazel eyes a brilliant topaz with the sheer force of it.

'And I won't tolerate any tyrannical behaviour,' she retaliated, uncaring of the tiny flaring from the centre of those hard brown eyes.

'I am here in the guise of an ally, not your enemy,' he reminded her implacably.

'And it would be much easier if I were amenable?' She felt as if she were on a roller-coaster, experiencing the tumult of emotional fear and exhilaration that went with the thrill of courting danger.

'While I can understand your aversion to men in general,' he drawled, 'you would be advised to re-member that I am not cast from the same mould as your ex-husband.'

'That doesn't mean I have to like you.' Her at-tempt at cool anger failed dismally in the face of his mocking cynicism.

'My dear Lexi, you don't know me well enough to judge.'

She wanted to lash out, physically *hit* him, and be damned to the consequences. One transgression had been ignored, and she knew without doubt that another would bring retaliation of a kind she'd be wise to avoid.

'Will you please leave?'

'I'll make the coffee.'

He appeared so indomitable, so in control, that it was almost more than she could bear, and she was consumed with boiling rage as she followed on his heels into the kitchen.

'This is *my* home, dammit,' Lexi vented furiously, 'and I want you out of it!'

Georg assessed the well-designed kitchen with one sweeping glance, then reached for the percolator, extracted a drip filter, and set about grinding the coffee beans.

Lexi viewed his back with angry vexation. '*Damn* you, don't you listen?' She reached for his arm in an attempt to drag him round to face her, and felt the sheer strength of well-honed muscle beneath her fingers.

'I heard you.' He transferred the percolator on to the element and switched it on.

'Don't you dare ignore me!'

Georg turned slowly to face her, and suddenly she was supremely conscious of his close proximity, the powerful breadth of shoulder beneath its civilised sheath of expensive tailoring.

'If you continue to behave like a belligerent child I'll treat you like one.' The words were silky-soft, and dangerous with the threat of intent.

'Oh? What particular form of punishment do you have in mind?' She was so angry that she really didn't care any more. 'Be warned that if you so much as touch me I'll have you up for assault.'

His eyes became almost black, and his mouth tightened into a thin line. Without warning he caught hold of her shoulders and drew her inextricably close. So close that she was made aware of every tautened muscle and sinew.

'Don't——'

It was far too late to bargain with him, and she cried out as his head lowered to hers, his mouth fastening with unerring accuracy over her own as he forced her tightly closed lips apart.

A silent moan failed to find voice as he initiated a brutal assault on her senses, and she struggled against him, beating her fists against his back, his ribs—anywhere she could reach.

Her jaw ached from the sheer force of his possession, and she could have screamed with frustrated rage as every attempt she made to struggle free was halted with effortless ease.

Timeless minutes later he relinquished her mouth, and she stood in shocked silence as she made a conscious effort to regain her breath, hardly aware that her face was waxen-pale and her eyes were large luminous pools mirroring a mixture of pain and disbelief.

His features appeared blurred behind the slow well of tears, and she blinked rapidly to dispel their threatened spill.

If he'd wanted to deliver a lesson in male superiority he had succeeded, although her spirit wouldn't permit him the satisfaction of knowing the depth of her shaken emotions.

Sheer unadulterated pride was responsible for the slight tilt of her chin, while a degree of dignity and self-respect lent her eyes a fiery blaze.

'If you don't leave I'll walk out of the door and book myself into a hotel for the night,' Lexi declared in a deadly calm voice.

His appraisal was swift and clinically analytical as he surveyed her beautiful features, and she hated the knowledge she glimpsed in his gaze, the sure, unabating regard that was a perplexing mixture of ruthlessness and shameless sensuality.

His eyes held hers for what seemed an age, then they slid slowly down to settle on the soft fullness of her mouth before lifting to meet her startled defiant gaze.

Then he turned and walked towards the door, opened it, and closed it quietly behind him.

Somehow she had expected him to overrule her, and, although she desperately wanted him gone, his departure was something of an anticlimax.

Damn him! She was so impossibly angry she almost wished he were still in the apartment so that she could vent some of her rage.

Except there was the pain of her ravaged mouth as a vivid reminder, and she felt a sudden chill shiver down the length of her spine in the knowledge that Georg Nicolaos would never allow himself to be subservient to any woman, much less *her*.

The frantic bubbling of the percolator penetrated her mind, and she reached forward to switch off the element, opting instead for hot milk with a generous dash of brandy.

When it was ready she carried it through to the lounge and sank into one of the large leather sofas, slipping off her shoes and nestling her feet up beneath her as she slowly sipped from the mug.

A heavy silence permeated the room, almost as if the man who had not long vacated it had left something of his presence behind, Lexi brooded as she gazed sightlessly into space.

He was everything she hated in a man, she decided with damning frustration: self-assured, arrogant, and impossibly iron-willed.

If it weren't for Jonathan she'd condemn Georg Nicolaos to the nether regions of hell without so much as a second thought.

A long heartfelt sigh escaped her lips. Five weeks, David had intimated. It would be a miracle if she survived the distance.

The brandy began to soothe her fractured nerves, and when the laced milk was finished she drifted into her bedroom, stripped off her clothes, removed her make-up, and slipped into bed to sleep deeply until seven when the alarm shrilled its loud insistent summons to the start of a new day.

CHAPTER THREE

THE photographic session went way over time, with endless extra shots being required—to such an extent that it was all Lexi could do to contain her impatience as she obediently performed for the camera.

As much as she admired Peter's professional expertise, this morning for some reason his seemingly endless search for perfection proved tiresome, and she longed for the moment he would call a halt.

'That's good, darling. Chin a fraction higher. Now turn slowly towards me. *Great*. Smile. Sultry, sexy—that's the look I want. Pout a little. Sweep down with those eyelashes. Good. Now open. Look at me.' The shutter clicked with increasing rapidity. 'That's it, darling. I've got all I need.'

With a sigh of relief Lexi stepped away from the backdrop with its concentration of lights angling in from various points on the set. The heat they generated added at least ten degrees to the temperature inside the studio, and she longed for a cool shower.

She quickly effected a change of clothes in a dressing-room at the rear of the set, and, aware of the time, Lexi simply caught up her bag and emerged to cast Peter and his two assistants a hasty grin.

'Got to dash. I'm due to model at a fashion auction at one. *Ciao.*'

It took ten minutes to reach her apartment, a further fifteen minutes to shower and dress, then she slipped back into the car and drove towards the exclusive suburb of Woollahra.

Traffic seemed unusually congested, and she managed to miss almost every set of traffic-lights at each consecutive intersection. Consequently, by the time she had parked the Mercedes she had five minutes to spare before the auction was due to begin.

Held in an exclusive boutique and organised by its owner to aid of one of Lexi's favoured charities, with guest attendance strictly by invitation, it was a twice-yearly event for which she waived her normal fee. Designer labels were displayed by three professional models and individually auctioned at a cost price reserve. Considered a 'must' by the social élite, it was definitely an occasion, with champagne and hors-d'oeuvres offered by hired staff, followed at the auction's conclusion by a sumptuous array of savouries and continental cakes served with coffee and tea.

Organised chaos reigned in the small changing-room, and Lexi murmured a quick apology as she began pulling on a pair of sheer tights.

'*Lexi*. For heaven's sake, we thought you weren't going to make it in time!'

Anxiety coloured the older woman's voice, and Lexi proffered a soothing smile. 'Relax, Renée. Jacqueline is just now beginning her welcoming introductory speech. It will be at least five minutes before she's ready to announce the first of the collection.' She stepped into a silk half-slip, then dressed in the stunning ensemble that represented an exotic and expensive line in resort wear. With skilled fingers she swept her hair up into a casually contrived knot atop her head, added adept strokes with shadow and liner to highlight her eyes, blusher to her cheeks, then outlined her mouth and brushed colour over the contour of her lips. 'There. All done.' A quick check in the mirror, a practised smile at her own reflection, then she slid her feet into slender-heeled pumps and stood waiting with poised assurance for Jacqueline's call.

Possessed of an ebullient personality and an enviable degree of showmanship, Jacqueline was very much in charge of the auction, which soon assumed the theatrics of a stage production. Without doubt she held her 'audience' in the palm of her hand, and, suitably relaxed by a generous flow of fine champagne, her guests entered into the spirit of it all with a display of friendly rivalry as they attempted to outbid each other in their race for a bargain purchase.

Elegant day-wear soon gave way to a sophisticated line of tailored business-wear, and was followed by the after-five range.

Lexi completed her walk, gave a final turn, then moved quickly into the changing-room, effecting a smooth exchange of garments with swift professional ease.

The background music was muted, a tasteful selection that didn't compete with Jacqueline's spirited auctioneering, and Lexi emerged on cue in an absolutely stunning creation that could easily have been created for her alone.

Adopting a practised smile, she moved with easy fluidity to pause, turn, then repeat the process at three-metre intervals until she'd completed the pre-arranged circuit.

As she turned to face the guests her eyes were caught by a tall figure standing on the periphery of her vision.

Georg Nicolaos. What the *hell* was he doing here?

Looking incredibly arresting in a dark business suit, his pale blue shirt worn with a sombre silk tie, he represented an alien force in what was surely a feminine sphere.

Lexi forced herself to meet his gaze and hold it for a few seconds before transferring her attention elsewhere as the bidding became fiercely competitive.

'Two hundred and fifty.'

'Four hundred.'

Heads turned as if in synchronisation at the sound of a deep masculine drawl, and Jacqueline, with immediate recognition and an impish sense of humour, broke into tinkling laughter.

'Darlings, we *are* honoured this afternoon. For those of you who haven't read this morning's papers, Georg and our darling Lexi are an item.' She paused slightly and made a delicate fluttering movement with her elegantly manicured hands. 'Don't you think it's just marvellous?' Her smile held genuine warmth as she turned towards Lexi. 'I'm so pleased for you both.' Turning back towards her guests, she lifted her hands in an expressive gesture. 'Now, ladies, is anyone going to compete with Georg?'

'Four hundred and fifty.'

'Six hundred.'

Lexi's eyes widened fractionally as she forced herself to maintain a slight smile. Inside, she could feel the onset of helpless frustration and anger at his deliberate actions.

'Seven,' followed in feminine determination.

'One thousand,' Georg drawled, lifting one eyebrow in a gesture of musing indulgence at the sound of a few gasps.

He was deliberately attempting to set a precedent in their purported relationship. His appearance here would be regarded as juicy gossip, Lexi seethed, and as such it would be discussed, embellished, and circulated with wildfire speed.

Damn him!

'Eleven hundred.'

'Twelve,' another feminine bidder added, while yet another topped it by a further two hundred dollars.

Dear lord in heaven. They were caught up with the need to outbid each other, turning a civilised event into a circus.

'Two thousand,' Georg called calmly, and there was a hushed silence.

Would anyone else dare bid? Somehow Lexi doubted it. Even the most frivolous of the women present would balk at paying three times the gown's wholesale price.

'Sold,' Jacqueline declared with a delighted clap of her hands. 'Thank you, Georg.' She turned towards Lexi and directed an ecstatic smile. 'You, too, darling.' With professional ease she commandeered her guests' attention. 'Now, ladies, please prepare yourselves for the evening-wear selection. Then I have a little surprise in store.'

Lexi escaped into the changing-room, and her fingers shook as she slid out of the gown and handed it to the assistant before donning a strapless and practically backless figure-hugging creation in patterned silk.

Any hopes she held that Georg might have made an unobtrusive exit were dashed as she re-emerged, and in silent defiance she directed him a deliberately sultry smile before veiling her eyes.

It was almost half an hour before the last evening gown was sold, and with each passing minute Lexi felt as if her nerves were being stretched to breaking point.

Georg had declined to make another bid, and his presence merely whipped speculation to fever pitch. Lexi's sensory perception was so acute that she could almost *hear* what they were thinking.

'Now, darlings, I've added an extra line as a little titillation.' Jacqueline paused, allowing her words to have maximum effect. 'What you've seen so far will certainly gain your favourite man's attention. Now, for the grand finale we'll play an ace with a range of sleep-wear guaranteed to raise his——' she hesitated with theatrical precision, then a husky voluptuous laugh escaped her lips '—blood-pressure.' From the degree of laughter filtering through to the changing-room, the guests were in fine form, their normal reserve loosened somewhat by several glasses of champagne.

Lexi cast the final rack an experienced eye, and inwardly cringed. Exclusive, ruinously expensive, the items displayed represented the finest in silk, satin and lace, and were guaranteed by the designer to be original and unduplicated.

Even attired in the exquisitely fashioned teddy, she would be just as adequately covered as if she were modelling a swim-suit. Yet there was a wealth of difference in the degree of projected provocativeness.

For a moment she considered refusing, but there were three models and consequently three of every line. If she opted out Georg, as well as every guest present, would be aware of it, and she was damned if she'd give him that satisfaction.

With professional panache she took each call, modelling first the satin lounge pyjamas, following them with a silk nightgown and négligé set in soft peach-coloured silk. The nightgown was so exquisitely designed it could easily have been worn as an evening gown, and she gave the patrons full benefit of its delightful lines by removing the négligé and completing another round.

The teddy, with an ankle-length wrap in matching satin, was left until last and presented as the *pièce de résistance*.

Lexi was the last of the three models to emerge, and she unconsciously lifted her chin a fraction higher as she moved slowly around the room, deliberately not casting so much as a glance in Georg's direction.

'Remove the wrap, darling,' Jacqueline instructed, and Lexi shook her head as she conjured forth a witching smile.

'I prefer a little mystique, Jacqueline.' The wrap had no ties, and she was careful to ensure that the lapels covered each peak of her satin-and-lace-clad breasts. Her long slim legs were beautifully smooth and lightly tanned, and with considerable grace she lifted a hand to her head, released the weight of her hair so that it cascaded in a rippling flow of thick curls down her back, then she held out the edges of her wrap and executed a slow turn before moving towards the changing-room, not caring that she was breaking with one of Jacqueline's preferred rules.

'One thousand dollars.'

No one glimpsed the flash of fury in her lovely golden eyes at the sound of that deep, faintly accented masculine voice, nor the faint tightening of her lips as she heard Jacqueline's subtle teasing and Georg's evocative drawl in response.

Instead she concentrated on changing into her own clothes, and deliberately ignored the other two models' curiosity as she re-fastened her hair into a casually elegant knot at her nape.

She would have given anything to have slipped out of the side-door and make good her escape, but Jacqueline, Lexi knew, preferred her models to mix and mingle for at least ten minutes, during which she presented each with a fashion accessory for donating their time without fee to such a worthy cause.

The social conclusion to the afternoon gave her assistants time to discreetly collect payment and distribute purchases.

Perhaps Georg had already left, Lexi decided darkly, for only the strongest man would opt to stay in a room full of animated chattering women.

She was wrong, of course. Worse, he didn't appear to be even vaguely ill at ease, and she took her time in joining him as she paused to talk with first one guest and then another as she slowly moved towards the door.

Eventually there was nowhere else for her to go, and she tilted her head slightly, centring her attention on the bridge of his aristocratic Grecian nose.

'Georg.' Her voice was a deliberately husky drawl, and she slanted one eyebrow in a gesture of teasing mockery. 'What *are* you doing here?'

His features creased into a seemingly warm, intimate smile, and his eyes were so dark it was impossible to read their expression. 'I patronise the charity organisation which benefits from this auction,' he informed her, and, lifting a hand, he casually pushed a stray tendril of hair back behind her ear. 'Knowing you were one of the models was sufficient incentive for me to put in a personal appearance.'

Dear heaven, he was good! Too damned good, she decided darkly, aware they were the focus of attention.

How had he known she'd be here this afternoon? David? As close as she was to her brother, she didn't communicate to him her every move. Therefore Georg must have deliberately sought to discover her whereabouts. The thought rankled unbearably.

'Another brilliantly calculated ploy?' Lexi arched with deliberate softness, and saw his eyes narrow fractionally.

'Five minutes,' he cautioned quietly. 'Then we'll leave.'

A slow sweet smile widened her provocatively curved mouth. 'Any longer and I won't be able to sheathe my claws.' She was so angry it was almost impossible to still the faint shakiness of her hand as she accepted a glass of chilled water from a dutiful waitress, and she kept her eyes veiled beneath long fringed lashes in an attempt to hide her true feelings.

If he so much as *dared* to present her with his purchases in front of all these women she'd be hard pressed not to throw them back at him!

A hollow laugh rose and died in her throat. It would be ironic if they weren't for her at all. No matter how much *she* hated him, there could be no doubt he was held in considerable awe by members of the opposite sex.

'You haven't forgotten we're dining with Jonathan this evening?'

Lexi spared him a level glance. 'No.' Thank heaven David would be there to act as a buffer, for sitting through an intimate family dinner would tax her acting ability to its very limit.

'News of our...relationship has reached my mother.' His eyes probed hers, seeing the faint flaring of defiance, the latent anger simmering beneath the surface of her control. 'I have been severely chastised for not having brought you to meet her.'

Her fingers tightened round the stem of her glass, and she took a steadying breath. 'I'm not sure I can stand such devotion to familial duty.'

'Lexi! *Georg!*'

It was too much to hope that they might be left alone, and Lexi had to stop herself from physically flinching as the man at her side altered his stance so that his arm pressed against her shoulder.

'Jacqueline,' he acknowledged. 'How are you?'

'Absolutely fine, darling.' Her smile was genuine, and she case Lexi a warm glance. 'You were outstanding, as always. That touch of originality at the end was quite stunning.' Her eyes lit with a hint of mischievous humour. 'Georg was suitably appreciative.'

'Overwhelmed,' he drawled in musing acknowledgment as he extracted and handed Jacqueline his cheque. 'And understandably anxious for a private encore.'

Lexi was dimly aware of Jacqueline's tinkling laughter as she proffered two gold signature-emblazoned carrier-bags.

'A lovely addition to your wardrobe, darling,' Jacqueline accorded, and, leaning forward, she brushed her lips lightly against Lexi's cheek. 'I couldn't be more delighted.'

Lexi had never felt more like screaming with vexation in her life. Yet she had to smile and pretend that Georg's gift was warmly received. The moment they were alone, she promised herself, she would verbally *slay* him.

'If you'll excuse us, Jacqueline?' Georg said smoothly.

Lexi murmured a farewell and followed it with a captivating smile, then she turned and preceded Georg from the boutique, waiting until they were on the pavement and at least ten paces from its doors before expelling a deep breath.

'You were utterly *impossible*!'

'Where are you parked?'

'Don't you *dare* ignore me!' Frustrated anger filled her voice, and, even though she pitched it low, there could be no doubt as to the extent of her fury.

'I have no intention of ignoring you,' Georg replied with deceptive calm. 'But the footpath of an exclusive shopping centre is hardly the place for a slanging match.' He directed her a look that held infinite mockery. 'Unless, of course, you have no objection to an audience of interested bystanders.'

'Where would you suggest?' she threw vengefully.

'Your apartment,' he drawled. 'After which we'll visit my mother and then join Jonathan for dinner.'

In a moment she'd erupt! 'I'm sure your mother is delightful, but I'd rather delay meeting her for a few days if you don't mind.'

'Ah, but I do mind.' He was so darned imperturbable that she felt like slapping him! 'She is expecting us at five.'

'You can call her and cancel.' Lexi walked quickly along the street in an attempt to out-pace him, and it irked her unbearably that his stride appeared leisurely by comparison.

'She is elderly and very fragile. She is also irascible, speaks her mind, and likes to have command over her children.' His voice held musing affection. 'We tend to indulge her.'

She reached the car park, and crossed to her silver Mercedes. 'Your mother may have issued a royal edict, but right now I've had about as much of you as I can stand.' She extracted her keys and unlocked the door. 'Believe that if I could opt out of dinner tonight with Jonathan, I would!' In one graceful movement she slid in behind the wheel and fired the engine.

Easing the vehicle forward, she sent it moving swiftly towards the exit without sparing so much as a glance in her rear-view mirror, and she headed towards Darling Point, uncaring as to whether he followed or not.

He really was the most insufferable, antagonistic, *frightening* man she'd ever met, Lexi fumed as she reached her apartment block and swept below street level to her allotted parking space.

Within minutes of her entering her apartment the doorbell pealed, and she flung the door open to see Georg's tall frame filling the aperture.

'How did you get past security?' she demanded instantly.

'I produced credentials, and exerted sufficient influence.' He extended two carrier-bags. 'Yours,' he declared with dangerous softness, and her eyes flared brilliantly alive with frustrated rage.

'I can't possibly accept them.'

There was a leashed quality about his stance as he entered the lounge, a silent warning evident that only a fool would choose to disregard. 'Consider them a gift.'

'For which you paid an exorbitant amount,' Lexi vented furiously, 'under the guise of a charitable donation.'

'The purchases were immaterial.'

'The main reason for your appearance at the boutique was abundantly clear,' she accorded bitterly. 'By tomorrow the society grapevine will have relayed every little detail plus embellishment and supposition.'

'Without doubt.'

Her eyes flashed. 'You don't give a damn, do you?'

He looked at her in silence, his gaze unwaveringly direct, and there was an element of ruthlessness apparent when he spoke. 'Go and get changed.'

She drew a deep, angry breath. 'I am not visiting your mother. At least, not today.'

'She's expecting us.'

He made her feel like a recalcitrant child, and she was neither. 'I don't like domineering, autocratic men who relegate women to second-class citizenship merely because of their sex.' She glimpsed a tiny flare of anger in the depths of his eyes, and chose to ignore it. 'Will you please leave? I'd like to shower and change.'

'What do you imagine I'll do if I stay?' Georg mocked cynically. 'Invade your bedroom and subject you to a display of unbridled passion?'

She managed to hold his gaze, although there was nothing she could do to prevent the soft tinge of pink that coloured her cheeks. Remembering the force of his kiss was sufficient to enable her to imagine precisely how uninhibited his lovemaking would be.

Effecting a careless shrug, she turned and walked towards the hallway, reaching her bedroom with seemingly unhurried steps where she carefully closed the door.

Damn him! Why did he ruffle her composure? Worse, why did she allow him to succeed?

Twenty minutes later she added the last touch to her make-up, then stood back from the mirror to view her image with critical assessment.

The slim-fitting dress of peacock-blue silk accentuated her slight curves, and provided a perfect foil for her dark auburn hair worn in a smooth knot at her nape with a small bow in matching blue.

Perfume, her favourite Givenchy, was sprayed to several pulse-points, then she gathered up her evening-bag and made her way to the lounge.

Georg was standing by the window, and he turned as she entered the room, his eyes conducting a sweeping appraisal that brought forth an unconscious lift of her chin as she issued coolly, 'Shall we go?'

Lexi didn't offer so much as a word as they took the lift down to street level, and she maintained an icy silence as Georg sent the Ferrari east towards Vaucluse.

As much as she wanted to rail against him, there seemed little point in continuing an argument she couldn't win.

Several butterflies inside her stomach began a series of somersaults as Georg eased the Ferrari into a wide circular driveway and brought it to a halt behind a large Mercedes.

'Relax,' he advised quietly as he slipped out from behind the wheel and moved round to open her door, and Lexi directed a brilliant smile at him as she stepped out, and walked at his side towards the imposing entrance.

'I'm perfectly relaxed,' she assured. Her eyes challenged his—wide, gold and apparently guileless.

The front door opened and they were welcomed inside by a formally suited man whose demeanour was politely deferential. 'The family are assembled in the lounge, if you would care to go through.'

Georg smiled at the butler. 'Thanks, Nathaniel.'

Lexi drew a calming breath, and drew courage from the strength of her convictions.

'Georgiou! You are late! Everyone else is here!'

A tiny figure attired entirely in black was the visual attestation of an elderly matriarch, and despite her advanced years her eyes were surprisingly alert behind gold-rimmed glasses as she sat rigidly upright in a straight-backed chair.

Lexi proffered a conciliatory smile. 'The fault is mine.'

The dark brown eyes sharpened and conducted a swift analytical assessment. 'Indeed?'

'Georg informed me less than an hour ago that you were expecting us.' Her eyebrows rose fractionally and she effected a deprecatory gesture with her hands. 'I had just finished a modelling assignment and I needed to go home and change.'

'Georgiou, are you not going to introduce this young woman to us all?'

'Of course, Mama,' Georg conceded with lazy humour. 'Lexi Harrison.'

'Lexi? What name is that?'

'My mother's favoured derivation of Alexis,' she informed her calmly, refusing to be fazed in the slightest.

'You are divorced.'

'Yes, I am.' What was this—an inquisition, for heaven's sake?

'Mama,' Georg admonished with musing indolence. 'You presume too much.'

'I agree,' a deep voice drawled, and an older version of Georg moved forward, his smile warm and welcoming. 'Lexi, how are you?'

'Alex,' Lexi acknowledged, allowing her answering smile to encompass the slim attractive-looking woman at his side.

'My wife Samantha,' he introduced. 'And this,' he paused to indicate the little girl cradled in the curve of his arm, 'is our daughter Leanne.'

'She's beautiful,' Lexi complimented, for it was true. The wide-eyed sable-haired imp was utterly adorable.

'Yes,' Alex agreed, and his eyes settled on his wife with such infinite warmth that Lexi almost caught her breath. 'I am a very fortunate man.'

'Anna and Nick are not able to be here,' Mrs Nicolaos informed them. 'Tomorrow night we will have a celebratory dinner.' Her eyes did not leave Lexi for a second. 'Precisely what do you model, young woman, and when and where did you meet Georgiou?'

The elderly woman was persistent, and 'irascible' wasn't the right word! 'Clothes,' Lexi answered with every semblance of outward calm. 'The winter, spring, summer and autumn collections of well-known designers; photographic stills for fashion magazines, and the occasional television commercial.' It wasn't in her nature to be outrageous, but the temptation to shock was irresistible. 'I don't pose in the nude, nor do I resort to the type of photography that portrays women in a state of provocative dishabille.'

Mrs Nicolaos didn't bat so much as an eyelid. 'Of course not. Your father would have disowned you.'

Lexi effected a slight moue in silent agreement. 'I met your son——'

'At a party,' Georg intervened smoothly. 'Lexi was accompanied by her brother.'

'Hmm. I do not approve of divorce.'

'Neither do I,' Lexi responded evenly. 'If I'd had any sense I would have lived in sin instead of opting for marriage. Then I could have walked away relatively unscathed.'

'And Georgiou? Do you intend walking away from him?'

This was getting worse by the minute! 'I would walk away from any man who mistreated me,' she said quietly. 'Whether he was your son or not.'

There was a palpable silence during which Lexi held the older woman's direct gaze, and for a brief moment she glimpsed a softening in those dark eyes before they moved to settle on her youngest son.

'Georgiou, open the champagne. Alexandros, relinquish my granddaughter so that she may sit with me a while.'

Leanne, who surely should have been terrified of her grandmother, ran to her side the instant Alex set her down on her feet, and the transformation on Mrs Nicolaos's face was unbelievable as Leanne caught hold of her hand. The elderly woman spoke softly in Greek, and the child gazed at her in open adoration.

'She's a darling,' Samantha said gently, interpreting Lexi's glance. 'She also guards her family like a lioness. If it's any consolation, she attempted to tear me apart the first time Alex brought me here.'

'Champagne,' Georg announced, handing Samantha and Lexi each a slim crystal flute, while Alex crossed to his mother's side.

'Sit down. Why is everyone standing?' Mrs Nicolaos demanded, directing both Alex and Georg a fierce look.

'Out of deference to you, Mama,' Alex declared gently. 'If it pleases you for us to be seated, then we shall do so for a short while. Then we will leave, and you must rest.'

'Bah! I am not an invalid!'

'You are infinitely precious to us all. That is why our visits are designed not to overtax your strength.' Alex leaned forward and brushed his lips against the lined cheek. 'Now, shall we have our champagne?'

It was almost six when they made their farewells, and, seated in the Ferrari, Lexi leaned back against the head-rest as Georg fired the engine and eased the car down the driveway behind Alex's Mercedes.

'You didn't tell me it was going to be the Nicolaos family *en masse*,' she berated him the instant the car entered the street.

He gave her a dark, penetrating glance before returning his attention to the road. 'Does it matter that Alex and Samantha were there?'

'This whole thing is beginning to getting out of hand,' she retaliated, hating the degree of deception involved. In the beginning it had seemed relatively uncomplicated, and now she wasn't so sure.

'Yet you were aware when you agreed that it was all or nothing,' Georg reminded her silkily.

'At the time I had little conception of what "all" would involve,' Lexi opined drily.

Only a few blocks separated his mother's home from Jonathan's exclusive residence, and they reached the elegant tudor-styled mansion in less than five minutes.

David's Ferrari was nowhere in sight, and Lexi wasn't sure whether to be relieved or disappointed at being the first to arrive.

'Before we go inside I suggest you slip this on.'

'This' was a brilliant square diamond set on a slender gold band, and she looked at him in consternation. 'You can't be serious?'

'Very.'

'Don't you think it's taking things a bit too far?'

'If we've been keeping our affair under wraps until your divorce was finalised, now that we've gone public surely the next logical step is a formal announcement of our forthcoming marriage?'

'*No.*'

'You don't think Jonathan will rest easy until he has proof that my intentions are honourable?'

Her eyes glittered with unspoken rage as he calmly slid the ring on to her finger. 'Damn you,' she accorded bitterly.

'Shall we go in?' There was an edge of mockery apparent. 'I imagine Sophie has heard us arrive, and your father will be curious as to why we're taking so long.'

CHAPTER FOUR

JONATHAN greeted them at the door, and Lexi returned his affectionate embrace with enthusiasm, smiling as he put her at arm's length.

'Come inside. I thought we'd relax out on the terrace. David will be delayed by about ten minutes, and Sophie has organised dinner for six-thirty.'

Home. The house where she had grown up, she mused as she followed Jonathan indoors. It was amazing how secure she felt within these walls, how protected.

It took only a few minutes for him to notice the significance of the ring on her finger. His pleasure brought her close to tears, and she could hardly protest when he brought out a bottle of Dom Perignon to celebrate the occasion.

'I'm delighted to have you both as my guests.'

The genuineness of her father's enthusiasm couldn't be doubted, and Lexi managed a suitable smile in response.

Georg, damn him, stayed close to her side, and even David's arrival did little to diminish his attention.

The warmth of his smile appeared so honest it was all she could do not to reel from its impact, and she was forced to suffer the touch of his hand on her elbow as he led her into dinner.

Sophie served the first course, a delicious beef consommé, and followed it with deep-fried prawns in a nest of finely shredded lettuce. The main course was a superb duck *à l'orange* with tiny roast potatoes, honeyed carrots, courgettes and beans.

David took care to ensure that the appropriate wine accompanied each course, although Lexi sipped at the contents of her glass and declined to have it refilled, opting for chilled water instead.

Conversation flowed, touching on a variety of subjects that pertained primarily to business and mutual acquaintances, and to all intents and purposes it appeared to be a convivial family gathering.

It proved, Lexi perceived a trifle wryly, what excellent actors they were.

'When do you go into hospital, Daddy?' It was a question she had to ask, and there was nothing she could do to mask her anxiety.

'Sunday week, darling,' Jonathan revealed gently. 'Surgery is scheduled for the following day.'

'You've always been so careful, eating the right foods, not smoking, exercising each day. I can't believe something like this could happen to you.'

'Let's admit it, Father is a human dynamo,' David declared with a slow smile. 'Always accepting a new challenge, fighting to make it succeed. Continually pitting his wits against unforeseen obstacles.'

Lexi captured her father's eyes and held them with her own. 'I think you'd better re-evaluate your life and slow down.' Without thought, she added with a light laugh, 'I want you around to appreciate your grandchildren.'

'Indeed,' Georg acceded with musing enthusiasm, and there was nothing Lexi could do in protest as he lifted her hand to his lips to kiss each finger in turn—a deliberately blatant gesture that taxed all her strength not to snatch her hand from his grasp.

'Grandchildren,' Jonathan repeated bemusedly. 'I like that idea.'

'You'll forgive me if I agree,' Georg declared with a husky chuckle, leaving no one in any doubt just where his thoughts lay.

Lexi reached out and deliberately traced the tip of her highly polished fingernail across the back of his left hand as she directed him a brilliantly warm smile. 'Steady, darling. I've only just accepted your engagement ring.'

As if sensing her protest Georg lifted a hand and his gaze was infinitely disturbed as he touched a finger to her lips. 'Something which has made me a very happy man.'

She wanted to *kill* him. Yet all she could do was smile.

'Have you made any plans for the wedding?'

'We thought a quiet affair, confined to family and close friends. Five weeks from now,' Georg indicated, and, on hearing Lexi's slightly audible gasp, he leant forward and bestowed a fleeting kiss on her as she opened her mouth to protest. 'If I had my way we'd obtain a special licence and marry within a matter of days.'

How could he sit there and announce such a thing? Lexi was so utterly furious that it was a wonder she didn't erupt with rage.

He turned towards Jonathan, totally ignoring her. 'That will give you time to recuperate sufficiently from surgery. Are you happy to leave all the arrangements to me?'

Her father couldn't have looked more delighted. 'Of course. I can't begin to tell you both how happy this makes me. Now I can enter hospital with a clear mind, knowing that if anything happens Lexi will be taken care of by someone who has my utmost respect.'

Oh, dear lord! After such fulsome enthusiasm how could she possibly refute it? Lexi groaned with frustration. But how far did it have to go? Surely specific arrangements for a wedding were hardly necessary?

'A church wedding, darling?'

'I don't think so, Daddy,' she negated quietly. 'I had all that before.' She lifted a hand and smoothed back a stray tendril of hair in a purely defensive gesture.

'The gardens are lovely—so colourful at this time of year,' Jonathan enthused. 'Would you consider marrying at home?'

'A marvellous idea,' Georg conceded, slanting Lexi such a warm glance that she almost reeled from its implied intimacy. 'Early afternoon? Followed by champagne and hors-d'oeuvres. Unless there is any objection, I would prefer the reception to be held in the restaurant. It is regarded as something of a family tradition, and would give my mother immense pleasure.'

The tension robbed her of her appetite, and she declined dessert and the cheeseboard, and opted instead for coffee laced with liqueur and cream.

Consequently her nerves had tightened almost to breaking point by the time they took their leave.

'Take good care of Lexi for me,' Jonathan bade Georg as he escorted them to the door.

'I fully intend to,' Georg declared with quiet emphasis, and Lexi was forced to suffer his arm about her waist as he led her down to the car.

Almost as soon as they were clear of the driveway she burst into angry, voluble speech.

'Did you *have* to be so——' she paused as words momentarily failed her '—proprietorial?' Her fingers clenched until the knuckles showed white as she gripped the clasp of her evening-bag. 'You sat there so damned *calmly*, looking at me as if...' She trailed to a frustrated halt, loath to say what Georg had no compunction in voicing.

'I couldn't wait to get you home and into bed?' he completed in a drawling tone, adding with cynical mockery, 'Is it so surprising that I might want to?'

'Discussing a wedding and prospective grand-children!' Outrage brought her anger to boiling point. 'It was totally ridiculous!'

'If I remember correctly, it was you who brought up the subject of grandchildren,' he alluded in droll tones, and she clenched her hands in an effort not to physically *hit* him!

'What on earth do you think you're *doing*, for heaven's sake?'

'Driving you home.'

An impossible fury rose within. 'Don't be facetious!'

'We'll discuss it rationally over coffee.'

'You're being deliberately evasive, skilfully utilising boardroom tactics to avoid the issue!' she accused heatedly.

'I am merely attempting to defuse your temper sufficiently until I'm in a position to satisfactorily deal with it.'

'Don't you dare patronise me. I won't stand for it!'

He didn't respond, and she sat in angry silence for several seconds before turning towards him. 'Stop the car. I'll hail a taxi.' She was so incensed that she reached for the door-handle without even caring that the car was travelling along the main arterial road towards Rose Bay.

'Don't be a fool!'

His words were harsh, demanding obedience, and she instinctively braced her body as he brought the Ferrari to a smooth halt alongside the kerb.

The handle refused to function, and she pulled at it fruitlessly for a number of seconds before becoming aware that he'd activated the locking mechanism.

'Release it, damn you!'

'I will, when you've calmed down,' Georg voiced implacably, switching off the engine and turning sideways to face her.

Incensed almost beyond endurance, she turned and lashed out at him, an action that was swiftly stilled as he caught hold of her hands and held them in a bone-crushing grip.

'You unspeakable fiend!' Topaz eyes glittered with fury as she made a futile attempt to break free.

His hands tightened, and she cried out in pain. 'You'll only succeed in hurting yourself.'

Part of her was appalled by the enormity of her actions while the other deplored the extent of her behaviour. 'Then let me go.'

His hard, intent stare played havoc with her nerve-ends, and she stifled a silent scream at the strength of purpose in those chilling depths. 'Your hands, yes,' he agreed, relinquishing them, and she rubbed them to ease the bruised bones.

She felt like a steel rope that had been rendered taut almost to breaking point. At any second she was in danger of snapping. Her mouth quivered as she drew a deep calming breath, and her hands shook uncontrollably.

'Perhaps you would care to tell me why you react so violently at the thought that a man might want to make love to you?'

Her thoughts scattered into a deep dark void where she couldn't retrieve them, and she stared blankly out of the windscreen, unable to summon her voice through the physical lump that had risen in her throat.

No one, not even Jonathan—dear lord, especially not Jonathan—knew just how deep were the scars from her association with Paul. The night she'd left him would be indelibly imprinted in her brain for as long as she lived. The explosive argument, one of many they'd had over money, had resulted in her expressing an intention to leave him and had ended in physical abuse of the worst kind. Paul had forced her to submit to sex, and afterwards she'd simply pulled on some clothes and ordered a taxi to take her to a motel. The next day she'd rung Jonathan and David and told them the marriage was over.

Lexi had little idea of the passage of time. It could have been five minutes or fifteen; she retained no recollection. At last she moved her head slightly, and her pale profile stood out in sharp contrast against the night's darkness.

'There's a beach not far from here. I'd like to walk for a while.'

Her voice sounded strangely quiet, almost disembodied, and she wasn't conscious of him reaching for the ignition until she heard the refined purr of the engine.

She sat in silence as he traversed the distance then pulled to a halt alongside a short flight of steps leading down on to the sandy foreshore.

Georg slid out from behind the wheel and walked round to open her door, watching with narrowed eyes as she slipped off her shoes.

He followed her actions, pushing the elegant hand-crafted imported shoes on to the floor before bending low to turn up the cuffs of his trousers. Then he straightened and locked the car, taking care to activate the alarm before moving to the head of the steps where he stood, impossibly tall and vaguely forbidding, silhouetted against the skyline.

The stretch of beach appeared deserted, and she longed for solitude. 'I can walk on my own.'

'I go with you, or you don't go at all,' Georg declared inflexibly.

Without a further word she moved past him, and, once down on the sand, she wandered out towards the gentle out-going tide, then began following its edge as the bay curved towards an outcrop of rocks.

There was a faint breeze, and she felt it tease loose a few strands of hair so that they brushed against her face.

The sand was wet beneath her bare feet, and there was just the soft sound of water lapping gently against the distant rocks. Every now and then a car sped past on the road, but the noise was far enough away not to intrude.

Somehow she expected Georg to attempt conversation, but he walked at her side in silence, and she was grateful for his perception.

On reaching the rocks, they turned as if by tacit agreement and began retracing their steps. Lexi felt the cool air on her face, and in an unbidden gesture she lifted her hand to her hair and freed the knot so that its length fell down her shoulders.

A sense of peace invaded her being, rather like the calm after a storm, and she tried to tell herself that it had nothing to do with the man at her side.

Instinct warned her that he was someone she would infinitely prefer to have as a friend than an enemy, for in opposition he'd prove a formidable force.

A slight shiver shook her slim frame, although it had nothing to do with feeling cold, and she gave a start of surprise when he shrugged off his jacket and placed it around her shoulders.

His fingers brushed her nape as he lifted her hair free, and Lexi spared him a quick glance, unable to read anything from his expression, and her murmured thanks sounded indistinct on the night air.

For some strange reason she felt as if she'd been enveloped in a security blanket, and she wasn't sure whether to feel alarmed or relieved.

The smooth jacket-lining was silky against her skin, and still held the warmth from his body. It was far too big for her, and its weight brought an awareness of his height and breadth. Evident, too, was the clean smell of the fine woollen material and the elusive woody tones of his cologne.

They reached the short flight of steps leading up on to the road far too quickly, and after dusting sand from their feet they each retrieved their shoes prior to sliding into the car.

Within a matter of minutes the Ferrari drew to a halt in the courtyard adjoining her apartment block, and she was powerless to prevent him from following her indoors.

Any argument seemed futile, and she simply extracted her key while they took the lift to her designated floor.

'Coffee?'

Lexi closed her eyes, then slowly opened them again in utter frustration. 'If you want coffee, *you* make it!'

He took the key from her fingers and unlocked the door, then he pushed her gently inside. 'I fully intend to,' he drawled. 'I merely asked if you would like some.'

'Oh—go to hell!'

His eyes speared hers, dark and fathoms deep with the silent threat of an emotion she didn't even begin to comprehend. 'Believe that I could take you there, and you would hate every second of it.'

Her whole body froze in seemingly slow motion, and her eyes became wide as they assumed a haunted, hunted quality. A glaze seemed to dull their expression as she stared sightlessly ahead, oblivious to her surroundings, the man a few feet distant—*everything* except a vivid event that would never be erased from her memory.

When he lifted a hand towards her she visibly flinched and averted her head to one side, instinctively shielding her face with her hands, and therefore missing the brief hardness that flared in his eyes.

'Cristos!' The harsh, softly husked oath sounded savage in the silence of the room, but it barely registered. He made a compulsive movement, then checked it as he demanded in a dangerously soft voice, 'Did Paul *hit* you?'

She blinked slowly, and the glaze gradually dissipated. A shiver shook her slender frame, and she hugged her arms together across her breasts in an attempt to contain it.

'Answer me, Lexi.'

The quietness of his voice didn't deceive her, and she stood, hesitant, loath to resurrect that fateful night.

'Yes.'

'Nothing more?'

She looked at him fearlessly as the silence between them became a palpable entity. Her breath hurt in her throat, constricting it almost beyond the ability to speak. 'Does it matter?'

She sensed his inner rage as he murmured something viciously explicit in his own language, and her chin lifted in an unbidden gesture as she sought a measure of strength.

'I think I'd like that coffee,' she indicated, meeting his compelling gaze with courage and dignity.

Georg's stance didn't alter for several heart-stopping seconds, then he turned and made his way towards the kitchen.

When he returned he placed a tall handled glass into her hands. 'Drink all of it.'

Lexi tasted the contents, and effected a faint grimace in recognition of the measure of brandy he'd added to the cream-topped brew. She almost never touched spirits, and it was more than a year since she'd had to resort to taking the occasional sleeping-pill. Obediently she sipped until the glass was empty, then set it down on a nearby table.

'Would you mind leaving now? It's late, and I'd like to go to bed.'

He slowly drained his glass, then held it between his hands. 'Have lunch with me tomorrow.'

'Today,' Lexi corrected absently. 'And no, I think I'd rather be alone.' The beginnings of a faint smile tugged one edge of her mouth. 'We're dining with your mother. I'll need to harness all my resources.'

'My family is not in the least formidable.'

She moved towards the lobby, and paused by the front door. 'That's a matter of opinion.'

Gentle fingers lifted her chin, and her lashes swiftly lowered as she felt his fingertips trace the outline of her mouth. Beneath his feather-light touch she was unable to control the slight trembling, and she stood very still as he brushed his lips against her temple.

'Be ready at six.'

As soon as he had gone she locked up and moved back into the lounge, activating the television set in a bid to discover a programme that would catch her interest until exhaustion set in and provided an escape into oblivion.

CHAPTER FIVE

LEXI chose to wear a stunning gown in emerald-green silk, its smooth lines hugging the delicate curves of her breasts, her waist, then flaring out from the hips to fall in generous folds to calf-length. Matching shoes and evening-bag completed the outfit, and her make-up was deliberately under-stated. In a last-minute decision she opted to leave her hair loose, using side-clips to hold its thick length away from her face.

The doorbell chimed just as she emerged into the lounge, and she moved quickly towards the lobby to answer its summons.

Georg stood framed in the aperture, attired in an immaculate dark suit and white linen shirt, and exuding a combination of dynamic masculinity and raw virility. 'Punctuality is one of your virtues,' he greeted her with a slow disturbing smile, and Lexi effected a faint shrug.

'Not always. Shall we leave?'

George headed the Ferrari towards Double Bay and slid to a halt adjacent to the shopping centre.

'Why are you stopping here?'

'Quite simply because this is where we're dining.'

'The restaurant? I thought we were dining with your mother,' Lexi said, faintly perplexed at the change in plan.

'Mama suggested that we celebrate according to Greek tradition,' Georg informed her smoothly. 'So tonight the restaurant is closed to all but family and close friends.'

'A party?'

'Specifically to celebrate our forthcoming marriage.'

She felt the nerves in her stomach clench in painful rejection. 'This entire débâcle gets worse with every passing day,' she opined wretchedly.

His appraisal was swiftly analytical as he raked her slim form. 'Relax.'

'How can I relax?' she retorted. 'Your family and friends will examine and dissect my every word as they attempt to determine whether I'm worthy of acceptance into the Nicolaos clan.'

'There can be no doubt that they will approve my choice,' he mocked, and she gave a short laugh.

'No one would dare oppose you.'

'You do,' he drawled.

'Only because you have the ability to make me impossibly angry!'

'We're almost there,' Georg declared imperturbably.

'And it's smile-time,' she said with a trace of bitterness.'

'You do it so well.'

'Oh, stop being so damned cynical!' She was almost at the end of her tether, and being faced with the prospect of a celebratory party where they would be the focus of attention was almost more than she could bear.

Yet somehow she managed to portray a combination of gracious sincerity and suitable bewitchment with the youngest Nicolaos son.

There was a variety of food to tempt the most critical palate, and sufficient of it to feed an army. Beneath Georg's persuasive touch, Lexi sampled several delicacies and followed it with a light white wine.

At times she thought she was a little over the top, and Georg merely compounded the situation by playing the part of adoring lover to the hilt.

Her ring was admired and commented upon, and inevitably the question arose as to a possible wedding date.

'The end of January,' Georg revealed, and laughed softly at Lexi's obvious surprise. 'Do you blame me? I have no intention of allowing her to slip through my fingers.'

'And the honeymoon?'

'Greece. Where else?'

Where else, indeed?

'Are you *mad*?' Lexi demanded in a subdued voice the instant they had a moment alone. To any onlookers they must appear a loving couple, drifting close together on the dance-floor. Bouzoukis played softly in the background a haunting melody that seemed filled with pathos, as were many of the Greek songs.

'All of these people are very dear friends,' Georg murmured close to her ear.

'There can be no mistake that they imagine this to be an engagement party.' She was so angry that her whole body shook with it. 'They've brought gifts, which will have to be returned. And why did you have to give out a wedding date?'

'In a few minutes the music will change. The women will sit at the tables and watch as the men take to the floor and dance.'

Lexi looked at him with helpless frustration. 'Including you?'

'Especially me,' he informed cynically, 'in an attempt to convince everyone I am a strong virile man who will promise his prospective wife many fine sons to carry the Nicolaos name.'

'The dance is a feat of strength?'

'Symbolic endurance,' George drawled, and his dark eyes gleamed with amusement as twin flags of colour stained her cheeks. 'Come, you will sit with my mother, Anna and Samantha.'

'I'll probably walk straight out the door.'

'Be sure that I will follow and drag you back.'

The threat of his intent was without doubt, and, unbidden, her eyes moved to rest on the sensual curve of his mouth, widening slightly and assuming momentary vulnerability in memory of the havoc he'd wrought the previous evening.

His gaze narrowed, then he lowered his head down to hers.

No one could possibly have heard what they were saying, and there wasn't one guest present who doubted the reason behind the brief seemingly passionate kiss the prospective bridegroom bestowed on his bride-to-be in the middle of the dance-floor before leading her to sit in the bosom of his family as the music assumed a traditional slow lilting beat.

Lexi sat perfectly still, a smile fixed permanently in place, as each of the men removed their jackets and rolled back their shirt-sleeves before taking up their positions on the dance-floor.

Together, with arms outstretched and in perfect unison, they began to move in time to the music, their steps quickening as the beat slowly increased, until only the very fit were able to sustain the rapid tempo.

Alex and Anna's husband Nick remained with Georg, as well as a few of the younger men, and Lexi found herself unconsciously holding her breath as the impossible beat continued.

There was a crash of broken crockery as a plate hit the wooden floor, quickly followed by another, until it was difficult to distinguish the sound of each plate.

'Lexi. Here is one for you.'

Turning, she saw the proffered plate extended in Samantha's hand.

'Throw it as a gesture of appreciation.'

'You're joking.'

'It will be noticed if you don't,' Samantha cautioned softly. 'By everyone.'

'Greek tradition?'

A mischievous smile lit Samantha's beautiful features. 'Feminine enthusiasm.'

Taking the plate, Lexi looked at Georg and calmly threw it on to the floor. For her it was a gesture of suppressed anger, and, without thinking, she picked up another for good measure and sent it following in the path of the first.

It was only when she had another plate pressed into her hand that she realised the significance of the numbers thrown.

Georg, damn him, merely laughed, his dark eyes alive with devilish humour, and Lexi wanted to curl up and die as Mrs Nicolaos took up a plate and extended it.

To refuse would have been incredibly rude, and, forcing a smile, she took it and sent it crashing to the floor.

'Well done,' Samantha accorded softly. 'You've now been officially accepted into the family.'

The music reached a crescendo, then abruptly stopped, and Lexi soon saw why as several waiters with brooms appeared and began clearing up the debris, while the men had glasses of wine pressed into their hands to quench their thirst.

It wasn't long before the bouzoukis were taken up again, and this time the men fetched their womenfolk on to the dance-floor.

Georg's skin felt warm beneath her fingers, his arms hard with corded muscle, and there was nothing Lexi could do to prevent being held close in against his body. She could feel the powerful beat of his heart, and sense the musky aroma of his cologne.

'Soon Alex and Samantha will take Mama home, then gradually everyone will leave,' Georg informed her as he led her among the dancing couples.

'Your mother is amazing,' she told him.

'Be sure that she has rested all day, and tomorrow will not be permitted to rise from her bed.'

'You're extremely protective of her.'

'Mama is a very special woman,' he accorded quietly. 'Her husband, his dreams; the children, and now the grandchildren. Together they have been her reason for living.' She sensed his faint smile. 'You have her approval.'

'Should I feel flattered?'

'Without question.'

'I wonder why,' Lexi mused. 'Could it be because I stand up for myself, and don't pretend you're God and any number of sacred saints all rolled into one?'

He slanted her a wry look that was tempered with humour. 'Perhaps she sees, as I do, a girl whose inner beauty surpasses her physical attributes.'

The breath caught in her throat. 'I don't think either of you knows me well enough to reach an adequate conclusion.'

'No?'

She felt defeated, and stiffened slightly as his lips brushed her temple. 'Please don't.'

'What a contrary combination of words,' Georg mocked. 'The first encourages, while the second is a refusal.'

'Perhaps I unconsciously chose them because I am a contrary creature!'

Gently he withdrew his arms, and her eyes reflected the sudden loss of security before she successfully masked their expression. 'Alex is about to leave with Mama,' he informed. 'Come, we will bid them goodnight, then stand together and thank our guests as they leave.'

It was an hour before they were able to get away, and in the car Lexi simply leaned well back and let her head sink against the head-rest. As Georg fired the engine, she closed her eyes, and didn't open them until he brought the car to a standstill outside the entrance to her apartment block.

'There's no need for you to come in.'

'Nevertheless, I will see you safely indoors.'

It was far too late to protest, and she was overcome with helpless frustration as she passed through the entrance lobby *en route* to the lifts.

'Don't you ever *listen*?' she burst out scant minutes later as he withdrew her set of keys, selected one and inserted it into the lock of her apartment.

'Always.'

'Then why are you *here*?'

He took time to close the door carefully before turning back to face her. 'Would you believe— because I want to be?'

Lexi closed her eyes, then slowly opened them again. 'Doesn't it matter that *I* don't want you here?'

He reached forward and brushed his fingers lightly along the edge of her jaw, then slipped to cup her chin. 'Precisely what are you afraid of?' Georg queried with cynical mockery, and her eyes assumed the hue of brilliant gold.

'Will you please leave? I'm tired and I want to go to bed.'

'Are you working tomorrow?'

'No. I intend sleeping in, then taking a picnic lunch to the beach, where I can enjoy a few hours of uninterrupted solitude.'

'In preparation for the party we're to attend tomorrow evening,' he drawled, and, leaning forward, he kissed her on the mouth, a hard, passionate possession that left her wide-eyed and faintly hurt. 'Sweet dreams, Lexi.'

Then he turned and left, closing the door quietly behind him.

* * *

Lexi chose a beach more than an hour's drive north of the city, and, with Christmas only a matter of days away, there were very few people electing to spend valuable shopping time lazing on a sandy foreshore.

For a number of hours she simply stretched out beneath the shade of a beach umbrella and read a thick paperback, then she applied a liberal dose of sunscreen and cautiously exposed herself to the sun's rays for a short space of time.

At four she packed everything into the boot of the Mercedes and drove back to Darling Point, where she showered and shampooed her hair in preparation for the evening ahead.

The party was a perfectly splendid affair, Lexi mused as she stood with apparent ease at Georg's side in a sumptuously appointed lounge of a harbourside mansion noted for being one of the city's finest. The guests numbered among the social élite, and each of the women appeared to have spent several hours, if not the entire day, on their appearance, so exquisitely perfect were their hair-styles and make-up. Collectively their designer clothes would have cost a small fortune, and a king's ransom was represented in jewellery.

She took a small sip of an innocuously mild spritzer, then gave a faint start of surprise as she saw Anaïs Pembleton moving determinedly towards them.

'Lexi, *darling*, how are you?' Without pausing for breath, the society matron greeted Georg. 'I'm so pleased you've managed to persuade this beautiful, beautiful girl back on to the social scene.'

'Anaïs,' Georg acknowledged, his expression politely bland.

'Congratulations are in order, I hear. May one ask when the wedding is to take place?'

'Oh, there's no hurry,' Lexi hastened to reply swiftly, only to be caught by Georg's look of musing indulgence.

'I am not a patient man,' he offered with a warm smile. 'If I had my way it would be tomorrow.'

Lexi seethed in silence, angry beyond belief at Georg's deliberate ploy. The sound of the society matron's laughter was the living end, and she gave into temptation and uttered sweetly, 'You know what they say about "once bitten, twice shy".'

'Oh, yes, darling. But this time, surely it's different?' The emphasis was there, and it succeeded in rousing her temper almost to boiling point. 'I mean, Georg is impossibly rich, whereas Paul . . .'

There was a faint pause, and Lexi finished with seeming sweetness, 'Was a Lothario and a leech?' Her eyes contained a dangerous sparkle. 'Why not say it to my face, Anaïs? It's no secret that it's been said behind my back.'

There was a faint gasp, then the older woman drew herself up to her full height as she mentally bore down on the slim young girl facing up to her with far more courage than she'd ever imagined possible. 'My dear Lexi,' she purred softly, 'you're surely not accusing me of anything?'

Lexi's smile was the epitome of innocence. 'Now why should you imagine that?'

'I am no rumour-monger,' Anaïs Pembleton assured with chilling hauteur.

'Merely a purveyor of purported fact.' Lexi attempted to defuse the strength of her stinging words with a solemn and faintly sad smile. 'If you'll excuse me, I really must powder my nose.' There was no need for any part of her exquisitely made-up features to be retouched, but if she didn't escape now she'd end up saying something totally regrettable.

The powder-room was empty, and Lexi withdrew several tissues, dampened them, then pressed the refreshingly cool pads against both temples before standing back to examine her features.

Her eyes looked incredibly large and luminous, and there were twin flags of colour high on each cheekbone. Her mouth looked far too full. Luscious, she decided, twisting the curved edges into an expression of self-derision.

She possessed the kind of looks most girls would have killed for, and a figure that was the envy of any self-respecting female. Nature, she accorded, had certainly been extremely gracious in her endowment. Add a successful career, bankability, considerable assets, and it all added up to something that was almost too good to be true.

On an impulse she lifted her hands and tore out the restraining pins from her hair, letting its length cascade down her back in a glorious thick mass of curls.

Gone was the slender-necked society belle with her air of fragility, for now Lexi resembled a contender in the promiscuity stakes.

A quirk of amusement lifted the edge of her lips. It was amazing what a different hairstyle and a change in expression could do! It remained to be seen whether Georg would appreciate the difference.

There was a gleam of defiance in her eyes as she entered the lounge, and she saw him at once, standing tall in a group of elegantly suited men.

It was marvellous how men gravitated towards each other on the pretext of discussing business. Jonathan was a prime example, as was David.

Perhaps it was time to give Georg a taste of his own medicine. A social occasion was meant to be exactly that—social, she determined, as she threaded her way through the guests to where he stood. And *she* could play charades equally as well as he could!

Deep in conversation, he turned slightly, then his gaze narrowed fractionally as he caught sight of her.

'Darling,' Lexi greeted, a deceptively soft smile parting her mouth as she placed fingers on the sleeve of his jacket. 'I'm dying of thirst.' Her eyes were wide and deep as she gazed up at him. 'Would you mind getting me another drink?'

'Of course,' Georg acceded as he excused himself from the group. 'Wine, or something stronger?'

'Stronger, definitely.'

'That bad?' he quizzed lightly. 'You sound as if you're planning an escape.'

Her lashes swept high and wide, and she attempted a singularly sweet smile. 'Only cowards cut and run, and I won't allow Anaïs Pembleton the pleasure.'

His gleaming gaze did strange things to her equilibrium. 'Then why not forgo the drink, and we'll drift out on to the terrace and dance?'

Lexi swallowed the sudden lump that had risen in her throat. 'No, I don't think so.'

'Afraid, *darling*?'

Her chin lifted fractionally. 'Of you, Georg?' She tilted her head slightly in the pretence of examining his features. 'You're so shockingly powerful, one derives the impression you have only to blink and the markets tremble. Yet I don't fear you.'

'Perhaps you should.'

Her eyes didn't waver. 'If you don't want to fetch me a drink I'll get one myself.'

Without a word he moved towards the bar, and returned with a vodka and orange juice.

'Did Jonathan never spank you as a child?' he queried mildly as she took the glass from his hand.

'He never had to,' Lexi retorted swiftly.

His mouth curved into a musing smile. 'The perfect juvenile, hmm? Picture-book pretty, with a complexion like porcelain, and impossibly long auburn hair bound in plaits.'

'Talk to David. He'll tell you I walked in his shadow, always wanting to play.'

'Did he allow you to?'

'Most of the time,' she answered, quietly reflective, yet her voice held a tinge of wryness. 'All his friends thought I was cute, and I survived puberty without braces or acne.'

'Is it such a handicap being beautiful?' he queried with soft cynicism, and she shot him a dark pensive glance.

'Sometimes I could scream for people to see beyond the façade, to be liked for *me*, everything that is Alexis Honore Harrison. Not simply Jonathan Harrison's daughter, or David Harrison's sister. Or even Lexi Harrison, model.' She effected a helpless shrug. 'There was a time when I thought of hiring a four-wheel drive and travelling north to Kakadu Reserve,' she continued broodingly as she sipped from her glass.

'Tracking kangaroos and crocodiles, dressed in khaki and wearing an akubra hat?' He lifted a hand and touched the tip of his forefinger to the edge of her nose. 'Living life in the rough and exposing this beautiful skin to the heat and dust and other unmentionable elements.' His finger slid down to the curve of her upper lip, then gently traced its outline. 'The trouble with running away is that eventually you have to return. And the problems you wanted to escape from still remain. It's better to stay and deal with them.' His smile was warm and completely disarming. 'Believe me.'

It was impossible to still the faint trembling of her mouth. 'You sound like Jonathan and David.'

He reached out and caught her arm in a light clasp. 'Come out on to the terrace. It's cooler, and we can talk without half the room watching our every move.'

He was weaving a subtle magical spell, and the crazy thing was that she drew great comfort from the touch of his hand. It was almost as if he represented a large stable rock to which she could cling, and be safe from the storm-tossed sea threatening to engulf her. Yet that in itself was a parody, for Georg Nicolaos represented a far bigger threat than she'd ever encountered, and she wasn't sure precisely how she was going to deal with it.

He was right, she accorded a few minutes later. The terrace was cooler, and it was nothing less than sheer bliss to be free of the surreptitious glances and the mild exasperation of knowing she was the subject of conjecture.

'Shall we dance?'

'Must we?'

He took the glass from her hand and placed it down on the wide ledge of the balustrading. 'I think so. I shan't bite,' he drawled with hateful mockery, and she stiffened as he drew her close.

'If you even dared,' Lexi warned with soft vehemence, 'I'd——'

'What? Bite me back?'

Damn him, he was amused! *'Yes!'*

'I'm almost tempted. The result could prove——' he paused deliberately '—interesting, shall we say?'

He held her impossibly close, and she felt consumed with futile anger. 'Damn you!' she burst out in a furious undertone. 'This isn't dancing!'

'Why not relax?' Georg queried imperturbably, restraining her efforts to wrest herself free with galling ease.

'The only way I can relax is when I'm ten feet away from you!' she declared vehemently.

'That's quite an admission. Have you stopped to consider why?'

His silky drawl was the very limit, and her head reared back as she sought to deliver a bitter invective. Except that the words never found voice as his mouth closed over hers in a kiss that took all her fine anger and tamed it into subdued submission.

'Don't ever do that again,' Lexi said shakily several long seconds after he'd relinquished her mouth. That long, infinitely slow possession had been one of the most evocative, erotic experiences of her life. Eyes closed, she had wanted it to go on and on, and never stop. And she'd wanted so much more than just the mere coupling of their mouths.

For the first time since those initial heady days with Paul she wanted, *needed* a complete satiation of the senses that went way beyond mere seduction. Not just with any man. *This* man, a tiny voice taunted.

And he knew. It was there in his eyes, the soft curve of his mouth, the possessiveness of his hands as they moved lightly down her back to curve her close against the hard length of his body.

She unconsciously pleaded with him, her eyes large luminous pools that shimmered with the threat of crystalline tears. 'Let me go.'

His gaze darkened fractionally, and his mouth moved to form a sensual curve. 'What if I refuse?'

She felt as if she were caught up in a swirling vortex of emotion so treacherous that she was in danger of drowning. 'Please.' The effort it cost her to summon a faint smile was beyond measure. 'I——' she hesitated, and her lips trembled slightly as her eyes silently beseeched him '—I don't want to play this particular game.'

His head lowered, and his lips brushed the length of her jaw to settle at the corner of her mouth. 'Who said it was a game?'

A single tear overflowed and slowly trickled down her cheek. 'You're not playing fair.'

'That depends on your definition of the word.'

If she didn't attempt to instil some levity into the situation she'd fragment into a thousand pieces. 'Shall we go back indoors?'

He lifted his head. 'Do you particularly want to?'

'I think so,' she said steadily. 'We've stayed out here sufficiently long to make our absence convincing.'

His eyes gleamed darkly in the shadowy light. 'One look at you will be enough to convince anyone,' he mocked gently as he lifted a hand and smoothed back a few wayward tresses.

For a moment she appeared stricken by his implication; then her features assembled an expressionless mask as she withdrew a tube of coloured gloss from her evening-bag and skilfully smoothed it over her lips.

Without a word she stepped away from him and walked slowly along the terrace to a double set of doors.

For what remained of the evening Georg was never far from her side, and she circulated among the guests, chatting, smiling with such conviction that it was doubtful anyone guessed that inside she was a mess of shattered nerves.

Everyone appeared to be enjoying themselves, but Lexi wondered darkly if it was just a façade. The smiles, the expressed interest all seemed so incredibly false, so artificial. Were any of them true friends, or merely trading as superficial acquaintances? A hollow laugh rose unbidden, then died in her throat. Should anyone present tonight suffer a change in financial status, their social standing would diminish to zero.

'Shall we leave?'

Lexi turned towards Georg and proffered a solemn smile. 'Is it awfully late?'

'Almost two.'

She managed an expression of mock surprise. 'Good heavens. I had no idea.'

A warm, sloping smile tugged at the corners of his mouth. 'Behave, Lexi,' he bade her, and, taking hold of her hand, he led her towards their hosts.

In the car he drove competently, slipping a cassette into the stereo system so that conversation wasn't a necessity, and when he drew to a halt outside her apartment block she made no demur as his hands closed over her shoulders.

She knew she should flee *now*, before she became lost, but it was far too late as his lips brushed hers, settling with unerring ease over their delicate curves, savouring the sensual softness; then she gasped as he caught hold of her lower lip and pulled it gently into his mouth. Her tongue darted forward in a gesture of protective defence, then sprang back in shocked disbelief as he caught its tip between his teeth and gently drew it forward.

She swallowed convulsively, and made a strangled demur in resistance, only to have his mouth open over her own as he took possession in a manner that left her in no doubt as to his ultimate intention.

She reached for his shoulders and used all her strength to push against him, gaining a slight degree of freedom only, she suspected, because he permitted it.

'Please.' The word came out as a tortured whisper.

'You could ask me in.'

'If I did,' she managed shakily, 'you'd read more into the invitation than I intended.'

'And you'd hate yourself in the morning?'

'Something like that.'

She could sense his faint smile a few seconds before his lips brushed hers, then she was free.

'We'll dine out tomorrow night.'

Lexi looked momentarily startled, and was about to refuse when she caught his faintly brooding smile. 'What if I've already made plans?'

'Cancel them,' he instructed cynically.

'I may not want to,' she felt empowered to state, and glimpsed the mockery evident in the depths of his eyes.

'Do it, Lexi. I'll collect you at seven.'

'Do you usually *tell* your female companions what your plans are, and expect them to pander to your every whim?'

His eyes became tinged with musing warmth, and a sloping smile tugged the corners of his mouth. 'For some reason they seem intent on pleasing me.'

She didn't doubt it for a minute. There was an inherent quality about him that was wholly sensual, and something else that made her want to run and hide. Except that she couldn't, and maybe that bothered her more than she was willing to admit.

It was almost as if he was playing a game, she decided with an intuitive flash of speculative knowledge. His manipulative force in the business sector was legendary, and the Press dutifully recorded his every move.

'Why wouldn't they?' Lexi returned sweetly, un-caring of his deep probing glance. 'You're an exceptionally wealthy man, you drive an exotic car, and you're reasonably attractive—if you happen to like a surfeit of brooding Greek magnificence.' She tilted her head to one side as she subjected him to a pensive appraisal. 'I hope I won't damage your ego when I say that it wouldn't really matter if you were fifty, paunchy and bald. The women would still flock to your side.'

One eyebrow slanted in musing cynicism, and she caught a gleam of laughter in the depths of his eyes. 'Perhaps I should return the compliment. There are any number of men waiting to beat a path to your door—if only you would let them.'

Her eyes widened fractionally, then became veiled by the swift downward sweep of her lashes. 'Now you're being facetious.'

'Perhaps we should be grateful that neither of us possess any illusions,' he drawled.

Lexi reached for the doorknob. 'Goodnight.'

She was totally unprepared as he leant forward and covered her mouth with his own.

This time there was no hard possession, more a mixture of evocative control and blatant intention.

She had no defence against the explorative probe of his tongue as it traversed the inner contours of her mouth, and an electrifying awareness tingled through her veins as his touch became so intensely erotic that she had to physically restrain herself from allowing her body its instinctive inclination to lean close in against him and deepen the kiss.

It was madness, and just as she thought she could stand it no longer he lifted his head and slowly pushed her to arm's length.

'Sleep well, Lexi,' he taunted lazily, and in her anxiety she didn't hesitate to escape.

He waited until she was safely through the security doors before restarting the engine, and Lexi walked towards the lift without so much as a backward glance.

How could she *sleep*? He aroused a complexity of emotions, and not one of them was enviable.

Her mouth felt slightly swollen, and she ran the tip of her tongue over the lower curve as she entered her apartment.

Damn Georg Nicolaos, she cursed irreverently. Damn him to hell.

CHAPTER SIX

'YOU'RE late,' Lexi greeted Georg the instant she opened the door the following evening.

He pulled back the cuff of his jacket and examined a distinctive gold Rolex. 'Seven minutes. Is it an unforgivable sin?'

It was immaterial that she hadn't been ready until two minutes ago, and she had no intention of informing him of that fact. 'I'm starving,' she declared truthfully, sweeping past him.

'Had a bad day?'

She wanted to hit him, and, enclosed within the confines of the lift, she wondered if there was some dark reason behind the temptation to resort to physical violence whenever she was in his company.

'Shall I start from the beginning?' Even to her own ears she sounded faintly harassed and on edge.

He unlocked the Ferrari and saw her seated inside before going round to slip in behind the wheel and fire the engine. 'Please do.'

'You're amused,' she accused him.

'Intrigued,' he amended as he concentrated on negotiating traffic.

Events of the totally chaotic day rose up to taunt her, and she grimaced in memory. 'The Mercedes had a flat tyre, and I changed it myself. So I was late. That disrupted Jacques's schedule. He swore so... graphically that I thought he was going to cancel the entire session. And nothing went right.

They sent the wrong-sized clothes, and the accessories didn't match. He ordered a few stills in black and white, then stormed out in a temper, leaving us to make the best of it. Monique blasted him with a blistered riposte that would have made a navvy blush.' Her mouth assumed a rueful moue. 'I missed lunch, discovered that the spare tyre I'd substituted this morning had developed a slow leak, and I had to catch a taxi into the city. The modelling academy kept me way beyond the projected time, and do you know how *impossible* it is to get a taxi between five and six?' She suddenly became aware of their whereabouts. 'Where are you taking me?'

'To my apartment.'

'For dinner?'

'Are you unaware that I am an accomplished chef?'

There was nothing she could do to guard against a sharp intake of breath. If she said she'd prefer to go to a restaurant he would imagine she was afraid to be alone with him. And she wasn't. At least, fear didn't motivate the state of her emotions.

'You've been slaving in the kitchen all afternoon?' she countered as he turned beneath an impressive apartment block and sent the Ferrari growling into a reserved bay. 'Don't you have to spend your weekend in an office directing a large slice of the city's finances?'

His smile was faintly cynical. 'I have access to hi-tech equipment in a number of offices, one of which is based in my apartment. Communication in the nineties is becoming increasingly portable. All it takes is the flick of an electronic button.' He switched off the ignition and slid out of the car, waiting until she joined him before walking towards the lifts. 'The restaurant is managed by a team of extremely competent chefs, who kindly permit me to work with them whenever I feel the inclination.' He jabbed the call-button and when the doors slid open he inserted a key to allow private access to the penthouse apartment. 'And slaving is scarcely applicable in preparing a dinner *à deux*,' he concluded as the lift came to a smooth halt.

The penthouse was magnificent, and she said so, complimenting him with genuine sincerity on the tasteful blend of cream, beige and muted shades of brown and Wedgwood blue skilfully used in the décor. Deep-buttoned leather furniture in chocolate brown lent a masculine touch, and contrasting colours were implemented in expensive works of art gracing the walls.

'Sit down,' Georg bade her, crossing to the cocktail bar. 'What can I get you to drink?'

Without doubt there would be wine to accompany their meal, and she had the feeling she needed to be in total control of her senses. 'Something long, cool and non-alcoholic.'

'Playing it safe, Lexi?'

Her eyes caught his, and her chin lifted a fraction in defiance of his drawling tones. 'It's the only way.'

'You sound defensive,' he accorded, slanting her a musing glance. 'Will it help if I assure you that you have nothing to fear?'

Maybe, just maybe she might have believed him if it wasn't for some elusive sixth sense that warned he was skilfully indulging in a contest where he was the mastermind and she merely a pawn. It was crazy, and totally without foundation, but the thought had infiltrated her mind and refused to be dislodged.

'You mean, I'm safe from any so-called "fringe benefits" you might consider your due as a participant in this diabolical scheme?'

His gaze didn't waver, although his eyes darkened measurably, and his voice when he spoke was deliberately mild, yet she detected an edge of steel beneath the velvet-smooth surface. 'As safe as you choose to be.'

If that was assurance it was unsuccessful, and she watched as he put ice in a tall glass, then added lime-juice, a dash of bitters and topped it with soda before handing it to her.

'Good luck.'

Educated in the best private schools, and fashionably 'finished', she was adept at dealing with almost any given situation, commanding an enviable repertoire of stock-in-trade social small talk. Yet with Georg Nicolaos she alternated between raging at him in temper and behaving like a tongue-tied teenager. It was ridiculous, she chided silently.

'Tell me about yourself.'

Lexi looked momentarily startled, and took an appreciative sip from her glass. 'A personal profile from birth until now?' Her lips widened to form a bitter-sweet smile. 'Including a run-down on my disastrous marriage?'

'I consider Paul to be immaterial,' Georg dismissed drily, and she felt a slight shiver feather its way down the length of her spine.

She looked at him carefully, noting the dark business suit, immaculate white linen shirt and sober navy blue silk tie. Character analysis just had to be his forte, for he appeared every inch the wealthy executive, exuding an animalistic sense of power with chilling ease.

'What made you decide to take up modelling?'

Lexi gave a careless shrug. 'It happened by accident. I attended a fashion parade with a friend three years ago. Just after I returned from two years abroad. The mother of another friend owned one of the boutiques supplying the parade with clothes. One of the models failed to show, and I was there— the right height and size. Before I knew it I was out on the catwalk trying to look as if I'd modelled clothes for years.'

'With obvious success,' Georg conceded.

'I enjoyed it,' she admitted. 'Sufficiently so to agree to participating in another fashion parade held a few days later. Jacques was there. He seemed to think I possessed a natural flair. So I began to look at it seriously, enrolling at a modelling academy to learn all the tricks of the trade, and, as they say—the rest is history.'

'It hasn't occurred to you to venture into the field of design?'

'No. It's a cut-throat trade, and you need to be a true artist. I prefer accessories. Matching up shoes, belts, whether to add a scarf and, if so, how it should be worn.' Her eyes had darkened with enthusiasm, and her voice held genuine warmth. 'Jewellery—even the right hairstyle, make-up. The entire composition. I often suggest changes, and Jacques usually goes along with them.'

'All in aid of making women appear beautiful.'

Lexi looked at him, deliberately searching for mockery, yet, if he had intended any, it was carefully hidden.

'A woman's true beauty comes from within,' she revealed slowly. 'It radiates through her skin, shows in her smile, and is reflected in her eyes. If she's not happy with herself, or lacks self-esteem, then it is generally apparent in mannerisms. Body language.' Her gaze became startlingly direct. 'With care and skill a woman can learn to make the best of her natural attributes, no matter what her size or age.'

'Gilding an outer shell, which, with expert marketing, grosses enormous profits for the various merchandisers.'

'Perhaps. But it isn't confined to women. Men like to present the outer trappings of their success in fine clothes.' She ran an experienced eye over his suit. 'Unless I'm mistaken, that's tailored by Ermenegildo Zegna. And your shoes are hand-stitched—either French or Italian imports.'

His smile proved to be a disruptive force, curving his mouth and lightening the harsh lines of his chiselled features. 'Are you implying that I project a required image?'

She responded with a winsome smile. 'Definitely.'

'Which is?'

'An astute entrepreneur,' she ventured quietly. 'Someone who wouldn't suffer fools gladly.'

'What about Georg Nicolaos, the man?'

For some reason she felt as if she'd skated on to dangerously thin ice. 'A contradiction between cruelty and kindness.'

'Ah—*honesty*.' Georg laughed softly, and one glance at those gleaming dark eyes revealed that he wasn't fooled in the slightest.

'Shall we have dinner?'

Lexi needed no second bidding, and she allowed him to lead her to the elegantly appointed dining-room, where within minutes he transferred serving dishes from the kitchen on to the table.

There was soup as a starter, a delicately flavoured leek and potato which tasted like liquid ambrosia, followed by luscious prawns in a delicate sauce served on a bed of rice.

The portions were temptingly small, so that she consumed every morsel, and the main course was an exquisite *coq au vin*.

There was wine—a clear sharp white—and chilled water, and dessert was a superb crème caramel.

'That was—perfect,' Lexi complimented, leaning back in her chair, fully replete.

'A compliment?'

'You can't possibly cook like that every night,' she declared in wistful disbelief, and caught his slow musing smile. 'Do you ever eat alone?' she asked, genuinely curious.

'Not often,' Georg responded indolently. 'I make a practice of dining with Mama once a week, and Samantha and Alex insist I join them on frequent occasions. Anna and Nick, also. Then, of course, the restaurant, and the inevitable social interludes...' He let his voice trail off as he effected an elegant shrug. 'However, there are times when I enjoy a quiet evening at home.'

'Samantha is charming,' Lexi voiced with sincerity.

'She is a very beautiful woman. Genuine, caring. Exceptional.'

Her eyes widened, and she glimpsed the darkness reflected in his own, then he smiled. 'Shall we have coffee?'

'Let's dispense with the dishes first,' she said, getting to her feet and beginning to stack plates together.

'Leave them. My housemaid, Carla, is due tomorrow. She'll attend to them.'

'It won't take long.' She spared him a quick glance. 'Unless you're particularly protective about a woman invading your kitchen?'

Shrugging off his jacket, he tossed it carelessly over a nearby chair, and she watched as he removed cufflinks and folded back the sleeves of his shirt.

'In that case, we'll do them together.'

The kitchen was a delight, spacious and boasting every modern convenience imaginable. Apart from a collection of saucepans drying in a dish-rack atop the draining-board, there wasn't a thing out of place.

'I'm impressed.'

'With the kitchen?'

His faint mockery did strange things to her equilibrium, and she concentrated on rinsing the crockery and cutlery while he stacked the dishwasher.

'What made you decide to be a chef?'

'My parents emigrated from Greece when Alex, Anna and I were very young. Papa owned three restaurants in Athens, and it was a natural progression for him to pursue the business here.' He filled the percolator with water, extracted a filter and spooned in freshly ground coffee beans. 'We all helped, waiting tables, the dishes, cleaning. Before school, after school, during semester breaks. Like all parents, they wanted great things for each of their children, and I followed Alex into university and studied for a business degree. Papa was taken ill not long after I graduated, and for a few years I worked in an office by day and managed the restaurant at night. Now we keep it for Mama's sake. It represents so many memories for us all.'

'She must be very proud of you.'

'We are a very close family.'

The strength of her own familial ties was such that she'd consented to an impossible charade with a man who was the antithesis of harmless.

'All done.' Lexi dried her hands, then watched as Georg set cups on to their saucers, then extracted sugar, liqueur and cream. His hands were large, and his forearms firmly muscled and liberally sprinkled with dark hair. Their actions displayed an economy of movement, and there was strength apparent as well as a degree of sensitivity.

'Come into the lounge.'

Said the spider to the fly, she echoed silently, wondering what quirk of cynical humour had promoted that thought to mind. 'I must leave soon,' she murmured out loud, and incurred his dark slanting glance.

'Must?'

'I need my beauty sleep,' she quipped lightly as she followed him and settled comfortably into a single armchair.

'We also need to plan the next week,' Georg indicated as he took an opposite chair. 'It was the reason I brought you here, so that we could discuss it rationally rather than risk argument in a public restaurant.'

'I don't argue,' Lexi retaliated, only to give a rueful smile as she caught his raised eyebrow. 'Well, not usually.'

'I'm the exception?'

She looked at him carefully. 'Just because I recognise the necessity for this...deception——' she paused deliberately '—doesn't mean I have to like it.'

The dark eyes sharpened, and for some inexplicable reason she had difficulty holding their concentrated gaze.

'You find me—dislikeable?'

She suddenly felt as if she'd stepped from the safe shallows into water way over her head. 'No,' she said honestly.

'Yet you're afraid.'

It was a statement she didn't deny. She had genuinely enjoyed his company tonight, even if she had been slightly on edge. And, if she was fair, she could only accord that fault as entirely her own.

'I don't feel entirely comfortable with you,' she admitted, and saw his eyelids droop slightly, successfully veiling his expression.

'Could that not be because we have yet to forge a friendship?'

Could a woman ever be mere *friend* to someone like Georg Nicolaos? Somehow she doubted it.

'You mentioned collaborating on our social calendar.' Lexi broached the subject in an attempt to steer the conversation into safer channels.

'There are the inevitable invitations issued at this time of year,' he drawled, 'few of which I usually accept. However, there is a party to be held at the home of a friend which I think we should attend. Samantha and Alex have requested that we join them at a society ball, the proceeds from which are donated to make Christmas a more joyful occasion for a number of terminally ill children. It is considered to be *the* social event of the season.'

'Good heavens,' Lexi said faintly. 'I'm due to fly to the Gold Coast on Thursday morning for a photographic shoot organised by the Mirage Resort. It will be followed early in the New Year by another at the sister resort in Port Douglas.'

Georg's eyes narrowed faintly. 'How long will you be away?'

She gave a slight shrug. 'Overnight, on each occasion.'

'Apart from that do you have any social obligations?'

She looked at him, noting the apparent indolence, and wasn't fooled in the slightest. 'Jonathan, David and I usually attend a few pre-Christmas functions together.' A faint sigh whispered from her lips. 'I think I prefer an evening of solitude with a good book, or tuned in to a VCR.'

'I can think of an infinitely more pleasurable way in which to spend the night hours,' Georg drawled, and saw the faint blush of pink that crept into her cheeks.

'I'm sure you can,' Lexi managed equably. With unhurried movements she stood to her feet. 'Would you mind if I phoned for a taxi?'

His eyes trapped her own for far too long, and she had to glance away from that disturbing gaze. 'You haven't finished your coffee.'

He was imperturbable, so maddeningly calm, and totally impervious to the agitation welling deep inside her. Lexi suddenly felt as if she were treading on eggshells.

'Please.' She attempted to keep her voice light and devoid of a degree of mounting tension. 'I'd really like to leave.'

'As soon as I finish my coffee I'll take you home.'

Reaching forward, she picked up the cup and saucer, spacing her movements so they appeared calm and unhurried as she sipped the remaining brew, then she carried the cup out to the kitchen and carefully rinsed it.

When she turned he was there, and her pulse began an erratic beat as he moved close to place his cup and saucer in the sink. It simply wasn't fair that she was overly sensitive to his potent brand of sexuality.

'Ready?'

She gave an indicative nod, and without a further word he turned and preceded her from the apartment.

In the car she sat in silence, consumed by an acute sense of vulnerability. A number of conversational gambits rose to mind, but she ventured none of them, and she sat trapped in silence for a few interminable seconds as he brought the Ferrari to a halt outside her apartment block.

'Thanks for dinner.' Good manners insisted that she acknowledge his hospitality.

'So—thank me.'

She looked at him carefully, and wondered why she should suddenly feel threatened. All she had to do was reach forward and place her lips to his cheek.

Except that he turned his head and her lips touched his mouth, and before she could retreat he lifted his hands to capture her head, and it was he who took command, *he* who turned what began as a casual salutation into an evocative embrace that made her aware of a magical, elusive alchemy.

A treacherous weakness invaded her limbs as he wrought havoc with a ravaging exploration that brought a thousand tiny nerve-endings leaping into pulsating life, arousing feelings too complex to distinguish any one as she clung to him unashamedly.

It was almost as if every pore of her skin became suffused with sweet aching pleasure beneath his mercilessly erotic plunder of her senses, and when at last he slowly released her she could only look at him in complete bewilderment.

Without a word she reached for the door-handle and slid out from the passenger seat.

The door snapped shut with a refined click, and she crossed to the main entrance without a backward glance, using her security card to gain access; it was only when she was safely indoors that she heard the muted roar of the Ferrari's engine as it purred down one half of the semi-circular driveway.

It was a relief to enter her apartment, and she secured the lock before crossing to the windows to close the curtains against the night sky.

She felt incredibly restless, and far too emotionally uptight to sleep. Perhaps a long, leisurely soak in the spa-bath might ease some of her tension, and without further thought she wandered into the bathroom and filled the capacious tub.

Half an hour later she emerged to towel herself dry, then, attired in a short cotton nightshirt, she slipped into bed to lie staring into the darkness for what seemed an age, before exhaustion finally claimed her in a deep, troubled sleep from which she woke late, dark-eyed and drained.

During the following few days Lexi deliberately maintained a low profile. She consulted with Jacques over the forthcoming shoot at the Gold Coast's tourist resort, met Jonathan for lunch, completed some Christmas shopping, and spent an hour stretched out on a lounger beside the pool each afternoon, perfecting a tan. For two consecutive evenings she conjured up a suitable excuse to avoid seeing Georg, and on the third night she answered the doorbell to find him standing in the hallway.

'Have you eaten yet?' he drawled, and Lexi looked at him with exasperation as he moved into the lounge.

'I planned on spending a quiet evening at home.'

One eyebrow slanted in quizzical disbelief. 'You've already done that two evenings in a row.'

She heaved a faint sigh. 'Is that an indication we should go out and play?'

'What if I say . . . you get to choose the venue?'

'You're taking an awful risk,' Lexi declared. 'I may decide on a rock concert.'

'Out of sheer perversity?'

'Yes, I think so.' Humour lent her hazel-gold eyes an impish sparkle and she tilted her head to one side. 'You'll have to change. Where we're going, anything else but jeans, T-shirt and joggers will be a fashion mis-statement.'

'You have tickets?'

A wide smile curved her mouth. 'Indeed. Jacques did an outrageously successful shoot a few years ago for one of the leading agencies in town. Ever since, they've presented him with half a dozen tickets to each top promotion.'

'I hardly dare ask which bands are featured,' he drawled, almost wincing as she named two; then she added insult to injury by following them with three artists known for their explosive style on stage. 'This is revenge, I gather?'

'I sat through *Madame Butterfly*,' she reminded him, and saw his eyes darken with cynical humour.

'I doubt there is any comparison.'

'It starts at eight.'

'You're determined?'

The thought of having him suffer through hours of impossibly loud rock music was too great a temptation to miss! 'Yes.'

'Then get changed, and we'll go back to my apartment.'

'After which, when you've changed into casual gear, we'll go straight on and grab a hamburger or eat something there.' She saw his look of disbelief and managed to appear completely guileless. 'Be a devil for once. I'm sure your digestive system will survive.'

'More pertinent: will my eardrums?'

'Oh, I think so,' Lexi declared solemnly. 'I've been to a number of rock concerts, and my hearing is still intact.' She gestured towards the drinks cabinet. 'Fix yourself something while I go change.'

Ten minutes later she emerged clad in faded denims, a white T-shirt, white jogging shoes, and a denim jacket slung casually across her shoulders. Make-up was minimal and she'd twisted her hair into an elaborate pleat at her nape.

'I suspect I'm in for a culture shock,' Georg drawled as he followed her out of the apartment, and she spared him a laughing glance.

The Ferrari traversed the short distance between Darling Point and Double Bay in record time, and Lexi watched the news on television while Georg effected a swift change of clothes.

'Hmm,' she accorded musingly as he re-entered the lounge a short while later. 'You look almost— human.'

He certainly looked different, having discarded the image of impeccably attired businessman for something infinitely more casual. Hip- and thigh-hugging jeans worn with a pale cotton shirt beneath a contrasting designer jacket was perfectly suitable attire in which to attend a rock concert. Yet somehow it failed to disguise the essence of the man and his innate ability to project an aura of power.

'It would take only minutes to grill steak and prepare a salad.'

'Hamburgers,' Lexi negated firmly, moving towards the lobby.

'Junk food.'

'Surveys report there's not as much junk in *junk* food as we're led to believe. It can actually be quite high in nutritional value.' She wrinkled her nose at him. 'Relax, Georg. You may just enjoy yourself.'

That Lexi did was without doubt. The music was loud, but the sound-effects were without distortion, emitted at their sophisticated best and an audible attestation to superb technology. She clapped and sang with the rest of the audience, oblivious for the most part to the man who sat at her side.

'Isn't he great?' Lexi enthused as one of Australia's better-known vocalists took the stage for a popular encore—a song that had won him an Entertainer of the Year award the previous year. He was married, a devoted husband and father, and affectionately held his doting public in the palm of his hand. 'He doesn't just *sing*—he puts everything into it and becomes a part of the music itself.' She turned towards Georg and was disconcerted to see that his attention was centred on her, not the band or the vocalist on stage. For a moment her breath locked in her throat as she became trapped by the expression in those dark eyes, then she swallowed and said fiercely, 'The proceeds of this concert go to charity.'

'You don't need to justify anything,' Georg drawled. 'And you're right. I am enjoying myself— watching you.'

She felt incredibly vulnerable, and everything else faded as she glimpsed something she dared not define before she managed to tear her gaze away.

The musicians caught her attention, but for the remainder of the evening she was supremely conscious of his presence.

It was late when the concert wound down, and the exits became jammed with a river of people attempting to vacate the venue. It was even worse trying to leave the car park.

Consequently it was after midnight before the Ferrari was able to move freely in traffic, and Lexi leaned well back in her seat and closed her eyes as she mentally reviewed the concert and its artists.

'Do you want to go somewhere for supper?'

She opened her eyes and turned to look at him. 'Are you hungry?'

'Peckish.'

'We're not exactly dressed for any of your usual haunts,' she ventured.

'I know of a place. Trust me.'

When the car slid to a halt she checked their whereabouts and shot him a cheeky grin. 'I don't believe this.'

'Come on. Out.' He slid from behind the wheel and went round to open her door. 'A fitting end to the evening, wouldn't you say?'

The café was intimately small and spotlessly clean, and the smell of food was tantalising. They sat opposite each other in a booth, and ordered steakburgers, fries and salad. Afterwards they washed it down with surprisingly good coffee, then Georg paid the bill and drove towards Darling Point.

It had been a wonderful evening, and she told him as much as he drew to a halt outside her apartment block.

'I agree.'

Something in the tone of his voice arrested her attention, and she turned towards him in seemingly slow motion as his hands caught hold of her shoulders.

'Georg—don't. Please,' she whispered as he impelled her forward, and the butterflies in her stomach began an erratic tattoo, making her frighteningly aware of the electric tension between them.

Lexi felt herself begin to tremble as he lowered his head and touched his lips briefly against her temple.

Any further protest became lost as his mouth slid down to cover hers in a kiss that was tantalising, tender, yet with a hint of controlled passion, and to her utter chagrin it left her feeling vaguely bereft and wanting more.

'I really must go,' she said a trifle shakily.

'Don't forget we're attending the charity ball tomorrow night,' Georg reminded her as she made to step out from the car. 'We're meeting Samantha and Alex there at eight. I'll pick you up at seven-thirty.'

She murmured agreement, then activated her security card to pass through the main doors, and when she turned back all she could see was the twin red tail-lights as the Ferrari swept down the street.

CHAPTER SEVEN

Lexi dressed with care, and her mirrored reflection gave visual satisfaction that her choice of gown was a success.

In midnight-blue silk, it accentuated her slim curves by hugging them shamelessly from breast to knee before flaring out in a generous fold that fell to ankle-length. Matching shoes and evening-bag completed the outfit, and for jewellery she'd opted to wear a glorious sapphire pendant encircled in diamonds and matching ear-studs.

Her hair was worn swept back from her face and caught together at one side so that a thick mass of curls cascaded down on to her left breast. Make-up had been skilfully applied to highlight her eyes, and a deep dusky rose coloured the generous curve of her mouth.

Perfume—Jean-Louis Scherrer—completed the required image, and at the sound of the doorbell she moved through the lounge to answer its summons.

'Beautiful,' Georg accorded softly, after conducting a slow appreciative appraisal that brought a defiant sparkle to her eyes.

'Wearing clothes is an acquired flair,' Lexi qualified with a faint defensive lift of her chin as she met his warm gaze.

'You do it extremely well.'

Perhaps she'd overdone it, she decided wryly. Except that tonight of all nights, given such an auspicious occasion, she felt the need to excel. The charity ball would be patronised by the cream of Sydney's society, and Lexi Harrison's affair with Georg Nicolaos was hot gossip. She would be examined in detail from the tip of her shoes to the top of her head, discussed and dissected, her behaviour observed and criticised. From the moment she stepped out of Georg's car she would need to *shine*.

'Would you like a drink?' she queried. 'Or shall we leave?'

'Oh, leave, I think,' Georg intimated with husky humour. 'Otherwise I shall probably be tempted to dissuade you from moving one step out of this apartment.'

The only way she could cope with him in this frame of mood was outright flippancy. 'And waste all the time and effort I've expended in adopting this glamorous image? Not on your life.'

'Shame,' he drawled. 'Now I shall have to exercise the utmost control during the entire evening.'

She proffered a wide sweet smile. 'I have no doubt you'll manage.'

He stood to one side, allowing her to precede him into the lobby.

The venue was a plush hotel in the inner city, and, although she had attended many such functions in the past, tonight it was impossible to dispel a feeling of nervousness.

Georg Nicolaos had a lot to answer for, she decided darkly as they moved into the foyer, where their tickets were scrutinised and marked off an impressive list before they were ushered into the elaborately decorated function-room.

Drinks and canapés were served by a bevy of hovering waiters, and Lexi drifted at Georg's side as they slowly mixed and mingled with a variety of acquaintances.

'Lexi; Georg.' Alex, with Samantha at his side looking incredibly lovely in black velvet. Lexi greeted them both warmly, accepted Samantha's compliment and promptly returned it. 'Shall we take our seats at the table?' Alex enquired. 'It looks as if most of the guests are intent on becoming seated.'

The food was superb, and Lexi forked a few mouthfuls from each course, declined wine in favour of mineral water, and opted for fresh fruit salad instead of the cheeseboard. There were the usual salutary speeches lauding the charity chairperson, the secretary, and a brief résumé of the charity's successful endeavours and anticipatory projections. Then it was clearly party-time as a band took up its position and began to play.

'Would you excuse me while I freshen up?' said Lexi.

'I'll come with you,' Samantha indicated, rising to her feet, and together they began threading their way across the room.

The powder-room was crowded, and it took considerable time before Samantha was able to occupy a spare cubicle. Lexi gave her place to an expectant mother who obviously needed to use the facilities more urgently than she did.

'Don't wait,' Lexi bade Samantha with a helpless smile. 'I'll rejoin you as soon as I can.'

It was at least five minutes before she emerged, and she paused as someone called her name, then stood politely as a woman she barely knew insisted on offering her congratulations.

An acquaintance of Jonathan's restricted her passage, enquiring after his health, and she turned to retrace her steps to the table.

Afterwards she couldn't recall quite what made her conduct a sweeping appraisal of the function-room and its guests. She certainly wasn't conscious of doing it deliberately. There had to be at least thirty people present whom she knew reasonably well, and more than fifty who were social acquaintances.

Even as her eyes skimmed the crowd, it never occurred to her that she might number her ex-husband among the invited guests.

Lexi felt the blood drain from her face at the sight of Paul standing on the far side of the room. Even from this distance she could see the wicked, faintly malevolent gleam in his eyes, the cynical twist of his mouth.

She saw him murmur to his companion, then he began threading his way through the gathered groups of guests.

'Well, hello,' Paul greeted softly, and she cringed beneath his deliberate raking appraisal. 'It's been ages, my sweet. I see you're inhabiting the social scene again,' he intoned hatefully. 'The gossip around town is that you and Georg Nicolaos are an item. Are you?'

Careful, she cautioned silently. The last thing she wanted was a scene. Perhaps if she was polite he'd be satisfied and leave her alone.

Lexi took her time in answering, letting her lashes sweep up as she met his stare with unblinking solemnity. 'Yes.'

His lips curved to form a vicious sickle. 'Why, Lexi, darling, whatever are you thinking of? Georg eats little girls for breakfast.'

'I'm no longer a little girl, Paul,' she said steadily. 'You personally saw to it that I grew up.'

'Do you imagine for one minute it will be any different with Georg Nicolaos? He's a hard corporate executive, too attuned to business interests to be much concerned with *you*, except when it suits him, of course.'

'As you were, Paul?'

'My, my,' he accorded with slow deliberation. 'Tell me, sweetie,' he began, pausing as he set his weapons ready for the figurative kill, 'are you still an inhibited, frigid little bitch in bed? Or hasn't Georg been able to persuade you into his yet?' He reached out a hand to push back a tendril of hair behind her ear, and laughed softly as she reared back from his touch as if from flame.

'You would be advised not to cause trouble, Ellis,' a too-familiar voice intimated with icy disdain, and Lexi felt faint.

'I have an invitation to this soirée,' Paul said mockingly, his eyes moving slowly from Georg to Lexi.

'Obviously,' Georg conceded with studied ruthlessness. 'Otherwise you would not have been admitted.' He paused, before adding with killing

softness, 'However, if I hear of your bothering Lexi
again I can promise that you will live to regret it.'

Lexi shivered at the degree of ice evident in
Georg's tone, and she glimpsed the malevolent
gleam in Paul's eye as he ventured cynically,
'Physical violence, my dear chap?'

'Nothing so uncivilised.'

Paul's gaze swept down to the ring on Lexi's
finger, then he lifted his head to slant her a mocking
glance. 'Congratulations, darling. Daddy will be
pleased.'

It was evident that Paul had deliberately sought
this very scene, and Lexi was supremely conscious
of the curious looks cast in their direction, the avid,
all-too-seeing eyes alight with speculative conjecture. Inside she was shattering into a thousand
pieces, but she was darned if she'd give Paul the
pleasure of glimpsing any visible signs of her
distress.

'Yes,' she agreed quietly, 'he is.'

'Better luck this time, sweetie.'

'We'll excuse you,' Georg said silkily. 'There can
be no doubt this conversation has reached its
conclusion.'

'I wouldn't dream of continuing it,' Paul declared
with ill-concealed mockery, then he turned and
strolled with apparent nonchalance to rejoin his
friends.

Pride was a damnable thing, and she lifted her
head, tilting her chin in an unconscious gesture of
defence. Georg's eyes seemed to tear down the
barriers she had erected, and after a few interminably long minutes she lowered her gaze to a
point somewhere above his left shoulder.

Without a word he reached out and caught hold of her hand, and she shifted her attention, meeting his unfathomable expression with a clear, direct gaze, hiding the pain buried deep inside. She even managed a slight smile, although she was unaware that it appeared to be tinged with sadness. 'The only regret I have where Paul is concerned is that I was foolish enough to be taken in by him in the first place.'

'You were young and susceptible, were you not?'

Lexi gave an imperceptible shrug. 'Nothing alters the fact that I made a terrible misjudgement of character, which was only compounded by my un-willingness to heed my father or David.'

'You paid for your mistake.'

It wasn't a query, merely a statement of fact, and her lashes swept down to shutter the sudden flaring of pain.

'Not all men are callous, insensitive brutes,' Georg offered quietly.

'Possibly not.' She paused, her eyes wide and startlingly direct. 'But I've never been sufficiently inclined to set out on a wild bedroom romp in an attempt to disprove Paul's accusations of my frigidity!'

'Ludicrous,' Georg drawled, and her eyes flashed with sudden animosity. 'That you could possibly be frigid,' he elaborated.

'And you're an expert on the sexual exploits of men and women?'

His faint smile held amused cynicism. 'I can guarantee that my experience is infinitely more vast than yours.'

'I wouldn't dream of doubting it!'

He lifted her hand to his lips and idly brushed her fingertips in a gesture that was blatantly evocative, and she felt so impossibly angry it was all she could do not to snatch her hand from his grasp.

'Stop opposing me,' he berated quietly.

'How can I *not* oppose you? At first it appeared I was agreeing to a simple collusion,' she said wretchedly. 'Now I'm wearing an engagement ring, and you've told Jonathan and the gossip columnists that we're getting married within weeks!'

'Would it be so disastrous if we did?'

Her eyes widened with incredulous disbelief. 'You can't be serious?'

'Very serious.'

'But—*why*?'

'Why not?' Georg countered smoothly. 'I look at Alex and Samantha and I know that I want what they have. A caring relationship; children.'

'That's no basis for marriage,' she responded, utterly shocked by his reasoning.

'Isn't it better to have a marriage based on friendship and mutual trust than chase an illusion?' His eyes were dark and fathomless. 'I have amassed considerable assets. Do you think for one moment that women solicit my attention for reasons other than with an eye to a generous expense account, travel, and the gift of limitless jewellery?' His query was wholly cynical, and she looked at him carefully.

'You would be content with such a relationship?'

'Yes.'

Her expression registered an entire gamut of emotions, and she struggled to contain them. Could she marry him? *Dared* she? Once she had chased a fairy-tale and fallen flat on her face. Maybe this time she should use her head instead of her heart.

He smiled, and everything else seemed to fade as he leant forward and brushed his lips against her forehead. 'I'll get you a drink,' he said solemnly. 'And then we'll mingle.'

Lexi accepted a glass of champagne, then walked at his side as they mixed with the guests, pausing to converse with one group and another before eventually rejoining Samantha and Alex.

'Shall we leave them to it?' Samantha queried with a cheeky grin as the two brothers became engaged in deep conversation, and Lexi agreed, watching as Samantha briefly touched Alex's shoulder.

Georg caught the unobtrusive gesture, and his eyes pierced Lexi's for a second before he returned his attention to the man at his side.

Together Samantha and Lexi threaded their way towards a table where two waitresses were dispensing coffee.

'Oh, this is heaven,' Samantha breathed as she sipped the aromatic brew. 'It has been a successful night. All the tickets were sold out last week.'

'Another notable charity,' Lexi accorded. 'Georg seems to be an active patron of several.'

'Georg is a very special man,' Samantha offered with deep sincerity.

'He complimented you in much the same manner.'

A dimpled smile turned Samantha's features into something quite beautiful. 'We are—*simpatico*. There was a time when Alex was impossibly jealous. Completely without foundation, I might add.'

'Of course.'

Samantha laughed. 'You sound so sure.'

'One has only to look at you and Alex together to know no one else in the world exists for either of you.'

'Yet it wasn't always like that.'

Lexi didn't know what to say, and sagely maintained her silence.

'I found myself married to Alex without any choice,' Samantha revealed quietly. 'I was very young, and at first I rebelled. Rather badly, I'm afraid. The first few months were——' she paused, effecting a faint grimace in memory '—difficult.'

'You weren't in love with him?'

'Not at first, no.'

'I find that very hard to believe.'

'Now I cannot imagine my life without him.'

Lexi looked at her carefully. 'What are you trying to tell me?'

'That Georg is the one man, aside from Alex, whom I would trust with my life,' Samantha said simply.

'You think I'm not sure of Georg?'

'I think,' Samantha corrected, 'you're unsure of yourself.'

'Oh, my,' Lexi declared with a defenceless little shrug. 'Next you'll say that love can come after the marriage, and I should leap in where any self-respecting angel would fear to tread!' Her eyes kindled with rueful cynicism, and Samantha laughed.

'Are we permitted to share the joke?' a deep voice drawled from behind, and Lexi turned to see Alex and Georg had rejoined them.

'Most definitely not.'

'Ah—woman-talk, I presume,' Alex declared, shooting his wife a dark probing glance that held latent warmth.

'We were talking about men,' Samantha reported gravely.

Her husband seemed interested, rivetingly so. 'Indeed?'

Georg began to laugh softly, and caught hold of Lexi's hand. 'I think we'll leave you two alone.' He tugged gently, and drew her towards the dance-floor.

'I'm not sure that I want to dance,' Lexi protested, yet somehow she was in his arms, and the music was slow, the lights low, and it was all too easy to forget everything except the moment.

His hold was less than conventional, and after a few minutes she gave in to temptation and let her head rest against the curve of his shoulder. If she closed her eyes she could almost imagine this was real, and somewhere deep inside was born the longing for it to be more than just a pretence.

There were as many reasons why she should marry him as there were reasons for her to refuse. She thought of Samantha and Alex, and their daughter Leanne; of a home, with Georg in the role of husband, lover, father.

'You're very quiet.'

Lexi lifted her head and gave him a rueful smile. 'I was just about to suggest we leave. It must be after midnight, and I have to catch an early-morning flight to the Gold Coast.'

'We'll find Samantha and Alex, and bid them goodnight,' Georg declared, relinquishing his hold.

Ten minutes later they were in the car, and Lexi sat in silence, listening to the slight swish of tyres traversing a road wet with a sudden summer shower of rain. The air smelt fresh and clean, and the sky was a clear indigo blue, almost black, and even as she looked there was a sprinkling of stars to herald the promise of a clear new day.

Georg brought the Ferrari to a halt outside the entrance to her apartment block and switched off the engine.

'I'll ring you as soon as I get back,' Lexi indicated as she released the seatbelt.

'Ring me when you arrive,' he drawled, releasing his own and shifting slightly to face her.

He seemed to loom large, a vaguely threatening force, and she mentally chided herself for possessing too vivid an imagination.

'I have to pack,' she said quickly.

'And you merely want to escape.'

She looked at him carefully, seeing his rough-chiselled features, the stark strength apparent. 'It's quite late.'

'Then kiss me goodnight, and run upstairs to bed.'

She felt her eyes widen, and wondered at the degree of indolent sensuality apparent in his voice.

'Why so hesitant, Lexi?' he drawled. 'Have I suddenly grown horns?'

She shook her head. 'Of course not,' she negated slowly.

'Yet you find it difficult, hmm?'

You can't begin to know *how* difficult, she longed to respond, then she gave herself a mental shake.

This was crazy. Tentatively she reached up to brush her lips against his cheek, and found he'd moved his head so that instead she encountered his mouth.

For a moment she froze, then she pressed her mouth lightly against his in a fleeting kiss.

'That isn't exactly what I had in mind.'

His faint mockery brought a flood of colour to her cheeks, and she opened her mouth to fling a stinging retort at him only to have it possessed by his in a kiss that rocked the very foundation of her being. 'Possessed' was the only word adequate to define it, and some devious alchemy had to be responsible for the traitorous way she began to respond. Her breathing became rapid and uneven, and she was aware of the pulse thudding at the base of her throat. Every inch of skin tingled alive, heightening her senses and making her feel achingly aware of him until she wanted more than a mere melding of mouths.

The restriction of clothes—his, *hers*—seemed an impossible barrier, and her fingers shook as they hovered close to his shirt buttons, then fell away in distracted dismay as she realised how close she was to wanting him totally.

With a murmur of distress Lexi tore her mouth away. Her eyes were impossibly wide and hauntingly luminous and her cheeks tinged with pink as she encountered his dark glittering gaze.

'If you don't want me to come upstairs and invade your bed I suggest you get out of the car before I discard my noble instincts,' Georg taunted with husky amusement.

Lexi needed no second bidding, and she heard his soft chuckle an instant before she closed the door behind her and ran lightly towards the entrance.

CHAPTER EIGHT

IT HAD been quite a day, one way and another, Lexi mused thoughtfully as she entered the luxurious apartment. The sun at its zenith had been hot—at least three degrees higher than Sydney temperatures, and she needed a cool shower and an icy drink.

The Gold Coast was one of her favourite places, its relaxed lifestyle and long hours of sunshine providing a magnet for the many tourists who flocked to the famed coastal strip in search of golden sands and sapphire-blue sea with spume-crested waves rolling in from the Pacific Ocean. Many of the shopping complexes favoured seven-day trading, and it was all too easy to lose track of time exploring exotic boutiques in any one of several malls.

With a faintly weary gesture Lexi reached a hand to the long thick length of her hair and lifted it away from her nape. The apartment's air-conditioning cooled the heat from her skin, which, despite liberal use of sunblock during the long hours spent in the sun, showed visible signs of exposure.

The photographic shoot had been successful, and a brief session in the morning should wrap it up, then she would be able to catch the next available flight home.

A strange anticipatory thrill coursed through her veins at the mere thought, and she was forced to admit reluctantly that Georg was the main cause.

His image was never far from her mind, and she had only to close her eyes to instantly recall his strong features, the depth of his eyes and the degree of lazy warmth in his smile.

Was it all merely a pretence in their scheme of make-believe? she wondered as she stripped off her clothes and stepped into the shower cubicle. Selecting shampoo, she began working it into the thick length of her hair.

There were times when she rather wistfully longed for their supposed romance to be real, yet that was akin to chasing an impossible dream. The reality was more...comfortable, she decided. If 'comfortable' was a description one could apply to Georg Nicolaos! He possessed the ability to set her emotions into pure turmoil with the least amount of effort.

Lexi sluiced shampoo from her hair, then repeated the process and worked in conditioning lotion.

It was impossible to dispel the fact that he probably regarded her as an attractive addition to his life; if they married she would assume the role of hostess and companion who conveniently fulfilled his sexual needs.

Could such an arrangement work? Would she be able to live with him, accept his physical love-making without becoming too emotionally involved?

Damn. The soft curse was lost beneath the sound of the shower as she deliberately cast such evocative thoughts aside and concentrated on completing her ablutions.

Several minutes later she donned a silk robe before plugging in the hairdrier to style her hair.

A time-consuming task, which she had almost completed when the doorbell rang, and a puzzled frown momentarily creased her forehead as she moved through the lounge. She hadn't ordered room-service, and she certainly wasn't expecting anyone.

The tall dark frame filling the aperture was incredibly familiar.

Her surprise was evident, and several differing emotions chased fleetingly across her expressive features. 'Georg! What are you doing here?'

'Aren't you going to ask me in?'

His slight smile did strange things to her equilibrium, and she stood aside at once. 'Of course.' She pushed a hand through her hair, and gave a faint grimace. Tumbled tresses, no make-up, and attired in only a robe. He couldn't have caught her at more of a disadvantage if he'd tried. 'I haven't long emerged from the shower.'

His eyes were strangely watchful as he reached forward and trailed his fingers down the smoothness of her cheek. 'You look about sixteen,' he said quietly, and she wrinkled her nose at him in silent admonition, feeling suddenly gauche at the degree of drawled amusement in his voice, and a little nervous.

'This is a surprise,' she declared lightly. 'Can I get you a drink?'

'I'll fix myself something while you get changed.'

Something in his tone ensured that he was the total focus of her attention, and her eyes flew to his with a mixture of concern and outright fear.

Unbidden, her hand rose towards him, then fluttered down to her side. 'It's Jonathan, isn't it?'

'He collapsed this afternoon,' Georg revealed gently. 'At this very moment he's in surgery. I chartered a private jet from Sydney, and a limousine is waiting outside. All you have to do is slip into some clothes.'

'David——'

'Is waiting for us at the hospital.' He leaned forward and brushed his lips against her temple. 'Jonathan will be fine,' he reassured. 'He has the best team of vascular surgeons in the country, and they're confident of success.'

There wasn't a thing she was capable of saying, and she turned away from him blindly, her movements completely automatic as she walked swiftly into the bedroom.

Retrieving a bag from the wardrobe, she hurriedly tore clothes from their hangers, then she slipped into clean underwear and donned eau de Nil cotton trousers and matching top, slid a brush through her hair and slipped her feet into casual shoes. She could attend to her make-up in the limousine, she decided, gathering up toiletries and her make-up bag.

'I've arranged your check-out,' Georg informed as she emerged into the lounge. 'Is there anyone here you should contact before we leave?'

'The cameraman. He's staying in a unit at the resort.'

'Give me his name, and we'll arrange for a message to reach him.'

Two hours later they arrived at Sydney airport, and it was after eight when they reached the hospital to find a weary, but mildly exuberant David waiting to greet them.

Lexi flew into his embrace at once, and was soundly hugged before being gently pushed to arm's length.

'Jonathan's OK,' David reassured her before she could voice the query. 'Surgery was successful, and he's in intensive care.'

Intensive care sounded vaguely frightening, and she stood still, hugging herself in a defensive gesture as she looked askance from one to the other in silence.

'Standard procedure,' Georg assured her quietly. 'They'll keep him there for a few days until he stabilises, I imagine.'

A shiver shook her slim frame. Life was so tenuous, so incredibly fragile. The thought of losing Jonathan was more than she could bear. 'Can I see him?'

'I'm sure the medical staff would advise against it,' Georg said gently. 'He'll be heavily sedated, and hooked up to various machines.'

She turned towards her brother. 'David?'

'Georg is right, sweetheart. There's nothing we can do.' He reached out and gave her shoulder a gentle squeeze. 'Let Georg take you home. The hospital has my number, and if there's even the slightest change I'll call you at once.'

In the car she sat in silence, and it was only when the Ferrari drew to a halt that she withdrew from reflective thought sufficiently to recognise her surroundings.

Indoors, she made for the lift, conscious that Georg walked at her side, and she made no demur when he took her keys and unlocked the apartment.

'Thank you,' she said with genuine gratitude. 'For ensuring that I reached Sydney as quickly as possible.'

'I'll fix a snack,' Georg indicated. 'You ate nothing on the plane.'

'I don't feel hungry.'

'Something light,' he insisted as he shrugged off his jacket, and, placing it over a nearby chair, he rolled up each sleeve-cuff and walked into the kitchen. 'An omelette?'

Lexi slowly followed him, watching as he deftly set the pan to heat, whisked eggs in a bowl, then sliced up bacon, cheese and tomato.

Within minutes she found herself seated at the table, forking delectable pieces of food into her mouth. It was delicious, and she said so, shooting him a slight smile as he made the coffee.

'You're more than just a handsome face,' she accorded lightly.

'Ah—a compliment,' he drawled as he poured the aromatic brew into two cups. 'Usually you are swift to upbraid me for some imagined misdemeanour.'

She spared him a direct look, and was disconcerted by his unwavering gaze. 'We—strike sparks off each other,' she ventured in explanation, and heard his husky laugh.

'Have you ever paused to consider *why*?'

'I resent you,' Lexi responded swiftly. 'For attempting to rule my life—*me*.' Replacing her cutlery on her plate, she pushed it towards the centre of the table. 'In a minute we'll be arguing again.'

'Something at which you seem to excel.'

She looked at him carefully, seeing the strength apparent and an indomitable measure of self-will. 'I don't feel inclined to be at cross purposes with you tonight.'

'In that case, let's take our coffee into the lounge and watch television together.'

She shrugged slightly. 'Why not?'

For the next hour they sat in separate chairs, watching the second half of a film, and when it finished Georg got to his feet.

A strange sense of desolation assailed her at the thought that he was about to leave, and she rose from the chair, then stood hesitantly as he took the few steps necessary to bring him within touching distance.

He had only to reach out, and she waited, almost afraid to breathe, alternately craving solace and unwilling to accept its price.

For a long time she just looked at him, watching with detached fascination as he lifted a hand and brushed his fingers across the delicate planes of her cheek, then lowered his head.

His kiss held an infinite degree of *tendresse*, and she felt the ache of tears. Never had she felt quite so alone or so incredibly forlorn, and she badly needed to hold on to his sheer physical presence.

He held her gaze, and she stood mesmerised, unable to look away from those deep dark depths as if her life depended on it. He tilted her face, framing it between his hands, and his gaze was steady. 'Do you want me to stay?'

'I—don't think I could bear to be alone,' she whispered, feeling shaky and ill-equipped to deal with him.

Her lips parted, trembling a little as he idly traced their lower curve. Unbidden, her eyes filled with tears, and he swore softly as they spilled over and ran slowly down each cheek. Lexi shook her head slightly, and rubbed the back of her hands across each cheek. 'It's just reaction.'

He pressed a forefinger against her mouth, and his eyes darkened as he felt her lips tremble beneath his touch.

'I'll heat some milk and brandy,' he said gently.

She was powerless to prevent the lump that rose in her throat, and she merely nodded in silent acquiescence, watching as he left the room.

Dear heaven, she was weary. If she could just close her eyes for a few minutes...

When Georg re-entered the lounge she was asleep, curled up on the sofa, looking as guileless as a young child.

A slow smile tugged at the edges of his mouth, and he carefully eased her slight body into his arms and carried her through to the bedroom.

She stirred faintly, but didn't wake as he slipped off her outer clothes and placed her between soft percale sheets.

He stood looking down at her for a very long time, then he moved quietly into the main bathroom and showered before switching off the lights with the exception of one in the hallway.

Lexi slept deeply, caught up in the spell of differing dreams, some more vivid and vaguely disturbing than others, and she was barely aware of a source of enveloping strength as she hovered increasingly closer to wakefulness.

There was something different apparent, but she was unable to pinpoint exactly what, until the powerful heartbeat beneath her cheek gradually penetrated her subconscious, and she froze, becoming aware with shocking clarity that she was not only in bed, but held lightly imprisoned against a male body. What was more, one of her arms curved across the hard musculature of his ribcage, while one of *his* closed possessively over her hip.

'You're awake.'

If she lay perfectly still maybe her immobility would persuade him he was mistaken.

'Don't pretend,' Georg drawled. 'Your heartbeat has just gone into overdrive.'

As if to prove his point he trailed a hand to the rapidly beating pulse at the base of her throat.

With infinite slowness her lashes swept slowly upwards. Her lips felt impossibly dry, and she drew in the lower curve in an attempt to moisten it. Inside she was as nervous as a kitten, and her eyes clung to his as he tilted her chin.

'What are you doing here?' Her voice quivered slightly, and her eyes widened as she viewed him with unblinking solemnity.

The reflection from the lighted hallway provided subdued illumination, and she glimpsed his faint smile.

'Your apartment, specifically, or your bed?'

Her throat ached, and the words came out in a husky undertone. 'Don't—tease.'

His fingers trailed a gentle exploratory path across the delicate hollows at the base of her throat.

His touch was familiar, and so very sure, that the blood drained from her face. He hadn't—surely they hadn't——? No, it wasn't possible. She would have woken, would have known——

'You think I would attempt to steal from you in sleep what you would not willingly give when you were in total possession of your senses?'

Dear lord, was she so transparent? Heat flooded her cheeks, and her lashes swept down to form a protective veil.

His warm breath fanned her temples. 'Lexi?'

She heard the softly voiced command, and was held immobile by the wealth of seduction apparent. She looked at him, and she wanted to cry, but no tears would come.

Capturing her head between his hands, he leant forward and covered her lips with his own, softly and with such tenderness that it made her catch her breath. There seemed no urgency to deepen the kiss as he gently traced the outline of her lips, savouring their sweet fullness until her mouth parted of its own volition.

Without conscious thought her hands slid to his shoulders, then crept up to encircle his neck, and his mouth hardened in possession as he sought a devastation that left her weak-willed and malleable.

It seemed an age before he relinquished her mouth, and he trailed his lips down the sensitive cord at her neck to explore the hollows at the base of her throat, then edged lower to the curve of her breast.

The top she wore was easily dispensed with, as was the silk and lace that comprised her bra, and she gasped as he captured one tender burgeoning peak between his teeth and rendered such exquisite pleasure that it was all she could do not to cry out. Her fingers raked through his hair, silently begging him to desist as her whole body began to pulsate with molten fire, and she became mindless, lost in a wealth of sensuality so intense that there was no room for anything else but the need to subside into the swirling vortex of emotion.

There could be no turning back, and she told herself that nothing else mattered, only *now*, as he gently removed every last vestige of her clothing.

His hands and his mouth became evocative instruments as he sought to awaken a tumultuous response, his lips grazing down over her ribcage on a destructive path towards the central core of her femininity.

Her shocked protest went unheeded, as with deliberate eroticism he taught her to enjoy an experience so fraught with sensual ecstasy that she cried out, alternately pleading for more and begging him to desist, until, just as she thought she could stand it no longer, his mouth began a slow upward trail, tantalising, teasing, tasting.

Slowly, with care, he gained entry with one sure thrust, then he deliberately sought a response she was afraid to give.

Her pleasure began as a spiralling sensation that swelled into an intense throbbing ache as she became completely and utterly absorbed in his deep rhythmic possession.

Mindlessly exultant, she scaled the heights of ecstasy and knew she never wanted to descend from this elusive sensory plateau where sheer sensation ruled.

Her faint whimper of distress was very real as he began to withdraw, and she held him close, unwilling to have it end.

His lips moved to her shoulder, caressing the delicate curves and hollows, before wandering with tactile sensuality to tease the edge of her mouth; then he lifted a hand to her chin and forced her to meet his gaze.

There wasn't a single word she was capable of uttering, and her eyes felt like huge liquid pools mirroring the degree of deep slumberous passion she'd experienced beneath his touch.

Gently he lifted her hand to his lips, and there was nothing she could do to prevent the slight quivering of her mouth as she glimpsed the warmth reflected in the depths of his eyes.

It was impossible for him to be unaware of her unbridled response to his lovemaking, and a faint tide of pink coloured her cheeks as she glimpsed his slight smile.

This, *this* was so different from Paul's selfish insensitivity, Lexi decided wondrously, feeling bewitched and bemused by the awakening of her own sensuality. She had read once that good lovemaking was nature's ultimate aphrodisiac, and it was true, for she felt tremendously and utterly *complete*.

Her eyes widened slightly as Georg slid out of the bed, and anything she might have said was lost beneath the brief pressure of his mouth; then he straightened and walked towards the *en suite* bathroom. She let her lashes drift, down, unwilling to move so much as an inch.

Minutes later her eyes flew wide open and she made a slight sound in protest as she was lifted out of the bed and carried into the bathroom.

Without any effort he stepped into the round spa-bath and lowered her to sit in front of him. Deliciously warm water lapped her shoulders, and it was pure reflex action that sent her hands to her hair, lifting, twisting its length into a knot atop her head.

She wasn't capable of uttering a single word as he collected soap and began slowly sponging her skin. The action was gently erotic, and she felt a traitorous warmth unfurl deep within and steal treacherously through her veins.

His lips grazed across her exposed nape and settled in the soft curve of her neck, then travelled to the tip of her shoulder and trailed back again. One hand cupped the slight fullness of her breast, while the other traced an evocative pattern across her ribcage, then ventured lower to settle with unerring ease on the nub of her femininity.

Nothing seemed to matter except the resurging desire spiralling through her body, emcompassing and all-consuming, and she gave a startled gasp as he lifted her round to face him.

He kissed her, gently at first, then with tantalising evocativeness, choosing not to allow her to deepen the kiss until she murmured a protest and captured his head with her hands.

His eyes gleamed with lazy passion as she moved forward, and he allowed her licence to initiate a foray that somehow became his to control, then he gently broke the kiss, smiling faintly at her disappointment.

For a moment she was unsure of his intention, and her eyes widened in disbelief as he carefully positioned her to accept his male length, and he watched several fleeting emotions chase expressively over her features as his manhood swelled inside her.

Then his hands slid to her breasts, shaping the soft curves before rendering exquisite torture to their engorged peaks.

Just as she thought she could stand it no longer, he slid one hand to her nape while the other tangled in the mass of her hair as he pulled her head down to his, and this time his kiss was an erotic possession that gave no quarter until she became a mindless supplicant in his arms.

It was a long time before they emerged to towel each other dry, then they walked arm in arm to the bedroom and slid into bed to continue the long slow exploration until sleep claimed them at the edge of a new day's dawn.

CHAPTER NINE

LEXI felt a featherlight touch tracing a delicate pattern along her collarbone, and she opened her eyes slowly, unwilling to come fully awake in case what she'd experienced last night had been little more than a figment of her vivid imagination.

'Wake up, sleepyhead.'

Dreams didn't have voices that sounded like a deep, teasing faintly accented drawl belonging to a certain Greek—at least, none of the dreams she'd ever experienced.

Slowly she let her eyelashes sweep upwards, and her eyes widened slightly as they met the lazy warmth reflecting in his.

'Good morning,' Georg greeted her gently.

She couldn't think of one coherent word to offer, and his mouth assumed a sensual curve that tripped her pulse-beat and sent it racing at a rapid rate.

Thanks, she wanted to say, for the most beautiful night of my life. Except that her throat was dry, and she doubted that any sound would emerge.

'Orange juice? Coffee?' he slanted musingly, shifting slightly to prop his head with one hand.

She wanted both, except she was loath to move, and he laughed softly as he reached out to push several tumbled tresses back behind her ear.

'Time to rise and shine,' he mocked huskily. 'I have a meeting to attend at nine-thirty, and I imagine you want to ring the hospital.'

Jonathan. Dear lord, how could she possibly have forgotten? Her eyes mirrored her anguish, and he leant forward to brush his lips across her mouth.

'David hasn't rung, so Jonathan's condition will be stable.' He pushed the sheet back and bent to bestow a lingering kiss on her breast. 'Let's take a shower, then we'll share breakfast.'

There was nothing she could do to prevent the faint tinge of pink that flew to her cheeks at the promise of shared intimacy, and the colour deepened as Georg slid out from the bed, unconcerned by his nakedness, and walked round to scoop her into his arms.

'Put me down,' Lexi protested half-heartedly, and he merely laughed as he carried her through to the bathroom.

Reaching into the shower-cubicle, he turned on the taps then let her slide to her feet in front of him.

'You're shy.'

As a statement of fact it was without equal, and she gave a slight ineffectual gesture of assent.

'Don't begin erecting barriers, Lexi.'

She felt utterly defenceless, and she swallowed convulsively as her mouth began to tremble. 'I'm not—used to this,' she said shakily.

His eyes flared, and she saw the pupils darken and change as he caught her close. Then his mouth opened over hers in a kiss that possessed every nuance of erotic mastery, skilfully absorbing her until nothing else mattered except *now*.

She had no idea how long they remained locked together, and when he slowly broke the kiss she could only stand in total bemusement as he reached for a shower-cap, pushed the mass of her curling hair beneath it and gently pulled her into the cubicle.

Half an hour later they were both dressed and seated opposite each other at the breakfast table.

Jonathan, the hospital reported, was stable and had spent a comfortable night. Visitors were limited to five minutes and restricted to immediate family.

Almost as soon as she had replaced the receiver David rang through with the same news and suggested she meet him for lunch.

'I'll see you tonight about seven,' Georg bade her as he drained the last of his coffee.

'Where?' Lexi queried idly as she walked with him towards the door, and he smiled down at her.

'My apartment . . . yours—does it matter?'

Her eyes lifted to meet his, and she looked unsure, not really wanting him to leave, yet knowing that he must.

'We'll discuss it tonight. Take care,' he said quietly as he opened the door.

Then he was gone, and Lexi closed the door behind him before wandering back into the kitchen.

The day held a dream-like quality as she attended to routine chores, made a few calls, rang David and confirmed arrangements for lunch, then drove to the hospital.

Jonathan was still heavily sedated, and, although he opened his eyes during her brief visit, she doubted her presence registered.

David was already seated when she entered the small restaurant, and he rose to his feet with a warm smile creasing his attractive features.

'I had trouble parking,' she explained with an expressive shrug as she brushed her lips to his cheek. He shook his head as he told her, 'I've only been waiting a few minutes. Will you have something to drink?'

'Mineral water.'

They each ordered from the menu, and Lexi opted for a garden salad followed with fresh fruit.

'How are you getting on with Georg?'

'Reasonably well,' Lexi acknowledged cautiously.

'Jonathan is absolutely delighted you've both opted for marriage,' David ventured, shooting her a deep probing look that didn't fool her in the slightest. 'You must know you have my blessing.'

She took a leisurely sip from her glass, then replaced it carefully down on the table. 'I'm sure you and Jonathan are immensely relieved.'

David appeared to choose his words carefully. 'We've both known the Nicolaos family for many years.'

'How is the business deal progressing with the Japanese consortium?'

'Extremely well. Alex and Georg have managed to elicit a signed preliminary agreement, which I have perused and sanctioned. As soon as Jonathan is well enough the documents will be presented for his signature.' He lifted his shoulders in an expressive gesture. 'Aside from time-consuming technicalities, it is virtually a *fait accompli*.'

She picked at her salad and forked a few morsels into her mouth before venturing, 'And Paul? Presumably you've managed to come to an amicable arrangement with him?'

'We're in a state of negotiation.'

'He's pressing for a larger settlement, and you're stalling,' Lexi deduced with a wry grimace.

'For a few more days, until the deal is due for a Press release,' David agreed.

'After which he will have no room for further negotiation.'

'Precisely.'

It was impossible to refrain from cynicism. 'And all loose ends will be successfully tied.'

'A propitious start to a productive new year.'

'It's Christmas the day after tomorrow,' Lexi murmured, and her expressive eyes dulled slightly as she became lost in reflective thought, remembering previous years at home with numerous gifts piled beneath an enormous decorated tree and Sophie dishing up a veritable feast of festive fare. 'It won't be the same with Jonathan in hospital.'

'I've already spoken with Sophie, and we'll have lunch together at the house, then spend time with Jonathan. Georg, I'm sure, will insist you share the evening with his family.'

She was gripped with a sudden need to confide her own doubts and insecurities. 'David...' she paused, unsure whether her choice of words would sound inane '...I'd rather this marriage was planned for months down the track, instead of the mere weeks Georg is insistent upon.'

Her brother assumed a look of professionally bland inscrutability. 'It's perfectly understandable you should experience doubts, given the circumstances. Why not discuss them with Georg?'

'Because he's equally clever as you, if not more so,' she acknowledged quietly, and he offered her a slightly whimsical smile.

'Shall we order coffee? I'm due in court at two.'

'David——'

'Marry him, Lexi,' he advised gently. 'I'm confident you'll never have cause to regret it.'

How could something appear so simple and logical, yet be fraught with innumerable complexities? Lexi pondered as she drove to the hospital and called in on Jonathan.

This time he was awake, but extremely drowsy, and she was cheered by his faint smile and the reassurance by nursing staff as to his progress.

What remained of the afternoon she spent shopping, and she returned to her apartment laden with various coloured carrier-bags and packages which she spilled on to the bed in the spare bedroom.

It was hot—so hot, in fact, that Lexi decided to change into a bikini and swim several leisurely lengths of the swimming-pool in an effort to cool off and relax, before returning to her apartment to shower and wash her hair.

Would Georg want to dine in, or go out? Out seemed infinitely safer, for she needed time to think about their shared intimacy and all that it implied before accepting a state of domesticity and shared domicile.

She was ready a few minutes before seven, dressed in an elegant cream strapless silk gown with matching accessories. A silk wrap completed the outfit, and she added a slim gold choker, bracelet and ear-studs. A last-minute check in the mirror lent reassurance that she'd made the right decision in adopting an intricate upswept hairstyle, and her make-up was understated, with skilled application of shadow and liner to emphasis her eyes.

For some reason she felt consumed by nervous tension, and when the doorbell pealed she took a deep breath before crossing the lounge.

Georg looked the epitome of the sophisticated executive, and she let her eyes sweep over the impeccable tailoring of his suit before lifting her gaze to meet his.

Then she immediately wished she hadn't, for she wasn't quite prepared for the lazy warmth evident in those dark eyes or the sensual curve of his mouth. It brought a vivid reminder of all that they'd shared through the night, and her senses leapt at the thought of what lay ahead at the evening's end.

'I wasn't sure what you had in mind,' Lexi offered helplessly, and a husky chuckle left his throat.

'Oh, just an enjoyable meal in your company,' he drawled, adding softly, 'for now.'

Her eyes widened at his unspoken implication, and she was powerless to prevent the feeling of acute vulnerability. 'Would you like a drink?'

His smile deepened, and her stomach seemed to execute a series of somersaults as he caught hold of her hand. 'If you're ready we'll leave.'

The restaurant Georg had chosen was one of the city's élite establishments, and he ordered expensive champagne, then asked her choice of food before selecting what proved to be an epicurean delight.

They conversed, discussing the highlights of each other's day among other things, and afterwards Lexi had no clear recollection of a single topic.

All she was aware of was Georg. His expressive features, the wide-spaced dark eyes, the broad well-defined bone-structure, and his mouth, which seemed to compel an almost hypnotic fascination.

It was after ten when they left, and Lexi was grateful when he slotted a tape into the cassette-player, for it meant she didn't have to search for something adequate by way of conversation.

On reaching her apartment block, he simply parked the car and together they took the lift to her designated floor. She was incapable of making any demur when he retrieved her keys, unlocked the door, then ushered her inside.

All evening she had been conscious of his indolent regard, the degree of latent passion evident, and now she felt like a finely tuned violin waiting for the maestro's touch. It was crazy to be so acutely aware of another human body and the effect it could have on her senses.

'You look so incredibly fragile I am almost afraid to touch you,' Georg mused as he lifted a hand and trailed his fingers down her cheek. He traced the curve of her mouth with a gentle forefinger, then lowered his head to bestow a fleeting kiss on her mouth.

Her lips parted involuntarily, trembling as she caught his indrawn breath, and she felt a sense of loss as he drew back and stood regarding her with disruptive sensuality.

'Will you object if I unpin your hair?'

She shook her head in silent acquiescence, and when the curls lay in a thick mass below her shoulders he slid his fingers through their length.

'I've wanted to do this all evening.'

And I've waited all day, she assured silently, and felt vaguely shocked at the truth of her thoughts.

Then he kissed her, gently at first, and afterwards she had little recollection of who was in command as passion flared and demanded assuagement.

With a husky exultant laugh Georg swept her into his arms and carried her through to the bedroom, where he took infinite care to remove every last vestige of her clothing before beginning on his own.

Lexi behaved like a shameless wanton beneath his touch as he sought to strike an unhitherto heard chord, and she cried out as the deep rhythm of his possession took her to the heights of ecstasy and beyond.

Long after he had fallen asleep at her side she lay awake, too caught up with introspection to cull an easy somnolence.

Even now it seemed a fantasy, some wild imaginative dream that had no part of reality. Potent, dangerous, and—in its aftermath—destructive.

Just as she'd thought the pain and degradation Paul had inflicted was unacceptable, this— passionate *possession* Georg evoked was everything she'd been led to believe, and more.

Had *he* felt like that? Was he able to command such a mindless response from every woman he took to bed? Or was it merely sexual chemistry at its zenith? She'd been so caught up with her own reactions that she hadn't given a thought to his.

A shudder shook her slender frame in the realisation that she'd taken everything he'd chosen to give, and given nothing in return. It had been *her* pleasure, her climactic orgasm that had been all-important, the desperate need to have him continue arousing those spiralling sensations until she felt almost *driven* by a wholly consuming desire.

In the night he stirred and reached for her, settling her into the curve of his body, and she woke late to find an empty space beside her and a scrawled note on the adjoining pillow, which read, 'Dinner tonight my apartment—I'll cook. Georg.'

Lexi showered, then, dressed in casual clothes, she drove to the supermarket, battling against weary mothers with young children and middle-aged matrons in an effort to traverse the numerous aisles and fill her trolley with necessary groceries. She visited Jonathan in hospital, then she returned home to tidy up before driving back to the hospital mid-afteroon.

It was almost six-thirty when she buzzed Georg's apartment from the lobby, and within minutes the lift descended to transport her to the uppermost floor.

She had elected to dress casually, choosing a straight black skirt and white knit top, and her hair was caught up at her nape with a fashionable black bow.

'Mmm, smells heavenly,' Lexi greeted him as soon as Georg opened the door, and she almost melted at the warmth reflected in his eyes.

'Tonight you will sample a selection of traditional Greek cuisine.'

'And afterwards can we watch the carol-singing on television?' she ventured, wriggling her nose at him as he slanted her a quizzical glance. 'It's Christmas Eve.'

He, too, was in casual attire: dressed in designer jeans and a cotton-knit shirt, he projected a raw virility that was arresting.

For a starter he served vine-wrapped parcels of minced lamb accompanied by a delicate sauce, which he followed with moussaka. Dessert was baklava, and afterwards they dispensed with the dishes before taking their coffee through to the lounge, where they watched a number of artists, accompanied by a choir, sing a variety of carols, recorded live from a large city park.

'I must go,' Lexi intimated when the programme came to a close.

'Why must you?' Georg drawled.

'Tomorrow is Christmas Day,' she said helplessly as he reached forward and undid the bow fastening her hair. 'I'm visiting Jonathan in the morning, and meeting David at the house at midday. After lunch we'll both go to the hospital, and——'

'Stay with me,' he interceded. 'And in the morning we will visit Jonathan together.'

She looked at him carefully, then opened her mouth to speak, only to have him press her lips closed.

'Indulge me. I cannot think of a nicer Christmas present than to wake and find you in my bed.'

A long time afterwards she wondered why she hadn't protested, but by then it was far too late to rationalise her decision.

Christmas Day was filled with love and laughter, the joy of gifts and giving, *family*. Hers, his. And Jonathan was progressing with such speed that it seemed there was little cause to doubt his ability to recover fully from surgery.

The days leading up to New Year passed all too quickly. Lexi spent each morning and afternoon visiting Jonathan, and the nights were spent with Georg, at his apartment or her own. Sometimes they ate out, dining with Samantha and Alex, or with Mrs Nicolaos, and when they stayed home they took it in turns to prepare the evening meal.

'I'll cook tonight,' Lexi declared as she followed him to the door of his apartment a few days before she was due to fly north for the photographic shoot at the Port Douglas Mirage Resort. She had something special in mind, and teased lightly as he moved towards the lift, 'Will you mind if I use your kitchen?'

'Carla is due to arrive about nine,' he warned as he pressed the call-button.

His housekeeper was Spanish, matronly, and came in two days a week to clean, stock up the pantry and refrigerator from Georg's list, and take care of the laundry. She was a delight, voluble, and possessed of a wicked sense of humour.

Lexi retreated into the kitchen and poured herself a second cup of coffee, then planned a menu and checked ingredients before making out a list of what she needed.

At ten she visited Jonathan, then went on to complete her shopping, and most of the afternoon was spent preparing food.

Carla left at five, and Lexi hurriedly changed into white evening culottes and a patterned top before returning to the kitchen to anxiously oversee the various dishes alternately simmering atop the elements and the oven. Then she was able to centre her attention on setting an elegant table in the dining-room.

When Georg arrived shortly after six everything was ready, and she felt inordinately pleased with the result.

'Hmm, is this is a sample of what I can look forward to in the future?' he drawled as he caught her close, and she returned his kiss with such fervour it left her slightly breathless.

'I felt like surprising you,' she said simply, and her bones seemed to melt at the warmth reflected in his eyes.

'Mental telepathy, perhaps?' Georg slanted as he moved across to the cabinet to pour them both a drink. 'I have decided to surprise you by having an agent line up a few properties for us to inspect tomorrow.'

Her expressive features portrayed a gamut of emotions. 'You intend buying a house?'

'Yes, Lexi. *Ours.*'

She took the slim crystal flute from his hand and sipped the contents. 'I assumed if we married that we'd live here.'

His gaze probed hers. '*When*, not if. And we shall live here until such time as the redecorating and refurbishing of the house is completed.'

The breath caught in her throat, and for a moment she was lost for words. 'I barely become accustomed to one concept when you confront me with another,' she managed shakily.

He reached out and tilted her chin. 'I thought I had managed to dispense with all your doubts.'

She gave a light shrugging gesture. 'Most of them.'

Gently he bent his head down to hers and trailed his lips over her cheek. 'Could it be that you need reassurance?'

'The kind of reassurance you have in mind will mean we get to miss dinner,' she reproved him with a helpless smile, and he laughed softly.

'Tonight you have gone to too much trouble for that, hmm?' His kiss was hard and brief, then he stepped back and caught hold of her hand. 'Let us eat.'

If not exactly of cordon bleu standard, the meal was a complete success, and Lexi basked in the glow of Georg's praise as he sampled one course after another before sitting back, replete, with a glass of superb port.

Together they dispensed with the dishes, and after a leisurely coffee Georg simply swung her into his arms and carried her through to the bedroom.

CHAPTER TEN

THERE was no doubt which house held the most appeal. Lexi fell in love with its Federation-style architecture and multi-coloured leaded windows, the many rooms with wide glass doors opening on to a magnificent terrace, and the panoramic view of the harbour. Possessed of an air of tranquillity, it seemed far removed from the city's hustle and bustle, and with its gardens pruned and replanted it would soon be restored to its former glory.

'This is it?' Georg queried, smiling at her enthusiasm.

'It has so much potential,' she breathed. 'What do *you* think?'

'I'll contact the agent this afternoon.'

'I have a few things to do,' Lexi declared as Georg headed the Ferrari towards Double Bay. 'Shopping.' She really could not leave selecting a suitable gown for the wedding any longer, and she knew of just the boutique where she might find exactly what she had in mind. 'And I'll call into the hospital to see Jonathan, then head back to my apartment.'

'Don't forget we're dining out tonight,' he reminded her. 'I'll collect you at six.'

It was after four when Lexi entered her apartment, and she moved through to the kitchen to retrieve a cool drink from the refrigerator. As much as she adored shopping, to do so in the heat of sub-tropical summer proved an enervating experience.

The insistent burr of the telephone sounded loud in the stillness of the apartment, and she quickly crossed the room and picked up the receiver.

'Lexi?'

The sound of Paul's voice was totally unexpected, and her fingers tightened until the knuckles showed white.

'You must know I have nothing whatsoever to say to you,' she reiterated hardily.

'You don't need to, darling. Just listen is all I ask.'

'Hurry up and get it over with, Paul. I haven't much spare time.'

'Jonathan's precious deal has gone through. Although I guess you know that. And I've been paid off,' he drawled. 'Not as handsomely as I'd like, but adequately enough.'

'Is that it?'

'Don't hang up, Lexi. This conversation is entirely for your benefit.'

She gave a heavy sigh. 'I find that almost impossible to believe.'

'Ah, but you see, darling,' Paul informed her hatefully, 'what you fail to comprehend is that the ultimate joke in this entire débâcle is on you. *Yes*, my sweet——' he paused to give his words sufficient emphasis '——a masterly scheme, conveniently compounded by *my* coincidental involvement, for, after your initial disastrous foray into matrimony with me, it became essential such an error was not repeated. Your dear father and brother, in cohorts with Georg, conspired to utilise

Jonathan's forthcoming surgery as a reason to arrange an eminently suitable marriage for you—with none other than Georg Nicolaos.' His laugh was totally without humour. 'And you, in your innocence, played right into their hands.'

She felt sickened, almost to the point of being physically ill. It took considerable effort to keep her voice calm, but she managed it—just.

'I don't have to listen to any of this.' She had surpassed anger, and was fast approaching a numbed state of limbo.

'Check it out with David,' Paul exhorted cynically. 'I doubt he'll deny it.' Lexi didn't bother to comment, and he continued in a hateful voice, 'Will you think me facetious if I wish you happiness in your second marriage? Such a pity its basis is no more to do with *love* than your first,' he accorded, and there was a slight click as he hung up.

Lexi stood where she was for several long seconds, then she depressed the call-button and punched out a succession of digits.

'David Harrison,' she requested as soon as the receptionist answered. 'Lexi Harrison speaking.'

'Mr Harrison is engaged with a client. Can I get him to call you?'

'It's urgent,' Lexi insisted, and seconds later David came on the line. 'Paul rang to tell me he'd been paid off,' she began without preamble. 'He insists Jonathan deliberately conspired with you and Georg to trap me into marriage. Is it true?'

There was an imperceptible silence, and her stomach gave a sickening lurch.

'Your happiness has always been Jonathan's prime concern,' David responded cautiously.

'Don't play the courtroom tactician with me, David,' she said tightly. 'At least have the decency to confirm or deny it.'

'It's clearly evident you and Georg are happy together.'

'Damn you!' she cursed. 'That doesn't excuse anything!'

'I'll call Georg——'

'Don't interfere,' she warned fiercely. 'If you do I'll never speak to you again!'

She replaced the receiver and almost immediately the telephone burred an insistent summons. For all of ten seconds she determined not to answer, and only the thought that it might be Jonathan motivated her to pick up the receiver.

'Lexi?' Georg's deep faintly accented voice sounded so close he could have been in the same room. 'I'll be delayed by about half an hour.'

Oh, heavens, they were supposed to be dining out! She closed her eyes, then slowly reopened them. 'I was just about to ring you,' she declared, inventing with no scruple whatsoever. 'I can't make it tonight. Jacques needs me. One of the models reported in sick.'

She closed her eyes momentarily against the slight throbbing that began in the region of her right temple.

'Where is the assignment? I'll meet you there.'

An inner voice screamed out in silent rejection. She couldn't face seeing him tonight. If she did she'd never contain the anger that was seething deep inside. 'No, Georg.' Time enough tomorrow to face a confrontation. By then she might have gathered sufficient courage to be able to adopt a cool rationale. 'I have to go. I'm running late.' She replaced the receiver before he had a chance to comment. Crossing into the bedroom, she stripped off her outer clothes, then selected designer jeans and a loose cotton top at random from her wardrobe. Dressed, she caught her hair into a loose knot, picked up her bag, and made her way out of the apartment.

Quite where she was heading she wasn't sure. Anywhere would do, as long as she had some time alone in which to think. Somewhere where no one could contact her.

In the car she slotted a compact disc into the music system, then sent the Mercedes up to street level. Taking a left turn, she simply drove, uncaring of her direction or destination.

Sheer driving skill and instinct kept her within the speed limit and observant of the road rules. Either that or divine guidance, she decided wryly as she finally brought the car to a halt on the side of the road.

She had no idea where she was, for how long or how far she'd travelled, and she rested her forehead on the steering-wheel in a gesture of infinite weariness.

Perhaps there was a motel somewhere nearby where she could book in for the night. It was either that or face a long drive back to her apartment.

A strange light-headedness assailed her, and she wound down the window to let in some fresh air. Now that she thought about it, the last time she'd eaten was at midday, and then it had only been a light salad.

A glance at her watch revealed that it was nine o'clock. She'd been driving for more than three hours.

It was hardly likely that anything would be open at this time of night, although she vaguely remembered passing a petrol station a short while ago. Maybe they ran a fast-food outlet where she could pick up hot coffee and a filled roll.

Without further thought she switched on the ignition and fired the engine, swinging the car in a semi-circle on to the northbound highway.

Half an hour later, suitably revived by two cups of strong coffee and a surprisingly wholesome meal, she made the decision to drive home.

It was almost one o'clock when she took the lift up to her apartment. As the doors slid open she stifled a yawn, weary almost beyond belief.

At first she didn't see the tall figure leaning against the wall outside her apartment door. It wasn't until a slight movement caught her attention that his presence registered, and she faltered mid-step, then froze as Georg's muscular frame unfolded.

Shock, resentment, *anger*—all those emotions seemed to register at once, and her tiredness vanished.

'What are you doing here?'

One eyebrow slanted in silent query. 'Whatever happened to "hello"?' His gaze was dark and infinitely formidable beneath its steady appraisal. 'I contacted Jacques, only to be told that, if there was a fashion parade on in the city tonight, he certainly wasn't running it.' His eyes seemed to mesmerise hers. 'If you didn't want to dine out you had only to say so.'

Lexi didn't blink. 'You would have asked questions and demanded answers.'

His silence accelerated her nervous tension to a point where she was sure he must see the pulse thudding at the base of her throat. 'Do you consider it so strange that I feel I have a right to know if something bothers you?'

His drawled query seemed like the last straw! Her anger snapped, and she could feel it erupt inside her like a volcano. *'Right?'* she exploded. 'You have no rights where I'm concerned!'

His gaze narrowed, and a muscle tensed along the edge of his jaw. 'The hallway is hardly the place for a slanging match. Where are your keys?'

Ignoring her protest, he took her bag and searched inside it until he discovered her keyring, then he calmly put an arm around her waist and hoisted her over his shoulder.

'Put me down, you fiend!' She tried to kick him and one of her shoes fell to the carpeted floor. 'Let me go, *damn you*!'

There was nothing she could do to stop him unlocking the front door, and, once inside, he closed it with an almost silent click before allowing her to slide down to her feet.

His eyes held hers, dark and incredibly watchful. 'Now, suppose you explain?' he demanded in a voice that was dangerously soft.

'Explain?' she vented, furious almost beyond belief. 'You thought you were very clever, didn't you? Together with Jonathan and David, you played both ends against the middle and manu-

factured a conspiracy in which you were not only a perpetrator, but a willing participant.' Her eyes gleamed with a fine rage. 'You conniving, uncaring, diabolical *bastard*! Who do you think you are, attempting to play God?' She took a step forward and began railing him with her fists, hitting him anywhere she could connect—his chest, his arms, his shoulders ... beating him with an anger that brought tears streaming down her cheeks until hard hands caught hold of her own, stilling their actions with galling ease.

'That's enough.'

'I hate you!' she stormed vehemently. '*Hate* you, do you understand?'

His hands tightened their grasp on her wrists, and she struggled powerlessly against him as he drew her close. Effortlessly he caught both her hands together, then slid his hand through the length of her hair, exerting sufficient pressure until there was no other option but for her to meet his gaze.

Lexi was aware of every muscle in the taut length of his body, and she wanted to scream and rage against him.

Broken dreams, a cynical inner voice taunted; the destruction of the hope that Georg could possibly feel about her the way she felt about him, that such a tenuous, precious emotion as *love* might be shared.

Yet pride forbade acceptance of any logic, and she pulled away from him, straining against hands that held her firmly at arm's length.

'Let me go,' she demanded, attempting to wrest free from his grasp and failing miserably.

'So that you can run away again?'

'I didn't run,' she disclaimed heatedly, and glimpsed the wry twist of his mouth.

'No?'

'Will you please leave?' she countered with un-accustomed hauteur. 'I'm tired, I have a headache, and I want to go to bed.' Her eyes resembled fiery shards of sheer topaz, a brilliance that refused to be daunted beneath his probing gaze. She felt mentally drained, and completely enervated. The headache was no fabrication, and she raised a shaky hand to her left temple in an attempt to ease the pain.

'I would have thought you impervious to any element of gossip,' Georg drawled with soft inflexibility.

Her eyes didn't waver from his for a second. 'Paul was terribly convincing.' She saw the dark flaring in the depths of his eyes, the faint bunching of muscle at the edge of his jaw. 'Yes, *Paul*. But then, you know, don't you? I have no doubt David called you, in spite of anything I said to the contrary.' She lifted a hand in an involuntary gesture as he would have spoken. 'Don't. Please don't compound the situation with any mean-ingless qualification.' She even managed a faint smile. 'It's amazing, really. Beneath the anger, the sheer *rage* that my life, my future, should be treated with such clinical detachment and utter high-handedness, I can still see the logic of it all from Jonathan's point of view. The youngest child, his adored little girl, couldn't be allowed to drift through life alone. A man had to be found: the *right* man. Someone above reproach, of considerable financial standing, and preferably of a similar calibre to Jonathan himself.' Her features assumed a deliberately winsome expression. 'Even fate took a hand in providing the perfect opportunity to have me collaborate. Bypass surgery is sufficiently serious to warrant respect and a willingness to ease the patient's mind. I can even understand Jonathan's need to tie it all up beforehand, so that *he* could undergo surgery safe in the knowledge there would be someone to care for me should things go wrong. What I fail to comprehend,' she continued slowly, 'is *your* involvement. You don't need my share of my father's money. You're so self-sufficient, you certainly don't need *me*. And I refuse to believe you'd consent to marry merely to honour the close friendship of a business partner.' She drew in a slight breath, not caring just how brutal her analytical dissection became. 'There is, of course, the possibility you had reached an age where you were inclined to make the clinical decision to take a wife and sire a son to follow in your footsteps. In that respect I guess I qualify. I'm from the right side of the track, educated, personable. We're even physically——'

'Compatible?'

Remembering exactly to what precise degree they were sexually in tune almost proved to be her undoing, and a faint tinge of pink rose to define her cheekbones. 'Yes.'

'Is that how you see me?'

Her chin lifted fractionally as she accorded without guile, 'I have to give you full marks for sensual expertise.'

His eyes seared hers, almost as if he could see through to her soul. 'You think that's all it was?' he demanded in a voice that sounded like steel razing silk asunder.

'Good sex,' she conceded matter-of-factly. Inside she was slowly dying. 'I doubt it comes any better.'

'The mechanical coupling of two consenting adults who indulge in an act of physical lust? Not making love, where each partner takes infinite care to caress and arouse until they ache with an awareness so acute it transcends mere pleasure? And even then the pleasure is extended until the fire becomes unbearable, like a mindless passion demanding the release that only they can give—to each other?'

Lexi wanted to close her eyes and shut out the images his voice evoked, to still the shivers that slithered across the surface of her skin as memory provided a graphic reminder of the nights they'd spent in each other's arms.

'Tomorrow I fly north to Cairns for the photographic shoot at Port Douglas. I plan to stay on at the resort for a few days.' She managed to hold his gaze without wavering. 'I need some peace and tranquillity in my life.'

'You imagine I'll let you walk away?'

Pride, together with an innate sense of self-preservation, was responsible for the steadiness of her voice. 'There is nothing you can do to stop me.'

He stood looking at her for what seemed an age, and the breath caught in her throat, seeming to formulate into a lump which made it impossible for her to swallow.

Dark eyes hardened with frightening anger, and for one heart-stopping moment she thought he was going to *shake* her.

'Have your time alone, if that's what you think you need.' His voice was controlled, yet as hard as tensile steel. 'However, if you intend opting out of our impending marriage, then *you* must be the one to tell Jonathan and rescind all the arrangements.'

Lexi closed her eyes against the compelling sight of him, then slowly opened them again, aware of a primeval instinct for survival as she became trapped in the prison of his penetrating gaze.

'That amounts to emotional blackmail,' she said shakily.

'I'll use any tool I can.'

'Why?'

A faint, slightly cruel smile curved from the edge of his mouth. 'You think you have all the answers. Work it out for yourself.'

Without a further word he turned and walked to the door, opened it, then pulled it closed behind him.

Lexi lifted her hand in an involuntary gesture as her subconscious mind sought to call him back, then she shook her head and gazed sightlessly around the room.

Crossing her arms, she hugged them tightly against her breasts. Never before had she felt quite so frighteningly alone, bereft, and, with an aching sense of loss so acute it took every ounce of effort to walk to the door, she attached the safety chain, activated the alarm system, then made her way to bed.

CHAPTER ELEVEN

THE PORT DOUGLAS resort was aptly named Mirage, for that was how it appeared after an hour's drive from Cairns along a road that alternately hugged the coastal foreshore then swung inwards to weave its way through dense rainforest.

The heat hit Lexi the moment she stepped out from the air-conditioned limousine, the high humidity of a tropical wet season making the air seem heavy and stultifying, and tiny beads of sweat began to dew on her skin in the brief few minutes it took for her to pay the driver.

Her reserved suite was cool, decorated in pale muted shades that were visually restful, and as soon as she was alone she headed for the bathroom and stripped off her clothes.

A leisurely shower proved refreshing, and she selected shorts and a sleeveless top before extracting a bottle of pineapple juice from the refrigerator.

It was deliciously icy, and, sipping it slowly, she moved to the large sliding glass doors to view the lush sculptured grounds bounded by enormous palms, and, beyond, the wide expanse of ocean.

She should rest, she thought, have a quiet evening meal, and follow it with an early night, so that she would be ready to sparkle beneath the all-revealing eye of the camera first thing in the morning. Except that she felt impossibly restless, and she prowled round the suite, then crossed to the phone in a determined bid to ring Jonathan and tell him of her safe arrival.

Georg's name wasn't even mentioned, much to her relief, and after she'd replaced the receiver she stood staring at the telephone in brooding silence.

A discreet rap at the door provided an interruption, and she accepted the long slim cellophaned box from the delivery-man. As soon as she was alone she hurriedly tore open the accompanying envelope, only to discover that the flowers were from the management, welcoming her to the hotel.

A wry smile tugged at her mouth. Why shouldn't they make a token gesture? The publicity from this shoot would arouse tremendous interest in the resort.

And she desperately tried to ignore an inner voice taunting unmercifully that she should even dare hope Georg might have despatched a floral tribute.

Dear heaven, why was she so contrary? If the roses had come from Georg she probably would have given them to one of the staff. And why should he send her anything when she'd virtually walked out on him?

She clenched her hands, then winced as the stone from her engagement ring dug into her finger. And that was another thing, she thought wretchedly as she adjusted the ring so that it rested squarely. She should have taken the ring off and given it back to him before she left Sydney. Except that she hadn't, and she began to wonder why.

Damn. There were no easy answers, and she was darned if she was to embark on a fact-and-find soul-searching mission *now*.

She'd come here for a reason: to work, and to follow it with a few extra days of relaxation. And that was exactly what she intended to do. Georg, and every facet of her involvement with him, could be successfully put on hold.

But it wasn't that easy. At least *work* presented few difficulties. The cameraman was easy to work with, and the clothes were superb. It was afterwards, when she was alone, that the problems began, for with so much time on her hands she began to pursue a path of destructive introspection.

The days were bad enough, but the nights were worse, for then she lay awake, aware with each passing hour of a deep, aching sense of loss.

When she finally did manage to fall asleep her dreams were vivid and heart-rendingly graphic. Inevitably she came sharply awake to discover that Georg's presence was a figment of a fertile imagination, and reality was an empty bed.

To spend so much time alone was detrimental, Lexi decided, and in a desperate need to fill her days she embarked on every recommended tour available.

She made friends with a few fellow guests, joining them for dinner on two occasions, and she spoke to her father by phone every day.

However, the one call she wanted, more than any other, never came, and somehow she was unable to summon sufficient courage to make the call herself.

Why didn't Georg ring? she agonised at least a dozen times every day. Had he decided, after all, to believe all those hateful things she'd flung at him in temper? Perhaps he had used this last week for a bit of introspection of his own.

Oh, lord, it would be terribly ironic if *he* opted to call the wedding off, just when extensive self-analysis of her emotions revealed she'd fallen irretrievably in love with him. For there could be no doubt it was *love*.

There was only one way to find out, and with new-found resolve she rang the airline, booked the next flight south, then packed her bag and checked out of the hotel.

Lexi arrived in Sydney, collected her holdall, then hired a taxi to take her to Darling Point, where she retrieved her mail and took the lift up to her apartment.

The answering-machine held a variety of messages, and she played the tape as she sifted through her mail.

One of the first things she must do was ring Jonathan, she thought, for she didn't want to cause him any anxiety should he phone the Port Douglas resort only to be told she'd already left.

'Come visit me this evening,' her father bade her after they'd exchanged a preliminary greeting. 'Bring Georg.' She almost heard the laughter in his voice as he teased, 'I won't expect you to stay long.'

Oh, heavens, how did she get of that? 'Georg doesn't know I'm back yet,' she responded lightly. 'Can I take a raincheck, and make it tomorrow night? I'll ring you in the morning.'

As soon as she'd concluded the call she depressed the reset button and dialled Georg's number before she had time to give the action any thought. If she hesitated she'd never summon the necessary courage.

But he wasn't at the restaurant, nor was he in his office.

'Would you care to leave a message?'

She hesitated for all of five seconds. 'No, I'll ring back.'

Fool, she accorded the instant she replaced the receiver. It would have been much simpler if she'd left her name. Except that then *she* would be the one waiting with bated breath for the phone to ring, and if he didn't call she'd be totally shattered. At least this way the ball was still in her court.

Or was it? Somehow she couldn't help thinking he was playing a very shrewd game, deliberately allowing her to think she had her freedom, while all the time aware she could never truly be free of him.

At five o'clock she emerged from the shower, and after completing her toilette she took painstaking care with her appearance, choosing the expensive lace-edged silk teddy Georg had bid impossibly highly for to wear beneath a cream silk ensemble of culottes, matching top and jacket.

Make-up was deliberately subtle, with emphasis on her eyes and mouth, and she caught her hair up in an elaborate chignon from which she teased free a few wispy tendrils for effect.

The end result was startling, as she had intended, and without pause for thought she collected a clutch-bag, her car-keys, then stepped out from the apartment without so much as a backward glance.

Halfway to Georg's apartment she decided she was quite mad. For all she knew, he could be at the restaurant, or dining with Alex and Samantha. He could be in any one of a dozen places, and least of all was he likely to be home.

Yet she had to start somewhere, she decided as she parked the car and walked towards the elegantly designed foyer of his exclusive apartment block.

Depressing the appropriate intercom buzzer, she waited anxiously for a response.

'Carla. Who is there, please?'

'Lexi,' she relayed into the microphone. 'Lexi Harrison.'

'Mr Georg is not here. You want to come up?'

Relief washed over her. 'Please.'

The buzzer sounded, and the security door slid open. Three minutes later Lexi walked out from the lift into the penthouse lobby.

'Ah, there you are,' Carla greeted her in accented English within seconds of Lexi's pressing the doorbell. 'You are lucky I am still here. Tonight I am late in leaving.' A broad grin creased her attractive matronly features, and her eyes sparkled. 'You wait here for Mr Georg?'

'Yes.' Lexi preceded the housekeeper into the lounge and sank into one of the soft leather chairs. 'Is he going to be long?'

'I don't know.' An eloquent shrug lifted broad capable shoulders. 'He ring before and tell me he cook for himself tonight. You want I should get you something? A drink, maybe? I can fix you a snack.'

'No,' Lexi refused with a kindly smile. 'Thanks all the same; I'll be fine. You go.'

'You sure? It's no trouble.'

'Sure,' Lexi assured her, touched by the older woman's concern.

As soon as she was alone she rose to her feet and crossed to the huge glass window where she stood staring sightlessly out at the view.

The harbour glistened against a backdrop of city buildings and clear azure sky. A tugboat bustled importantly out to meet an incoming liner, and two ferries passed each other as they forged in opposite directions to their different destinations. Houses and apartment blocks dotted the foreshore, with trees and landscaped gardens covering numerous hills rising high from the sea.

In midsummer, with the advantage of daylight saving, there was still evidence of a heat haze lingering in the air, and it would be several hours before dusk would provide a gradually darkening shroud. Then the city would come alive with a galaxy of light, myriad pinpricks of electricity providing a veritable fairyland to complement the brilliantly flashing neon from city buildings.

It was a similar view to the one Lexi enjoyed from her own apartment, and she had become so accustomed to the visual beauty's being on constant display that it failed to register as she became lost in contemplation.

Would Georg be pleased to see her? Her features paled at the thought that he might not. Dear lord in heaven! How was she supposed to live without him? Oh, *why* did she have to suffer such a conflict of emotions? she cursed helplessly.

The faint sound of a key being turned in the lock momentarily froze her limbs, then she slowly swung round to face the door.

One glance at Georg's tall dark-suited frame was sufficient for the nerves in her stomach to begin a painful somersault, and she stood in mesmerised silence as he entered the room.

Her eyes flew to his face, seeing the dark set of his jaw, the broad chiselled cheekbones assembled into an unfathomable mask.

Everything she wanted to say remained locked in her throat, and she simply stood still as he carefully closed the door behind him.

Then he turned towards her, and she nearly died at the hard implacability evident.

'Lexi.'

His voice was a cynical world-weary drawl, and she drew a deep calming breath in defence against the agonising shaft of pain that ripped through her body.

'Hello, Georg,' she greeted him quietly, her eyes wide and clear as he moved further into the room. 'Carla let me in.'

He paused, surveying her with detached inscrutability for what seemed an age, then crossed to the drinks cabinet. 'Can I get you a drink?'

Lexi doubted she'd be able to lift the glass to her lips without spilling its contents, and if she so much as swallowed anything she'd choke! 'No—thanks,' she added with extreme politeness, watching as he selected a glass, added ice, a measure of whisky and a generous splash of soda before turning to face her.

'When did you get back?'

'This afternoon.'

He moved across to where she stood. 'You could have phoned.'

'I rang the office, but you weren't in.'

'A message would have reached me.'

The deep drawling voice sent goose-pimples scudding over the surface of her skin, and she had to steel herself against actually shivering. A spark of defiance lifted her chin and tilted it fractionally. 'You're not going to make this easy for me, are you?'

His eyes seared hers, hardening with frightening intensity. 'Can you give me any reason why I should?'

Lexi closed her eyes against the compelling sight of him, then slowly opened them again. The air between them seemed alive with latent emotion, and her heart gave a lurch as she glimpsed a muscle tensing along his jaw.

She was dangerously close to tears, and she looked at him, silently begging for his understanding. 'I spent every waking minute thinking about you while I was away, remembering, examining everything you said, all that had happened between us,' she began slowly. Her eyes unconsciously beseeched him to understand, but his expression remained an inscrutable mask. 'I even managed to persuade myself *before* Paul's revelation that marriage to you would have its compensations.' A hollow laugh rose in her throat to escape as a strangled sound, and she lifted her hands in a gesture of self-deprecation. 'Heaven knows, I'd rushed into my first marriage ignoring everything except my heart. There seemed to be some sense in using some caution with regard to a second attempt, and at least you had Jonathan's whole-hearted approval. I even dared to think we might be happy together, and I began to relax, lulled into a state of contented acceptance. I felt I could trust you, and I became very——' she hesitated, hardly wanting to lay bare her heart '—fond of you.' Oh, dear lord, if only he knew just *how* fond!

She waited for him to say something, to give her some reassurance, but he remained silent.

'After Paul, I didn't want to trust any man again. I didn't even feel I could trust myself.' She swallowed painfully, and felt the ache of unshed tears as she gathered the strength to continue. 'I hated having to live a lie, even for Jonathan's sake, and I especially hated you for taking me through the threshold of pain and showing me what pleasure could be.' Her mouth trembled as it tried for a smile and lost miserably. 'Must you have it all?' she demanded shakily, and it seemed a lifetime before he spoke.

'Yes.'

It took an inordinate amount of courage to continue, but she managed—just.

'When I discovered there was a deliberate conspiracy I was so angry, so disillusioned, so incredibly—hurt,' Lexi admitted poignantly.

His eyes never left hers for a second. 'And now?'

This was no time to be faint-hearted, and with a sense of trepidation she took the greatest gamble of her life. She lifted a shaky hand, then let it fall helplessly down to her side, and her eyes shimmered with the force of her emotion. 'I discovered I can't live without you.' She attempted a faint smile and failed miserably as her lips trembled. 'Don't you understand? *I love you.*' The words were torn out of her in a flow of wretched emotion, and she looked at him blindly through a well of tears. 'What more do you want?'

Georg carefully placed his glass down on a nearby table, then he caught hold of her shoulders and pulled her close, lifting a hand to catch hold of her chin and tilting it so that she had no option but to look at him.

'*You,*' he accorded softly. 'As my wife, by my side, always.'

There was no way she could still the silent trickling flow of tears as they spilled and ran slowly down each cheek, and her mouth shook almost beyond control.

His eyes darkened until they were almost black. 'Don't,' he groaned, gathering her close. '*Cristos*, don't cry!'

His hands were gentle as they slid through her hair to hold fast her head, and his mouth lowered to nuzzle the sweet curve of her neck, his lips caressing the softly throbbing vein until he felt the faint tremor in her throat; then he began a tantalisingly slow path to her mouth. He kissed her gently at first, then with increasing hunger as he sought to remove every last vestige of doubt.

It seemed an age before he relinquished her lips, and she could only look at him in total bemusement as he trailed a finger down the slope of her nose, and traced the soft, swollen contours of her mouth.

She was unable to prevent the slight shiver that raked her slender body, and he slid his hands up to frame her face.

'You're beautiful,' he accorded gently. 'So generous and warm and giving. A joy only a fool would discard.' He smiled as her eyes widened, and his thumb gently probed the tremulous curves of her mouth, then began tracing their outline with tactile exploration. 'It was impossible for me not to be aware of your existence,' he owned huskily. 'You intrigued me, and I wanted to get to know you better. Under normal circumstances Jonathan would have arranged for us to be formally introduced over dinner at his home, but both he and David knew you would see it as a deliberate guise. As soon as I learned of Jonathan's ill-health it was *my* suggestion to involve you in attempt to halt Paul's meddling.' His mouth moved to form a wry smile. 'I knew within days of going public with our supposed romance that only the reality would suffice, and I used every weapon at my command.' He laughed softly at her expression of disbelief. 'I knew I had insufficient time to afford you a gentle seduction. My pursuit had to be swift and blatant.' He paused to bestow a brief hard kiss to her soft mouth, thereby preventing any response she might have made. 'In my arms your body was its own traitorous mistress, alive and gloriously vibrant beneath my touch, and every time we made love I was sure you must know the extent of my feelings.' His lips touched hers, light and as fleeting as a butterfly's wings.

'I was sufficiently naïve to think it was merely sexual expertise,' Lexi admitted with a faint smile.

'I wanted to kill Paul,' Georg went on to reveal, and his eyes hardened with latent anger. 'A few days ago I had to physically restrain myself from going after him and committing serious bodily harm,' he asserted bleakly, and there was an inflexible quality evident in those tautly chiselled features that she longed to ease.

'It doesn't matter. *He* doesn't matter,' Lexi assured him, conscious of his darkening gaze.

'He'll never have the opportunity to hurt you again.'

She looked at him, loving the strength, the sheer animal magnificence that set him apart from other men. Her heart swelled, and her lips parted to form a soft tremulous smile.

'You're determined to play the role of my guardian angel?' she couldn't resist teasing, and received a husky growl in response as he gathered her close against him.

'Husband; lover,' he corrected, his expression softening miraculously, and she felt herself begin to drown in the warmth of his eyes. 'Friend; confidant,' he added, moulding her slim curves against his hardened frame. '*Yours*, for a lifetime.'

Her eyes clung to his, and for a moment she was unable to speak, then any words she might have said were lost as he lowered his head and kissed her with such gentle evocativeness that she almost cried.

'I love you,' he accorded gently. 'So much. These past few days have been hell. When I arrived home tonight and found you here I was so desperately afraid you had come to demand your freedom.'

Lexi lifted a hand to his lips, and her eyes widened measurably as he caressed each finger in turn, drawing first one, then the other into his mouth and gently biting each tender tip. A shaft of exquisite pleasure unfurled deep inside her, slowly radiating throughout her whole body until she was filled with delicious expectant warmth.

'Will you do something for me?'

His smile held such a degree of latent passion that she melted into a thousand pieces.

'What is this thing you want me to do?' He leaned forward and brushed his lips against the corner of her mouth in an evocative, deliberately tantalising gesture. 'Tell me.'

For a moment she almost hesitated, wondering if it was really important any more. 'Would you *ask* me to marry you?' Her voice was serious, and as he lifted his head she looked into his eyes, begging him to understand. In a defensive, unbidden gesture she edged the tip of her tongue over the soft curve of her mouth.

He stood regarding her in silence, his expression unusually grave. 'It means that much to you?'

'Yes.'

He caught hold of her hand and placed it against his chest so that she could feel the strong beat of his heart. 'Dear, sweet Lexi. Will you marry me? Let me love you, treasure you for the rest of my life?'

Her mouth shook a little, and her eyes ached with the wealth of her own emotion. 'Yes. *Yes.*' She slid her arms up round his neck and pulled his head down to hers. Then she kissed him, glorying in taking the initiative for a few long minutes before he became caught up with the strength of his own passion, wreaking a devastating assault on her feelings, plundering until she clung to him, unashamedly as anxious as he for a complete satiation of the senses.

It seemed an age before he slowly broke the kiss, and she gave a murmur in protest as he disentangled her arms from around his neck.

'Carla said you were going to cook,' she voiced reluctantly, wanting only to be close to him.

With infinite care he slid the jacket from her shoulders, then set about loosening her top.

'We'll have a midnight snack, and wash it down with champagne.' His hands slipped inside the waistband of her silk trousers and pushed them gently down over the slight curve of her hips. 'But right now all I want to do is feast myself on you,' he husked emotively, and she almost died at the wealth of passion evident in those dark eyes so close to her own.

Lexi gave a soft delighted laugh, and an inner radiance was responsible for the twinkle of utter bewitchment in the depths of her beautiful eyes. 'Here, in the lounge?'

With an exultant chuckle he swept her into his arms and carried her effortlessly down the hall to the master suite where he let her slip to her feet mere inches from the large bed.

'In my bed, minx,' he chided gently, shrugging out of his jacket in one easy movement. Her fingers began undoing the buttons on his shirt, dealing deftly with the belt buckle, and as she reached for the zip fastening on his trousers a long shudder shook his powerful frame.

Unbidden, she traced a slow pattern through the dark springy hair whorling on his chest, beginning a tactile exploration that brought a strangled sound from the depths of his throat.

'Do you have any conception of what you're doing to me?'

A shaft of exquisite pleasure exploded deep within her, radiating through every nerve until she felt incredibly alive, for it was a heady experience to imagine she held any power over him.

'I think the feeling is mutual,' she managed shakily some minutes later as his lips trailed an evocative path to her breasts, and she cried out as his tongue savoured one taut roseate peak, then drew it gently between his teeth to suckle, creating such delicious torture that it was almost impossible not to cry out at the degree of ecstacy spiralling through her body.

Gently he pulled her down on to the bed, and their loving became a long slow pacing of each other's pleasure that surpassed anything they'd previously shared.

Afterwards they rose and shared a leisurely bath, delighting in creating new depths of sensual arousal, and it was a long time later, cradled close in the protective circle of Georg's arms, that Lexi lifted her head towards his to voice quietly, 'Thank you.'

His lips trailed gently across her forehead to settle at her temple. 'For what, specifically?'

'Loving me,' she accorded simply. She felt his mouth begin a slow caressing path down to her cheek until it reached the curve of her lips.

'You're so unbelievably beautiful that you take my breath away.'

She smiled beneath the witching touch of his mouth, and a delicious laugh bubbled to the surface. 'Do you think you can summon sufficient energy to sizzle two steaks while I toss a salad?'

'*Sizzle?*' He caught her lower lip between his teeth in subtle punishment, and growled softly, 'A gourmet chef creates magic with food.'

'Not merely with food,' she declared solemnly, slipping easily from his grasp, but only, she suspected, because he let her.

She walked unselfconsciously into the *en suite* bathroom and plucked a large bath-sheet to wrap sarong-style round her slim curves, then she emerged into the bedroom to see he'd risen from the bed and was in the process of donning a silk robe.

Georg held out his hand and she placed hers into that strong warm enveloping grasp, then together they walked out of the room.

All the self-doubts, the pain, were gone, and in its place was love—everlasting.

BEST SELLER ROMANCE

Helen Bianchin

YESTERDAY'S SHADOW

Harlequin Mills & Boon

SYDNEY ❀ AUCKLAND ❀ MANILA
LONDON ❀ TORONTO ❀ NEW YORK
PARIS ❀ AMSTERDAM ❀ HAMBURG ❀ MILAN
STOCKHOLM ❀ MADRID ❀ ATHENS ❀ BUDAPEST
WARSAW ❀ SOFIA ❀ PRAGUE ❀ TOKYO ❀ ISTANBUL

First Published 1984
This Edition 1998
ISBN 0 733 51143 0

Published by
Harlequin Mills & Boon
3 Gibbes Street
Chatswood, NSW 2067
Australia

HARLEQUIN MILLS & BOON and the Rose Device are trademarks used under
license and registered in Australia, New Zealand, Philippines, United States
Patent & Trademark Office and in other countries.

Printed and bound in Australia by
McPherson's Printing Group

CHAPTER ONE

THE sun was a distant glowing orb in an azure sky, with none of its promised heat evident at this relatively early morning hour.

Natalie leaned back against the cushioned headrest and endeavoured to conjure some interest in the panoramic vista beyond the smoke-tinted window as the bus eased on to the Gold Coast highway at Southport and began its smooth run towards the centre of Surfer's Paradise.

This coastal stretch of south-east Queensland was truly golden, with sand the colour of clover honey. High-rolling waves crashed to its shores in spuming magnificence, providing sought-after surfing conditions, which, coupled with record sunshine hours, brought an abundance of tourists and holidaymakers throughout the year. Innumerable towering high-rise buildings lined the foreshore, bearing evocative names that stirred the imagination and tempted an alternative lifestyle.

With an impartial, slightly jaundiced eye, Natalie observed the changes that had taken place during her three-year absence. Many of the houses along the highway had gone, and in their place stood modern architecturally-designed high-rise that added to a rapidly growing concrete jungle.

The faint hiss of hydraulic brakes coupled with the driver's announcement of arrival prompted Natalie to her feet, and she joined the general exodus of alighting passengers.

A quick glance at her watch confirmed that she would have time for a much-needed cup of coffee.

It had been hours since she had checked out of the hotel in Brisbane, and her stomach demanded sustenance even though her nerves screamed rejection.

The decision to return had taken considerable courage, and for the umpteenth time she damned fate for being so cruel. A slow gnawing fear manifested itself and played havoc with her composure. Given a choice, she would gladly have opted out of the whole wretched scheme— but there was no choice. It was a case of 'damned if you do, damned if you don't'! she conceded wryly. Like it or not—and she didn't, not at *all* —she was committed to confronting a man she had vowed never to have anything to do with for the rest of her life. All her instincts screamed for her to escape while she could, and only determined resolve forced her into a nearby coffee lounge, where she ordered coffee and a light snack.

'Are you on holiday?'

Natalie glanced up as the young waiter placed the food before her. 'No,' she disclaimed shortly, directing him an icy glare from smoky-grey eyes. Heaven preserve her from a self-assured male on the make!

'Would you like cream for the cappucino?' He was persistent, his smile openly speculative as dark Latin eyes, liquid with admiration, roved slowly over her delectable curves.

'No—nor do I need anything else.' She spoke with deceptive softness, but her meaning was unmistakable, and with a philosophical shrug he moved away.

The coffee was aromatic, and she sipped it appreciatively, aware of a soothing effect which, coupled with a serving of toasted bacon and cheese

fingers, calmed her digestive juices and helped
bolster her morale.

A few minutes after nine o'clock she emerged
into the morning sunshine and turned towards
the main street. The office building she sought
lay three blocks distant, and she deliberately set
a brisk pace, oblivious to the frank admiring
glances her diminutive five-feet-three-inch form
received.

Slim, with curves in all the right places, she
possessed an enviable peaches-and-cream complexion that moulded a delicate bone structure.
Eyes that lightened or darkened with each change
of mood were an intriguing feature, and were
fringed with thick dark lashes. Long shoulder-
length blonde hair resembling liquid silk shot with
streaks of gold owed nothing to artifice and swung
softly with every move she made.

A slight breeze tempered the sun's warmth as
she crossed the street, zig-zagging her way between
traffic, and on reaching the pavement she paused
momentarily to draw a calming breath. Ahead of
her lay the towering edifice housing the offices of
Marshall Associates, and with a glint of defiance
she moved towards the electronically-controlled
glass doors.

The elegant marble façade echoed the luxuriously appointed interior, its design and décor a
visual masterpiece, and she experienced a sense of
icy fatalism as she crossed the foyer and entered
the elevator. Selecting the appropriate button, she
jabbed it with unnecessary force, and was
immediately transported with swift precision to
her designated level.

Heaven help her, she had *arrived*! Celestial
assistance was never more warranted, she decided
grimly, and summoning her features into a cool

polite mask she crossed the thick-piled carpet towards reception.

'Mr Marshall, please.' Her voice held clipped detachment, and she met the receptionist's quick assessing stare with equanimity.

'May I have your name?'

'Maclean—Natalie Maclean,' she responded evenly, and her stomach muscles tightened as the girl picked up an inter-office phone. If Ryan Marshall refused to see her, her task would be made doubly difficult.

'Mr Marshall has several appointments this morning,' the young girl related efficiently. 'However, there's a possibility that he can fit you in around midday. Will that be suitable?'

The reprieve couldn't be ignored, and Natalie inclined her head in silent acquiescence. She had come too far to wreck whatever chance she had by demanding instant attention. 'Thank you.'

Her self-confidence descended to an all-time low as she turned and walked towards the elevator. Dear God, three hours to fill in!

On reaching the ground level she stepped out into the warm sunshine with no definite purpose in mind. There were not a great number of people around at this relatively early hour as March was not a peak tourist season, and she wandered idly window-shopping, explored a new arcade, then entered a new complex where she spent her time leisurely browsing in several exclusive boutiques. With a further hour until midday, she purchased the daily newspaper and thoroughly scanned its pages over coffee.

It was five minutes to twelve when Natalie presented herself at the reception desk, and this time she was directed to a sumptuously furnished lounge with views over the Nerang River.

'Please take a seat. Mr Marshall shouldn't be long.'

Natalie selected a velvet-upholstered sofa positioned near an expanse of plate-glass. Every minute seemed an hour, despite the wide variety of magazines provided, and the slightest sound succeeded in sending her stomach into a series of painful somersaults.

'Miss Maclean? If you would care to come with me, Mr Marshall will see you now.' The smile was perfunctory, and Natalie stood to her feet, dazed by the effort it took to control her wayward nerves.

Marshall—she hated the name, almost as much as she hated the man who bore it.

Her entire respiratory system seemed out of control, making breathing difficult as she followed in the secretary's wake, and each step taken down that long carpeted corridor seemed to accelerate her inner tension.

'Miss Maclean.' The announcement was professionally delivered, and with the actions of an automaton Natalie moved into the room, hardly aware of the almost silent click of the door as it closed behind her.

Like a magnet her eyes swept to the tall frame positioned indolently at ease behind a central executive desk. Three years had wrought little change—if anything he appeared more dynamic than ever. Broad shoulders tapering to slim taut hips exuded leashed strength beneath casual yet elegantly tailored attire, and there was a rugged, almost animalistic sense of power—an inherent vitality, that was unequalled. Thick, well-groomed light-brown hair held no hint of grey, and the dark golden, almost tigerish, eyes wore an expression of deliberate insolence as they subjected her to a slow encompassing appraisal.

'Maclean?' Ryan Marshall taunted with dangerous softness, and Natalie felt an unaccustomed frisson of fear slither its way down her spine.

'It is my name,' she managed with deceptive calmness, and saw the edge of his mouth twist with sardonic cruelty.

'I seem to recall you acquired another.'

She swallowed with difficulty, feeling intensely vulnerable—*exposed*, beneath the intense, almost electric masculinity the man projected. It took incredible effort to instil a semblance of steadiness into her voice. 'That's something I try very hard to forget.'

One dark eyebrow rose in wry cynicism. 'Are you successful?'

No, *damn* you! she wanted to scream. She had spent too many wakeful nights remembering to ever be able to forget. Aloud, she indicated with infinite civility, 'I don't want to take up too much of your valuable time.'

He shifted slightly, moving with lithe pantherish grace round the desk to lean on its edge. His eyes bored into her own, dissecting and assessing, as if they possessed a licence to her soul.

'Your reason for instigating this—confrontation intrigues me.' He indicated one of several deep-seated armchairs with an indolent sweeping gesture. 'Sit down.'

Determination, coupled with an inborn sense of wariness, lifted her chin as a stoic denial left her lips. 'I'd prefer to stand.'

The edge of his mouth formed a wry twist. 'Thereby assuming a position of near-flight?'

The first stirring of anger darkened her eyes to a stormy grey. 'You're not making this very easy,' she began, and he demanded with deceptive softness,

'My dear Natalie, are you daring to suggest that I should?'

Resentment washed over her, leaving a tide of weariness. Personalities, however provocative, mustn't be permitted to intervene. 'My father is ill,' she stated flatly. 'A terminal disease that requires surgery and expensive treatment.'

There wasn't so much as a flicker of emotion apparent in those rugged features, and the ensuing silence seemed to reverberate around the room. Natalie was conscious of every breath she took, sure that the loud hammering of her heart must be audible.

Ryan Marshall's regard was swift and analytical, his eyes never leaving hers for a second. 'You have my sympathy.'

'But not your support,' Natalie stated with a tinge of bitterness, recognising no relenting in his manner.

'I wasn't aware that it had been requested,' he countered silkily, and she drew a deep calming breath.

'I didn't want to come here, much less appeal for help.' Her eyes regarded him steadily. 'You are my last resort, believe me.'

'How—flattering,' he acknowledged sardonically, and she met his gaze unwaveringly, seeing the inflexibility evident, and hated him afresh.

'Must I *beg*?'

'Would you?'

'Is that what you want?' she demanded bitterly.

There was a swift gleam in those tigerish eyes, and a cynical smile twisted the edge of his mouth. 'The inclination to see you on your knees is almost impossible to ignore.'

'My God, you're despicable!' Natalie asserted

with considerable force, and her eyes flashed as she rounded on him. 'I never imagined it possible to hate anyone as much as I hate you!'

'Have you finished?' he drawled imperturbably, although there was a warning softness evident that she refused to heed.

'Yes, *damn* you!' Anger set her features alive, her entire body seeming to reverberate with it. 'I was mad to come here—*insane* to think I might succeed.' She turned towards the door, filled with an incredible silent rage.

'Not so fast.' Somehow he was there before her, a towering formidable wall.

At such close proximity he was unsettling, the atmosphere between them charged with electrical force, and the knowledge that he still possessed the power to disturb her rose like bitter gall in her throat.

'You walked out of my life,' Ryan essayed softly—dangerously, and it took all Natalie's courage to stand quiescent beneath the force of his silent anger. 'Disappeared, seemingly without trace,' he continued ominously. 'No word— nothing, for three years.' One eyebrow lifted in silent mockery. 'And now you expect a simple "yes" or "no" answer to what amounts to a considerable sum of money?'

Put like that, it sounded ludicrous—something she had recognised from the start. Except that Andrea's subtle persuasion plus observance of her father's steady decline into ill-health, watching him deteriorate almost daily, had swept aside any misgivings.

'I should never have come,' she declared with resignation. Now, more than ever, she was convinced of it. With as much dignity as she could muster she made to move past him.

'There is a solution.'

Ryan's drawling tones brought her to a halt, and she slowly lifted her head.

'I hardly dare ask.' Her grey eyes were openly suspicious, and she schooled her composure to appear outwardly calm—an impossible task when her pulse-beat was accelerating crazily, and she lifted a hand to her throat in an attempt to hide its visible thudding.

'It's relatively simple,' he related quietly as he subjected her to a slow sweeping appraisal, his gaze fixed disturbingly on the soft outline of her mouth. 'We effect a reconciliation.'

Some inner voice screamed an agonised refusal, and for a wild moment she thought she had cried out that single monosyllabic negation. All vestige of colour left her features, leaving them pale and tense. It took every reserve of strength to remain civil, and the words came out stiffly—'I'm not that desperate!'

Ryan's eyes darkened until they resembled chips of topaz, and she felt an icy shiver scud down her spine at his dangerous compelling expression. Only a fool would dare cross a man such as he—yet she couldn't, *daren't*, agree to his proposition. Suddenly she was frighteningly aware of her own vulnerability—sure in the knowledge of his anger and the lengths to which his power could extend.

'No?'

That softly-voiced demand brought a momentary return of anger. *'No!'* Dear God, this was a thousand times worse than she had ever imagined possible.

'So emphatic,' Ryan mocked quietly, and without thought her hand flew to his face, the sound as it connected seeming unnecessarily loud in the stillness of the room.

The ensuing silence seemed interminable. A muscle tensed along his jaw, the only visible sign of his temper, and she wondered at her own temerity in providing provocation.

'I think I'd better leave,' she evinced in a strangled whisper, fear of subsequent retribution making escape imperative.

'If you don't,' Ryan bit out tersely, 'I'm liable to do something regrettable.'

How she managed to vacate the building without collapsing into an unenviable heap seemed a minor miracle. Inwardly she was shaking like a leaf, her composure torn to shreds at what had transpired, and in a trance she retraced her steps to the bus depot, purchased the necessary ticket and caught the next bus back to Brisbane where she was able to connect with another to Sydney.

Natalie reached the small country town of Casterton, located on the south-west Victorian border, utterly weary in both body and spirit. Having spent the past forty-eight hours travelling in cramped conditions and with insufficient rest, the thought of having to impart failure to her optimistic stepmother was almost the last straw. Andrea had been so positive an appeal to Ryan would succeed—the mere transition nothing less than a necessary formality.

A drawn-out sigh left Natalie's lips as she scanned the adjacent car park. It would have been nice to have been met, but the journey had been expensive enough without the additional expense of a trunk call notifying her arrival. A taxi was out, for she didn't possess sufficient money for the fare. In fact, she hadn't eaten since early that morning in an effort to conserve her funds. Calculating the evening's approaching dusk, she set out on foot, confident she would reach home before nightfall.

The wooden gate creaked as she passed through, and the lighted windows ahead were a welcoming sight as she mounted the steps.

Andrea's response to the doorbell was instantaneous. *'Natalie!'* Her perfectly-moulded features reflected an avid curiosity, demanding instant knowledge. 'How did you get on?'

Natalie had trouble summoning even a ghost of a smile. 'Don't I get offered a restoring cup of coffee first?' she countered with mild reproach. 'The last meal I had was breakfast.' She entered the small lounge and made for the kitchen. 'Is Dad asleep?'

'Likewise Michelle.' Andrea was right behind her, a faint murmur of apology on her lips. 'There's nothing left from dinner—I didn't know when to expect you.'

'I'll make do with a sandwich,' Natalie conceded, extracting a few slices of bread and selecting a filling from the refrigerator as Andrea set about making coffee.

'Well?'

Natalie met her stepmother's anxious gaze across the table and first took a bite from her sandwich, then a reviving gulp of steaming coffee.

There was no delaying the inevitable, and little point in embroidering unpleasant news. 'I'm sorry,' she said quietly, hating the disbelief that flickered across Andrea's face.

'You saw Ryan?'

'Yes, I saw him,' she agreed wearily.

'And he *refused*?'

'It wasn't a pleasant meeting.'

'But, dear God, he's your husband!' Andrea declared, appalled.

'We're separated, remember?' Natalie corrected wryly.

'You're still his legal wife,' her stepmother reminded her unnecessarily. 'If he knew about Michelle——'

'He doesn't,' Natalie interjected quickly, fixing the older woman with a warning look. 'And as long as I live, he'll never get the opportunity to lay claim to her.'

'You're a fool,' Andrea disclaimed vehemently. 'No one dismisses wealth in favour of poverty.'

Natalie felt weary beyond measure, her head ached, and she needed to catch up on some much-needed sleep. 'How has Dad been?' Her voice almost cracked with tiredness, and for a moment Andrea relented.

'Worse. I had to call the doctor twice while you were away. If he doesn't have surgery soon——' her voice trailed to a wretched halt, and Natalie saw the shine of unshed tears before the older woman managed to control them. 'For heaven's sake, go to bed—you look as if you're going to drop with fatigue. We'll talk tomorrow.'

The attic at the top of the narrow flight of stairs had been converted into a suite of rooms for Natalie more than seven years previously when her father had remarried. An only child, she had been sensitive to the relationship between her father and new stepmother, and enjoyed the feeling of independence in having her own private niche. It comprised a sitting-room, bedroom and adjoining bathroom, and she had been entirely responsible for the décor, and during the past three years she had never been more grateful for the retreat it offered.

Loath to disturb the sleeping child, Natalie didn't switch on the light, and she quietly gathered up a nightgown before moving through to the bathroom where she showered, then, refreshed, slipped beneath crisp cool sheets to drift within minutes into sweet oblivion.

Having been granted a week's leave of absence, the next few days were busy, for Natalie found a veritable pile of work awaiting her return. Her desk overflowed with it, necessitating minimum lunch breaks and often as much as an hour or two added on to her usual finishing time. Her employer was an elderly solicitor of indeterminate age, whose office she ran with single-handed efficiency. He had been so good about granting compassionate leave that she could hardly refuse to work doubly hard in an effort to bring her work up to date.

Consequently the time spent at home during Michelle's waking hours was minimal. There wasn't much opportunity to do more than look in on her father for more than ten minutes in the morning, and a further fifteen at night. If John Maclean had deduced a reason behind his daughter's sudden desire for a short vacation he gave no sign, and merely enquired if she had enjoyed herself. He appeared to tire more easily as each day passed, and watching him slowly fade filled her with a sense of helpless rage.

Saturday morning dawned bright and clear, promising sunshine in a contrary southern autumn climate, and after completing a few major chores Natalie strapped Michelle into the car-seat, then drove into town to pick up essential groceries.

It was a weekly ritual she enjoyed, although traversing each aisle with an increasingly mischievous two-year-old child had become something of an endurance test, requiring unlimited patience and a firm hand!

Having lived all her life in this small town—apart from a disastrous three months—Natalie knew every resident by name, and as was the pattern with country towns, knowledge of everyone's business was commonplace. Shopping in the town's centre was never a simple affair, as it inevitably involved several exchanges of conversation from the state of her father's health, Michelle's new tooth, a neighbour's rheumatism, to the state of the world in general.

Consequently it was almost one o'clock when she drove the small, rather careworn Mini into the garage and began unloading her purchases. Michelle had become fractious, the result of hunger and tiredness, and it took almost an hour before order was restored and blissful peace reigned as the little girl slept.

'Coffee, or a cool drink?'

'Coffee,' Natalie answered without hesitation, giving a faint smile as she regarded her stepmother across the kitchen table. 'I need reviving.'

'I'll have one, too,' Andrea agreed, standing to her feet. 'I'll make it. You look tired.'

'I didn't think it showed that much,' she murmured with self-mockery. They had just finished a light lunch, and suddenly noticing her father's tray wasn't resting on the servery, Natalie moved away from the table with the intention of retrieving it.

'John isn't here,' Andrea said quickly. 'He's been taken for a drive.'

Natalie stopped in her tracks, surprise uppermost. 'Is that wise? He was in a great deal of pain this morning.'

The kettle whistled and Andrea poured boiling

water over instant coffee, then placed the cups on the table.

'Sit down, Natalie.'

Something in her stepmother's tone brought a slight frown, and Natalie gave her a sharp look. 'What's the matter?' Her eyes narrowed, then widened with sudden disbelieving comprehension. 'You didn't——'

'Contact Ryan?' her stepmother completed defensively. 'Yes. Two days ago.'

'You had no right!' The words tumbled from Natalie's lips in a rush of anger, and she saw the older woman's mouth tighten into a determined line.

'I consider I had ever right,' Andrea insisted, and sank down into a chair, her fingers shaking as she extracted a cigarette from its packet and lit it, then she exhaled a stream of smoke as if the nicotine alone could supply a measure of courage. Her eyes beseeched Natalie to understand. 'Can't you see I had no choice?'

'You could have told me first!' Natalie cried indignantly, only to hear her stepmother's voice say quietly,

'So that you could run away—again? Eventually you'll run out of places to hide. Then what?' she queried a trifle grimly. 'Ryan has a right to know of Michelle's existence,' she added, her eyes glittering with indignation.

'*Rights!*' Natalie demanded in utter condemnation. 'What about *my* rights? Don't they deserve some consideration?'

Andrea released an angry puff of smoke and threw her stepdaughter an angry glare. 'We've sheltered you for three years, Natalie—fabricated lies concerning your whereabouts during the initial enquiries Ryan made after you'd left him.' Her eyes softened slightly, silently pleading. 'You've had every support we could offer. Now I have to think of your father.'

'At my expense,' Natalie declared bitterly, then could have bitten her tongue. 'I'm sorry,' she apologised, instantly contrite. 'That was a selfish thing to say.'

A long-drawn-out sigh left the older woman's lips. 'Ryan rang this morning while you were out, confirming arrangements he had made for your father. Late this morning an ambulance transported John to the nearest airport, where he'll be flown to Sydney and admitted to hospital. By this evening he'll be in the care of one of the finest medical teams in the country.'

Natalie felt as if a hand was tightly squeezing her heart. 'You'll follow Dad, of course,' she said matter-of-factly.

'I fly out tomorrow,' Andrea revealed slowly. 'I have a sister in one of the inner city suburbs with whom I can stay.'

'How will you get on for money?' It was a question Natalie had to ask, even though she already knew the answer.

For an instant her stepmother wavered, then defended with hardly a trace of guilt, 'Ryan has advanced sufficient funds to release me of any worry.'

Natalie felt her stomach contract, and her whole body began to ache with an inexplicable pain. 'In return, he gets Michelle,' she pronounced through white lips.

'Don't be ridiculous,' Andrea protested. 'He can't abduct her.'

Natalie directed the older woman a levelling glance. 'Can't he?' Her voice was totally sceptical. 'Ryan Marshall is a law unto himself!'

'He struck me as a fair-minded man,' Andrea defended, and Natalie gave a derisive laugh.

'He's hard, and totally without any scruples,' she declared.

'Nonsense. I don't believe——'

'Michelle is *mine*, and nobody, not even Ryan, is going to take her away from me.' Natalie stood blindly to her feet. 'I'm going to pack, and leave—*now*.' Plans raced willy-nilly through her brain. 'The Mini—you won't need it for the next few months——'

The insistent peal of the doorbell provided an interruption, sounding unnecessarily loud to her tautly stretched nerves, and she swung back towards Andrea, her eyes stark with fear.

'You're too late.' There was an element of regret in the older woman's voice, a sense of concern, and her eyes clouded as Natalie said bitterly,

'Thanks, Andrea. Your timing is lousy!'

'Won't you at least let him in?' Andrea entreated.

'The hell I will!' she refused vehemently. 'It's your house, *you* let him in. I'm going upstairs.' She had almost left the room when the doorbell pealed a further summons, and Andrea stood to her feet, smoothed her hair, then attempted to ease some of the tension from her features.

'Michelle's asleep,' she warned quietly, and Natalie hardly paused as she crossed the hall and ascended the stairs.

'With the battle about to be fought,' she shot pitilessly, 'I imagine she'll wake, regardless!'

On reaching her suite of rooms she quietly closed the door and leaned against it, momentarily shutting her eyes in an attempt to dispel the blind panic that drained her face of any vestige of colour.

Slowly she opened her eyes and for a moment their expression was blank, then she stirred herself sufficiently to walk into the bedroom where her daughter lay sleeping in a white-painted bed beneath the window.

A fierce protectiveness filled her breast as she gazed down at the child, cherubic in sleep. Light wispy blonde hair and pale creamy skin, she was Natalie in miniature—except for a pair of knowing gold-hazel eyes that, when open, were entirely Ryan's.

A short double knock on the outer door jolted her into awareness, and with a deep steadying breath Natalie slowly moved from the bedroom to the cheerfully-furnished sitting-room.

Just as she reached the door it swung open, and Natalie felt a frisson of fear slither down her spine at the sight of the man filling its aperture. Of its own volition her chin lifted in silent defiance, and for one unguarded second she glimpsed naked savagery in his expression before it was successfully masked.

Silence rebounded around the room until it became unbearable, and she almost choked attempting to swallow the lump that rose unbidden to her throat.

CHAPTER TWO

'SHALL we dispense with any pleasantries, and go straight into battle?' Natalie heard her voice, shaky with anger, and wondered dispassionately if it belonged to someone else. There was a strange feeling of unreality about the scene. Ryan—*here*. Something she had had recurring nightmares about during the past few years, waking in a cold sweat that he had managed to elicit information leading to her whereabouts—worse, discovered the wild passion they had once shared had borne fruit in the form of a child. Hers, but indisputably *his*.

A muscle tensed along his powerful jaw, adding emphasis to a profile that was arresting.

'I didn't come here to fight,' Ryan declared with clipped cynicism, and she uttered a disbelieving laugh.

'You surprise me!'

'Aren't you going to ask me in?' he countered, and with an exaggerated gesture she stood to one side.

'By all means, let's be civil about the whole thing.'

'Andrea saw fit to contact me,' Ryan declared with an edge of mockery as he moved to the centre of the room, and Natalie met his hard gaze with a touch of defiance.

'So I've just been informed.' Her grey eyes resembled the bleakness of a storm-tossed sea. 'My father gets taken care of—one can only presume in the best of private hospitals. Andrea has all burden of debt lifted from her shoulders.'

Bitterness clouded her features, intermingled with angry rejection. 'I can understand Andrea's methods, but I won't pretend to condone them.'

For a moment Ryan's eyes gleamed with anger, and when he spoke his voice was dangerously soft. 'How do you think I reacted on discovering I have a child?'

Sparks flew from her eyes as she threw wildly, 'If it had been left to me, you'd never have known of her existence!'

'I could strangle you with my bare hands,' Ryan intimated mercilessly, and for a few heartstopping seconds she experienced genuine fear. He looked capable of anything, his superior strength reducing her to a state of defenceless impotence.

'Assault is a punishable offence,' Natalie declared warily.

It seemed an age before he spoke, and when he did his voice was devoid of any emotion. 'I want my daughter.'

Anger erupted from her throat like lava from an active volcano. 'You can't have her!' Her eyes flashed with bitter enmity as she lashed, 'I'll fight you in every court in the country!'

'Any judge would award me custody,' Ryan declared silkily, 'on the grounds that my ability to provide for her well-being is far superior to yours.'

Each word hammered home with chilling finality, and Natalie's voice rasped with disbelieving incredulity. 'I won't let you take her,' she whispered. 'You'll hand her over to a highly competent nanny, then bundle her off to boarding school the minute she becomes eligible.' The words had difficulty getting past the lump in her throat, and her body seemed racked with pain. 'What kind of monster are you?'

'A very human one,' he answered quietly, his eyes holding hers unwaveringly. 'I want you back.'

She looked at him, aghast. 'You can't be serious?'

'Utterly.'

'What is this—*revenge*?'

'Call it whatever you like.'

'And if I refuse?'

'You won't.' His smile was singularly humourless. 'Michelle is my trump card.'

'You—bastard,' Natalie whispered futilely.

'Such language!' Ryan chastised mockingly, and Natalie rounded on him in utter fury.

'Go to hell!'

'Be careful I don't take you with me,' he taunted softly.

'Words fail to express how much I hate you!'

'My heart bleeds,' he drawled sardonically, his lips moving to form a cynical smile. 'Our—er—reconciliation won't be without its compensations.'

'I don't give a damn for any so-called compensations!'

His expression hardened measurably. 'We fly out tomorrow, Natalie,' he declared with marked inflexibility. 'Andrea will accompany us as far as Sydney. I suggest you begin packing.'

'You're joking!' she exclaimed, horrified as her brain began whirling at the implications such a transition involved.

'Not in the least,' Ryan denied wryly, regarding her through narrowed eyes.

'The house can't be left unattended——'

'It's all been arranged, Natalie,' he told her cynically, and she gave a bitter laugh.

'Of course—forgive me. I'm merely a pawn in this diabolical charade.'

'Hardly a charade,' he reminded her sardonically, and she forced herself to speak with a semblance of civility.

'Having acquainted me of the details, will you please leave?'

One eyebrow slanted with mocking cynicism. 'This room, or the house?'

'Both!'

'Andrea is very hospitable,' Ryan disclosed dispassionately. 'She offered me a bed for the night.'

'Not *mine*,' Natalie declared vehemently, and his lips twisted into a faint smile.

'So adamant, my darling wife. I vividly recall a time when you leapt at the chance.'

'I was a besotted fool,' she muttered in an unsteady voice, fixing her gaze on a spot to the left of his shoulder.

'Three years, Natalie,' he mused cynically. 'Dare I hope you've grown up?'

Resentment welled up inside her, sharpening her tongue. 'If by growing up you mean I might condone a mistress or two, or more, then you're sadly mistaken!'

Ryan's expression became keenly alert. 'What the hell are you talking about?'

'Simone Vesey.' Natalie revealed with succinct sarcasm, and an eyebrow slanted in a gesture of mockery.

'What do you want? A blow-by-blow account of every woman I've bedded since puberty?'

'My word!' she breathed unevenly. 'You mean, you remember them *all*?'

The air crackled with latent animosity, a reminder of his temper evident in the chilling glint from his topaz eyes, and she unconsciously held her breath, waiting for an inevitable verbal onslaught.

'Is there anything to be gained in pursuing this conversation?' he demanded dryly, and she released a long-drawn-out sigh.

'I admire your adroitness in escaping the issue.'

'I wasn't aware Simone Vesey *was* an issue.'

'Oh really, Ryan,' Natalie mocked with derision, 'I didn't come down with the last shower of rain!'

'I could slap you, do you know that?' he declared silkily after a measurable silence.

'My goodness, is that a threat?' she countered sweetly, and saw his eyes darken ominously.

'Don't tempt me,' he began hardily. 'I have a thin rein on my temper as it is.'

'Why?' she demanded huskily. 'Is your ego dampened to discover the child you fathered is female, rather than a coveted son?'

For a moment Natalie thought he would explode, and she wondered at her own temerity in rousing his anger. The result wasn't an enviable quality, and she retained too vivid a memory of past retributions to want to incur any repeat.

'What you're doing amounts to coercion,' she proffered shakily, and he arched a sardonic eyebrow.

'Do you want to change your mind?'

With an unconscious movement she lifted a hand and smoothed back a stray tendril of hair behind her ear. There was no defiance in her manner, just a kind of desperate curiosity. 'What would you do if I did?'

'Take Michelle.' There was a terrible finality in those words that didn't bear thinking about.

'You're despicable,' Natalie whispered, appalled. 'I'm her mother!'

'I'm also her father.'

The words tumbled forth with choked incoherency. 'I'll never forgive you for this!'

His slow smile was a mere facsimile. 'My heart bleeds.

He was nothing less than a callous *brute,* and she was about to tell him so when a thin piercing cry erupted from the adjoining room, rapidly ascending to a fractious wail, and without a word Natalie turned in escape to tend to her daughter's needs.

Michelle was sitting up in bed, her lips puckered in distress, two large tears slowly wending their way down her childish cheeks. The instant she caught sight of Natalie her small arms reached out and her face became wreathed in a full-dimpled smile.

'Had a nice nap, darling?' Natalie asked, crossing to take the little girl into her arms. Her lips moved down to nuzzle the sweet crease at Michelle's neck. No one, not even Ryan, was going to deprive her of the most important possession in her life.

With easy adeptness Natalie changed the little tot into her clothes, then she swung her into her arms for a customary cuddle. Michelle responded by chuckling with delight.

'May I?'

Natalie hadn't heard a sound, nothing to indicate that Ryan had followed her into the bedroom, and she turned slowly, her arms shielding her daughter as if from some predatory aggressor.

His eyes met hers unwaveringly, silently demanding she comply, and her chin lifted of its own volition. Her hold on Michelle instinctively tightened as she glimpsed his savage anger.

Heaven knew what would have happened next if Michelle, fascinated by the sight of a strange man, hadn't suddenly decided to proffer Ryan a singularly sweet smile.

'Hello there,' he greeted her quietly, his lips widening into a slow lopsided smile, and immediately was rewarded with a gurgling chuckle.

'I usually take her downstairs for a glass of milk and a cereal biscuit,' Natalie put in stiffly.

'Then I suggest you let me do so. Andrea can supply the sustenance while I become better acquainted with my daughter.'

'While I do—what?'

The smile was still evident, but his eyes were dark golden chips. 'Pack,' he instructed succinctly, daring her to defy him as he moved and took Michelle from her arms.

The door opened, then closed quietly behind him, and it was with a supreme effort that Natalie managed to control the urge to throw something in his wake! She would have taken much satisfaction in the action—no matter how futile!

Impotent rage clouded her gaze as she retrieved a suitcase from the wardrobe, and flinging it on to the bed she threw clothes into it with no compunction for their neatness. Michelle's favourite toys were placed into a large overnight bag, then she did a quick mental check that no necessities had been overlooked.

At the lower edge of the narrow staircase Natalie paused and drew a deep steadying breath before moving towards the lounge. Her eyes were suspiciously bright as she met Andrea's quick darting gaze, and the tight little smile she summoned forth didn't fool anyone.

Ryan was seated comfortably in an armchair with Michelle positioned on one powerful thigh, the little girl appearing totally enchanted with the new man in her life as she busily attempted to unbutton his shirt.

Learning at an early age, Natalie thought silently, and caught the faint cynicism in his gleaming eyes. Damn him—he had always been adept at reading her mind!

'How about a drink?' Andrea suggested brightly.

'Ryan? Whisky, if I remember correctly. And Natalie, a light sherry?'

Oh, for the sanity of preserving the conventions, Natalie mocked silently as she accepted the glass of amber liquid.

'I've organised dinner,' Andrea prattled, aware that the tension within the room could be sliced with a proverbial knife. 'You will dine with us, Ryan?'

He inclined his head in silent acquiescence. 'Thank you.'

Natalie darted him a glance that held thinly-veiled venom, and was met with an expression of musing mockery. Damn him! He seemed bent on deliberately making things as awkward for her as possible! Her mood verged on dangerous anti-pathy, and the alcohol gave her the impetus to query, 'Perhaps one of you would care to enlighten me as to the extent of the information Dad has been given regarding the sudden availability of funds?' Her eyes burned with ill-concealed fury as she evinced with deliberate sarcasm, 'After all, our stories should match, don't you think?'

Andrea glanced nervously at Ryan, who asserted with silky smoothness,

'John has been told the truth.' He paused deliberately, then continued blandly, 'Your recent—holiday was instrument in achieving a reconciliation. Naturally, upon learning of my father-in-law's illness, I insisted on assuming responsibility for any medical expenses.'

'*Naturally*,' Natalie echoed dryly. She could only admire their conspiracy. It had all been carefully planned, and doubtless Andrea felt justified in sparing John any unpleasantness. It was the one thing that was commendable in the entire misadventure!

'Sarcasm doesn't suit you,' Ryan slanted

imperturbably, and she gave a wry laugh, emptying the contents of her glass before crossing to the cabinet to refill it from the decanter.

'What do you expect? Polite conversation?'

Andrea shifted slightly on her chair, attempting to deal with an awkward situation as best she knew how. 'We've had a very mild summer,' she began, directing her attention to Ryan. 'How has the weather been on the Coast?'

'Oh, by all means,' Natalie intervened facetiously, 'let's discuss the weather.'

'Contrary,' Ryan answered, blandly ignoring his wife. 'With the highest rainfall recorded in more than a decade.'

'Interesting how the seasons appear to have changed over the years,' Andrea commented, as if the topic consumed a vital interest, and Natalie felt stifled by the banality of the situation.

'If you'll excuse me,' she said abruptly, 'I'll leave the two of you to discuss the state of the world.' She glanced towards Andrea. 'I'll unpeg the washing from the line, and prepare Michelle's vegetables.' Offering a bright smile, she barely skimmed Ryan with her gaze, hating the ease with which Michelle had accepted him. 'I'm sure the two of you can manage quite well without me.'

Dinner was not the dreaded event Natalie had imagined it might be, for with sophisticated adroitness Ryan managed to maintain a conversational flow, despite her often monosyllabic response. It didn't seem to bother him a whit whether she participated or not.

At the end of the meal, Natalie rose to her feet with alacrity. 'I'll attend to the dishes.' She collected plates and began stacking them, refusing to meet those dark musing eyes across the table.

'Irish coffee, Ryan?' Andrea suggested, appearing relaxed and at ease. 'A nice finishing touch, don't you agree?'

'I'll set the coffee on to perk.' Natalie escaped into the kitchen with a sense of relief, despite the seemingly mountainous pile of saucepans, crockery and cutlery that needed to be washed. Andrea had really surpassed herself with dinner, applying all her culinary skills and succeeding beautifully— although dealing with the aftermath took considerable time before order was restored.

With the coffee made, its tantalising aroma teased the tastebuds as Natalie placed three mugs on to a tray and carried it into the lounge, whereupon Andrea looked up with a trace of guilt.

'I should have given you some help.'

'Nonsense,' Natalie dismissed. 'You couldn't neglect our guest.'

'Good heavens,' the older woman exclaimed in mild amazement, 'Ryan is more than a mere guest?'

Natalie chose silence, deliberately avoiding his gaze as he took a mug from the proffered tray, then seating herself in a single armchair on the opposite side of the room she pondered just how soon she could decently retire without making her exit too glaringly obvious.

'Will it be convenient if we leave around seven in the morning?'

She glanced up at the sound of that drawling voice, centring her attention somewhere in the vicinity of his left ear. 'I'm surprised you bother to ask.' A tinge of cynicism entered her voice. 'I imagined you'd have the arrangements made, without referring to me as to their suitability.'

'You didn't answer the question.'

Her smoky grey eyes shifted to meet his. 'How are we travelling?' she asked levelly, and felt her heart give a sudden lurch as Andrea stood to her feet, for all the world intent on declaring her need for an early night.

'You will excuse me, won't you?' Andrea's smile encompassed them both. 'I'll leave you to settle the finer details. Goodnight.'

Don't go! Natalie wanted to scream. For God's sake, don't leave me alone with him! But it was too late, for the older woman was already at the door, her departing smile a stark reminder of Natalie's vulnerability.

Ryan regarded her steadily, his expression enigmatic. He appeared totally at ease, and it was all she could do not to turn and flee.

After what seemed an interminable silence, he informed her in a lazy drawl. 'A chartered Lear jet will take us to Sydney. After ensuring that Andrea is safely met by her sister, we'll fly on to Coolangatta.'

'Where your car is waiting,' she concluded, and glimpsed his wry smile.

'Yes.'

Standing to her feet, Natalie collected the mugs and the tray with the intention of taking them through to the kitchen.

'In such a hurry to escape my company?' His mocking drawl brought forth a surge of latent anger.

'It's been a very wearying day,' she retorted with asperity, spearing him with a stormy glance. 'Tomorrow won't be any better, travelling from dawn to sunset. I intend getting a full night's sleep.'

Ryan's mouth twisted into a sardonic smile. 'Your last alone, Natalie. Enjoy it.'

For a heartstopping moment she was tempted to throw the tray and its contents at his hateful head, then sanity prevailed. Without bothering to look at him, she walked from the room, and in the kitchen she rinsed the mugs and put them to drain, then replaced the tray.

There was no means by which to reach the stairs without going through the lounge, and she studiously avoided glancing at Ryan as she moved towards the hall.

'Andrea failed to indicate where I'm to sleep.' His voice reached her just as she was about to open the door, and she turned to see the lazy mockery evident in his expression.

'The guest room is to the right of the stairs,' Natalie told him bleakly. 'I'll check that the bed has been made up.'

The fact that it hadn't filled her with silent rage. Damn Andrea for placing her in such an invidious position! It was all Natalie could do not to fling the necessary sheets and blankets on to the bed and instruct Ryan to make it up himself.

The chore was completed in a matter of minutes, and her face was a stony mask as she attempted to move past him.

The elusive woodsy tang of his aftershave teased her nostrils as she drew close. Every last nerve-end tingled into awareness, making her shockingly aware of him, and there was no willpower in the world able to halt the faint tinge of pink that crept over her cheeks. Three years—more than a thousand *nights*, hadn't dimmed the electrifying hunger, the *need*, that she had deliberately buried deep inside herself.

Dear God, what was the matter with her! How could she respond like this when she hated him— *hated*, with every fibre in her body! It was madness, some temporary form of insanity. It *had* to be!

A slight movement alerted her attention, and with a sense of terrible fascination she watched as Ryan lifted a hand and idly traced the outline of her lips.

'Are you staying?'

The soft drawl acted like a douche of cold water, and she wrenched away, filled with sickening despair. 'No—*no*!'

She reached the safety of her room, hardly aware of having ascended the stairs, and leaned against the closed door, her breathing as heavy and spasmodic as if she had just run a mile.

It was a long time before she roused herself sufficiently to move towards her bedroom, where she slowly and mechanically went through the motions of preparing for bed.

Slipping between the sheets, she buried her head into the pillow with an audible groan as painful memories came flooding back in a sequence of hauntingly vivid events, making sleep impossible.

CHAPTER THREE

IT had begun with a carefree holiday Natalie shared with two girl friends, each taking three weeks' annual leave, and intent on enjoying as much fun and sun as the famed Queensland coastal resort of Surfer's Paradise claimed to provide.

On the fourth evening, *Thursday*—dear God, she could even remember the day, the *hour*—they had elected to visit a disco, where during the course of the evening she had been unable to deter the amorous clutches of her partner and had signalled her friends that she intended to leave.

Thinking nothing of walking the two blocks to the hotel, she had viewed the four young revellers ahead with scant regard until they surrounded her, jostling and jeering as they halted her progress. At first she had smiled and stepped aside, then when they refused to let her pass she unloosed a few pithy words with little effect, and just as things began to get out of hand a tall lean stranger appeared on the scene, and in a matter of seconds the youths were gone.

'Thank you,' Natalie proffered gratefully, turning to her rescuer with a slight smile. 'That was fast becoming a sticky situation.'

'You're a visitor to the Coast?'

It was more a statement than a query, and she gave a light chuckle. 'Is it that obvious?' In the dimly-lit side-street all she could determine was a tall well-built frame.

'It isn't wise to walk alone here at night,' her

rescuer drawled. 'If you must, choose one of the main streets where there are plenty of people.'

'I didn't think,' Natalie found herself saying with total honesty. 'The hotel is only a short distance away, and the Esplanade seemed the quickest route.'

'If you don't want a recurrence of that nasty episode, I suggest you allow me to drive you back to your hotel.'

'And jump from the frying pan straight into the fire?' she retorted with a faint laugh. 'Thanks—but no, thanks.'

'Such independence!' he mocked quizzically, and she responded cautiously,

'Having just delivered a warning on "stranger-danger", you contradict yourself by suggesting I get into your car.'

He was walking beside her, within touching distance, and he laughed—a deep throaty chuckle that made her turn and look at him.

The illumination from a nearby street light threw his features sharply into focus, outlining a broad-chiselled profile with an arresting quality that sent shock-waves slithering down the length of her spine.

'So—no car,' he mocked, and his firm sen-suously-moulded mouth widened into a smile. 'By your own admittance, the hotel isn't far. We'll walk.'

Natalie gave a faint shrug. 'It really isn't necessary.'

'Call it my good deed for the day.'

She wrinkled her nose at him, and her eyes danced with ill-concealed humour. 'You don't look the Boy Scout type.'

His answering smile did strange things to her equilibrium. 'Just what *do* I look like?'

Her head tilted to one side as she regarded him. 'Hmm—sophisticated,' she proffered pensively. 'Successful, I'd say. You have that certain air. And popular with the fairer sex.'

'Not trustworthy? Reliable?'

Natalie laughed, and it was a sweet melodic sound, without pretention. 'I'd have to know you a lot better before I'd dare to pass comment on those qualities.'

'Have dinner with me tomorrow night.' It wasn't a question, it was a statement—expecting acceptance.

'I'm holidaying with two friends,' she refused politely.

'Who can surely spare you for one night?'

'No—thank you. I don't know you—anything about you,' she explained carefully. They had almost reached the end of the second block, and her hotel lay just across the street, its entrance ablaze with light.

'Do you have a name?'

She looked at him squarely, sensing a dangerous, compelling quality—an inherent determination to conquer any obstacle that stood in his way. Accepting a date with him would be akin to diving off a jetty into unknown depths in the dark of night! 'I don't think my name is important,' she said quietly. 'Thank you for providing an escort. Goodnight.'

Not waiting for his response, she stepped from the pavement and crossed to the hotel, entering its portals and summoning the elevator without so much as a backward glance.

During the following few days the three girls alternately shopped and sunbathed, electing on Saturday night to take in a much-advertised floorshow held at an international hotel.

It was halfway through the evening during an intermission that Natalie experienced a strange prickling sensation at the base of her nape, and turning slowly to discover the cause she came face to face with none other than her tall dynamic rescuer. Her smile was little more than a polite acknowledgment. of his presence before she turned back to converse with her friends.

What happened next was unexpected, but afterwards she could only view the encounter with musing resignation.

'May I offer to get you a drink?' The deep drawling voice from close behind simultaneously accompanied his light touch at her elbow, and even before she turned she could see the effect his presence was having on both her friends.

Susan, the more vivacious of the three, recognising an opportunity too good to let slip through her fingers immediately rose to the occasion and accepted with gracious alacrity.

The inevitable introductions were effected, and it seemed a refusal to join his .table was unavoidable—impossible, when Susan had already accepted on their behalf!

Ryan Marshall proved himself to be an attentive host, and without being aware of it Natalie found she had been subtly included in an invitation to his home the following evening.

After the show he insisted on driving the three girls back to their hotel, and on parting instructed that they be ready at seven the next evening.

'We'll get a taxi,' Natalie said a trifle desperately, only to be foiled in the attempt by his insistence that he would call for them.

Choosing what to wear and the ensuing preparations for the evening ahead seemed to take most of the day, although despite all opposition

Natalie elected to wear a simply-cut dress in aquamarine silk, its bodice gathered at the waist, creating a blouson effect, the skirt falling a few inches below her knees. The colour highlighted the fairness of her hair and gave her lightly tanned skin an added glow. High-heeled strappy sandals and a matching white clutch purse were a perfect complement, and although she applied make-up with care, she chose an understated look, using a minimum of eyeshadow and mascara, and merely smoothed a shiny gloss over her lips.

She settled into the front seat of the luxurious vehicle with a sense of trepidation. Ryan Marshall was no ordinary man. The car he drove was an expensive foreign model, and it seemed her worst fears were confirmed when he took the turn-off leading to an exclusive inner island suburb.

Cronin Island was the smallest and perhaps the most prestigious of the island developments, for Surfer's Paradise was a long coastal strip whose inner islands lay along the meandering Nerang River and were linked to the mainland by several bridges. Developers had had the foresight to gauge the Coast's potential, and over the years had developed the small islands into canal estates, continuing canal development on to the mainland fringes. The result was unique, providing highly sought-after real estate. No visit to the tourist mecca was complete without taking a cruise along the canal waterways, receiving colourful commentary on the history of the canal development, and an opportunity to view some of the more famous millionaire residences.

The evening possessed an unreal quality from the moment Ryan swept the car between high electronically-controlled wrought-iron gates and brought it to a halt in the forecourt of what could only be described as a mansion. Guests began arriving shortly after eight, and during the ensuing hours Natalie was supremely conscious of his every glance, the slight almost secretive smile he gave her whenever their eyes seemed to meet—which was often. Some form of elusive magic was pulling them together, and she appeared powerless to stop it. Common sense screamed for her to run as fast and as far as she could. Ryan Marshall, whatever—*whoever* he was, was a thousand light years apart from the life she led, and to become involved with him in any way was asking for heartache.

It was Natalie's insistence that resulted in the three girls getting a taxi back to the hotel. Her polite refusal to have Ryan drive them drew forth a faint teasing smile, and when the taxi drew up outside the gates he leant out a hand and idly brushed his fingers down her cheek in a strangely gentle gesture.

'Goodnight, Natalie.' His voice was a soft seductive drawl, and despite the warm evening air, she shivered.

At nine the following morning he phoned with an invitation to dinner that evening. Politely but firmly, she refused, and put down the receiver.

When the girls returned from the beach that afternoon there was a cellophane-wrapped florist's box containing one single red rose, and a card indicating that he would call at six-thirty.

'No,' Natalie insisted, when she was alternately pleaded with and berated by her friends.

'For heaven's sake—he's *gorgeous*!' Susan wailed in despair. 'What have you got to lose?'

My sanity—among other things! she wanted to scream. Instead she said calmly, 'I'm not going out with him.'

'You mean you'll stay here and tell him so when he arrives?'

'No.' She wasn't that brave! 'I'll leave a message at the desk.' She wrinkled her nose at them, inveigling, 'How about dinner at the Pizza Hut, or McDonald's—followed by a movie?'

They complied, albeit reluctantly, returning to the hotel after eleven, and the next morning there was a further floral tribute—this time the message read, 'I'm serious. Seven this evening. Ryan'. Half an hour later the phone rang.

'It's for you,' Susan announced, holding the receiver out towards Natalie, who shook her head, mouthing a silent message relaying her absence from the apartment.

Ten minutes later there was a knock at the door, and Natalie flew into the bedroom. 'If it's who I think it is——' she paused, her eyes wide as a gamut of emotions darkened their depths, 'I'm down at the beach—or in the pool—anywhere,' she finished blindly.

It didn't do any good. Three minutes later the door opened, and Ryan was in the room, his lengthy frame leaning with indolent ease against the wall.

'You can't come in—this is a bedroom,' Natalie almost stammered, her eyes wide with consternation as she gazed at him.

'Correction,' he drawled. 'It's a room in which there are two beds—somewhere you've escaped in order to avoid me. Why?'

'Can't you accept that I won't go out with you?' she countered, her grey eyes serious.

'You don't wear a ring proclaiming any man's right of possession,' Ryan declared quietly. 'Is it possible you're afraid of me?'

He was too perceptive by far! 'Yes,' she

admitted starkly. Worse, afraid of myself, she added silently.

His voice was deep and wholly serious. 'I'd like the opportunity to get to know you.'

A choking, faintly scornful laugh left her lips. 'Don't you mean "get me into bed"?'

Dark golden eyes flared briefly with anger, then his mouth twisted into a wry smile. 'That, too.'

Natalie had difficulty in swallowing. 'I don't go in for transient relationships,' she responded steadily, and his eyebrow slanted in quizzical appraisal.

'Meaning that I do?'

'Look,' she began desperately, 'you're probably a very nice man. In fact, you look——' she searched for an appropriate word, and failed. 'Susan would go out with you in a flash,' she rushed, throwing her hands out in a gesture of despair. 'Why *me*?'

'Dinner tonight,' Ryan insisted softly. 'If you don't agree, I'll bundle you into the car *now*.'

She felt her eyes widen into large pools of incredulity. 'You can't do that!'

'Can't I?' he mocked lightly, and she made one last attempt.

'What about your job—you must work at something!'

'I've decided to delegate responsibility today.' He moved from the door and advanced slowly towards her. 'We're going out. No,' he paused, and placed a finger to her lips, 'no arguments.'

'My friends——'

'If having them along means I get *you*, by all means ask them.'

It was an enjoyable day, as Ryan drove to out-of-the-way spots, places the tourist buses rarely frequented, and if he intended that the time spent in his company might melt her resistance, he succeeded.

The restaurant was small and secluded, eliciting the patronage of the socially élite, and it wasn't until Natalie had sipped a full glass of wine that she began to relax a little.

'Tell me about yourself.'

She glanced at the man opposite and proffered a slight smile. 'Age, rank and serial number?' she quipped lightly. 'Really, I'm very uninteresting. From an ordinary middle-class family, comprising father, stepmother—no brothers or sisters. I've lived all my life in a small country town near the south-west border of Victoria. I'm nineteen years of age, and I work for an elderly solicitor.' The wine was giving her courage—perhaps she should have some more! 'Your turn.'

'Thirty-two, a family well scattered in several different countries throughout the world. Development and construction is my business.'

Her eyes sparkled with hidden laughter. 'Very concisely compiled. You must be very successful,' she added, and met his thoughtful gaze.

'Yes. Does it bother you?'

'Wealth can't buy health or happiness,' she said slowly.

'It helps,' he assured her with mocking cynicism.

'I imagine it does,' Natalie agreed seriously. 'Although I'd hate to be unsure whether my friends liked me for myself, or merely for the material possessions my wealth could provide.'

His eyes narrowed thoughtfully. 'You're too clever by far—do you know that?'

Very carefully she lifted her glass and took a tentative sip. 'This is an excellent wine.'

A slow smile teased the edges of his mouth, and he raised his glass in a silent mocking toast.

The food surpassed anything she had ever tasted, and as the evening progressed she began to view its end with mixed emotions. Sure that she needed all her faculties alert and not undermined by alcohol, she refused to have her glass refilled. It didn't elude her that Ryan was well aware of the reason why, and what was more, found the fact amusing.

In the car she was silent, unable to think of a thing to say that wouldn't come out as inane or inconsequential. It took all of four minutes to reach the hotel, yet each one seemed like an hour, and when Ryan brought the vehicle to a halt she sat still, longing to flee from his presence yet not quite able to summon the courage to do so.

'Is it all men who have this effect—or just me?'

Natalie endeavoured to evade the issue. 'Thank you for a pleasant evening.' She reached for the door clasp, only to be forestalled.

'You're trembling—why?' he demanded softly. 'I haven't the slightest intention of harming so much as a hair on your beautiful head.'

'It's late,' she ventured a trifle desperately, and he smiled. Without a word he leaned an arm along the back of her seat and bent towards her. His warm breath fanned her cheek, then his lips touched an earlobe before trailing slowly down the edge of her jaw to the corner of her mouth.

It was a gentle caress, provocative and faintly teasing, momentary, and leaving her with a strange bereft feeling as he reached for the clasp to unlatch her door.

'Goodnight, Natalie.' His voice bore a trace of mockery, and she slipped from the car, her reciprocal murmur lost in the sound of the soft clunk as the door closed behind her.

In a daze she walked to the entrance and

inserted her key into the security lock, and when
the doors slid shut behind her she turned and
caught a glimpse of gleaming paintwork as the
racy Ferrari slipped out on to the road.

For some unknown reason she wanted to cry. He
had made no mention of ringing, nor had he
suggested another date. She tried to tell herself she
didn't care, but how else could she explain the
strange ache deep inside her?

With the dawn came reason and a resolve to
forget the compelling Ryan Marshall. Natalie was
evasive when begged to relate every detail of the
previous evening, and dispelled the inclination to
stay close to the phone in case it rang, choosing
instead to spend the day at the beach. There were
no messages at reception on their return, and with
a feeling of desperation she suggested they eat out,
attend a nightclub—anything, in an attempt to be
caught up in noise and laughter so that her
attention was diverted away from the man who
had begun to fill her thoughts to such a degree
that it was vaguely frightening.

The next morning she was dragged from sleep
by the sound of the phone ringing, and she flew to
answer it, unsuspecting in a state of half-
wakefulness as to who might be calling at such an
early hour.

'Natalie?'

She slumped against the wall, unable to find her
voice for a few seconds, and Ryan's deep drawl
held amusement.

'Did I get you out of bed?'

Hastily she consulted her watch. 'It's seven
o'clock.'

'And you're standing there in a demure cotton
shift with your hair all tousled,' he mused, and she
could sense the laughter in his voice.

'I have no intention of telling you anything about my sleeping attire,' she declared unsteadily, and heard a deep-throated chuckle in response.

'I'll be back early this evening. Will you have dinner with me?'

'Back from where?' The words were out before she could stop them, and she cursed herself for appearing inquisitive.

'Sydney. I flew down yesterday.'

'Oh.'

'Shall we say seven?'

She wanted to say no, but a single monosyllabic acceptance left her lips of its own volition, and it was only after she had replaced the receiver that she cursed herself for being a fool in arranging to see him again.

The hours through the day dragged, and she was ready a good ten minutes before the appointed time, her nerves setting her stomach into an impossible knot as she waited. Twice she considered changing her attire, undecided whether the simple cream silk blouse and pencil-slim skirt were suitable for what he had in mind. A slight hysterical bubble burst in self-derisive mockery. What Ryan Marshall had in mind was undoubtedly to remove her clothing as skilfully and unobtrusively as possible!

His arrival created havoc with her finely-tuned senses, and the sight of his lengthy frame attired in an opened-necked black silk shirt and expensively-tailored cream trousers almost robbed her of the ability to speak.

In the car she sat in silence, and it was only when he turned from Chevron Island and headed towards Cronin Island that her worst fears were realised.

'We're dining at your home?'

Ryan's glance was swift and analytical. 'I prefer not to share your company with a room full of strangers.'

The butterflies in Natalie's stomach set up a frightening tattoo and she endeavoured to inject a steadiness into her voice. 'I think you'd better take me back to the hotel.'

The car slowed and turned into the wide sweeping driveway, coming to a halt outside the entrance. Carefully Ryan switched off the engine, then he turned towards her, resting an elbow on the steering wheel as he allowed his gaze to rove slowly over her expressive features.

Natalie forced her eyes to remain steady during that intense scrutiny, hating him for placing her in such an invidious position—hating herself equally for being so vulnerable.

'I have any number of female acquaintances with whom I can indulge a bedroom romp,' he informed her cynically, then pursued relentlessly, 'My housekeeper has prepared an excellent meal. The eating of it, in your company, is all I have in mind.'

'You expect me to believe that?'

'Get out of the car, Natalie.' His voice held a silky threat that sent shivers of apprehension slithering down the length of her spine, and she complied without so much as a word.

With a mounting sense of trepidation she preceded him through the wide panelled doors into the foyer, allowing herself to be led into a spacious lounge, and it wasn't until she had taken a few reviving sips of some excellent wine that she had the courage to take note of her surroundings.

The neutral clover-shaded carpet was thick-piled and luxurious, providing a perfect background for the dark laquered cane furniture whose soft-plumped cushions were covered in apricot silk. Expensive paintings adorned pale cream textured walls, and large sliding glass doors were smoke-tinted, providing privacy as well as acting as a filter for the strong Queensland sunlight.

'You have a beautiful home,' Natalie accorded sincerely, and glimpsed the faint sardonic cynicism in the tigerish eyes some distance from her own.

'Very politely spoken,' Ryan acknowledged with an edge of mockery. 'If I offer to show you the rest of it, doubtless you'll read some ulterior motive into the invitation.'

'Not at all,' she responded civilly. 'I'd find it a fascinating experience.'

Without a word he crossed the room, and taking the glass from her hand he placed it down on to a nearby glass-topped table. An eyebrow slanted in quizzical amusement as he glanced at her. 'Are you sure it's my home you're referring to?'

The wine had given her the necessary confidence to arm herself against him. 'Of course. I have your word that you have no ulterior motive in mind.'

His response was an echo of silent laughter, bringing an answering smile to her lips as she allowed herself to be led on a tour of inspection.

The house comprised three levels, two of which were evident from the front entrance. The lower level was at the rear overlooking the Nerang River, and it was in this large room that the party had been held. Slate-paved floors, brick and alternate timber feature walls provided a stunning background for the cane furniture, and sliding glass doors ran the entire length of one wall, opening out on to a paved courtyard where a magnificent swimming pool reposed, its translucent waters tinged a cool blue by exquisite tiling. The grounds were lit by inconspicuous lighting, revealing an outdoor barbecue area and perfect landscaping.

A formal dining room adjoined the lounge on the ground level, and opposite the main entrance foyer was an informal television lounge with comfortable sprawling chairs and settees, electronic stereo equipment, and a video recorder. There was also a study, a second informal dining room, beyond which was a kitchen containing every conceivable labour-saving electrical device, including a microwave oven.

The upper level comprised no fewer than five bedrooms, each with en suite facilities. The housekeeper's living quarters were a self-contained suite of rooms and were situated above the garages to the left of the house.

'Very impressive,' Natalie murmured as they reached the lounge. She had been conscious of Ryan's close proximity and aware of its effect on her equilibrium.

'Another drink?'

Dared she? There would be wine to accompany the meal, and somehow she had to get through the evening with all of her faculties intact. 'No, thank you,' she refused quietly. 'But don't let me stop you from having another.'

Ryan shook his head. 'Let's go in to dinner, shall we?'

Afterwards Natalie had no clear recollection of what she ate, other than that the food was excellent, the wine a palatable complement. They talked, touching on a wide variety of subjects, listened to music, and at midnight, in almost Cinderella fashion, she elected to leave.

Quite how she managed to find herself in Ryan's arms was a mystery, but it felt right to be there, and his mouth was gentle on hers, tasting the sweetness of her lips with a curious lightness that made her ache for more. Hardly aware of what she was doing, she let her arms creep up to clasp behind his neck as she unconsciously moved close against him.

A soft intake of breath was the only warning she received, then his mouth became hard and demanding, mastering her own in a kiss that was devastating. In a total annihilation of her senses, it left her weak-willed and malleable beneath his experienced hands, and when he finally released her she was barely able to stand.

'Home, I think,' Ryan decreed enigmatically, taking in her bemusement with a narrowed, slightly speculative gaze.

In the car outside her hotel he bestowed a brief hard kiss, then leaned across and opened her door.

To say Natalie floated through the entrance foyer was an understatement, and his image filled her dreams, haunting her through the following day until his phone call confirmed that he wanted to see her again—after hours spent convincing herself she was too young, too naïve—too *inexperienced*, for him to be the slightest bit interested.

They dated frequently—constantly, was perhaps more apt, and Natalie spent each day torn between the deep wealth of feeling Ryan was able to evoke, and the knowledge that it could never be anything more than a holiday romance. She managed to keep her head—barely. Each ensuing occasion became a subtle battle of willpower, and never before had she been made so shockingly aware just how easy it was to succumb to the moment, or to lose sight of the moral principles she considered so important.

The days flew, each signalling one less to be

spent in Ryan's company, and Natalie became
filled with bitter-sweet agony as the close of her
holiday drew near. The last evening commanded
every ounce of strength she possessed, and she
prepared for it carefully, taking an inordinate
amount of time with her make-up, even going so
far as to wear a new dress bought especially for the
occasion.

When she stepped into the Ferrari her greeting
was over-bright, her smile wide as she fastened the
seatbelt. If Ryan noticed, he made no comment,
and he eased the powerful car into the stream of
traffic.

Natalie was too numb to take much notice of
where they were going, and it was only when the
car swept to a halt in the curved driveway that
she realised he had brought her to his home.
Given a choice, she would have opted for a large
restaurant where the patronage and floorshow
would provide an essential distraction. A quiet
intimate candlelit dinner might very well be her
downfall!

The wine and the food were excellent, and she
savoured each mouthful much as a condemned
prisoner might regard his final meal. Coffee was
served in the lounge, and it required both hands to
hold the cup steady as he sipped the delicious
brew.

'I'd like to thank you for making my holiday
such an enjoyable one,' Natalie ventured evenly,
amazed she hadn't stumbled over the words—
despite having rehearsed the trite little phrase
countless times throughout the day.

'Will you marry me?'

'It's been very kind of you to give up so much of
your time,' she continued, then realisation dawned
as the full intent of his words sank in. 'Would you

mind—repeating that?' she uttered faintly, and glimpsed his silent laughter.

'Do I need to?'

Her eyes were wide and unblinking, and she could have sworn her heart stopped beating. 'I think so,' she said carefully.

Without a word Ryan extracted a small velvet jeweller's box, snapped open the lid, then slid the exquisite solitaire diamond on to the appropriate finger of her left hand.

'It's beautiful,' Natalie whispered, in awe of its magnificence. Large clear grey eyes regarded him seriously. 'Are you sure you want me to have it?'

'Shall I go down on bended knee and declare my unswerving devotion?' Ryan parried gently, holding her gaze.

'That might be expecting too much,' she began unsteadily. 'Although the temptation is almost irresistible.' A mischievous sparkle lit her eyes. 'Perhaps I should insist. I may never see you so humbled again.'

'Minx,' he murmured wryly, pulling her into his arms. I've a good mind to render a punishment that will have you begging for mercy!'

His mouth settled on hers with passionate intensity, searing as he branded his possession, and when she thought her lungs might burst his hold slackened.

'I think it's just as well I'm going home tomorrow,' Natalie voiced shakily as she rested her head against his hard chest. The thought of being apart from him, even for a day, seemed too much to bear.

'I'm flying down with you tomorrow to convince your father my intentions are honourable.' She sensed the smile she knew to be on his lips. 'Also to convince him that a short engagement is essential. Anything more than a week, and I'll be on the brink of insanity.'

'A *week*——'

'If it could be arranged in less time, believe me, it would be tomorrow.' He took her chin between thumb and forefinger, lifting it so she had no option but to look at him. 'I have no intention of allowing you out of my sight until we've exchanged our nuptial vows.' His eyes darkened with emotion, and his voice held cynical amusement. 'Left alone, you just might invent any number of reasons why we shouldn't marry. It's a risk I'm not prepared to take.' He lowered his head to kiss her—thoroughly, and when she surfaced again she was far too bemused to demur.

The week that followed retained a haziness that disallowed time for reflection, taken up as it was with countless arrangements, a trip to Melbourne for a wedding gown, time-consuming phone calls to friends, issuing invitations. Even the day itself held an elusive quality—Natalie could recall laughing, *crying*, displaying a gamut of emotions as she said goodbye to family and friends and boarded the private chartered jet with Ryan for an undisclosed destination.

An idyllic honeymoon on Green Island, off the coast from Cairns, was everything Natalie imagined it might be—and more. Ryan's love-making surpassed her wildest imagination, as beneath his skilful expertise she scaled the heights of emotional sensuality. She loved, believed herself to be loved in return, and was incapable of thinking anything could destroy her happiness.

Their return to Surfer's Paradise resulted in a seemingly endless stream of parties as Ryan's friends and business associates demanded an introduction to his bride.

A building contractor and developer, Ryan had a finger in several projects, among which numbered no fewer than three high-rise buildings along the coastal foreshore. The head of a well-established construction empire, he possessed an instinct to be in the right place at the right time, willing to take the calculated risks necessary to turn a successful business into a multi-million-dollar consortium. A respected member of the community, he was on the board of directors of more than one corporation, and socially much in demand.

It was at one such party that Natalie came into contact with Simone Vesey—a dark-haired, creamy-skinned model whose tall willowy frame was a human clothes peg for several designers, her classical features photographed and included in several of the world's leading fashion magazines.

Whether by invitation or design, Simone was an inclusion at every function Natalie and Ryan attended, and it didn't take any imagination at all to understand that the glamorous woman was a veritable man-eater, or that her prime target was the highly desirable Ryan Marshall. His new bride was regarded as easily dismissable, and little more bothersome than a tiresome insect!

Well-meaning matrons hinted that Ryan was a bit of a rake—reformed, of course, with the advent of his marriage—and if gossip could be relied upon, his past had been anything but exemplary.

It hadn't taken long for the first seeds of doubt to take root in Natalie's mind. Ryan's dedication to work was something she could understand, and although he always endeavoured to be home for dinner when they were not entertaining or being entertained, there were occasions when business intervened. At first she took little notice of the phone calls saying he would be late, not to wait dinner as he had to entertain a business associate.

Simone's subtle innuendoes became a steady drip of poison, conspiring to make Natalie feel insecure, resulting in several pleas to lessen their social obligations—something Ryan resisted, then as she began to persist he grew increasingly impatient, and the arguments began.

With no friend in whom to confide her misgivings, Natalie began to view each social occasion as a silent battle—more a war of nerves, with Simone steadily emerging the winner.

After one terrible argument Natalie found it impossible to bear Ryan's intolerance a moment longer and quietly packed a bag and left, returning home to Casterton where, sworn to secrecy, her father and Andrea had disavowed any knowledge of her whereabouts.

The discovery that she might be pregnant came within weeks of her return home, and despite all opposition she chose to keep Ryan in ignorance, destroying unopened the letters that arrived for forwarding, and a month later she instructed a solicitor in Melbourne to write to Ryan on her behalf stating that there was no possibility of a reconciliation and that she desired no further contact.

Choosing to lead a quiet restrained life, almost to the point of seclusion, she managed to get through the months prior to Michelle's birth, and afterwards she had made the child her reason for living, showering love and attention with enviable maternal devotion.

CHAPTER FOUR

THE first leg of the flight was over. Natalie freshened up and attended to Michelle's needs, then rejoined Ryan in the airport lounge.

'Ready?'

Too choked to utter so much as a word, she merely nodded, and it wasn't until they were on the tarmac and about to board the jet that she dared trust herself to speak.

'I won't make a willing captive,' she warned in a dark undertone.

'My dear Natalie,' he drawled, sparing her a mocking glance, 'I didn't for one minute imagine you would.'

Inside the small cabin she sank into a seat and settled Michelle, checking their seatbelts, and was all too aware of Ryan's presence directly opposite.

The small plane began taxiing out towards the runway, its passage smooth.

'How are you going to explain my sudden return to the Marshall household?' Natalie queried with a note of defiance. The ruthless set of his compelling features was daunting, yet something goaded her on, blotting out all rational thought. 'Your current—er——' she paused with seeming delicacy, 'girl-friend isn't going to like the fact that your ex-wife is about to be reinstated.'

The silence inside the cabin seemed to reverberate until it became almost a tangible entity.

'*Ex*-wife, Natalie?' he demanded with silky detachment.

The screaming pitch of the jet's engines

precluded an immediate reply, and she waited until they were airborne before offering to comment.

'We've been apart for three years,' she defended. 'That constitutes a separation.'

'I prefer to call it an estrangement.'

Natalie let out a heartfelt sigh. 'So what explanation is going to be given in view of our supposed reconciliation? In the interests of feasibility we should both stick to the same story.'

'My private life is my own,' Ryan asserted irrefutably, and she didn't doubt he could fend off the most curious of queries with a chilling stare, whereas she would founder like a gasping fish in the face of the more formidable of his acquaintances.

'And Michelle?' she persisted. 'Her presence will doubtless raise more than an eyebrow or two.'

'I don't give a damn.'

A tiny devil tempted her further. 'Suppose it's implied she's not your child?'

A muscle tensed along his jaw, and the blazing glance he threw her was filled with icy rage. 'Be thankful for Michelle's presence. If it weren't for her, I'd thrash you to within an inch of your life,' he vowed mercilessly.

'Jealous, Ryan?'

His expression was implacable as he put a rein on his temper. 'There will come an hour when we're alone,' he inclined pitilessly. 'Will you be so brave then, I wonder?'

'What do you intend?' she muttered, hating him as the butterflies in her stomach began an erratic tattoo. 'Am I to suffer some torture of the damned now you've found me again?'

'Is that what you think?'

'I feel like a recalcitrant child hauled before the headmistress for having dared played truant from school,' she vented defensively, and he laughed, a deep-throated sound totally devoid of humour.

'I'm not sure I approve the comparison,' Ryan acknowledged dryly.

'I would hardly expect you to,' Natalie sighed with resignation, and turned to check that Michelle hadn't attempted to tamper with her seatbelt.

The little tot was happily engrossed with her favourite toy and appeared oblivious to everything else. An amenable child, she was used to amusing herself and adored travelling, rarely becoming fractious whenever Natalie ventured out—which wasn't often.

Like a sleek silver bird, the jet steadily transported Natalie towards another world, and she suppressed a shiver of apprehension as to whether she could cope with the faster paced lifestyle, the constant social round of parties and formal dinners—more important, the people who made up Ryan's circle of friends and acquaintances. The inherent backstabbing and one-upmanship beneath the thin veneer of charm was a factor she found difficult to condone.

'Second thoughts?'

She turned at the sound of that deep voice, and deliberately avoided Ryan's penetrating gaze. A sense of fatalism invaded her bones, and she was unable to suppress the feeling that she was embarking on a journey from which there could be no return.

The first opalescent glow of dusk was beginning to tinge the early evening sky as the small jet circled Coolangatta airport prior to its descent.

For the remainder of the flight Ryan had chosen to devote most of his attention to his daughter, who, contrary to Natalie's expressed will to become fractious, had done little else but laugh and indulge in an endless patter of barely comprehensible chatter. For all the notice Natalie's presence received, she might as well not even have been there! A secret part of her silently screamed at Michelle's downright fickle behaviour. Damn Ryan! He possessed the power to charm any female regardless of age, and Michelle was no exception.

An elegant Daimler stood in solitary splendour near the entrance to the car park, and Natalie evinced little surprise when Ryan moved towards the opulent vehicle and unlocked the passenger door.

'What happened to the Ferrari?' It was an idle query and meant to convey sarcasm.

'I still have it,' Ryan answered dryly, shooting her a dark glance. 'However, you'll have to agree that it's hardly a suitable vehicle in which to transport a young child, plus luggage.'

She uttered a deprecatory laugh. 'I suppose Jenkins uses the Daimler to do the shopping.'

'As a matter of fact, he does.'

'My God!' she declared with pious disregard. 'You've become even more of an autocratic plutocrat than ever!'

An eyebrow slanted in her direction. 'Are you going to hold it against me?'

How could she? He had worked long hard hours from an early age, using what capital he earned to invest in property, then building, selling, achieving capital gains for reinvestment. From employing one labourer, he now headed one of the largest construction companies on the Gold Coast. Ryan Marshall was a self-made man who deserved his hard-earned success.

Michelle began to cry, the first pitiful whimper

rapidly becoming an indignant wail that refused to be soothed.

At Ryan's faintly raised eyebrow, Natalie had to forcibly restrain a self-satisfied smile. It would do him good to realise his daughter wasn't all sweetness and light!

'She's hungry,' she explained, trying to console the upset infant without success. 'And apart from a short doze on the plane, she hasn't had her usual afternoon sleep.'

'We'll be home in thirty minutes.' Ryan slid in behind the wheel and ignited the engine, easing the large vehicle out into the steady stream of traffic moving northwards along the main highway.

'Young children are sticklers for routine,' Natalie said dryly. 'It's fifteen minutes after her mealtime. I doubt she'll last half an hour without something. There's a few pieces of fruit and a packet of cereal biscuits in my bag,' she told him, looking for it, and seeing it was neither at her feet nor on the rear seat. 'Damn!' The exclamation fell from her lips without thought. 'You must have stowed it in the boot with everything else.'

Ryan threw her a sharp darting glance. 'I'll pull over as soon as I can get into the left lane. Good grief!' he exclaimed as Michelle let out a yell. 'Is she usually this noisy?'

Natalie's smile was a mere facsimile, and she ventured sweetly, 'As far as obstinacy and getting her own way are concerned, she's every bit her father's daughter.'

Five minutes later Michelle had finished a banana and was happily munching a cereal biscuit as the car sped swiftly through Burleigh on the main coastal highway.

It seemed all too soon that numerous high-rise buildings encroached the darkening skyline, a

myriad winking lights providing a panoramic
fairyland that competed with brightly flashing
neon as they reached the outskirts of the tourist
resort.

'The Chevron have added a new accommodation
tower to their complex,' Ryan told her as they
passed a brightly lit entrance, and seconds later
they negotiated the Chevron bridge, slowing
imperceptibly to adapt to a lower speed limit.

As they reached Cronin Island the Daimler
swept through the gates and the illuminated
driveway cast shadows over the splendid landscaped grounds as Ryan brought the car to a halt
before the impressive entrance.

'I've instructed Martha to serve dinner at eight,'
he told her as he slid out and crossed to open her
door. 'I imagine that will give you time to feed,
bath and put Michelle down for the night?'

Natalie felt her stomach muscles tighten at the
thought *bed* evoked—more particularly, *his* bed,
and the fact that he would insist she share it.

'In a strange house she may not settle
immediately,' she warned, cradling the little girl
close as she stepped out from the car. 'I'd like a
shower, and a change of clothes, if I may?'

'This is your home, Natalie,' Ryan reminded her
dryly, and she cast him a sceptical glance.

'No,' she corrected evenly. 'It's where you're
forcing me to live. This grandiose—mansion was
never intended to be anyone's *home*. It's an
elegantly appointed showplace in which to entertain and impress, with never a speck of dust in
evidence or a cushion out of place.'

His expression was deliberately enigmatic. 'Shall
we go inside? I imagine Martha and Jenkins are
anxious to renew their friendship.'

Natalie mounted the few steps ahead of him,

summoning a slight smile as the solid oak-panelled door swung open. Jenkins' usually solemn features relaxed with genuine pleasure, and he ventured cordially,

'It's good to have you back, if I may say so miss.'

'You haven't changed, Jenkins,' she told him, unable to still the dancing light in her eyes. Possessing a droll sense of humour that never surfaced in the presence of guests, the manservant and his wife were more friends than employees, running Ryan's home with enviable efficiency and loving care. Doubtless he had been given a christian name, but Natalie had never heard it, and even Martha referred to her husband by his surname.

'You'll find everything just as you left it,' Jenkins revealed, regarding Michelle with undisguised interest. 'Martha has prepared a room opposite the main suite for the little one, and she has a meal ready, whenever you wish to feed her.'

'Thank you,' Natalie responded gratefully, aware that Ryan had come to stand beside her.

'Smooth flight, I presume?' Jenkins enquired of his employer. 'There were three calls. I've left details in your study.'

'I'll attend to them later,' Ryan drawled, taking hold of Natalie's elbow. 'First, we need to get this young lady settled into her new home.'

'Delightful little thing, isn't she?' the older man observed with a smile. 'I daresay she's hungry.'

'She was,' Ryan said dryly, and Jenkins chuckled as he shot Natalie a conspiratorial grin.

'Cried, did she?'

'With earsplitting velocity!'

'It's something must young children do when they're tired and hungry,' Natalie defended, trying to extricate herself from her husband's grasp. 'Tell Martha I'll be ready to feed Michelle in about five minutes. I'll just wash her face and hands first.'

Jenkins was right, she perceived on reaching the upper floor. Nothing had changed. Not even the colour of the towels placed in the bathroom. Almost as if in the presence of a ghost, she shivered as memories returned to haunt her. Just by closing her eyes it was all too easy to remember those few laughter love-filled months she had spent in this house, loving and being loved as she'd never dreamed possible. Beneath Ryan's infinite expertise she'd learnt to shed every last inhibition, incredulous that any two people had the right to be so happy. Even then she had been aware that one day the beautiful bubble might burst, but nothing had prepared her for the resultant pain, the devastating agony that followed in its wake. Like a wounded animal she had run away to hide until the scars could heal.

Now, coming here had merely made her more aware of the reason she had left. How could she live in the same house as Ryan, hating him as she did? When every waking minute she wanted to hurt him as he had hurt her? It could only result in a fiasco, with Michelle caught in the middle. A child should be surrounded with love, guided by discipline, not the means by which two people were flung together.

Dear Lord! she groaned audibly. Ryan had ensured he held all the winning cards. There would be no second escape.

Michelle's disgruntled whimper brought Natalie out of her reverie, and with a determined smile she attended to the little tot's needs before scooping her back into her arms, then she returned downstairs.

There was no sign of Ryan, and Natalie breathed a sigh of relief as she made her way to the kitchen, experiencing a slight wariness at the initial meeting with Martha.

The faint coolness soon evaporated as the older woman clucked and exclaimed over Michelle, and whatever her private thoughts regarding Natalie's flight and subsequent return, they were carefully hidden.

'She's adorable!' she smiled.

'Most of the time,' Natalie acceded as she helped her daughter scrape the last of her vegetables from the plate. The little girl began to rock back and forth, signifying her desire to leave the table.

'I'll take her upstairs for a bath,' Natalie decided, lifting the child into her arms. 'Then, with the help of some warm milk, she'll probably go off to sleep.'

Michelle waved her hand when they reached the door, much to Martha's delight, then in a fit of unaccustomed shyness the toddler buried her head against her mother's neck.

Bathtime invariably involved a variety of splashing games, and this evening was no exception. Natalie cast a rueful glance at her dampened clothes, and shook her head as Michelle attempted to send another spray of water her way.

'That's enough, my girl!' she remonstrated with a grin, plucking the protesting child from the water.

Michelle emitted a peal of laughter as she was enveloped in a large fluffy towel, wriggling for all she was worth in an attempt to prolong her bedtime.

Slipping on vest and nightgown required split-second timing for success. 'Rascal!' Natalie scolded when the task was completed. 'Now, into your nice bed with Teddy, while I go fetch your milk. Okay?'

Halfway down the stairs she met Ryan, and there was nothing she could do about her sudden erratic heartbeat at the sight of him. Gone was the formal jacket, and the three top buttons of his shirt were undone, revealing a glimpse of golden curling hair between the vee of blue silk. Her breathing became faintly uneven and she steeled herself against the dynamic masculinity he exuded, hating the way all her nerve-ends prickled in sheer awareness of his presence.

'You look like a drowned kitten,' he drawled, subjecting her to a lingering scrutiny that paused over-long on the damp patches on her blouse.

Too late Natalie remembered the absence of a bra, and as if he could read her mind Ryan uttered a soft sensual laugh that brought colour flying to her cheeks. She was suddenly aware of damp tendrils of hair that had escaped the smooth knot pinned on top of her head, the faint clean smell of baby powder that clung to her clothes, and with a muttered exclamation she hastily brushed past him.

Damn! she cursed silently as she made her way to the kitchen. Her hands were decidedly shaky as she filled the clean beaker Martha had left beside the small saucepan of warm milk. She felt so tense and overwrought it wasn't funny!

When she reached Michelle's bedroom it was to find Ryan sitting on the side of the bed intent on amusing the little girl. With an easy laugh he extracted the tot from the bed and carried her to a nearby chair.

'I usually sit her on the floor when she drinks,' Natalie said stiltedly, and received a wry glance as he complied by placing Michelle down on to the carpet. 'She's very good usually, and rarely spills a drop.'

'Am I a usurper in this domain?'

'How can you be, when this is your home?'

'Ours, Natalie,' he drawled, and she cast him a withering glance.

'Don't remind me!'

Michelle seemed lost to the task of finishing her milk, and already her eyes looked heavy, the lids drooping in tiredness.

'Go and have your shower,' Ryan bade quietly. 'I'll stay with her until she's asleep.'

'What if she cries?' Natalie asked doubtfully, and he arched an eyebrow in quizzical amusement.

'Afraid I won't be able to cope? There's always Martha to come to my rescue.'

'In that case,' she responded sweetly, 'I'll leave you to it.' She blew Michelle a kiss, then turned and left the room.

In the main suite she extracted clean underwear and a slim-fitting dress of crease-resistant lilac silk, then moved through to the bathroom.

The warm needle-spray had a soothing effect, and she stayed longer than necessary before turning off the water and stepping from the shower stall. Five minutes later she was dressed, and after applying a minimum of make-up she crossed the hallway and checked on Michelle before descending the stairs.

'Shall I pour you a drink?'

Natalie moved into the lounge and selected a solitary armchair before sinking into it with more than a little trepidation. An elegant crystal glass part filled with light amber liquid was held in one hand, and Ryan looked formidable and slightly menacing.

'A Martini, please.' Heaven knew she needed

something to bolster her morale! A slanted eyebrow greeted the request, and when she took the glass from his hand she swallowed the contents within minutes, extending it to be refilled without batting an eyelid.

Already the painful knot of nerves inside her stomach was beginning to relax, lending a false calmness to her manner.

'I imagine we're supposed to be frightfully civil,' Natalie began politely. 'Can you suggest a safe topic of conversation we can pursue? I'm afraid I've lost touch with the current political situation, and I can't recall a thing to relate that might be of interest.'

'It would help if you stopped regarding me as an animal about to pounce on its prey,' Ryan drawled, and she effected a faint grimace.

'But you will, won't you?' she declared wryly. 'You're not a man to be crossed lightly, and I've no doubt you'll exact some form of revenge.' She took a generous sip, amazed at the lucidity the alcohol appeared to have in transferring thoughts to words! 'Three years, Ryan,' she pondered deliberately, subjecting him to an unwavering scrutiny. 'I imagine a bevy of delectable women have vied for your company, eager to assuage any—er—loneliness.' Even the mere thought of that lean hard body making love to any other nubile female froze her features into a dispassionate mask. 'I doubt my absence has even been noticed.'

'Don't try my patience too far,' he warned silkily. 'I can promise you won't like the consequences.'

'I'm trembling already.' The sarcasm was an echo of the truth, and he knew it.

'So you should,' he opined softly, and Natalie stood quickly to her feet.

'I've lost my appetite. In fact, I'm sure any food would stick in my throat.' She turned, and had taken no more than three steps when hard hands caught hold of her arms, halting her flight, and Ryan swung her round to face him in one easy movement.

'Oh no, you don't,' he drawled, and his eyes narrowed fractionally as she began to struggle. 'Be still, for the love of heaven!' The directive was explosive, and his fingers bit into her soft flesh.

'You're hurting me!' Her bitterness wasn't feigned, and with an angry oath he released his grip.

'Three years ago I could have strangled you without the slightest hesitation,' he revealed with wry cynicism.

Natalie swallowed compulsively. 'How do you think I felt,' she began a trifle shakily, 'when I discovered the "loving husband" image you projected was just that—an image?' Her eyes filled with anger. 'An elusive non-existent entity,' she brooded, gaining courage as she met his steady enigmatic gaze. 'I was an easy target—a real innocent babe.' A soundless laugh of derision left her lips. 'You had it all, Ryan, and I, poor fool, thought it was love!' An edge of mockery entered her voice. 'Amazing that you proposed marriage— something, I gathered from the ever-lovely Simone, you'd never been known to offer in the past.'

His expression was inscrutable, and the edge of his mouth lifted in a gesture of sardonic cynicism. 'It didn't occur to you to regard Simone's revelations in the light of "Hell hath no fury like a woman scorned"?'

Her gaze was incredibly steady. 'At first—yes. I wasn't too naïve not to recognise that she would go to any lengths to get you. If it had been just

Simone——' she faltered slightly, then went on, 'But there were others only too willing to testify to having shared a torrid affair.' Her faint laugh sounded slightly off-key. 'I was surrounded by vicious, envious women intent on pressing home their painful barbs. I was even given proof,' she disclosed dispassionately. 'The opportunity to discover for myself that one of your supposed "business dinners" was nothing less than a cover for an——' she paused, then added with contrived delicacy—'extra-marital liaison with Simone.'

It seemed an age before Ryan spoke, and she shivered at the icy rage evident beneath the silkiness of his voice. 'By heaven, you seem bent on inviting the wrath of God—whose patience is doubtless more provident than mine!'

For a heartstopping moment Natalie thought he meant to strike her, and she drained her glass in one long swallow, then carefully placed it down on a nearby table. 'If you'll excuse me, I'll go upstairs.'

'We'll eat dinner—together,' Ryan insisted hardily, quelling her retort with a pitiless glare. 'You had almost nothing for breakfast, and hardly touched any lunch.' He subjected her slim curves to an analytical scrutiny, and muttered with exasperation, 'God knows, you're little more than skin and bone.'

'Thanks!' she acknowledged bitterly. 'I've never been voluptuous.'

'A few weeks of Martha's cooking will soon add essential kilos,' he declared brutally, leading her towards the dining room, and when she was seated he uncorked the wine and filled her glass.

'Salute.'

Natalie didn't acknowledge the mocking toast, and merely sipped at the contents of her glass as she viewed the variety of covered dishes on the table. Gleaming silver and fine bone china reposed on white damask, and Martha had arranged an attractive floral centrepiece that was a perfect foil for the exquisite candelabrum.

Without reference to her taste, Ryan placed a portion from each dish on to her plate, and when she toyed with it, added a sharp admonition.

'I'm not a child!' she snapped resentfully.

His glance speared her mercilessly. 'Then stop behaving like one.'

'You can't force me to eat.'

For a few fateful seconds they warred a silent battle, then Ryan said quietly, 'Martha has gone to a lot of trouble to ensure that your first evening home is an enjoyable one. If you don't eat, she'll take it as a personal affront to her culinary skills.'

'Bravo,' Natalie said bleakly. 'I have little option but to concede defeat.' Without a further word she picked up the appropriate cutlery and set about doing justice to the food on her plate.

Every mouthful seemed to require painstaking effort, and she was conscious that it was taking her an inordinate amount of time to complete the meal. When it was finally over, she almost slumped back in her seat with relief. The nerves in her stomach were beginning to play havoc with her digestion, and there was nothing she wanted more than to leave the room and Ryan's hateful company.

Summoning a taut smile, she folded her napkin and rose to her feet. 'If you'll excuse me, I'll for go coffee.'

'In such a hurry to go to bed, Natalie?'

Her insides began to shake, but she managed to keep her voice steady. 'We've been travelling since early morning. I'm tired.' And scared stiff, she added silently. Not only of Ryan, but her own wayward emotions.

'Just be sure which bed you occupy,' he warned with dangerous softness.

'I've been there, and back—remember?' she reminded him with a trace of weary bitterness, and without a further word she left the room, crossing the spacious foyer to the stairs.

In the main suite she entered the bathroom and removed her make-up, then brushed her teeth and picked up the brush to render her customary number of strokes, following a ritual so familiar it required no conscious thought.

Retracing her steps to the bedroom, she saw that her suitcase had disappeared, and investigation revealed that Martha had competently restored its contents to one of the walk-in wardrobes.

Selecting a nightgown, Natalie removed her clothes and donned the filmy creation—noting with wry resignation that the utilitarian cotton shifts she had packed had been successfully hidden—doubtless by the romantically-inclined housekeeper. Anything further from a romantic reconciliation couldn't be imagined!

The large bed seemed to mock her silently, and she closed her eyes in an effort to shut out the sight of it and all it signified. She couldn't slip beneath the sheets and lie waiting for Ryan to materalise—it simply wasn't possible! And where are you going to run to? a tiny imp jeered. There's nowhere he won't find you within this huge house, and any thought of going into the grounds would only invite disaster!

With the actions of an automaton, Natalie crossed to the bedside cabinet and switched on the lamp before closing the main overhead light.

A strange restlessness made it impossible for her to settle to anything, and without being aware of it she began to pace back and forth, oblivious to all but an overwhelming feeling of desperation. If it wasn't too ridiculous a comparison, she felt like a condemned prisoner awaiting final condemnation!

Dear heaven, if only he'd hurry up, so that it could be over and done with! But it was all part of a game, a cruel play on her emotions. As revenge, however subtle, it was totally effective, for she couldn't remember ever being such a quivering mass of nerves!

Damn Ryan—*damn* him to hell! she muttered inaudibly as anger rose to the fore, filling her with towering rage. Who did he think he was—a feudal lord? And she a shivering grateful waif? The devil she'd wait for his appearance!

The soft swish of silk was the only sound to signify her movement as she swept from the room, and without hesitation she made for a guestroom at the furthest end of the hall.

Cool satin sheets felt inordinately luxurious, and she laid her head against the pillow, closing her eyes in the hope that sleep would overtake her.

It didn't, of course, and she tossed restlessly, her head filled with too many haunting memories to induce somnolence.

Natalie wasn't sure when Ryan entered the room, only that some sixth sense warned he was there, and she watched in mesmerised fascination as he moved toward the bed.

In the semi-darkness he towered large and infinitely formidable, his features appearing harsh as a thin stream of moonlight highlighted the broad planes and angles of his face.

'You little fool,' he drawled in a dangerously

quiet voice. Without the slightest effort he pulled
back the covers and lifted her into his arms.

'Put me down!' she hissed vehemently, and
began pummelling his hard chest with her fists.
'I'm quite capable of walking!'

In the main suite he allowed her to slide to her
feet, and she gave a silent cry of pain as his hands
caught her shoulders in a bruising grip.

'Why make things worse for yourself?' he
rasped, his eyes dark with anger, and Natalie
retaliated without thought to the consequences.

'Did you honestly expect to find me *here*?' She
cast her glance wildly round the luxuriously
appointed room, and her voice shook with rage.
'My God! What do you think I am? A masochist?'

Ryan's expression subtly changed to assume
sardonic cynicism. 'I retain a vivid memory of a
sweet biddable girl who became a witching wanton
in my arms.'

She suddenly had great difficulty in swallowing,
and it took considerable effort to meet and hold
his gaze. 'That girl grew up,' she offered steadily.
'You saw to it—personally.'

His eyes narrowed fractionally, and she sensed
the latent anger lying dormant beneath the surface
of his control. 'Are you going to fight me every
inch of the way?'

'What else do you expect?'

'Not compliance,' he admitted with an edge of
mockery, and Natalie raised solemn grey eyes to
his, taking in the hard planes of his chiselled
features as she sought to gauge his mood.

'You intend that I shall.' It was a statement that
hardly conceded defeat, and his mouth gave a wry
twist.

'You know it.'

'Why?' she demanded simply. 'What possible

satisfaction can you derive?'

'What would you know about my satisfaction?' Ryan taunted, and his hands impelled her close so that she was made all too aware of his arousal.

'I don't like being a subject of lust!'

His warm breath fanned her temple, teasing loose a few curling blonde tendrils. 'You have the damnedest way of deploying words. Why not relax?'

'So that it will make you feel better when you take me?' She met his gaze steadily. 'Sorry, but I'm not that charitable.'

Gold eyes gleamed with inimical anger. 'By heaven,' he breathed ominously, 'you'd tempt the devil himself!'

Natalie drew a deep unsteady breath, and managed to keep her voice even with the greatest difficulty. 'What will it prove? Other than your need to exact some form of revenge?'

'What in hell would you suggest?' he demanded, and his hands tightened over her delicate shoulder bones, making her wince with pain. 'I have an irresistible urge to make you pay,' he muttered with dangerous softness, giving her an ungentle shake, and her eyes blazed with bitter anger.

'Do you imagine I haven't?' She felt sick with the tumult of her emotions. 'It wasn't easy for me to return home and admit to a failed marriage, nor was it exactly a picnic being pregnant without a husband's support. I cursed you a thousand times when my body was racked with the agony of trying to give birth, until the doctors decided on a Caesarian.' Her grey eyes clouded with remembered pain. 'For more than two years I've lived with the fear that you might discover Michelle's existence, knowing that if you did, I'd be forced to part with her.' She gave a choked laugh. 'God knows, Ryan—I've *paid*!'

His hands tightened into an excruciating grip that made her cry out, and with a muffled oath he thrust her from him. A muscle tensed along his jaw, and she shivered in the force of his barely suppessed fury.

'Dammit, Natalie,' he swore with explosive force, 'what do you want from me? Remorse for getting you pregnant? For not being there like any other expectant father?' His eyes became bleak with bitterness. 'You didn't give me the opportunity.'

'And if I had?' she demanded with agonised incredulity. 'You'd have had a team of highly proficient lawyers extricate Michelle before I'd regained the strength to fight you!'

For interminable seconds Ryan just stood there regarding her in total silence, his features an inscrutable mask, then he gave an inaudible mocking laugh. 'Your opinion of me isn't very flattering.'

Natalie had the greatest difficulty in swallowing the lump in her throat. 'I haven't had reason to think otherwise.'

'Yet you're here,' Ryan reminded her sardonically. 'At my insistence.' His eyes lanced her to the bone. 'Pleasant dreams,' he said with quiet mockery, and turning away he moved towards the door to leave the room without so much as a backward glance.

CHAPTER FIVE

NATALIE woke to hear the muted sound of running water, indicative of someone occupying the shower in the adjoining bathroom. A glance at her watch revealed that it was barely six, and she gave an inaudible groan before burying her head beneath the pillow.

Seconds later she was fully awake and mentally alert. There was only one person who would utilise the bedroom's en suite facilities, and her eyes flew to the empty space beside her, seeing at once the cast-back covers and the imprint on the pillow.

'You slept here!' she accused on a note of hysteria the instant Ryan appeared through the doorway.

He looked fresh and compellingly vital, his muscle frame whipcord-hard and aggressively male, the towel hitched carelessly about his hips a mere concession to the bounds of decency.

'My room, my bed,' he drawled with imperturbable calm. 'Where else would I sleep?'

'There are other rooms,' she hissed in outrage, and catching the direction of his slow lazy appraisal she hastily drew the sheets up to her chin.

'And give Jenkins and Martha reason to suspect our reconciliation might be a sham?' he enquired with studied mockery.

'The conventions must be observed at all costs,' Natalie sneered with noted sarcasm, her mind in a turmoil at the thought of having spent the night in the same bed with him. Worse, to have been unaware of it.

'You're here to stay,' Ryan stated brusquely. 'The sooner you come to terms with that fact, the better.'

'Even though I find it utterly hateful?'

His expression assumed cynical mockery. 'Consider the alternative.' He turned and walked with pantherish grace towards a large capacious wardrobe and slid open the door, extracted essential items of clothing, then proceeded to dress.

Natalie quickly averted her gaze from his lithe muscled torso, a faint tinge of pink colouring her cheeks as she caught his soft chuckle.

'You can look now,' he murmured sardonically, and she swung round to face him, a fiery sparkle kindling her eyes.

'Will you please get out of here.'

He buttoned his shirt and tucked it into snug-fitting suede trousers, his expression lazily amused. 'Why?'

Fury erupted inside her like molten lava. 'Because I want to get out of bed, that's why!'

One eyebrow rose in mocking query. 'My dear Natalie—*modesty*?' A slight smile tugged the corners of his sensually-moulded mouth. 'After three years of marriage, and having borne my child?'

'We lived as man and wife for only three *months*, and you know it!' she blazed, and his eyes narrowed fractionally.

'A fact I intend to remedy before long.'

'I won't let you.' Fine words, when she didn't stand a chance against his superior strength, or the degree of sensual expertise at his command.

As if he knew the pattern of her thoughts he gave a slight smile. 'Do you really think you could stop me?'

'No,' she answered steadily. 'But I doubt if you'd enjoy making love to a block of ice.'

His hard intent stare played havoc with her composure, and she stifled a silent scream at the strength of purpose in those chilling depths.

With slow unhurried movements he unbuttoned his shirt, pulling it free from the waistband of his trousers, and when his fingers released the zip she burst into incredulous speech.

'What do you think you're doing?' Her eyes widened into large stormy pools that relayed fear as he casually thrust his discarded clothes on to a nearby chair, and her throat constricted, choking off any sound that might otherwise have been emitted.

He moved with indolent ease towards the bed, his dark gaze hard and unwavering, and she couldn't have looked away if her life depended on it.

'Don't—please!' The words were wrung from her throat in a tortured whisper, and she cried out as he reached for the sheet and tore it from her grasp.

His appraisal of her thinly-clad body in its silken gown was indolently insolent, and she scrambled across the width of the bed, only to be caught and held with dismaying ease.

Natalie began to struggle in earnest, twisting to lash out at him, pummelling the sinewy shoulders, his ribs, chest—anywhere she could manage to connect her flailing fists.

Without any effort at all Ryan caught first one arm, then the other, and held them above her head.

'You unspeakable fiend!'

Topaz eyes glittered with latent anger. 'Let's see how long you can remain an icicle, my sweet wife,' he drawled with hateful cynicism, and Natalie cried out as he put a hand to the neckline of her nightgown and ripped it cleanly to its hem.

'You can't do this,' she whispered, her voice coming out in an agonised rush, and he took hold of her chin, forcing it high.

'Destroy a dispensable bit of cloth?' His mouth moved to form a wry smile. 'There are several to replace it, in drawers, exactly where you left them.' A slow sweeping glance took in every inch of her, and she writhed beneath its analytical appraisal.

'I hate——' The words were lost as his mouth crushed hers, bruising in its intensity, and she groaned inaudibly as he forced her lips apart to sear the sweetness within. It was a brutal invasion of her senses which numbed and shocked, and she was scarcely aware when the pressure eased and took on a persuasive quality.

With a slow featherlight touch, Ryan began to caress each vulnerable hollow, trailing his lips along a familiar path that had in the past led her towards an ultimate explosion of ecstasy.

Natalie closed her eyes and willed her body not to respond as his tongue teased an exploratory circle of one rosy-peaked breast before tantalising the other. All her fine body hairs prickled in awareness of his sensual arousal, and her whole body began to vibrate with an emotion she was unable to control.

Not content, his mouth travelled back to cover her own, and this time there was a wealth of seduction in his touch as he employed subtle persuasion in a manner that was impossible to ignore.

A slow ache started in the region of her stomach and steadily spread to her loins, and she threshed restlessly against the encompassing passion that ran like quicksilver through her veins, totally at variance with her brain and her desperate resolve not to succumb.

Like a maestro Ryan played the delicate sensory pulse-beats with virtuoso mastery, exacting the very response she had sworn not to give, and Natalie was scarcely aware of her voice begging the release only his body could assuage until the climax had been reached and subsided, and she lay spent beside him.

'I loathe you,' she declared shakily, trying to move away without success.

'Be quiet.' It was a husky admonition delivered close to her ear, and his hand lifted to smooth back the length of her hair in a strangely gentle gesture.

Of their own volition her lips began to tremble. 'Damn you—*damn* you,' she whispered with impotent rage, the hate inside rising to give her eyes a fiery sparkle. She felt tormented, *tortured*, and most damning of all—betrayed. 'You planned that—seduction scene, didn't you?' she voiced bitterly, hating him with a depth of feeling that was vaguely frightening.

'Yes,' Ryan revealed with brutal frankness, and grasping hold of her chin he forced her to look at him. 'Hate me for it if you must, but there was no other way.'

'You could have given me time,' Natalie cried, sorely tried, and glimpsed his wry smile.

'Providing provocation, but unwilling to deliver?' There was mocking cynicism evident in the compelling features so close to her own. 'I won't be manipulated, Natalie—not even by you.'

'That's a horrible thing to say,' she said in slightly strangled tones, and his eyes narrowed speculatively.

'Yet you would take pleasure in deliberately baiting me, withholding so-called sexual favours,' he drawled. 'Something, I imagine, you'd regard as a form of divine punishment.'

She was goaded to retaliate, and she did so with scarcely a thought to the possible consequences. 'And being the egotistical male that you are, it has to be your hand that wields the power—like some sort of human god!'

'My equation of sexual equality doesn't permit otherwise.'

'Oh, go to hell!' she muttered impotently, unable to deal with the force of his masculinity a moment longer.

'You can fight me as often, and for as long as you like,' Ryan intimated heartlessly. 'Just remember I always intend to be the victor.'

The tip of her tongue edged its way along her lower lip in a purely nervous gesture. 'What if you're wrong?' Ridiculous to imagine a man of Ryan's calibre could ever make a false judgment! 'Would you concede defeat?'

'Elaborate, Natalie,' he drawled, and her gaze was remarkably steady.

'What if things don't work out?' she queried bravely. 'Or suppose neither treatment nor surgery for my father is successful? What then?'

'If you mean—will I let you go? The answer is no.'

'How can you say that?' she demanded. 'John's life-span is limited. You know it as well as I do.'

The pressure on her chin increased, and her eyes became stormy at the pain he was inflicting.

'The bond that ties us together is Michelle,' he told her with brooding savagery. 'Anything to do with your father's health is merely incidental.'

'So you won't——'

'Tolerate divorce,' he finished silkily, adding, 'or any form of separation. Be sure of it.'

'But that's a——'

'Lifetime sentence,' he elucidated with chilling finality, and Natalie shivered involuntarily.

'You're nothing less than an unfeeling monster!'

'Whom you hate, eh?'

'Utterly,' she responded succinctly, and incurred his mocking amusement.

'It wasn't hate you experienced in my arms a short while ago.'

'I can't stop you possessing my body,' she offered quietly. 'But my mind is entirely my own.'

'And you can't conceive a time when they might both be in accord?'

'Never!'

The edges of his mouth twisted into a cynical smile. 'We shall see.'

She swallowed the sudden lump that rose in her throat, and bravado alone was responsible for the words that left her lips. 'If you've finished with me, I'd like to get up. I need a shower.'

His eyes narrowed in sudden anger, and for a moment she thought he meant to exact retribution, then with a careless shrug he released her, allowing her to slide from the bed where she caught hold of the first thing that came to hand to cover herself before making for the adjoining bathroom.

There, she turned on the water and slipped beneath its cascading, cleansing warmth, and she soaped herself liberally in an effort to be rid of any reminder of Ryan's body.

Dear God! Her limbs began to shake at the thought of what had transpired and her reaction to his lovemaking. Every nerve-end seemed to pulsate in a resurgence of erotic ecstasy, and she relentlessly scrubbed every square inch of her flesh before closing off the water.

He was a brute—an unfeeling, callous *barbarian*! He had successfully ensured that she was chained to him for as long as Michelle was dependent. A horrifying thought suddenly struck—what if there were more children? She would be irretrievably chained for more years than she cared to contemplate. Condemned to a life she couldn't condone with a man she could only hate, subjected to the bittersweet torment of physical lust that was at total variance with her tender emotions. She wanted to scream and rage against fate for being so cruel.

With hurried movements she completed her toilette and slipped into a cool sleeveless cotton dress, tugged a brush through the length of her hair, then crossed the hall to where Michelle had spent the night.

The little girl's bedroom was bathed with early morning sunlight, and Natalie's eyes flew to the far side of the room where Michelle could be seen indulging in what she obviously regarded to be a highly amusing game with her father.

'Martha has already given her a glass of milk,' Ryan informed her calmly, sitting back on his heels. 'Breakfast will be ready in half an hour.'

Michelle sent Natalie a beatific smile across the room, then turned her attention back to Ryan. 'Daddy, Mummy—play!'

For a child whose vocabulary hadn't included 'Daddy' until yesterday, she was adjusting extremely well, Natalie conceded wryly.

'We're endeavouring to build a castle,' Ryan explained. 'Will you help sort out the blocks?'

It was an invitation she had the power to ignore, and despite the fact that all her maternal instincts screamed for her to snatch Michelle into her arms and run as far from Ryan as her legs would carry her, she hesitated to destroy the little girl's newly-acquired trust in the man who would ultimately play a large part in her life.

'Is it to be a round or square castle?' she queried with a faint smile, and crossed the room to sink gracefully down on to her knees. A box containing wooden blocks of all shapes and sizes lay before them—together with a wide variety of toys Natalie had not seen before. It appeared that upon learning he had a child, Ryan had gone out and ordered largely from the toy department in a city store.

'Square will undoubtedly be less complicated,' Ryan declared, setting down a row of foundation blocks. His eyes met hers across the top of Michelle's head, and there was nothing Natalie could do to prevent the erratic thudding pulse at the base of her throat. The edges of his mouth were slanted to form a humorous smile, and his eyes were warm.

Michelle was enchanted to have two adults at her command, and went into a peal of delicious giggles when Ryan hoisted her high onto his shoulder some twenty minutes later.

'I think this young lady is hungry. I know I am!' His deep throaty chuckle did strange things to Natalie's composure, and the laughing smile her daugher received made her oddly wistful. Three years ago *she* had been the recipient of such open affection, and the knowledge seemed to reopen an old wound.

She didn't want his affection, much less his love. So why was she feeling so—resentful? A tiny mirthless laugh bubbled up in her throat. Dear God, she couldn't be jealous of her own daughter! Such a thought was ludicrous!

Breakfast was a convivial meal, with Michelle behaving beautifully. She fed herself with the minimum of fuss, and virtually accident-free twixt spoon and mouth.

Expecting Ryan to leave for the office, Natalie could hardly contain her surprise when he indicated no such intention, electing instead to spend the day getting better acquainted with his wife and daughter.

'Do you think that's wise?' Natalie found herself asking, and incurred a faint mocking smile by return.

'I employ extremely capable men,' Ryan slanted cynically. 'The business won't founder if I'm absent for a day.'

'That wasn't what I meant, and you know it,' she returned civilly.

'Precisely what do you mean?' There was sardonic amusement in his glance, and she had to restrain herself from hurling the first thing that came to hand.

'You're a novelty,' she explained bluntly, and at the sudden flaring in those golden eyes she lifted a hand and pushed a few stray locks of hair behind her ear. It was an outward sign of nervousness, and it irked her that he was aware of it. 'I think Michelle should get used to you gradually,' she ventured slowly, meeting his gaze unflinchingly. 'Young children are very susceptible individuals, and if you're with her constantly for a few days, then absent for five, she's bound to be confused.' Conviction that she was right added strength to her voice. 'She's too young to understand what "Daddy" means, never having known any man except my father, whom she calls "Poppa".' She eyed him steadily, unsure of his mood, for his expression was deliberately enigmatic. 'She may call you Daddy, but it's merely a word without meaning as yet.' She let her hand encompass the room. 'All this—opulence makes a dramatic change from our more humble surroundings. And her room——' she gestured helplessly. 'It's like being let loose in a toyshop! You may feel you're making up for lost time, but I won't have her spoilt.'

'I have no intention of spoiling her, as you call it,' Ryan drawled. 'As for confusing her, I disagree. The transition itself will prove confusing, but I don't see how my presence over the next few days can add to it.'

'Is child psychology one of your attributes? Along with everything else?'

He appeared to hold his temper in check, yet his voice was dangerously soft as he said, 'Natalie, if you want to fight, I'll oblige. But save it for when we're alone. Your talk of children being susceptible to atmosphere doesn't hold much weight when you give every appearance of defying your own dictum.'

'Forgive me,' she managed with implied sarcasm. 'I'd quite forgotten how inflexible and arrogant you can be when crossed!'

His gaze was startlingly direct. 'My, my,' he drawled quietly, 'you are a scratchy bundle of fur this morning!'

'I'm not in the mood to purr,' she snapped, and a gleam of amusement lit his eyes.

'This morning——'

'Was a mistake,' she intercepted swiftly. 'One that I won't permit to be repeated.'

'Indeed?'

Natalie drained the last of her coffee, then replaced the cup on to its saucer before standing to her feet. 'If you'll excuse me? I need some fresh air.' She didn't bother looking at him, merely scooped Michelle from her chair and walked quickly from the room.

On ascending the spiral staircase to the lower level, she unlatched the door that led out to the pool. At this relatively early hour the full impact of the sun's strength was not in evidence, and she let Michelle down to walk while retaining a firm handclasp, witnessing the little girl's delight as they slowly traversed the pool's surround before moving towards the river at the lower edge of the garden. A large cabin cruiser was moored to the pontoon at the end of the jetty, and Natalie made her way slowly towards it.

'Boat,' Michelle pronounced knowledgeably, adding, 'Daddy's boat.'

Whose else could it be but Ryan's? Natalie pondered wryly. The sureness with which Michelle was accepting each and every one of her father's possessions was slightly daunting.

'Ride in Daddy's boat?'

She glanced down at her daughter's blonde locks and caught the open-eyed wonderment in those guileless eyes raised so solemnly, and slowly shook her head. 'Not today, darling.'

'Why?'

'Because, my sweet, your daddy's a busy man. He'll take us for a ride another day.' Obviously a diversion was needed to distract the tot's attention, and with practised adroitness Natalie pointed to a large tabby cat sunning itself on the steps leading to the gazebo, adjacent the pool. 'Come and meet Sasha.'

The cat was a familiar sight, and belonged to Martha, who had adopted him as stray several years before, and he lived an idyllic life bathed in affection, with the run of the grounds and that of

Martha and Jenkins' living quarters.

It was some further ten minutes before they retraced their steps, and on reaching the glass sliding doors Natalie saw Ryan lounging against the aperture. His expression was impossible to discern, and clothed in hip-hugging levis and an open-necked shirt left unbuttoned almost to the waist, he appeared aggressively male and a definite threat to her peace of mind.

'Enjoy your walk?'

To the casual observer his words were an interested query, but Natalie perceived the faint emphasis and substituted 'escape' for 'walk'. He was too perceptive by far, and she longed to retaliate with a sarcastic rejoinder.

'Ride in Daddy's boat,' Michelle demanded with childish candour, and Natalie could only admire her singlemindedness—something that was assuredly inherited from her father!

'Well now,' Ryan drawled, his smile faintly crooked as he slanted a brief enquiring eyebrow towards Natalie before lowering his height with one fluid movement to rest on his haunches, 'I guess we could do that.' His eyes twinkled with warm humour as Michelle viewed him with unblinking solemnity.

'Mummy says Daddy too busy,' the little tot revealed carefully.

'It's a beautiful morning,' Ryan indicated, appearing to give the matter consideration. 'Much too nice to spend indoors. The boat it is, infant.' The corners of his eyes crinkled with laughter as he swept the little girl into the circle of his arm and lifted her high on to his shoulder. 'We'll find Martha and ask her to prepare a picnic lunch.'

Natalie wanted to scream that she didn't want to go—least of all spend the entire day in such

close proximity to her indomitable husband. She
felt like a puppet, with both Ryan and Michelle
manipulating the strings. Yet there was little she
could do but appear to give in gracefully. Like it
or not, Michelle had the right to become better
acquainted with her father, and Ryan was taking
steps to ensure that the transition was carried out
as smoothly as possible. It was important that
there be no apparent dissension if the little girl was
to accept their changed circumstances, and much
of the success lay with Natalie's attitude. No
matter how much she hated to admit it, Ryan was
right. Any fights had to be conducted in private—
and there would be many!

Weatherwise, it was an idyllic day, with the
slightest breeze coming off the Bay to temper the
sun's late summer heat. Armed with a bountifully
supplied picnic basket, they set off just after ten,
Jenkins taking charge behind the wheel as he eased
the large cabin cruiser along the Nerang River.

Natalie had taken a similar cruise in those
halcyon days just after their marriage, and had
been impressed then with the waterways and
existing development. Now she viewed the vast
changes with interest, especially Paradise Waters
and Sorrento, whose blocks bore prestige homes
reflecting differing architectural designs. Sparkling
swimming pools of various shapes and sizes set in
landscaped grounds, the large number of boats
and cabin cruisers moored to private jetties,
attested to the Coast's affluent society.

Colour abounded in glorious profusion, with the
poinciana vying with the bauhinia and the trumpet
flower. Clematis and banksia, hibiscus and
frangipani provided an exotic background for the
splendid stand of tropical palm trees glimpsed in
most gardens. Overall, it was a visual paradise,

and since it offered such a pleasant climate, little wonder so many people elected to spend and end their days along this coastal strip.

Michelle was more intrigued with the cruiser itself, and Jenkins' handling of it. Between the two men, she was entertained to her delight, and Natalie was inclined to reflect that her own presence was little more than a perfunctory inclusion.

At that precise moment Ryan looked up and caught her gaze, the expression in his tigerish eyes faintly mocking, and she felt a momentary shaft of pain. He was deliberately entrenching himself in Michelle's affections, making any thoughts of a separation untenable. It was almost as if he was forcing her to accept that she could never part them; that he could provide in a way she alone would find impossible. The chains that bound her to Michelle were now forged with steel, and the knowledge that he *knew* rankled unbearably.

Natalie watched in idle fascination as Ryan caught Michelle in his arms and trod with easy, lithe movements to where she stood.

'Feeling neglected?'

She swallowed quickly. 'No. Why should I be?'

He bent forward, lowering his head slightly. 'Liar,' he said softly, and without any warning his lips brushed her temple, then slid down to tease the edge of her mouth before claiming it with a sensuous gentleness that made her ache for more.

The knowledge made her resentful of her own emotions, and her eyes sparked dangerously as she drew back. 'Michelle——'

'Is our daughter,' Ryan interjected sardonically, his eyes agleam with amusement. 'We are responsible for her existence. Eventually she will become aware of it, and all that it implies.'

'She's a little young for a lesson in procreation,' Natalie snapped, and saw a flash of white teeth as he gave a twisted smile.

'Agreed. But evidence of her parents' affection is essential, don't you think?'

Her response was tinged with acrimony. 'You profess to be the expert. Why even consider my opinion?'

The smile didn't reach his eyes, and she felt a shiver of apprehension slither its way from the base of her neck down the length of her spine. 'Behave, Natalie. Otherwise I'll ensure that you regret it.'

'I'm hopelessly outmatched,' she returned lightly, although her eyes were dark and stormy as she met his implacable gaze. 'Perhaps we should stick to the mundane—such as where you intend to stop for lunch, and when.' Her smile was falsely bright. 'Children have an inbuilt clock when it comes to mealtimes!'

Ryan spared the elegantly slim gold watch on his wrist a cursory glance. 'There's a picnic area adjacent the Council grounds at Evandale. We can be there in ten minutes.'

'Excellent,' she concurred with every evidence of charming acceptance. 'I'll take Michelle while you tell Jenkins.'

It was a victory that was really no victory at all, for Michelle's fascination with Ryan meant a few fractious tears when Natalie attempted to retrieve her from her father's arms.

On reflection, it was a pleasant day, despite Natalie's conviction that the hours spent in Ryan's company could only prove disastrous. Jenkins' presence, plus that of Michelle, ensured restraint, and it was something of a relief when the cruiser berthed at the lower edge of the Cronin Island residence in the late afternoon.

Michelle's eyes were drooping as she fought off sleep, and within minutes of entering the house Natalie carried her upstairs, gave her a quick wash, slipped off her outer clothes, then tucked the little girl into bed.

'Have a nice nap, sweetheart,' she bade softly, bending down to bestow a kiss, then with a smile she turned and left the room, closing the door quietly behind her.

The effects of sea-spray and the sun on her skin and hair made her long for a cool refreshing shower, and she crossed the hall, entering the main bedroom to find Ryan in the process of discarding his clothes.

'Oh!' The surprised monosyllable left her lips before she could halt it, and he slanted her a mocking glance.

'We do share a bedroom. Or had you forgotten?'

How could she possibly *forget*? Electing to ignore him, she walked to the capacious wardrobe running the length of one entire wall, slid open a mirrored door and extracted clean underwear. She turned, her eyes widening as she saw Ryan had moved and was standing less than a foot distant. There was a towel slung carelessly about his hips, and the faint male scent of him was flagrantly evocative, stirring her senses so that she was shockingly aware of the sheer animal magnetism he projected.

The hand that reached out and lifted her chin was firm, forcing recognition of his relentless gaze. 'Don't resort to a childish fit of the sulks,' he drawled, and immediately resentment flared.

'I'm not,' she denied, and saw his eyes narrow fractionally.

'No? I find that hard to believe.'

At such proximity he was dangerous—to her peace of mind, and the dictates of her flesh. Already each separate nerve-end tingled alive, craving his touch, and the ache that began deep inside slowly encompassed her body, threatening the slim thread of control she sought so desperately to maintain.

'I'm not used to sharing a room,' she explained, aiming for civility. Nervousness was responsible for the faint parting of her lips, and without conscious thought the edge of her tongue licked slowly along her lower lip. Something flared in those dark golden eyes, and she hastened into speech, the words tumbling forth in an incoherent jumble. 'You startled me—I didn't expect——'

'Michelle has shared your room for more than two years,' Ryan interjected smoothly, letting his gaze rove slowly over her features, noting the heightened colour tinging her cheeks.

'That's—different.'

'It's an incurable addiction, isn't it?' he drawled, making no attempt to free her.

'I don't know what you're talking about,' Natalie responded shakily, and he uttered a soundless derisory laugh.

'Liar! Your body screams for my possession almost as much as mine demands release.'

'Any one would imagine you're the only man who can——'

'Take you to the heights—and beyond?' he finished, cupping her face with both hands, drawing her closer with no effort at all.

'I could have had other lovers,' Natalie voiced the words with contrived conviction, and glimpsed the brief flaring of terrible anger as his eyes searched deep into her very soul, stripping away the protective layers she had spent three years rebuilding with such painstaking care.

'Have you?'

The desire to wound as she had been wounded made her cry out a single monosyllabic affirmative. '*Yes*—damn you! A wild, senseless succession of men only too willing to oblige!'

For a few timeless seconds Ryan looked capable of murder, then his eyes hardened until they resembled topaz chips. 'You have precisely one minute to rescind the reckless folly of those words, and be warned—the truth, this time!'

The seconds pounded with numerical relentlessness through her brain, and as she reached the lower fifties his hold shifted to her shoulders, crushing the delicate bones until she cried out in pain. 'You're hurting me!'

His expression was without mercy, and frighteningly pitiless. At that moment he looked capable of anything, and the words left her lips in a tortured gasp. 'No! No one.' The agonising pressure eased, but only slightly, and she closed her eyes tightly against the damning well of tears threatening to spill in an ignominious stream down her cheeks. Her mouth was trembling so much she could hardly control it, and of their own volition her hands crept up to cover her face.

Natalie had little recollection how long she remained like that, for she seemed locked in a timeless void, conscious only of a feeling of utter devastation.

Slowly, yet with remarkable ease, her hands were prised loose, then her lips were taken, possessed, in a kiss that was punishingly cruel. Without askance, Ryan's mouth forced hers apart, invading its sweetness, plundering, until she could taste the saltiness of her own blood as

the soft inner tissue grazed and split against her
teeth.

Not content, Ryan sought the zip fastening of
her dress, and when it was free, he removed the
thin cotton from her body very simply by tearing it
to the hem. With deliberate detachment he
released the clip of her bra, then tossed it to the
carpet. Bare seconds later they were joined by her
slip and briefs.

Natalie clutched her arms together in an attempt
to cover her breasts, but such effort was soon
dashed as he swung her high and carried her to the
bed, dropping her unceremoniously down on to its
silken coverlet.

He towered over her, large and incredibly
menacing, and never had she seen him so
consumed with rage. There was controlled violence
in the way he looked at her, his eyes raking her
nudity with a savage ruthlessness that made her
want to shrivel up and die.

'I'm sorry.' The words were scarcely more than
a whisper and brought a bitter twist to his mouth.

'You will be, by the time I finish with you!' Hard
and implacable, he lowered his body on to the bed
beside her, trapping her slimness with his own. His
mouth covered hers, insensitive to the pain he was
inflicting as he began a ravishment of her senses
that sought and punished each sensual pulse and
hollow before fastening with devastating intent
over the rosy peak of her breast, consuming and
alternatively teasing until she uttered a low
guttural plea for mercy. Not content, his lips
trailed to its twin, his teeth and tongue wreaking
havoc until she almost screamed out for him to
desist. Like a crazed, demented being she twisted
and turned in an effort to escape that torturing
mouth, then she gave a whimper of despair as it

travelled lower to create a leisurely, ultimate devastation.

She was floating and utterly mindless when Ryan took possession with one single aggressive thrust, and the tiny animal sounds were stilled in her throat as his mouth closed over hers.

Later—although how much later, she was unaware—Ryan carried her into the bathroom, and beneath the warm needle-spray of the shower he soaped and cleansed her body, his touch oddly gentle, before attending to his own needs, then towelled her dry and enveloped her in a silky robe, and with a towel hitched around his hips he dried her hair, brushing it first, then combing it until it flowed like pale silk to her shoulder-blades.

Throughout it all Natalie stood quiescent, her eyes closed against the terrible humiliation and pain she felt deep inside. She wanted to cry, but the tears wouldn't come. At some stage she knew herself to be alone, but she was incapable of moving.

'Drink this.'

It was a command that couldn't be ignored, and when the rim of a glass touched her lips she simply sipped its contents like an obedient child.

The spirits were potent, but palatable, and ran through her veins like warm quicksilver, making her feel strangely weightless.

'Rest for an hour or so,' Ryan instructed brusquely. 'I'll have Martha attend to Michelle. Between us we can feed her and put her to bed.' He lifted a hand and tucked a lock of hair back behind her ear, and without its partially protective curtain Natalie felt exposed and vulnerable. 'We have a dinner engagement,' he told her, his expression inscrutable. 'You remember Rick?'

She did, for he was one of the few of Ryan's

business associates with whom she had felt at ease. A financier based in Melbourne, Rick Andreas had interests in southern Queensland and regularly commuted to the Coast, where he owned a penthouse suite atop one of the more prestigious apartment blocks.

'He married several months ago,' Ryan continued. 'Lisa is anxious to meet you. You'll get on well together.'

Dear lord! *Tonight*? How could she go out and socially shine in company—even if it was only a foursome? Slowly she lifted her eyes to his, seeing little more than a keen intensity in his gaze. 'What time do we leave?' The query was stilted, and she had the strangest feeling someone else had spoken, for the voice didn't seem to be her at all.

A muscle tautened along his jaw, making his features appear harsh and formidable. 'Dammit, Natalie——!' he began explosively.

'Don't worry, Ryan,' she assured him with unaccustomed cynicism, 'I haven't the strength to oppose you.'

'You want an apology for something you deliberately provoked?' he demanded hardily, stifling an oath. 'How the hell did you expect me to react?'

She still felt raw, and an icy numbness seemed to have invaded her bones despite the warm summer heat. 'I can only plead temporary amnesia,' she voiced dully, holding his gaze unwaveringly. 'I should have remembered you possess a wicked temper.'

He remained silent for what seemed an age, and his voice when he spoke was dangerously quiet. 'You have the damnedest ability to arouse a complexity of emotions—some of which are totally unenviable. I'm constantly at odds whether to strangle you or sweep you into wild passionate oblivion.' His eyes were enigmatic as he paused imperceptibly. 'We once shared something beautiful—something that will forever be remembered by Michelle's very existence.'

'That was a long time ago,' Natalie said sadly, suddenly finding it difficult to swallow the lump that had risen to her throat. With a gesture of utter weariness she lifted a hand and massaged her temple in an attempt to ease the dull throbbing there. 'If you don't mind, I'd like to be alone for a while.'

His eyes kindled with a mixture of anger and regret, then became hooded as he turned towards the wardrobe, selecting briefs, immaculate tan trousers and a beige silk shirt. 'I'll ensure you're not disturbed until six. We're meeting Rick and Lisa in the bar of the Lotus Inn at seven.'

CHAPTER SIX

THE restaurant was crowded, and at first glance all
the tables appeared to be taken. The smiling
waitress was most profuse with her apologies, her
manner deferential as she referred to the patrons
hugging the bar. 'Mr Andreas is already seated at
the table, Mr Marshall. He suggests we serve your
drinks there.'

Ryan gave an affirmative nod, and with his arm
creating a protective arc about Natalie's waist, he
moved aside to follow in the Chinese girl's wake.

Natalie drew a deep steadying breath and
uttered a silent prayer for divine assistance to get
her through the ensuing few hours. Outwardly she
gave the appearance of being a well-dressed
socialite; the silky emerald-coloured dress with its
swathed bodice and softly-gathered skirt accentuated her slim curves and was a perfect
complement to her lightly-tanned skin and striking
blonde hair.

Beside her, Ryan was every inch the dominant,
successful male. Immaculately groomed in dark
hip-hugging trousers and a cream silk shirt left
unbuttoned at the neck, he wore the mantle of
sophistication with ease. There was a hint of
leashed power beneath his rugged exterior, an
elusive aura that went with extreme wealth, adding
to a whole that would always draw attention—
unwanted or not.

'Natalie—Ryan,' a deep voice murmured, its
intonation bearing a slight, almost imperceptible
accent, and Natalie forced a warm smile as she

greeted the tall dark-haired man who had risen to his feet.

'Hello, Rick,' she managed with sincerity. 'It's good to see you again.'

'And you,' he responded quietly, then turning to the young woman seated on his right he gave a slow eloquent smile. 'This is Lisa, my wife.'

Natalie experienced a shaft of envy at his depth of regard for the slim dark-haired girl whose serene features were brought alive by a pair of sparkling dark eyes.

'I'm pleased to meet the woman responsible for Ryan's downfall,' Lisa began, sparing Ryan a twinkling glance. 'I hope we can be friends, Natalie.'

'Thank you—I'd like that.' Natalie took the seat Ryan held out for her, and accepted the slim fluted glass of wine Rick placed on the table before her. It was a light palatable Riesling, and provided a much-needed boost to her sadly low morale.

'It's a little crowded,' Rick remarked, allowing his gaze to encompass the room and its occupants. 'But the food more than compensates.' His eyes were oddly thoughtful as they rested on Natalie. 'I hope this evening will be the first of many we can enjoy together.'

'It will be,' Ryan said smoothly, and he reached out a hand and trailed his fingers down the length of Natalie's arm, then interlaced his fingers with hers. His glance was warm and his smile gentle, and to any onlooker he appeared an adoring husband. 'Natalie and I plan on having a week to ourselves before beginning the inevitable round of entertaining.' He gave a slight shrug and offered a slow teasing smile. 'If the going proves too heavy, I may load up the cruiser and take her off to some remote tropic isle for a while.'

Nick's white teeth flashed in a wicked grin. 'I know just the place. In fact, I own it.' His eyes twinkled with devilish humour as he raised his glass in a silent mocking toast. 'It's yours to use any time you require it.'

Natalie controlled a telling tide of colour which threatened to tinge her cheeks, and threw him a faintly cynical glance. 'You haven't changed, Rick.'

'Ah, but I have,' he declared with a quizzical smile, and Lisa broke in with a musical laugh.

'There's nothing worse than a reformed rake!'

'Alas, I have been tamed. The once-proud lion now permits himself to be led on a chain he has no intention of breaking.' Ryan's eyes held amusement as he spared Lisa a faintly mocking glance, and in an oddly touching gesture he picked up her hand and carried it to his lips.

'You'll have Natalie think I crack a proverbial whip!' his wife protested. 'When, in fact, it was the opposite.'

'Indeed,' he concurred quietly, and Ryan interjected with customary smoothness.

'Shall we order?'

The next few hours passed with reasonable swiftness, the conversational flow maintained with practised ease, so that there was little chance for Natalie to indulge in introspection.

They had been served with a variety of dishes, each kept at an even temperature atop individual silver burners, and replaced at regular intervals with a further selection.

'Dessert?'

'I couldn't,' Natalie refused, more than replete, and Rick cast Lisa a quizzical glance.

'I shouldn't, but I'll have a banana fritter with cream,' his wife decided with a rueful grin. 'I've developed a sweet tooth.'

'Need I enquire why?' Ryan teased, his eyes ablaze with silent laughter, and Lisa picked up her napkin and threatened to throw it at him.

'Wretch!' she laughed. 'I imagine in another month it will be perfectly obvious.'

'I shall be a doting uncle,' he assured her, lifting his glass in a silent salute. 'I couldn't be more happy for you both.'

Lisa turned towards Natalie. 'You have a daughter.' Her eyes became faintly wistful. 'I'd love a little girl. Not that I mind, either way, as long as it comes into the world healthy.' She spared her husband a soft look. 'Rick, like most men, would prefer a son. But a little girl,' she trailed off with a sigh. 'Think of all the pretty clothes, and the fun involved in dressing her!'

'I'm sure I can manage to provide you with both, given time,' her husband declared. 'Meanwhile, you'll have to be patient and see what fate has decreed to send us.' He leaned sideways and bestowed a lingering kiss to her temple. 'I'm going to beg Natalie for a dance while you eat your dessert.'

What else could Natalie do but accept? To refuse would seem churlish, and Rick was too much a friend to offend.

The dance floor was small, the artist and his music a shade too loud, and it was so long since she had danced that at first she stumbled and lost her step.

'Don't apologise,' Rick murmured, pulling her closer to ensure better guidance.

'You're being kind,' she acknowledged with a rueful smile, and incurred his penetrating glance.

'May I say that it's good to see you and Ryan together again?'

Are we? she queried silently. We live in the same

house, share the same table—even the same bed.
Yet we couldn't be more apart than if a thousand
miles separated us.

'Have I offended you?'

She came out of her reverie and flashed him a
bright humourless smile. 'No, of course not.'
Heaven help her, she would have to summon forth
every reserve of strength. 'You'll have to forgive
me, Rick' she began quietly. 'I developed a
shocking headache just before we left, and the pills
I took have had a rather numbing effect.' The
smile reached her eyes as she added sincerely,
'Allow me to congratulate you. Lisa is a lovely
girl.'

Rick wasn't fooled, and she knew it, but innate
good manners prevented him from probing, and
for this she was supremely thankful.

'She's my life,' he revealed softly, and Natalie
was unable to prevent the faint prick of tears at
the depth of emotion in his voice.

They circled the floor in silence, and when the
music paused Rick led her back to their table.

The expression in Ryan's eyes was impossible to
discern, and she deliberately avoided his glance,
turning instead to Lisa and offering a faint laugh.

'I'm sadly out of practice, I'm afraid. If Rick
has sore toes tomorrow, you'll know the reason
why!'

'Is that an indirect accusation, darling?' Ryan
drawled, and she cast him a sweet smile.

'How could it be?' she countered evenly, lifting
her partly-filled glass and savouring the excellent
wine. She met his eyes over the rim and wrinkled
her nose. 'Although I'd rather it were your toes,
and not Rick's, that have to suffer.' The barb was
there, but accompanied with a laugh she doubted
Rick or Lisa realised its intention.

'In that case, I'd better remedy any remission without delay,' Ryan slanted mockingly, and draining his glass he stood to his feet in one fluid movement.

Natalie could have screamed at her own folly in taunting him. She didn't want to dance, and especially not with her indomitable husband. Yet to refuse would undoubtedly gain an attention she had at all costs to avoid. With the best grace she could muster she allowed him to lead her towards the dance floor, and as his arms closed around her she strained against the inevitable body contact.

'For God's sake, relax,' Ryan bade with accustomed bluntness.

'You have to be joking,' she retaliated swiftly, hating the way he effortlessly moulded her body close to his. 'Do you have to act so convincingly proprietorial?' she demanded seconds later as she felt his fingers trail a tantalising exploratory path over the length of her back.

'Am I?' he demanded lazily, and she felt his lips brush her temple. 'I'm merely following my instincts.'

'And we know what they are!' she retorted, and heard his faint throaty laugh.

'What a little vixen you are, Natalie! You tease, then run, and scream when you're caught.' He slanted her a sardonic twisted smile. 'You're a chameleon, reverting from child to woman and back again at the slightest provocation.'

'And you're totally insufferable!' she hissed, attempting to wriggle out of his grasp. Being so close to him like this made her aware of his muscular hardness, and already his potent magnetism drew her to him like a moth to flame. Every nerve-end quivered vibrantly alive, and she shook her head in a gesture of utter despair. 'I hate you,' she whispered in vengeful avowal. 'I never imagined myself capable of hating anyone as much as I hate you!'

'Stop it,' Ryan warned. 'You've already suffered one painful lesson. Don't give me reason to give you another.'

'And you would,' she retorted bitterly. 'I have to be made to conform—whatever the cost!'

'I'd prefer to conduct our wrangling without a public audience,' he evinced hardily. 'But continue any further and I'm liable to do something regrettable.'

'In a room full of people, your scope is limited,' she retorted with a touch of truculence, and caught the flare of anger that hardened his eyes.

She didn't have time to cry out as his mouth closed over hers in a kiss that was leisurely enough, and as shattering to her equilibrium as he intended.

When he lifted his head she had to cling on to him so that she didn't fall, and seconds later she turned her head into his shoulder in an attempt to hide her humilation.

The music increased in volume and tempo, but Ryan kept to the outer fringe of the floor, his head bent low so that his cheek brushed hers, and to any observers they must have appeared totally engrossed in each other.

It seemed an age before he disentangled his arms and led her back to the table. Her emotions were numbed, and she felt as listless as a rag doll. If Rick or Lisa noticed they had the good sense not to comment, and by mutual consent they ordered coffee, then chose to leave almost immediately.

'I'll ring you,' Lisa declared gently as they reached the street. 'We'll meet for lunch.'

Natalie murmured an appropriate rejoinder,

then, conscious of Ryan's firm grasp at her elbow, she bade them both goodnight and allowed him to lead her towards the car.

Seated inside its luxurious interior, she went through the motions of fastening her seatbelt with the movements of an automaton, dimly aware that he had slipped in behind the wheel and was intent on manoeuvring the large vehicle into the stream of traffic.

Wearily she leaned her head back against the headrest and closed her eyes. She felt an emotional wreck, and so physically tired she was ill-equipped to face the inevitable recriminations that would follow once they reached home.

It took five minutes to gain access to the small bridge that led to Cronin Island, and a further minute for the car to sweep through the remote-controlled gates and halt inside the garage.

Without a word she slid out of her seat and followed him into the house, crossing the large entrance foyer to the stairs, mounting each step with an odd sense of fatalism as they led her ever nearer to the upper floor and ultimately to their bedroom.

The decisive click of the door as it closed behind her had a strange effect on her nerves, making them jangle in painful discord, and she turned to face him in an oddly defensive movement.

In the shadowed half-light from a distant bedlamp Ryan appeared large and formidable, his stance vaguely menacing as he moved towards her.

Suddenly Natalie didn't care any more, and she closed her eyes in an attempt to shut out the sight of him. Maybe if she prayed very hard, when she opened her eyes it would be to discover all this was part of a nightmare. Silly, stupid tears welled up behind her lids and seeped through to trickle slowly down each cheek until they came to rest at the edge of her chin.

She sensed rather than heard him move, and felt the featherlight brush of his fingers as they trailed the path of her tears.

'You sweet fool,' Ryan muttered with wry gentleness, and tilting her chin he slid a hand beneath the heavy swathe of her hair to hold fast her head, then his lips touched each closed eyelid in turn before slipping to her temple and teasing a downward path to the softly-beating pulse at the base of her neck.

Slowly and with infinite care he removed her dress, and she shivered as her slip, then her bra and briefs fell to the floor.

A barely-stifled oath left Ryan's lips as he saw the faint bruising evident on her delicate skin, and she swayed beneath his touch as he brushed his lips to each painful bruise in turn.

Despite a despondent lethargy her traitorous body began to respond, and she groaned in despair. 'Don't—please!' Her voice trailed off in an aching sob. 'I couldn't bear any more.'

His mouth covered hers, his tongue teasing an evocative path along her lower lip. 'I'm going to put you to bed,' he murmured, his warm breath invading her mouth.

'But not alone,' she said sadly, unable to open her eyes, and she felt his lips twist beneath hers.

'Do you want to be alone?'

She started to nod, then gave a slow shake of her head. 'I want to sleep.' A convulsive sob choked in her throat. What was the use of begging? He was immune to any plea she might make.

In a single movement he lifted her into his arms and carried her to the large bed, then lowered her between the sheets. She could hear the faint rustle of clothing, then the edge of the bed depressed as he slid in beside her, and in the darkness he reached out, drawing her close and cradling her into the curve of his body. As a hand covered her breast she stiffened, then as he made no attempt to caress she gradually relaxed, her breathing steadying until its even rise and fall revealed a slip into blissful somnolent oblivion.

The following few days were a delight, for with Ryan absent from eight in the morning until six at night, Natalie was able to devote the daylight hours to Michelle. Together they swam in the pool, explored the garden and grounds, then with Jenkins' escort—at Ryan's insistence—the little girl was introduced to the first of the Coast's entertainment facilities. With such a variety, it was difficult to choose, but Sea World won the day, and Michelle was entranced with the performing dolphins, the sea-lions and tiny penguins.

'More, more!' she demanded when it was time to leave, and Natalie declared firmly that they would come another day. It would prove all too easy to indulge her. As it was, being Ryan's daughter, she would soon grow accustomed to luxury and the material possessions that wealth could provide. It was essential to establish and maintain an even balance, especially as Michelle was a very perceptive child and able to distinguish a difference between her former and her present lifestyle.

Without Ryan's disturbing presence Natalie was able to relax, although the evenings were something she preferred not to give much thought to. She came to anticipate the time he was due to return, unconsciously listening for the sound of the car in the driveway, the closing of a door followed by his entrance into the house. Together with Michelle, who had been fed an hour before, she would wait for him in the lounge. There they would share a drink while Ryan questioned them about their day, and the increasing rapport between father and daughter was something Natalie could only reluctantly admire, even though it hurt unbearably that the little girl's affections could be so easily won. At seven, amidst giggles and delighted shrieks of laughter, Michelle was lifted high on to her father's shoulders and carried upstairs to bed, where, with predictable delaying tactics, she managed to extend her bedtime for a further fifteen minutes as she alternately begged a drink or stressed the necessity for another visit to the bathroom.

Dinner was served at seven-thirty, and after settling Michelle, Ryan would shower and change his clothes, then escort Natalie down to the dining room. This was the time she came to dread, for inevitably before the main course was halfway through he had managed to put her on the defensive, making it almost impossible for her to maintain civility. By the time coffee was served, they were engrossed in verbal battle—not that she was any match for his brand of sardonic cynicism.

On Thursday evening, exactly a week from the day she had returned to Ryan's household, he emerged from the shower and entered the bedroom with lithe easy movements, his tall frame bare apart from the towel hitched casually about his hips.

'Change into something more sophisticated,' he ordered without preamble. 'We're dining out.' He crossed to the wardrobe, and Natalie watched in idle fascination as he extracted dark trousers and a dark silk-print shirt, then began the process of dressing.

'Where?' she queried, and instantly incurred a dark slanting glance.

'Does it matter?'

'I don't possess anything terribly sophisticated,' she responded evenly, meeting his gaze. 'Fashions have changed over the past three years, and I haven't been able to afford to compete with the latest trend.'

One eyebrow rose in quizzical mockery. 'You mean you haven't already indulged in a madly expensive spending spree?'

'I left all those plastic credit cards behind, if you remember?' she countered sweetly, and his eyes narrowed with an angry gleam.

'Why the hell didn't you ask? Jenkins has instructions to give you any money you might need.'

'Oh, Jenkins has been discretion itself,' Natalie declared in swift defence. 'However, I could hardly ask him for an advance on my clothing allowance.'

'You could have asked me.'

She flicked a stray lock of hair back behind her ear, and met his gaze fearlessly. 'I once begged you to give me financial assistance to help my father, and you refused. I'll never put myself in the invidious position of having to ask anything of you again!'

His answering silence held an element of danger, and she involuntarily tensed, unconsciously holding her breath as he subjected her to a long analytical appraisal before saying in a quiet voice that sent icy shivers slithering down her spine, 'That particular request rapidly transgressed into a verbal battle.' His eyes resembled hard topaz chips that speared her mercilessly. 'I was in no mood to grant your request.'

'Perhaps I should have been more forthcoming

and offered my body,' Natalie heard the words slip from her lips before she had given them conscious thought.

Ryan gave every appearance of keeping a tight rein on his temper. 'I'll forget you said that.'

She closed her eyes momentarily, then turned away with a gesture of weariness. 'I'll get changed,' she said quietly. Fighting him could only lead to destruction—hers. Perhaps it was better to concede defeat before he gained an invaluable foothold on her emotions. Heaven knew it was difficult enough to cope with each physical onslaught without providing additional provocation. Yet subconsciously some tiny imp seemed to urge her into fresh battle at almost every turn, and it galled her unbearably that he continually triumphed.

Crossing to her wardrobe, she selected a slim-skirted black sleeveless dress with a draped bodice whose neckline was anything but demure, plunging as it did almost to her waist at the back and front. Slim-high-heeled black sandals gave her added height, and she fastened a silver locket that had belonged to her grandmother around her neck, then attended to her make-up before brushing her hair so that it swung loose about her shoulders. A light spray of perfume to several pulse-spots, and she collected an evening purse from a drawer, slipped in lipstick, comb, powder compact and a handkerchief, then turned towards the door.

'I'm ready.'

Ryan stood seemingly relaxed and at ease, his eyes hooded, making his expression difficult to discern. He opened the door and stood aside, following as she walked down the hall to the stairs.

Jenkins had already brought the car around, and he bade them goodnight as they left the house.

It was warm outside after the air-conditioned interior of the house, and Natalie slid into the passenger seat of the waiting Ferrari, reached for the safety-belt and fastened it as Ryan slipped in behind the wheel.

'Where are we going?'

The powerful car had negotiated the Chevron bridge and was purring with leashed ease past the golf course, heading west towards the hills.

'Nerang.'

'Good heavens,' she exclaimed. 'You are informative!'

His eyes didn't shift from the road. 'There's an old renovated homestead that has been converted into a restaurant,' he explained with seeming patience. 'The food is excellent, and the atmosphere quiet and intimate. It's a little different from the usual, and I think you'll enjoy it.'

The dusk of evening had disappeared and the car's powerful headlights picked out the surrounding bush-clad terrain, which in turn gave way to housing developments.

Natalie took in the changes with interest. The last time she had passed along this particular road there was scarcely a house to be seen. Now there were factories and houses at irregular intervals, giving credence to the Coast's industrial growth over the past few years.

'Are we dining alone?' She voiced the query idly, more as something to say than a desire for knowledge.

'Yes.'

'Oh.'

Ryan spared her a swift glance. 'Such enthusiasm,' he mocked sardonically. 'Do you find my sole company so daunting?'

She swallowed quickly and gave a slight shrug. 'Whenever we're alone, we usually quarrel.'

'I'm sure we'll manage to maintain a modicum of civility,' he drawled. 'There'll be others present. The place is well patronised.'

Natalie retreated into silence as he brought the car to a smooth halt at a busy intersection. After gaining a pause in the traffic he swung the wheel with smooth efficiency and eased into a parking space.

Switching off the ignition, he reached into the rear compartment and withdrew two bottles. 'It isn't licensed, so we bring our own,' he explained with an edge of mockery, and she slid out to walk at his side towards the nondescript cottage, whose only claim to being an exclusive eatery was its sparkling neon sign.

The contrast inside was dramatic. Dark-stained timbered walls and ceilings, soft lighting, heavy lace curtaining masking the windows, all lent an olde-wordle atmosphere. Immaculate white linen and gleaming silverware created an elegance that was matched by the attentive staff.

Their table was tucked away in a quiet corner, and Natalie took a sip of excellent German Riesling as she perused the blackboard menu.

'Any particular preference?'

She glanced towards that drawling voice and tried to ignore the way her senses leapt at the mere sight of him. It was crazy how she could alternate between dislike and its antithesis with such rapidity. 'Mmn,' she deliberated, scanning the dishes offered. 'I'll have fish, I think, barramundi meuniere, with no starter.'

'My appetite is a little more substantial than yours,' said Ryan, giving her order. 'I'll start with peppered prawns, and have scallopini with mushrooms to follow. Vegetables, no salad. Natalie?'

'Oh, salad, thank you.'

His faint amusing gleam put her slightly on the defensive.

'I happen to like salad.'

'Did I suggest that you didn't?'

'I've come a long way since the days when I followed your every lead,' she said lightly, taking the sting out of her words with a slight smile.

The waitress arrived with a small wooden board containing a crusty loaf and a pot of garlic butter, which she placed beside Ryan.

He lifted the serrated knife and proceeded to cut it into slices, which he buttered, then placed one on to Natalie's plate.

'I could have done that,' she protested, accepting the slice, and promptly bit into it, finding it delicious.

'Indulge me. I'm in an attentive mood.'

'My goodness!' She allowed her eyes to widen deliberately. 'This moment will have to be recorded for posterity.'

'Drink your wine,' he drawled, refilling her glass, and she wrinkled her nose at him.

'I know your game. You're trying to lull me into a warm dreamy state, so that I won't have the inclination to argue.'

He lifted his glass and touched its rim to hers, his eyes faintly mocking. 'Here's to us.'

'I'm not sure I should drink to that.'

'Why ever not?'

'It might lead to my downfall.'

'Would that be so very bad?' he queried with unaccustomed gentleness, and she nodded.

'Oh yes,' she said sadly. 'I fell in love with you once. It was like being enclosed in a beautiful bubble, flying higher and higher with the rays of the sun shooting its translucent film with a myriad pretty colours. I thought I was immune from the rest of the world, protected, and infinitely precious.' She met his gaze unflinchingly. 'One day the bubble burst, and I crashed painfully down to earth.' She lifted her glass and stared at its contents. 'It isn't an experience I want to repeat.'

'Fate is an incredible entity,' Ryan began after a measurable silence, and anything further he might have said was lost by the presence of the waitress as she deposited a dish of peppered prawns before him.

The aroma tantalised her nostrils, activating her taste-buds, and as he lifted the first prawn to his mouth he caught her faintly wistful expression.

'Like to try one?'

She watched as he replaced the fork into the dish, and when he lifted a succulent morsel and fed it into her mouth she didn't refuse. With a strange fascination she accepted two more mouthfuls, aware of the blatant sensuality in sharing his food and the same utensil. It was almost as if he was deliberately attempting to establish that they shared something more tangible than mere food, and the knowledge was so profound she didn't dare dwell on it.

'You're treating me like a child,' she breathed shakily, and was unable to glance away from the depth of his probing gaze.

'Am I?' There was no mockery evident, and for a moment she was totally oblivious to everyone else in the room.

With a sense of mounting panic she reached for her glass and resolutely sipped its contents. Dear God, what was the matter with her? The wine, the food, Ryan's manner, all seemed part of a flagrant seduction. She had only to close her eyes and the past three years might never have been.

'Have another slice of bread.'

Natalie regarded the proffered board, and shook her head. It was perhaps as well that at that precise moment the waitress returned to clear Ryan's dish and set their main course before them.

The barramundi fillet melted in her mouth, and the delicate sauce was a perfect complement.

'Dessert?'

Natalie shook her head and finished the last of her wine. 'No. Thank you.'

'Irish coffee? Or perhaps a Royale?' Ryan suggested, leaning well back in his chair. 'An excellent way to finish off a meal, don't you agree?'

Rich black coffee spiced with spirits and topped with cream had a definite appeal, and she nodded in silent acquiescence.

With calm unhurried movements he extracted cigarettes and a lighter, then when the slim tube was lit to his satisfaction he exhaled the smoke with every evidence of pleasure.

'It's only ten. Would you like to take in a show after we leave here?'

The thought of crowds of people, bright glaring lights and noise after these peaceful surroundings prompted her to refuse. 'Besides, you have work tomorrow,' she added, sipping the delicious hot coffee from its pottery goblet. She felt sated with good food and wine, relaxed, and vaguely sleepy.

'I'm taking the day off,' Ryan informed her blandly, and through a haze of smoke his expression was difficult to discern.

She managed a slight smile. 'Any particular reason?'

'A shopping excursion—yours and Michelle's.'

'We're to be suitably fitted out in a style accustomed to your standing,' she declared evenly. 'May I point out that Michelle will become tired and fractious after an hour or two?'

'I hadn't bargained on bringing her along. Martha is quite capable of looking after her.'

'I didn't realise my clothes were so sadly lacking.'

'Your clothes are fine,' Ryan asserted, his dark golden eyes giving evidence of an appreciative appraisal as they swept down the deep vee of her bodice. 'You simply need more. We're having a few people in for dinner on Saturday evening.'

Natalie felt her heart sink, and she finished the rest of her coffee before flashing him a brilliant smile. 'In that case a shopping spree is definitely in order. It will be very important that I shine and dazzle effectively, and for that I must dress the part.'

'Shall we go?'

His hand was firm on the back of her waist as they threaded their way to the front desk, and outside he saw her seated in the car before crossing round to slip in behind the wheel.

The drive home was accomplished in what seemed a very short time. Why was it that the return journey always appeared to be *less*? Natalie mused as she followed Ryan into the house.

She crossed the carpet to the stairs, and paused to slip off her sandals before ascending to the upper floor with the straps dangling from her fingers. In the bedroom she switched on the light and moved to the bathroom, cleansed her skin of make-up, brushed her teeth, then retraced her steps.

Ryan was standing near the window, the scene beyond the partially curtained glass apparently holding his attention. One hand was thrust into his trouser pocket, and in the dim glow cast from a solitary bedlamp he appeared to tower even taller than his six feet three inches.

Natalie extracted a filmy nightgown from beneath her pillow and donned it after shedding her clothes, then she crossed to the mirrored dresser and picked up her brush.

She was halfway through the customary number of strokes when the brush was taken from her hand, and she gave Ryan's shadowy reflection a startled glance as he began to stroke the brush through the length of her hair.

'It's like pale spun silk,' he murmured, letting it slip slowly through his fingers as if the feel fascinated him.

There was an odd familiarity in his touch that brought a return of the past, and Natalie closed her eyes in an effort to dispel the memory it evoked. As if encased in a magical hypnotic spell she sat quiescent as he lifted a swathe of hair and gently brushed his lips against her nape. She was powerless to move away, or even speak, and as his mouth trailed to a vulnerable hollow at the base of her throat she gave an inaudible moan, aware of the slow pulsing ache that threatened her treacherous emotions, yet she was powerless to stop their response.

In a dreamlike trance she felt him lift and turn her so that she stood resting against his hard lean frame, and as his mouth closed over hers she let her arms slowly encircle his neck.

His mouth created its own havoc, filling her senses with bittersweet warmth until she clung to him like a wild untamed creature craving fulfilment. Nothing else mattered but the satisfaction of his possession, and like a priceless musical instrument he played her emotions to their fullest extent before staking his claim in an action that soared them both high to a plateau of mutual ecstasy.

CHAPTER SEVEN

RYAN was as good as his word, and early next morning they drove into Surfer's Paradise, where, within a very short space of time, the back seat and the boot of the Daimler were filled with a variety of boxes in all shapes and sizes.

Natalie's head spun at the speed with which it was all accomplished, and when Ryan suggested a drink, she allowed him to lead her into a small but select coffee lounge.

'Hmn, I needed that,' she murmured appreciatively as she sipped a superbly-brewed cappuccino. Her eyes were drawn to his, and she was unable to prevent the query, 'Who have you invited to dinner tomorrow night?'

His eyes gleamed with hidden mockery. 'Scared?'

She grimaced slightly. 'Apprehensive. I doubt I'll ever make a serene hostess.'

'There aren't many around,' he allowed cynically. 'It's all a clever façade. Inside, they're desperately afraid, and only practice and maturity brings a semblance of serenity.'

'So,' she declared ruefully. 'Forewarned is forearmed. Are Rick and Lisa coming?'

'They are, together with the Richardsons, a few business associates and their partners.'

'Not Simone?' The words were out before she could stop them, and it took considerable courage to hold his gaze.

'Not to my knowledge,' Ryan responded evenly. 'However, it's possible she could partner either of two associates.' His eyes narrowed slightly until they resembled topaz chips. 'I don't doubt you can handle it if she does turn up.'

'Oh, I'm sure she will,' she said with a brittle smile. 'Turn up, I mean. In fact, I wouldn't put it past her to deliberately manipulate the invitation.'

Throughout the next day Natalie was a mass of nerves, and she showered and changed into one of her new dresses—a soft synthetic material in subtle shades of pink, lilac and grey that highlighted her blonde hair and glowing skin. Her make-up was applied with time-consuming care, and a liberal spray of Miss Dior to several pulse-beats added the finishing touch.

'Very pleasing,' Ryan drawled as he entered the bedroom from the bathroom, and she inclined her head in a mocking acceptance of his compliment.

'Thank you, kind sir.' She let her eyes wander over his dark trousers and immaculate pale shirt. 'You, too, will pass muster.'

One eyebrow slanted in cynical appraisal. 'I think you could do with a drink. Shall we go downstairs?'

'Into battle,' Natalie inclined impishly, and allowed him to take her elbow.

It was amazing what a glass of wine could do to boost her morale, she mused some fifteen minutes later, and when Jenkins escorted Nick and Lisa Andreas into the lounge she went forward to greet them with genuine warmth.

Within the space of ten minutes all but two of their guests had arrived, and Natalie felt the tension knot in her stomach as Jenkins ushered in a tall dark-haired man whose face appeared vaguely familiar, and the knot tightened when she saw his companion.

Simone Vesey was sophistication personified,

from the top of her elegantly-coiffured dark head
to the tip of her imported shoes. Attired in black,
her make-up superb, she drew the attention of
every pair of eyes in the room.

Good manners alone carried Natalie through
the ensuing ten minutes, and afterwards she could
not have recounted a word as she smiled and
exchanged polite small-talk with their guests.

It was a relief when dinner was announced, and
throughout the numerous courses she strived to
act out a part in which she felt totally ill at ease,
and it was mostly due to Lisa and Rick Andreas,
seated close by, that her attention was averted
from Simone's blatant attempt to flirt with Ryan.

To give him his due, he didn't respond, but it
rankled nonetheless, and Natalie felt her eyes
being drawn more and more often towards them.

How she managed to get through the remainder
of the evening was a mystery, although the
assistance of several glasses of wine no doubt
helped! The room, the guests—all seemed cloaked
with a sense of *déjà vu*, and brought back a vivid
recollection of several evenings in the past when
she and Ryan had entertained guests, several of
whom were present tonight.

After coffee had been served in the lounge, one
couple then another began to disperse, until only
Simone and Gordon White remained.

'Darling, I must congratulate you on effecting a
reconcilation with Ryan,' smiled Simone with
superficial civility, but there was only enmity
evident in those brilliant dark eyes as she fixed
Natalie with a raking stare.

'Thank you,' Natalie managed evenly, aware
that Ryan and Gordon were deep in conversation
and therefore partly oblivious to what was taking
part between Simone and herself.

'I'm sure you worked very hard.'

Natalie gave a polite smile. 'If you choose to think so.'

A thin stream of smoke rose from the slender cigarette Simone held, and she lifted it to her mouth, took a long inhalation, then expelled the smoke with every evidence of satisfaction. 'He was on the point of instigating divorce before you hit him with your—er—*pièce de résistance*, shall we say? So convincing to be able to produce a child.' Her eyes glittered angrily. 'It's to be hoped Ryan took the precaution of checking the blood grouping. Subtler tricks than yours have been worked in the past, and he is a very wealthy man.'

'You haven't changed, Simone,' Natalie remarked wryly.

'No, darling—and I never will,' the dark-haired woman breathed with thinly disguised emnity.

Natalie caught Ryan's narrowed glance and offered him a brilliant smile, then crossed to his side. 'Simone was just saying they must leave.' She let her gaze shift to his companion. 'It's been a pleasure meeting you, Gordon.'

It seemed natural to move towards the door, and she could hardly believe it was all over as she stood at Ryan's side in the foyer and bade them goodnight.

The instant the door closed she turned and made for the stairs. 'I'm going to bed.'

'Nothing more to drink?' Ryan slanted, and she rounded on him with a hollow laugh.

'Are you trying to suggest I've had more than I can handle?'

'Did I say that?' he queried with a bland inscrutability, and anger rose to the fore with a vengeance.

'Oh, go to hell, Ryan! I'm tired, and after

fielding Simone's vicious innuendoes, I'm in no mood to continue with yours!'

'You hardly spoke to her all evening,' he commented with a narrowed glance, and she erupted into angry speech.

'You more than made up for my lapse in that direction!' she spat furiously, and his eyes gleamed with mocking cynicism.

'I do believe you're jealous. Are you?'

'You have to be kidding!'

She watched in idle fascination as he crossed to her side, and his husky laugh was more than she could bear.

'I think you protest too much, my darling wife,' he uttered quizzically, and without thought her hand flew to his face.

'Oh no,' Ryan cautioned softly as he caught it in mid-air, then deftly twisted it behind her back. 'If you want to fight, we'll do it in the privacy of our bedroom. Then there'll be no doubt as to its conclusion.'

'I hate you,' she breathed bitterly. 'My God, you don't know how much!'

Without another word he swung her into his arms and carried her up the stairs, oblivious to the fists she rained against his powerful back, and in their room he threw her on to the bed, then joined her there.

What followed remained indelibly imprinted in her brain, and even as she begged for mercy her traitorous body arched and twisted beneath his, silently urging him towards a tumultuous, raging, almost raping, possession.

She slept deeply, haunted by dreams in which she was a shadowy participant, yet when she woke she retained no recollection of those somnolent sequences. Only Ryan and the events of the previous evening flooded forth with dreadful clarity, and she turned her head cautiously only to see that she was alone in the large bed. A glance at her watch revealed that it was after eight, and she breathed a small sigh of relief that he would already have breakfasted and left for the golf course.

She rose and showered, then dressed and went downstairs to join Michelle for the first meal of the day.

'Swim, Mummy!'

Natalie sipped her coffee and bit into her toast. 'After, sweetheart. It's going to be a lovely warm day. We'll sit out by the pool, and you can draw some pictures while I read the newspaper. Then we'll swim, okay?'

'Yes, please.'

They finished their breakfast, then changed into swimsuits before going downstairs to the pebbled courtyard adjoining the pool. Natalie smoothed some sunscreen cream over the little girl's skin, then rendered a similar treatment to her own.

The time passed swiftly, and after giving Michelle a swimming lesson she stretched out on a canvas chair and let the sun's warmth dry the moisture from her skin.

A slight sound alerted her, and she looked up to see Martha hurrying forward, her pleasant features faintly anxious.

'A long-distance call, Natalie, from Mrs Maclean.'

Natalie stood to her feet in one fluid movement. 'I'll take it on the bar extension,' she declared, her eyes darting to the tiny figure happily engrossed with toys not too far distant from the pool's edge. 'Will you watch Michelle?'

Her feet almost flew across the pebbled

courtyard, and she picked up the receiver with shaky fingers. 'Andrea?'

'I'm at the hospital,' her stepmother declared without preamble. 'They're preparing John for surgery immediately. I'll ring you the minute he comes out.'

'How is he?'

'As fit as he'll ever be to withstand the operation. The light's flashing, Natalie, and I haven't any more coins.'

'I'll catch the next flight down,' Natalie declared, voicing the words even as the intention entered her head, then the line bleeped and went dead. 'Damn!' She replaced the receiver and reached for the telephone directory, finding the number she wanted with the minimum of effort. Dialling the digits, she waited impatiently for the airline to answer. 'Hello? This is an emergency. I want a seat on the first flight to Sydney. I can be at the airport in less than an hour.' She listened attentively, then said a decisive 'Thanks'. God— three-quarters of an hour was cutting it fine! Especially as she hadn't even packed! 'Martha?'

That good woman almost ran in her haste to give assistance, a protesting Michelle scooped against an ample bosom.

'Can you tell Jenkins to get the car ready, then help me pack? We'll have to achieve a minor miracle if I'm to make that flight out of Coolangatta on time!'

'Are you taking Michelle?'

Natalie didn't even pause as she ran towards the stairs. 'Of course. I couldn't leave her behind.'

The next fifteen minutes were a mixture of well-organised confusion and total chaos, but unbelievably there were two suitcases stowed in the boot of the powerful Daimler, both she and

Michelle were presentably clothed, and Jenkins was handling the powerful car with skilful efficiency as it sped down the coastal highway.

The jet was actually warming up on the tarmac when they reached the airport, and with Jenkins' help they made it—just, being last to board.

An hour later they landed at Sydney's Mascot airport, and were immediately whisked by taxi to the hospital.

'You brought Michelle?' Andrea queried, faint disapproval creasing her brow. 'Natalie, she would have been better left at home. A hospital isn't the place for young children.'

'I just packed and left without thinking about it,' she answered. 'Any news yet?'

'He's still in surgery. Oh, dear Lord, it's been so long!' Tears welled up behind tired blue eyes, and Natalie felt a surge of compassion for the older woman.

'Hey, he's my father,' she said gently. 'I love him too.'

Andrea nodded in silence. 'He's all I have,' she declared brokenly.

'Shall I get you a cup of coffee? Have you had anything to eat?' Her own stomach felt empty, for she had been too engrossed with feeding Michelle to bother about her own needs. 'You take Michelle while I ask at reception.'

She was back in five minutes carrying a tray on which reposed two steaming cups of coffee and a plate of sandwiches. 'We'll both feel better when we've had this.'

Andrea undid a sachet of sugar and stirred her coffee abstractedly, her eyes darting to the front desk at every sound or movement from that direction.

'Have something to eat,' Natalie cajoled. 'Even

when Dad comes out from theatre, it will be at least an hour or two before the anaesthetic begins to wear off, and even then he'll drift in and out of sleep for several hours. You don't want his first glimpse of you to cause him any concern.'

'Do I look that bad?' Andrea asked ruefully. 'I haven't slept for the past two nights worrying about the outcome of all this.'

'It shows—a little,' Natalie agreed with a slight grin. 'But you're far from appearing haggard. Now, please—eat. For Dad's sake, if not for your own.'

The hours seemed interminable, and keeping Michelle suitably amused proved something of a distraction—a not unwelcome one, for conversation was at a low ebb.

It was almost four o'clock when a gowned, bespectacled man entered the waiting room, and Andrea immediately sprang to her feet wearing an agonisingly anxious expression.

'John—is he all right? Please——'

'Mr Maclean is in the recovery room,' the surgeon soothed with the ease of long practice. 'He'll be taken to his suite in about half an hour. Sister will allow you to see him very briefly, but I must warn you that it will be several hours before he'll regain full consciousness.' His eyes kindled with professional warmth. 'I would advise that you go home, have a meal, then return later this evening.'

'Has the operation been a success?' Andrea's eyes were almost stark with fear, and Natalie held her breath for his reply.

'It's much too early to be conclusive, Mrs Maclean. Several factors have to be considered before I'm prepared to give an assessment. Rest assured he's in the best possible hands.'

It was professional ambiguity at best, and Natalie sensed Andrea's inner anguish at not having her worst fears either confirmed or denied.

'I'll stay with you,' she reassured her, and the older woman nodded her silent appreciation.

'You'd better ring Ryan.'

Ryan? She hadn't even thought to leave a message, although Martha or Jenkins would inform him of her whereabouts. A wry smile tugged the corners of her mouth. This episode would merely be another in a rapidly-growing string of events to be chalked up against her. She seemed to anger him at every turn—as he angered *her*. Whenever they were together the air was fraught with latent animosity. Some devilish imp impelled her to behave in a manner that was totally alien to her nature, delighting in being as deliberately perverse as possible, so that his resultant wrath heaped retribution upon her hapless head.

'I'll ring him this evening from the hotel,' Natalie murmured, delaying the inevitable.

'Where are you staying?' Andrea asked him in an abstracted manner, and Natalie gave a rueful laugh.

'Would you believe—I don't know? I came straight here from the airport.' She picked up the magazine Michelle had dropped and re-opened the pages. 'I'll beg some assistance from the receptionist. Maybe she can recommend a reasonable place. Otherwise, I'll simply pick something at random from the directory.'

'Natalie?'

She turned slightly, waiting, and Andrea said quietly, 'Thank you for coming.'

'It never occurred to me not to,' she responded

gently, then resumed her way to the reception
desk.

'Mrs Marshall?'

Natalie nodded in faint puzzlement.

'I have Mr Marshall on the line. Will you take
the call from this phone?' She indicated a
telephone set at the edge of her desk, and Natalie
drew a deep steadying breath as she crossed to pick
up the receiver.

'Ryan?'

'I'm at the airport.' His voice was unnecessarily
brusque. 'Stay at the hospital until I get there.'

He hung up before she had a chance to say
anything, and immediately resentment rose to the
fore. Of all the nerve! Calmly ignoring his
directive, she set about arranging accommodation
for herself and Michelle, then returned to resume
her seat beside Andrea.

Almost twenty minutes later an officious-
looking Sister entered the waiting-room and
summoned Andrea. 'Only a few minutes, Mrs
Maclean,' she insisted, sparing Natalie a quick
glance. 'Alone, I'm afraid.'

Natalie gave her stepmother an encouraging
smile, and watched as both women disappeared
from view.

'Hungry, Mummy,' Michelle asserted with
childish candour, and Natalie cast a swift glance at
the clock on the wall.

'Soon, sweetheart.'

Andrea's features were pale when she returned,
and Natalie stood to her feet at once, concern
uppermost.

'I'll ring for a taxi. It can drop you at your
sister's house, then take us on to the hotel.'

Mercifully, they were able to leave the hospital
in a very short space of time, and after depositing

Andrea, Natalie directed the driver to the address in King's Cross.

After checking in to her room, food was the first consideration, and Natalie dialled room service to place an order.

Michelle was irritable and tired, as well as being hungry, and had become almost impossible to manage.

'Darling, don't cry,' she begged, attempting to soothe the little girl. 'Let's go the bathroom and wash, then we'll switch on the television, and before you know it there'll be a knock on the door and our dinner will be here.'

'Daddy!' Michelle wailed, and Natalie momentarily closed her eyes before crossing to the bathroom.

Within minutes there was a knock on the outer door, and she gave a sigh of relief. Food, at last!

Expecting to see the waiter, she took a few speechless seconds to register Ryan's tall frame as she opened the door.

'What are you doing here?'

Dark slim-fitting trousers and a dark patterned shirt lent him a grim implacable air, and anger emanated beneath the surface of his control. 'I could ask you the same question.'

'Daddy!' Michelle's tiny body hurtled towards them and almost flew into the arms that reached to lift her high against a powerful chest.

At that precise moment the waiter appeared with a covered tray, adding to the general confusion, and it was a few minutes before the door closed after his retreating figure.

'Hungry,' the little girl insisted mournfully, looking from one parent to the other with big reproachful eyes, and Ryan crossed to the table, set his daughter in a chair and proceeded to feed her.

'I can do that,' Natalie protested, eyeing him warily.

'Ring room service and order another meal,' he instructed hardily.

She drew a deep breath, then crossed to the phone. 'What do you want?'

'Anything. I'm not fussy.'

The order placed, she moved to the table and sat down. Suddenly she wasn't hungry any more, and she toyed with the food on her plate, pushing it back and forth like a child confronted with food deemed obnoxious to its palate.

Her hunger sustained, Michelle scrambled down to sit happily on the carpet in front of the television set, oblivious to all but the flickering screen.

'Is this——' Ryan cast a glance at the room before swinging back to fix her with an unwavering glare, 'another act of defiance?'

'You had no need to race after me,' Natalie hissed through clenched teeth. 'I'm quite capable of looking after myself.'

'Did I imply that you weren't?'

'Then why are you here?' she demanded truculently.

'Depending on the outcome of the operation, I thought you might need my support,' he declared dryly, and her eyes moved to a point beyond his right shoulder.

'Such concern,' she mocked lightly, ignoring the angry tensing of his jaw as she met his gaze. 'For a moment I believed you'd come to check that I hadn't absconded with Michelle.'

Hard topaz chips gleamed beneath his partially hooded lids, and her stomach muscles tightened into a painful knot at the anger evident.

'You wouldn't escape me a second time.' The threat was there, and she shivered involuntarily.

'Andrea phoned this morning.'

Ryan leaned against the back of his chair in a deliberately indolent pose that reminded her of a jungle beast poised for attack. One false move, and she'd be in the midst of a battle! 'So Jenkins told me.'

'I was just able-to catch a flight by the skin of my teeth.'

A knock at the door ensured a timely interruption, and Natalie watched as Ryan crossed the carpet.

'Tell reception Mrs Marshall will be checking out in fifteen minutes,' he instructed the waiter after taking the tray. 'We should be through here by then.'

'What do you mean—checking out?' she demanded the instant the door closed behind the uniformed figure.

'I have an apartment in Double Bay,' Ryan declared smoothly, seating himself at the table before sparing her a compelling glance. 'We'll stay there.'

'I'm not moving anywhere,' she insisted stormily. 'Michelle is tired and so am I. We're staying here. *You* stay at your apartment.'

His appraisal was swift and impenetrable. 'You'll come with me, even if I have to carry you.'

'Do you know what you are?' she cried, sorely tried, and became positively incensed as a lazy smile creased his rough-hewn features.

'My imagination boggles,' he accorded dryly, and she burst into restrained expostulatory speech.

'A diabolical, feudal—tyrant! You give orders and expect instant blind obedience, and if anyone should dare to so much as question them, you employ force without a thought to the consequences!' Her voice lowered to a vengeful whisper. 'Well—*damn* you, Ryan Marshall! If you want me out of this hotel, you *can* darned well carry me!'

'You think I won't?' he queried silkily, and she gave a bitter laugh.

'You're going to look pretty silly if you do!'

His eyes held a tigerish gleam. 'Oh, I think I'll evoke some misguided sympathy—a child held against one shoulder, and a wife hauled over the other. They'll imagine you as something of a shrew in need of a sound slap or two—and envy me the experience,' he concluded in a hateful drawl.

Anger made her splutter incredulously, 'You wouldn't dare!'

'Try me.'

The temptation to pick up something and hurl it at him was almost too much to resist, and it was only Michelle's presence that put a cautionary brake on her temper. She stood with impotent rage as Ryan calmly ate his meal, then polished it off with the glass of wine which the waiter had thoughtfully supplied.

'Are you ready?'

Natalie threw him a venomous glare. 'No!'

'Pity,' Ryan drawled, his expression lightly mocking. 'I no longer feel in the mood to fight. But since you insist,' he finished with a slight shrug, standing to his feet.

She took an involuntary step backwards as he crossed to the telephone, and she watched in mesmerised fascination as he dialled the required digits before instructing quietly, 'Will you send a porter to Room——' he checked the number from the key-tab and repeated it. 'And call a taxi.' He replaced the receiver and turned towards Natalie. 'Which is it to be?'

There was no choice if she was to retain a

vestige of dignity, and with an angry toss of her head she crossed to the divan and collected her shoulderbag, then stood in angry silence as he scooped Michelle into his arms and preceded her from the room.

In the taxi she maintained an icy silence, and when it despatched them outside a prestigious apartment block she merely took Michelle and followed as he carried their bags.

The elevator rose with swift electronic precision to the uppermost floor, and with a sense of fatalism Natalie moved past him to wait beside the only visible door in sight.

Inside, it reflected an interior decorator's skilful flair, blending essential masculine colours to achieve an understated elegance. Beige thick-tufted carpet and cream textured walls provided an excellent background for the chocolate-brown velour-covered sofas with camel velvet scatter cushions. Splashes of contrast were interspersed on the walls in the form of bold framed prints.

Natalie strolled towards a deep-cushioned sofa and deposited Michelle, then slid the strap of her bag off her shoulder. 'This is what is commonly referred to as the ultimate in bachelor pads,' she observed with thinly-veiled sarcasm. 'I'm almost afraid to ask, but perhaps you'll indulge me— where is the bedroom?'

Ryan slipped a set of keys into his trouser pocket and crossed to an elegantly assembled bar. 'There are two at the end of the hall,' he informed her dryly, reaching for a glass and pouring himself a drink. 'Will you have one?'

'I'll bath Michelle first and settle her down.' She picked up the smaller of the two bags and glanced back at her daughter.

'Go ahead, I'll bring her.'

'Daddy,' Michelle insisted sleepily, fighting to keep her eyes open, and with a husky laugh Ryan left the bar and crossed to the sofa.

'Come on, sleepyhead, he bade, lifting the little girl into his arms. 'Bath and bed, hm?'

The task became a joint effort, and there was a strange aching sensation around the region of her heart as Natalie watched those tiny arms wind themselves up round Ryan's neck as he bent to bestow a goodnight kiss. Even as they moved back from the bed, the drooping eyelids flickered shut, and her breathing tempered into an even beat denoting sleep.

In the lounge she chose a solitary cushioned chair and sank into it to view him warily as he crossed to the bar and retrieved his glass.

'A light wine—or something stronger?'

'Stronger,' she declared succinctly, and saw one eyebrow rise with sardonic amusement.

'On an empty stomach, is that wise?'

Natalie lifted a hand and let her fingers thread through the length of her hair. 'I'm not in the mood for wisdom.' She watched as he poured a measure of spirits into a glass and added a generous splash of soda water before handing it to her.

'It would have been easier if you'd left Michelle with Martha.'

'You sound an echo of Andrea,' she said stiltedly, taking a tentative sip, and she grimaced slightly as the spirits hit the back of her throat.

'The hospital has this number,' Ryan assured her, and took a generous swallow, his eyes enigmatic as they noted each fleeting expression on her delicate features. 'They'll call if there's any change.'

'When are you going back?'

'So eager to be rid of me?' he parried, and she gave an expressive sigh.

'I can't even ask a simple question without it being turned against me!'

'I have to be back on the Coast by Wednesday.'

She raised cool grey eyes to meet his impenetrable gaze. 'I'd like to stay longer. Preferably until Dad is out of hospital.'

'No deal, Natalie,' he refused. 'That could run into several weeks, and I've no intention of permitting your absence for anything approaching that length of time.'

'But I'm his daughter,' she argued. 'I have a right——'

'You're also my wife,' Ryan declared inflexibly, and she uttered a hollow laugh.

'Whose husband doesn't hesitate to exert *his* rights whenever and wherever he pleases!'

'The pleasure isn't exactly one-sided,' he reminded her with droll cynicism, and her action was purely instinctive as she tossed the contents of her glass towards his hateful face.

There was a frightening deliberation in the way he set his glass down on a nearby table, and Natalie watched with hypnotic fascination as he moved towards her. Something in his eyes made her want to scream, but no sound came out.

Without a word he reached for her, drawing her upright and hoisting her over one shoulder to carry her wildly struggling to the bedroom. She rained blows against his back, to any part of that powerful frame that she could reach, and all to no avail, as with a backwards kick with one foot he set the door closed behind him.

'Put me down, you—you *fiend*!'

He allowed her to slide down to her feet, and she winced as his fingers bit painfully into the soft flesh of her arms.

'God help me! You'd try the patience of a saint!' he bit out with barely controlled fury, and the next instant she was hauled with appalling ease across one powerful thigh as he gave her a thorough spanking.

It was an annihilating experience, and one she wouldn't care to have repeated. As Ryan stood her upright she actually felt her body shake with a mixture of suppressed indignation and downright resentment as such high-handedness. She had behaved like a recalcitrant child, and he had reacted accordingly.

'I consider that was long overdue,' Ryan growled harshly, totally unrepentant, and her eyes resembled a storm-tossed sea as she glared up at him.

'You—bastard!' she whispered with bitter vengeance, hating him in that moment to such a degree that it was vaguely frightening. Of all the emotions he was capable of arousing, this was the least enviable.

His smile was totally without humour. 'Be thankful I kept a rein on my temper,' he drawled sardonically. 'My initial instinct was to inflict something far worse.'

'Rape?' Natalie arched with careless disregard. 'I wouldn't let you.'

Something flared in those topaz depths, chilling her to the bone. 'You couldn't stop me.'

An unbidden lump rose to her throat, and she swallowed convulsively. 'Ryan——' Her eyes widened until they resembled huge pools in which genuine fear was reflected.

'Shut up,' he directed with brooding savagery, and his hands closed over the delicate bones of her shoulders as he impelled her forward, then his mouth closed over hers with deadly intent, and the soundless scream remained locked in her throat.

The hardness of his lips crushed hers, forcing them apart, in a ravaging invasion that made her want to cry and rage against him.

To stand quiescent beneath such an onslaught was intolerable, and Natalie beat her fists against his ribs, anywhere she could connect, in an effort to get him to desist. With an ease that was galling Ryan captured first one hand, then the other, and held them together behind her back. Held fast against his hard frame, there was little she could offer by way of resistance, and she suffered his bruising force for what seemed an age before the pressure altered subtly and began to assume a persuasive quality.

Unbidden, a slow fire began to course through her veins, bringing awareness to each separate nerve-end until they tingled with life and appeared to reach out, clamouring for his touch.

Slowly, of their own volition, her arms crept up to encircle his neck, and her fingers curled into the hair that grew low at the base of his nape, caressing, holding his head down to hers in a gesture that betrayed all too vividly her need of him.

Beginning a wild evocative path, his mouth left hers and trailed along her jaw to tease a sensitive earlobe, then pressed a light kiss to each closed eyelid before seeking a tell-tale hammering pulse at the base of her throat. As his mouth wandered slowly downwards she gave an audible moan and arched herself against him, revelling in the depth of emotion he was able to arouse.

One by one, her clothes slowly fell to the floor, and his deep husky laugh greeted her efforts to unbutton his shirt.

'I'll help you,' he husked deeply, and at her faint blush he bent and bestowed a swift hard kiss to her trembling mouth. Moments later he lifted her into his arms and carried her to the bed, where he led her with consummate ease to the very brink of ecstasy, pacing her pleasure with his own, until she wept from the sheer joy of it.

Afterwards she lay within the circle of his arms, too enervated to move, and she gave a slight sigh as sleep threatened to claim her. Once again Ryan had proved that on a physical level they were in perfect accord. Yet how could their relationship survive by lust alone? Gradually her eyes closed, the lashes barely flickering as she gave herself up to somnolent oblivion.

CHAPTER EIGHT

DURING the next few days Natalie spent most of her time with Andrea at the hospital, providing comfort simply by being there.

Ryan astounded her by completely taking over Michelle, even to supplying an evening meal, and never had she been so grateful for his presence.

On Tuesday afternoon there was a slight change for the better and by evening John Maclean had shown steady improvement. Andrea was still cautious, but her expression held hope that was borne out by the hospital's medical team the next morning.

'Andrea, that's wonderful!' Natalie declared as the news was imparted by phone. 'Yes, I'll tell Ryan. I'll meet you at the hospital in an hour.' She put the receiver down and turned towards the table where Ryan was intent in absorbing the financial section of the daily newspaper.

He looked up as she crossed the room, and his expression was curiously intent. 'Dad's going to be okay,' she told him with a relieved smile, and he inclined his head in silent acknowledgment.

'Good. I'll arrange a late morning flight to Coolangatta.'

Her eyes widened fractionally and a slight frown creased her brow. 'Ryan, I have to stay, surely you must see that?'

'Until Sunday—not a day longer.' His eyes met hers steadily. 'Is that understood?'

She grabbed the reprieve with both hands, agreeing without thought. 'Sunday will be fine.'

'I'll take Michelle with me. The hospital won't allow her in to see John,' he said decisively.

Natalie wasn't sure she liked the idea, but she had to concede that it had some merit. 'All right,' she agreed reluctantly. 'I'll pack' she added, looking at him gravely, knowing she would miss him. Part of her wanted to cry out, 'Don't go', but she overcame the desire to voice those damning words. It wouldn't do to let him think she was falling in love with him again. That way could only lead to disaster. Michelle was something else again, for they had never been apart for longer than a day, and never a night. She felt torn in two, a victim of divided loyalties. Yet she knew there was no other course. She was compelled to stay near her father for a few more days at least.

Ryan crossed to the phone and made two calls, one of them long-distance, while Natalie deftly sorted clothes into a suitcase.

'I'll arrange your flight back,' he told her as they rode the elevator to the ground floor. 'Michelle will be fine,' he added gently as he glimpsed the faint shimmer of tears that threatened to overflow, and she nodded.

'I know. Between Martha and Jenkins, she'll be thoroughly spoiled!' The doors slid open, and a waiting taxi could be seen stationary outside the main glassed entrance. 'I'll phone.'

Ryan paused, shooting her a dark inscrutable glance. 'Dammit, Natalie, this is a hell of a time to become weepily sentimental!' His head bent and he placed a bruising, possessive kiss on her trembling mouth, then he swept through the door without a backward glance and all she could see as the taxi moved away was Michelle's tiny hand waving a frantic farewell.

Damn, damn, *damn*! she muttered to herself,

retracing her steps to the elevator, and she jabbed the button with unnecessary force. She should be rejoicing in her new-found freedom, yet already she felt bereft—almost as if she were a limb that had just been severed from its stalwart trunk. In the weeks since Ryan had forced this ill-fated reconciliation she had prayed for its end—or at least a temporary respite. Now she had it, she found she didn't want it. A sigh escaped her lips. How contrary could she be? One advantage in being alone was that she would have time to evaluate her own emotions. Yet she already knew the answer, and the knowledge didn't help matters at all.

In the apartment she went into the bedroom and attended to her make-up, then after running a brush through the length of her hair she caught up her bag and made for the front door. Scorning the use of a taxi, she walked to the end of the street and caught a bus into the city.

As her father began to improve Natalie limited her visits to fit in with visiting hours, and she often left the apartment early after breakfast to spend the morning exploring the city shops. Andrea would sometimes join her, then after lunch they inevitably caught a taxi to the hospital.

The days were easy to fill. It was the evenings and the long dark hours that appeared to drag. Magazines, books, even the television screen failed to provide more than a fleeting interest, and after spending one night tossing sleeplessly alone in the main bedroom, Natalie moved her things to the smaller guest room.

Michelle's voice on the phone each evening was little more than an excited incomprehensible chatter that was succeeded by Ryan's lazy drawl, and each call caused Natalie to feel more restless than ever. It was Saturday evening, the day before she was due to leave, that the last of Ryan's calls came, and she answered the phone in a breathless rush.

'Natalie? What took you so long?'

Who did he think he was, for heaven's sake? 'I was in the shower,' she explained. 'It's been raining down here, and I got wet walking back from the bus stop.'

There was an infinitesimal silence. 'What the hell were you doing in a bus?'

'I like riding in buses,' she responded civilly, and lifted the towel to rub her hair dry. 'Besides, there wasn't a taxi in sight.'

'Next time, wait for one.' His voice crackled forcibly down the line, and she felt her hackles begin to rise.

'Aren't you being a bit ridiculous?'

'It's a failing where you're concerned,' he drawled. 'Just do as I say, hm?'

'I'll catch a bus if I want to,' she returned sharply, and heard him muffle an oath.

'Your flight leaves at seven tomorrow evening. Check with reservations. They're holding your ticket.'

'I've changed my mind.' The words were out before she had time to think about them. 'I'm not coming back tomorrow.'

'The hell you're not!' he bit out explosively.

'I've decided to stay on a few extra days. Shopping,' she explained sweetly.

'Be on that plane, Natalie,' Ryan directed hardily. 'Or answer to the consequences!'

'What else can you do to me?' she queried simply. Suddenly her act of defiance seemed to lose its appeal. 'You have Michelle,' she continued quietly. 'That alone should be sufficient guarantee that I'll return. Andrea wants to do some shopping, and I'd like to be with her. I'll be back on Tuesday.' She replaced the receiver before he had a chance to comment, and she stood in reflective silence.

What on earth was the matter with her? She wanted to be with Ryan more than anything in the world, yet she had just postponed her return by a further forty-eight hours.

With total disregard for any restraint, Natalie dragged Andrea through a multitude of boutiques on a shopping spree that saw her purchasing another suitcase in which to pack the selection of clothes, shoes and various other sundry items she had bought. Credit cards were produced with careless abandon, and she didn't once give a thought to the size of the bills Ryan would receive as a result. Any pangs of guilt were quickly dampened by the knowledge that he could well afford it!

However, a sense of trepidation descended as the powerful jet touched down at Coolangatta on Tuesday evening, and the butterflies in her stomach began an erratic painful tattoo as she crossed the tarmac with her fellow passengers and entered the airport lounge.

Natalie scanned the large room and its occupants, searching for a familiar head, praying inwardly that it might be Jenkins and not Ryan who had come to meet her. Then a tiny hysterical laugh burst forth from her lips. Maybe no one had come, and she would have to utilise the airport bus to Surfer's Paradise, and catch a taxi home!

It was at that precise moment that she glimpsed a well-groomed head atop a pair of powerful shoulders, and even as she began making her way towards him, Ryan turned and she caught the full force of his tigerish gaze.

All she wanted to do was run and be engulfed in his embrace and feel the warmth of his mouth against her own, but as she drew close she could see a hardness evident in those topaz depths that precluded an affectionate reunion.

Somehow she summoned a smile, an artificial concession that was a mere facsimile, and walked at his side when he crossed to retrieve her bags from the luggage bay.

'I had a wonderful time,' Natalie evinced to no one in particular, and incurred a dark slanting glance.

'I expected another suitcase, at least,' Ryan allowed in an indolent mocking drawl.

'I'm not by nature a big spender,' she offered in explanation. 'However, I'll endeavour to do better next time.'

They reached the car, and Natalie slipped into the passenger seat while Ryan slung her bags into the boot, then he slid in beside her and switched the engine into powerful life.

'How is Michelle?'

'Struggling to stay awake when I left.' He eased out of the parking area and joined the steady stream of traffic moving north along the highway.

'I thought you might have brought her with you. I've missed her.'

'Undoubtedly,' he allowed dryly.

She gave him a quick glance. 'Is that meant to convey censure?'

His shrug was slight. 'What makes you think that?'

Natalie smoothed a stray lock of hair back behind her ear, and let her attention centre on the road ahead. 'You were angry I stayed on an extra few days.'

'Not exactly,' he replied in clipped tones. 'I

don't begrudge you time spent with Andrea, or for that matter, a shopping expedition. I was annoyed because you used it as an excuse for a further act of defiance.'

'You'd prefer me to be an amenable, meek little mouse,' she proclaimed bleakly, and incurred a deep husky laugh by way of response.

'God forbid!'

'And yet there was a time when I bowed to your every wish,' she mused pensively, then slanted him a deep probing glance. 'Now, I seem hell-bent on providing provocation at the least invitation.'

'You do, indeed,' Ryan drawled. 'Have you given a thought to the reason *why*, I wonder?'

Natalie grimaced slightly in the semi-darkness. 'You're the one with all the answers. *You* tell me.'

'Oh no, my sweet. That's one discovery you're going to have to make all on your own.'

There was nothing adequate she could think of by way of reply, and she refrained from commenting for the remainder of the drive home. Ryan, too, appeared in a reflective mood, and after reaching Cronin Island he garaged the car, took her bags from the boot, and followed her indoors.

Jenkins took charge of the luggage at that point, and Ryan indicated the lounge with an indolent sweep of his arm.

'Let's have a drink. I could do with one.'

Natalie stifled the refusal that sprang to her lips, and managed a slight smile. 'I'd like to look in on Michelle first.' She moved towards the stairs, and spared him a glance over her shoulder. 'I'll have something long and cool. I won't be long.' She almost ran upstairs in her haste to escape his disturbing presence, hating herself for the way her contrary senses were behaving at the sight and nearness of him. Wanting to appear cool, calm and collected, she was a shivering mass of nerves knowing that an hour or two from now she would be in his bed.

The door to Michelle's room was closed, and Natalie carefully turned the knob so as not to disturb the little girl as she lay sleeping, her small face angelic in repose, a doll and golliwog flanking her slight body as she lay beneath the covering sheet. A shaft of exultant emotion shot through Natalie as she gazed her fill before bending to bestow the softest of fleeting kisses to the tiny brow, then, content, she retraced her steps and closed the door quietly behind her.

Ryan was standing indolently at ease on the far side of the lounge when she entered it a few brief minutes later, and she crossed to his side and took the glass from his outstretched hand.

'If it's too strong, let me know and I'll add more soda,' he murmured, and she couldn't discern much from his engimatic expression as she took a tentative sip.

'Thank you. It's fine.'

He took a long swallow from the contents of his glass, then cast her an oddly speculative glance. 'I have to fly to the States tomorrow for a few days. Business, I'm afraid. Rick Andreas is coming with me.'

'The wheels of big business, one presumes?'

'What else?' Ryan parried with assumed urbanity, although his eyes were keenly alert, and she proffered a sweet smile.

'I like Lisa. I'll give her a call while you're away, and maybe we can get together for coffee.'

He gave a slight indicative nod of approval. 'She'd enjoy that.'

There was a lengthy silence, and one Natalie felt

she had to break. 'How was Michelle while I was away?'

'Fine. No problems.' His slow smile did strange things to her composure. 'She's a beautiful, well-mannered child.'

Her eyes flickered upward. 'Am I supposed to take that as a compliment?'

'Why not?'

'My goodness,' she managed with every semblance of humour, 'a compliment from the great man himself !'

'Don't be sassy,' he cautioned. 'I may just retaliate!'

'Is that a threat or a promise?'

'Whichever way you choose to take it,' he drawled, and Natalie emptied the contents of her glass in one long swallow before replacing it down on to a nearby table.

'If you'll excuse me, I'm going to take a shower, then go to bed. It's been an exhausting week.'

'No doubt you're relieved at the outcome of your father's operation?'

'Of course,' Natalie responded at once, meeting his penetrating gaze. 'I have to thank you.'

'I shall see that you do,' he slanted lazily, and she felt an unwelcome blush tinge her cheeks.

'Naturally,' she added with droll cynicism, 'I fully expect to have to pay my—er—*dues*, shall we say?'

For a split second his eyes flashed brilliant golden fire, then he bade mockingly, 'Go up to bed, Natalie. I'll join you soon.'

A strangled sound left her throat, then without a further word she turned and walked from the room, gained the stairs, then the upper floor, before closing the door to their room and leaned against it.

Slowly her eyes encompassed the large room with its magnificent furnishings before coming to rest on the silken spread covering the bed. A faint grimace pulled the edges of her mouth. Bed—or rather, *Ryan's* bed—was the reason for her downfall. For it was there that she came alive, exulting in the touch of his hand, his lips, eager to please and be pleased—lost and mindless in the tumult of emotion only he could arouse. It was earth-shattering that one man possessed such power—equally devastating to realise that it could be taken away, as it had three years ago. Yet she had survived. Or had she? She had functioned during that time, but only barely. Now she was akin to a ball back in play on the court, totally at the mercy of the players who directed it, yet at odds at being given no choice.

With a drawn-out sigh she crossed the room and went into the bathroom, discarding clothes with unaccustomed slowness as she turned on the shower, then she stepped beneath its warm spray to cleanse her skin and ease the tension that had set up a slow throbbing ache at the base of her nape.

The whole of life was a game, she mused as she lathered soap over every inch of her body. Something that was manipulated by /fate—forces over which there was no control.

If she had never accompanied her friends on holiday to Surfer's Paradise more than three years ago, she wouldn't have met Ryan, and by now she would quite possibly be happily married to someone else. Or maybe she would have made a career for herself and have travelled beyond the fringes of this large continent.

A long shiver slid down her spine, and with a shaky hand she reached out and turned off the

water, then sought a nearby towel with which to
dry herself. The thought of never having known
Ryan was enough to throw her into a state of
confused introspection, and the knowledge made
her angry. How was it possible to love and hate a
man both at the same time? It was crazy!

Towelled dry, she completed her toilette, then
slipped a silky nightgown over her head, and
emerged into the bedroom to slide beneath the
covers. A hand reached out and switched off the
bedside lamp, then she closed her eyes against the
darkness and drifted within minutes into a
dreamless sleep, oblivious to the man who slid in
beside her some hours later, and when she woke it
was daylight, with the sun filtering warmly
through the closed curtains, and all that remained
as evidence of her bed having been shared was the
thrown-back covers and an imprint on the
adjoining pillow.

Natalie greeted Ryan's absence with a sense of
relief, grateful for the breathing space it provided.
If it hadn't been for her palatial surroundings she
could almost believe the past few weeks were a
figment of her imagination. Her routine assumed
its previous pattern, in that she devoted most of
her time to Michelle's welfare as she sought to
instil a rudimentary learning programme in
preparation for when the little girl would attend
kindergarten. She made it a sharing, caring
experience and delighted in her daughter's response.

More than anything, Natalie wanted Michelle to
grow up as normally as possible—something that
would prove difficult when evidence of wealth was
all around her. It would be too easy to shower
gifts and possessions with careless abandon, and in

so doing allow her daughter to believe she could demand anything at will. A careful balance must be preserved at all costs, otherwise a spoilt little termagant would be the result.

Jenkins' presence behind the wheel of the powerful Daimler merely added to the reality of Ryan's status, and Natalie dismissed his insistence to act as chauffeur with a negligent wave of her hand.

'I'm quite capable of driving,' she added in an attempt to appease him. 'My Queensland licence is still current, and besides,' she paused, wrinkling her nose with an impish grin, 'you maintain the illusion of grandeur. If I don't adopt a down-to-earth approach, Michelle will mistakenly believe she's a princess at least!'

'I've been instructed to accompany you,' Jenkins persisted in mild rebuke, and Natalie gave a wry grimace.

'Any particular reason why?'

The manservant chose his words carefully. 'Unemployment is high among the youths frequenting the surfing beaches. They need money to support their carefree lifestyle, and many arrive from out-of-State full of dreams and soon have little more than empty pockets. Security among the wealthy residents is a necessity, not an indulgence.'

Natalie put her head slightly to one side, and subjected him to a steady scrutiny. 'Are you trying to suggest that kidnapping, or abduction, is a possibility?'

'My presence is a precaution against any eventuality,' he responded evenly, and she shook her head slowly.

'I think you're being overly dramatic. This isn't Europe, and Ryan isn't that much of a plutocrat—is he?'

'It isn't my position to comment, except to request you allow me to follow his wishes.'

'Orders, don't you mean?'

'Very well—orders.'

She drew a shaky hand through her hair. 'And if I choose to disregard them?'

'I strongly advise against it,' he responded quietly, and she threw up her hands in a gesture of mute despair.

'Jenkins! I don't want to get you into any trouble, but honestly, all I want to do is browse among the shops in town, then perhaps drive to one of the amusement parks—even explore the outskirts, like Nerang.' Her eyes beseeched him to understand. 'I can't keep you hanging around for most of the day at my beck and call. It isn't fair,' she protested. 'You have plenty of other more worthwhile things to do.'

'Looking after your welfare, and that of your daughter, is what I'm paid to do.'

'As well as attending to the grounds, maintaining all three cars, the shopping——' Natalie reeled off in a rush. 'How can you do any of those things if you're out with me for most of the day?'

'There are any number of private contractors on call for maintenance of the grounds. Ryan's orders were most specific. You have first priority.' Jenkins tempered the words with a kindly smile, but she wasn't amused.

'No matter what he says, I won't be treated like a pampered pet,' she muttered in retort, then offered a conciliatory smile. 'It has nothing to do with you personally. I really enjoy your company.'

'Then why not comply?'

'Because it's a matter of principle,' Natalie insisted stubbornly.

'The car will be ready if you'd care to let me know what time you want to leave.'

'Oh!' she expelled her breath in an angry sigh. 'You're just as bad as he is!'

'It's for your own protection, Natalie. Please believe that,' the older man said gently, and she shrugged her shoulders in defeat.

'If you insist. Shall we say—half an hour?'

The morning was pleasant, with Michelle on her best behaviour, so that the time passed with amazing speed as they strolled through the many arcades before venturing on to the beach for a walk along the sandy foreshore.

As a threesome, they were the recipients of more than idle speculation from several passers-by, and Natalie felt a light laugh erupt with gurgling mirth.

'They're not sure what to make of us,' she giggled softly. 'Are you my father? A doting uncle, perhaps? My—er—benefactor? Or my husband, so much more mature than I, and whom I could only possibly have married for money. For shame!' she mocked, unabashed.

'I prefer to think of you as the daughter I never had,' Jenkins said gently, and she stopped in her tracks and turned towards him.

'Why, Jenkins, how very sweet!' On impulse she leant forward a gave his cheek a quick kiss. 'I'm flattered.'

'I must say how pleased I am that you're back with Ryan again. Martha and I were very upset when you left.'

'It was—just one of those things,' she said a trifle sadly.

There was a slight pause, then he said quietly, 'I'm sorry if I offended you.'

'Good grief, how could you do that?'

'By mentioning something that's none of my business.'

She gave a slight shrug. 'It's all water under the bridge, Jenkins. What counts is that we're together.'

'Have you any plans for this afternoon?'

It was a tactful attempt to divert the conversation, and Natalie was grateful.

'Oh, I'm sure I'll manage to think of something,' she grinned, and he gave a warm smile.

'If you've had enough of the beach, may I suggest we walk along the Esplanade?'

She spared him a quick encompassing glance, then burst into laughter. 'You long-suffering man—I bet you've got sand in your shoes! Own up!'

'You're right,' he grimaced ruefully. 'I'm not exactly dressed for this particular caper.'

'Then back to civilisation and asphalt paving,' Natalie grinned, and scooping Michelle into her arms she turned and led the way to a short flight of steps on her left.

They were about to turn into Orchid Avenue when a bright voice hailed them, and Natalie turned at once to see an attractively dressed young woman crossing the road towards them.

'Lisa, how nice to see you,' she greeted warmly, and received an answering smile in response.

'Likewise. And this must be Michelle.' She gave the little girl a teasing grin. 'Have you been in town long?'

'About an hour and a half,' Jenkins told her, and Lisa tilted her head to one side.

'Would you consider joining me for lunch?'

'I'd love to, but this young lady has a sleep directly after her midday meal,' Natalie proffered with regret, and Jenkins intervened mildly,

'If I might make a suggestion? Allow me to take Michelle home. Martha can feed her and put her to bed, and you can ring me when you want to be brought home.'

'How about it?' asked Lisa, her eyes twinkling with enthusiasm, and Natalie accepted without demur.

'We'll walk to the car,' she declared, her spirits lifting at the thought of a few hours spent in Lisa's company. It would be nice to talk to someone her own age, browse among the boutiques without being conscious of Michelle's distracting presence.

The little girl didn't blink an eyelid on being strapped into her car-seat, and smiled as she waved goodbye when the large car drew away from its parking space.

'Martha and Jenkins have become surrogate parents,' Natalie told him. 'Or perhaps I should amend that to a combination of grandparents and babysitters-in-chief.'

'Do you mind?'

'Not really,' she said. 'It takes a little getting used to. I've had her all to myself for almost two and a half years.'

'Is there anywhere you'd like to go in particular for lunch?' Lisa questioned, and Natalie grinned.

'There are so many new restaurants I'm unaware of, so you lead, and I'll simply follow.'

'You might regret that statement. I have a penchant for seafood, so be warned,' Lisa declared lightly.

'Seafood is fine.'

They ordered a light Moselle, and sipped it tentatively while perusing the menu, then ordered after a leisurely deliberation.

'I've been meaning to call you,' Lisa began. 'I guess you know Rick has gone with Ryan to the States?'

'He did mention it, yes.'

'I was going with them, but flying is out at the moment.' Her eyes positively sparkled. 'It's considered unwise at this crucial stage of pregnancy.'

Natalie's response was genuinely warm. 'I imagine Rick is very pleased.'

'Faintly bemused,' Lisa amended. 'With a history of twins on both sides of the family, I've been warned there's a likelihood I'll follow suit. It's a little too soon to tell, but I'm mentally prepared to buy two of everything!'

The waiter served them each with a starter of prawn salad, refilled their glasses, and discreetly retreated.

'Mmm,' Lisa accorded with evident enjoyment. 'I'll have to watch what I eat, otherwise I'll be adding a few extra unwanted kilos!'

'You're as slim as a reed,' Natalie declared, and the other girl laughed.

'Only because I endeavour to stay that way. Too much indulgence, and I'll have to buy a new wardrobe.'

'I'm sure Rick wouldn't mind,' Natalie opined idly, and gave her attention to the delectable food placed before her. Crumbed scallops and salad greens excellently prepared were a delight to the palate, and followed by a compôte of fresh fruit topped with a dollop of cream served to complete an extremely enjoyable meal.

'Coffee?'

'I don't think I could find room for it, now,' Natalie sighed. 'Perhaps we could have one later?'

'Good idea. Now, I'll take care of the bill,' Lisa determined, and as Natalie made to demur, she smilingly shook her head. 'I insist. Next time I'll allow you to do the honours.'

'In that case, I'll give in gracefully.'

Once outside, they walked to the nearest arcade and idly browsed among the several boutiques before heading for a nearby coffee lounge sporting umbrellaed tables set up outdoors.

'Ah, this is nice.' Lisa sank into a chair and smiled at Natalie. 'We must do this fairly often.'

'I'd love to. Really,' Natalie assured her, and the other girl broke into an engaging grin.

'Rick and Ryan have been friends, as well as business associates, for a long time. It's an added bonus that their respective wives get on well together.' Lisa wrinkled her nose and gave a slight grimace. 'A lot of the women I meet socially are superficial and too wrapped up in themselves to be interested in anyone or anything else.'

'I couldn't agree more,' Natalie said with feeling. 'I can't help thinking I'm on display.'

Lisa laughed. 'You, too?' She gave a slight shrug. 'The first few months after I married Rick are something I wouldn't want to repeat.'

Natalie sipped the last of her coffee and replaced her cup down on to its saucer, enjoying the slight breeze that had sprung up.

'I'm afraid I'm going to have to leave within the next few minutes,' Lisa excused herself regretfully as she spared a glance at her watch. 'I've an appointment with my gynaecologist. His rooms are not far from here.' She drained her coffee and stood to her feet. 'The men are due back the day after tomorrow. I'll get Rick to arrange something with Ryan, and we'll get together for dinner. I'll ring and let you know.'

Natalie caught hold of her shoulderbag and paid the hovering waitress, then walked with Lisa to the main highway where they parted to go in opposite directions.

It was such a nice day—too nice to bother

Jenkins again with the car. In any case, she felt like walking, and it wasn't far. The exercise would do her good!

She set off at a leisurely pace and reached the Chevron bridge, glimpsing the sparkling waters of the river flowing below as she crossed to the other side. Small craft sped noisily towards the river's mouth, and there was a cruise boat in the distance en route to the many waterways that were a tourist feature of the Coast.

The main shopping centre on Chevron Island was busy with traffic, and she took care before crossing at a main intersection, then turned into the street leading to Cronin Island.

She hadn't walked one block when a slight noise alerted her attention, and turning, she caught sight of a car travelling at considerable speed very close to the kerb. It was a large nondescript sedan with tinted windows, and a split second later she gave a cry of alarm as it appeared to head straight for her, neither slowing nor attempting to stop.

It had to be out of control, and in a moment of blind horror she sidestepped out of its oncoming path, feeling a rush of air whoosh past as she fell to the ground.

Then it was gone, and she lay still, unaware of any pain, but feeling slightly dazed and very shaken. Slowly she rose to her feet and reached down to retrieve her shoulderbag, then she cast a glance up the street to see if there were any witnesses, but there were none. Not a solitary soul in sight! she thought hysterically.

Gingerly she stepped forward. The small bridge leading to Cronin Island was just up ahead beyond the slight curve in the road, and once she reached that she was barely one hundred metres from home.

Five minutes later she pressed the intercom button beside the locked gates, and leaned against the solid concrete wall as she waited for Jenkins or Martha to answer.

'Marshall residence. Would you please state your name?'

'It's Natalie, Martha,' she said shakily. 'Can you let me in?'

'Good heavens——'

Those were the last words she heard as a black inky void descended, and she slid to the ground in a crumpled heap.

CHAPTER NINE

WHEN Natalie came to she was lying in bed, and there was a strange man holding her hand.

'Who are you?' Did she speak those words? They sounded strange, almost as if they belonged to someone else, and as for her head—it felt light and woolly, not her own at all!

'Dr Henson, Mrs Marshall,' he told her quietly. 'How do you feel?'

'I'm not sure,' she owned shakily, and he gave a slight smile of reassurance.

'I'll conduct a thorough examination now that you're awake. Are you in any pain?'

Was she? She moved cautiously, but nothing hurt. 'No.'

'Can you remember what happened?'

Natalie gave a brief nod, then revealed what had transpired. Martha stood in the background, her kind features creased with anxiety, and Natalie spared her a smile. 'I'm all right—honestly. Just a bit shaken.'

'We'll see, shall we?' The doctor began his examination, and when it was completed he stood to his feet and closed his bag. 'You've been very lucky, in my opinion. A few grazes, some bruising, and shock. Bedrest for the next eighteen hours,' he instructed, then gave a slight smile. 'You'll have a few aches and pains tomorrow, but I'll check on those when I call in the morning.'

Natalie's lids flickered wide. 'Is that necessary?'

'I'm sure Mr Marshall will think so,' he declared, then he turned towards Martha. 'There's no concussion, but if you're concerned at all, you have my number.'

Jenkins could be seen hovering in the hall as Martha opened the door, and Natalie shook her head in disbelief. 'Such a fuss! I'm perfectly fine. You heard the doctor.'

'Would you like something to drink? A nice hot cup of tea with plenty of sugar will do you good,' the older woman suggested as she crossed to the bed.

'Is Michelle still asleep?' On receiving an affirmative nod, Natalie gave a sigh of relief. 'Thank heavens for that! I suppose Jenkins carried me inside?'

'That he did,' Martha declared. 'You gave us both the shock of our lives!'

'It was such a nice day, I thought I'd walk,' Natalie explained. 'I didn't anticipate being the inadvertent victim of some lunatic driver.'

'Ryan won't be pleased.'

'Does he have to know?'

Martha slowly shook her head. 'Jenkins is going to put a call through as soon as the doctor leaves. I'll go and make that tea. I could do with a cup myself!'

With a bit of luck, Ryan would be unreachable and therefore remain in ignorance until his return home. Natalie did a swift mental calculation, and came up with Saturday—which was *tomorrow*.

Despite all opposition, Martha insisted on serving Natalie dinner on a tray in bed, and afterwards Michelle was allowed to visit her for a while. The little girl's eyes were huge as she stood solemnly beside the bed, and it took some persuasion before she could be led to her own room across the hall.

Natalie idly leafed through some magazines

Martha provided, but she couldn't settle to do more than scan a few of the articles before discarding one glossy scribe after another. Even the portable television Jenkins had set up on a stand at the end of the bed didn't hold her interest for long, and shortly after eight she slipped out of bed and went into the bathroom with the intention of having a shower. A few aches were beginning to make themselves felt as the bruising started to come out, and the hot water would surely ease them a little.

Her eyes fell on the oval bathtub with its gold-plated taps, the bottles of essence, and she changed her mind. A quick turn of her wrist and water gushed out of the taps, filling the room with steam, and she added essence before slipping out of her nightgown, then she stepped into the hot fragrant water.

She soaked until the water cooled and she was on the verge of adding more hot water when there was a soft knock at the door.

'Ryan is on the phone,' Martha called, and Natalie gave a prodigious sigh.

'Tell him I'm in the bath.' She knew it wouldn't make the slightest difference, but maybe she could put off the inevitable.

'He insists on speaking to you,' the older woman declared.

'Couldn't I be asleep? I don't feel up to answering a whole lot of questions.'

'Jenkins has already given him all the details. Being so far away, it's only natural he wants to hear from you personally.'

Natalie stood up and reached for a towel, and after drying most of the excess moisture from her body she wrapped the towel sarong-wise round her slim curves and opened the door.

Martha's face showed concern, and a certain amount of compassion. 'Get back into bed. There's an extension there.' Her smile was kindly. 'I'll bring up some warm milk and brandy. It will help you sleep.'

Natalie crossed to the bed and sat down, then with a sense of trepidation she reached for the receiver. 'Ryan? How are you?'

'More to the point—how are *you*?' His voice held restrained anger, and she resorted to flippancy by way of defense.

'I'm still in one piece, if that's what you want to know. No damage to report, just a few scratches and some bruising. In other words, I'm fine.'

'Bill Henson assures me you were fortunate to have come off so lightly,' he drawled, and she demanded incredulously—

'Did you ring him?'

'Of course. Did you expect me not to?'

'Why? Jenkins gave a full report.'

'Assuredly,' Ryan said abruptly. 'He rang me immediately.'

Natalie changed the receiver to her other hand and pushed back her hair from where it had fallen to cover part of her face. 'It had nothing to do with Jenkins,' she began quietly. 'I hope you haven't implied that he was in any way to blame.'

'Dammit, Natalie,' he groaned softly, 'why *walk* home, for God's sake?'

His tone made her stomach muscles contract with tension, and a slow-burning anger came to the surface in retaliation. 'Can't you leave the post-mortem until tomorrow? Your concern is gratifying, but quite honestly, you're giving me a headache!'

His muffled oath was barely audible, and she didn't wait for him to comment further. 'I'm rather tired. Goodnight.' With that she replaced the receiver, then sat staring at the phone half expecting it to ring, and when after several minutes it didn't, she rose and extracted a nightgown, then returned and slid into bed.

'I've brought you some Paracetamol tablets to ease the pain,' Martha told her as she entered the room. 'Make sure you drink the milk. If you take my advice, you'll try to get some sleep.'

Natalie pulled a face, but obediently took the glass from the proffered tray. 'I feel like a child,' she grumbled, tempering the words with a slight smile.

'I'm going to sleep in the next room. Then if you need anything, or Michelle wakes during the night, I'll be close by.'

The older woman's kindness overwhelmed her, and her eyes filled with tears. 'Thank you.' She took the glass and sipped its contents, swallowed the tablets, then when the glass was empty she placed it on to the tray and slid down into a comfortable position. 'I feel drowsy already,' she murmured. 'Goodnight. And—thank you,' she added gently. 'You're very kind.'

When Natalie woke in the morning she felt stiff and sore. The slightest movement made her wince with pain, and she ran a tub full of hot water in which to soak.

Martha brought her breakfast shortly after eight, and Michelle put in an appearance the minute she was permitted. Dr Henson called at nine, examined her and pronounced her fit enough to get up after lunch.

The day passed slowly, although as evening drew near Natalie was aware of a build-up of nervous tension. Ryan's arrival was imminent, and she dreaded the initial confrontation. Jenkins left with the car at eight, and within minutes she elected to retire upstairs on the pretext of going to bed.

It was sheer cowardice, she knew, but the thought of facing him was more than she could bear. With a bit of luck, she would be asleep when he returned.

Instead, she tossed and turned, unable to get comfortable, and instead of relaxing, she grew more tense with every passing minute.

The lights of the car as it swung into the driveway threw a momentary beam that reflected through the drapes at the window, filling the room with a subdued glow, then it was gone, and she turned on her side, facing away from the door in the hope that when he did enter the room he would assume she was asleep.

It didn't work that way, and she cursed herself for being such a fool in thinking that it might.

Minutes later the door opened and she sensed rather than heard him come in. A switch clicked as the bedside lamp sprang to light, then the side of the bed depressed with his weight.

'Natalie?'

Pretence was an ineffectual weapon, and she didn't attempt to use it. 'I was trying to get to sleep.'

'I'm sure you were,' Ryan drawled enigmatically, and she responded waspishly,

'Then why disturb me?'

'Your claws are showing, kitten,' he mocked sardonically, and leaning towards her he placed a hand either side of her shoulders. 'I do believe you're all right, after all.'

'Do you want to inspect the evidence? Count every scratch and bruise?' she demanded tritely, and heard his soft chuckle.

'What an interesting idea. Would you comply, I wonder?'

'Like hell!' she responded inelegantly, and swallowed the sudden lump that rose to her throat as his fingers trailed down her cheek.

'My sweet little idiot,' he murmured gently. 'I'm almost afraid to leave you alone. Do you know how fortunate you were not to be seriously hurt?'

'I'm sorry if I caused you concern,' she said stiffly, and Ryan gave an audible groan, then bent low to place his mouth against the side of her neck.

'Next time I go away, I'm taking you with me. At least then I can keep an eye on you.'

'I'm not a child to be watched and guarded every waking moment,' she retorted, then was unable to say anything further as his mouth moved to close over her own in a kiss that was gently possessive.

Minutes later he gathered her on to his lap, and she was unable to prevent a faint gasp of pain as his hands closed over her ribs.

She saw his eyes narrow, then her own widened into huge grey pools as he carefully slid aside the straps of her nightgown.

'Sweet mother in heaven!' Ryan breathed emotively as he caught sight of the dark bruises over most of her ribcage. 'Are there any more like that?'

'I haven't really looked,' Natalie professed, then she gave a startled gasp as he leant down and gently kissed each and every mark. It was a tantalisingly evocative experience, and one that stirred her senses, bringing them alive until they pulsated with latent warmth.

'In a few days' time, we're going away,' Ryan told her quietly. 'Just the two of us. Rick owns a small island off the Great Barrier Reef. It's remote, yet possesses an excellent deep anchorage harbour. Jenkins will stock up the cruiser, and we'll spend a few lazy days on board. Does that hold any appeal?'

The thought of spending every hour in each twenty-four with him sounded warning bells of a kind Natalie daren't ignore. He was capable of weaving his own potent brand of magic— something she could deal with in small doses. But several days was something else, let alone the *nights*!

'Indulge me, Natalie,' he smiled gently. 'I'm in need of a holiday.'

She swallowed compulsively, knowing that fate played a large part in her destiny. What lay between them had to be resolved one way or another. 'In that case,' she said shakily, 'who am I to refuse?'

The cruiser edged its way along the Nerang River, then negotiated the tricky channels by the Spit before heading north.

It was a beautiful day, hot, yet a light breeze did much to ease the sting of the sun's rays.

Natalie had elected to wear a bikini, with a wrap-around skirt which could be removed if it got too hot later on. Ryan looked totally at ease at the controls, his powerful torso bare except for a pair of cotton shorts. Despite working indoors he had managed to acquire a deep tan, and the sight of him almost took her breath away.

She felt relaxed and at ease, almost as if these few days held something special. It was strange, but she knew that whatever had happened before had become a thing of the past. There was only *now*, and the prospect of their future together.

It took five hours to reach the small island—one among so many others, that Natalie wondered how Ryan could possibly claim it to be their intended destination.

'Shall we eat?' she asked as he secured the controls and released the anchor.

'Hungry, are you?' Ryan smiled, and she wrinkled her nose at him.

'Aren't you?'

'Hmm—but not for food.' His glance roved over her slim curves with apparent appreciation, and she blushed at his intended meaning.

'I'm not sure this holiday is a good idea. All this fresh air and sunshine, with too much time on our hands and nothing to do.'

Ryan's eyes were filled with laughter as he gazed at her. 'I can think of plenty!'

She reached for her discarded towel and bunched it into a ball and threw it at him. 'Wretch! I'm going down into the galley to prepare some lunch. You can watch the seagulls.'

'I'd much rather watch *you*.'

Shaking her head slowly, she turned and made for the short flight of steps leading down into the well-appointed cabin. She took iced cans from the refrigerator, lemonade for herself and beer for Ryan, then set about making a salad to go with the cold meat Martha had provided. Crunchy bread rolls completed the meal, and she set the small table with a cloth before adding cutlery, then called that it was ready.

'Mmm, that looks good,' Ryan murmured as he slid his lengthy frame into the cushioned seat, and she gave a slight shrug.

'It isn't Cordon Bleu fare, but it should taste all right.'

'As good as you?'

'Really, you have a one-track mind!' She slid in opposite him and picked up her knife and fork.

'The wounds of the past go deep. Too deep, Natalie?'

The softness of his voice was deceptive, but there was no advantage in pretending. 'A week ago I would have said yes,' she began slowly.

'And now?'

'I don't know.' She looked at him, meeting his steady gaze, and offered quietly, 'A lot has happened since I came back. I need time to think.'

'We also need to talk.'

There was a measurable silence, and one Ryan broke by stating irrefutably, 'First, let's get rid of the largest bogey of all—Simone.' His gaze was startlingly direct.

Natalie took a sip of lemonade in an attempt to give herself the breathing space necessary. 'Perhaps it's best left alone,' she voiced a trifle shakily.

'I don't agree.'

'Couldn't we leave it until tomorrow?' Or the day after, or maybe not at all, she begged silently, not sure she wanted to pursue the subject. It brought back too many painful memories.

'That particular young woman almost destroyed our marriage,' he voiced hardily.

'That was a long time ago,' she said steadfastly. 'I was very young—not only in years, but in experience.'

'I was confident I could shield you from anything and everything,' Ryan said quietly, and she drew a deep calming breath.

'Simone can be very convincing.'

'You ran away. Have you any conception what I went through trying to find you?'

There was one question she had to ask, and courage gave her the necessary impetus. 'Did you never once consider divorce?'

His eyes didn't waver. 'No '

'I—see,' she said slowly, and he gave a wry smile.

'Do you, Natalie?'

Her eyes became faintly pensive, and she flicked back a stray lock of hair in a purely defensive gesture. 'I feel as if I'm caught up in a whirlpool!'

His eyes gleamed with devilish humour, and a husky laugh sounded deep in his throat. 'You'll come out of it soon. I give you my word.'

The weather proved idyllic, and although a few clouds banked up in the sky, the sun triumphed, bestowing in its benevolence a warm basking glow.

Natalie fished with Ryan, teasing him mercilessly when her catch outweighed his, and they swam, sunbathed, ate, made love, then when the sun went down they made love again, delighting in the pleasure each was able to give the other.

On the third day they lifted anchor and made for the northern point of Stradbroke Island, where they spent a further two days, then regretfully set a course for home.

CHAPTER TEN

MICHELLE was overjoyed to see them, and Ryan listened to her childish, and for the most part indistinguishable chatter with apparent solemnity, sparing Natalie a quick musing gleam across the table as he endeavoured to give his daughter and his breakfast equal attention.

Natalie was unable to prevent the faint tingling blush that stole over her cheeks as she met his smiling gaze, and her eyes were wise and luminous when he rose to his feet minutes later and bestowed a brief hard kiss prior to leaving the house.

Michelle scrambled on to her knee and reached for a finger of toast left on Natalie's plate, consuming it with relish. 'Daddy gone to work,' she chanted in a sweet sing-song voice, and Natalie hugged the small body close.

'Yes, darling. He'll be back in time for tea.'

Solemn wide eyes regarded her unblinkingly. 'We stay home?'

'Well,' Natalie deliberated with a wide smile, 'we could go out, if you like. Suppose we get Jenkins to take us to the shopping centre close to Broadbeach?'

'Cake and fishes,' Michelle declared promptly, and Natalie laughed, hugging her close.

'Very well, imp. We'll have lunch out on the verandah of the coffee shop so that you can watch the fishes in the pond. Then home for a nap, okay?'

' 'kay,' the tot agreed engagingly.

They left shortly after ten-thirty in the Daimler with Jenkins at the wheel and were deposited outside one of the large department stores in the Pacific Fair shopping complex.

'Twelve-thirty will be fine,' Natalie advised as the older man retrieved Michelle's stroller from the boot and set it upright on the pavement.

'I'll be here before that, just in case the little one gets overtired.' He smiled and returned Michelle's wave before slipping in behind the wheel, and Natalie slung the strap of her bag over her shoulder and eased her way with the stroller towards the complex centre.

It was a beautiful day. The sun was hot, but not unpleasantly so. Shoppers wandered the bricked lanes without any sense of haste, and Natalie kept their pace, pausing now and then to browse at an attractive window display before moving on.

'Drink,' Michelle began, adding a plaintive, 'please!'

They were close to a replica of a Cotswold cottage which specialised in Devonshire cream teas and had several tables and chairs set up outdoors beneath a large canopy, and Natalie crossed the small bridge beneath which water flowed from a picturesque waterwheel towards the main pond. She chose a table close to the fenced area and set Michelle on a chair where she could see the goldfish, then ordered a can of lemonade and an iced coffee.

They had visited this complex on two previous occasions, and now she listened attentively as Michelle pointed with excitement to one par-ticularly large red fish they had affectionately named 'Granddaddy'. The fact that there were several fish equally large was something Natalie didn't reveal. There was time enough for the loss of childish fantasy.

The drink consumed, they completed a circle of the shops before heading for the terraced verandah overlooking the pond for lunch. The coffee lounge was well patronised, and after selecting sandwiches Natalie secured an empty table.

The past hour and a half had passed swiftly. In a further five hours Ryan would be home, and she was unable to still the faint smile that softened her lips at the thought his presence evoked. The few days they had spent on Rick's island had been idyllic, something she would treasure for the rest of her life. There was a tremendous feeling of well-being in having come full circle from love, through all the misunderstandings, the bitterness, to the wealth of happiness they now shared. Perhaps it was a lesson one had to learn in the school of life, she perceived, that love is a gift to be treated with the utmost care to ensure it continued to flourish. Something beyond the physical and spiritual emotions, becoming an inextricable entity inter-woven with trust and fidelity.

'More fish, Mummy!'

Natalie came out of her reverie, and smiled down at the little girl happily finishing the last of her sandwich. 'Yes, darling.' She drained her coffee, then steadied Michelle's glass so that it didn't spill. 'When you've had your drink we'd better go.' She spared a glance at her watch and saw that it was almost twelve-thirty. 'Jenkins will be waiting for us.'

He was, but with the utmost patience, and Michelle obediently scrambled into her car-seat, her face wreathed in smiles as Natalie fastened the straps.

The stroller placed in the boot, Jenkins slipped

behind the wheel, and almost immediately the little girl regaled him with the morning's events in a ceaseless childish spiel which lasted until the moment he brought the large vehicle to a halt in the driveway.

'Right, my girl,' Natalie grinned as she released the tot and scooped her into her arms. 'Face, hands, teeth, then into bed with you!' She walked to the door, then crossed the foyer towards the stairs. 'When you wake, we'll swim in the pool and I'll give you another lesson. Just think how surprised Daddy will be when he finds out you can swim.'

'Like the fishes,' Michelle giggled, and Natalie laughed and buried her face against the little girl's neck.

'You wriggle like a fish,' she declared as she set the child down to her feet in the bathroom. Within minutes she had her clean, then divested of outer clothing, she carried her through to the bedroom and slipped the small body between cool sheets before crossing to draw the drapes at the window. 'Sleep tight, angel.'

' 'bye, Mummy.'

Natalie retraced her steps to the lower ground floor where she collected a pad and pen with which to write a letter to her father and Andrea. Sliding open the screened door, she crossed the courtyard and sat down at one of the outdoor tables.

It was pleasantly warm beneath the shady canvas umbrella, and she flipped open the pad and began to record a newsy account of the past week, adding in detail various anecdotes related to Michelle.

'Excuse me, Natalie but there's someone to see you.'

She glanced up with faint surprise at the sound of Martha's voice, and caught the older woman's slight perplexion.

'It's Miss Vesey.'

Natalie gave a slight grimace, uttering a barely audible 'Damn!' as she laid down her pen. 'I suppose I can't be out?' she hazarded ruefully, not relishing the prospect of seeing Simone, let alone attempting to entertain her.

' 'fraid not, sweetie,' a brightly pitched voice drawled from the wide screen door, and into the sunshine walked its elegantly-clad owner. 'I decided not to wait,' she explained with considerable hauteur to Martha, then encountered Natalie with a wide brittle smile. 'After all, I know this house like the back of my hand.'

Martha's expression was civil, but only just, and her displeasure was evident by the faint tightening of her lips the instant before she turned back towards Natalie.

'Would you like me to bring something cool to drink?'

'Do that,' Simone instructed with a careless fluttering hand as she crossed to sit at the table opposite Natalie. 'You know what I usually have.'

The older woman was politely stoical. 'You'll have to refresh my memory, Miss Vesey. It's some time since you last visited this house.'

A soft tinkling laugh was at variance with the annoyance expressed in those brilliant dark eyes. 'Really, Martha,' she chided with a slight moue, 'there's no need to be discreet! Natalie knows all about Ryan's fascination for me.' She arched a sparkling glance towards her victim, and taunted, 'Don't you, darling?'

Dear Lord, what was this viperous witch up to? Natalie took in the over-bright eyes, the slender scarlet-tipped nails engaged in extracting a cigarette from its elegant gold case, and drew a deep steadying breath. If Simone had possessed the foreknowledge to time her attack for the previous week, it might have had the desired effect, but she was that many days too late.

'I'll have iced soda water, Martha,' Natalie said quietly. She needed a clear head to deal with the enemy—for Simone was surely that!

'Make mine vodka on ice with a splash of bitters and lime.'

Martha's obvious reluctance to leave them alone was oddly touching, and Natalie swung slowly back to meet Simone's brittle gaze.

'Is this a social visit?' Her voice was incredibly polite, and distant.

'My dear—*no*,' the other woman denied, and exhaling a stream of smoke into the air she leaned forward so that her elbows rested on the table. 'Surely you've guessed why I'm here?' A malevolent gleam lanced the distance between them. 'You're not exactly dumb.'

Natalie unconsciously eased back against her chair until she felt its support and endeavoured to appear relaxed. 'May I take that as a compliment?'

'You don't learn, do you?' Simone demanded acidly.

'On the contrary,' Natalie answered with considerable poise, 'I've learned a great deal.'

'Oh, I'll concede you're three years older,' her aggressor agreed with a derogatory laugh. 'But you're still incredibly naïve.'

'I think you'll find I'm somewhat more mature than you give me credit for,' Natalie managed evenly, treading the verbal distance with care.

Simone tilted her head slightly and fixed Natalie

with an unwavering stare that was unnerving to say the least. 'Really?'

The tension was broken by Martha's return, and Natalie gave the older woman a grateful smile as the tray of drinks was placed on the table.

'Would you care for something to eat? I've just taken a batch of scones from the oven.'

'Nothing,' Simone refused with chilling dismissal, and a perverse streak caused Natalie to voice with warm enthusiasm,

'I'd love one, split, with jam and cream, if it isn't too much trouble.'

'Of course not.

'Really, Natalie!' Simone chided with thinly-veiled sarcasm. 'Martha is merely a servant. Treat her like a friend, and you'll find she'll take over.'

Natalie picked up the frosted glass and took a long cool sip before replacing it back on to the table. 'Jenkins and Martha have been with Ryan for a long time,' she said steadily. 'As for running the house, Martha does that with the utmost efficiency, and completely to my satisfaction.'

Simone sipped at her vodka, and eyed Natalie with an odd speculative gleam over its rim. 'My, my! Perhaps you have grown up a little. Your claws are showing!'

You ain't seen nothing yet! Natalie jeered silently. A tiny smile lifted the edges of her mouth, and her eyes were clear and without guile. 'You'll find they're quite sharp.'

'Is that a warning of some sort?'

Natalie lifted her glass and took another appreciative sip before responding. 'If you care to think so.'

Anger tightened the other woman's face into an unattractive mask. 'I don't take threats lightly.'

Natalie's head lifted slightly as she met Simone's smouldering gaze. 'Neither do I.'

'How am I threatening you?'

'Aren't you?'

'You silly little bitch!' Simone snapped viciously. 'The only reason you're here is because of a stupid mistake.'

'Apparently I'm guilty of several,' Natalie said a trifle flippantly. 'Perhaps you'd care to elucidate?'

'Michelle,' the other declared succinctly. 'Your daughter, and supposedly Ryan's.' She gave a high-pitched laugh that sounded faintly off-key. 'In these modern times, you certainly goofed, didn't you, sweetie?' Her eyes glittered dangerously. 'Or was it all part of a carefully thought out plan?'

It was perhaps as well that Martha came on the scene at that precise moment, or Natalie's reserve of patience might have flown the coop!

'Will that be all?' the valued servant queried, her face creased with anxiety, and Simone snapped out,

'Oh, for God's sake! Leave us alone, will you?'

The older woman drew herself to her fullest height, and her bosom fairly quivered with rage. 'I take my orders from Mrs Marshall, not the likes of you!'

'Thank you for the scones, Martha,' Natalie said quietly, her eyes remarkably steady. 'Would you mind checking on Michelle for me? She's due to wake soon.'

For a moment Martha appeared doubtful whether she should leave, then ignoring Simone she gave Natalie a troubled smile. 'If she wakes, I'll keep her amused inside the house.'

'Do that,' Simone declared viciously. 'I can't stand little brats.'

Obviously that was too much for Martha, for
with considerable aplomb she turned and subjected
Simone to a raking stare. 'Praise God, Ryan had
the good sense not to marry you.'

'If he had, you certainly wouldn't still be here!'

Martha's mouth tightened into a thin line, then
exercising great restraint she made a dignified exit,
and the minute she was out of sight Simone burst
into furious speech.

'That woman is just too much!'

'I think you've outstayed your welcome,'
Natalie observed, standing to her feet. 'I'll see you
to the door.'

'I haven't said what I came to say.'

'Forgive me. I consider you've already said too
much.'

'Oh, darling, I haven't even started yet!'

Natalie refrained from saying so much as a
word, then after a measurable silence she sank
back into her chair. 'I'm all ears, Simone. Get
whatever it is off your chest, then leave.'

Out came the cigarettes and lighter, and not
until one slim tobacco tube was lit to her
satisfaction did the words flow.

'It's relatively simple. I want Ryan.'

Natalie's eyes were remarkably level as she
viewed the dark-haired sophisticated beauty. 'Does
Ryan want you?'

'I wouldn't be here if he didn't.'

'Am I supposed to fit in with your scheme and
lamely offer to divorce him?'

'It would help. However, he's wealthy enough to
employ someone to manufacture evidence against
you.'

'Adultery?'

An elegant stream of smoke slowly wafted
between them, and Simone reached for her half-

empty glass and proceeded to drain its contents. 'You catch on fast.'

'What if I won't comply?'

'You will. I supplied you with sufficient evidence three years ago. Your return hasn't changed anything.'

'Have you never heard the adage—"once bitten, twice shy"?'

'Are you going to be difficult?' Winged eyebrows arched with sardonic cynicism. 'I wouldn't advise it, sweetie.' A vengeful gleam entered Simone's eyes, making them appear malevolent and infinitely dangerous. 'Next time you're out walking I'll ensure you get more than a fright!'

Comprehension gave way to concern. 'You put my life at risk, deliberately! That's a criminal offence.'

'You'd have to prove it first.'

'You must want Ryan very badly,' Natalie said quietly, and Simone gave a hollow laugh.

'I had him, once. Then you came on the scene.' Her eyes gleamed with a mixture of molten fire and ice. 'A silly teenager from the country. God! You had *nothing* compared to what I could give him.'

'Except, maybe—love?'

'What has that got to do with it?'

'Everything, I imagine,' Natalie said dryly.

'I satisfied him on a physical level.' A look of pure enmity made Simone's features appear ugly. 'Whereas *you*, so lily-white and virginal, could hardly have known what it was all about!'

'Ryan is an excellent tutor,' Natalie remarked, not really wanting to pursue with such invective. Yet this was war, if only a verbal one, and had to be led to its ultimate conclusion.

'I'm sure I could provide more titillating tricks than you ever dreamed were possible!'

'Lust alone is an empty emotion. Only when it's accompanied by love does it become something beautiful.'

'Don't hand me that sentimental rubbish! Look around you,' Simone spat vengefully. 'This house, the cars, apartments—even the cruiser goes into a cool six figures! Who cares about *love*?'

'I do,' Natalie said with quiet conviction, and for a moment she looked incredibly sad. 'Whatever you believe to the contrary, it was Ryan who made the running in our relationship. Even when I expressed doubts, he overruled them.' Courage gave her the strength to go on. 'I was overwhelmed in those first few crucial months after Ryan married me. I'd never met anyone like him, and all these trappings appeared like a giant fairytale. Instead of deriving pleasure from them, they rose between us like an insurmountable barrier. Given a choice, I'd have preferred to have been without them. At least then I could have felt able to compete on an equal level.' A drawn-out sigh left her lips, and she forced a slight smile. 'As it was, I became confronted at every turn with sophisticated socialites who for the most part didn't care a fig about me personally. I knew that, and so did you. What was more, you wanted what I appeared to have—*Ryan*. Or rather, Ryan's possessions. You played your hand well, Simone. Like a gullible fool, I believed every word you said and ran as far and as fast as my legs would carry me.' She paused, and idly traced the pattern on the wrought-iron table with her finger. 'However, this time I'm not running.'

'You'll stay and be humiliated?'

'Why should I be humiliated?' she parried.

'I can take Ryan from you as easily as——'
Simone clicked her fingers in the air with a decisive
snap—'that.'

'If that's true, why didn't he instigate a legal
separation and then divorce me?'

'Because he was embittered with marriage,'
Simone vented furiously. 'However, given time, I
could have won him round.'

'Well, your time just ran out,' Natalie said
carefully, making sure she enunciated her words
with clear distinction as she continued, 'I love
him—very much. There's Michelle, whom neither
of us would give up easily. And there'll be another
child before the years's end, unless I'm mistaken.'

The fury in Simone's face was something
frightening to see, and for a moment Natalie
fought an instinctive desire to back away. Quietly
she stood her ground, her gaze unwavering,
outwardly calm yet defensively on the alert.

Even so, she was unprepared for the hand that
snaked out and dealt a stinging blow to her left
cheek, almost unbalancing her. Blindly she
reached for the edge of the table in an attempt to
steady herself, and felt her vision blur as tears
welled at the pain Simone had managed to inflict.

'You smart, conniving little bitch! I hate you—
hate you, do you hear?' The words streamed out
with low guttural invective, and Natalie lifted a
shaky hand to brush the excess moisture from her
eyes.

'I think you'd better leave.'

Natalie heard Jenkins' voice and slowly turned
to face him, seeing the silent anger expressed in his
usually kind features. Thank God for his
intervention! Simone had gone beyond rage to the
brink of not being responsible for her actions.

'I'll leave when I damn well please!' Dark hair

swung in a slow arc as her head turned towards the manservant. 'Now get out. I haven't finished yet.'

'You are no longer welcome in this house, Miss Vesey,' Jenkins asserted with calm inflexibility, and Natalie saw him move until he stood between her and Simone. 'If you won't leave of your own accord, I shall have to employ force.'

'Lay a finger on me, and I'll have you up for assault!'

'I don't think so,' a deep drawling voice intervened, and Natalie's eyes flew to the tall figure moving towards them.

'Ryan! Oh, thank God you've come!' Simone cried, and a whole flood of words flowed from her lips, interspersed with convulsive sobs. 'It's been awful—she's been so horrible—saying terrible things——'

Natalie stood in stunned silence, part of her brain registering with devilish humour that Simone was stealing *her* lines! Like an invisible spectator she observed the tableau, noting the two men's stance with interest. One defensive; the other dangerous, resembling a jungle tiger about to spring. Simone's acting excelled itself. Indeed, if Natalie hadn't been an unwilling participant and evidenced for herself such bitter invective, she would have believed every word that came out of the other woman's mouth!

Ryan appeared to listen, but his eyes were on Natalie, not Simone. When the torrent of words came to a halt, his voice was almost deadly in its intent as he stressed with chilling abruptness,

'Jenkins will escort you to your car. If you so much as come within speaking distance of my wife again, or attempt to threaten her in any way, I will personally see to it that you never receive an

invitation from any of the Coast's social echelon.'
His eyes were pitiless and totally without mercy. 'If
you possess an ounce of sense, you'll re-locate
yourself elsewhere.'

'But you loved me! I know you did!'

His silence became an almost tangible thing, and
Natalie unconsciously held her breath.

'I used you, in much the same manner you used
me,' he corrected with silky detachment. 'It was
over many years ago—long before Natalie first
came on the scene.'

'But we were good for each other!' Simone
cried. 'You know we were. Everyone said so!'

'Everyone was wrong. There is only one woman
in this life who means anything and everything to
me.'

'She'll never be your equal,' Simone hissed.
'*Never!*'

Ryan turned slightly, although his eyes were
wary and didn't shift as he instructed quietly,
'Jenkins, escort Miss Vesey from the house, and
ensure that she doesn't set foot in it again.'

'Yessir! It will be a pleasure.'

'You can't do this to me!'

'I just have, Simone.'

Jenkins stepped forward and took her arm,
leading her across the pebbled courtyard, and
Natalie watched until they disappeared indoors.

'Did she harm you in any way?'

Dear Lord! Invidious words, a slap that had
almost rocked her from her feet? 'I'm all right,' she
managed quietly, aware that Ryan had moved to
stand in front of her.

'Are you?' His voice was faintly sceptical, and
her eyelids instinctively lowered as he lifted her
chin. 'Look at me, Natalie.'

Slowly she opened her eyes, meeting and

holding his gaze, and swallowed convulsively as he gently brushed his fingers over her cheek. 'You're home early.' She had to say something, otherwise she would burst into stupid childish tears.

His smile did strange things to her equilibrium, and some of the compelling formidability left his features. 'Is that all you have to say?'

'I'm temporarily lost for words.'

Gently he bent his head down to hers and trailed his lips over her cheek. 'Martha rang me,' he said close to her mouth.

'She did?'

His lips teased a trail along her jaw and sought an earlobe. 'Uh-huh. Both she and Jenkins are very protective of their ewe lamb.'

'Oh.'

His mouth closed over hers in a gentle provocative gesture, seeking an elusive response she was at that moment unable to give, and he reluctantly lifted his head.

'Neither of them were prepared to stand by and see Simone make another attempt to wreck our marriage.'

More than anything Natalie wanted to fling herself into his arms and have them hold her close. 'How much did you overhear?' she ventured at last, and glimpsed a faint speculative gleam in the eyes that surveyed her.

'Why? What did you say to her?'

Natalie felt oddly inarticulate. 'Simone did most of the talking.'

'While you sat in docile silence?'

'Not—exactly,' she conceded, fixing her gaze on the uppermost button of his black silk shirt.

'But you don't want to tell me, is that it?'

Something in his voice made her look at him, and she slowly shook her head—not in negation, but as a gesture of self-mockery at her lack of perception. 'I don't want to play games any more,' she began a trifle sadly, and his eyes narrowed fractionally.

'What are you talking about?'

'You and me,' she stated simply.

'Elaborate, Natalie,' he bade after a measurable silence, and her grey eyes were remarkably clear as she held his gaze.

'I'm tired of pretending.'

'Ah, I see.'

'Do you?'

'Shall we go inside?' he countered, and she raised her hand in an impotent gesture.

'We can talk here.'

A warm smile curved his generous mouth, reaching up to his eyes so that they crinkled with silent laughter. 'I don't imagine the *talking* will last very long. Do you want to shock the neighbours?'

'It's the middle of the afternoon,' Natalie protested, and he gave a deep throaty laugh.

'Do you want to mete out some sort of punishment by making me wait until tonight?'

'Would you?'

He reached out and tilted her chin. 'If you asked me.'

Her lower lip began to tremble. 'I love you. I never stopped.'

'I know,' Ryan said gently.

'I wanted to hurt you, the way *I* was hurt.'

'It's past, darling. Between us, we'll ensure that it never happens again.' He placed a brief hard kiss on her upturned mouth, then bent to bestow a more lingering caress before fitting her into the curve of his shoulder and leading her indoors. 'We have each other. Michelle is a bonus.'

A tiny secret smile curved her lips. 'How would you view an extra bonus?'

His glance speared her guileless features. 'Are you trying to tell me something?'

'I think I'm going to have another child,' she said quietly.

His eyes darkened measurably, and his voice sounded slightly strained. 'Do you mind?'

'Do you?' she countered slowly.

'How can you ask that?' Ryan demanded huskily as he swept her into his arms to carry her effortlessly up the stairs to their room.

Gently he lowered her to her feet, then cupped her face so that she had to look at him. 'I should have been more careful.'

'Why?' she asked simply, and saw a muscle tense along his jaw.

'You had a difficult time with Michelle.'

'Just holding her in my arms made it all worth while,' Natalie ventured quietly. 'A warm living being conceived out of love—yours and mine.'

'You're beautiful, do you know that?' he groaned emotively, and his hands slid up to her temples to hold her head. 'Will you stay with me, sleep with me, and share the rest of the days of my life?'

An impish desire to tease him a little got the better of her. 'Only the *days*, Ryan?'

'Wretch,' he laughed with glittering warmth. 'I should make you pay for that!'

'Mmm,' she whispered pensively, running the edge of her tongue along her lower lip in a deliberately provocative gesture. 'That sounds promising.'

Emotion flared in the dark golden eyes above her own, then his mouth was on hers, possessing it with a deep consuming passion that had her clinging to him unashamedly.

Slowly and with infinite gentleness he undressed

her, smiling as she helped him remove his clothes, then together they reached for each other, delighting in a mutual exploratory pleasure of all the tantalising sensory nerve-ends until only total possession could ease their aching need.

Afterwards, they rose from the bed and bathed together, then, clothed they emerged from the room and descended the stairs, arm in arm.

Natalie leaned her head momentarily against Ryan's hard shoulder and felt the answering pressure as his hand curved over her hip. She felt warm and infinitely loved, and she gave a soft bubbly laugh and raised her face for the kiss he bent low to bestow, exulting in the passion she knew would remain with them for the rest of their lives. At last, all the shadows of yesterday were gone.

Harlequin Mills & Boon

Next months
Mills & Boon romances

MILLS AND BOON

Just For A Night
by Miranda Lee

Outback Heat
by Emma Darcy

Honeymoon Baby
by Susan Napier

The Baby Bond
by Sharon Kendrick

Man About The House
by Alison Kelly

The Ideal Father
by Rosalie Ash

Bride For Sale
by Susanne McCarthy

A Man Worth Waiting For
by Helen Brooks

The Temptation Trap
by Catherine George

The Diamond Dad
by Lucy Gordon

Undercover Husband
by Rebecca Winters

Look-Alike Fiancé
by Elizabeth Duke

Gentlemen Prefer...Brunettes
by Liz Fielding

Charlie's Dad
by Alexandra Scott

Hevenly Husband
by Carolyn Greene

Ready-Made Bride
by Janelle Denison

The Baby Came C.O.D.
by Marie Ferrarella

The Irresistible Prince
by Lisa Kaye Laurel

MEDICAL

Country Remedy
by Joanna Neil

A Family To Share
by Gill Sanderson

Tomorrow's Child
by Lilian Darcy

Contract Dad
by Helen Shelton

BESTSELLERS
(Four In One)

Such Dark Magic
by Robyn Donald

Tiger Eyes
by Robyn Donald

Island Enchantment
by Robyn Donald

The Colour Of Midnight
by Robyn Donald

Take 4 bestselling love stories FREE

And get a gorgeous FREE gift too!

Harlequin Mills & Boon

AVAILABLE NOW

Captive Heart
CAROLINE ANDERSON

Hijacked Honeymoon
MARION LENNOX

Promises To Keep
JOSIE METCALFE

Wedding At Gold Creek
MEREDITH WEBBER

Harlequin Mills & Boon

Best Actress Competition

Test your knowledge of female actors in the latest romance films!!! Firstly fill in the blanks to reveal the actresses who appear in the films below. Once you've filled in all the blanks unjumble the circled letters to find the BEST ACTRESS award winner at the 1998 Oscars!!!

THE BODYGUARD

W _ _ _ _ _ _   H _ _ _ _ _ _

TITANIC

K _ _ W _ _ _ _ _ _

FRENCH KISS

M _ _   R _ _ _ _

ROMEO & JULIET

C _ _ _ _ _ _   D _ _ _ _

BEST ACTRESS AWARD GOES TO...

H _ _ _ _ H _ _ _

Once you have solved the Harlequin Mills & Boon BEST ACTRESS competition, simply complete your name and address details overleaf and send this page to the given address by the 31st December 1998.

The first three correct entries drawn will each WIN a years FREE SUPPLY OF ROMANCE NOVELS in the series of the winners choice.

DON'T MISS OUT! POST YOUR ENTRY TODAY

How To Enter

Harlequin Mills & Boon

Best Actress Competition

The first three correct entries drawn will each WIN a years supply of romance novels in the series of the winners choice. First solve the puzzle overleaf to reveal the best actress at the 1998 Oscars. Then complete your NAME and ADDRESS details below (make sure you send it in before the 31st December 1998) and send to:

BEST ACTRESS COMPETITION
★ Locked Bag 2
Chatswood NSW 2067

Name (Mrs/Miss/Ms/Mr) _____

Address _____

_____ Postcode_____

Daytime Tel. No. (__) _____

* New Zealand Address: Private Bag 92122, Auckland 1020
Competition is open to residents of Australia and New Zealand only.
You may be sent promotional mailings as a result of this entry.

PLEASE TICK BOX IF YOU ARE A READER
SERVICE SUBSCRIBER ☐

ONLY ONE ENTRY PER HOUSEHOLD PLEASE!!!!